Collected Stories

Hanif Kureishi was born and brought up in Kent. He read philosophy at King's College, London. In 1981 he won the George Devine Award for his plays *Outskirts* and *Borderline*, and in 1982 he was appointed Writer in Residence at the Royal Court Theatre. In 1984 he wrote *My Beautiful Laundrette*, which received an Oscar nomination for Best Screenplay. His second screenplay, *Sammy and Rosie Get Laid* (1987), was followed by *London Kills Me* (1991), which he also directed. *The Buddha of Suburbia* won the Whitbread Prize for Best First Novel in 1990 and was made into a four-part drama series by the BBC in 1993. His version of Brecht's *Mother Courage* has been produced by the Royal Shakespeare Company and the Royal National Theatre. His second novel, *The Black Album*, was published in 1995. With Jon Savage he edited *The Faber Book of Pop* (1995). His first collection of short stories, *Love in a Blue Time*, was published in 1997. His story 'My Son the Fanatic', from that collection, was adapted for film and released in 1998. *Intimacy*, his third novel, was published in 1998, and a film of the same title, based on the novel and other stories by the author, was released in 2001 and won the Golden Bear award at the Berlin Film Festival. His play *Sleep With Me* premiered at the Royal National Theatre in 1999. His second collection of stories, *Midnight All Day*, was published in 2000. *Gabriel's Gift*, his fourth novel, was published in 2001. *The Body and Seven Stories* and *Dreaming and Scheming*, a collection of essays, were published in 2002. His screenplay *The Mother* was directed by Roger Michell and released in 2003. In 2004 he published his play *When the Night Begins* and a memoir, *My Ear at His Heart*. A second collection of essays, *The Word and the Bomb*, followed in 2005. His screenplay *Venus* was directed by Roger Michell in 2006. His latest novel, *Something to Tell You* was published to great critical acclaim in 2008. In 2009 the National Theatre staged an adaptation of his strikingly prescient and acclaimed novel, *The Black Album*. He has been awarded the Chevalier de l'Ordre des Arts des Lettres and a CBE for services to literature and his work has been translated into thirty-six languages.

Collected Stories

HANIF KUREISHI

faber and faber

This collection of stories first published in 2010
by Faber and Faber Ltd
Bloomsbury House
74–77 Great Russell Street
London WC1B 3DA

Typeset by RefineCatch Limited, Bungay, Suffolk
Printed in England by CPI Mackays, Chatham

A CIP record for this book
is available from the British Library

ISBN 978–0–571–24980–0

2 4 6 8 10 9 7 5 3 1

Contents

CONTENTS

LOVE IN A BLUE TIME

First published in 1997

In a Blue Time

When the phone rings, who would you most like it to be? And who would you hate it to be? Who is the first person that comes into your mind, Roy liked to ask people, at that moment?

The phone rang and Roy jumped. He had thought, during supper in their new house, with most of their clothes and books in boxes they were too weary to unpack, that it would be pleasant to try their new bed early. He looked across the table at Clara and hoped she'd let the phone run on to the answering machine so he could tell who it was. He disliked talking to his friends in front of her; she seemed to scrutinise him. Somehow he had caused her to resent any life he might have outside her.

She picked up the phone, saying 'Hallo' suspiciously. Someone was speaking but didn't require or merit a reply. Roy mouthed at her, 'Is it Munday? Is it him?'

She shook her head.

At last she said, 'Oh God,' and waved the receiver at Roy.

In the hall he was putting on his jacket.

'Are you going to him?'

'He's in trouble.'

She said, 'We're in trouble, and what will you do about that?'

'Go inside. You'll get cold standing there.'

She clung to him. 'Will you be long?'

'I'll get back as soon as I can. I'm exhausted. You should go to bed.'

'Thank you. Aren't you going to kiss me?'

He put his mouth to hers, and she grunted. He said, 'But I don't even want to go.'

'You'd rather be anywhere else.'

At the gate he called, 'If Munday rings, please take his number. Say that otherwise I'll go to his office first thing tomorrow morning.'

She knew this call from the producer Munday was important to him, indeed to both of them. She nodded and then waved.

It wouldn't take him more than fifteen minutes to drive to the house in Chelsea where his old friend Jimmy had been staying the last few months. But Roy was tired, and parked at the side of the road to think. To think! Apprehension and dread swept through him.

Roy had met Jimmy in the mid-seventies in the back row of their university class on Wittgenstein. Being four years older than the other students, Jimmy appeared ironically knowing compared to Roy's first friends, who had just left school. After lectures Jimmy never merely retired to the library with a volume of Spinoza, or, as Roy did, go disappointedly home and study, while dreaming of the adventures he might have, were he less fearful. No – Jimmy did the college a favour by popping in for an hour or so after lunch. Then he'd hang out impressing some girls he was considering for his stage adaptation of *Remembrance of Things Past*.

After he'd auditioned them at length, and as the sky darkened over the river and the stream of commuters across Blackfriars Bridge thinned, Jimmy would saunter forth into the city's pleasures. He knew the happenin' cinemas, jazz clubs, parties. Or, since he ran his own magazine, *Blurred Edges*, he'd interview theatre directors, photographers, tattooists and performance artists who, to Roy's surprise, rarely refused. At that time students were still considered by some people to be of consequence, and Jimmy would light a joint, sit on the floor and let the recorder run. He would print only the trifling parts of the tape – the gossip and requests for drinks – satisfying his theory that what people were was more interesting than their opinions.

Tonight Jimmy had said he needed Roy more than he'd ever needed him. Or rather, Jimmy's companions had relayed that message. Jimmy himself hadn't made it to the phone or even to his feet. He was, nevertheless, audible in the background.

On the doorstep Roy hesitated. Next morning he had a critical breakfast meeting with Munday about the movie Roy had written and was, after two years of preparation, going to direct. He was also, for the first time, living with Clara. This had been a sort of choice, but its consequences – a child on the way – had somehow surprised them both.

He couldn't turn back. Jimmy's was the voice Roy most wanted to hear on the phone. Their friendship had survived even the mid-eighties, that vital and churning period when everything had been forced forward with a remorseless velocity. Roy had cancelled his debts to anyone whose affection failed to yield interest. At that time, when Roy lived alone, Jimmy would turn up late at night, just to talk. This was welcome and unusual in Roy's world, as they didn't work together and there was no question of loss or gain between them. Jimmy wasn't impressed by Roy's diligence. While Roy rushed between meetings Jimmy was, after all, idling in bars and the front of girls' shirts. But though Jimmy disappeared for weeks – one time he was in prison – when Roy had a free day, Jimmy was the person Roy wanted to spend it with. The two of them would lurch from pub to pub from lunchtime until midnight, laughing at everything. He had no other friends like this, because there are some conversations you can only have with certain people.

Roy pushed the door and cautiously made his way down the uncarpeted stairs, grasping the banister with feeble determination as, he realised, his father used to do. Someone seemed to have been clawing at the wallpaper with their fingernails. A freezing wind blew across the basement: a broken chair must have travelled through a window.

There was Jimmy, then, on the floor, with a broken bottle beside him. The only object intact was a yellowing photograph of Keith Richards pinned to the wall.

Not that Jimmy would have been able to get into his bed. It was occupied by a cloudy-faced middle-aged woman with well-cut hair who, though appearing otherwise healthy, kept nodding out. Cradled into her was a boy of around sixteen with a sly scared look, naked apart from a Lacoste crocodile tattooed onto his chest. Now and again the woman seemed to achieve a dim consciousness and tried shoving him away, but she couldn't shift him.

Jimmy lay on the floor like a child in the playground, with the foot of a bully on his chest. The foot belonged to Marco, the owner of the house, a wealthy junkie with a blood-stained white scarf tied around his throat. Another man, Jake, stood beside them.

'The cavalry's arrived,' Jake said to Marco, who lifted his boot.

Jimmy's eyes were shut. His twenty-one-year-old girlfriend Kara, the daughter of a notable bohemian family, who had been seeing Jimmy for a year, ran and kissed Roy gratefully. She was accompanied by an equally young friend, with vivid lips, leopard-skin hat and short skirt. If Roy regretted coming, he particularly regretted his black velvet jacket. Cut tight around the waist, it was long and shining and flared out over the thighs. The designer, a friend for whom Roy had shot a video, had said that ageing could only improve it. But wherever he wore it, Roy understood now, it sang of style and money, and made him look as if he had a job.

Kara and the girl took Roy to one side and explained that Jimmy had been drinking. Kara had found him in Brompton Cemetery with a smack dealer, though he claimed to have given that up. This time she was definitely leaving him until he sorted himself out.

'They're animals,' murmured Jimmy.

Marco replaced his foot on his chest.

The kid in the bed, who had now mounted the woman, glared over his shoulder, saying to Jimmy, 'What the fuck, you don't never sleep here no more. You got smarter people to be with than us.'

Jimmy shouted, 'It's my bed! And stop fucking that woman, she's overdosing!'

There was nothing in the woman's eyes.

'Is she all right?' Roy asked.

'She still alive,' the boy explained. 'My finger on her pulse.'

Jimmy cried, 'They stole my fucking booze and drunk it, found my speed and took it, and stole my money and spent it. I'm not having these bastards in my basement, they're bastards.'

Jake said to Roy: 'Number one, he's evicted right now this minute. He went berserk. Tried to punch us around, and then tried to kill himself.'

Jimmy winked up at Roy. 'Did I interrupt your evening, man? Were you talking about film concepts?'

For years Roy had made music videos and commercials, and directed episodes of soap operas. Sometimes he taught at the film school. He had also made a sixty-minute film for the BBC, a story about a black girl singer. He had imagined that this would be the start of something considerable, but although the film received decent reviews, it had taken him no further. In the mid-eighties he'd been considered for a couple of features, but like most films, they'd fallen through. He'd seen his contemporaries make films in Britain, move to LA and buy houses with pools. An acquaintance had been nominated for an Oscar.

Now at last his own movie was in place, apart from a third of the money and therefore the essential signed contracts and final go-ahead, which were imminent. In the past week Munday had been to LA and New York. He had been told that with a project of this quality he wouldn't have trouble raising the money.

Kara said, 'I expect Roy was doing some hard work.' She turned to him. 'He's too much. Bye-bye, Jimmy, I love you.'

While she bent down and kissed Jimmy, and he rubbed his hand between her legs, Roy looked at the picture of Keith Richards and considered how he'd longed for the uncontrolled life, seeking only pleasure and avoiding the ponderous difficulties of keeping every-thing together. He wondered if that was what he still wanted, or if he were still capable of it.

When Kara had gone, Roy stood over Jimmy and asked, 'What d'you want me to do?'

'Quote the lyrics of "Tumblin' Dice".'

The girl in the hat touched Roy's arm. 'We're going clubbing. Aren't you taking Jimmy to your place tonight?'

'What? Is that the idea?'

'He tells everyone you're his best friend. He can't stay here.' The girl went on. 'I'm Candy. Jimmy said you work with Munday.'

'That's right.'

'What are you doing with him, a promo?'

From the floor Jimmy threw up his protracted cackle.

Roy said, 'I'm going to direct a feature I've written.'

'Can I work on it with you?' she asked. 'I'll do anything.'

'You'd better ring me to discuss it,' he said.

Jimmy called, 'How's the pregnant wife?'

'Fine.'

'And that young girl who liked to sit on your face?'

Roy made a sign at Candy and led her into an unlit room next door. He cut out some coke, turned to the waiting girl and kissed her against the wall, smelling this stranger and running his hands over her. She inhaled her line, but before he could dispose of his and hold her again, she had gone.

Marco and Jake had carted Jimmy out, stashed him in Roy's car and instructed him to fuck off for good.

Roy drove Jimmy along the King's Road. As always now, Jimmy was dressed for outdoors, in sweaters, boots and heavy coat. In contrast, Roy's colleagues dressed in light clothes and would never inadvertently enter the open air: when they wanted weather they would fly to a place that had the right kind. An overripe gutter odour rose from Jimmy, and Roy noticed the dusty imprint of Marco's foot on his chest. Jimmy pulled a pair of black lace-trimmed panties from his pocket and sniffed at them like a duchess mourning a relative.

This was an opportunity, Roy decided, to use on Jimmy some of the honest directness he had been practising at work. Surely it would be instructive and improving for Jimmy to survive without constant assistance. Besides, Roy couldn't be sucked into another emotional maelstrom.

He said, 'Isn't there anywhere you can go?'

'What for?' said Jimmy.

'To rest. To sleep. At night.'

'To sleep? Oh I see. It's okay. Leave me on the corner.'

'I didn't mean that.'

'I've slept out before.'

'I meant you've usually got someone. Some girl.'

'Sometimes I stay with Candy.'

'Really?'

Jimmy said, 'You liked her, yeah? I'll try and arrange something. Did I tell you she likes to stand on her head with her legs open?'

'You should have mentioned it to Clara on the phone.'

'It's a very convenient position for cunnilingus.'

'Particularly at our age when unusual postures can be a strain,' added Roy.

Jimmy put his hand in Roy's hair. 'You're going grey, you know.'

'I know.'

'But I'm not. Isn't that strange?' Jimmy mused a few seconds. 'But I can't stay with her. Kara wouldn't like it.'

'What about your parents?'

'I'm over forty! They're dying, they make me take my shoes off! They weep when they see me! They –'

Jimmy's parents were political refugees from Eastern Europe who'd suffered badly in the war, left their families, and lived in Britain since 1949. They'd expected, in this city full of people who lived elsewhere in their minds, to be able to return home, but they never could. Britain hadn't engaged them; they barely spoke the language. Meanwhile Jimmy fell in love with pop. When he played the blues on his piano his parents had it locked in the garden shed. Jimmy and his parents had never understood one another, but he had remained as rootless as they had been, never even acquiring a permanent flat.

He was rummaging in his pockets where he kept his phone numbers on torn pieces of cigarette packet and ragged tube tickets. 'You remember when I brought that girl round one afternoon –'

9

'The eighteen-year-old?'

'She wanted your advice on getting into the media. You fucked her on the table in front of me.'

'The media got into her.'

'Indeed. Can you remember what you wore, who you pretended to be, and what you said?'

'What did I say?'

'It was your happiest moment.'

'It was a laugh.'

'One of our best.'

'One of many.'

They slapped hands.

Jimmy said, 'The next day she left me.'

'Sensible girl.'

'We'd exploited her. She had a soul which you were disrespectful to.' Jimmy reached over and stroked Roy's face. 'I just wanted to say, I love you, man, even if you are a bastard.'

Jimmy started clapping to the music. He could revive as quickly as a child. Nevertheless, Roy determined to beware of his friend's manipulations; this was how Jimmy had survived since leaving university without ever working. For years women had fallen at Jimmy's feet; now he collapsed at theirs. Yet even as he descended they liked him as much. Many were convinced of his lost genius, which had been perfectly preserved for years, by procrastination. Jimmy got away with things; he didn't earn what he received. This was delicious but also a provocation, mocking justice.

Roy had pondered all this, not without incomprehension and envy, until he grasped how much Jimmy gave the women. Alcoholism, unhappiness, failure, ill-health, he showered them with despair, and guiltlessly extracted as much concern as they might proffer. They admired, Roy guessed, his having made a darkness to inhabit. Not everyone was brave enough to fall so far out of the light. To Roy it also demonstrated how many women still saw sacrifice as their purpose.

Friendship was the recurring idea in Roy's mind. He recalled some remarks of Montaigne. 'If I were pressed to say why I love him, I feel that my only reply could be, "because it was he, because it was I".' Also, 'Friendship is enjoyed even as it is desired; it is bred, nourished and increased only by enjoyment, since it is a spiritual thing and the soul is purified by its practice.' However, Montaigne had said nothing about the friend staying with you, as Jimmy seemed set on doing; or about dealing with someone who couldn't believe that, given the choice, anyone would rather be sober than drunk, and that once someone had started drinking they would stop voluntarily before passing out – the only way of going to sleep that Jimmy found natural.

Roy no longer had any clue what social or political obligations he had, nor much idea where such duties could come from. At university he'd been a charged conscience, acquiring dozens of attitudes wholesale, which, over the years, he had let drop, rather as people stopped wearing certain clothes one by one and started wearing others, until they transformed themselves without deciding to. Since then Roy hadn't settled in any of the worlds he inhabited, but only stepped through them like hotel rooms, and, in the process, hadn't considered what he might owe others. Tonight, what love did this lying, drunken, raggedy-arsed bastard demand?

'Hey.' Roy noticed that Jimmy's fingers were tightening around the handbrake.

'Stop.'

'Now?' Roy said.

'Yes!'

Jimmy was already clambering out of the car and making for an off-licence a few steps away. He wasn't sober but he knew where he was. Roy had no choice but to follow. Jimmy was asking for a bottle of vodka. Then, as Jimmy noticed Roy extracting a £50 note – which was all, to his annoyance, that he was carrying – he added a bottle of whisky to his order. When the assistant turned his back Jimmy swiped four beer cans and concealed them inside his jacket. He also collected Roy's change.

Outside, a beggar extended his cap and mumbled some words of a song. Jimmy squatted down at the man's level and stuffed the change from the £50 into his cap.

'I've got nothing else,' Jimmy said. 'Literally fuck-all. But take this. I'll be dead soon.'

The man held the notes up to the light. This was too much. Roy went to snatch them back. But the bum had disappeared them and was repeating, 'On yer way, on yer way . . .'

Roy turned to Jimmy. 'It's my money.'

'It's nothing to you, is it?'

'That doesn't make it yours.'

'Who cares whose it is? He needs it more than us.'

'. . . on yer way . . .'

'He's not our responsibility.'

Jimmy looked at Roy curiously. 'What makes you say that? He's pitiful.'

Roy noticed two more derelicts shuffling forward. Further up the street others had gathered, anticipating generosity.

'. . . on yer way . . .'

Roy pulled Jimmy into the car and locked the doors from inside.

Along from Roy's house, lounging by a wall with up-to-something looks on their faces, were two white boys who occupied a nearby basement. The police were often outside, and their mother begging them to take them away; but the authorities could do nothing until the lads were older. Most mornings when Roy went out to get his *Independent* he walked across glass where cars had been broken into. Several times he had greeted the boys. They nodded at him now; one day he would refuse his fear and speak properly. He didn't like to think there was anyone it was impossible to contact in some way, but he didn't know where to begin. Meanwhile he could hardly see out of his house for the bars and latticed slats. Beside his bed he kept a knife and hammer, and was mindful of not turning over too strenuously for fear of whacking the red alarm button adjacent to his pillow.

'This the new house? Looks comfortable,' said Jimmy. 'You didn't invite me to the house-warming, but Clara's gonna be delighted to see me now. Wished I owned a couple of suitcases so I could stand at the door and tell her I'm here for a while.'

'Don't make too much noise.'

Roy led Jimmy into the living room. Then he ran upstairs, opened the bedroom door and listened to Clara breathing in the darkness. He had wanted to fuck her that night. When the phone rang he was initiating the painstaking preparatory work. It was essential not to offend her in any way since a thumbs-down was easy, and agreeable, to her. He had been sitting close by her and sending, telepathically – his preferred method of communication – loving sensual messages. As they rarely touched one another gratuitously, immediate physical contact – his hand in her hair – would be a risk. But if he did manage to touch her without a setback and even if, perhaps, he persuaded her to pull her skirt up a little – this made him feel as if he had reached the starting-gate, at least – he knew success was a possibility. Bearing this in mind he would rush upstairs to bed, changing into his pyjamas so as not to alarm her with uncovered flesh. He had, scrupulously, to avoid her getting the right idea.

He tried to anticipate which mood would carry her through the bedroom door. If there was something he'd neglected to do, like lock the back door or empty the dishwasher, arduous diplomacy would be imperative. Otherwise he would observe her undressing as she watched TV, knowing it would be only moments before his nails were in the bitch's fat arse.

But wait: she had perched on the end of the bed to inspect her corns while sucking on a throat pastille and discussing the cost of having the front of the house repointed. His desire was boiling, and he wanted to strike down his penis, which by now was through the front of his pyjamas, with a ruler.

As she watched TV beside him and he played with her breasts, she continued to pretend that this was not happening; perhaps, for her, it wasn't. She did, though, appear to believe in foreplay, at least for herself. After a time she would even remove all her clothes, though not without a histrionic shiver to demonstrate that sex altered one's temperature. At this encouragement he would scoot across the floor and hunt, in the back of a drawer, for a pair of crumpled black nylon French knickers. Rolling her eyes at the tawdry foolishness of men she might, if his luck was in, pull them on. He knew she was finally conquered when she stopped watching television. Unfortunately, she used this opportunity, while she had his attention, to scold him for minor offences. He could, with pleasure, have taped over her mouth.

In all this there must have been, despite their efforts, a unifying pleasure, for next morning she liked to hold him, and wanted to be kissed.

Roy could only close the door now. Before returning to Jimmy he went into the room next door. Clara had bought a changing table on which lay pairs of mittens, baby boots, little red hats, cardigans smaller than handkerchiefs. The curtains were printed with airborne elephants; on the wall was a picture of a farmyard.

What had he done? She puzzled him still. Never had a woman pursued him as passionately as Clara over the past five years. Not a day would pass, at the beginning, when she didn't send him flowers and books, invite him to concerts and the cinema, or cook for him. Perhaps she had been attempting, by example, to kindle in him the romantic feeling she herself desired. He had accepted it like a pasha. At other times he'd attempted to brush her away, and had always kept other women. He saw now what a jejune protest that was. Her love had been an onslaught. She wanted a family. He, who liked to plan everything, but had really only known what sort of work he sought, had complied in order to see what might occur. He had been easily overrun; the child was coming; it gave him vertigo.

He was tugging at a mattress leaning against the wall. Jimmy would be cosy here, perhaps too cosy, reflected Roy, going downstairs without it.

14

Jimmy was lying with his feet on the sofa. Beside him he had arranged a beer, a glass and a bottle of Jack Daniels taken from the drinks cupboard. He was lighting a cigarette from the matches Roy had collected from the Royalton and the Odeon, smart New York restaurants, and kept to impress people.

There was no note from Clara about Munday, and no message on the machine.

Roy said, 'All right, pal?' He decided he loved his friend, envied his easy complacency, and was glad to have him here.

Jimmy said, 'Got everything I need.'

'Take it easy with the Jack. What about the bottle we bought?'

'Don't start getting queenie. I didn't want to break into them straight away. So – here we are together again.' Jimmy presented his glass. 'What the fuck?'

'Yeah, what the fuck!'

'Fuck everything!'

'Fuck it!'

The rest of the Jack went and they were halfway through the vodka the next time Roy pitched towards the clock. The records had come out, including Black Sabbath. A German porn film was playing with the sound turned off. The room became dense with marijuana smoke. They must have got hungry. After smashing into a tin of baked beans with a hammer and spraying the walls, Roy climbed on Jimmy's shoulders to buff the mottled ceiling with a cushion cover and then stuffed it in Jimmy's mouth to calm him down. Roy didn't know what time the two of them stripped in order to demonstrate the Skinhead Moonstomp or whether he had imagined their neighbour banging on the wall and then at the front door.

It seemed not long after that Roy hurried into Soho for buttered toast and coffee in the Patisserie Valerie. In his business, getting up early had become so habitual that if, by mistake, he woke up after seven, he panicked, fearing life had left without him.

Before ten he was at Munday's office where teams of girls with Home Counties accents, most of whom appeared to be wearing

cocktail dresses, were striding across the vast spaces waving contracts. Roy's arrival surprised them; they had no idea whether
Munday was in New York, Los Angeles or Paris, or when he'd be
back. He was 'raising money'. Because it had been on his mind,
Roy asked seven people if they could recall the name of Harry
Lime's English friend in *The Third Man*. But only two of them had
seen the film and neither could remember.

There was nothing to do. He had cleared a year of other work to
make this film. The previous night had sapped him, but he felt
only as if he'd taken a sweet narcotic. Today he should have few
worries. Soon he'd be hearing from Munday.

He drifted around Covent Garden, where, since the mid-eighties,
he rarely ventured without buying. His parents had not been badly
off but their attitude to money had been, if you want something
think whether you really need it and if you can do without it. Well,
he could do without most things, if pushed. But at the height of
the decade money had gushed through his account. If he drank
champagne rather than beer, if he used cocaine and took taxis from
one end of Soho to the other five times a day, it barely dented the
balance. It had been a poetic multiplication; the more he made the
more he admired his own life.

He had loved that time. The manic entrepreneurialism, prancing
individualism, self-indulgence and cynicism appealed to him as
nothing had for ten years. Pretence was discarded. Punk disorder and
nihilism ruled. Knowledge, tradition, decency and the lip-service
paid to equality; socialist holiness, talk of 'principle', student clothes,
feminist absurdities, and arguments defending regimes – 'flawed
experiments' – that his friends wouldn't have been able to live under
for five minutes: such pieties were trampled with a Nietzschean
pitilessness. It was galvanising.

He would see something absurdly expensive – a suit, computers,
cameras, cars, apartments – and dare himself to buy it, simply to
discover what the consequences of such recklessness might be.
How much fun could you have before everything went mad? He
loved returning from the shops and opening the designer carrier

bags, removing the tissue paper, and trying on different combinations of clothes while playing the new CDs in their cute slim boxes. He adored the new restaurants, bars, clubs, shops, galleries, made of black metal, chrome or neon, each remaining fashionable for a month, if it was lucky.

Life had become like a party at the end of the world. He was sick of it, as one may grow sick of champagne or of kicking a dead body. It was over, and there was nothing. If there was to be anything it had to be made anew.

He had lived through an age when men and women with energy and ruthlessness but without much ability or persistence excelled. And even though most of them had gone under, their ignorance had confused Roy, making him wonder whether the things he had striven to learn, and thought of as 'culture', were irrelevant. Everything was supposed to be the same: commercials, Beethoven's late quartets, pop records, shopfronts, Freud, multi-coloured hair. Greatness, comparison, value, depth: gone, gone, gone. Anything could give some pleasure; he saw that. But not everything provided the sustenance of a deeper understanding.

His work had gone stale months ago. Whether making commercials, music videos or training films, Roy had always done his best. But now he would go along with whatever the client wanted, provided he could leave early.

Around the time he had begun to write his film, he started checking the age of the director or author if he saw a good movie or read a good book. He felt increasingly ashamed of his still active hope of being some sort of artist. The word itself sounded effete; and his wish seemed weakly adolescent, affected, awkward.

Once, in a restaurant in Vienna during a film festival, Roy saw that Fellini had come in with several friends. The maestro went to every table with his hands outstretched. Then the tall man with the head of an emperor sat down and ate in peace. And what peace it would be! Roy thought often of how a man might feel had he made, for instance, *La Dolce Vita*, not to speak of *8 1/2*. What insulating spirit this would give him, during breakfast, or waiting

17

to see his doctor about a worrying complaint, enduring the empty spaces that boundary life's occasional rousing events!

Bergman, Fellini, Ozu, Wilder, Cassavetes, Rosi, Renoir: the radiance! Often Roy would rise at five in the morning to suck the essential vitamin of poetry in front of the video. A few minutes of *Amarcord,* in which Fellini's whole life was present, could give him perspective all day. Certain sequences he examined scores of times, studying the writing, acting, lighting and camera movements. In commercials he was able to replicate certain shots or the tone of entire scenes. 'Bit more Bergman?' he'd say. 'Or do you fancy some Fellini here?'

In New York he went to see *Hearts of Darkness*, the documentary about Coppola's making of *Apocalypse Now*. He was becoming aware of what he wouldn't do now: parachute from a plane or fight in a war or revolution; travel across Indonesia with a backpack; go to bed with three women at once, or even two; learn Russian, or even French, properly; or be taught the principles of architecture. But for days he craved remarkable and noble schemes on which everything was risked.

What would they be? For most of his adult life he'd striven to keep up with the latest thing in cinema, music, literature and even the theatre, ensuring that no one mentioned an event without his having heard of it. But now he had lost the thread and didn't mind. What he wanted was to extend himself. He tormented himself with his own mediocrity. And he saw that, apart from dreams, the most imaginative activity most people allowed themselves was sexual fantasy. To live what you did – somehow – was surely the point.

In his garden in the mornings, he began to write, laying out the scenes on index cards on the grass, as if he were playing patience. The concentration was difficult. He was unused to such a sustained effort of dreaming, particularly when the outcome was distant, uncertain and not immediately convertible into a cheque or interest from colleagues. Why not begin next year?

After a few days' persistence his mind focused and began to run in unstrained motion. In these moments – reminded of himself even as he got lost in what he was doing – the questions he had asked about life, its meaning and direction, if any, about how best to live, could receive only one reply. To be here now, doing this.

That was done. He was in a hurry to begin shooting. Private satisfactions were immaterial. The film had to make money. When he was growing up, the media wasn't considered a bright boy's beat. Like pop, television was disparaged. But it had turned out to be the jackpot. Compared to his contemporaries at school, he had prospered. Yet the way things were getting set up at home he had to achieve until he expired. He and Clara would live well: nannies, expensive schools, holidays, dinner parties, clothes. After setting off in the grand style, how could you retreat to less without anguish?

All morning his mind had whirled. Finally he phoned Clara. She'd been sick, and had come downstairs to discover Jimmy asleep on the floor amid the night's debris, wrapped in the table-cloth and the curtains, which had become detached from the rail. He had pissed in a pint glass and placed it on the table.

To Roy's surprise she was amused. She had, it was true, always liked Jimmy, who flirted with her. But he couldn't imagine her wanting him in her house. She wasn't a cool or loose hippie. She taught at a university and could be formidable. Most things could interest her, though, and she was able to make others interested. She was enthusiastic and took pleasure in being alive, always a boon in others, Roy felt. Like Roy, she adored gossip. The misfortunes and vanity of others gave them pleasure. But it was still a mostly cerebral and calculating intelligence that she had. She lacked Jimmy's preferred kind of sentimental self-observation. It had been her clarity that had attracted Roy, at a time when they were both concerned with advancement.

Cheered by her friendliness towards Jimmy, Roy wanted to be with him today.

Jimmy came out of the bathroom in Roy's bathrobe and sat at the table with scrambled eggs, the newspaper, his cigarettes and 'Let It

Bleed' on loud. Roy was reminded of their time at university, when, after a party, they would stay up all night and the next morning sit in a pub garden, or take LSD and walk along the river to the bridge at Hammersmith, which Jimmy, afraid of heights, would have to run across with his eyes closed.

Roy read his paper while surreptitiously watching Jimmy eat, drink and move about the room as if he'd inhabited it for years. He was amazed by the lengthy periods between minor tasks that Jimmy spent staring into space, as if each action set off another train of memory, regret and speculation. Then Jimmy would search his pockets for phone numbers and shuffle them repeatedly. Finally, Jimmy licked his plate and gave a satisfied burp. When Roy had brushed the crumbs from the floor, he decided to give Jimmy a little start.

'What are you going to do today?'

'Do? In what sense?'

'In the sense of . . . to do something.'

Jimmy laughed.

Roy went on, 'Maybe you should think of looking for work. The structure might do you good.'

'Structure?'

Jimmy raised himself to talk. There was a beer can from the previous night beside the sofa; he swigged from it and then spat out, having forgotten he'd used it as an ashtray. He fetched another beer from the fridge and resumed his position.

Jimmy said, 'What sort of work is it that you're talking about here?'

'Paying work. You must have heard of it. You do something all day –'

'Usually something you don't like to do –'

'Whatever. Though you might like it.' Jimmy snorted. 'And at the end of the week they give you money with which you can buy things, instead of having to scrounge them.'

This idea forced Jimmy back in his seat. 'You used to revere the surrealists.'

'Shooting into a crowd! Yes, I adored it when –'

'D'you think they'd have done anything but kill themselves laughing at the idea of salaried work? You know it's serfdom.'

Roy lay down on the floor and giggled. Jimmy's views had become almost a novelty to Roy. Listening to him reminded Roy of the pleasures of failure, a satisfaction he considered to be unjustly unappreciated now he had time to think about it. In the republic of accumulation and accountancy there was no doubt Jimmy was a failure artist of ability. To enlarge a talent to disappoint, it was no good creeping into a corner and dying dismally. It was essential to raise, repeatedly, hope and expectation in both the gullible and the knowing, and then to shatter them. Jimmy was intelligent, alertly bright-eyed, convincing. With him there was always the possibility of things working out. It was an achievement, therefore, after a calculated build-up, to bring off a resounding fuck-up. Fortunately Jimmy would always, on the big occasion, let you down: hopelessness, impotence, disaster, all manner of wretchedness – he could bring them on like a regular nightmare.

Not that it hadn't cost him. It took resolution, organisation, and a measure of creativity to drink hard day and night; to insult friends and strangers; to go to parties uninvited and attempt to have sex with teenage girls; to borrow money and never pay it back; to lie, make feeble excuses, be evasive, shifty and selfish. He had had many advantages to overcome. But finally, after years of application, he had made a success, indeed a triumph, of failure.

Jimmy said, 'The rich love the poor to work, and the harder the better. It keeps them out of trouble while they're ripped off. Everyone knows that.' He picked up a porn magazine, *Peaches*, and flipped through the pages. 'You don't think I'm going to fall for that shit, do you?'

Roy's eyes felt heavy. He was falling asleep in the morning! To wake himself up he paced the carpet and strained to recall the virtues of employment.

'Jimmy, there's something I don't understand about this.'

'What?'

'Don't you ever wake up possessed by a feeling of things not done? Of time and possibility lost, wasted? And failure . . . failure in most things – that could be overcome. Don't you?'

Jimmy said, 'That's different. Of mundane work you know nothing. The worst jobs are impossible to get. You've lived for years in the enclosed world of the privileged with no idea what it's like outside. But the real work you mention, I tell you, every damn morning I wake up and feel time rushing past me. And it's not even light. Loneliness . . . fear. My heart vibrates.'

'Yes! and don't you think, this is a new morning, maybe this day I can redeem the past? Today something real might be done?'

'Sometimes I do think that,' Jimmy said. 'But most of the time . . . to tell you the truth, Roy, I know nothing will get done. Nothing, because that time is past.'

When the beer was gone they went out, putting their arms around one another. On the corner of Roy's street was a rough pub with benches outside, where many local men gathered between March and September, usually wearing just shorts. They'd clamber from their basements at half past ten and by eleven they'd be in place, chewing a piece of bread with their beer, smoking dope and shouting above the traffic. Their women, who passed by in groups, pushing prams laden with shopping, were both angrier and more vital.

One time Roy walked past and heard Springsteen's hypodermic cry 'Hungry Heart' blaring from inside. He'd lingered apprehensively: surely the song would rouse the men to some sudden recklessness, the desire to move or hunt down experience? But they merely mouthed the words.

He thought of the books which had spoken to him as a teenager and how concerned they were with young men fleeing home and domesticity, to hurl themselves at different boundaries. But where had it led except to self-destruction and madness? And how could you do that kind of thing now? Where could you run?

Roy's preferred local was a low-ceilinged place with a semicircular oak bar. Beyond, it was long and deep, broken up by booths, corners and turns. Men sat alone, reading, staring, talking to themselves, as if modelling for a picture entitled 'The Afternoon Drinkers'. There was a comfortable aimlessness; in here nothing had to happen.

Jimmy raised his glass. Roy saw that his hand trembled, and that his skin looked bruised and discoloured, the knuckles raw, fingers bitten.

'By the way, how was Clara this morning?'

'That was her, right?' said Jimmy.

'Yeah.'

'She's big outfront but looking great. A bit like Jean Shrimpton.'

'You told her that?'

Jimmy nodded.

Roy said, 'That's what did the trick. You'll be in with her for a couple of days now.'

'Still fuck her?'

'When I can't help myself,' said Roy. 'You'd think she'd appreciate the interest but instead she says that lying beside me is like sleeping next to a bag of rubbish that hasn't been collected for a fortnight.'

'She's lucky to have you,' said Jimmy.

'Me?'

'Oh yes. And she knows it too. Still, thank Christ there's plenty of pussy back on stream now that that Aids frenzy has worn off.'

Roy said, 'All the same, it's easy to underestimate how casual and reassuring married love can be. You can talk about other things while you're doing it. It isn't athletic. You can drift. It's an amicable way of confirming that everything is all right.'

'I've never had that,' said Jimmy.

'You're not likely to, either.'

'Thanks.'

After a time Jimmy said, 'Did I mention there was a phone call this morning. Someone's office. Tuesday?'

'Tuesday?'

'Or was it Wednesday?'

'Munday!'

'Munday? Yeah, maybe it was . . . one of those early days.'

Roy grasped him by the back of the neck and vibrated him a little. 'Tell me what he said.'

Jimmy said, 'Gone. Everything vaporises into eternity – all thoughts and conversations.'

'Not this one.'

Jimmy sniggered, 'The person said he's in the air. Or was. And he's popping round for a drink.'

'When?'

'I think it was . . . today.'

'Christ,' said Roy. 'Finish your pint.'

'A quick one, I think, to improve our temper.'

'Get up. This is the big one. It's my film, man.'

'Film? When's it on?'

'Couple of years.'

'What? Where's the hurry? How can you think in those kinda time distances?'

Roy held Jimmy's glass to his lips. 'Drink.'

Munday might, Roy knew, swing by for a few minutes and treat Roy as if he were a mere employee; or he might hang out for five hours, discussing politics, books, life.

Munday embodied his age, particularly in his puritanism. He was surrounded by girls; he was rich and in the film business; everywhere there were decadent opportunities. But work was his only vice, with the emphasis on negotiating contracts. His greatest pleasure was to roar, after concluding a deal: 'Course, if you'd persisted, or had a better agent, I'd have paid far more.'

He did like cocaine. He didn't like to be offered it, for this might suggest he took it, which he didn't, since it was passé. He did, nevertheless, like to notice a few lines laid accidentally out on the table, into which he might dip his nose in passing.

Cocaine would surely help things go better. As Roy guided Jimmy back, he considered the problem. There was a man – Upton

Turner – who was that rare thing, a fairly reliable dealer who made home visits and occasionally arrived on the stated day. Roy had been so grateful for this – and his need so urgent – that when Turner had visited in the past, Roy had enquired after his health and family, giving Turner, he was afraid, the misapprehension that he was a person as well as a vendor. He had become a nuisance. The last time Roy phoned him, Turner had flung the phone to one side, screaming that the cops were at the door and he was 'lookin' at twenty years!' As Roy listened, Turner was dumping thousands of pounds worth of powder down the toilet, only to discover that the person at the door was a neighbour who wanted to borrow a shovel.

Despite Turner's instability, Roy called him. Turner said he'd come round. At once Munday's office then rang.

'He's coming to you,' they said. 'Don't go anywhere.'

'But when?' Roy whined.

'Expect him in the near future,' the cool girl replied, and added, with a giggle, 'This century, definitely.'

'Ha, ha.'

They had some time at least. While listening for Upton's car, Roy and Jimmy had a few more drinks. At last Roy called Jimmy over to the window.

'There.'

'No!' Jimmy seized the curtain to give him strength. 'It's a wind-up. That isn't Turner. Maybe it's Munday.'

'It is our man, without a doubt.'

'Doesn't he feel a little conspicuous – in his profession?'

'Wouldn't you think so?'

'Jesus, Roy, and you're letting this guy into your new home?'

They watched Turner trying to land the old black Rolls in a space, his pit-bull sitting up front and music booming from the windows. He couldn't get the car in anywhere, and finally left it double-parked in the road with the traffic backing up around it, and rushed into the house with the noisy dog. Turner was small, balding and middle-aged, in a white shirt and grey suit that clung to his backside and flared at the ankles. He saw Jimmy drinking at the table and came to an abrupt standstill.

'Roy, son, you're all fucking pissed. You should have said we're having a bit of a laugh, I'd have brought the party acid.'

'This is Jimmy.'

Turner sat down, parting his legs and sweeping back his jacket, exposing his genitals outlined by tight trousers as if he anticipated applause. He reached into his pocket and tossed a plastic bag onto the table containing fifty or sixty small envelopes. Jimmy was rubbing his hands together in anticipation.

Turner said, 'How many of these are you having? Eh?'

'Not sure yet.'

'Not sure? What d'you mean?'

'Just that.'

'All right,' Turner conceded. 'Try it, try it.'

Roy opened one of the envelopes.

'Never seen so many books an' videos as you got in these boxes,' Turner said, pacing about. He halted by a pile and said, 'Alphabetical. A mind well ordered. As a salesman I evaluate the people from looking at their houses. Read 'em all?'

'It's surprising how many people ask that,' Roy said with relaxed enjoyment. 'It really is. Turner, d'you want a drink or something else?'

'You must know a lot then,' Turner insisted.

'Not necessarily,' Jimmy said. 'It doesn't follow.'

'I know what you mean.' Turner winked at Jimmy and they laughed. 'But the boy must know something. I'm gonna offer credit where it's due, I'm generous like that.' He lit a cigarette in his cupped hand and surveyed the kitchen. 'Nice place. You an' the wife getting the builders in?'

'Yeah.'

'Course. I bet you have a pretty nice life, all in all. Plays, travel, posh friends. The police aren't looking for you, are they?'

'Not like they are for you, Turner.'

'No. That's right.'

'Turner's looking at fifteen. Isn't that right, man?'

'Yeah,' said Turner. 'Sometimes twenty. I'm looking at –' He noticed Jimmy suppressing a giggle and turned to see Roy smirking. He said, 'I'm looking at a lot of shit. Now, Mister Roy, if you know so fucking much I'll try and think if there's something I need to ask you, while I'm here.'

Jimmy said to Roy, 'Are you ready for Mr Turner's questions?'

Roy tapped his razor blade on the table and organised the powder into thick lines. He and Jimmy hunched over to inhale. Turner sat down at last and pointed at the envelopes.

'How many of them d'you want?'

'Three.'

'How many?'

'Three, I said.'

'Fuck.' Turner banged his fist on the table. 'Slags.'

Roy said, 'You want a piece of pie?'

'That I could go for.'

Roy cut a piece of Clara's cherry pie and gave it to Turner. Turner took two large bites and it was inside him. Roy cut another piece. This time Turner leaned back in his chair, raised his arm and hurled it across the kitchen as if he were trying to smash it through the wall. The dog thrashed after it like a shoal of piranhas. It was an aged creature and its eating was slobbery and breathless. The second it had finished, the dog ran back to Turner's feet and planted itself there, waiting for more.

Turner said to Roy, 'Three, did you say?'

'Yeah.'

'So I have come some considerable miles at your instant command for fuck-all. You know,' he said sarcastically, 'I'm looking at eighteen.'

'In that case four. All right. Four g's. Might as well, eh, Jimmy?'

Turner slapped the dog. 'You'll get another go in a minute,' he told it. He looked at Jimmy. 'What about ten?'

'Go for it,' said Jimmy to Roy. 'We'll be all right tomorrow. Ten should see us through.'

'Smart,' said Turner. 'Planning ahead.'

'Ten?' Roy said. 'No way. I don't think you should hustle people.'

Turner's voice became shrill. 'You saying I hustle you?'

Roy hesitated. 'I mean by that . . . it's not a good business idea.'

Turner raised his voice. 'I'm doing this to pay off my brother's debts. My brother who was killed by scum. It's all for him.'

'Quite right,' murmured Jimmy.

'Hey, I've got a fucking question for you,' Turner said. 'Little Roy.'

'Yes?'

'Do you know how to love life?'

Jimmy and Roy looked at one another.

Turner said, 'That's stumped you, right? I'm saying here, is it a skill? Or a talent? Who can acquire it?' He was settling into his rap. 'I deal to the stars, you know.'

'Most of them introduced to you by me,' Roy murmured.

'And they the unhappiest people I seen.'

'It's still a difficult question,' said Roy.

He looked at Turner, who was so edgy and complicated it was hard to think of him as a child. But you could always see the light of childhood in Jimmy, he was luminous with curiosity.

'But a good one,' said Jimmy.

'You're pleased with that one,' Roy said to Turner.

'Yeah, I am.' Turner looked at Jimmy. 'You're right. It's a difficult question.'

Roy put his hand in his jeans pocket and dragged out a wad of £20 notes.

'Hallo,' Turner said.

'Jesus,' said Jimmy.

'What?' Roy said.

'I'll take a tenner off,' Turner said. 'As we're friends – if you buy six.'

'I told you, not six,' said Roy, counting the money. There was plenty of it, but he thumbed through it rapidly.

Turner reached out to take the whole wad and held it in his fist, looking down at the dog as his foot played on its stomach.

'Hey,' Roy said and turned to Jimmy who was laughing.

'What?' said Turner, crumpling the money in his hand. Roy pulled the cherry pie towards him and cut a slice. His hand was shaking now. 'You are in a state,' Turner said. He took the mobile phone out of his pocket and turned it off.

'Am I?' Roy said. 'What are you going to do with that money?'

Turner got up and took a step towards Roy. 'Answer the fucking question!'

Roy put up his hands. 'I can't.'

Turner pushed three small envelopes towards Jimmy, put all the money in his pocket, yanked away his drug bag, and, pursued by the dog, charged to the door. Roy ran to the window and watched the Rolls take off down the street.

'You wanker,' he said to Jimmy. 'You fucking wanker.'

'Me?'

'Christ. We should have done something.'

'Like what?'

'Where's the knife! You should have stuck it in the bastard's fucking throat! That pig's run off with my money!'

'Thing is, you can't trust them proles, man. Sit down.'

'I can't!'

'Here's the knife. Go after him then.'

'Fuck, fuck!'

'This will calm you down,' said Jimmy.

They started into the stuff straight away and there was no going back. Roy attempted to put one gram aside for Munday but Jimmy said, why worry, they could get more later. Roy didn't ask him where from.

Roy was glad to see Upton go. He'd be glad, too, to see the end of the chaos that Jimmy had brought with him.

'What are your plans?' he asked. 'I mean, what are you going to be doing in the next few days?'

Jimmy shook his head. He knew what Roy was on about, but ignored him, as Roy sat there thinking that if he was capable of love he had to love all of Jimmy now, at this moment.

It was imperative, though, that he clear his mind for Munday. The drug got him moving. He fetched a jersey and clean socks for Jimmy, thrust Jimmy's old clothes into a plastic bag, and, holding them at arm's length, pushed them deep into the rubbish. He showered, got changed, opened the windows and prepared coffee.

It was only when Munday, who was ten years younger than him and Jimmy and far taller, came through the door, that Roy realised how spaced he and Jimmy were. Fortunately Clara had said she'd be out that evening. Munday, who had just got off the plane, wanted to relax and talk.

Roy forced his concentration as Munday explained his latest good news. His business, for which Roy had made many music videos, was in the process of being sold to a conglomerate. Munday would be able to make more films and with bigger budgets. He would be managing director and rich.

'Excellent,' said Roy.

'In some ways,' Munday said.

'What do you mean?'

'Let's have another drink.'

'Yes, we must celebrate.' Roy got up. 'I won't be a moment.'

At the door he heard Jimmy say, 'You might be interested to hear that I myself have attempted a bit of writing in my time . . .'

It was that 'I myself' that got him out.

Roy went to buy champagne. He was hurrying around the block. Powerful forces were keeping him from his house. His body ached and fluttered with anxiety; he had Aids at least, and, without a doubt, cancer. A heart attack was imminent. On the verge of panic, he feared he might run yelling into the road but was, at that moment, unable to take another step. He couldn't, though, stay where he was, for fear he might lie down and weep. In a pub he ordered a half but took only two sips. He didn't know how long he'd been sitting there, but he didn't want to go home.

Munday and Jimmy were sitting head to head. Jimmy was telling him a 'scenario' for a film about a famous ageing film director and a drifting young couple who visit him, to pay homage. After they've eaten with him, praised his percipience and vision, admired his awards and heard his Brando stories, they enquire if there is anything they can do for him. The director says he wants to witness the passion of their love-making, hear their conversation, see their bodies, hear their cries and look at them sleeping. The girl and her earnest young man co-operate until . . . They become his secretaries; they take him prisoner; maybe they murder him. Jimmy couldn't remember the rest. It was written down somewhere.

'It's a decent premise,' said Munday.

'Yes,' agreed Jimmy.

Munday turned to Roy, who had rejoined them. 'Where's this guy been hiding?'

He was durable and unsubtle, Munday; and, in spite of his efforts, kindness and concern for others were obvious.

'In the pub,' said Roy.

'Artist on the edge,' said Jimmy.

'Right,' said Munday. 'Too much comfort takes away the hunger. I'll do this . . .' he said.

He would advance Jimmy the money to prepare a draft.

'How much?' asked Jimmy.

'Sufficient.'

Jimmy raised his glass. 'Sufficient. Brilliant – don't you think, Roy?'

Roy said he had to talk to Munday in the kitchen.

'OK,' said Munday. Roy closed the door behind them. Munday said, 'Terrific guy.'

'He used to be remarkable,' said Roy in a low voice, realising he'd left the champagne in the pub. 'Shame he's so fucked now.'

'He has some nice ideas.'

'How can he get them down? He's been dried out three times but always goes back on.'

'Anyhow, I'll see what I can do for him.'

'Good.'

'I meet so few interesting people these days. But I'm sorry to hear about your condition.'

'Pardon?'

'It happens to so many.'

'What happens?'

'I see. You don't want it to get around. But we've worked together for years. You're safe with me.'

'Is that right? Please tell me,' Roy said, 'what you're talking about.'

Munday explained that Jimmy had told him of Roy's addiction to cocaine as well as alcohol.

'You don't believe that, do you?' Roy said.

Munday put his arm around him. 'Don't fuck about, pal, you're one of my best video directors. It's tough enough as it is out there.'

'But you don't, do you?'

'He predicted you'd be in denial.'

'I'm not in fucking denial!'

Munday's eyes widened. 'Maybe not.'

'But I'm not – really!'

Nevertheless, Munday wouldn't stop regarding him as if he were contriving how to fit these startling new pieces into the puzzle that Roy had become.

He said, 'What's that white smear under your nose? and the blade on the table? You will always work, but not if you lie to my face. Roy, you're degrading yourself! I can't have you falling apart on a shoot. You haven't been giving one hundred per cent and you look like shit.'

'Do I?'

'Sure you feel okay now? Your face seems to be twitching. Better take some of these.'

'What are they?'

'Vitamins.'

'Munday –'

'Go on, swallow.'

'Please –'

'Here's some water. Get them down. Christ, you're choking. Lean forward so I can smack you on the back. Jesus, you won't work for me again until you've come out of the clinic. I'll get the office to make a booking tonight. Just think, you might meet some exciting people there.'

'Who?'

'Guitarists. Have you discussed it with Clara?'

'Not yet.'

'If you don't, I will.'

'Thank you. But I need to know what's happening with the film.'

'Listen up then. Just sip the water and concentrate – if you can.'

Later, at the front door Munday shook Jimmy's hand and said he'd be in touch. He said, 'You guys. Sitting around here, music, conversation, bit of dope. I'm going back to the airport now. Another plane, another hotel room. I'm not complaining. But you know.'

The moment Munday got in his Jag and started up the street, Roy screamed at Jimmy. Jimmy covered his face and swore, through his sobs, that he couldn't recall what he'd told Munday. Roy turned away. There was nothing to grasp or punish in Jimmy.

They stopped at an off-licence and drank on a bench in Kensington High Street. A young kid calling himself a traveller sat beside them and gave them a hit on some dope. Roy considered how enjoyably instructive it could be to take up such a position in the High Street, and how much one noticed about people, whereas to passers-by one was invisible, pitied or feared. After a while they went morosely into a pub where the barman served everyone else first and then was rude.

Roy's film would be delayed for at least eighteen months, until Munday was in a stronger position to argue for 'unconventional' projects. Roy doubted it would happen now.

For most of his adult years he'd wanted success, and thought he knew what it was. But now he didn't. He would have to live with himself as he was and without the old hope. Clara would be ashamed of him. As his financial burdens increased his resources had, in a few minutes, shrunk.

As the dark drew in and the street lights came on and people rushed through the tube stations, he and Jimmy walked about, stopping here and there. There seemed, in London, to be a pub on every corner, with many men on red plush seats drinking concentratedly, having nothing better to do. Occasionally they passed restaurants where, in the old days, Roy was greeted warmly and had passed much time, too much – sometimes four or five hours – with business acquaintances, now forgotten. Soon Roy was lost, fleeing with the energy of the frustrated and distressed, while Jimmy moved beside him with his customary cough, stumble and giggle, fuelled by the elation of unaccustomed success, and a beer glass under his coat.

At one point Jimmy suddenly pulled Roy towards a phone box. Jimmy ran in, waited crouching down, and shot out again, pulling Roy by his jacket across the road, where they shrank down beside a hedge.

'What are you doing?'

'We were going to get beaten up.' Though shuddering and looking about wildly, Jimmy didn't stop his drinking. 'Didn't you hear them swearing at us? Poofs, poofs, they said.'

'Who, who?'

'Don't worry. But keep your head down!' After a while he said, 'Now come on. This way!'

Roy couldn't believe that anyone would attempt such a thing on the street, but how would he know? He and Jimmy hastened through crowds of young people queuing for a concert; and along streets lined with posters advertising groups and comedians whose names he didn't recognise.

There was a burst of laughter behind them. Roy wheeled round, but saw no one. The noise was coming from a parked car – no, from across the road. Then it seemed to disappear down the street like the tail of a typhoon. Now his name was being called. Assuming it was a spook, he pressed on, only to see a young actor he'd given work to, and to whom he'd promised a part in the film. Roy was aware of his swampy loafers and stained jacket that stank of pubs. Jimmy stood beside him, leaning on his shoulder, and they regarded the boy insolently.

'I'll wait to hear, shall I?' said the actor, after a time, having muttered some other things that neither of them understood.

They settled in a pub from which Roy refused to move. At last he was able to tell Jimmy what Munday had said, and explain what it meant. Jimmy listened. There was a silence.

'Tell me something, man,' Jimmy said. 'When you prepared your shooting scripts and stuff –'

'I suppose you're a big film writer now.'

'Give me a chance. That guy Munday seemed okay.'

'Did he?'

'He saw something good in me, didn't he?'

'Yes, yes. Perhaps he did.'

'Right. It's started, brother. I'm on the up. I need to get a room – a bedsitter with a table – to get things moving in the literary department. Lend me some money until Munday pays me.'

'There you go.'

Roy laid a £20 note on the table. It was all the cash he had now. Jimmy slid it away.

'What's that? It's got to be a grand.'

'A grand?'

Jimmy said, 'That's how expensive it is – a month's rent in advance, a deposit, phone. You've avoided the real world for ten years. You don't know how harsh it is. You'll get the money back – at least from him.'

Roy shook his head. 'I've got a family now, and I haven't got an income.'

'You're a jealous bastard – an' I just saved your life. It's a mistake to begrudge me my optimism. Lend me your pen.' Jimmy made a note on the back of a bus ticket, crossed it out and rejigged it. 'Wait and see. Soon you'll be coming to my office an' asking me for work. I'm gonna have to examine your CV to ensure it ain't too low-class. Now, do you do it every day?'

'Do what?'

'Work.'

'Of course.'

'Every single day?'

'Yes. I've worked every day since I left university. Many nights too.'

'Really?' Jimmy read back what he'd scrawled on the ticket, folded it up, and stuck it in his top pocket. 'That's what I must do.' But he sounded unconvinced by what he'd heard, as if, out of spite, Roy had made it sound gratuitously laborious.

Roy said, 'I feel a failure. It's hard to live with. Most people do it. I s'pose they have to find other sources of pride. But what – gardening? Christ. Everything's suddenly gone down. How am I going to cheer myself up?'

'Pride?' Jimmy sneered. 'It's a privilege of the complacent. What a stupid illusion.'

'You would think that.'

'Why would I?'

'You've always been a failure. You've never had any expectations to feel let down about.'

'Me?' Jimmy was incredulous. 'But I have.'

'They're alcoholic fantasies.'

Jimmy was staring at him. 'You cunt! You've never had a kind word for me or my talents!'

'Lifting a glass isn't a talent.'

'You could encourage me! You don't know how indifferent people can be when you're down.'

'Didn't I pick you up and invite you to stay in my house?'

'You been trying to shove me out. Everything about me is wrong or despised. You threw my clothes away. I tell you, you're shutting the door on everyone. It's bourgeois snobbery, and it is ugly.'

'You're difficult, Jimmy.'

'At least I'm a friend who loves you.'

'You don't give me anything but a load of trouble.'

'I've got nothing, you know that! Now you've stolen my hope! Thanks for robbing me!' Jimmy finished his drink and jumped up. 'You're safe. Whatever happens, you ain't really going down, but I am!'

Jimmy walked out. Roy had never before seen Jimmy leave a pub so decisively. Roy sat there another hour, until he knew Clara would be home.

He opened the front door and heard voices. Clara was showing the house to two couples, old friends, and was describing the conservatory she wanted built. Roy greeted them and made for the stairs.

'Roy.'

He joined them at the table. They drank wine and discussed the villa near Perugia they would take in the summer. He could see them wearing old linen and ancient straw hats, fanning themselves haughtily.

He tilted his head to get different perspectives, rubbed his forehead and studied his hands, which were trembling, but couldn't think of anything to say. Clara's friends were well off, and of unimaginative and unchallenged intelligence. About most things, by now, they had some picked-up opinion, sufficient to aid party conversation. They were set and protected; Roy couldn't imagine them overdosing on their knees, howling.

The problem was that at the back of Roy's world-view lay the Rolling Stones, and the delinquent dream of his adolescence – the idea that vigour and spirit existed in excess, authenticity and the romantic unleashed self: a bourgeois idea that was strictly anti-bourgeois. It had never, finally, been Roy's way, though he'd played at it. But Jimmy had lived it to the end, for both of them.

The complacent talk made Roy weary. He went upstairs. As he undressed, a cat tripped the security lamps and he could see the sodden garden. He'd barely stepped into it, but there were trees and grass and bushes out there. Soon he would get a table and chair for the lawn. With the kid in its pram, he'd sit under the tree, brightened by the sun, eating Vignotte and sliced pear. What did one do when there was nothing to do?

He'd fallen asleep; Clara was standing over him, hissing. She ordered him to come down. He was being rude; he didn't know how to behave. He had 'let her down'. But he needed five minutes to think. The next thing he heard was her saying goodnight at the door.

He awoke abruptly. The front door bell was ringing. It was six in the morning. Roy tiptoed downstairs with a hammer in his hand. Jimmy's stringy body was soaked through and he was coughing uncontrollably. He had gone to Kara's house but she'd been out, so he'd decided to lie down in her doorway until she returned. At about five there had been a storm, and he'd realised she wasn't coming back.

Jimmy was delirious and Roy persuaded him to lie on the sofa, where he covered him with a blanket. When he brought up blood Clara called the doctor. The ambulance took him away not long after, fearing a clot on the lung.

Roy got back into bed beside Clara and rested his drink on her hard stomach. Clara went to work but Roy couldn't get up. He stayed in bed all morning and thought he couldn't ever sleep enough to recover. At lunchtime he walked around town, lacking even the desire to buy anything. In the afternoon he visited Jimmy in the hospital.

'How you feeling, pal?'

A man in his pyjamas can only seem disabled. No amount of puffing-up can exchange the blue and white stripes for the daily dignity which has been put to bed with him. Jimmy hardly said hallo. He was wailing for a drink and a cigarette.

'It'll do you good, being here.' Roy patted Jimmy's hand. 'Time to sort yourself out.'

Jimmy almost leapt out of bed. 'Change places!'

'No thanks.'

'You smug bastard – if you'd looked after me I wouldn't be in this shit!'

A fine-suited consultant, pursued by white-coated disciples, entered the ward. A nurse drew the curtain across Jimmy's wounded face.

'Make no mistake, I'll be back!' Jimmy cried.

Roy walked past the withered, ashen patients, and towards the lift. Two men in lightweight uniforms were pushing a high bed to the doors on their way to the operating theatre. Roy slotted in behind them as they talked across a dumb patient who blinked up at the roof of the lift. They were discussing where they'd go drinking later. Roy hoped Jimmy wouldn't want him to return the next day.

Downstairs the wide revolving door swept people into the hospital and pushed him out into the town. From the corner of the building, where dressing-gowned patients had gathered to smoke, Roy turned to make a farewell gesture at the building where his friend lay. Then he saw the girl in the leopard-skin hat, Kara's friend.

He called out. Smiling, she came over, holding a bunch of flowers. He asked her if she was working and when she shook her head, said, 'Give me your number. I'll call you tomorrow. I've got a couple of things on the go.'

Before, he hadn't seen her in daylight. What, now, might there be time for?

She said, 'When's the baby due?'

'Any day now.'

'You're going to have your hands full.'

He asked her if she wanted a drink.

'Jimmy's expecting me,' she said. 'But ring me.'

He joined the robust street. Jimmy couldn't walk here, but he, Roy, could trip along light-headed and singing to himself – as if it were he who'd been taken to hospital, and at the last moment, as the anaesthetic was inserted, a voice had shouted, 'No, not him!', and he'd been reprieved.

Nearby was a coffee shop where he used to go. The manager waved at him, brought over hot chocolate and a cake, and, as usual, complained about the boredom and said he wished for a job like Roy's. When he'd gone, Roy opened his bag and extracted his newspaper, book, notebook and pens. But he just watched the passers-by. He couldn't stay long because he remembered that he and Clara had an antenatal class. He wanted to get back, to see what was between them and learn what it might give him. Some people you couldn't erase from your life.

We're Not Jews

Azhar's mother led him to the front of the lower deck, sat him down with his satchel, hurried back to retrieve her shopping, and took her place beside him. As the bus pulled away Azhar spotted Big Billy and his son Little Billy racing alongside, yelling and waving at the driver. Azhar closed his eyes and hoped it was moving too rapidly for them to get on. But they not only flung themselves onto the platform, they charged up the almost empty vehicle hooting and panting as if they were on a fairground ride. They settled directly across the aisle from where they could stare at Azhar and his mother.

At this his mother made to rise. So did Big Billy. Little Billy sprang up. They would follow her and Azhar. With a sigh she sank back down. The conductor came, holding the arm of his ticket machine. He knew the Billys, and had a laugh with them. He let them ride for nothing.

Mother's grey perfumed glove took some pennies from her purse. She handed them to Azhar who held them up as she had shown him.

'One and a half to the Three Kings,' he said.

'Please,' whispered Mother, making a sign of exasperation.

'Please,' he repeated.

The conductor passed over the tickets and went away.

'Hold onto them tightly,' said Mother. 'In case the inspector gets on.'

Big Billy said, 'Look, he's a big boy.'

'Big boy,' echoed Little Billy.

'So grown up he has to run to teacher,' said Big Billy.

'Cry baby!' trumpeted Little Billy.

Mother was looking straight ahead, through the window. Her voice was almost normal, but subdued. 'Pity we didn't have time to get to the library. Still, there's tomorrow. Are you still the best reader in the class?' She nudged him. 'Are you?'

'S'pose so,' he mumbled.

Every evening after school Mother took him to the tiny library nearby where he exchanged the previous day's books. Tonight, though, there hadn't been time. She didn't want Father asking why they were late. She wouldn't want him to know they had been in to complain.

Big Billy had been called to the headmistress's stuffy room and been sharply informed – so she told Mother – that she took a 'dim view'. Mother was glad. She had objected to Little Billy bullying her boy. Azhar had had Little Billy sitting behind him in class. For weeks Little Billy had called him names and clipped him round the head with his ruler. Now some of the other boys, mates of Little Billy, had also started to pick on Azhar.

'I eat nuts!'

Big Billy was hooting like an orang-utan, jumping up and down and scratching himself under the arms – one of the things Little Billy had been castigated for. But it didn't restrain his father. His face looked horrible.

Big Billy lived a few doors away from them. Mother had known him and his family since she was a child. They had shared the same air-raid shelter during the war. Big Billy had been a Ted and still wore a drape coat and his hair in a sculpted quiff. He had black bitten-down fingernails and a smear of grease across his forehead. He was known as Motorbike Bill because he repeatedly built and rebuilt his Triumph. 'Triumph of the Bill,' Father liked to murmur as they passed. Sometimes numerous lumps of metal stood on rags around the skeleton of the bike, and in the late evening Big Bill revved up the machine while his record player balanced on the windowsill repeatedly blared out a 45 called 'Rave On'. Then everyone knew Big Billy was preparing for the annual bank holiday run to the coast. Mother and the other neighbours were forced to shut their windows to exclude the noise and fumes.

Mother had begun to notice not only Azhar's dejection but also his exhausted and dishevelled appearance on his return from school. He looked as if he'd been flung into a hedge and rolled in a puddle – which he had. Unburdening with difficulty, he confessed the abuse the boys gave him, Little Billy in particular.

At first Mother appeared amused by such pranks. She was surprised that Azhar took it so hard. He should ignore the childish remarks: a lot of children were cruel. Yet he couldn't make out what it was with him that made people say such things, or why, after so many contented hours at home with his mother, such violence had entered his world.

Mother had taken Azhar's hand and instructed him to reply, 'Little Billy, you're common – common as muck!'

Azhar held onto the words and repeated them continuously to himself. Next day, in a corner with his enemy's taunts going at him, he closed his eyes and hollered them out. 'Muck, muck, muck – common as muck you!'

Little Billy was as perplexed as Azhar by the epithet. Like magic it shut his mouth. But the next day Little Billy came back with the renewed might of names new to Azhar: sambo, wog, little coon. Azhar returned to his mother for more words but they had run out.

Big Billy was saying across the bus, 'Common! Why don't you say it out loud to me face, eh? Won't say it, eh?'

'Nah,' said Little Billy. 'Won't!'

'But we ain't as common as a slut who marries a darkie.'

'Darkie, darkie,' Little Billy repeated. 'Monkey, monkey!'

Mother's look didn't deviate. But, perhaps anxious that her shaking would upset Azhar, she pulled her hand from his and pointed at a shop.

'Look.'

'What?' said Azhar, distracted by Little Billy murmuring his name.

The instant Azhar turned his head, Big Billy called, 'Hey! Why don't you look at us, little lady?'

She twisted round and waved at the conductor standing on his platform. But a passenger got on and the conductor followed him upstairs. The few other passengers, sitting like statues, were unaware or unconcerned.

Mother turned back. Azhar had never seen her like this, ashen, with wet eyes, her body stiff as a tree. Azhar sensed what an effort she was making to keep still. When she wept at home she threw herself on the bed, shook convulsively and thumped the pillow. Now all that moved was a bulb of snot shivering on the end of her nose. She sniffed determinedly, before opening her bag and extracting the scented handkerchief with which she usually wiped Azhar's face, or, screwing up a corner, dislodged any stray eyelashes around his eye. She blew her nose vigorously but he heard a sob.

Now she knew what went on and how it felt. How he wished he'd said nothing and protected her, for Big Billy was using her name: 'Yvonne, Yvonne, hey, Yvonne, didn't I give you a good time that time?'

'Evie, a good time, right?' sang Little Billy.

Big Billy smirked. 'Thing is,' he said, holding his nose, 'there's a smell on this bus.'

'Pooh!'

'How many of them are there living in that flat, all squashed together like, and stinkin' the road out, eatin' curry and rice!'

There was no doubt that their flat was jammed. Grandpop, a retired doctor, slept in one bedroom, Azhar, his sister and parents in another, and two uncles in the living room. All day big pans of Indian food simmered in the kitchen so people could eat when they wanted. The kitchen wallpaper bubbled and cracked and hung down like ancient scrolls. But Mother always denied that they were 'like that'. She refused to allow the word 'immigrant' to be used about Father, since in her eyes it applied only to illiterate tiny men with downcast eyes and mismatched clothes.

Mother's lips were moving but her throat must have been dry: no words came, until she managed to say, 'We're not Jews.'

There was a silence. This gave Big Billy an opportunity. 'What you say?' He cupped his ear and his long dark sideburn. With his other hand he cuffed Little Billy, who had begun hissing. 'Speak up. Hey, tart, we can't hear you!'

Mother repeated the remark but could make her voice no louder.

Azhar wasn't sure what she meant. In his confusion he recalled a recent conversation about South Africa, where his best friend's family had just emigrated. Azhar had asked why, if they were to go somewhere – and there had been such talk – they too couldn't choose Cape Town. Painfully she replied that there the people with white skins were cruel to the black and brown people who were considered inferior and were forbidden to go where the whites went. The coloureds had separate entrances and were prohibited from sitting with the whites.

This peculiar fact of living history, vertiginously irrational and not taught in his school, struck his head like a hammer and echoed through his dreams night after night. How could such a thing be possible? What did it mean? How then should he act?

'Nah,' said Big Billy. 'You no Yid, Yvonne. You us. But worse. Goin' with the Paki.'

All the while Little Billy was hissing and twisting his head in imitation of a spastic.

Azhar had heard his father say that there had been 'gassing' not long ago. Neighbour had slaughtered neighbour, and such evil hadn't died. Father would poke his finger at his wife, son and baby daughter, and state, 'We're in the front line!'

These conversations were often a prelude to his announcing that they were going 'home' to Pakistan. There they wouldn't have these problems. At this point Azhar's mother would become uneasy. How could she go 'home' when she was at home already? Hot weather made her swelter; spicy food upset her stomach; being surrounded by people who didn't speak English made her feel lonely. As it was, Azhar's grandfather and uncle chattered away in Urdu, and when Uncle Asif's wife had been in the country, she had, without prompting, walked several paces behind them in the street. Not wanting to side with either camp, Mother had had to position herself, with Azhar, somewhere in the middle of this curious procession as it made its way to the shops.

Not that the idea of 'home' didn't trouble Father. He himself had never been there. His family had lived in China and India; but since he'd left, the remainder of his family had moved, along with hundreds of thousands of others, to Pakistan. How could he know if the new country would suit him, or if he could succeed there? While Mother wailed, he would smack his hand against his forehead and cry, 'Oh God, I am trying to think in all directions at the same time!'

He had taken to parading about the flat in wellington boots with a net curtain over his head, swinging his portable typewriter and saying he expected to be called to Vietnam as a war correspondent, and was preparing for jungle combat.

It made them laugh. For two years Father had been working as a packer in a factory that manufactured shoe polish. It was hard physical labour, which drained and infuriated him. He loved books and wanted to write them. He got up at five every morning; at night he wrote for as long as he could keep his eyes open. Even as they ate he scribbled over the backs of envelopes, rejection slips and factory stationery, trying to sell articles to magazines and newspapers. At the same time he was studying for a correspondence course on 'How To Be A Published Author'. The sound of his frenetic typing drummed into their heads like gunfire. They were forbidden to complain. Father was determined to make money from the articles on sport, politics and literature which he posted off most days, each accompanied by a letter that began, 'Dear Sir, Please find enclosed . . .'

But Father didn't have a sure grasp of the English language which was his, but not entirely, being 'Bombay variety, mish and mash'. Their neighbour, a retired school-teacher, was kind enough to correct Father's spelling and grammar, suggesting that he some-times used 'the right words in the wrong place, and vice versa'. His pieces were regularly returned in the self-addressed stamped enve-lope that the *Writers' and Artists' Yearbook* advised. Lately, when they plopped through the letter box, Father didn't open them, but tore them up, stamped on the pieces and swore in Urdu, cursing the English who, he was convinced, were barring him. Or were they? Mother once suggested he was doing something wrong and should study something more profitable. But this didn't get a good response.

In the morning now Mother sent Azhar out to intercept the postman and collect the returned manuscripts. The envelopes and parcels were concealed around the garden like an alcoholic's bottles, behind the dustbins, in the bike shed, even under buckets, where, mouldering in secret, they sustained hope and kept away disaster.

At every stop Azhar hoped someone might get on who would discourage or arrest the Billys. But no one did, and as they moved forward the bus emptied. Little Billy took to jumping up and twanging the bell, at which the conductor only laughed.

Then Azhar saw that Little Billy had taken a marble from his pocket, and, standing with his arm back, was preparing to fling it. When Big Billy noticed this even his eyes widened. He reached for Billy's wrist. But the marble was released: it cracked into the window between Azhar and his mother's head, chipping the glass. She was screaming. 'Stop it, stop it! Won't anyone help! We'll be murdered!'

The noise she made came from hell or eternity. Little Billy blanched and shifted closer to his father; they went quiet.

Azhar got out of his seat to fight them but the conductor blocked his way.

Their familiar stop was ahead. Before the bus braked Mother was up, clutching her bags; she gave Azhar two carriers to hold, and nudged him towards the platform. As he went past he wasn't going to look at the Billys, but he did give them the eye, straight on, stare to stare, so he could see them and not be so afraid. They could hate him but he would know them. But if he couldn't fight them, what could he do with his anger?

They stumbled off and didn't need to check if the crêpe-soled Billys were behind, for they were already calling out, though not as loud as before.

As they approached the top of their street the retired teacher who assisted Father came out of his house, wearing a three-piece suit and trilby hat and leading his Scottie. He looked over his garden, picked up a scrap of paper which had blown over the fence, and sniffed the evening air. Azhar wanted to laugh: he resembled a phantom; in a deranged world the normal appeared the most bizarre. Mother immediately pulled Azhar towards his gate.

Their neighbour raised his hat and said in a friendly way, 'How's it all going?'

At first Azhar didn't understand what his mother was talking about. But it was Father she was referring to. 'They send them back, his writings, every day, and he gets so angry . . . so angry . . . Can't you help him?'

'I do help him, where I can,' he replied.

'Make him stop, then!'

She choked into her handkerchief and shook her head when he asked what the matter was.

The Billys hesitated a moment and then passed on silently. Azhar watched them go. It was all right, for now. But tomorrow Azhar would be for it, and the next day, and the next. No mother could prevent it.

'He's a good little chap,' the teacher was saying, of Father.

'But will he get anywhere?'

'Perhaps,' he said. 'Perhaps. But he may be a touch –' Azhar stood on tiptoe to listen. 'Over hopeful. Over hopeful.'

'Yes,' she said, biting her lip.

'Tell him to read more Gibbon and Macaulay,' he said. 'That should set him straight.'

'Right.'

'Are you feeling better?'

'Yes, yes,' Mother insisted.

He said, concerned, 'Let me walk you back.'

'That's all right, thank you.'

Instead of going home, mother and son went in the opposite direction. They passed a bomb site and left the road for a narrow path. When they could no longer feel anything firm beneath their feet, they crossed a nearby rutted muddy playing field in the dark. The strong wind, buffeting them sideways, nearly had them tangled in the slimy nets of a soccer goal. He had no idea she knew this place.

At last they halted outside a dismal shed, the public toilet, rife with spiders and insects, where he and his friends often played. He looked up but couldn't see her face. She pushed the door and stepped across the wet floor. When he hesitated she tugged him into the stall with her. She wasn't going to let him go now. He dug into the wall with his penknife and practised holding his breath until she finished, and wiped herself on the scratchy paper. Then she sat there with her eyes closed, as if she were saying a prayer. His teeth were clicking; ghosts whispered in his ears; outside there were footsteps; dead fingers seemed to be clutching at him.

For a long time she examined herself in the mirror, powdering her face, replacing her lipstick and combing her hair. There were no human voices, only rain on the metal roof, which dripped through onto their heads.

'Mum,' he cried.

'Don't you whine!'

He wanted his tea. He couldn't wait to get away. Her eyes were scorching his face in the yellow light. He knew she wanted to tell him not to mention any of this. Recognising at last that it wasn't necessary, she suddenly dragged him by his arm, as if it had been his fault they were held up, and hurried him home without another word.

The flat was lighted and warm. Father, having worked the early shift, was home. Mother went into the kitchen and Azhar helped her unpack the shopping. She was trying to be normal, but the very effort betrayed her, and she didn't kiss Father as she usually did.

Now, beside Grandpop and Uncle Asif, Father was listening to the cricket commentary on the big radio, which had an illuminated panel printed with the names of cities they could never pick up, Brussels, Stockholm, Hilversum, Berlin, Budapest. Father's typewriter, with its curled paper tongue, sat on the table surrounded by empty beer bottles.

'Come, boy.'

Azhar ran to his father who poured some beer into a glass for him, mixing it with lemonade.

The men were smoking pipes, peering into the ashy bowls, tapping them on the table, poking them with pipe cleaners, and relighting them. They were talking loudly in Urdu or Punjabi, using some English words but gesticulating and slapping one another in a way English people never did. Then one of them would suddenly leap up, clapping his hands and shouting, 'Yes – out – out!'

Azhar was accustomed to being with his family while grasping only fragments of what they said. He endeavoured to decipher the gist of it, laughing, as he always did, when the men laughed, and silently moving his lips without knowing what the words meant, whirling, all the while, in incomprehension.

D'accord, Baby

All week Bill had been looking forward to this moment. He was about to fuck the daughter of the man who had fucked his wife. Lying in her bed, he could hear Celestine humming in the bathroom as she prepared for him.

It had been a long time since he'd been in a room so cold, with no heating. After a while he ventured to put his arms out over the covers, tore open a condom and laid the rubber on the cardboard box which served as a bedside table. He was about to prepare another, but didn't want to appear over-optimistic. One would achieve his objective. He would clear out then. Already there had been too many delays. The waltz, for instance, though it made him giggle. Nevertheless he had told Nicola, his pregnant wife, that he would be back by midnight. What could Celestine be doing in there? There wasn't even a shower; and the wind cut viciously through the broken window.

His wife had met Celestine's father, Vincent Ertel, the French ex-Maoist intellectual, in Paris. He had certainly impressed her. She had talked about him continually, which was bad enough, and then rarely mentioned him, which, as he understood now, was worse.

Nicola worked on a late-night TV discussion programme. For two years she had been eager to profile Vincent's progress from revolutionary to Catholic reactionary. It was, she liked to inform Bill – using a phrase that stayed in his mind – indicative of the age. Several times she went to see Vincent in Paris; then she was invited

51

to his country place near Auxerre. Finally she brought him to London to record the interview. When it was done, to celebrate, she took him to Le Caprice for champagne, fishcakes and chips.

That night Bill had put aside the script he was directing and gone to bed early with a ruler, pencil and *The Brothers Karamazov*. Around the time that Nicola was becoming particularly enthusiastic about Vincent, Bill had made up his mind not only to study the great books – the most dense and intransigent, the ones from which he'd always flinched – but to underline parts of and even to memorise certain passages. The effort to concentrate was a torment, as his mind flew about. Yet most nights – even during the period when Nicola was preparing for her encounter with Vincent – he kept his light on long after she had put hers out. Determined to swallow the thickest pills of understanding, he would lie there muttering phrases he wanted to retain. One of his favourites was Emerson's: 'We but half express ourselves, and are ashamed of that divine idea which each of us represents.'

One night Nicola opened her eyes and with a quizzical look said, 'Can't you be easier on yourself?'

Why? He wouldn't give up. He had read biology at university. Surely he couldn't be such a fool as to find these books beyond him? His need for knowledge, wisdom, nourishment was more than his need for sleep. How could a man have come to the middle of his life with barely a clue about who he was or where he might go? The heavy volumes surely represented the highest point to which man's thought had flown; they had to include guidance.

The close, leisurely contemplation afforded him some satisfaction – usually because the books started him thinking about other things. It was the part of the day he preferred. He slept well, usually. But at four, on the long night of the fishcakes, he awoke and felt for Nicola across the bed. She wasn't there. Shivering, he walked through the house until dawn, imagining she'd crashed the car. After an hour he remembered she hadn't taken it. Maybe she and Vincent had gone on to a late-night place. She had never done anything like this before.

He could neither sleep nor go to work. He decided to sit at the kitchen table until she returned, whenever it was. He was drinking brandy, and normally he never drank before eight in the evening. If anyone offered him a drink before this time, he claimed it was like saying goodbye to the whole day. In the mid-eighties he'd gone to the gym in the early evening. For some days, though, goodbye was surely the most suitable word.

It was late afternoon before his wife returned, wearing the clothes she'd gone out in, looking dishevelled and uncertain. She couldn't meet his eye. He asked her what she'd been doing. She said 'What d'you think?' and went into the shower.

He had considered several options, including punching her. But instead he fled the house and made it to a pub. For the first time since he'd been a student he sat alone with nothing to do. He was expected nowhere. He had no newspaper with him, and he liked papers; he could swallow the most banal and incredible thing provided it was on newsprint. He watched the passing faces and thought how pitiless the world was if you didn't have a safe place in it.

He made himself consider how unrewarding it was to constrain people. Infidelities would occur in most relationships. These days every man and woman was a cuckold. And why not, when marriage was insufficient to satisfy most human need? Nicola had needed something and she had taken it. How bold and stylish. How petty to blame someone for pursuing any kind of love!

He was humiliated. The feeling increased over the weeks in a strange way. At work or waiting for the tube, or having dinner with Nicola – who had gained, he could see, a bustling, dismissive intensity of will or concentration – he found himself becoming angry with Vincent. For days on end he couldn't really think of anything else. It was as if the man were inhabiting him.

As he walked around Soho where he worked, Bill entertained himself by thinking of how someone might get even with a type like Vincent, were he so inclined. The possibility was quite remote but this didn't prevent him imagining stories from which he emerged with some satisfaction, if not credit. What incentive, distraction, energy and interest Vincent provided him with! This was almost the only creative work he got to do now.

A few days later he was presented with Celestine. She was sitting with a man in a newly opened café, drinking cappuccino. Life was giving him a chance. It was awful. He stood in the doorway pretending to look for someone and wondered whether he should take it.

Vincent's eldest daughter lived in London. She wanted to be an actress and Bill had auditioned her for a commercial a couple of years ago. He knew she'd obtained a small part in a film directed by an acquaintance of his. On this basis he went over to her, introduced himself, made the pleasantest conversation he could, and was invited to sit down. The man turned out to be a gay friend of hers. They all chatted. After some timorous vacillation Bill asked Celestine in a cool tone whether she'd have a drink with him later, in a couple of hours.

He didn't go home but walked about the streets. When he was tired he sat in a pub with the first volume of *Remembrance of Things Past*. He had decided that if he could read to the end of the whole book he would deserve a great deal of praise. He did a little underlining, which since school he had considered a sign of seriousness, but his mind wandered even more than usual, until it was time to meet her.

To his pleasure Bill saw that men glanced at Celestine when they could; others openly stared. When she fetched a drink they turned to examine her legs. This would not have happened with Nicola; only Vincent Ertel had taken an interest in her. Later, as he and Celestine strolled up the street looking for cabs, she agreed that he could come to her place at the end of the week.

It was a triumphant few days of gratification anticipated. He would do more of this. He had obviously been missing out on life's meaner pleasures. As Nicola walked about the flat, dressing, cooking, reading, searching for her glasses, he could enjoy despising her. He informed his two closest friends that the pleasures of revenge were considerable. Now his pals were waiting to hear of his coup.

Celestine flung the keys, wrapped in a tea-towel, out of the window. It was a hard climb: her flat was at the top of a run-down five-storey building in West London, an area of bedsits, students and itinerants. Coming into the living room he saw it had a view across a square. Wind and rain were sweeping into the cracked windows stuffed with newspaper. The walls were yellow, the carpet brown and stained. Several pairs of jeans were suspended on a clothes horse in front of a gas fire which gave off an odour and heated parts of the room while leaving others cold.

She persuaded him to remove his overcoat but not his scarf. Then she took him into the tiny kitchen with bare floorboards where, between an old sink and the boiler, there was hardly room for the two of them.

'I will be having us some dinner.' She pointed to two shopping bags. 'Do you like troot?'

'Sorry?'

It was trout. There were potatoes and green beans. After, they would have apple strudel with cream. She had been to the shops and gone to some trouble. It would take ages to prepare. He hadn't anticipated this. He left her there, saying he would fetch drink.

In the rain he went to the off-licence and was paying for the wine when he noticed through the window that a taxi had stopped at traffic lights. He ran out of the shop to hail the cab, but as he opened the door couldn't go through with it. He collected the wine and carried it back.

He waited in her living room while she cooked, pacing and drinking. She didn't have a TV. Wintry gales battered the window. Her place reminded him of rooms he'd shared as a student. He was about to say to himself, thank God I'll never have to live like this again, when it occurred to him that if he left Nicola, he might, for a time, end up in some unfamiliar place like this, with its stained carpet and old, broken fittings. How fastidious he'd become! How had it happened? What other changes had there been while he was looking in the other direction?

He noticed a curled photograph of a man tacked to the wall. It looked as though it had been taken at the end of the sixties. Bill concluded it was the hopeful radical who'd fucked his wife. He had been a handsome man, and with his pipe in his hand, long hair and open-necked shirt, he had an engaging look of self-belief and raffish pleasure. Bill recalled the slogans that had decorated Paris in those days. 'Everything Is Possible', 'Take Your Desires for Realities', 'It Is Forbidden to Forbid'. He'd once used them in a TV commercial. What optimism that generation had had! With his life given over to literature, ideas, conversation, writing and political commitment, ol' Vincent must have had quite a time. He wouldn't have been working constantly, like Bill and his friends.

The food was good. Bill leaned across the table to kiss Celestine. His lips brushed her cheek. She turned her head and looked out across the dark square to the lights beyond, as if trying to locate something.

He talked about the film industry and what the actors, directors and producers of the movies were really like. Not that he knew them personally, but they were gossiped about by other actors and technicians. She asked questions and laughed easily.

Things should have been moving along. He had to get up at 5.30 the next day to direct a commercial for a bank. He was becoming known for such well-paid but journeyman work. Now that Nicola was pregnant he would have to do more of it. It would be a struggle to find time for the screenwriting he wanted to do. It was beginning to dawn on him that if he was going to do anything worthwhile at his age, he had to be serious in a new way. And yet when he considered his ambitions, which he no longer mentioned to anyone – to travel overland to Burma while reading Proust, and other, more 'internal' things – he felt a surge of shame, as if it was immature and obscene to harbour such hopes; as if, in some ways, it was already too late.

He shuffled his chair around the table until he and Celestine were sitting side by side. He attempted another kiss.

She stood up and offered him her hands. 'Shall we dance?'

He looked at her in surprise. 'Dance?'

'It will 'ot you up. Don't you . . . dance?'

'Not really.'

'Why?'

'Why? We always danced like this.' He shut his eyes and nodded his head as if attempting to bang in a nail with his forehead.

She kicked off her shoes.

'We dance like this. I'll illustrate you.' She looked at him. 'Take it off.'

'What?'

'This stupid thing.'

She pulled off his scarf. She shoved the chairs against the wall and put on a Chopin waltz, took his hand and placed her other hand on his back. He looked down at her dancing feet even as he trod on them, but she didn't object. Gently but firmly she turned and turned him across the room, until he was dizzy, her hair tickling his face. Whenever he glanced up she was looking into his eyes. Each time they crossed the room she trotted back, pulling him, amused. She seemed determined that he should learn, certain that this would benefit him.

'You require some practice,' she said at last. He fell back into his chair, blowing and laughing. 'But after a week, who knows, we could be having you work as a gigolo!'

It was midnight. Celestine came naked out of the bathroom smoking a cigarette. She got into bed and lay beside him. He thought of a time in New York when the company sent a white limousine to the airport. Once inside it, drinking whisky and watching TV as the limo passed over the East River towards Manhattan, he wanted nothing more than for his friends to see him.

She was on him vigorously and the earth was moving: either that, or the two single beds, on the juncture of which he was lying, were separating. He stuck out his arms to secure them, but with each lurch his head was being forced down into the fissure. He felt as if his ears were going to be torn off. The two of them were about to crash through onto the floor.

He rolled her over onto one bed. Then he sat up and showed her what would have happened. She started to laugh, she couldn't stop.

The gas meter ticked; she was dozing. He had never lain beside a lovelier face. He thought of what Nicola might have sought that night with Celestine's father. Affection, attention, serious talk, honesty, distraction. Did he give her that now? Could they give it to one another, and with a kid on the way?

Celestine was nudging him and trying to say something in his ear.

'You want what?' he said. Then, 'Surely . . . no . . . no.'

'Bill, yes.'

He liked to think he was willing to try anything. A black eye would certainly send a convincing message to her father. She smiled when he raised his hand.

'I deserve to be hurt.'

'No one deserves that.'

'But you see . . . I do.'

That night, in that freezing room, he did everything she asked, for as long as she wanted. He praised her beauty and her intelligence. He had never kissed anyone for so long, until he forgot where he was, or who they both were, until there was nothing they wanted, and there was only the most satisfactory peace.

He got up and dressed. He was shivering. He wanted to wash, he smelled of her, but he wasn't prepared for a cold bath.

'Why are you leaving?' She leaped up and held him. 'Stay, stay, I haven't finished with you yet.'

He put on his coat and went into the living room. Without looking back he hurried out and down the stairs. He pulled the front door, anticipating the fresh damp night air. But the door held. He had forgotten: the door was locked. He stood there.

Upstairs she was wrapped in a fur coat, looking out of the window.

'The key,' he said.

'Old man,' she said, laughing. 'You are.'

She accompanied him barefoot down the stairs. While she unlocked the door he mumbled, 'Will you tell your father I saw you?'

'But why?'

He touched her face. She drew back. 'You should put something on that,' he said. 'I met him once. He knows my wife.'

'I rarely see him now,' she said.

She was holding out her arms. They danced a few steps across the hall. He was better at it now. He went out into the street. Several cabs passed him but he didn't hail them. He kept walking. There was comfort in the rain. He put his head back and looked up into the sky. He had some impression that happiness was beyond him and everything was coming down, and that life could not be grasped but only lived.

With Your Tongue down My Throat

1

I tell you, I feel tired and dirty, but I was told no baths allowed for a few days, so I'll stay dirty. Yesterday morning I was crying a lot and the woman asked me to give an address in case of emergencies and I made one up. I had to undress and get in a white smock and they took my temperature and blood pressure five times. Then a nurse pushed me in a wheelchair into a green room where I met the doctor. He called us all 'ladies' and told jokes. I could see some people getting annoyed. He was Indian, unfortunately, and he looked at me strangely as if to say, 'What are you doing here?' But maybe it was just my imagination.

I had to lie on a table and they put a needle or two into my left arm. Heat rushed over my face and I tried to speak. The next thing I know I'm in the recovery room with a nurse saying, 'Wake up, dear, it's all over.' The doctor poked me in the stomach and said, 'Fine.' I found myself feeling aggressive. 'Do you do this all the time?' I asked. He said he did nothing else.

They woke us at six and there were several awkward-looking, sleepy boyfriends outside. I got the bus and went back to the squat.

A few months later we got kicked out and I had to go back to Ma's place. So I'm back here now, writing this with my foot up on the table, reckoning I look like a painter. I sip water with a slice of lemon in it. I'm at Ma's kitchen table and there are herbs growing in pots around me. At least the place is clean, though it's shabby

60

and all falling apart. There are photographs of Ma's women friends from the Labour Party and the Women's Support Group and there is Blake's picture of Newton next to drawings by her kids from school. There are books everywhere, on the Alexander Method and the Suzuki Method and all the other methods in the world. And then there's her boyfriend.

Yes, the radical (ha!) television writer and well-known toss-pot Howard Coleman sits opposite me as I record him with my biro. He's reading one of his scripts, smoking and slowly turning the pages, but the awful thing is, he keeps giggling at them. Thank Christ Ma should be back any minute now from the Catholic girls' school where she teaches.

It's Howard who asked me to write this diary, who said write down some of the things that happen. My half-sister Nadia is about to come over from Pakistan to stay with us. Get it all down, he said.

If you could see Howard now like I can, you'd really laugh. I mean it. He's about forty-three and he's got on a squeaky leather jacket and jeans with the arse round his knees and these trainers with soles that look like mattresses. He looks like he's never bought anything new. Or if he has, when he gets it back from the shop, he throws it on the floor, empties the dustbin over it and walks up and down on it in a pair of dirty Dr Martens. For him dirty clothes are a political act.

But this is the coup. Howard's smoking a roll-up. He's got this tin, his fag papers and the stubby yellow fingers with which he rolls, licks, fiddles, taps, lights, extinguishes and relights all day. This rigmarole goes on when he's in bed with Ma, presumably on her chest. I've gone in there in the morning for a snoop and found his ashtray by the bed, condom on top.

Christ, he's nodding at me as I write! It's because he's so keen on ordinary riff-raff expressing itself, especially no-hoper girls like me. One day we're writing, the next we're on the barricades.

Every Friday Howard comes over to see Ma.

To your credit, Howard the hero, you always take her somewhere a bit jazzy, maybe to the latest club (a big deal for a poverty-stricken teacher). When you get back you undo her bra and hoick your hands up her jumper and she warms hers down your trousers. I've walked in on this! Soon after this teenage game, mother and lover go to bed and rattle the room for half an hour. I light a candle, turn off the radio and lie there, ears flapping. It's strange, hearing your ma doing it. There are momentous cries and gasps and grunts, as if Howard's trying to bang a nail into a brick wall. Ma sounds like she's having an operation. Sometimes I feel like running in with the first-aid kit.

Does this Friday thing sound remarkable or not? It's only Fridays he will see Ma. If Howard has to collect an award for his writing or go to a smart dinner with a critic he won't come to see us until the next Friday. Saturdays are definitely out!

We're on the ninth floor. I say to Howard: 'Hey, clever boots. Tear your eyes away from yourself a minute. Look out the window.'

The estate looks like a building site. There's planks and window frames everywhere – poles, cement mixers, sand, grit, men with mouths and disintegrating brick underfoot.

'So?' he says.

'It's rubbish, isn't it? Nadia will think we're right trash.'

'My little Nina,' he says. This is how he talks to me.

'Yes, my big Howard?'

'Why be ashamed of what you are?'

'Because compared with Nadia we're not much, are we?'

'I'm much. You're much. Now get on with your writing.'

He touches my face with his finger. 'You're excited, aren't you? This is a big thing for you.'

It is, I suppose.

All my life I've been this only child living here in a council place with Ma, the drama teacher. I was an only child, that is, until I was eleven, when Ma says she has a surprise for me, one of the nicest I've ever had. I have a half-sister the same age, living in another country.

'Your father had a wife in India,' Ma says, wincing every time she says *father*. 'They married when they were fifteen, which is the custom over there. When he decided to leave me because I was too strong a woman for him, he went right back to India and right back to Wifey. That's when I discovered I was pregnant with you. His other daughter Nadia was conceived a few days later but she was actually born the day after you. Imagine that, darling. Since then I've discovered that he's even got two other daughters as well!'

I don't give my same-age half-sister in another country another thought except to dislike her in general for suddenly deciding to exist. Until one night, suddenly, I write to Dad and ask if he'll send her to stay with us. I get up and go down the lift and out in the street and post the letter before I change my mind. That night was one of my worst and I wanted Nadia to save me.

On some Friday afternoons, if I'm not busy writing ten-page hate letters to DJs, Howard does imagination exercises with me. I have to lie on my back on the floor, imagine things like mad and describe them. It's so sixties. But then I've heard him say of people: 'Oh, she had a wonderful sixties!'

'Nina,' he says during one of these gigs, 'you've got to work out this relationship with your sister. I want you to describe Nadia.'

I zap through my head's TV channels – Howard squatting beside me, hand on my forehead, sending loving signals. A girl materialises sitting under a palm tree, reading a Brontë novel and drinking yogurt. I see a girl being cuddled by my father. He tells stories of tigers and elephants and rickshaw wallahs. I see . . .

'I can't see any more!'

Because I can't visualise Nadia, I have to see her.

So. This is how it all comes about. Ma and I are sitting at breakfast, Ma chewing her vegetarian cheese. She's dressed for work in a long, baggy, purple pinafore dress with black stockings and a black band in her hair, and she looks like a 1950s teenager. Recently Ma's gone blonde and she keeps looking in the mirror. Me still in my T-shirt and pants. Ma tense about work as usual, talking about school for hours on the phone last night to friends. She tries to interest me in child abuse, incest and its relation to the GCSE. I say how much I hate eating, how boring it is and how I'd like to do it once a week and forget about it.

'But the palate is a sensitive organ,' Ma says. 'You should cultivate yours instead of –'

'Just stop talking if you've got to fucking lecture.'

The mail arrives. Ma cuts open an airmail letter. She reads it twice. I know it's from Dad. I snatch it out of her hand and walk round the room taking it in.

Dear You Both,

It's a good idea. Nadia will be arriving on the 5th. Please meet her at the airport. So generous of you to offer. Look after her, she is the most precious thing in the entire world to me.

Much love.

At the bottom Nadia has written: 'Looking forward to seeing you both soon.'

Hummmm . . .

Ma pours herself more coffee and considers everything. She has these terrible coffee jags. Her stomach must be like distressed leather. She is determined to be businesslike, not emotional. She says I have to cancel the visit.

'It's simple. Just write a little note and say there's been a mis-understanding.'

And this is how I react: 'I don't believe it! Why? No way! But why?' Christ, don't I deserve to die, though God knows I've tried to die enough times.

'Because, Nina, I'm not at all prepared for this. I really don't know that I want to see this sister of yours. She symbolises my betrayal by your father.'

I clear the table of our sugar-free jam (no additives).

'Symbolises?' I say. 'But she's a person.'

Ma gets on her raincoat and collects last night's marking. You look very plain, I'm about to say. She kisses me on the head. The girls at school adore her. There, she's a star.

But I'm very severe. Get this: 'Ma. Nadia's coming. Or I'm going. I'm walking right out that door and it'll be junk and prostitution just like the old days.'

She drops her bag. She sits down. She slams her car keys on the table. 'Nina, I beg you.'

2

Heathrow. Three hours we've been here, Ma and I, burying our faces in doughnuts. People pour from the exit like released prisoners to walk the gauntlet of jumping relatives and chauffeurs holding cards: Welcome Ngogi of Nigeria.

But no Nadia. 'My day off,' Ma says, 'and I spend it in an airport.'

But then. It's her. Here she comes now. It is her! I know it is! I jump up and down waving like mad! Yes, yes, no, yes! At last! My sister! My mirror.

We both hug Nadia, and Ma suddenly cries and her nose runs and she can't control her mouth. I cry too and I don't even know who the hell I'm squashing so close to me. Until I sneak a good look at the girl.

You. Every day I've woken up trying to see your face, and now you're here, your head jerking nervously, saying little, with us drenching you. I can see you're someone I know nothing about. You make me very nervous.

You're smaller than me. Less pretty, if I can say that. Bigger nose. Darker, of course, with a glorious slab of hair like a piece of chocolate attached to your back. I imagined, I don't know why (pure prejudice, I suppose), that you'd be wearing the national dress, the baggy pants, the long top and light scarf flung all over. But you have on FU jeans and a faded blue sweatshirt – you look as if you live in Enfield. We'll fix that.

Nadia sits in the front of the car. Ma glances at her whenever she can. She has to ask how Nadia's father is.

'Oh yes,' Nadia replies. 'Dad. The same as usual, thank you. No change really, Debbie.'

'But we rarely see him,' Ma says.

'I see,' Nadia says at last.

'So we don't,' Ma says, her voice rising, 'actually know what "same as usual" means.'

Nadia looks out of the window at green and grey old England. I don't want Ma getting in one of her resentful states.

After this not another peep for about a decade and then road euphoria just bursts from Nadia.

'What good roads you have here! So smooth, so wide, so long!'

'Yes, they go all over,' I say.

'Wow. All over.'

Christ, don't they even have fucking roads over there?

Nadia whispers. We lean towards her to hear about her dear father's health. How often the old man pisses now, running for the pot clutching his crotch. The sad state of his old gums and his obnoxious breath. Ma and I watch this sweetie compulsively, wondering who she is: so close to us and made from my substance, and yet so other, telling us about Dad with an outrageous intimacy we can never share. We arrive home, and she says in an accent as thick as treacle (which makes me hoot to myself when I first hear it): 'I'm so tired now. If I could rest for a little while.'

'Sleep in my bed!' I cry.

Earlier I'd said to Ma I'd never give it up. But the moment my sister walks across the estate with us and finally stands there in our flat above the building site, drinking in all the oddness, picking up Ma's method books and her opera programmes, I melt, I melt. I'll have to kip in the living room from now on. But I'd kip in the toilet for her.

'In return for your bed,' she says, 'let me, I must, yes, give you something.'

She pulls a rug from her suitcase and presents it to Ma. 'This is from Dad.' Ma puts it on the floor, studies it and then treads on it.

And to me? I've always been a fan of crêpe paper and wrapped in it is the Pakistani dress I'm wearing now (with open-toed sandals – handmade). It's gorgeous: yellow and green, threaded with gold, thin summer material.

I'm due a trip to the dole office any minute now and I'm bracing myself for the looks I'll get in this gear. I'll keep you informed.

I write this outside my room waiting for Nadia to wake. Every fifteen minutes I tap lightly on the door like a worried nurse.

'Are you awake?' I whisper. And: 'Sister, sister.' I adore these new words. 'Do you want anything?'

I think I'm in love. At last.

Ma's gone out to take back her library books, leaving me to it. Ma's all heart, I expect you can see that. She's good and gentle and can't understand unkindness and violence. She thinks everyone's just waiting to be brought round to decency. 'This way we'll change the world a little bit,' she'd say, holding my hand and knocking on doors at elections. But she's lived on the edge of a nervous breakdown for as long as I can remember. She's had boyfriends before Howard but none of them lasted. Most of them were married because she was on this liberated kick of using men. There was one middle-class Labour Party smoothie I called Chubbie.

'Are you married?' I'd hiss when Ma went out of the room, sitting next to him and fingering his nylon tie.

'Yes.'

'You have to admit it, don't you? Where's your wife, then? She knows you're here? Get what you want this afternoon?'

You could see the men fleeing when they saw the deep needy well that Ma is, crying out to be filled with their love. And this monster kid with green hair glaring at them. Howard's too selfish and arrogant to be frightened of my ma's demands. He just ignores them.

What a job it is, walking round in this Paki gear!

I stop off at the chemist's to grab my drugs, my trancs. Jeanette, my friend on the estate, used to my eccentricities – the coonskin hat with the long rabbit tail, for example – comes along with me. The chemist woman in the white coat says to Jeanette, nodding at me when I hand over my script: 'Does she speak English?'

Becoming enthralled by this new me now, exotic and interior. With the scarf over my head I step into the Community Centre and look like a lost woman with village ways and chickens in the garden.

In a second, the communists and worthies are all over me. I mumble into my scarf. They give me leaflets and phone numbers. I'm oppressed, you see, beaten up, pig-ignorant with an arranged marriage and certain suttee ahead. But I get fed up and have a game of darts, a game of snooker and a couple of beers with a nice lesbian.

Home again I make my Nadia some pasta with red pepper, grated carrot, cheese and parsley. I run out to buy a bottle of white wine. Chasing along I see some kids on a passing bus. They eyeball me from the top deck, one of them black. They make a special journey down to the platform where the little monkeys swing on the pole and throw racial abuse from their gobs.

'Curry breath, curry breath, curry breath!'

The bus rushes on. I'm flummoxed.

She emerges at last, my Nadia, sleepy, creased around the eyes and dark. She sits at the table, eyelashes barely apart, not ready for small talk. I bring her the food and a glass of wine which she refuses with an upraised hand. I press my eyes into her, but she doesn't look at me. To puncture the silence I play her a jazz record – Wynton Marsalis's first. I ask her how she likes the record and she says nothing. Probably doesn't do much for her on first hearing. I watch her eating. She will not be interfered with.

She leaves most of the food and sits. I hand her a pair of black Levi 501s with the button fly. Plus a large cashmere polo-neck (stolen) and a black leather jacket.

'Try them on.'

She looks puzzled. 'It's the look I want you to have. You can wear any of my clothes.'

Still she doesn't move. I give her a little shove into the bedroom and shut the door. She should be so lucky. That's my best damn jacket. I wait. She comes out not wearing the clothes.

'Nina, I don't think so.'

I know how to get things done. I push her back in. She comes out, backwards, hands over her face.

'Show me, please.'

She spins round, arms out, hair jumping.

'Well?'

'The black suits your hair,' I manage to say. What a vast improvement on me, is all I can think. Stunning she is, dangerous, vulnerable, superior, with a jewel in her nose.

'But doesn't it . . . doesn't it make me look a little rough?'

'Oh yes! Now we're all ready to go. For a walk, yes? To see the sights and everything.'

'Is it safe?'

'Of course not. But I've got this.'

I show her.

'Oh, God, Nina. You would.'

Oh, this worries and ruins me. Already she has made up her mind about me and I haven't started on my excuses.

'Have you used it?'

'Only twice. Once on a racist in a pub. Once on some mugger who asked if I could spare him some jewellery.'

Her face becomes determined. She looks away. 'I'm training to be a doctor, you see. My life is set against human harm.'

She walks towards the door. I pack the switch-blade.

Daddy, these are the sights I show my sister. I tow her out of the flat and along the walkway. She sees the wind blaring through the busted windows. She catches her breath at the humming bad smells. Trapped dogs bark. She sees that one idiot's got on his door: *Dont burglar me theres nothin to steel ive got rid of it all.* She sees that some pig's sprayed on the wall: *Nina's a slag dog.* I push the lift button.

69

I've just about got her out of the building when the worst thing happens. There's three boys, ten or eleven years old, climbing out through a door they've kicked in. Neighbours stand and grumble. The kids've got a fat TV, a microwave oven and someone's favourite trainers under a little arm. The kid drops the trainers.

'Hey,' he says to Nadia (it's her first day here). Nadia stiffens. 'Hey, won't yer pick them up for me?'

She looks at me. I'm humming a tune. The tune is 'Just My Imagination'. I'm not scared of the little jerks. It's the bad impression that breaks my heart. Nadia picks up the trainers.

'Just tuck them right in there,' the little kid says, exposing his armpit.

'Won't they be a little large for you?' Nadia says.

'Eat shit.'

Soon we're out of there and into the air. We make for South Africa Road and the General Smuts pub. Kids play football behind wire. The old women in thick overcoats look like lagged boilers on little feet. They huff and shove carts full of chocolate and cat food.

I'm all tense now and ready to say anything. I feel such a need to say everything in the hope of explaining all that I give a guided tour of my heart and days.

I explain (I can't help myself): this happened here, that happened there. I got pregnant in that squat. I bought bad smack from that geezer in the yellow T-shirt and straw hat. I got attacked there and legged it through that park. I stole pens from that shop, dropping them into my motorcycle helmet. (A motorcycle helmet is very good for shoplifting, if you're interested.) Standing on that corner I cared for nothing and no one and couldn't walk on or stay where I was or go back. My gears had stopped engaging with my motor. Then I had a nervous breakdown.

Without comment she listens and nods and shakes her head sometimes. Is anyone in? I take her arm and move my cheek close to hers.

'I tell you this stuff which I haven't told anyone before. I want us to know each other inside out.'

She stops there in the street and covers her face with her hands.

'But my father told me of such gorgeous places!'

'Nadia, what d'you mean?'

'And you show me filth!' she cries. She touches my arm. 'Oh, Nina, it would be so lovely if you could make the effort to show me something attractive.'

Something attractive. We'll have to get the bus and go east, to Holland Park and round Ladbroke Grove. This is now honeyed London for the rich. Here there are *La* restaurants, wine bars, bookshops, estate agents more prolific than doctors, and attractive people in black, few of them ageing. Here there are health food shops where you buy tofu, nuts, live-culture yogurt and organic toothpaste. Here the sweet little black kids practise on steel drums under the motorway for the Carnival and old blacks sit out in the open on orange boxes shouting. Here the dope dealers in Versace suits travel in from the suburbs on commuter trains, carrying briefcases, trying to sell slummers bits of old car tyre to smoke.

And there are more stars than beggars. For example? Van Morrison in a big overcoat is hurrying towards somewhere in a nervous mood.

'Hiya, Van! Van? Won't ya even say hello!' I scream across the street. At my words Van the Man accelerates like a dog with a winklepicker up its anus.

She looks tired so I take her into Julie's Bar where they have the newspapers and we sit on well-woven cushions on long benches. Christ only know how much they have the cheek to charge for a cup of tea. Nadia looks better now. We sit there all friendly and she starts off.

'How often have you met our father?'

'I see him every two or three years. When he comes on business, he makes it his business to see me.'

'That's nice of him.'

'Yes, that's what he thinks. Can you tell me something, Nadia?' I move closer to her. 'When he'd get home, our father, what would he tell you about me?'

71

If only I wouldn't tempt everything so. But you know me: can't live on life with slack in it.

'Oh, he was worried, worried, worried.'

'Christ. Worried three times.'

'He said you . . . no.'

'He said what?'

'No, no, he didn't say it.'

'Yes, he did, Nadia.'

She sits there looking at badly dressed television producers in linen suits with her gob firmly closed.

'Tell me what my father said or I'll pour this pot of tea over my head.'

I pick up the teapot and open the lid for pouring-over-the-head convenience. Nadia says nothing; in fact she looks away. So what choice do I have but to let go a stream of tea over the top of my noddle? It drips down my face and off my chin. It's pretty scalding, I can tell you.

'He said, all right, he said you were like a wild animal!'

'Like a wild animal?' I say.

'Yes. And sometimes he wished he could shoot you to put you out of your misery.' She looks straight ahead of her. 'You asked for it. You made me say it.'

'The bastard. His own daughter.'

She holds my hand. For the first time, she looks at me, with wide-open eyes and urgent mouth. 'It's terrible, just terrible there in the house. Nina, I had to get away! And I'm in love with someone! Someone who's indifferent to me!'

'And?'

And nothing. She says no more except: 'It's too cruel, too cruel.'

I glance around. Now this is exactly the kind of place suitable for doing a runner from. You could be out the door, halfway up the street and on the tube before they'd blink. I'm about to suggest it to Nadia, but, as I've already told her about my smack addiction, my two abortions and poured a pot of tea over my head, I wouldn't want her to get a bad impression of me.

'I hope,' I say to her, 'I hope to God we can be friends as well as relations.'

Well, what a bastard my dad turned out to be! Wild animal! He's no angel himself. How could he say that? I was always on my best behaviour and always covered my wrists and arms. Now I can't stop thinking about him. It makes me cry.

This is how he used to arrive at our place, my daddy, in the days when he used to visit us.

First there's a whole day's terror and anticipation and getting ready. When Ma and I are exhausted, having practically cleaned the flat with our tongues, a black taxi slides over the horizon of the estate, rarer than an ambulance, with presents cheering on the back seat: champagne, bicycles, dresses that don't fit, books, dreams in boxes. Dad glows in a £3,000 suit and silk tie. Neighbours lean over the balconies to pleasure their eyeballs on the prince. It takes two or three of them working in shifts to hump the loot upstairs.

Then we're off in the taxi, speeding to restaurants with menus in French where Dad knows the manager. Dad tells us stories of extreme religion and hilarious corruption and when Ma catches herself laughing she bites her lip hard – why? I suppose she finds herself flying to the magnet of his charm once more.

After the grub we go to see a big show and Mum and Dad hold hands. All of these shows are written, on the later occasions, by Andrew Lloyd Webber.

This is all the best of life, except that, when Dad has gone and we have to slot back into our lives, we don't always feel like it. We're pretty uncomfortable, looking at each other and shuffling our ordinary feet once more in the mundane. Why does he always have to be leaving us?

After one of these occasions I go out, missing him. When alone, I talk to him. At five in the morning I get back. At eight Ma comes into my room and stands there, a woman alone and everything like that, in fury and despair.

'Are you involved in drugs and prostitution?'

I'd been going with guys for money. At the massage parlour you do as little as you can. None of them has disgusted me, and we have a laugh with them. Ma finds out because I've always got so much money. She knows the state of things. She stands over me.

'Yes.' No escape. I just say it. Yes, yes, yes.

'That's what I thought.'

'Yes, that is my life at the moment. Can I go back to sleep now? I'm expected at work at twelve.'

'Don't call it work, Nina. There are other words.'

She goes. Before her car has failed to start in the courtyard, I've run to the bathroom, filled the sink, taken Ma's lousy leg razor and jabbed into my wrists, first one, then the other, under water, digging for veins. (You should try it sometime; it's more difficult than you think: skin tough, throat contracting with vomit acid sour disgust.) The nerves in my hands went and they had to operate and everyone was annoyed that I'd caused such trouble.

Weeks later I vary the trick and swallow thirty pills and fly myself to a Surrey mental hospital where I do puzzles, make baskets and am fucked regularly for medicinal reasons by the art therapist who has a long nail on his little finger.

Suicide is one way of saying you're sorry.

With Nadia to the Tower of London, the Monument, Hyde Park, Buckingham Palace and something cultured with a lot of wigs at the National Theatre. Nadia keeps me from confession by small talk which wears into my shell like sugar into a tooth.

Ma sullen but doing a workmanlike hospitality job. Difficult to get Nadia out of her room most of the time. Hours she spends in the bathroom every day experimenting with make-up. And then Howard the hero decides to show up.

Ma not home yet. Early evening. Guess what? Nadia is sitting across the room on the sofa with Howard. This is their first meeting and they're practically on each other's laps. (I almost wrote lips.) All afternoon I've had to witness this meeting of minds.

They're on politics. The words that ping off the walls are: pluralism, democracy, theocracy and Benazir! Howard's senses are on their toes! The little turd can't believe the same body (in a black cashmere sweater and black leather jacket) can contain such intelligence, such beauty, and yet jingle so brightly with facts about the Third World! There in her bangles and perfume I see her speak to him as she hasn't spoken to me once – gesticulating!

'Howard. I say this to you from my heart, it is a corrupt country! Even the revolutionaries are corrupt! No one has any hope!'

In return he asks, surfacing through the Niagara of her conversation: 'Nadia, can I show you something? Videos of the TV stuff I've written?'

She can't wait.

None of us has seen her come in. Ma is here now, coat on, bags in her hands, looking at Nadia and Howard sitting so close their elbows keep knocking together.

'Hello,' she says to Howard, eventually. 'Hiya,' to Nadia. Ma has bought herself some flowers, which she has under her arm – carnations. Howard doesn't get up to kiss her. He's touching no one but Nadia and he's very pleased with himself. Nadia nods at Ma but her eyes rush back to Howard the hero.

Nadia says to Howard: 'The West doesn't care if we're an undemocratic country.'

'I'm exhausted,' Ma says.

'Well,' I say to her. 'Hello, anyway.'

Ma and I unpack the shopping in the kitchen. Howard calls through to Ma, asking her school questions which she ignores. The damage has been done. Oh yes. Nadia has virtually ignored Ma in her own house. Howard, I can see, is pretty uncomfortable at this. He is about to lift himself out of the seat when Nadia puts her hand on his arm and asks him: 'How do you create?'

'How do I create?'

How does Howard create? With four word-kisses she has induced in Howard a Nelson's Column of excitement. 'How do you create?' is the last thing you should ever ask one of these guys.

'They get along well, don't they?' Ma says, watching them through the crack of the door. I lean against the fridge.

'Why shouldn't they?'

'No reason,' she says. 'Except that this is my home. Everything I do outside here is a waste of time and no one thanks me for it and no one cares for me, and now I'm excluded from my own flat!'

'Hey, Ma, don't get –'

'Pour me a bloody whisky, will you?'

I pour her one right away. 'Your supper's in the oven, Ma.' I give her the whisky. My ma cups her hands round the glass. Always been a struggle for her. Her dad in the army; white trash. She had to fight to learn. 'It's fish pie. And I did the washing and ironing.'

'You've always been good in that way, I'll give you that. Even when you were sick you'd do the cooking. I'd come home and there it would be. I'd eat it alone and leave the rest outside your door. It was like feeding a hamster. You can be nice.'

'Are you sure?'

'Only your niceness has to live among so many other wild elements. Women that I know. Their children are the same. A tragedy or a disappointment. Their passions are too strong. It is our era in England. I only wish, I only wish you could have some kind of career or something.'

I watch her and she turns away to look at Howard all snug with the sister I brought here. Sad Ma is, and gentle. I could take her in my arms to console her now for what I am, but I don't want to indulge her. A strange question occurs to me. 'Ma, why do you keep Howard on?'

She sits on the kitchen stool and sips her drink. She looks at the lino for about three minutes, without saying anything, gathering herself up, punching her fist against her leg, like someone who's just swallowed a depth charge. Howard's explaining voice drifts through to us.

Ma gets up and kick-slams the door.

'Because I love him even if he doesn't love me!'

Her tumbler smashes on the floor and glass skids around our feet.

'Because I need sex and why shouldn't I! Because I'm lonely, I'm lonely, okay, and I need someone bright to talk to! D'you think I can talk to you? D'you think you'd ever be interested in me for one minute?'

'Ma –'

'You've never cared for me! And then you brought Nadia here against my wishes to be all sweet and hypercritical and remind me of all the terrible past and the struggle of being alone for so long!'

Ma sobbing in her room. Howard in with her. Nadia and me sit together at the two ends of the sofa. My ears are scarlet with the hearing of Ma's plain sorrow through the walls. 'Yes, I care for you,' Howard's voice rises. 'I love you, baby. And I love Nina, too. Both of you.'

'I don't know, Howard. You don't ever show it.'

'But I'm blocked as a human being!'

I say to Nadia: 'Men are pretty selfish bastards who don't understand us. That's all I know.'

'Howard's an interesting type,' she says coolly. 'Very open-minded in an artistic way.'

I'm getting protective in my old age and very pissed off.

'He's my mother's boyfriend and long-standing lover.'

'Yes, I know that.'

'So lay off him. Please, Nadia. Please understand.'

'What are you, of all people, accusing me of?'

I'm not too keen on this 'of all people' business. But get this.

'I thought you advanced Western people believed in the free intermingling of the sexes?'

'Yes, we do. We intermingle all the time.'

'What then, Nina, is your point?'

'It's him,' I explain, moving in. 'He has all the weaknesses. One kind word from a woman and he thinks they want to sleep with him. Two kind words and he thinks he's the only man in the world. It's a form of mental illness, of delusion. I wouldn't tangle with that deluded man if I were you!'

All right!

A few days later.

Here I am slouching at Howard's place. Howard's hole, or 'sock' as he calls it, is a red-brick mansion block with public-school, stately dark oak corridors, off Kensington High Street. Things have been getting grimmer and grimmer. Nadia stays in her room or else goes out and pops her little camera at 'history'. Ma goes to every meeting she hears of. I'm just about ready for artery road.

I've just done you a favour. I could have described every moment of us sitting through Howard's television *œuvre* (which I always thought meant *egg*). But no – on to the juicy bits!

There they are in front of me, Howard and Nadia cheek to cheek, within breath-inhaling distance of each other, going through the script.

Earlier this morning we went shopping in Covent Garden. Nadia wanted my advice on what clothes to buy. So we went for a couple of sharp dogtooth jackets, distinctly city, fine brown and white wool, the jacket caught in at the waist with a black leather belt; short panelled skirt; white silk polo-neck shirt; plus black pillbox, suede gloves, high heels. If she likes something, if she wants it, she buys it. The rich. Nadia bought me a linen jacket.

Maybe I'm sighing too much. They glance at me with undelight.

'I can take Nadia home if you like,' Howard says.

'I'll take care of my sister,' I say. 'But I'm out for a stroll now. I'll be back at any time.'

I stroll towards a café in Rotting Hill. I head up through Holland Park, past the blue sloping roof of the Commonwealth Institute (or Nigger's Corner as we used to call it) in which on a school trip I pissed into a wastepaper basket. Past modern nannies – young women like me with dyed black hair – walking dogs and kids.

The park's full of hip kids from Holland Park School, smoking on the grass; black guys with flat-tops and muscles; yuppies skimming frisbees and stuff; white boys playing Madonna and Prince. There are cruising turd-burglars with active eyes, and the usual

London liggers, hang-gliders and no-goodies waiting to sign on. I feel outside everything, so up I go, through the flower-verged alley at the end of the park, where the fudge-packers used to line up at night for fucking. On the wall it says: *Gay solidarity is class solidarity.*

Outside the café is a police van with grilles over the windows full of little piggies giggling with their helmets off. It's a common sight around here, but the streets are a little quieter than usual. I walk past an Asian policewoman standing in the street who says hello to me. 'Auntie Tom,' I whisper and go into the café.

In this place they play the latest calypso and soca and the new Eric Satie recording. A white Rasta sits at the table with me. He pays for my tea. I have chilli with a baked potato and grated cheese, with tomato salad on the side, followed by Polish cheesecake. People in the café are more subdued than normal; all the pigs making everyone nervous. But what a nice guy the Rasta is. Even nicer, he takes my hand under the table and drops something in my palm. A chunky chocolate lozenge of dope.

'Hey. I'd like to buy some of this,' I say, wrapping my swooning nostrils round it.

'Sweetheart, it's all I've got,' he says. 'You take it. My last lump of blow.'

He leaves. I watch him go. As he walks across the street in his jumble-sale clothes, his hair jabbing out from his head like tiny bedsprings, the police get out of their van and stop him. He waves his arms at them. The van unpacks. There's about six of them surrounding him. There's an argument. He's giving them some heavy lip. They search him. One of them is pulling his hair. Everyone in the café is watching. I pop the dope into my mouth and swallow it. Yum yum.

I go out into the street now. I don't care. My friend shouts across to me: 'They're planting me. I've got nothing.'

I tell the bastard pigs to leave him alone. 'It's true! The man's got nothing!' I give them a good shouting at. One of them comes at me.

'You wanna be arrested too!' he says, shoving me in the chest.

'I don't mind,' I say. And I don't, really. Ma would visit me.

Some kids gather round, watching the rumpus. They look really straggly and pathetic and dignified and individual and defiant at the same time. I feel sorry for us all. The pigs pull my friend into the van. It's the last I ever see of him. He's got two years of trouble ahead of him, I know.

When I get back from my walk they're sitting on Howard's Habitat sofa. Something is definitely going on, and it ain't cultural. They're too far apart for comfort. Beadily I shove my aerial into the air and take the temperature. Yeah, can't I just smell humming dodginess in the atmosphere?

'Come on,' I say to Nadia. 'Ma will be waiting.'

'Yes, that's true,' Howard says, getting up. 'Give her my love.'

I give him one of my looks. 'All of it or just a touch?'

We're on the bus, sitting there nice and quiet, the bus going along past the shops and people and the dole office when these bad things start to happen that I can't explain. The seats in front of me, the entire top deck of the bus in fact, keeps rising up. I turn my head to the window expecting that the street at least will be anchored to the earth, but it's not. The whole street is throwing itself up at my head and heaving about and bending like a high rise in a tornado. The shops are dashing at me, at an angle. The world has turned into a monster. For God's sake, nothing will keep still, but I've made up my mind to have it out. So I tie myself to the seat by my fists and say to Nadia, at least I think I say, 'You kiss him?'

She looks straight ahead as if she's been importuned by a beggar. I'm about to be hurled out of the bus, I know. But I go right ahead.

'Nadia. You did, right? You did.'

'But it's not important.'

Wasn't I right? Can't I sniff a kiss in the air at a hundred yards?

'Kissing's not important?'

'No,' she says. 'It's not, Nina. It's just affection. That's normal. But Howard and I have much to say to each other.' She seems depressed suddenly. 'He knows I'm in love with somebody.'

'I'm not against talking. But it's possible to talk without r-r-rubbing your tongues against each other's tonsils.'

'You have a crude way of putting things,' she replies, turning sharply to me and rising up to the roof of the bus. 'It's a shame you'll never understand passion.'

I am crude, yeah. And I'm about to be crushed into the corner of the bus by two hundred brown balloons. Oh, sister.

'Are you feeling sick?' she says, getting up.

The next thing I know we're stumbling off the moving bus and I lie down on an unusual piece of damp pavement outside the Albert Hall. The sky swings above me. Nadia's face hovers over mine like ectoplasm. Then she has her hand flat on my forehead in a doctory way. I give it a good hard slap.

'Why are you crying?'

If our father could see us now.

'Your bad behaviour with Howard makes me cry for my ma.'

'Bad behaviour? Wait till I tell my father –'

'Our father –'

'About you.'

'What will you say?'

'I'll tell him you've been a prostitute and a drug addict.'

'Would you say that, Nadia?'

'No,' she says, eventually. 'I suppose not.'

She offers me her hand and I take it.

'It's time I went home,' she says.

'Me, too,' I say.

3

It's not Friday, but Howard comes with us to Heathrow. Nadia flicks through fashion magazines, looking at clothes she won't be able to buy now. Her pride and dignity today is monstrous. Howard hands me a pile of books and writing pads and about twelve pens.

'Don't they have pens over there?' I say.

'It's a Third World country,' he says. 'They lack the basic necessities.'

Nadia slaps his arm. 'Howard, of course we have pens, you stupid idiot!'

'I was joking,' he says. 'They're for me.' He tries to stuff them all into the top pocket of his jacket. They spill on the floor. 'I'm writing something that might interest you all.'

'Everything you write interests us,' Nadia says.

'Not necessarily,' Ma says.

'But this is especially . . . relevant,' he says.

Ma takes me aside: 'If you must go, do write, Nina. And don't tell your father one thing about me!'

Nadia distracts everyone by raising her arms and putting her head back and shouting out in the middle of the airport: 'No, no, no, I don't want to go!'

My room, this cell, this safe, bare box stuck on the side of my father's house, has a stone floor and whitewashed walls. It has a single bed, my open suitcase, no wardrobe, no music. Not a frill in the grill. On everything there's a veil of khaki dust waiting to irritate my nostrils. The window is tiny, just twice the size of my head. So it's pretty gloomy here. Next door there's a smaller room with an amateur shower, a sink and a hole in the ground over which you have to get used to squatting if you want to piss and shit.

Despite my moans, all this suits me fine. In fact, I requested this room. At first Dad wanted Nadia and me to share. But here I'm out of everyone's way, especially my two other half-sisters: Gloomie and Moonie I call them.

I wake up and the air is hot, hot, hot, and the noise and petrol fumes rise around me. I kick into my jeans and pull my Keith Haring T-shirt on. Once, on the King's Road, two separate people came up to me and said: 'Is that a Keith Haring T-shirt?'

Outside, the sun wants to burn you up. The light is different too: you can really see things. I put my shades on. These are cool shades. There aren't many women you see in shades here.

The driver is revving up one of Dad's three cars outside my room. I open the door of a car and jump in, except that it's like throwing your arse into a fire, and I jiggle around, the driver laughing, his teeth jutting as if he never saw anything funny before.

'Drive me,' I say. 'Drive me somewhere in all this sunlight. Please. Please.' I touch him and he pulls away from me. Well, he is rather handsome. 'These cars don't need to be revved. Drive!'

He turns the wheel back and forth, pretending to drive and hit the horn. He's youngish and thin – they all look undernourished here – and he always teases me.

'You stupid bugger.'

See, ain't I just getting the knack of speaking to servants? It's taken me at least a week to erase my natural politeness to the poor.

'Get going! Get us out of this drive!'

'No shoes, no shoes, Nina!' He's pointing at my feet.

'No bananas, no pineapples,' I say. 'No job for you either, Lulu. You'll be down the Job Centre if you don't shift it.'

Off we go then, the few yards to the end of the drive. The guard at the gate waves. I turn to look back and there you are standing on the porch of your house in your pyjamas, face covered with shaving cream, a piece of white sheet wrapped around your head because you've just oiled your hair. Your arms are waving not goodbye. Gloomie, my suddenly acquired sister, runs out behind you and shakes her fists, the dogs barking in their cage, the chickens screaming in theirs. Ha, ha.

We drive slowly through the estate on which Dad lives with all the other army and navy and air force people: big houses and big bungalows set back from the road, with sprinklers on the lawn, some with swimming pools, all with guards.

We move out on to the Superhighway, among the painted trucks, gaudier than Chinese dolls, a sparrow among peacocks. What a crappy road and no fun, like driving on the moon. Dad says the builders steal the materials, flog them and then there's not enough left to finish the road. So they just stop and leave whole stretches incomplete.

The thing about this place is that there's always something happening. Good or bad it's a happening place. And I'm thinking this, how cheerful I am and everything, when bouncing along in the opposite direction is a taxi, an old yellow and black Morris Minor stuck together with sellotape. It's swerving in and out of the traffic very fast until the driver loses it, and the taxi bangs the back of the car in front, glances off another and shoots off across the Superhighway and is coming straight for us. I can see the driver's face when Lulu finally brakes. Three feet from us the taxi flies into a wall that runs alongside the road. The two men keep travelling, and their heads crushed into their chests pull their bodies through the windscreen and out into the morning air. They look like Christmas puddings.

Lulu accelerates. I grab him and scream at him to stop but we go faster and faster.

'Damn dead,' he says, when I've finished clawing him. 'A wild country. This kind of thing happen in England, yes?'

'Yes, I suppose so.'

Eventually I persuade him to stop and I get out of the car.

I'm alone in the bazaar, handling jewellery and carpets and pots and I'm confused. I know I have to get people presents. Especially Howard the hero who's paying for this. Ah, there's just the thing: a cage the size of a big paint tin, with three chickens inside. The owner sees me looking. He jerks a chicken out, decapitates it on a block and holds it up to my face, feathers flying into my hair.

I walk away and dodge a legless brat on a four-wheeled trolley made out of a door, who hurls herself at me and then disappears through an alley and across the sewers. Everywhere the sick and the uncured, and I'm just about ready for lunch when everyone starts running. They're jumping out of the road and pulling their kids away. There is a tidal wave of activity, generated by three big covered trucks full of soldiers crashing through the bazaar, the men standing still and nonchalant with rifles in the back. I'm half knocked to hell by some prick tossed off a bike. I am tiptoeing my way out along the edge of a fucking sewer, shit lapping against my shoes. I've just about had enough of this country, I'm just about to call for South Africa Road, when –

'Lulu,' I shout. 'Lulu.'

'I take care of you,' he says. 'Sorry for touching.'

He takes me back to the car. Fat, black buffalo snort and shift in the mud. I don't like these animals being everywhere, chickens and dogs and stuff, with sores and bleeding and threats and fear.

'You know?' I say. 'I'm lonely. There's no one I can talk to. No one to laugh with here, Lulu. And I think they hate me, my family. Does your family hate you?'

I stretch and bend and twist in the front garden in T-shirt and shorts. I pull sheets of air into my lungs. I open my eyes a moment and the world amazes me, its brightness. A servant is watching me, peeping round a tree.

'Hey, peeper!' I call, and carry on. When I look again, I notice the cook and the sweeper have joined him and they shake and trill.

'What am I doing?' I say. 'Giving a concert?'

In the morning papers I notice that potential wives are advertised as being 'virtuous and fair-skinned'. Why would I want to be unvirtuous and brown? But I do, I do!

I take a shower in my room and stroll across to the house. I stand outside your room, Dad, where the men always meet in the early evenings. I look through the wire mesh of the screen door and there you are, my father for all these years. And this is what you were doing while I sat in the back of the class at my school in Shepherd's Bush, pregnant, wondering why you didn't love me.

In the morning when I'm having my breakfast we meet in the living room by the bar and you ride on your exercise bicycle. You pant and look at me now and again, your stringy body sways and tightens, but you say fuck all. If I speak, you don't hear. You're one of those old-fashioned romantic men for whom women aren't really there unless you decide we are.

Now you lie on your bed and pluck up food with one hand and read an American comic with the other. A servant, a young boy, presses one of those fat vibrating electric instruments you see advertised in the *Observer* Magazine on to your short legs. You look up and see me. The sight of me angers you. You wave furiously for me to come in. No. Not yet. I walk on.

In the women's area of the house, where visitors rarely visit, Dad's wife sits sewing.

'Hello,' I say. 'I think I'll have a piece of sugar cane.'

I want to ask the names of the other pieces of fruit on the table, but Wifey is crabby inside and out, doesn't speak English and disapproves of me in all languages. She has two servants with her, squatting there watching Indian movies on the video. An old woman who was once, I can see, a screen goddess, now sweeps the floor on her knees with a handful of twigs. Accidentally, sitting there swinging my leg, I touch her back with my foot, leaving a dusty mark on her clothes.

'Imagine,' I say to Wifey.

I slip the sugar cane into my mouth. The squirting juice bounces off my taste buds. I gob out the sucked detritus and chuck it in front of the screen goddess's twigs. You can really enjoy talking to someone who doesn't understand you.

'Imagine my dad leaving my ma for you! And you don't ever leave that seat there. Except once a month you go to the bank to check up on your jewellery.'

Wifey keeps all her possessions on the floor around her. She is definitely mad. But I like the mad here: they just wander around the place with everyone else and no one bothers you and people give you food.

'You look like a bag lady. D'you know what a bag lady is?'

Moonie comes into the room. She's obviously heard every word I've said. She starts to yell at me. Wifey's beaky nozzle turns to me with interest now. Something's happening that's even more interesting than TV. They want to crush me. I think they like me here for that reason. If you could see, Ma, what they're doing to me just because you met a man at a dance in the Old Kent Road and his French letter burst as you lay in front of a gas fire with your legs up!

'You took the car when we had to go out to work!' yells Moonie. 'You forced the driver to take you! We had to sack him!'

'Why sack him?'

'He's naughty! Naughty! You said he drives you badly! Nearly killed! You're always causing trouble, Nina, doing some stupid thing, some very stupid thing!'

Gloomie and Moonie are older than Nadia and me. Both have been married, kicked around by husbands arranged by Dad, and separated. That was their small chance in life. Now they've come back to Daddy. Now they're secretaries. Now they're blaming me for everything.

'By the way. Here.' I reach into my pocket. 'Take this.'

Moonie's eyes bulge at my open palm. Her eyes quieten her mouth. She starts fatly towards me. She sways. She comes on. Her hand snatches at the lipstick.

'Now you'll be able to come out with me. We'll go to the Holiday Inn.'

'Yes, but you've been naughty.' She is distracted by the lipstick. 'What colour is it?'

'Can't you leave her alone for God's sake? Always picking on her!' This is Nadia coming into the room after work. She throws herself into a chair. 'I'm so tired.' To the servant she says: 'Bring me some tea.' At me she smiles. 'Hello, Nina. Good day? You were doing some exercises, I hear. They rang me at work to tell me.'

'Yes, Nadia.'

'Oh, sister, they have such priorities.'

For the others I am 'cousin'. From the start there's been embarrassment about how I am to be described. Usually, if it's Moonie or Gloomie they say: 'This is our distant cousin from England.' It amuses me to see my father deal with this. He can't bring himself to say either 'cousin' or 'daughter' so he just says Nina and leaves it. But of course everyone knows I am his illegitimate daughter. But Nadia is the real 'daughter' here. 'Nadia is an impressive person,' my father says, on my first day here, making it clear that I am diminished, the sort with dirt under her nails. Yes, she is clever, soon to be doctor, life-saver. Looking at her now she seems less small than she did in London. I'd say she has enough dignity for the entire government.

'They tear-gassed the hospital.'

'Who?'

'The clever police. Some people were demonstrating outside. The police broke it up. When they chased the demonstrators inside they tear-gassed them! What a day! What a country! I must wash my face.' She goes out.

'See, see!' Moonie trills. 'She is better than you! Yes, yes, yes!'

'I expect so. It's not difficult.'

'We know she is better than you for certain!'

I walk out of all this and into my father's room. It's like moving from one play to another. What is happening on this set? The room is perfumed with incense from a green coiled creation which burns outside the doors, causing mosquitoes to drop dead. Advanced telephones connect him to Paris, Dubai, London. On the video is an American movie. Five youths rape a woman. Father – what do I call him, Dad? – sits on the edge of the bed with his little legs sticking out. The servant teases father's feet into his socks.

'You'll get sunstroke,' he says, as if he's known me all my life and has the right to be high-handed. 'Cavorting naked in the garden.'

'Naked is it now?'

'We had to sack the driver, too. Sit down.'

I sit in the row of chairs beside him. It's like visiting someone in hospital. He lies on his side in his favourite mocking-me-for-sport position.

'Now –'

The lights go out. The TV goes off. I shut my eyes and laugh. Power cut. Father bounces up and down on the bed. 'Fuck this motherfucking country!' The servant rushes for candles and lights them. As it's Friday I sit here and think of Ma and Howard meeting today for food, talk and sex. I think Howard's not so bad after all, and even slightly good-looking. He's never deliberately hurt Ma. He has other women – but that's only vanity, a weakness, not a crime – and he sees her only on Friday, but he hasn't undermined her. What more can you expect from men? Ma loves him a lot – from the first moment, she says; she couldn't help herself. She's still trusting and open, despite everything.

Never happen to me.

Dad turns to me: 'What do you do in England for God's sake?'

'Nadia has already given you a full report, hasn't she?'

A full report? For two days I gaped through the window lip-reading desperately as nose to nose, whispering and giggling, eyebrows shooting up, jaws dropping like guillotines, hands rubbing, Father and Nadia conducted my prosecution. The two rotund salt and pepper pots, Moonie and Gloomie, guarded the separate entrances to this room.

'Yes, but I want the full confession from your mouth.'

He loves to tease. But he is a dangerous person. Tell him something and soon everyone knows about it.

'Confess to what?'

'That you just roam around here and there. You do fuck all full time, in other words.'

'Everyone in England does fuck all except for the yuppies.'

'And do you go with one boy or with many?' I say nothing. 'But your mother has a boy, yes? Some dud writer, complete failure and playboy with unnatural eyebrows that cross in the middle?'

'Is that how Nadia described the man she tried to –'

'What?'

'Be rather close friends with?'

The servant has a pair of scissors. He trims Father's hair, he snips in Father's ear, he investigates Father's nostrils with the clipping steel shafts. He attaches a tea-cloth to Father's collar, lathers Father's face, sharpens the razor on the strop and shaves Father clean and reddish.

'Not necessarily,' says Father, spitting foam. 'I use my imagination. Nadia says eyebrows and I see bushes.'

He says to his servant and indicates me: 'An Englisher born and bred, eh?'

The servant falls about with the open razor.

'But you belong with us,' Dad says. 'Don't worry, I'll put you on the right track. But first there must be a strict course of discipline.'

The room is full of dressed-up people sitting around Dad's bed looking at him lying there in his best clothes. Dad yells out cheerful slanders about the tax evaders, bribe-takers and general scumbags who can't make it this evening. Father obviously a most popular man here. It's better to be entertaining than good. Ma would be drinking bleach by now.

At last Dad gives the order they've been waiting for.

'Bring the booze.'

The servant unlocks the cabinet and brings out the whisky.

'Give everyone a drink except Nina. She has to get used to the pure way of life!' he says, and everyone laughs at me.

The people here are tractor dealers (my first tractor dealer!), journalists, landowners and a newspaper tycoon aged thirty-one who inherited a bunch of papers. He's immensely cultured and massively fat. I suggest you look at him from the front and tell me if he doesn't look like a flounder. I look up to see my sister standing at the window of Dad's room, straining her heart's wet eyes at the Flounder who doesn't want to marry her because he already has the most pleasant life there is in the world.

Now here's a message for you fuckers back home. The men here invite Nadia and me to their houses, take us to their club, play tennis with us. They're chauvinistic as hell, but they put on a great show. They're funny and spend money and take you to their farms and show you their guns and kill a snake in front of your eyes. They flirt and want to poke their things in you, but they don't expect it.

Billy slides into the room in his puffy baseball jacket and pink plimsolls and patched jeans. He stands there and puts his hands in his pockets and takes them out again.

'Hey, Billy, have a drink.'

'OK. Thanks . . . Yeah. OK.'

'Don't be shy,' Dad says. 'Nina's not shy.'

So the entire room looks at shy Billy and Billy looks at the ground.

'No, well, I could do with a drink. Just one. Thanks.'

The servant gets Billy a drink. Someone says to someone else: 'He looks better since he had that break in Lahore.'

'It did him the whole world of damn good.'

'Terrible what happened to the boy.'

'Yes. Yes. Ghastly rotten.'

Billy comes and sits next to me. Their loud talking goes on.

'I've heard about you,' he says under the talking. 'They talk about you non-stop.'

'Goody.'

'Yeah. Juicy Fruit?' he says.

He sits down on the bed and I open my case and give him all my tapes.

'Latest stuff from England.'

He goes through them eagerly. 'You can't get any of this stuff here. This is the best thing that has ever happened to me.' He looks at me. 'Can I? Can I borrow them? Would you mind, you know?' I nod. 'My room is on top of the house. I'll never be far away.'

Oh, kiss me now! Though I can see that's a little premature, especially in a country where they cut off your arms or something for adultery. I like your black jeans.

'What's your accent?' I say.

'Canadian.' He gets up. No, don't leave now. Not yet. 'Wanna ride?' he says.

In the drive the chauffeurs smoke and talk. They stop talking. They watch us. Billy puts his baseball cap on my head and touches my hair.

91

'Billy, push the bike out into the street so no one hears us leave.'

I ask him about himself. His mother was Canadian. She died. His father was Pakistani, though Billy was brought up in Vancouver. I turn and Moonie is yelling at me. 'Nina, Nina, it's late. Your father must see you now about a strict discipline business he has to discuss!'

'Billy, keep going.'

He just keeps pushing the bike, oblivious of Moonie. He glances at me now and again, as if he can't believe his luck. I can't believe mine, baby!

'So Pop and I came home to live. Home. This place isn't my home. But he always wanted to come home.'

We push the bike up the street till we get to the main road.

'This country was a shock after Vancouver,' he says.

'Same for me.'

'Yeah?' He gets sharp. 'But I'd been brought here to live. How can you ever understand what that's like?'

'I can't. All right, I fucking can't.'

He goes on. 'We were converting a house in 'Pindi, Pop and me. Digging the foundations, plastering the walls, doing the plumbing . . .'

We get on the bike and I hold him.

'Out by the beach, Billy.'

'Yeah. But it's not simple. You know the cops stop couples and ask to see their wedding certificates.'

It's true but fuck it. Slowly, stately, the two beige outlaws ride through the city of open fires. I shout an Aretha Franklin song into the night. Men squat by busted cars. Wild maimed pye-dogs run in our path. Traffic careers through dust, past hotels and air-line buildings, past students squatting beside traffic lights to read, near where there are terrorist explosions and roads melt like plastic.

To the beach without showing our wedding certificate. It's more a desert than a beach. There's just sand: no shops, no hotels, no ice-creamers, no tattooists. Utterly dark. Your eyes search for a light in panic, for safety. But the curtains of the world are well and truly pulled here.

I guide Billy to the Flounder's beach hut. Hut – this place is bigger than Ma's flat. We push against the back door and we're in the large living room. Billy and I dance about and chuck open the shutters. Enter moonlight and the beach as Billy continues his Dad rap.

'Pop asked me to drill some holes in the kitchen. But I had to empty the wheelbarrow. So he did the drilling. He hit a cable or something. Anyway, he's dead, isn't he?'

We kiss for a long time, about forty minutes. There's not a lot you can do in kissing; half an hour of someone's tongue in your mouth could seem an eternity, but what there is to do, we do. I take off all my clothes and listen to the sea and almost cry for missing South Africa Road so. But at least there is the light friction of our lips together, barely touching. Harder. I pull the strong bulk of his head towards mine, pressing my tongue to the corner of his mouth. Soon I pass through the mouth's parting to trace the inside curve of his lips. Suddenly his tongue fills my mouth, invading me, and I clench it with my teeth. Oh, oh, oh. As he withdraws I follow him, sliding my tongue into the oven of his gob and lie there on the bench by the open shutters overlooking the Arabian Sea, connected by tongue and saliva, my fingers in his ears and hair, his finger inside my body, our bodies dissolving until we forget ourselves and think of nothing, thank fuck.

It's still dark and no more than ninety minutes have passed, when I hear a car pulling up outside the hut. I shake Billy awake, push him off me and pull him across the hut and into the kitchen. The fucking door's warped and won't shut so we just lie down on the floor next to each other. I clam Billy up with my hand over his gob. There's a shit smell right next to my nose. I start to giggle. I stuff Billy's fingers into my mouth. He's laughing all over the place too. But we shut up sharpish when a couple come into the hut and start to move around. For some reason I imagine we're going to be shot.

The man says: 'Curious, indeed. My sister must have left the shutters open last time she came here.'

The other person says it's lovely, the moonlight and so on. Then there's no talking. I can't see a sausage but my ears are at full stretch. Yes, kissing noises.

Nadia says: 'Here's the condoms, Bubble!'

My sister and the Flounder! Well. The Flounder lights a lantern. Yes, there they are now, I can see them: she's trying to pull his long shirt over his head, and he's resisting.

'Just my bottoms!' he squeals. 'My stomach! Oh, my God!'

I'm not surprised he's ashamed, looking in this low light at the size of the balcony over his toy shop.

I hear my name. Nadia starts to tell the Flounder – or 'Bubble' as she keeps calling him – how the Family Planning in London gave me condoms. The Flounder's clucking with disapproval and lying on the bench by the window looking like a hippo, with my sister squatting over his guts, rising and sitting, sighing and exclaiming sometimes, almost in surprise. They chat away quite naturally, fucking and gossiping and the Flounder talks about me. Am I promiscuous, he wants to know. Do I do it with just anyone? How is my father going to discipline me now he's got his hands on me? Billy shifts about. He could easily be believing this shit. I wish I had some paper and a pen to write him a note. I kiss him gently instead. When I kiss him I get a renewal of this strange sensation that I've never felt before today: I feel it's Billy I'm kissing, not just his lips or body, but some inside thing, as if his skin is just a representative of all of him, his past and his blood. Amour has never been this personal for me before!

Nadia and the Flounder are getting hotter. She keeps asking Bubble why they can't do this every day. He says, yes, yes, yes, and won't you tickle my balls? I wonder how she'll find them. Then the Flounder shudders and Nadia, moving in rhythm like someone doing a slow dance, has to stop. 'Bubble!' she says and slaps him, as if he's a naughty child that's just thrown up. A long fart escapes Bubble's behind. 'Oh, Bubble,' she says, and falls on to him, holding him closer.

Soon he is asleep. Nadia unstraddles him and moves to a chair and has a little cry as she sits looking at him. She only wants to be held and kissed and touched. I feel like going to her myself.

When I wake up it's daylight and they're sitting there together, talking about their favourite subject. The Flounder is smoking and she is trying to masturbate him.

'So why did she come here with you?' he is asking. Billy opens his eyes and doesn't know where he is. Then he sighs. I agree with him. What a place to be, what a thing to be doing! (But then, come to think of it, you always find me in the kitchen at parties.)

'Nina just asked me one day at breakfast. I had no choice and this man, Howard –'

'Yes, yes,' the Flounder laughs. 'You said he was handsome.'

'I only said he had nice hair,' she says.

But I'm in sympathy with the Flounder here, finding this compliment a little gratuitous. The Flounder gets up. He's ready to go.

And so is Billy. 'I can't stand much more of this,' he says. Nadia suddenly jerks her head towards us. For a moment I think she's seen us. But the Flounder distracts her.

I hear the tinkle of the car keys and the Flounder says: 'Here, put your panties on. Wouldn't want to leave your panties here on the floor. But let me kiss them first! I kiss them!'

There are sucky kissing noises. Billy is twitching badly and drumming his heels on the floor. Nadia looks at the Flounder with his face buried in a handful of white cotton.

'And,' he says with a muffled voice, 'I'm getting lead in my pencil again, Nadia. Let us lie down, my pretty one.'

The Flounder takes her hand enthusiastically and jerks it towards his ding-dong. She smacks him away. She's not looking too pleased.

'I've got my pants on, you bloody fool!' Nadia says harshly. 'That pair of knickers you've sunk your nose in must belong to another woman you've had here!'

'What! But I've had no other woman here!' The Flounder glares at her furiously. He examines the panties, as if hoping to find a name inside. 'Marks & Spencers. How strange. I feel sick now.'

'Marks & Spencers! Fuck this!' says Billy, forcing my hands off his face. 'My arms and legs are going to fucking drop off in a minute!'

So up gets Billy. He combs his hair and turns up the collar of his shirt and then strolls into the living room singing a couple of choruses from The The. I get up and follow him, just in time to see Nadia open her mouth and let off a huge scream at the sight of us. The Flounder, who has no bottoms on, gives a frightened yelp and drops my pants which I pick up and, quite naturally, put on. I'm calm and completely resigned to the worst. Anyway, I've got my arm round Billy.

'Hi, everyone,' Billy says. 'We were just asleep in the other room. Don't worry, we didn't hear anything, not about the condoms or Nina's character or the panties or anything. Not a thing. How about a cup of tea or something?'

I get off Billy's bike midday. 'Baby,' he says.

'Happy,' I say, wearing his checked shirt, tail out. Across the lawn with its sprinkler I set off for Dad's club, a sun-loved white palace set in flowers.

White-uniformed bearers humble as undertakers set down trays of foaming yogurt. I could do with a proper drink myself. Colonels with generals and ladies with perms, fans and crossed legs sit in cane chairs. I wish I'd slept more.

The old man. There you are, blazer and slacks, turning the pages of *The Times* on an oak lectern overlooking the gardens. You look up. Well, well, well, say your eyes, not a dull day now. Her to play with.

You take me into the dining room. It's chill and smart and the tables have thick white cloths on them and silver cutlery. The men move chairs for the elegant thin women, and the waiters take the jackets of the plump men. I notice there are no young people here.

'Fill your plate,' you say, kindly. 'And come and sit with me. Bring me something too. A little meat and some dhal.'

I cover the plate with food from the copper pots at the buffet in the centre of the room and take it to you. And here we sit, father and daughter, all friendly and everything.

'How are you today, Daddy?' I say, touching your cheek.

Around us the sedate upper class fill their guts. You haven't heard me. I say once more, gently: 'How are you today?'

'You fucking bitch,' you say. You push away your food and light a cigarette.

'Goody,' I say, going a little cold. 'Now we know where we are with each other.'

'Where the fuck were you last night?' you enquire of me. You go on: 'You just fucked off and told no one. I was demented with worry. My blood pressure was through the roof. Anything could have happened to you.'

'It did.'

'That bloody boy's insane.'

'But Billy's pretty.'

'No, he's ugly like you. And a big pain in the arse.'

'Dad.'

'No, don't interrupt! A half-caste wastrel, a belong-nowhere, a problem to everyone, wandering around the face of the earth with no home like a stupid-mistake-mongrel dog that no one wants and everyone kicks in the backside.'

For those of you curious about the menu, I am drinking tear soup.

'You left us,' I say. I am shaking. You are shaking. 'Years ago, just look at it, you fucked us and left us and fucked off and never came back and never sent us money and instead made us sit through fucking *Jesus Christ Superstar* and *Evita*.'

Someone comes over, a smart judge who helped hang the Prime Minister. We all shake hands. Christ, I can't stop crying all over the place.

It's dusk and I'm sitting upstairs in a deckchair outside Billy's room on the roof. Billy's sitting on a pillow. We're wearing cut-off jeans and drinking iced water and reading old English newspapers that we pass between us. Our washing is hanging up on a piece of string we've tied between the corner of the room and the television aerial. The door to the room is open and we're listening again and again to 'Who's Loving You' – very loud – because it's our favourite record. Billy keeps saying: 'Let's hear it again, one mo' time, you know.' We're like an old couple sitting on a concrete patio in Shepherd's Bush, until we get up and dance with no shoes on and laugh and gasp because the roof burns our feet so we have to go inside to make love again.

Billy goes in to take a shower and I watch him go. I don't like being separated from him. I hear the shower start and I sit down and throw the papers aside. I go downstairs to Nadia's room and knock on her door. Wifey is sitting there and Moonie is behind her.

'She's not in,' Moonie says.

'Come in,' Nadia says, opening her door, I go in and sit on the stool by the dressing table. It's a pretty room. There is pink everywhere and her things are all laid out neatly and she sits on the bed brushing her hair and it shines. I tell her we should have a bit of a talk. She smiles at me. She's prepared to make an effort, I can see that, though it surprises me. She did go pretty berserk the other day, when we came out of the kitchen, trying to punch me and everything.

'It was an accident,' I tell her now.

'Well,' she says. 'But what impression d'you think it made on the man I want to marry?'

'Blame me. Say I'm just a sicko Westerner. Say I'm mad.'

'It's the whole family it reflects on,' she says.

She goes to a drawer and opens it. She takes out an envelope and gives it to me.

'It's a present for you,' she says kindly. When I slip my finger into the flap of the envelope she puts her hand over mine. 'Please. It's a surprise for later.'

Billy is standing on the roof in his underpants. I fetch a towel and dry his hair and legs and he holds me and we move a little together to imaginary music. When I remember the envelope Nadia gave me, I open it and find a shiny folder inside. It's a ticket to London.

I'd given my ticket home to my father for safe-keeping, an open ticket I can use any time. I can see that Nadia's been to the airline and specified the date, and booked the flight. I'm to leave tomorrow morning. I go to my dad and ask him what it's all about. He just looks at me and I realise I'm to go.

4

Hello, reader. As I'm sure you've noticed by now, I, Howard, have written this Nina and Nadia stuff in my sock, without leaving the country, sitting right here on my spreading arse and listening to John Coltrane. (And rolling cigarettes.) Do you think Nina could have managed phrases like 'an accent as thick as treacle' and 'But the curtains are well and truly pulled here' and especially 'Oh, oh, oh'? With her education? So all along, it's been me, pulling faces, speaking in tongues, posing and making an attempt on the truth through lies. And also, I just wanted to be Nina. The days Deborah and I have spent beating on her head, trying to twist her the right way round, read this, study dancing, here's a book about Balanchine and the rest of it. What does she make of all this force feeding? So I became her, entered her. Sorry.

Nina in fact has been back a week, though it wasn't until yesterday that I heard from her when she phoned to tell me that I am a bastard and that she had to see me. I leave straightaway.

At Nina's place. There she is, sitting at the kitchen table with her foot up on the table by her ashtray in the posture of a painter. Deborah not back from school.

'You look superb,' I tell her. She doesn't recoil in repulsion when I kiss her.

'Do I look superb?' She is interested.

'Yeah. Tanned. Fit. Rested.'

'Oh, is that all?' She looks hard at me. 'I thought for a moment you were going to say something interesting. Like I'd changed or something. Like something had happened.'

We walk through the estate, Friday afternoon. How she walks above it all now, as if she's already left! She tells me everything in a soft voice: her father, the servants, the boy Billy, the kiss, the panties. She says: 'I was devastated to leave Billy in that country on his own. What will he do? What will happen to that boy? I sent him a pack of tapes. I sent him some videos. But he'll be so lonely.' She is upset.

The three of us have supper and Deborah tries to talk about school while Nina ignores her. It's just like the old days. But Nina ignores Deborah not out of cruelty but because she is elsewhere. Deborah is thinking that probably Nina has left her for good. I am worried that Debbie will expect more from me.

The next day I fly to my desk, put on an early Miles Davis tape and let it all go, tip it out, what Nina said, how she looked, what we did, and I write (and later cross out) how I like to put my little finger up Deborah's arse when we're fucking and how she does the same to me, when she can comfortably reach. I shove it all down shamelessly (and add bits) because it's my job to write down the things that happen round here and because I have a rule about no material being sacred.

What does that make me?

I once was in a cinema when the recently uncovered spy Anthony Blunt came in with a friend. The entire cinema (but not me) stood up and chanted 'Out, out, out' until the old queen got up and left. I feel like that old spy, a dirty betrayer with a loud-speaker, doing what I have to.

I offer this story to you, Deborah and Nina, to make of it what you will, before I send it to the publisher.

Dear Howard,

How very kind of you to leave your story on my kitchen table casually saying, 'I think you should read this before I publish it.' I was pleased: I gave you an extra kiss, thinking that at last you wanted me to share your work (I almost wrote world).

I could not believe you opened the story with an account of an abortion. As you know I know, it's lifted in its entirety from a letter written to you by your last girlfriend, Julie. You were conveniently in New York when she was having the abortion so that she had to spit out all the bits of her broken heart in a letter, and you put it into the story pretending it was written by my daughter.

The story does also concern me, our 'relationship' and even where we put our fingers. Your portrait of me as a miserable whiner let down by men would have desperately depressed me, but I've learned that unfeeling, blood-sucking men like you need to reduce women to manageable clichés, even to destroy them, for the sake of control.

I am only sorry it's taken me this long to realise what a low, corrupt and exploitative individual you are, who never deserved the love we both offered you. You have torn me apart. I hope the same thing happens to you one day. Please never attempt to get in touch again.

Deborah

Someone bangs on the door of the flat. I've been alone all day. I'm not expecting anyone, and how did whoever it is get into the building in the first place?

'Let me in, let me in!' Nina calls out. I open up and she's standing there soaked through with a sports bag full of things and a couple of plastic bags under her arm.

'Moving in?' I say.

'You should be so lucky,' she says, barging past me. 'I'm on me way somewhere and I thought I'd pop by to borrow some money.'

She comes into the kitchen. It's gloomy and the rain hammers into the courtyard outside. But Nina's cheerful, happy to be back in England and she has no illusions about her father now. Apparently he was rough with her, called her a half-caste and so on.

'Well, Howard, you're in the shit, aren't you?' Nina says. 'Ma's pissed off no end with you, man. She's crying all over the shop. I couldn't stand it. I've moved out. You can die of a broken heart, you know. And you can kill someone that way too.'

'Don't talk about it,' I say, breaking up the ice with a hammer and dropping it into the glasses. 'She wrote me a pissed-off letter. Wanna read it?'

'It's private, Howard.'

'Read it, for Christ's sake, Nina,' I say, shoving it at her. She reads it and I walk round the kitchen looking at her. I stand behind her a long time. I can't stop looking at her today.

She puts it down without emotion. She's not sentimental; she's always practical about things, because she knows what cunts people are.

'You've ripped Ma off before. She'll get over it, and no one reads the shit you write anyway except a lot of middle-class wankers. As long as you get paid and as long as you give me some of it you're all right with me.'

I was right. I knew she'd be flattered. I give her some money and she gathers up her things. I don't want her to go.

'Where are you off to?'

'Oh, a friend's place in Hackney. Someone I was in the loony bin with. I'll be living there. Oh, and Billy will be joining me.' She smiles broadly. 'I'm happy.'

'Wow. That's good. You and Billy.'

'Yeah, ain't it just!' She gets up and throws back the rest of the whisky. 'Be seeing ya!'

'Don't go yet.'

'Got to.'

At the door she says: 'Good luck with the writing and every-thing.'

I walk to the lift with her. We go down together. I go out to the front door of the building. As she goes out into the street running with sheets of rain, I say: 'I'll come with you to the corner,' and walk with her, even though I'm not dressed for it.

At the corner I can't let her go and I accompany her to the bus stop. I wait with her for fifteen minutes in my shirt and slippers. I'm soaked through holding all her bags but I think you can make too much of these things. 'Don't go,' I keep saying inside my head.

Then the bus arrives and she takes her bags from me and gets on and I stand there watching her but she won't look at me because she is thinking of Billy. The bus moves off and I watch until it disappears and then I go inside the flat and take off my clothes and have a bath. Later. I write down the things she said but the place still smells of her.

Blue, Blue Pictures of You

I used to like talking about sex. All of life, I imagined – from politics to aesthetics – merged in passionate human conjunctions. A caress, not to speak of a kiss, could transport you from longing to Russia, on to Velazquez and ahead to anarchism. To illustrate this fancy, I did, at one time, consider collecting a 'book of desire', an anthology of outlandish, melancholy and droll stories about the subject. This particular story was one, had the project been finished – or even started – I would have included. It was an odd story. Eshan, the photographer who told it to me, used the word himself. At least he said it was the oddest request he'd had. When it was put to him by his pub companion, his first response was embarrassment and perplexity. But of course he was fascinated too.

At the end of the street where Eshan had a tiny office and small dark room, there was a pub where he'd go at half past six or seven, most days. He liked to work office hours, believing much discipline was required to do what he did, as if without it he would fly off into madness – though he had, in fact, never flown anywhere near madness, except to sit in that pub.

Eshan though he liked routine, and for weeks would do exactly the same thing every day, while frequently loathing this decline into habit. In the pub he would smoke, drink and read the paper for an hour or longer, depending on his mood and on whether he felt sentimental, guilty or plain affectionate towards his wife and two children. Sometimes he'd get home before the children were asleep, and carry them around on his back, kick balls with them, and tell them stories of pigs with spiders on their heads. Other times he would turn up late so he could have his wife make supper, and be free of the feeling that the kids were devouring his life.

Daily, there were many hapless people in that bar: somnolent junkies from the local rehab, the unemployed and unemployable, pinball pillocks. Eshan nodded at many of them, but if one sat at his table without asking, he could become truculent. Often, however, he would chat to people as he passed to and fro, being more grateful than he knew for distracting conversation. He had become, without meaning to, one of the bar's characters.

Eshan's passion was to photograph people who had produced something of significance, whose work had 'meaning'. These were philosophers, novelists, painters, film and theatre directors. He used only minimal props and hard, direct lighting. The idea wasn't to conceal but to expose. The spectator could relate the face to what the subject did. He called it the moment of truth in the features of people seeking the truth.

He photographed 'artists' but also considered himself, in private only, to be 'some sort' of an artist. To represent oneself – a changing being, alive with virtues and idiocies – was, for Eshan, the task that entailed the most honesty and fulfilment. But although his work had been published and exhibited, he still had to send out his portfolio with introductory letters, and harass people about his abilities. This was demeaning. By now he should, he reckoned, have got further. But he accepted his condition, imagining that overall he possessed most of what he required to live a simple but not complacent life. His wife illustrated children's books, and could earn decent money, so they got by. To earn a reasonable living himself, Eshan photographed new groups for the pop press – not that he was stimulated by these callow faces, though occasionally he was moved by their ugliness, the stupidity of their innocence, and their crass hopes. But they wanted only clichés.

A young man called Brian, who always wore pink shades, started to join Eshan regularly. The pub was his first stop of the day after breakfast. He was vague about what he did, though it seemed to involve trying to manage bands and set up businesses around music. His main occupation was dealing drugs, and he liked supplying Eshan with different kinds of grass that he claimed would make him 'creative'. Eshan replied that he took drugs in the evenings to stop himself getting creative. When Eshan talked about surrealism, or the great photographers, Brian listened with innocent enthusiasm, as if these were things he could get interested in were he a different person. It turned out that he did know a little about the music that Eshan particularly liked, West Coast psychedelic music of the mid-sixties, and the films, writing and politics that accompanied it. Eshan talked of the dream of freedom, rebellion and irresponsibility it had repre-sented, and how he wished he'd had the courage to go there and join in.

'You make it sound like the past few years in London,' Brian said. 'Except the music is faster.'

A couple of months after Eshan started seeing him in the pub, Brian parted from his casual girlfriends. He went out regularly – it was like a job; and he was the sort of man that women were attracted to in public places. There was hope; every night could take you somewhere new. But Brian was nearly thirty; for a long time he had been part of everything new, living not for the present but for the next thing. He was beginning to see how little it had left him, and he was afraid.

One day he met a girl who used to play the drums in a trip-hop group. Any subject – the economy, the comparative merits of Paris, Rome or Berlin – would return him to this woman. Every day he went to some trouble to buy her something, even if it was only a pencil. Other times it might be a first-edition Elizabeth David, an art deco lamp from Prague, a tape of Five Easy Pieces, a bootleg of Lennon singing 'On The Road to Rishikesh'. These things he would anxiously bring to the pub to ask Eshan's opinion of. Eshan wondered if Brian imagined that because he was a photographer he had taste and judgement, and, being married, had some knowledge of romance.

After a few drinks Eshan would go home and Brian would start phoning to make his plans for the night ahead. In what Eshan considered to be the middle of the night, Brian and Laura would go to a club, to someone's house, and then on to another club. Eshan learned that there were some places that only opened at nine on Sunday morning.

Lying in bed with his wife as they watched TV and read nineteenth-century novels while drinking camomile tea, Eshan found himself trying to picture what Brian and Laura were doing, what sort of good time they were having. He looked forward to hearing next day where they'd been, what drugs they'd taken, what they wore and how the conversation had gone. He was particularly curious about her reaction to each gift; he wanted to know whether she was demanding more and better gifts, or if she appreciated the merits of each one. And what, Eshan enquired with some concern, was Brian getting in return?

'Enough,' Brian inevitably replied.

'So she's good to you?'

Unusually, Brian replied that no lover had ever shown him what she had. Then he leaned forward, glanced left and right, and felt compelled to say, despite his loving loyalty, what this was. Her touch, her words, her sensual art, not to mention her murmurs, gasps, cries; and her fine wrists, long fingers and dark fine-haired bush that stood out like a punk's back-combed mohican – all were an incomparable rapture. Only the previous evening she had taken him by the shoulders and said –

'Yes?' Eshan asked.

'Your face, your hands, you, all of you, you . . .'

Eshan dried his palms on his trousers. Sighing inwardly, he listened, while signalling a detached approval. He encouraged Brian to repeat everything, like a much-loved story, and Brian was delighted to do so, until they were no longer sure of the facts.

Perhaps Eshan envied Brian his lover and their pleasure, and Brian was beginning to envy Eshan his stability. Whatever it was between them, Brian involved Eshan in his new love. It was, Eshan was pleased to see, agonising. Laura drew out Brian's best impulses; tenderness, kindness, generosity. He became more fervent as a dealer so as to take her to restaurants most nights; he borrowed money and took her to Budapest for a week.

But in love each moment is magnified, and every gesture, word and syllable is examined like a speech by the President. Solid expectation, unfurled hope, immeasurable disappointment – all are hurled together like a cocktail of random drugs that, quaffed within the hour, make both lovers reel. If she dressed up and went to a party with a male friend, he spent the night catatonic with paranoia; if he saw an old girlfriend, she assumed they would never speak again. And surely she was seeing someone else, someone better in every way? Did she feel about him as he did her? To love her was to fear losing her. Brian would have locked her in a bare room to have everything hold still a minute.

One day when Eshan went to the bar he returned to see that Brian had picked up a folder Eshan had left on the table, opened it, and was holding up the photographs. Brian could be impudent, which was his charm, and Eshan liked charm, because it was rare and good to watch as a talent. But it also exposed Brian as a man who was afraid; his charm was charged with the task of disarming people before they damaged him.

'Hey,' said Eshan.

Brian placed his finger on a picture of Doris Lessing. Laura was reading *The Golden Notebook*; could he buy it for her? Eshan said, yes, and he wouldn't charge. But Brian insisted. They agreed on a price and on a black frame. They drank more and wondered what Laura would think. A few days later Brian reported that though Laura would never finish the book – she never finished any book, the satisfaction was too diffuse – she had been delighted by the picture. Could she visit his studio?

'Studio? If only it was. But yes, bring her over – it's time we met.'

'Tomorrow, then.'

They were more than two hours late. Eshan had been meditating, which he did whenever he was tense or angry. You couldn't beat those Eastern religions for putting the wet blanket on desire. When he was turning out the lights and ready to leave, Brian and Laura arrived at the door with wine. Eshan put out his work for Laura. She looked closely at everything. They smoked the dope he had grown on his balcony from Brian's seeds, lay on the floor with the tops of their heads touching, and watched a Kenneth Anger film. Brian and Laura rang some people and said they were going out. Would he like to come? Eshan almost agreed. He said he would like to have joined them, but that he got up early to work. And the music, an electronic blizzard of squeaks, bleeps and beats, had nothing human in it.

'Yes, that's right,' Laura said. 'Nothing human there. A bunch of robots on drugs.'

'You don't mean that,' said Brian.

A few days after the visit Brian made the strange request.

'She enjoyed meeting you,' he was saying, as Eshan read his newspaper in the pub.

'And me her,' Eshan murmured without raising his eyes. 'Anyone would.'

It cheered Brian to hear her praised. 'She's pretty, eh?'

'No, beautiful.'

'Yes, that's it, you've got the right word.'

He picked up his phone. 'She wants to ask you a favour. Can she join us?'

'I've got to go.'

'Of course, you've got to put the kids to bed, but I think you'll find it an interesting favour.'

Laura arrived within fifteen minutes. She sat down at their table and began.

'What we want is for you to photograph us.'

Eshan nodded. Laura glanced at Brian. 'Naked. Or we could wear things. Rings through our belly buttons or something. But anyway – making love.' Eshan looked at her. 'You photograph us fucking,' she concluded. 'Do you see?'

Eshan didn't know what to say.

She asked, 'What about it?'

'I am not a pornographer.'

It must have sounded pompous. She gave him an amused look. 'I've seen your stuff, and we haven't the nerve for pornography. It isn't even beauty we want. And I know you don't go for that.'

'No. What is it?'

'You see, we go to bed and eat crackers and drink wine and caress one another and chatter all day. We've both been through terrible things in our lives, you see. Now we want to capture this summer moment – I mean we want you to capture it for us.'

'To look back on?'

She said, 'I suppose that is it. We all know love doesn't last.'

'Is that right?' said Eshan.

Brian added, 'It might be replaced by something else.'

'But this terrible passion and suspicion . . . and the intensity of it . . . will get domesticated.' She went on, 'I think that when one has an idea, even if it is a queer one, one should follow it through, don't you?'

Eshan supposed he agreed with this.

Laura kissed Brian and said to him, 'Eshan's up for it.'

'I'm not sure,' said Brian.

Eshan had picked up his things, said goodbye and reached the door, before he returned.

'Why me?'

She was looking up at him.

'Why? Brian has run into you with your children. You're a kind father, a normal man, and you will surely understand what we want.' Eshan looked at Brian, who had maintained a neutral expression. She said, 'But . . . if it's all too much, let's forget it.'

It was an idea they'd conceived frivolously. He would give her the chance to drop the whole thing. She should call in the morning.

He thought it over in bed. When Laura made the request, though excited, she hadn't seemed mad or over-ebullient. It was vanity, of course, but a touching, naive vanity, not a grand one; and he was, more than ever, all for naivety. Laura was, too, a woman anyone would want to look at.

An old upright piano and guitar; painted canvases leaning against the wall; club fliers, rolling papers, pills, a razor blade, beer bottles empty and full, standing on a chest of drawers. Leaning against this, a long mirror. The bed, its linen white, was in the centre of the room.

Laura pulled the curtains, and then half-opened them again.

'Will you have enough light?'

'I'll manage,' Eshan whispered.

Brian went to shave. Then, while Eshan unpacked his things, he plucked at the guitar with his mouth open, and drank beer. The three of them spoke in low voices and were solicitous of one another, as if they were about to do something dangerous but delicate, like planting a bomb.

A young man, covered in spots, wandered into the room.

'Get out now and go to bed,' Laura said. 'You've got chickenpox. Everyone here had it?' she asked.

They all laughed. It was better then. She put a chair against the door. They watched her arrange herself on the bed. Eshan photographed her back; he photographed her face. She took her clothes off. The breeze from the open window caressed her. She stretched out her fingers to Brian.

He walked over to her and they pressed their faces together. Eshan photographed that. She undressed him. Eshan shot his discomfort.

Soon they were taking up different positions, adjusting their heads, putting their hands here and there for each shot. Brian began to smile as if he fancied himself as a model.

'It's very sweet, but it ain't going to work,' Eshan told them. 'There's nothing there. It's dead.'

'He might be right,' Laura told Brian. 'We're going to have to pretend he's not here.'

Eshan said, 'I'll put film in the camera now, then.'

Eshan didn't go to bed but carried his things through the dark city back to his studio. He developed the material as quickly as he could and when it was done went home. His wife and children were having breakfast, laughing and arguing as usual. He walked in and his children kept asking him to take off his coat. He felt like a criminal, though the only laws he'd broken were his own, and he wasn't sure which ones they were.

Unusually he had the pictures with him and he went through them several times as he ate his toast, keeping them away from the children.

'Please, can I see?' His wife put her hand on his shoulder. 'Don't hide them. It's a long time since you've shown me your work. You live such a secret life.'

'Do I?'

'Sometimes I think you're not doing anything at all over there but just sitting.'

She looked at the photographs and then closed the folder.

'You stayed out all night without getting in touch. What have you been doing?'

'Taking pictures.'

'Don't talk to me like that. Who are these people, Eshan?'

'People I met in the pub. They asked me to photograph them.'

They went into the kitchen and she closed the door. She could be very disapproving, and she didn't like mysteries.

'And you did this?'

'You know I like to start somewhere and finish somewhere else. It wasn't an orgy.'

'Are you going to publish or sell them?'

'No. They paid me. And that's it.'

He got up.

'Where are you going?'

'Back to work.'

'Is this the same kind of thing you'll be doing today?'

'Ha ha ha.'

He tried to resume his routine but couldn't work, or even listen to music or read the papers. He could only look at the pictures. They were not pornography, being too crude and unembellished for that. He had omitted nothing human. All the same, the images gave him a dry mouth, exciting and distressing him at the same time. He wouldn't be able to start anything else until the material was out of the studio.

He thought Brian would have gone back to his place, but wasn't certain. However, he couldn't persuade himself to ring first. He took a chance and walked all the way back there again. He was exhausted but was careful to cross the road where he crossed it before.

She came to the door in her dressing gown, and was surprised to see him. He said he'd brought the stuff round, and proffered the folder as evidence.

He went past her and up the stairs. She tugged her dressing gown around herself, as if he hadn't seen her body before. Upstairs they sat on the broken sofa. She was reluctant to look at the stuff, but knew she had to. She held up the contact sheets, turning them this way and that, repeatedly.

'Is that what you wanted?' he asked.

'I don't know.'

'Is that what you do on a good day?'

'I should thank you for the lovely job you've done. I don't know what I can do in return.' He looked at her. She said, 'How about a drum lesson?'

'Why not?'

She took him into a larger room, where he noticed some of Brian's gifts. Set before a big window, with a view of the street and the square, was her red spangled kit. She showed him how she played, and demonstrated how he could. Soon this bored her and she made lunch. As he ate she returned to the photographs, glanced through them without comment, and went back to the table. He wasn't certain that she wanted him there. But she didn't ask him to go away and seemed to assume that he had nothing better to do. He didn't know what else he would do anyway, as if something had come to an end.

They started to watch television, but suddenly she switched it off and stood up and sat down. She started agitatedly asking him questions about the people he knew, how many friends he had, what he liked about them, and what they said to one another. At first he answered abruptly, afraid of boring her. But she said she'd never had any guidance, and for the past few years, like everyone else, had only wanted a good time. Now she wanted to find something important to do, wanted a reason to get out of bed before four. He murmured that fucking might be a good excuse for staying in bed, just as the need to wash was an excuse for lying in the bath. She understood that, she said. She hardly knew anyone with a job; London was full of drugged, useless people who didn't listen to one another but merely thought all the time of how to distract themselves and never spoke of anything serious. She was tired of it; she was even tired of being in love; it had become another narcotic. Now she wanted interesting difficulty, not pleasure or even ease.

'And look, look at the pictures . . .'

'What do they say?'

'Too much, my friend.'

She hurried from the room. After a time she returned with a bucket which she set down on the carpet. She held the photographs over it and invited him to set fire to them.

'Are you sure?' he said.

'Oh yes.'

They singed the carpet and burned their fingers, and then they threw handfuls of ash out of the window and cheered.

'Are you going to the pub now?' she asked as he said goodbye.

'I don't think I'll be going there for a while.'

He told her that the next day he was going to photograph a painter who had also done record covers. He asked her to come along, 'to have a look'. She said she would.

Leaving the house he crossed the street. He could see her sitting in the window playing. When he walked away he could hear her all the way to the end of the road.

My Son the Fanatic

Surreptitiously the father began going into his son's bedroom. He would sit there for hours, rousing himself only to seek clues. What bewildered him was that Ali was getting tidier. Instead of the usual tangle of clothes, books, cricket bats, video games, the room was becoming neat and ordered; spaces began appearing where before there had been only mess.

Initially Parvez had been pleased: his son was outgrowing his teenage attitudes. But one day, beside the dustbin, Parvez found a torn bag which contained not only old toys, but computer discs, video tapes, new books and fashionable clothes the boy had bought just a few months before. Also without explanation, Ali had parted from the English girlfriend who used to come often to the house. His old friends had stopped ringing.

For reasons he didn't himself understand, Parvez wasn't able to bring up the subject of Ali's unusual behaviour. He was aware that he had become slightly afraid of his son, who, alongside his silences, was developing a sharp tongue. One remark Parvez did make, 'You don't play your guitar any more,' elicited the mysterious but conclusive reply, 'There are more important things to be done.'

Yet Parvez felt his son's eccentricity as an injustice. He had always been aware of the pitfalls which other men's sons had fallen into in England. And so, for Ali, he had worked long hours and spent a lot of money paying for his education as an accountant. He had bought him good suits, all the books he required and a computer. And now the boy was throwing his possessions out!

The TV, video and sound system followed the guitar. Soon the room was practically bare. Even the unhappy walls bore marks where Ali's pictures had been removed.

Parvez couldn't sleep; he went more to the whisky bottle, even when he was at work. He realised it was imperative to discuss the matter with someone sympathetic.

Parvez had been a taxi driver for twenty years. Half that time he'd worked for the same firm. Like him, most of the other drivers were Punjabis. They preferred to work at night, the roads were clearer and the money better. They slept during the day, avoiding their wives. Together they led almost a boy's life in the cabbies' office, playing cards and practical jokes, exchanging lewd stories, eating together and discussing politics and their problems.

But Parvez had been unable to bring this subject up with his friends. He was too ashamed. And he was afraid, too, that they would blame him for the wrong turning his boy had taken, just as he had blamed other fathers whose sons had taken to running around with bad girls, truanting from school and joining gangs.

For years Parvez had boasted to the other men about how Ali excelled at cricket, swimming and football, and how attentive a scholar he was, getting straight 'A's in most subjects. Was it asking too much for Ali to get a good job now, marry the right girl and start a family? Once this happened, Parvez would be happy. His dreams of doing well in England would have come true. Where had he gone wrong?

But one night, sitting in the taxi office on busted chairs with his two closest friends watching a Sylvester Stallone film, he broke his silence.

'I can't understand it!' he burst out. 'Everything is going from his room. And I can't talk to him any more. We were not father and son – we were brothers! Where has he gone? Why is he torturing me!'

And Parvez put his head in his hands.

Even as he poured out his account the men shook their heads and gave one another knowing glances. From their grave looks Parvez realised they understood the situation.

'Tell me what is happening!' he demanded.

The reply was almost triumphant. They had guessed something was going wrong. Now it was clear. Ali was taking drugs and selling his possessions to pay for them. That was why his bedroom was emptying.

'What must I do then?'

Parvez's friends instructed him to watch Ali scrupulously and then be severe with him, before the boy went mad, overdosed or murdered someone.

Parvez staggered out into the early morning air, terrified they were right. His boy – the drug addict killer!

To his relief he found Bettina sitting in his car.

Usually the last customers of the night were local 'brasses' or prostitutes. The taxi drivers knew them well, often driving them to liaisons. At the end of the girls' shifts, the men would ferry them home, though sometimes the women would join them for a drinking session in the office. Occasionally the drivers would go with the girls. 'A ride in exchange for a ride,' it was called.

Bettina had known Parvez for three years. She lived outside the town and on the long drive home, where she sat not in the passenger seat but beside him, Parvez had talked to her about his life and hopes, just as she talked about hers. They saw each other most nights.

He could talk to her about things he'd never be able to discuss with his own wife. Bettina, in turn, always reported on her night's activities. He liked to know where she was and with whom. Once he had rescued her from a violent client, and since then they had come to care for one another.

Though Bettina had never met the boy, she heard about Ali continually. That late night, when he told Bettina that he suspected Ali was on drugs, she judged neither the boy nor his father, but became businesslike and told him what to watch for.

'It's all in the eyes,' she said. They might be bloodshot; the pupils might be dilated; he might look tired. He could be liable to sweats, or sudden mood changes. 'Okay?'

Parvez began his vigil gratefully. Now he knew what the problem might be, he felt better. And surely, he figured, things couldn't have gone too far? With Bettina's help he would soon sort it out.

He watched each mouthful the boy took. He sat beside him at every opportunity and looked into his eyes. When he could he took the boy's hand, checking his temperature. If the boy wasn't at home Parvez was active, looking under the carpet, in his drawers, behind the empty wardrobe, sniffing, inspecting, probing. He knew what to look for: Bettina had drawn pictures of capsules, syringes, pills, powders, rocks.

Every night she waited to hear news of what he'd witnessed.

After a few days of constant observation, Parvez was able to report that although the boy had given up sports, he seemed healthy, with clear eyes. He didn't, as his father expected, flinch guiltily from his gaze. In fact the boy's mood was alert and steady in this sense: as well as being sullen, he was very watchful. He returned his father's long looks with more than a hint of criticism, of reproach even, so much so that Parvez began to feel that it was he who was in the wrong, and not the boy!

'And there's nothing else physically different?' Bettina asked.

'No!' Parvez thought for a moment. 'But he is growing a beard.'

One night, after sitting with Bettina in an all-night coffee shop, Parvez came home particularly late. Reluctantly he and Bettina had abandoned their only explanation, the drug theory, for Parvez had found nothing resembling any drug in Ali's room. Besides, Ali wasn't selling his belongings. He threw them out, gave them away or donated them to charity shops.

Standing in the hall, Parvez heard his boy's alarm clock go off. Parvez hurried into his bedroom where his wife was still awake, sewing in bed. He ordered her to sit down and keep quiet, though she had neither stood up nor said a word. From this post, and with her watching him curiously, he observed his son through the crack in the door.

The boy went into the bathroom to wash. When he returned to his room Parvez sprang across the hall and set his ear at Ali's door.

A muttering sound came from within. Parvez was puzzled but relieved.

Once this clue had been established, Parvez watched him at other times. The boy was praying. Without fail, when he was at home, he prayed five times a day.

Parvez had grown up in Lahore where all the boys had been taught the Koran. To stop him falling asleep when he studied, the Moulvi had attached a piece of string to the ceiling and tied it to Parvez's hair, so that if his head fell forward, he would instantly awake. After this indignity Parvez had avoided all religions. Not that the other taxi drivers had more respect. In fact they made jokes about the local mullahs walking around with their caps and beards, thinking they could tell people how to live, while their eyes roved over the boys and girls in their care.

Parvez described to Bettina what he had discovered. He informed the men in the taxi office. The friends, who had been so curious before, now became oddly silent. They could hardly condemn the boy for his devotions.

Parvez decided to take a night off and go out with the boy. They could talk things over. He wanted to hear how things were going at college; he wanted to tell him stories about their family in Pakistan. More than anything he yearned to understand how Ali had discovered the 'spiritual dimension', as Bettina described it.

To Parvez's surprise, the boy refused to accompany him. He claimed he had an appointment. Parvez had to insist that no appointment could be more important than that of a son with his father.

The next day, Parvez went immediately to the street where Bettina stood in the rain wearing high heels, a short skirt and a long mac on top, which she would open hopefully at passing cars.

'Get in, get in!' he said.

They drove out across the moors and parked at the spot where on better days, with a view unimpeded for many miles by nothing but wild deer and horses, they'd lie back, with their eyes half closed, saying 'This is the life.' This time Parvez was trembling. Bettina put her arms around him.

'What's happened?'

'I've just had the worst experience of my life.'

As Bettina rubbed his head Parvez told her that the previous evening he and Ali had gone to a restaurant. As they studied the menu, the waiter, whom Parvez knew, brought him his usual whisky and water. Parvez had been so nervous he had even prepared a question. He was going to ask Ali if he was worried about his imminent exams. But first, wanting to relax, he loosened his tie, crunched a popadom and took a long drink.

Before Parvez could speak, Ali made a face.

'Don't you know it's wrong to drink alcohol?' he said.

'He spoke to me very harshly,' Parvez told Bettina. 'I was about to castigate the boy for being insolent, but managed to control myself.'

He had explained patiently to Ali that for years he had worked more than ten hours a day, that he had few enjoyments or hobbies and never went on holiday. Surely it wasn't a crime to have a drink when he wanted one?

'But it is forbidden,' the boy said.

Parvez shrugged. 'I know.'

'And so is gambling, isn't it?'

'Yes. But surely we are only human?'

Each time Parvez took a drink, the boy winced, or made a fastidious face as an accompaniment. This made Parvez drink more quickly. The waiter, wanting to please his friend, brought another glass of whisky. Parvez knew he was getting drunk, but he couldn't stop himself. Ali had a horrible look on his face, full of disgust and censure. It was as if he hated his father.

Halfway through the meal Parvez suddenly lost his temper and threw a plate on the floor. He had felt like ripping the cloth from the table, but the waiters and other customers were staring at him. Yet he wouldn't stand for his own son telling him the difference between right and wrong. He knew he wasn't a bad man. He had a conscience. There were a few things of which he was ashamed, but on the whole he had lived a decent life.

'When have I had time to be wicked?' he asked Ali.

In a low monotonous voice the boy explained that Parvez had not, in fact, lived a good life. He had broken countless rules of the Koran.

'For instance?' Parvez demanded.

Ali hadn't needed time to think. As if he had been waiting for this moment, he asked his father if he didn't relish pork pies?

'Well . . .'

Parvez couldn't deny that he loved crispy bacon smothered with mushrooms and mustard and sandwiched between slices of fried bread. In fact he ate this for breakfast every morning.

Ali then reminded Parvez that he had ordered his own wife to cook pork sausages, saying to her, 'You're not in the village now, this is England. We have to fit in!'

Parvez was so annoyed and perplexed by this attack that he called for more drink.

'The problem is this,' the boy said. He leaned across the table. For the first time that night his eyes were alive. 'You are too implicated in Western civilisation.'

Parvez burped; he thought he was going to choke. 'Implicated!' he said. 'But we live here!'

'The Western materialists hate us,' Ali said. 'Papa, how can you love something which hates you?'

'What is the answer then?' Parvez said miserably. 'According to you.'

Ali addressed his father fluently, as if Parvez were a rowdy crowd that had to be quelled and convinced. The Law of Islam would rule the world; the skin of the infidel would burn off again and again; the Jews and Christers would be routed. The West was a sink of hypocrites, adulterers, homosexuals, drug takers and prostitutes.

As Ali talked, Parvez looked out of the window as if to check that they were still in London.

'My people have taken enough. If the persecution doesn't stop there will be *jihad*. I, and millions of others, will gladly give our lives for the cause.'

'But why, why?' Parvez said.

'For us the reward will be in paradise.'

'Paradise!'

Finally, as Parvez's eyes filled with tears, the boy urged him to mend his ways.

'How is that possible?' Parvez asked.

'Pray,' Ali said. 'Pray beside me.'

Parvez called for the bill and ushered his boy out of the restaurant as soon as he was able. He couldn't take any more. Ali sounded as if he'd swallowed someone else's voice.

On the way home the boy sat in the back of the taxi, as if he were a customer.

'What has made you like this?' Parvez asked him, afraid that somehow he was to blame for all this. 'Is there a particular event which has influenced you?'

'Living in this country.'

'But I love England,' Parvez said, watching his boy in the mirror. 'They let you do almost anything here.'

'That is the problem,' he replied.

For the first time in years Parvez couldn't see straight. He knocked the side of the car against a lorry, ripping off the wing mirror. They were lucky not to have been stopped by the police: Parvez would have lost his licence and therefore his job.

Getting out of the car back at the house, Parvez stumbled and fell in the road, scraping his hands and ripping his trousers. He managed to haul himself up. The boy didn't even offer him his hand.

Parvez told Bettina he was now willing to pray, if that was what the boy wanted, if that would dislodge the pitiless look from his eyes.

'But what I object to,' he said, 'is being told by my own son that I am going to hell!'

What finished Parvez off was that the boy had said he was giving up accountancy. When Parvez had asked why, Ali had said sarcastically that it was obvious.

'Western education cultivates an anti-religious attitude.'

And, according to Ali, in the world of accountants it was usual to meet women, drink alcohol and practise usury.

'But it's well-paid work,' Parvez argued. 'For years you've been preparing!'

Ali said he was going to begin to work in prisons, with poor Muslims who were struggling to maintain their purity in the face of corruption. Finally, at the end of the evening, as Ali was going to bed, he had asked his father why he didn't have a beard, or at least a moustache.

'I feel as if I've lost my son,' Parvez told Bettina. 'I can't bear to be looked at as if I'm a criminal. I've decided what to do.'

'What is it?'

'I'm going to tell him to pick up his prayer mat and get out of my house. It will be the hardest thing I've ever done, but tonight I'm going to do it.'

'But you mustn't give up on him,' said Bettina. 'Many young people fall into cults and superstitious groups. It doesn't mean they'll always feel the same way.'

She said Parvez had to stick by his boy, giving him support, until he came through.

Parvez was persuaded that she was right, even though he didn't feel like giving his son more love when he had hardly been thanked for all he had already given.

Nevertheless, Parvez tried to endure his son's looks and reproaches. He attempted to make conversation about his beliefs. But if Parvez ventured any criticism, Ali always had a brusque reply. On one occasion Ali accused Parvez of 'grovelling' to the whites; in contrast, he explained, he was not 'inferior'; there was more to the world than the West, though the West always thought it was best.

'How is it you know that?' Parvez said, 'seeing as you've never left England?'

Ali replied with a look of contempt.

One night, having ensured there was no alcohol on his breath, Parvez sat down at the kitchen table with Ali. He hoped Ali would compliment him on the beard he was growing but Ali didn't appear to notice.

The previous day Parvez had been telling Bettina that he thought people in the West sometimes felt inwardly empty and that people needed a philosophy to live by.

'Yes,' said Bettina. 'That's the answer. You must tell him what your philosophy of life is. Then he will understand that there are other beliefs.'

After some fatiguing consideration, Parvez was ready to begin. The boy watched him as if he expected nothing.

Haltingly Parvez said that people had to treat one another with respect, particularly children their parents. This did seem, for a moment, to affect the boy. Heartened, Parvez continued. In his view this life was all there was and when you died you rotted in the earth. 'Grass and flowers will grow out of me, but something of me will live on –'

'How?'

'In other people. I will continue – in you.' At this the boy appeared a little distressed. 'And your grandchildren,' Parvez added for good measure. 'But while I am here on earth I want to make the best of it. And I want you to, as well!'

'What d'you mean by "make the best of it"?' asked the boy.

'Well,' said Parvez. 'For a start . . . you should enjoy yourself. Yes. Enjoy yourself without hurting others.'

Ali said that enjoyment was a 'bottomless pit'.

'But I don't mean enjoyment like that!' said Parvez. 'I mean the beauty of living!'

'All over the world our people are oppressed,' was the boy's reply.

'I know,' Parvez replied, not entirely sure who 'our people' were, 'but still – life is for living!'

Ali said, 'Real morality has existed for hundreds of years. Around the world millions and millions of people share my beliefs. Are you saying you are right and they are all wrong?'

Ali looked at his father with such aggressive confidence that Parvez could say no more.

One evening Bettina was sitting in Parvez's car, after visiting a client, when they passed a boy on the street.

'That's my son,' Parvez said suddenly. They were on the other side of town, in a poor district, where there were two mosques.

Parvez set his face hard.

Bettina turned to watch him. 'Slow down then, slow down!' She said, 'He's good-looking. Reminds me of you. But with a more determined face. Please, can't we stop?'

'What for?'

'I'd like to talk to him.'

Parvez turned the cab round and stopped beside the boy.

'Coming home?' Parvez asked. 'It's quite a way.'

The sullen boy shrugged and got into the back seat. Bettina sat in the front. Parvez became aware of Bettina's short skirt, gaudy rings and ice-blue eyeshadow. He became conscious that the smell of her perfume, which he loved, filled the cab. He opened the window.

While Parvez drove as fast as he could, Bettina said gently to Ali, 'Where have you been?'

'The mosque,' he said.

'And how are you getting on at college? Are you working hard?'

'Who are you to ask me these questions?' he said, looking out of the window. Then they hit bad traffic and the car came to a standstill.

By now Bettina had inadvertently laid her hand on Parvez's shoulder. She said, 'Your father, who is a good man, is very worried about you. You know he loves you more than his own life.'

'You say he loves me,' the boy said.

'Yes!' said Bettina.

'Then why is he letting a woman like you touch him like that?'

If Bettina looked at the boy in anger, he looked back at her with twice as much cold fury.

She said, 'What kind of woman am I that deserves to be spoken to like that?'

'You know,' he said. 'Now let me out.'

'Never,' Parvez replied.

'Don't worry, I'm getting out,' Bettina said.

'No, don't!' said Parvez. But even as the car moved she opened the door, threw herself out and ran away across the road. Parvez shouted after her several times, but she had gone.

Parvez took Ali back to the house, saying nothing more to him. Ali went straight to his room. Parvez was unable to read the paper, watch television or even sit down. He kept pouring himself drinks.

At last he went upstairs and paced up and down outside Ali's room. When, finally, he opened the door, Ali was praying. The boy didn't even glance his way.

Parvez kicked him over. Then he dragged the boy up by his shirt and hit him. The boy fell back. Parvez hit him again. The boy's face was bloody. Parvez was panting. He knew that the boy was unreachable, but he struck him nonetheless. The boy neither covered himself nor retaliated; there was no fear in his eyes. He only said, through his split lip: 'So who's the fanatic now?'

The Tale of the Turd

I'm at this dinner. She's eighteen. After knowing her six months I've been invited to meet her parents. I am, to my surprise, forty-four, same age as her dad, a professor – a man of some achievement, but not that much. He is looking at me or, as I imagine, looking me over. The girl-woman will always be his daughter, but for now she is my lover.

Her two younger sisters are at the table, also beautiful, but with a tendency to giggle, particularly when facing in my direction. The mother, a teacher, is putting a soft pink trout on the table. I think, for once, yes, this is the life, what they call a happy family, they've asked to meet me, why not settle down and enjoy it?

But what happens, the moment I'm comfortable I've got to have a crap. In all things I'm irregular. It's been two days now and not a dry pellet. And the moment I sit down in my better clothes with the family I've got to go.

These are good people but they're a little severe. I am accompanied by disadvantages – my age, no job, never had one, and my . . . tendencies. I like to say, though I won't tonight – unless things get out of hand – that my profession is failure. After years of practice, I'm quite a success at it.

On the way here I stopped off for a couple of drinks, otherwise I'd never have come through the door, and now I'm sipping wine and discussing the latest films not too facetiously and my hands aren't shaking and my little girl is down the table smiling at me warm and encouraging. Everything is normal, you see, except for this gut ache, which is getting worse, you know how it is when you've got to go. But I won't get upset, I'll have a crap, feel better and then eat.

I ask one of the sisters where the bathroom is and kindly she points at a door. It must be the nearest, thank Christ, and I get across the room stooping a little but no way the family's gonna see me as a hunchback.

I sit down concerned they're gonna hear every splash but it's too late: the knotty little head is already pushing out, a flower coming through the earth, but thick and long and I'm not even straining, I can feel its soft motion through my gut, in one piece. It's been awaiting its moment the way things do, like love. I close my eyes and appreciate the relief as the corpse of days past slides into its watery grave.

When I'm finished I can't resist glancing down – even the Queen does this – and the turd is complete, wide as an aubergine and purplish too. It's flecked with carrot, I notice, taking a closer look, but, ah, probably that's tomato, I remember now, practically the only thing I've eaten in twenty-four hours.

I flush the toilet and check my look. Tired and greying I am now, with a cut above my eye and a bruise on my cheek, but I've shaved and feel as okay as I ever will, still with the boyish smile that says I can't harm you. And waiting is the girl who loves me, the last of many, I hope, who sends me vibrations of confidence.

My hand is on the door when I glance down and see the prow of the turd turning the bend. Oh no, it's floating in the pan again and I'm bending over for a better look. It's one of the biggest turds I've ever seen. The flushing downpour has rinsed it and there is no doubt that as turds go it is exquisite, flecked and inlaid like a mosaic depicting, perhaps, a historical scene. I can make out large figures going at one another in argument. The faces I'm sure I've seen before. I can see some words but I haven't got my glasses to hand.

I could have photographed the turd, had I brought a camera, had I ever owned one. But now I can't hang around, the trout must be cooling and they're too polite to start eating without me. The problem is, the turd is bobbing.

I'm waiting for the cistern to refill and every drip is an eternity, I can feel the moments stretching out, and outside I can hear the murmuring voices of my love's family but I can't leave that submarine there for the mother to go in and see it wobbling about. She knows I've been in the clinic and can see I'm drinking again; I've been watching my consumption, as they say, but I can't stop and she's gonna take her daughter to one side and . . .

I've been injecting my little girl. 'What a lovely way to take drugs,' she says sweetly. She wants to try everything. I don't argue with that and I won't patronise her. Anyhow, she's a determined little blonde thing, and for her friends it's fashionably exciting. I can tell she's made up her mind to become an addict.

It took me days to hunt out the best stuff for her, pharmaceutical. It's been five years for me, but I took it with her to ensure she didn't make a mistake. Except an ex-boyfriend caught up with us, took me into a doorway and split my face for corrupting her. Yet she skips school to be with me and we take in Kensington Market and Chelsea. I explain their history of fashion and music. The records I tell her to listen to, the books I hold out, the bands I've played with, the creative people I tell her of, the deep talks we have, are worth as much as anything she hears at school, I know that.

At last I flush it again.

Girls like her . . . it is easy to speak of exploitation, and people do. But it is time and encouragement I give them. I know from experience, oh yes, how critical and diminishing parents can be, and I say try, I say yes, attempt anything. And I, in my turn, am someone for them to care for. It breaks my heart but I've got, maybe, two years with her before she sees I can't be helped and she will pass beyond me into attractive worlds I cannot enter.

I pray only that she isn't pulling up her sleeve and stroking her tracks, imagining her friends being impressed by those mascots, the self-inflicted scars of experience; those girls are dedicated to the truth, and like to show their parents how defiant they can be.

I'm reaching for the door, the water is clear and I imagine the turd swimming towards Ramsgate. But no, no, no, don't look down, what's that, the brown bomber must have an aversion to the open sea. The monstrous turd is going nowhere and nor am I while it remains an eternal recurrence. I flush it again and wait but it won't leave its port and what am I going to do, this must be an existential moment and all my days have converged here. I'm trembling and running with sweat but not yet lost.

I'm rolling up the sleeve of my Italian suit, it's an old suit, but it's my best jacket. I don't have a lot of clothes, I wear what people give me, what I find in the places I end up in, and what I steal.

I'm crying inside too, you know, but what can I do but stick my hand down the pan, into the pissy water, that's right, oh dark, dark, dark, and fish around until my fingers sink into the turd, get a muddy grip and yank it from the water. For a moment it seems to come alive, wriggling like a fish.

My instinct is to calm it down, and I look around the bathroom for a place to bash it, but not if it's going to splatter everywhere, I wouldn't want them imagining I'm on some sort of dirty protest.

By now they must have started eating. And what am I doing but standing here with a giant turd in my fist? Not only that, my fingers seem to adhere to the turd; bits of my flesh are pulled away and my hand is turning brown. I must have eaten something unusual, because my nails and the palms are turning the colour of gravy.

My love's radiant eyes, her loving softness. But in all ways she is a demanding girl. She insists on trying other drugs, and in the afternoons we play like children, dressing up and inventing characters, until my compass no longer points to reality. I am her assistant as she tests the limits of the world. How far out can she go and still be home in time for tea? I have to try and keep up, for she is my comfort. With her I am living my life again, but too quickly and all at once.

And in the end, to get clear, to live her life, she will leave me; or, to give her a chance, I must leave her. I dream, though, of marriage and of putting the children to bed. But I am told it is already too late for all that. How soon things become too late, and before one has acclimatised!

I glance at the turd and notice little teeth in its velvet head, and a little mouth opening. It's smiling at me, oh no, it's smiling and what's that, it's winking, yes, the piece of shit is winking up at me, and what's that at the other end, a sort of tail, it's moving, yes, it's moving, and oh Jesus, it's trying to say something, to speak, no, no, I think it wants to sing. Even though it is somewhere stated that truth may be found anywhere, and the universe of dirt may send strange messengers to speak to us, the last thing I want, right now in my life, is a singing turd.

I want to smash the turd back down into the water and hold it under and run out of there, but the mother – when the mother comes in and I'm scoffing the trout and she's taking down her drawers I'm gonna worry that the turd lurking around the bend's gonna flip up like a piranha and attach itself to her cunt, maybe after singing a sarcastic ditty, and she's going to have an impression of me that I don't want.

But I won't dwell on that, I'm going to think constructively where possible even though its bright little eyes are glinting and the mouth is moving and it has developed scales under which ooze – don't think about it. And what's that, little wings . . .

I grab the toilet roll and rip off about a mile of paper and start wrapping it around the turd, around and around, so those eyes are never gonna look at me again, and smile in that way. But even in its paper shroud it's warm and getting warmer, warm as life, and practically throbbing and giving off odours. I look desperately around the room for somewhere to stuff it, a pipe or behind a book, but it's gonna reek, I know that, and if it's gonna start moving, it could end up anywhere in the house.

There's a knocking on the door. A voice too – my love. I'm about to reply 'Oh love, love' when I hear other, less affectionate raised voices. An argument is taking place. Someone is turning the handle; another person is kicking at the door. Almost on me, they're trying to smash it in!

I will chuck it out of the window! I rest the turd on the sill and drag up the casement with both hands. But suddenly I am halted by the sky. As a boy I'd lie on my back watching clouds; as a teenager I swore that in a less hectic future I would contemplate the sky until its beauty passed into my soul, like the soothing pictures I've wanted to study, bathing in the colours and textures of paint, the cities I've wanted to walk, loafing, the aimless conversations I've wanted to have – one day, a constructive aimlessness.

Now the wind is in my face, lifting me, and I am about to fall. But I hang on and instead throw the turd, like a warm pigeon, out out into the air, turd-bird awayaway.

I wash my hands in the sink, flush the toilet once more, and turn back to life. On, on, one goes, despite everything, not knowing why or how.

Nightlight

'There must always be two to a kiss.'
R. L. Stevenson, 'An Apology for Idlers'

She comes to him late on Wednesdays, only for sex, the cab
waiting outside. Four months ago someone recommended her
to him for a job but he has no work she can do. He doesn't
even pay himself now. They talk of nothing much, and there are
silences in which they can only look at one another. But neither
wants to withdraw and something must be moving between them,
for they stand up together and lie down beside the table, without
speaking.

Same time next week she is at the door. They undress immediately. She leaves, not having slept, but he has felt her dozing before
she determinedly shakes herself awake. She collects herself quickly
without apology, and goes without looking back. He has no idea
where she lives or where she is from.

Now she doesn't come into the house, but goes straight down
into the basement he can't afford to furnish, where he has thrown
blankets and duvets on the carpet. They neither drink nor play
music and can barely see one another. It's a mime show in this
room where everything but clarity, it seems, is permitted.

At work his debts increase. What he has left could be taken away,
and no one but him knows it. He is losing his hold and does it
matter? Why should it, except that it is probably terminal; if one
day he feels differently, there'll be no way back.

For most of his life, particularly at school, he's been successful, or en route to somewhere called Success. Like most people he has been afraid of being found out, but unlike most he probably has been. He has a small flat, an old car and a shabby feeling. These are minor losses. He misses steady quotidian progress, the sense that his well-being, if not happiness, is increasing, and that each day leads to a recognisable future. He has never anticipated this extent of random desolation.

Three days a week he picks up his kids from school, feeds them, and returns them to the house into which he put most of his money, and which his wife now forbids him to enter. Fridays he has dinner with his only male friend. After, they go to a black bar where he likes the music. The men, mostly in their thirties, and whose lives are a mystery to him, seem to sit night after night without visible discontent, looking at women and at one another. He envies this, and wonders if their lives are without anxiety, whether they have attained a stoic resignation, or if it is a profound uselessness they are stewing in.

On this woman's day he bathes for an hour. He can't recall her name, and she never says his. She calls him, when necessary, 'man'. Soon she will arrive. He lies there thinking how lucky he is to have one arrangement which costs nothing.

Five years ago he left the wife he didn't know why he married for another woman, who then left him without explanation. There have been others since. But when they come close he can only move backwards, without comprehending why.

His wife won't speak. If she picks up the phone and hears his voice, she calls for the kids, those intermediaries growing up between immovable hatreds. A successful woman, last year she found she could not leave her bed at all. She will have no help and the children have to minister to her. They are inclined to believe that he has caused this. He begins to think he can make women insane, even as he understands that this flatters him.

Now he has this inexplicable liaison. At first they run tearing at one another with middle-aged recklessness and then lie silently in the dark, until desire, all they have, rekindles. He tells himself to make the most of the opportunity.

When she's gone he masturbates, contemplating what they did, imprinting it on his mind for ready reference: she on her stomach, him on the boat of her back, his face in her black hair for ever. He thinks of the fluffy black hairs, flattened with sweat, like a toff's parting, around her arsehole.

Walking about later he is both satisfied and unfulfilled, disliking himself for not knowing why he is doing this – balked by the puzzle of his own mind and the impossibility of grasping why one behaves so oddly, and why one ends up resenting people for not providing what one hasn't been able to ask for. Surely this new thing is a web of illusion, and he is a fool? But he wants more foolishness, and not only on Wednesdays.

The following weeks she seems to sense something. In the space where they lie beneath the level of the street, almost underground – a mouse's view of the world – she invites him to lie in different positions; she bids him touch different parts of her body. She shows him they can pore over one another.

Something intriguing is happening in this room, week after week. He can't know what it might be. He isn't certain she will turn up; he doesn't trust her, or any woman, not to let him down. Each week she surprises him, until he wonders what might make her stop.

One Wednesday the cab doesn't draw up. He stands at the window in his dressing gown and slippers for three hours, feeling in the first hour like Casanova, in the second like a child awaiting its mother, and during the third like an old man. Is she sick, or with her husband? He lies on the floor where she usually lies, in a fever of desire and longing, until, later, he feels a presence in the room, a hanging column of air, and sits up and cries out at this ghost.

He assumes he is toxic. For him, lacking disadvantages has been a crime in itself. He grasps the historical reasons for this, since his wife pointed them out. Not that this prevented her living off him. For a while he did try to be the sort of man she might countenance. He wept at every opportunity, and communicated with animals wherever he found them. He tried not to raise his voice, though for her it was 'liberating' to get wild. Soon he didn't know who he was supposed to be. They both got lost. He dreaded going home. He kept his mouth shut, for fear of what would come out; this made her search angrily for a way in.

Now he worries that something has happened to this new woman and he has no way of knowing. What wound or hopelessness has made her want only this?

Next week she does come, standing in the doorway, coat-wrapped, smiling, in her early thirties, about fifteen years younger than him. She might have a lover or husband; might be unemployed; might be disillusioned with love, or getting married next week. But she is tender. How he has missed what they do together.

The following morning he goes downstairs and smells her on the sheets. The day is suffused with her, whoever she is. He finds himself thinking constantly of her, pondering the peculiar mixture of ignorance and intimacy they have. If sex is how you meet and get to know people, what does he know of her? On her body he can paint only imaginary figures, as in the early days of love, when any dreams and desires can be flung onto the subject, until reality upsets and rearranges them. Not knowing, surely, is beautiful, as if everything one learns detracts from the pleasures of pure imagination. Fancy could provide them with more satisfaction than reality.

But she is beginning to make him wonder, and when one night he touches her and feels he has never loved anything so much – if love is loss of the self in the other then, yes, he loves her – he begins to want confirmation of the notions which pile up day after day without making any helpful shape. And, after so many years of living, the expensive education, the languages he imagined would be useful, the books and newspapers studied, can he be capable of love only with a silent stranger in a darkened room? But he dismisses the idea of speaking, because he can't take any more disappointment. Nothing must disturb their perfect evenings.

You want sex and a good time, and you get it; but it usually comes with a free gift – someone like you, a person. Their arrangement seems an advance, what many people want, the best without the worst, and no demands – particularly when he thinks, as he does constantly, of the spirit he and his wife wasted in dislike and sniping, and the years of taking legal and financial revenge. He thinks often of the night he left.

He comes in late, having just left the bed of the woman he is seeing, who has said she is his. The solid bulk of his wife, her back turned, is unmoving. His last night. In the morning he'll talk to the kids and go, as so many men he knows have done, people who'd thought that leaving home was something you did only once. Most of his friends, most of the people he knows, are on the move from wife to wife, husband to husband, lover to lover. A city of love vampires, turning from person to person, hunting the one who will make the difference.

He puts on the light in the hall, undresses and is about to lie down when he notices that she is now lying on her back and her eyes are open. Strangely she looks less pale. He realises she is wearing eyeshadow and lipstick. Now she reaches out to him, smiling. He moves away; something is wrong. She throws back the covers and she is wearing black and red underwear. She has never, he is certain, dressed like this before.

'It's too late,' he wants to cry.

He picks up his clothes, rushes to the door and closes it behind him. He doesn't know what he is doing, only that he has to get out. The hardest part is going into the children's room, finding their faces in the mess of blankets and toys, and kissing them goodbye.

This must have turned his mind, for, convinced that people have to take something with them, he hurries into his study and attempts to pick up his computer. There are wires; he cannot disconnect it. He gathers up the television from the shelf. He's carrying this downstairs when he turns and sees his wife, still in her tart garb, with a dressing gown on top, screaming, 'Where are you going? Where? Where?'

He shouts, 'You've had ten years of me, ten years and no more, no more!'

He slips on the step and falls forward, doubling up over the TV and tripping down the remaining stairs. Without stopping to consider his injuries, he flees the house without affection or dislike and doesn't look back, thinking only, strange, one never knows every corner of the houses one lives in as an adult, not as one knew one's childhood house. He leaves the TV in the front garden.

The woman he sees now helps kill the terrible fear he constantly bears that his romantic self has been crushed. He feels dangerous but wants to wake up in love. Soft, soft; he dreams of opening a door and the person he will love is standing behind it.

This longing can seize him at parties, in restaurants, at friends' and in the street. He sits opposite a woman in the train. With her the past will be redeemed. He follows her. She crosses the street. So does he. She is going to panic. He grabs her arm and shouts, 'No, no, I'm not like that!' and runs away.

He doesn't know how to reach others, but disliking them is exhausting. Now he doesn't want to go out, since who is there to hold onto? But in the house his mind devours itself; he is a cannibal of his own consciousness. He is starving for want of love. The shame of loneliness, a dingy affliction! There are few creatures more despised than middle-aged men with strong desires, and desire renews itself each day, returning like a recurring illness, crying out, more life, more!

At night he sits in the attic looking through a box of old letters from women. There is an abundance of pastoral description. The women sit in cafés drinking good coffee; they eat peaches on the patio; they look at snow. Everyday sensations are raised to the sublime. He wants to be scornful. It is easy to imagine 'buzzes' and 'charges' as the sole satisfactions. But what gratifies him? It is as if the gears of his life have become disengaged from the mechanisms that drove him forward. When he looks at what other people yearn for, he can't grasp why they don't know it isn't worth wanting. He asks to be returned to the ordinary with new eyes. He wants to play a child's game: make a list of what you noticed today, adding desires, regrets and contentments, if any, to the list, so that your life doesn't pass without your having noticed it. And he requires the extraordinary, on Wednesdays.

He lies on his side in her, their mouths are open, her legs holding him. When necessary they move to maintain the level of warm luxury. He can only gauge her mood by the manner of her love-making. Sometimes she merely grabs him; or she lies down, offering her neck and throat to be kissed.

He opens his eyes to see her watching him. It has been a long time since anyone has looked at him with such attention. His hope is boosted by a new feeling: curiosity. He thinks of taking their sexuality into the world. He wants to watch others looking at her, to have others see them together, as confirmation. There is so much love he almost attempts conversation.

For several weeks he determines to speak during their love-making, each time telling himself that on this occasion the words will come out. 'We should talk,' is the sentence he prepares, which becomes abbreviated to 'Want to talk?' and even 'Talk?'

However his not speaking has clearly gladdened this woman. Who else could he cheer up in this way? Won't clarity wreck their understanding, and don't they have an alternative vocabulary of caresses? Words come out bent, but who can bend a kiss? If only he didn't have to imagine continually that he has to take some action, think that something should happen, as if friendships, like trains, have to go somewhere.

He has begun to think that what goes on in this room is his only hope. Having forgotten what he likes about the world, and think-ing of existence as drudgery, she reminds him, finger by finger, of the worthwhile. All his life, it seems, he's been seeking sex. He isn't certain why, but he must have gathered that it was an important thing to want. And now he has it, it doesn't seem sufficient. But what does that matter? As long as there is desire there is a pulse; you are alive; to want is to reach beyond yourself, into the world, finger by finger.

Lately

After Chekhov's story 'The Duel'

1

At eight, those who'd stayed up all night, and those who'd just risen, would gather on the beach for a swim. It had been a warm spring and was now a blazing, humid summer, the hottest of recent times, it was said. The sea was deliciously tepid.

When Rocco, a thin dark-haired man of about thirty, strolled down to the sea in his carpet slippers and cut-off Levi's, he met several people he knew, including Bodger, a local GP who struck most people, at first, as being unpleasant.

Stout, with a large close-cropped head, big nose, no neck and a loud voice, Bodger didn't appear to be an advertisement for medicine. But after they had met him, people began to think of his face as kind and amiable, even charming. He would greet everyone and discuss their medical and even psychological complaints in the pub or on the street. It was said that people took him their symptoms to give him the pleasure of attempting to cure them. The barbecues he held, at unusual and splendid locations, were famous. But he was ashamed of his own kindness, since it led him into difficulties. He liked to be curt.

'I've got a question for you,' said Rocco, as they made their way across the mud flats. 'Suppose you fell in love. You lived with the woman for a couple of years and then – as happens – stopped loving her, and felt your curiosity was exhausted. What would you do?'

'Get out, I'd say, and move on.'

'Suppose she was on her own and had nowhere to go, and had no job or money?'

'I'd give her the money.'

'You've got it, have you?'

'Sorry?'

'Remember, this is an intelligent woman we're talking about.'

'Which intelligent woman?' Bodger enquired, although he had already guessed.

Bodger swam vigorously according to his routine; Rocco stood in the waves and then floated on his back.

They dressed at the base of the cliffs, Bodger shaking sand from his shoes. Rocco picked up the papers he'd brought with him, an old copy of the *New York Review of Books* and the *Racing Post*.

'It's a nightmare living with someone you don't love, but I wouldn't worry about it,' advised the doctor, in his 'minor ailments' voice. 'Suppose you move on to another woman and find she's the same? Then you'll feel worse.'

They went to a vegetarian café nearby, where they were regulars. The owner always brought Bodger his own mug and a glass of iced water. Bodger enjoyed his toast, honey and coffee. The swimming gave him an appetite.

Unfortunately, Rocco craved almond croissants, which he'd once had in a café in London; every morning he'd raise his hand and ask the manager to bring him some. Of course, in their town they'd never seen such things, and each request annoyed the manager more. Bodger could see that one day Rocco would get a kick up his arse. He wished he had the nerve to make such enjoyable trouble.

'I love this view.' Bodger craned to look past Rocco at the sea. Rocco was rubbing his eyes. 'Didn't you sleep?'

'I must tell someone. Things with Lisa are bad.' Rocco ignored the fact that Bodger was drumming his fingers on his unopened newspaper. 'I've lived with her two years. I loved her more than my life. And now I don't. Maybe I never loved her. Maybe I was deluded.

Perhaps I am deluded about everything. How can people lead sensible lives while others are a mess? You know what Kierkegaard said? Our lives can only be lived forward and only understood backwards. Living a life and understanding it occupy different dimensions. Experience overwhelms before it can be processed.'

'Kierkegaard! I've been intending to read him. Is he great?'

'Perhaps I enjoyed stealing her from her husband. What?'

'Which book of his should I start with?'

Rocco said, 'She was always up for sex, and I was always hard. We fucked so often we practically made electricity.'

Bodger leaned forward. 'What was that like?'

'We wanted to leave London. The people. The pollution. The expense. We came here . . . to get a bit of land, grow stuff, you know.'

'The dope?'

'Don't be fatuous. Vegetables. Except we haven't got them in yet.'

'It's a little late.'

'Maybe you or your friend Vance would have started a business and a family and all that. But this town is getting me down. And Lisa is always . . . always . . . about the place. That's what I'm saying.'

'I wouldn't leave a beautiful woman like that.'

'Even if you didn't love her?'

'Not her. Romance doesn't last. But respect and co-operation do. I'm a doctor. I recommend endurance.'

'If I wanted to test my endurance I'd go to the gym like that idiot Vance. I think I've got Alzheimer's disease.'

The doctor laid his hand on Rocco's forehead. It was damp. Rocco seemed to be sweating alcohol. Bodger was about to inform him that his T-shirt was inside out and back to front, but he remembered that when his friend's shirts became too offensive he reversed them.

'I don't think so. Does she love you?'

Rocco sighed. 'She thinks she's one of those magazine independent women, but without me she'd be all over the place. She's useless really. What can she do? She has irritating ways.'

'Like what?' said Bodger with interest.

Rocco tried to think of a specific illustration that wasn't petty. He couldn't tell Bodger he hated the way she poked him in the stomach while trying to talk to him; or the way she blew in his nostrils and ears when they were having sex; or the way she applied for jobs she'd never get, and then claimed he didn't encourage her; how she always had a cold and insisted, when taking her temperature, that insertion of the thermometer up the backside was the only way to obtain a legitimate reading; or how she was always losing money, keys, letters, even her shoes, and falling off her bicycle. Or how she'd take up French or singing, but give up after a few weeks, and then say she was useless.

Rocco said, 'What can you do when you're with a person you dislike, but move on to another person you dislike? Isn't that called hope? I'm off.'

'Where?'

'Back to London. New people, new everything. Except we've got no money, nothing.'

Bodger said, 'You're intelligent, that's the problem.'

Rocco was biting his nails. 'I miss the smell of the tube, the crowds in Soho at night, men mending the road outside your window at eight in the morning, people pissing into your basement, repulsive homunculi in ill-fitting trousers shouting at strangers. In the city anything can turn up. There's less time to think there. My mind won't shut up, Bodger.'

The doctor collected his things. 'Nor will my patients.'

'Don't mention this, because I'm not telling her yet.' Rocco pulled out a letter. 'Yesterday this arrived. It fell open – accidentally. Her husband's not well.'

Bodger leant over to look at it, but stopped himself. 'What's wrong with him?'

'He's dead.'

'Aren't you going to show it to her?'

'She'll get upset and I won't be able to leave her for ages.'

'But you took her away from her husband, for God's sake. Marry her now, Rocco, please!'

'That's a good idea, when I can't bear the girl and couldn't fuck her with my eyes closed.'

Bodger paid, as he always did, and the two friends walked along the top of the cliff. When they parted Bodger told Rocco how he wished he had a woman like Lisa, and that he didn't understand why she would live with Rocco and not with him.

'Those shoulders, those shoulders,' he murmured. 'I'd be able to love her.'

'But we'll never know that for sure, will we?' said Rocco. 'Thanks for the advice. By the way, have you ever lived with a woman?'

'What? Not exactly.'

Rocco sauntered off.

Bodger hoped he wouldn't be thinking of Rocco and Lisa all morning. Occasions like this made him want to appreciate what he had. He would do this by thinking of something worse, like being stuck in a tunnel on the District Line in London on the hottest day of the year. Yes, he liked this seaside town and the sea breeze, particularly early in the morning, when the shops and restaurants were opening and the beach was being cleaned.

'Karen, Karen!' he called to Vance's wife who was jogging on the beach. She waved back.

2

When Rocco got home Lisa had managed to dress and had even combed her hair. She wore a long black sleeveless dress and knee-high leather boots. The night before she'd been at a party on the beach. Most people had been stoned. She couldn't see the point of that any more, everyone out of it, dancing in their own space. She had got away and rested in the dunes. Now she sat at the window drinking coffee and reading a magazine she'd read before.

'Would it be okay if I went swimming this morning?' she asked.

She was supposed to sign on but had obviously forgotten. Rocco was about to remind her but preferred the option of blaming her later.

'I don't care what you do.'

'I only asked because Bodger told me to take it easy.'

'Why, what's wrong with you now?'

She shrugged. He looked at her bare white neck and the little curls on the nape he had kissed a hundred times.

He went into the bedroom. His head felt damp, as if sweat was constantly seeping from his follicles. He was too exhausted to even gesture at the ants on the pillow. They were all over the house. If you sat down they crawled up your legs; if you opened a paper they ran across the pages. But neither of them did anything about it.

He lay down. Almost immediately, though, he groaned. He could hear, through a megaphone, a voice intoning Hail Marys. The daily procession of pilgrims to the local shrine, one of Europe's oldest, had begun. They came by coach from all over the country. People in wheelchairs, others on crutches, the simple, the unhappy and the dying limped up the lane past the cottage. A wooden black madonna was hoisted on the shoulders of the relatively hearty; others embraced rosaries and crucifixes. The sound echoed across the fields of grazing cattle. Cults, shamans, mystics; the hopeless searched everywhere. To everyone their own religion, these days. Who was not deranged, from a certain point of view? Who didn't long for help?

In their first weeks in the cottage, he and Lisa had played a game as the pilgrims passed. Rocco would put on a Madonna record, run up the steps of their raised garden, and piss over the hedge onto the shriners, crying, 'Holy water, holy water!' Lisa would rush to restrain him and they would fuck, laughing, in the garden.

The day was ahead of him and what did he want to do? He thought that having intentions, something in the future to move towards, might make the present a tolerable bridge. But he couldn't think of any projects to want.

Rereading the letter he looked up and saw Lisa observing him. He was about to stuff it back in his pocket, but how would she know what it contained?

Three years ago he had fallen in love. Lisa wasn't only pretty; plenty of women were pretty. She was graceful, and everything about her had beauty in it. She was self-aware without any vanity; and, most of the time, she knew her worth, without conceit. With her, he would make an attempt at monogamy, much vaunted as a virtue, apparently, by some. She would curb his desire. Running away with her would also represent an escape from futility. Now, however, he felt that all he had to do was abandon her, flee and somehow achieve the same thing.

He said, 'I'll ask Bodger if you can swim. I need some advice myself.'

'About what?'

'Everything.'

Rocco knew he was talented: he could play and compose music; he could direct in the theatre and on film; he could write. To release his powers he had to get away. Action was possible. That, at least, he'd decided. This cheered him, but not as much as it should, because he didn't even have the money to travel to the next railway station. And, of course, before he got out he'd have to settle things with Lisa. He needed a longer discussion with Bodger.

At twelve they had lunch because there was nothing else to do. He and Lisa always had the same thing, tinned tomato soup with cheese on toast, followed by jelly with condensed milk. It was cheap and they couldn't argue about what to have.

'I love this soup,' he said, and she smiled at him. 'It's delicious.' It was too much, being nice. He didn't think he could keep it up. Not even the thought of her dead husband brought on compassion. 'How do you feel today? Or have I asked you that already?'

She shook her head. 'Stomach pains again, but okay.'

'Take it easy then.'

'I think so.'

The sound of her slurping her jelly, which he hoped that just this once she would spare him, made him see how husbands murdered their wives. He pushed away his bowl and ran out of the cottage. She watched him go, the spoon at her lips.

3

'Scum. Rocco is scum,' said Vance. 'He really is. And I can tell you why.'

'You had better,' said Bodger.

Bodger was studying Feather, the local therapist who lived nearby, because he was drawing her.

Vance was glancing at himself in Bodger's mirror, not so much to admire his crawling sideburns, floral shirt, ever-developing shoulders, and thick neck, but to reassure himself that his last, satisfying impression had been the correct one.

He ran the town's hamburger restaurant, a big place with wooden floors, loud seventies music and, on the walls, rock posters and a T-Rex gold disc. In the basement he had recently opened the Advance, a club. Nearby he owned a clothes shop.

Vance was the most ambitious man in the town. It was no secret that his appetite extended further than anything or anyone in front of him. Looking over their heads, he was going places. But it was here, to his perpetual pique, that he was starting from.

Like numerous others, he often dropped by Bodger's place in the afternoon or late at night, to gossip. Most surfaces in Bodger's house were covered with bits of wood that he'd picked up on walks, or with his drawings or notebooks. There were towers of annotated paperbacks on astronomy, animals, plants, psychology; collapsing rows of records; and pieces of twisted metal he'd discovered in skips. The chairs were broken, but had a shape he liked; his washing, which he did by hand as 'therapy', hung in rows across the kitchen. To Vance it was detritus, but every object was chosen and cherished.

Vance said, 'Did you know what he said about this shirt? He asked if I were wearing the Nigerian or the Ghanaian flag.'

Feather started to laugh.

'Yes, it's hilarious,' said Vance. 'He provokes me and then wants my respect.'

Bodger said, 'I saw him this morning and felt sorry for him.'

'He's rubbish.'

'Why say that of someone?'

Vance said, 'Did you know – he's probably told you several times – that he's got two degrees in philosophy? He's had one of the best educations in the world. And who paid for it? Working people like me, or my father. And what does he do now? He drinks, hangs around, borrows money, and sells dope that gives people nightmares. Surely we should benefit from his brilliant education? Or was it just for him?'

'Is it the education that's useless, or just Rocco?' Feather asked.

'Exactly,' said Bodger.

'Both, probably. Thank God this government's cutting down on it.' Vance turned to Feather. 'Can't you therapise him into normality?'

'Suppose he turned out worse?'

Vance went on, 'You know what he said to me? He called me greedy and exploitative. And no one has fucked more of my waitresses. Did I tell you, he was in bed with one and she asked him if he'd liked it. I teach them to be polite, you see. He said . . . what was it? "The whole meaning of my life has coalesced at this timeless moment."' Neither Feather nor Bodger laughed. 'How idiotic can you get? Last time he came into the restaurant, he raised his arse and farted. The customers couldn't breathe.'

'Stop it,' said Bodger to Feather, who was laughing now.

'The worst thing is, girls fall for him. And he's got nothing! Can you explain it?'

'He knows how to look at them,' said Feather.

She herself had a steady gaze, as if she were deciphering what people really meant.

'What d'you mean?' asked Vance.

'Women look into his eyes and see his interest in them. But he also lets them see his unhappiness.'

Vance couldn't see why anyone would find Rocco's unhappiness amatory, but something about the idea puzzled him, and he considered it.

When they'd first come to the town, Vance had welcomed Lisa and Rocco. He didn't let them pay for their coffee, ensured they had the best table, and introduced them to the local poets and musicians, and to Bodger. She was attractive; he was charming. This was the sort of café society he'd envisaged in his restaurant, not people in shorts with sandy feet and peeling noses.

Bodger was drawing. 'Calling the man scum – well, that's just unspeakable and I don't agree with it.'

'His problem is,' said Feather, 'he loves too many people.'

Vance started up again. 'Why defend someone who sleeps with people's girlfriends – and gives them diseases – borrows money, never works, is stoned all the time and tells lies? These days people don't want to make moral judgements. They blame their parents, or society, or a pain in the head. He came to my place every day. I liked him and wanted to give him a chance. People like him are rubbish.'

Bodger threw down his pencil. 'Shut up!'

Feather said, 'The desire for pleasure plays a large part in people's lives.'

'So?' Vance stared at her. 'Suppose we all did what we wanted the whole time. Nothing would get done. I'll tell you what riles me. People like him think they're superior. He thinks that doing nothing and discussing stupid stuff is better than working, selling, running a business. How does he think the country runs? Lazy people like him should be forced to work.'

'Forced?' said Bodger.

This was one of Vance's favourite subjects. 'Half the week, say. To earn his dole. Sweeping the streets, or helping pensioners get to the shops.'

'Forcibly?' said Bodger. 'The police carrying him to the dustcart?'

'And to the pensioners,' said Vance. 'I'd drag him to them myself.'

'Not everyone can be useful,' said Feather.

'But why shouldn't everyone contribute?'

'I've lost my concentration,' said Bodger.

They went out into his garden where everything grew as it wanted. It was hot but not sunny. Cobwebs hung in the bushes like hammocks. The foliage was dry and dusty, the trees were wilting, the pond dry.

The liquefying heat debilitated them; they drank water and beer. Bodger fell asleep in a wicker chair with a handkerchief over his face.

Feather and Vance went out of the back gate arm in arm. He asked her to have a drink with him at the restaurant.

'I would, but I've got a client,' she said.

'More dreams?'

'I hope so.'

'Don't you get sick of all those whingeing people and their petty problems? Send them to me for a kick, it'll be cheaper.'

'People's minds are interesting. More interesting than their opinions. And certainly, as Rocco might have said, as interesting as hamburgers.'

She was smiling. They had always amused one another. She didn't mind if he mocked what she did. In fact it seemed to stimulate her. She liked him in spite of his personality.

'Come to me for a couple of sessions,' she said. 'See what sort of conversations we might have.'

'I'll come by for a massage but I'll never let you tinker with my brain. Words, words. How can talking be the answer to everything? There's nothing wrong with me. If I'm sick, God help everyone else.' After a while he added, 'Rocco's dangerous because he uses other people and gives them nothing in return.'

'Some people like being used.'

'I'm giving you notice, Feather, I'm going to kill that bastard.'

'As long as there's good reason for it,' she said, walking away.

4

Too weak to move, ravers from the previous night sat on the beach in shorts. Some slept, others swigged wine, one had set up a stall selling melons. A woman, a regular who came every morning with her cat in a box, walked it on a lead while the kids barked at her.

Lisa snoozed on the sand until she thought she'd boil, and then raced into the sea.

She loved her black dress. It was almost the only thing that fitted her. She put on her large straw hat with its broad brim pressed down so tightly over her ears that her face seemed to be looking out of a box. As she passed them the boys called after her. She was tall, with a long neck and a straight back. She walked elegantly, with her head up. In another age a man would be holding a parasol for her.

Nearby sat a middle-aged woman, a TV executive, who kept a cottage nearby, commuted to Los Angeles, and read scripts on the beach. She had most of what anyone could want, but was always alone. She dressed expensively but she was plump and her looks had faded. The boys, barking at the cat, also barked at her. Lisa shuddered. Men wanted young women – what a liberated age it was!

Maybe Lisa would ask her for a job. But working like that would bore her after a few weeks. How would she have time to learn the drums? At least . . . at least she had Rocco.

What conversations they had had, hour after hour, as they walked, loved, ate, sat. If she imagined the perfect partner, who would see her life as it was meant to be seen, absorbing the most secret confessions and most trivial incidents in a wise captivated mind, then he had been the one. What serenity and unstrained ease, without shame or fear, there had been, for a time.

Lately he had been hateful. She would have threatened to leave him, except his mood was her fault; she had to cure him. It was she who'd insisted they leave London, imagining a place near the sea, with the countryside nearby. They would grow their own food and read and write; there would be languorous stoned evenings.

There had been. Now they were going down. She'd spent too much on jewellery, bags, and clothes in Vance's. The manager, Moon, had 'loaned' her Ecstasy too, which she and Rocco had taken or given away. She owed Moon too much. Beside, she was wasting her life here, where very little happened. But what were lives for? Who could say? She didn't want to start thinking about that.

She and Rocco rarely fucked now. If they did, he would smack her face before he came. She was always left in a rage. But he was curious about her body. He watched her as she did up her shoes; he would lift her skirt as she stood at the sink; he would look her over as she lay naked on the bed, and would touch her underwear when she was out. But she ached for sex. Her nipples wanted attention; she would pinch them between her fingers as she drank her tea. She felt desire but didn't know how to deliver herself of it.

She walked through the town. Vance's shop was beside two shops selling religious paraphernalia; there was nothing of use to buy in the high street. The pubs were priest-ridden; the most common cause of argument was Cardinal Newman.

Several of the local boys who worshipped Rocco, including the most fervent, a lad called Teapot, liked to hang around the shop. They copied Rocco's mannerisms and peculiar dress sense, wearing, for instance, a jean jacket over a long raincoat or fingerless gloves; they carried poetry, and told girls that the meaning of life had coalesced over their breasts.

Fortunately Teapot's group were still on the beach and only Moon was sitting in Vance's tenebrous shop, fiddling with his decks. He spent more time deciding which music to play than organising the stock. Sometimes Vance let him DJ at the Advance.

The blinds were down. A fan stirred and rippled the light fabrics. Moon had a mod haircut and wore little blue round shades. Lisa wanted to wave, so uncertain was she that he could see her, or anything.

She moved around the shop, keeping away from him as she asked if he had any E. She was going somewhere that she couldn't face straight and needed the stuff today.

'How will you pay me?' he asked outright, as she dreaded he would.

'Moon –'

'Leave aside the money you owe me, what about the money you owe the shop? The leather jacket.'

'It was lifted from the pub.'

'That's not my fault. Vance is going to find out.'

'Rocco's sold an article to the *New Statesman*. He'll come by to pay you.'

Moon snorted. 'Look.' He scattered some capsules on the counter, along with a bag of his own brand of grass, with a bright 'Moon' logo printed on it. 'Is it right to play games with someone's head?'

If she found a man attractive she liked to kiss him. This 'entertained' her. She would explain that there was no more to it than that, but the men didn't realise she meant it. She had had to stop it.

'You made me like you. You opened your legs.'

He came towards her and put his hand inside the front of her dress. She let him do it. He started kissing her breasts.

He was keen to hang his 'back in five minutes' sign on the door for an hour. But, unusually, some kids came in. She snatched up the caps from the counter and got out.

From the door he yelled, 'See you later!'

'Maybe.'

'At the Rim.'

She stopped. 'You coming, then?'

'Why not? By the way, don't mess with me. You don't want me spreading stuff about you, do you?'

5

They would drive five miles out of town along the south-bound road, stop at a pub at the main junction, and then head up to the Rim.

Rocco, Bodger and Moon led the way in Bodger's Panda, followed by Karen, Vance, Feather – holding her cat – and Lisa in Vance's air-conditioned Saab. The boot was full of food and drink.

'Two years from now,' Vance was telling Feather, 'when I've raised the money, I'll – I mean we –' he added, nodding at his wife Karen. 'We'll be off to Birmingham. Open a place there.'

'If we can ever afford it,' said Karen. 'I can't see the bank allowing it.'

'Shut your face,' said Vance. 'I've explained. I'm not making the mistake of going straight to London. I need experience. Coming with us?'

Feather stroked her cat. 'Whatever for?'

'Because however comfortable you are now, rubbing your pussy and listening to people moaning about mum and dad, in five years you'll be bored. And older. There's a lot of people there need serious head help.'

Karen cried out, 'Look!'

They were speeding along a road carved out of a sheer cliff. Everyone felt they were racing along a shelf attached to a high wall and that at any moment they would go hurtling over into the abyss. On the right stretched the sea, while on the left was a rugged brown wall covered in creeping roots.

They had several drinks in the pub garden, before moving on.

'I don't know what I'm doing here,' said Rocco. 'I should be on the train to London.'

'What about the view?' said Bodger.

Rocco shrugged. 'I have a busy internal life.'

As they walked back to the car, Vance said, 'Why does Rocco have to come with us? He spoils everything with his moaning.'

'You've got to come to terms with Rocco,' said Feather. 'He's obviously doing something to you. What is it?'

'It's making me mad.'

They drove through quiet villages and past farms. Tractors blocked their way. Dogs barked at them. They left the road for a dirt track. Then they had to unpack the cars and walk up the chalky hill to the Rim. Moon carried his music box and bag of tapes, Bodger a pile of blankets and his ice box, and the others brought the provisions. Soon, to one side, the town and the sea were below them, and on the other the hills looked brown, pink, lilac, suffused with light.

Karen threw up her arms and danced. 'What a brilliant idea! It's so quiet.'

'Yes, it is beautiful,' said Rocco. Sometimes he talked to Karen in the restaurant. He felt sorry for her, married to Vance. 'But I like it when you dance.'

'Always the flattterer,' said Vance.

Rocco knew Vance didn't like him, and he was afraid of him too. When Vance was around he felt awkward. Ignoring this last remark he walked away and regretted having come.

Bodger called after him, 'Everyone – get some wood for the fire!'

They wandered off at random, leaving Karen and Moon behind. Moon, with a sleepy look, like he'd been woken against his will, spread out the blankets and set out the spliff, wine and beer. When Vance had gone Karen smoked grass as if she were holding a long cigarette at a cocktail party, and then lay down with her head nearly inside the music.

Lisa wanted to skip, laugh, shout, flirt and tease. In her cotton dress with blue dots and the straw hat, she felt light and ethereal. She had stopped bleeding at last. A few days ago Bodger had told her she was having a miscarriage. She hadn't understood how it had happened. It had been Moon. Her body had bled for him, her heart for Rocco.

She climbed a hill through prickly bushes, and sat down. They'd been late getting away. Dusk was approaching. Down below a bonfire was already burning. Feather's shadow moved in a radius around the fire as she piled on wood and stirred the pot with a spoon tied to a long stick.

Bodger fussed around the fire as though at home in his own kitchen.

'Where's the salt?' he called. 'Don't say we've forgotten it! Don't laze about, everyone. Have I got to do everything?'

Vance and Karen were having a casually bitter argument, looking away from one another, as if just chatting.

Feather began unpacking the basket, but stopped and walked off, looking at the sea. After a while some strangers came into view. It was impossible to make them all out in the flickering light and bonfire smoke, but she saw a woollen cap and grey beard, then a dark blue shirt, and a swarthy young face. About five of these people were squatting in a circle: travellers. Shortly after the people struck up a slow-moving song, like those sung in church during Lent.

Moon clambered up the path. Lisa was aware of him behind her. Had there actually been a time when this boy had attracted her?

'It was a mistake,' she said immediately. How could she explain that she wanted him for some things and not others?

'I'll wait until you want me,' he said.

'Do that.'

It became an amusing game again. She still owed him, of course. They had made a baby. For a short while, in the weeks of her pregnancy, she had been a woman and had imagined that people were beginning to take her seriously. She had stood in front of the mirror, sticking out her stomach and stroking it, imagining herself big.

'I must go now.'

She walked quickly, so that Moon knew not to follow her; when she turned she saw him taking another route. But after a few minutes walking she heard a sound and was frightened. She took a few more steps.

'How are you feeling?' said Bodger.

She was startled. He seemed to have concealed himself behind a tree and jumped out on her, surely an unusual practice for a doctor.

'Not physically bad,' she said, grateful for the enquiry. 'Strong again, in that way. But I'm lost.' He was looking at her strangely. 'I liked the last medicine you gave me, but what prescription can anyone give for lostness?'

'A kiss.'

'Sorry?'

'Let me kiss you.'

He closed his eyes, awaiting her reply, as if it were the most important question he'd ever asked.

She left him standing in that position. Down below the soup was ready. They poured it into the bowls and drank it with that air of ritual solemnity exclusive to picnics, and declared they never tasted anything so appetising at home.

They lay in a jumble of napkins, water bottles and paper plates. It got dark; the bonfire was dying. Everyone felt too sluggish to get up and put on more wood. Lisa drank beer after beer and let Moon watch her.

Rocco felt awkward sitting there. His back was hot from the fire, while Vance's loathing was directed at his chest and face. The hatred made him feel weak and humiliated.

'A great picnic and enchanting evening,' said Rocco.

'Glad you liked it.'

In a cringing voice he said, 'You know, Vance, occasionally I envy your certainty about everything.'

Lisa interrupted. 'I don't. I'll never know how anyone can have so much when so many people have almost nothing.'

Vance shook his head at both of them and Lisa got up and ran away. Rocco stared into the distance.

6

It was past one when they got into the cars. Everyone was ready for bed, apart from Moon and Lisa, who were chasing one another in the woods.

'Hurry up!' shouted Bodger, who had become irritable.

'Too stoned,' said Vance, jangling his keys. 'I'm off.'

Exhausted by the picnic, by Vance's hatred of him, and by his own thoughts, Rocco went to find Lisa. She was in high spirits; when she seized him by both hands and laid her head on his chest, breathlessly laughing out loud, he said, 'Don't be vulgar.'

She lost heart. She climbed into the car feeling stupid.

'Typical of the sentimental unemployed,' Vance said, closing his eyes, the better to concentrate on his opinions. Karen was driving. 'They think people are suffering because I've taken their money. They think I don't care. That I see an unemployed man and woman who can't feed their kids or pay the mortgage, and I fall about laughing. Meanwhile he swaggers around at exhibitions, museums and theatres, passing judgement, puffing himself up.'

'Music and books,' said Bodger. 'The best things in life. Reason for living. What men and women make. The best. And what will remain of us, if anything.'

Vance went on, 'You'll never find one of these people – whose dole I provide – sticking out their hand and saying, thank you for wanting to be rich, thank you for making this country run and for taking risks! There's more and more of them about. People don't contribute. What we'll do with them is the problem of our time.'

Bodger said, 'Lisa. She said something simplistic. And you're jumping on her because you hate Rocco. But she's a lovely woman!'

'Bodger, if you met a man who giggled all day and never worked, you'd say, a job will do you good. But you let her off because she's a beautiful woman.'

'What would you do with her, then? Hit her?'

Vance said, 'I might let her peel my potatoes.'

7

It would be too hot to sleep. Even with the windows open the air was not disturbed. Lisa sat down and looked at Rocco.

'Why did you speak to me like that? Rocco, please.' He was pulling something from his pocket. 'What's that?'

'It came for you.'

'When?'

'The other day.'

'Which day?'

'Read it.'

He went into the bedroom and lay down in the dark.

She was weeping. 'Rocco.' Thinking he was standing behind her chair, she sobbed, 'Why didn't you tell me this? I wouldn't have gone on the rotten picnic and laughed like that. Moon said such dirty things to me. I think I'm losing my mind.'

He was suffocating. He put his fingers in his ears. Then he climbed through the window, over the fence, and went down the street. Above his head a brightly lit train shot across a bridge.

Rocco peeped through Bodger's windows.

'Are you asleep? Hey. What's happening?'

He heard some coughing. Then, 'What d'you think I'm doing at this time?'

Bodger stood there in his underpants scratching.

'I'm going to kill myself, Bodger.'

'Thanks for the information.'

'Put the light on! I can't stay at home. You're my only friend and my only hope. Bodger, I've got to get away from here.'

Bodger let him in and put three bottles of wine and a bowl of cherries on the table.

'I want to talk.'

It was a monologue, of course, but Bodger – unfortunately for him – considered Rocco to be the only person in town worth talking to.

'How much frustration can a person bear?' Rocco asked. 'How much should one bear? Is stoicism a great or a foolish thing? Without it life would be unliveable. But if there's too much of it, nothing happens, and you can only ask, why are you stopping new shapes forming?' Without waiting for Bodger to express an opinion, he said, 'Please lend me the money to get away. I only need enough to last a few weeks, until I get a room or a flat. If you can lend me a grand, I'd be grateful.'

'One thousand pounds!'

'London's expensive. Seven hundred and fifty would do it.'

'You already owe me more than that.'

'You think I don't know that?'

Bodger said, 'I'll have to borrow it myself. I haven't got any loose cash. I went on that holiday. I've got the mortgage, my mother, and I bought the car. I –'

Rocco could tell that his friend didn't want to let him down. To cheer him up, Rocco offered Bodger one of the cherries and poured him some of his own wine.

'What about Lisa?' said Bodger. 'She's not staying here, is she?'

'I'm going to set things up in London for her. She'll join me after. If there's two of us there at first, it'll cost twice as much.'

'I'll miss you both,' said Bodger.

He raised his glass. 'You're a good man. I love you. Come with us.'

'Oh God, why do you have to be so weak? Can't you make up with Vance before you go?'

'I'm going to try. But I'm too lazy and useless for him. The only thing is, you don't know how he treats his staff. He's the sort of person who thinks that the more ruthless, cruel and domineering they are, the better boss they'll be. You wouldn't work five minutes for him. Poor Vance, why doesn't someone tell him the eighties are over?'

Rocco drank and ate the cherries cheerfully. 'People exist for him not as interesting human beings, but as entities to work. I'm surprised he hasn't suggested the weak be exterminated. And all this to make our society more affluent, more rationalised, more efficient. Will that bring happiness to people?'

'Aren't you trying to exterminate Lisa?'

Rocco sat back. 'I don't understand your problem, Bodger. One only sees these things as tragic if one has a certain view of relationships. That they mustn't end. That their ending is tragic rather than painful. That the duration of a relationship is the only measure of its success. Why see it like that?'

'People aren't disposable items, are they? It's chilling, Rocco. You sound rational and ruthless at the same time, not always a propitious combination, as you surely know.'

'Certain people are good for certain things and not for others. One wants something from some people, and they want something from you. You go on until there's nothing more.'

'Vance would agree with you.'

'Yes. I see that. I'm not saying it's not painful. Only tonight I believe in another possible future. Will it kill you to give me that chance?'

'Not immediately.' He started to put the drinks away. 'I must go to bed.'

Rocco was lying across the sofa with a bottle in his hand. 'Can I stay?'

He would sit up all night and listen to Bodger's classical records. Even though Rocco would weep at certain musical passages, Bodger liked having someone there.

8

Three days after the picnic Lisa opened the door to find Karen standing there with her son. When she saw Lisa was in, she sent the boy to play football in the garden and stepped inside. It was the first time Karen had been inside the cottage, and even as she looked around disapprovingly she was saying, 'Is it true, your husband died?'

Lisa wondered why she had come. They had never been friends. In fact Karen had often been condescending towards her. Perhaps there was something she had to tell her. But what?

Lisa said, 'It is true.'

'Is that terrible?'

Lisa shrugged.

'Oh God, Lisa.' For a moment Karen hugged her. 'It makes me think of Vance dying.' Looking over Lisa's shoulder she said, 'Books everywhere. Didn't you go to college?'

'University.'

'Is there a difference? I'm a pea brain. I expect you've noticed. What did you do there?'

'Had a lovely time at parties. And read – stuff I'd never read again.'

'Poetry?'

'Psychology. My husband – the, er, dead man – was a lecturer.'

'I'd like to read books. Except I don't know where to start. People who read too much are snobby, though.'

Lisa said, 'I know I didn't make enough of it. All that free education, and no one told me not to waste it. No one had my best interests at heart – least of all me. Isn't that funny?'

Karen said, 'You can get married to Rocco now.'

'But I haven't lived yet.'

'I'll tell you, from experience – marriage will make you secure. I know I'm all right with Vance and he'll take care of me. If I ask for something he writes a cheque.'

Lisa just laughed.

Karen look startled. 'You think he'll run off with someone else?'

'Do you?'

'Soon we're going to get out of here. In the next few years.'

'So are we.'

'But when though, when? Vance keeps saying we will but I know it won't happen!' Karen stood watching her son in the garden. She began to tug at her hair. 'The worst marriages – they aren't the most violent or stifling. Or the cruellest even. You could take action then. It would be obvious. The worst are the ones that are just wrong. People stay because it takes ten years to realise it, and those years are thrown away and you don't know where.'

Lisa murmured, 'I woke up startled the other night. He was kissing me.'

'Who?'

'He didn't know he was doing it. All over my face. Rocco's at his sweetest when he's unconscious.'

'You know, he did this thing with me once,' Karen said. Lisa looked up at her. 'He was carrying a book of poems. I said, "What's that junk about?" "Listen," he said, and read me this one song. It made me feel strange. He made me see what it was about. Vance never liked Rocco. Or you.'

'Have we ever harmed anyone? Vance can be very hard.'

'D'you think so?'

'How d'you stand all that rushing about?' asked Lisa. 'More like thrashing about, actually.'

'We went to the Caribbean. But Vance was always busy. He says I'm out of focus. Men only think about work . . . they never think about love, only sex. I always get up before Vance, to clean my teeth and shower so he won't see me looking ugly. He doesn't like my accent.'

'What d'you mean?'

'He hears me in front of other people, in a restaurant in London, or in front of you –'

'Me?'

'And he looks at me as if he's never seen me before. He says we've got to change if we're going to get anywhere.' Suddenly she cried out, 'What's that?'

'Where?'

'There – on the table.'

'An ant.'

'Kill it!'

Lisa smiled.

Karen stood up. 'They're swarming everywhere! It's unsanitary!' She sat down again and tried not to look around, but said, in her confusion, 'Don't you ever want to . . . to go to bed with another person, someone else?'

'Sorry?'

'Just to try another body. Another thingy. You know.'

Lisa was about to say something but only cleared her throat.

Karen said, 'Is that your only dress? Haven't you got anything else? Moon says you're always in the shop.'

'I like this dress. It's cool.'

'Vance might have to close that place. You're the only person who goes in there.'

'And the club?'

'Vance doesn't tell me much.' She said, 'A lot of the men round here go for you. Like Moon.'

'Oh Moon,' sighed Lisa. 'As Rocco said, Moon's on another planet. Men think that if they put their hands on you or say filthy things you'll want them.'

'Only if you ask for it,' Karen replied sharply. 'What will you live on in London?'

'I'll . . . I'll do journalism. I've been thinking about some ideas.'

Karen nodded. 'A single woman in London. That's a popular scenario. Thing is,' she said, 'however much a woman wants a career, for most of us it's a load of day-dreams. We aren't going to make enough to have a top-class life. The only way to get that is to marry the right guy. You might be brainy, but without money you can't do nothing.'

'Money! Why do people have to have so much of it?'

'People are so envious, it's dirty envy, it makes me mad. They want what we have but won't do anything to get it.'

Waves of heat rolled through Lisa's body; if only the top of her head were hinged and she could let them out.

She said, 'People say of the young people in this town . . . that we don't want to do anything. It's not true. Just give us a chance, we say.' Before Karen could speak again, Lisa went on, 'Did you come for any reason?'

Karen looked surprised. 'Only to talk.'

Lisa was thinking of other things. Her demeanour changed. 'I want to do so much. To learn to sing and dance. To paint. To row on the river. To play guitar and drums. I can't wait to begin my life!'

When she left Karen insisted on kissing Lisa again.

Lisa felt dizzy and feverish. She stepped out of her dress and rolled herself into a ball, under a sheet. She was thirsty, but there was no one to bring her a drink.

She awoke to find Rocco apologising for his rudeness at the picnic.

She cried out, 'Oh God, that woman Karen has done me in!'

'What was she here for? What did she say?'

Rocco noticed the blood on the sheet and went immediately to fetch Bodger.

'Did they teach you at medical school to hold onto your patients' hands that long, while whispering in their ears?' enquired Rocco when Bodger came out of the room.

'So you're jealous?' said Bodger. 'You don't want me to go out with her?'

'If you sorted out the money and I got out, you'd be welcome to have a go.'

'I'm trying to get the money,' said Bodger, glancing back at the door in embarrassment. 'But I'm a doctor, not a financier.'

'I've never known a doctor to be short of money.'

Bodger's voice squeaked. 'You're arrogant! I haven't had time to go to the bank. Are you still sure you want to get out?'

'If I can't get away by Saturday I'm going to go insane!'

'All right, all right!'

'What about by Friday morning?' Rocco put his mouth close to Bodger's ear and whispered. 'When I'm gone, she's all yours. If you knew how I've been praising you!'

'Have you?'

'Oh yes. She likes men. A lot of women do.'

'Yes?'

'But they keep it to themselves – for fear of encouraging the wrong sort.'

Bodger couldn't help believing him.

9

'You don't look well,' said Vance as Bodger came into the restaurant. 'Shall I call a doctor?'

'I thought I'd see the enterprise culture at work,' shouted Bodger over the music, removing his bicycle clips and putting his hands over his ears. 'Without conversation, clearly. What, er, are you up to?'

'Creating work, satisfying demand, succeeding.'

'Lend me £300, will you, Vance? No, £400.'

Vance put his arm around him.

'The place next door is for sale. Come and look. I'm thinking of buying it and knocking through. Put the kitchen in there. More tables here.' While Bodger looked around the almost empty restaurant Vance spoke to a waitress. 'Better food, too.' The waitress returned; Vance put the money on the table with his hand on top of it. 'If it's for Rocco you can forget it.'

'What if it is? That would be none of your business!'

'I won't let you lend money to any sad sack.'

Bodger waved his arms. 'It is for him! But no one tells me what to do!'

'Shhh . . . People are eating.'

Feather, who was writing her journal at the next table, started laughing.

Bodger said, 'Don't be inhumane. You think you're letting people be independent, but really you're just letting them down. How can it be wrong to help others?'

'But I'm all for charity. Is Rocco going away?' Bodger nodded. 'Without her?'

'At first.'

'The bastard's doing a runner. With my money! He's going to leave her behind. You'll get stuck with her.'

'Will I?'

Vance regarded him beadily. 'You want her?' Bodger gulped. 'Do you?'

'I would love her.'

'I can't guarantee to lay on love, but she'll sleep with you.'

'Are you certain? Did she mention it?'

'She'd do it with anyone. Haven't you asked her yet?'

'Asked?' Bodger was shivering. 'Once I'd said it . . . if she said yes, I'd be too excited, you know, to do anything. I sort of imagine that there are, out there, people who know how to ask for everything they want. They're not afraid of being rejected or laughed at, or of being so nervous that they can't even speak. But I'm not one of them.'

'You'll soon get sick of Lisa. She'll be so expensive to run. Can't imagine her working. High ideals and no prospects. Your great friend Rocco is making you an idiot.'

'I'll make him promise to take her with him.'

'Promise! In a year you'll run into him in London doing your Christmas shopping, and he'll be with another woman saying this time it's true love.'

Bodger put his head in his hands.

Vance said at last, 'You're a good man and people respect you. But this is weakness.' He passed the money over. 'There's one condition. Lisa goes with him. If she doesn't, I'll kick his backside into the sea.'

10

Next day, a Thursday, Karen closed a part of the restaurant and held a small party for her son's birthday. When Rocco and Lisa arrived Vance was giving the boy his present.

'He's going to be a businessman,' Vance told Bodger. 'But not in this country.'

'What's wrong with this country?'

Vance was looking across at Rocco and Lisa.

'That woman doesn't know she is about to be betrayed, does she? Or have you spoken to him?'

'Not yet.'

Vance told the waitress to give them drinks and then said, 'Sometimes I look around and think I'm the only person working in England – keeping everyone else alive, paying ridiculous taxes. Maybe I'll just give up too, chuck it all in, and sit in the pub.'

'Someone's got to run the pub, Vance.'

'You're exactly right.'

Rocco was greeting people; he smiled unctuously at Vance. They shook hands. Then Rocco guided Bodger into a quiet corner.

'Tomorrow is Friday.' He was biting his nails. 'Did you get me the loan?'

'Some of it. I'll get the rest later.'

'Thank God!'

'No, thank me.'

'Yes, yes. You've saved me.'

Bodger said, 'Look at Lisa! How could you go anywhere without those shoulders?'

'We owe so much money here, we can't leave. And where will we both stay in London? I've got friends, but I can't impose her on people. How come you've suddenly got a problem with our agreement? Have you been talking to someone? It's Vance, isn't it? I thought you had a mind of your own.'

Bodger blurted out, 'Take her with you, or I'll give you no more money.'

'Don't you know how to love a friend?'

'Don't you know how to love Lisa?'

Karen came over with her son. 'Am I interrupting? Rocco, look at this.'

She made the boy show Rocco his essays and drawings. 'Excellents' and 'very goods' danced before Rocco's eyes. Karen remarked in the posh voice she adopted on these occasions. 'They push them hard at private schools.'

'I know,' said Rocco. 'I am hoping, in the next few years, to make a partial recovery.'

He wanted his freedom; he didn't want Lisa. If he stayed the bills would mount up. He would get more frustrated. Other people wanted you to live lives as miserable as theirs. This they considered moral behaviour.

He thought of the moment the train would pull away and how he would open a bottle of beer to celebrate. Of course, when Lisa did get to London he would have to squirm and lie to get rid of her: as if everyone didn't lie at times, as if the lie were not protecting something, the integrity of a life. Lying was an underrated and necessary competence.

From across the room Lisa felt Moon's eyes on her. She wanted to go with him to the beach. And then she felt she had no control over herself. Her desire made her want to leave Rocco. He would protest, of course. He needed her more than he acknowledged. But she would make plans secretly, and then announce them. It was time to get away.

Moon and Rocco nodded at one another and went outside to try some weed Moon had been growing using a new method involving human shit. Moon was intending to set up as a dealer, and move to London. He was awaiting Rocco's opinion.

Rocco's bloodshot eyes had closed. Then he started chuckling. Moon nodded confidentially. 'Cool, cool.' But after a time Rocco was clucking, and his head started to thrash as he reacted to some welling disturbance or internal storm. He started looking at people with a wild, frightened disposition, as if he feared they would attack him, his guffaws became shriller until he sounded like a small dog. He tried to get up from the table but his legs would not obey him and his right arm started jumping about on the table. Bodger was so alarmed that he and a frightened Moon led Rocco downstairs, supporting his head from behind while Feather held a glass against his teeth, and water spilled onto his chest.

Lisa was clutching the back of the chair, afraid she would fall, terrified that Moon had told Rocco about them.

She went to Bodger. 'What's wrong with him?'

'He's smoked too much.'

'Not more than normal,' said Moon hastily.

'What is it, the stuff you gave him?'

'Mellow Wednesday. Because it's mellow.'

'I'm still alive,' Rocco moaned, and said quietly to Bodger, 'If I can get out of here I'll be okay.'

Later, they all walked along the front under a violet sky.

Fearing that Moon might try and talk to her, Lisa tried to stay close to Karen and her son. Fear and dejection weakened her; she could hardly move her legs. But she didn't go home, thinking Moon would try and accompany her. They went down to the beach.

11

'I'm going,' said Rocco at last.

Lisa took his arm. 'Me too.'

Rocco said, 'Thanks for the smoke, Moon. I'll do the same for you some day.'

Moon said he was going in her direction. What a fool she'd been to provoke Moon, but she had been stupefied by desire. Now she had to take the consequences.

Rocco turned away. 'I've got stuff to do. See you later.'

'I must talk to you,' said Moon, when he'd gone. 'You're playing games with me.'

Lisa said, 'But I'm depressed.'

'That's not going to stop me fucking you this evening. Otherwise what you've been doing will get around. People round here will certainly be interested, you know what they're like. In fact I think I'm going to fuck you today and tomorrow. After, you can do what you want.'

Lisa stopped at her front door. It was getting dark. She listened to the steady sea roar, glanced up at the star-strewn sky and felt she wanted to finish with everything.

'You're right, I've messed you around.'

She walked rapidly away and then turned up a side street leading away from the town. Pale patches of light from illuminated windows lay here and there on the road and she felt like a fly, perpetually falling into an inkpot and then crawling out again into the light. Moon was following her. At one point he stumbled, fell, and started laughing.

She turned. 'Not in my house.'

12

Rocco had decided to spare Lisa all the lies at once. He would spread them out. He had also had another brilliant idea: to tell Bodger that she was going to accompany him, and, at the last moment, announce that she wasn't well enough. If Bodger wouldn't give him the money he'd leave anyway, hitch-hiking to London and sleeping on the street. After yesterday's embarrassing paranoid fit, staying in the town was impossible.

Having decided this he felt better. He would visit Bodger for lunch, and charm him, and put him at ease. As soon as he walked in he saw Vance and Feather.

Before Rocco could get out, Vance said, 'How d'you feel after your little fit? I thought only women had hysterics.'

'Hysteria is ridiculous, yes. But most people recognise that paranoia is a kind of language, speaking to us but in a disguised way.'

Vance was looking at him with contempt. 'You're hopeless. Always scrounging money and talking rubbish.'

'What? What did you say?'

'You heard.'

Rocco went into the kitchen where Bodger was preparing lunch.

He began to yell, 'If you haven't got the money, just say that. But don't go round town telling everyone about my problems! Don't you know how to keep a confidence? I suppose, as a doctor, you tell everyone about your patients' illnesses!'

Bodger threw a wooden spoon at him. 'Come back later!'

Rocco rushed out of the kitchen.

'Everyone's spying on me now!' he cried. 'There's nothing better for people to talk about! I borrow money! I ask someone to help me! And for that I am crucified! Then people say I get paranoid . . . End this surveillance now – that's all I'm asking!'

Bodger followed him out of the kitchen, red-faced with rage. 'No one accuses me of such shit!'

Feather began to laugh.

Rocco shouted at Bodger, 'Just leave me alone!' He looked at Vance. 'Particularly you – you fascist Burger Queen.'

'Sorry? Did I hear you right? I think I might have to kick your head in.'

'Try it.'

This was the moment Vance had been waiting for. He took it slowly.

'Not your head. Maybe I'll break a few fingers, or an arm. It'll be educational for you.'

Vance moved towards Rocco with his fists up. Rocco stood there. Bodger extended his arms between them.

'But you can't even fight,' Vance told Rocco across Bodger. 'I don't think there's anything you can do.'

'No? Burger Queen – bring me some French fries too. Two French fries and a knickerbocker glory! Ha, ha ha!'

Vance said, 'I'm tempted, but I'm not going to fight you now – because I might kill you. I'll fight you tomorrow.'

'I used to be a skinhead.'

'Ha! See you tomorrow morning. On the Rim. No rules, skinhead.'

'Bastard, I'm going to stick your head in a bun and eat it with onions and relish! Ha, ha, ha!'

Vance smacked his fist into his palm. 'I'm afraid you're going to get damaged. Badly. Oh, oh, oh, you're going to cry!'

'Can't wait,' said Rocco. 'And by the way, can I have a green salad on the side?'

A few drinks made Rocco feel even better. And when his mood declined he had only to recall Vance's sneering face, manicured hands and Nigerian shirt to lift himself. How could a fool from a nothing place upset him? He would get the first punch in, and stamp on the bastard.

Teapot was in the pub and when Rocco told him about the fight they went into a field and practised karate kicks. It had been some time since Rocco had kicked anything but Lisa out of bed, and he kept tripping over even as he imagined his boot meeting Vance's balls.

Struggling for breath, he got up and declared, 'It's desperation not technique that's required. I'm going to rely on insanity.'

'That's right,' said Teapot. 'Go mental.'

'Now fuck off.'

He was glad to be alone. But when it got dark he became uneasy. He wanted to be in bed, but knew the night would be sleepless. He would have to think about Vance and prepare the lies he had to tell to Lisa. It was better to go from pub to pub.

He had been doing this for some time when Teapot tracked him down.

'I've been looking everywhere for you,' said the teenager. 'Come here!'

Rocco tried to swat him away. 'I'm saving my energy for tomorrow.'

Teapot almost picked him up and dragged him out of the pub. Rocco had no idea why Teapot should be in such a hurry. Teapot pushed him through the town's narrow streets to the beach and along the wall. There, Teapot took his hand and told him to be quiet.

Bewildered, Rocco followed him, and was helped onto the top of the wall. They lay down; at a sign from the ever-helpful Teapot they peered over the top. In the gloom Rocco could see Moon lying with his head between a woman's legs. Looking at the sky, she was humming to herself, as she liked to. He had imagined she only did that for him.

13

Bodger was ashamed of his outburst. He wanted to apologise to his friend and explain that fighting was childish.

Searching the pubs he stopped and sat down several times, recognising that it had been Rocco who'd insulted him and that he'd always done everything he could to help him.

When he opened the door of his house, Bodger heard Vance and Feather.

'Tomorrow there's going to be a fight,' Vance declared. 'We're civilised people, but we want to beat each other's brains to porridge. The strongest will triumph. Love and peace – out of the window! The thought of a fight – it's frightening . . . but don't we love it?'

Feather said, 'Strength and wisdom aren't the same.'

Bodger hurried in. 'The weather will spoil everything anyway.' He sat down. 'We have to care for one another. Yes! Otherwise we lose our humanity.'

Vance went on, 'We have the weak – people like Rocco – dominating the strong with their whingeing. They want others to do everything for them. But they will deplete our strength and drag us down. Selfishness, wanting something for oneself, is the law of reality. But if I benefit, others will benefit.'

Feather took all this equably. 'Who says who is weak and who is strong, and in what sense?'

'Him, presumably,' said Bodger. 'The new God enterprise.'

'Get real,' said Vance. 'Half the people who drag themselves to your surgery are skivers. They watch soap operas day and night. Why should we spend valuable resources keeping them alive?' He turned to Feather. 'I hope you're coming tomorrow.'

'I'm a pacifist.'

He smacked his fist into his palm.

'That's just voluntary ignorance. You should come and see what life is like.'

14

Rocco lay on the sofa and became aware of an unusual clattering sound. Wondering if children had got in upstairs, he ran to the stairs. No, it couldn't be that – the entire atmosphere had altered, as if there'd been a collision in space and the world would be extinguished. He moved to the window. The earth had turned grey. It was raining on the hard ground. Tonight, surely, was the end of summer. The evenings would draw in; no one would lie on the beach or gather at the War Memorial; the coach parties and foreign tourists would leave. Only they would remain.

For most of his life, at this time of year, he would be returning to school, and a new term.

He remembered as a kid running into the garden with two girls and getting soaked. They had snuggled up to one another in fear. No longer was he afraid of thunderstorms and now he ruined girls. Never had he planted one tree and never had he denied himself the opportunity to say something cutting or cruel, but he'd only wrecked everything.

Already aching from the exercises he had attempted with Teapot, he would feel worse tomorrow. What did it matter? He would encourage Vance to do him in, not only to break his arms – which wouldn't affect his brain – but to destroy his spirit and remaining hopes. It would be a relief.

It seemed not long after that Teapot turned up with his motor-bike and spare helmet. He and Rocco smoked some of Moon's Mellow Wednesday, practised some kicks, and went off.

Lisa had returned as it was getting light and had fallen asleep on the sofa with a coat over her. Rocco kissed her face and smoothed her hair.

There had been a moment – Moon was lapping between her legs and her mind was running free – when she'd projected herself into the future and looked back. She saw that these people, like the teachers and children at her first school – all pinches, curses, threats and boisterous power – were in retrospect just pathetic or ordinary, and nothing to be afraid of. She knew, at that moment, that she had already left.

When she thought of what she'd been through she didn't know how she hadn't gone mad. Her own strength surprised her. How much more of it might she have?

15

Feather rose early, meditated restlessly, and started out with a rucksack and stick. Why was she going? It was ridiculous for a pacifist to be present at such an event. But she was curious. She thought of Rocco. He had suffered; he understood something about life; he liked people. There was no cruelty in him; yet he fucked everyone up. And the person he made suffer the most was himself.

She stopped on the way to eat and drink; she washed in a rain-filled stream. For a change the air was moist. She wondered why this journey wasn't more enjoyable and when she sat and thought about it she realised she was tired of being alone; it was time to find a lover, particularly with winter on its way.

The others drove as far as they could and then walked up the chalk downs, until they could see the town in the distance, and the sea beyond.

She was walking up the Rim when a car approached. It was Karen, who was distressed. But Feather didn't want a lift.

She walked to the very top, a flat area with a pagan pedestal. The first thing she saw was Vance unpacking new running shoes. He wore sweatbands around his head and wrists, a singlet and a pair of shorts. Rocco hadn't given a thought to what he would wear, and had turned up in his ordinary clothes. He noticed that Bodger had arrived, but refused to acknowledge him.

Teapot rushed over to Vance. 'Please, Mr Vance, Rocco's terrified. He's shaking all over. Don't hurt him. He's had some Mellow Wednesday. You can't beat up a man in that condition.'

'I'll teach him a lesson,' said Vance, hawking and spitting. 'After the beating he'll be an improved person.'

'Look at him.'

Vance glanced over at Rocco and guffawed. 'He's disgusting, it's true. But that doesn't change anything.'

Teapot said, 'And he's upset.'

'So?'

Bodger was standing nearby with his doctor's bag. 'What about?'

'He saw his girlfriend being fucked – last night.'

'Who by?'

Teapot leaned towards them. 'Moon.'

Bodger went pale.

Across the way, practising his kicks and trying to make himself usefully mad, Rocco twisted his ankle. Teapot helped him up, but Rocco could barely walk and, when everyone was ready, Teapot had to cart him to the fighting place. Rocco stood there on one foot, breathing laboriously.

Karen stood a few feet away, tugging at her hair. She was watching her husband but seemed, also, to be thinking about something else.

Vance was dancing around and when he turned away to give Karen the thumbs up, Rocco, windmilling an arm as he'd seen guitarists do, took a tremendous swing at him, which missed. Then he hobbled towards Vance and attempted a flying kick.

Rocco collapsed and lay there shouting, 'Beat me, Burger Queen. Kick my head in. Kick, kick, kick!'

'Get up. I'm not ready yet. Get up, I said!'

Vance reached out a hand to him, and Rocco got up. Then he tried, once more, to attack Vance who danced around him until, taking aim, he landed a nice punch in the centre of Rocco's face. Rocco fell down and Vance bestrode him, picking up his arm and bending it back over his knee. Rocco refused even to whimper but his face was screaming.

Bodger, with his hand over his mouth, murmured, 'Don't, don't . . .'

'A fight's a fight, ain't it?' said Vance.

'Please, Vance, you're just making more work for me.'

'Kill me, kill me, Queen,' begged Rocco.

'Don't worry,' said Vance. 'I'm on my way.'

Suddenly there was a sound from the bushes. Feather, naked but covered in dirt and mud, rushed screeching into the space and began to dance. Vance stared at her, as they all did, but decided to take no notice – until Feather took up a position in front of him and held up her hands.

'I'm breaking my fingers,' she said.

Vance continued his bending work.

Feather snapped her little finger and waved it at everyone.

'Now the next,' she said. 'And the next.'

'No, no, no!' said Bodger.

'What the hell is going on?' cried Vance. 'Get her out of here!'

Bodger rushed into the centre of the fight and threw himself on Vance.

Rocco had thought, somehow, that he would never get home again and had no idea that he'd be so glad to be back. The books, records and pictures in his house and the light outside seemed new to him. He thought he might read, listen to music and then go and look at the sea. Vance had been right, the fight had done him good.

Lisa, pale and thin, didn't understand why he was being so gentle. Somehow she had thought he would never come back. She was prepared for that. But he had returned.

He stroked her face and hair, looked into her eyes and said, 'I've only got you.'

After, they sat in the garden.

16

It had been raining. A strong sea was running. It was early evening when Bodger, Feather and Vance came up the lane past Lisa and Rocco's house. Bodger carried a couple of bottles of wine and Feather some other provisions. They were on their way to her place. She had arranged to massage both Bodger and Vance, but now her right hand was bandaged. All day Vance had been fussing around her, both contrite and annoyed, and kept touching her reassuringly, as if to massage her.

'I'm not apologising to them,' said Vance.

'I wonder what they're doing,' said Feather. 'Stop for a minute.'

'Just for a second,' said Bodger.

They all looked over the hedge.

'Well, well.' Vance said. 'Who would have believed it?'

Rocco had dragged a couple of suitcases outside and was attempting to throw the contents – papers and notebooks – onto a shambolic bonfire. As the papers caught fire, the wind blew them across the garden. In the doorway Lisa, with a cardigan thrown over her shoulders, was folding her clothes and placing them in a pile. As they worked, she and Rocco chatted to one another and laughed.

'It's true,' said Feather.

Bodger turned to Vance. 'You're a bloody fucking fool.'

Vance said, 'What's wrong with you?'

'This didn't have to happen!'

Feather said, 'Go and tell them.'

'It's too late,' Vance said.

'Tell me if this pleases you!' Bodger cried. 'Be glad then – and dance!'

'Bodger, they've been wanting to get out for weeks. And I'm paying for it.' Vance added, 'It's amazing, he's actually doing something. And we're left behind.'

He turned and saw Moon scurrying up the lane, calling out, 'I'm not too late, am I?'

'You're always late, you little shite. Who's minding the shop?'

'Vance, please,' said Moon. 'I've shut it for a few minutes.'

'Get back there and open up – before I open you up!'

Moon looked over the hedge. Vance was about to grab him when Feather gave him a look; Vance noticed that Moon was crying under his shades.

Rocco had seen them by now, but he didn't look up. He stood by the fire flinging balls of paper into the flames.

Wearing her black dress and straw hat Lisa stood in the doorway smiling. In a strange, abstract motion, she raised her flat hand and waved to all of them. Vance turned and walked away up the lane, lowering his head and shoulders into the wind. Lisa went back into the house. Without moving, the others stood in a line watching Rocco until it began to drizzle and the fire went out. At last they went away, wondering what they would do now. It was raining hard.

The Flies

'We hadn't the pleasure now of feeling we were starting a new life,
only a sense of dragging on into a future full of new troubles.'
Italo Calvino, 'The Argentine Ant'

One morning after a disturbed night, a year after they moved into
the flat, and with their son only a few months old, Baxter goes into
the box-room where he and his wife have put their wardrobes,
opens the door to his, and picks up a pile of sweaters. Unfolding
them one by one, he discovers that they all appear to have been
crocheted. Not only that, the remaining threads are smeared with
a viscous yellow deposit, like egg yolk, which has stiffened the
remains of the ruined garments.

He shakes out the moths or flies that have gorged on his clothes,
and stamps on the tiny crisp corpses. Other flies, only stupefied,
dart out past him and position themselves on the curtains, where
they appear threateningly settled, just out of reach.

Baxter hurriedly rolls up the clothes in plastic bags, and, retch-
ing, thrusts them into the bottom of a dustbin on the street. He
goes to the shops and packs his wardrobe with fly killer; he sprays
the curtains; he disinfects the rugs. He stands in the shower a
long time. With water streaming down him nothing can adhere to
his skin.

He doesn't tell his wife about the incident, thinking, at first, that
he won't bother her with such an unimportant matter. He has,
though, spotted flies all over the flat, which his wife, it seems, has

not noticed. If he puts mothballs in his pockets, and has to mask this odour with scents, and goes about imagining that people are sniffing as he passes them, he doesn't care, since the attack has troubled him.

He wants to keep it from himself as much as from her. But at different times of the day he needs to check the wardrobe, and suddenly rips open the door as if to surprise an intruder. At night he begins to dream of ragged bullet-shaped holes chewed in fetid fabric, and of creamy white eggs hatching in darkness. In his mind he hears the amplified rustle of gnawing, chewing, devouring. When this wakes him he rushes into the box-room to shake his clothes or stab at them with an umbrella. On his knees he scours the dusty corners of the flat for the nest or bed where the contamination must be incubating. He is convinced, though, that while he is doing this, flies are striking at the bedsheets and pillows.

When one night his wife catches him with his nose against the skirting board, and he explains to her what has happened, she isn't much concerned, particularly as he has thrown away the evidence. Telling her about it makes him realise what a slight matter it is.

He and his wife acquired the small flat in a hurry and consider themselves fortunate to have it. For what they can afford, the three rooms, with kitchen and bathroom, are acceptable for a youngish couple starting out. Yet when Baxter rings the landlord to enquire whether there have been any 'outbreaks' before, he is not sympathetic but maintains they carried the flies with them. If it continues he will review their contract. Baxter, vexed by the accusation, counters that he will suspend his rent payments if the contagion doesn't clear up. Indeed, that morning he noticed one of his child's cardigans smeared and half-devoured, and only just managed to conceal it from his wife.

Still, he does need to discuss it with her. He asks an acquaintance to babysit. They will go out to dinner. There was a time when they would have long discussions about anything – they particularly enjoyed talking over their first impressions of one another – so happy were they just to be together. As he shaves, Baxter reflects

that since the birth of their child they have rarely been to the theatre or cinema, or even to coffee shops. It has been months since
they ate out. He is unemployed and most of their money has been
spent on rent, bills, debts, and the child. If he were to put it plainly,
he'd say that they can hardly taste their food; they can't even watch
TV for long. They rarely see their friends or think of making new
ones. They never make love; or, if one of them wants to, the other
doesn't. Never does their desire coincide – except once, when, at the
climax, the screams of their child interrupted. Anyhow, they feel
ugly and their bodies ache. They sleep with their eyes open; occasionally, while awake, they are actually asleep. While asleep they
dream of sleep.

Before the birth, they'd been together for a few months, and
then serious lovers for a year. Since the child their arguments have
increased, which Baxter imagines is natural as so much has happened to them. But their disagreements have taken on a new tone.
There was a moment recently when they looked at one another
and said, simultaneously, that they wished they had never met.

He had wanted a baby because it was something to want; other
people had them. She agreed because she was thirty-five. Perhaps
they no longer believed they'd find the one person who would
change everything.

Wanting to feel tidy, Baxter extracts a suit from his wardrobe.
He holds it up to the light on its hanger. It seems complete, as it did
the last time he looked, a couple of hours before. In the bathroom
his wife is taking longer than ever to apply her make-up and curl
her hair.

While removing his shoes, Baxter turns his back. When he looks
again, only the hanger remains. Surely a thief has rushed into the
room and filched his jacket and trousers? No; the suit is on the
floor, a small pyramid of charred ash. His other suits disintegrate
at one touch. Flies hurl themselves at his face before chasing into
the air.

He collects the ash in his hands and piles it on the desk
he's arranged in the box-room, where he has intended to study

something to broaden his understanding of life now that he goes out less. He has placed on the desk several sharpened but unused pencils. Now he sniffs the dirt and sifts it with the pencils. He even puts a little on his tongue. In it are several creamy ridged eggs. Within them something is alive, hoping for light. He crushes them. Soot and cocoon soup sticks to his fingers and gets under his nails.

Over dinner they drink wine, eat good food and look around, surprised to see so many people out and about, some of whom are smiling. He tells her about the flies. However, like him, she has become sarcastic and says she's long thought it time he acquired a new wardrobe. She hopes the involuntary clear-out will lead to sartorial improvement. Her own clothes are invariably protected by various guaranteed ladies' potions, like lavender, which he should try.

That night, tired by pettiness and their inability to amuse one another, she sits in the box-room and he walks the child up and down in the kitchen. He hears a cry and runs to her. She has unlocked her wardrobe to discover that her coats, dresses and knitwear have been replaced by a row of yellowish tatters. On the floor are piles of dead flies.

She starts to weep, saying she has nothing of her own left. She implies that it is his fault. He feels this too, and is ready to be blamed.

He helps her to bed, where the child sleeps between them. Just as they barely kiss now when they attempt love, he rarely looks into her eyes; but as he takes her arm, he notices a black fly emerge from her cornea and hop onto her eyelash.

Next morning he telephones a firm of exterminators. With unusual dispatch, they agree to send an Operative. 'You need the service,' they say before Baxter has described the symptoms. He and his wife obviously have a known condition.

They watch the van arrive; the Operative opens its rear doors and strides into their hall. He is a big and unkempt man, in green overalls, with thick glasses. Clearly not given to speaking, he listens keenly, examines the remains of their clothes, and is eager to see the pyramidal piles of ash which Baxter has arranged on newspaper. Baxter is grateful for the interest.

At last the Operative says, 'You need the total service.'

'I see,' says Baxter. 'Will that do it?'

In reply the man grunts.

Baxter's wife and the baby are ordered out. Baxter runs to fetch a box in order to watch through the window.

The Operative dons a grey mask. A transparent bottle of greenish liquid is strapped to his side. From the bottle extends a rubber tube with a metal sieve on the end. Also feeding into the sieve is a flat-pack of greyish putty attached to a piece of string around the man's neck. On one thigh is a small engine which he starts with a bootlace. While it runs, he strikes various practised poses and holds them like a strangely attired dancer. The rattling noise and force is terrific; not a living cretin could proceed through the curtains of sprayed venom.

The Operative leaves behind, in a corner, an illuminated electrified blue pole in a flower pot, for 'protection'.

'How long will we need that?' Baxter enquires.

'I'll look at it the next couple of times. It'll have to be recharged.'

'We'll need the full Operative service again?'

The Operative is offended. 'We're not called Operatives now. We're Microbe Consultants. And we are normally invited back, when we are available. Better make an appointment.' He adds, 'We're hoping to employ more qualified people. By the way, you'll be needing a pack too.'

'What is that?'

From the van he fetches a packet comprising of several sections, each containing different potions. Baxter glances over the interminable instructions.

'I'll put it on the bill,' says the Operative. 'Along with the curtain atomiser, and this one for the carpet. Better take three packs, eh, just in case.'

'Two will be fine, thanks.'

'Sure?' He puts on a confidential voice. 'I've noticed, your wife looks nice. Surely you want to protect her?'

'I do.'

'You won't want to run out at night.'

'No. Three then.'

'Good.'

The total is formidable. Baxter writes the cheque. His wife leans against the door jamb. He looks with vacillating confidence into her tense but hopeful eyes, wanting to impress on her that it will be worth it.

She puts out the potions. The caustic smell stings their eyes and makes them cough; the baby develops red sores on its belly. But they rub cream into the marks and he sleeps contentedly. Baxter goes to the shops; his wife cooks a meal. They eat together, cuddle, and observe with great pleasure the saucers in which the dying flies are writhing. The blue pole buzzes. In the morning they will clear out the corpses. They are almost looking forward to it, and even laugh when Baxter says, 'Perhaps it would have been cheaper to play Bulgarian music at the flies. We should have thought of that!'

The next morning he clears the mess away and, as there are still flies in the air, puts out more saucers and other potions. Surely, though, they are through the worst. How brought down he has been!

Lately, particularly when the baby cries, he has been dawdling out on the street. A couple of the neighbours have suggested that the new couple stop by for a drink. He has noticed lighted windows and people moving across holding drinks. Leaving his wife and child in safety, he will go out more, that very night in fact, wearing whatever he can assemble, a suit of armour if need be.

His wife won't join him and she gives Baxter the impression that he hasn't brought them to the right sort of neighbourhood. But as he is only going to be five minutes away, she can't object. He kisses her, and after checking that the blue pole is functioning correctly, he begins at the top of the street, wearing an acrylic cardigan purchased from the charity shop, inedible combat trousers and a coat.

The first couple Baxter visits have three young children. Both adults work, designing household objects of some kind. Kettles, Baxter presumes, but it could be chair legs. He can't remember what his wife has said.

He rings the bell. After what seems a considerable amount of hurried movement inside, a bearded man opens the door, breathing heavily. Baxter introduces himself, offering, at the same time, to go away if his visit is inconvenient. The man demurs. In his armchair he is drinking. Baxter, celebrating that night, joins him, taking half a glass of whisky. They discuss sport. But it is a disconcerting conversation, since it is so dark in the room that Baxter can barely make out the other man.

The woman, harassed but eager to join in, comes to the foot of the stairs before the children's yells interrupt. Then she stomps upstairs again, crying out, 'Oh right, right, it must be my turn again!'

'Will they never stop?' shouts the man.

'How can they sleep?' she replies. 'The atmosphere is suffocating them.'

'All of us!' says the man.

'So you've noticed!'

'How could I not?'

He drinks in silence. Baxter, growing accustomed to the gloom, notices a strange gesture he makes. Dipping his fingers into his glass, the bearded man flicks the liquid across his face, and in places rubs it in. He does the same with his arms, even as they talk, as if the alcohol is a lotion rather than an intoxicant.

The man stands up and thrusts his face towards his guest.

'We're getting out.'

'Where?'

He is hustling Baxter by the arm of his black PVC coat towards the door. Immediately the woman flies down the stairs like a bat and begins to dispute with her husband. Baxter doesn't attend to what they are saying, although other couples' arguments now have the ability to fascinate him. He is captivated by something else. A fly detaches itself from the end of the man's protuberant tongue, crawls up the side of his nose, and settles on his eyebrow, where it joins a companion, unnoticed until now, already grazing on the hairy ridge. It is time to move on.

Taking a wrong turn in the hall, Baxter passes through two rooms, following a smell he recognises but can't identify. He opens a door and notices an object standing in the bath. It is a glowing blue pole, like the one in his flat, and it seems to be pulsating. He looks closer and realises that this effect is caused by the movement of flies. He is reaching out to touch the thing when he hears a voice behind him, and turns to see the bearded man and his wife.

'Looking for something?'

'No, sorry.'

He doesn't want to look at them but can't help himself. As he moves past they drop their eyes. At that moment the woman blushes, for shame. They give off a sharp bleachy odour.

He isn't ready to go home but can't stay out on the street. Further down the road he sees figures in a window, before a hand drags the curtain across. He has barely knocked on the door before he is in the room with a glass in his hand.

It is a disparate crowd, comprising, he guesses, shy foreign students, the sorts of girls who would join cults, an oldish man in a tweed suit and rakish hat, people dancing with their shoes off, and others sitting in a row on the sofa. In the corner is a two-bar electric fire and a fish tank. Baxter has forgotten what exactly he is wearing and when he glimpses himself in a mirror and realises that no one minds, he is thankful.

His neighbour is drunk but oddly watchful. She puts her arms around his neck, which discomfits him, as if there is some need in him that she has noticed, though he can't see what it is.

'We didn't think you'd come. Your wife barely speaks to any of us.'

'Doesn't she?'

'Well, she's charming to some people. How is the flat?'

'It's fine . . . Not too bad.'

Becoming aware of an itching on his forehead, he slaughters a fly between finger and thumb.

She says, 'Sure?'

'Why not?'

He feels another fly creeping across his cheek. She is looking at him curiously.

'I'd like it if you would dance with me,' she says.

He dislikes dancing but suspects that movement is preferable to stasis. And tonight – why not? – he will celebrate. She points out her husband, a tall man standing in the doorway, talking to a woman. Warm and fleshy, she shakes her arse, and he does what he can.

Then she takes the index finger of his right hand and leads him into a conservatory at the back. It is cold; there is no music. She shoves down her clothes, bends forward over the arm of a chair and he slides the finger she's taken possession of, and two others, into her. It is a luxurious and well-deserved oblivion. Surely happiness is forgetting who you are! But too soon he notices a familiar caustic smell. He looks about and sees bowls of white powder placed on the floor; another contains a greenish-blue sticky substance. Injured specks move drowsily in the buckets.

He extracts his hand and holds it out. Up at the wrist it is alive with flies.

She looks round. 'Oh dear, the little babies are hungry tonight.' She flaps at them unconcernedly.

'Isn't there a remedy?' he asks.

'People live with it.'

'They do?'

'That is the best thing. It is also the worst. They work incessantly. Or drink. People all over the world endure different kinds of bacteria.'

'But surely, surely there is a poison, brew or . . . blue light that will deter them for ever?'

'There is,' she says. 'Of a kind.'

'What is it?'

She smiles at his desperation. 'The potions do work, for a period. But you have to replace them with different makes. Imported is best, but expensive. Try the Argentinian. Then the South African, in that order. I'm not sure what they put in that stuff, but . . . Course, the flies get used to it, and it only maddens and incites them. You might need to go on to the Madagascan.' Baxter must be looking disheartened because she says, 'In this street this is how we keep them away – passion!'

'Passion?'

'Where there is passion you don't notice anything.'

He lies over her from behind. He says he can't believe that these things are just inevitable; that there isn't, somewhere, a solution.

'We'll see to it – later,' she grunts.

After, in the living room, she whispers, 'Most of them have got flies round here. Except the newly-weds and adulterers.' She laughs. 'They got other things. Eighteen months, it takes. If you're lucky you get eighteen months and then you get the flies.' She explains that the flies are the only secret that everyone keeps. Other problems can be paraded and boasted of, but this is an unacceptable shame. 'We are poisoned by ourselves.' She looks at him. 'Do you hate her?'

'What?'

'Do you, yet? You can tell me.'

He whispers that it is dawning on him, as love dawns on people, that at times he does hate her; hates the way she cuts up an apple; hates her hands. He hates her tone of voice and the words he knows she'll use; he hates her clothes, her eyelids, and everyone she knows; her perfume makes him nauseous. He hates the things he's loved about her; hates the way he has put himself in thrall to her; hates the kindnesses she shows him, as if she is asking for something. He sees, too, that it doesn't matter that you don't love someone, until you have a child with them. And he understands, too, how important hatred is, what a strong sustaining feeling it is; a screen perhaps, to stop him pitying her, and himself, and falling into a pit of misery.

His neighbour nods as he shivers with shame at what she has provoked him into saying. She says, 'My husband and I are starting a microbe business ourselves.'

'Is there that much call for it?'

'You can't sing to them, can you?'

'I suppose not.'

'We've put a down payment on our first van. You will use only us, won't you?'

'We're broke, I'm afraid. Can't use anyone.'

'You can't let yourself be invaded. You'll have to work. You haven't been using the Microbe Consultants, have you?'

'They have passed by, yes.'

'They didn't sell you a pack?'

'Only two.'

'Useless, useless. Those men are on commission. Never let them in the house.'

She holds him. Dancing in the middle of the night, while he is still conscious, she puts her mouth to his ear and murmurs, 'You might need Gerard Quinn.'

'Who?'

'Quinn has been hanging around. He'll be in touch. Meanwhile, behind that door' – she points at a wooden door with a steel frame, with a padlock hanging from it – 'we are working on a combination potion, a deadly solution. It's not yet ready, but when we have a sample, I'll bring it.' He looks at her sceptically. 'Yes, everyone would be doing it. But the snag is, what prevents a definitive remedy is that husbands and wives give the stuff to their partners.' Baxter feels as if he will fall over. 'Have you actually mixed it in with her cereal yet, or are you still considering it?'

'One time I did do that, but I put it down the drain.'

'People use it to commit suicide too. One can't be too careful, you see.'

She leaves him. He notices that the bearded man has arrived, and is laughing and sprinkling himself with alcohol beside the fish tank. He raises his hand in acknowledgement of Baxter. Later, before Baxter passes out, he sees the bearded man and the female neighbour go into the conservatory together.

Early in the morning his neighbour's husband carries Baxter home.

Baxter is still asleep beside the bed, where he has collapsed, when the landlord visits. Fortunately he has forewarned them, and Baxter's wife has stuffed the blue pole, potions and any devoured items into a cupboard. The man is susceptible to her; when necessary she can be both charming and forceful. Even though a fly lands on his lapel as they are talking, she convinces him that the problem is 'in remission'.

After lunch, Baxter empties the full saucers once more, and sets out new ones. Once more the flies begin to die. But it is no longer something he can bear to look at. He stands in the bedroom and tells his wife that he will be out for the afternoon, and will take the kid with him. No, she says, he has always been irresponsible. He has to insist, as if it is his last wish, until she gives in.

It has made her sullen, but it is an important victory. He has never been alone with his son. In its sling, weighted against his body, he carries this novelty about the city. He sits in cafés, puts it on his knee and admires its hands and ears; he flings it in the air and kisses it. He strolls in the park and on the grass gives it a bottle. People speak to him; women, particularly, seem to assume he is not a bad character. The child makes him more attractive. He likes having this new companion, or friend, with him.

He thinks of what else they might do. His lover's phone number comes into his mind. He calls her. They cross the river on the bus. At her door he wants to turn back but she is there immediately. He holds up the child like a trophy, though Baxter is fearful that she will be unnerved by the softened features of the other woman alive between them.

She invites them in. She is wearing the ear-rings he gave her; she must have put them on for him. They find themselves sighing at the sight of one another. How pleased she is to see them both; more pleased than he has allowed himself to imagine. She can't stop herself slipping her hands inside his coat, as she used to. He wraps her up and kisses her neck. She belongs in this position, she tells him. How dispirited she has been since he left last time, and hasn't been in touch. Sometimes she hasn't wanted to go out. At times she has thought she would go mad. Why did he push her away when he knew that with her everything seemed right? She has had to find another lover.

He doesn't know how to say he couldn't believe she loved him, and that he lacked the courage to follow her.

She holds the baby, yet is unsure about kissing him. But the boy is irresistible. She hasn't changed a nappy before. He shows her. She wipes the boy down, and rubs her cheeks against his skin. His soother stops twitching and hangs from his lips.

They take off their clothes and slip into bed with him. She caresses Baxter from his fingertips to his feet, to make him hers again. She asks him to circle her stomach with kisses. He asks her to sit on her knees, touching herself, showing herself to him, her thumbs touching her pubic bone, making a butterfly of her hands. They are careful not to rock the bed or cry out suddenly, but he has forgotten how fierce their desire can become, and how much they can laugh together, and he has to stuff his fingers in her mouth.

As she sleeps he lies looking at her face, whispering words he has never said to anyone. This makes him more than peaceful. If he is away from his wife for a few hours he feels a curious warmth. He has been frozen, and now his love of things is returning, like a forgotten heat, and he can fall against any nearby wall and slide down it, so soft does he feel. He wants to go home and say to his wife, why can't we cover each other in affection for ever?

Something is brushing his face. He sits up to see a fly emerging from his lover's ear. Another hangs in his son's hair. His leg itches; his hand, too, and his back. A fly creeps from the child's nose. Baxter is carrying the contagion with him, giving it to everyone!

He picks up the sleeping child and wakes the dismayed woman. She attempts to reason with him, but he is hurrying down the street as if pursued by lunatics, and with the desire to yell heartless words at strangers.

He passes the child to his wife, fearing he is looking at her a little wildly. It has all rushed back, what he owes her: kindness, succour, and something else, the details elude him; and how one can't let people down merely because one happens, one day, to feel differently.

Not that she notices his agitation, as she checks the baby over.

He take a bath, the only place in the flat they can feel at peace. Drinking wine and listening to the radio, he will swat away all thoughts. But the vows he made her aren't affection, just as a signature isn't a kiss, and no amount of promises can guarantee love. Without thinking, he gave her his life. He valued it less then, and now he wants it back. But he knows that retrieving a life takes a different courage, and is crueller.

At that moment his heart swells. He can hear her singing in the kitchen. She claps too. He calls her name several times.

She comes in irritably. 'What do you want?'

'You.'

'What for? Not now.' She looks down at him. 'What a surprise.'

'Come on.'

'Baxter –'

He reaches out to stroke her.

'Your hands are hot,' she says. 'You're sweating.'

'Please.'

She sighs, removes her skirt and pants, gets in the bath and pulls him onto her.

'What brought that on?' she says after, a little cheered.

'I heard you singing and clapping.'

'Yes, that's how I catch the flies.' She gets out of the bath. 'Look, there are flies floating on the water.'

A few days later, when the blue pole has flickered and died – and been smashed against the wall by Baxter – and the bowls of powder have been devoured, leaving a crust of frothing corpses, the Operative is at the door. He doesn't seem surprised by the failure of his medicaments, nor by Baxter's fierce complaints about the hopeless cures.

'It's a course,' he insists. 'You can't abandon it now, unless you want to throw away the advances and go back to the beginning.'

'What advances?'

'This is a critical case. What world are you living in, thinking it'll be a simple cure?'

'Why didn't you say that last time?'

'Didn't I? I'd say you're the sort who doesn't listen.'

'The blue pole doesn't work.'

He speaks as if to a dolt. 'It draws them. The vibration makes them voracious. Then they eat. And perish for ever. But not if you kick it to pieces like a child. I passed your wife on the doorstep. She's changed since the last time. Her eyes –'

'All right!'

'I've seen it before. She is discouraged. Don't think she doesn't know what's going on!'

'What is going on?'

'You know.'

Baxter puts his head in his hands.

The Operative sweeps up the remains of the blue pole and offers Baxter a bag of grey crystals. 'Watch.' He pours them into a bowl – the sound is a whoosh of hope – and rests it on the floor. The flies land on it and, after a taste, hop a few inches, then drop dead.

The Operative kisses his fingers.

'This is incomparable.'

'Argentinian?' asks Baxter. 'Or South African?'

The Operative gives him a mocking look.

'We never disclose formulas. We have heard that there are people who are mixing their own poisons at home. This will make your skin bubble like leprosy, and your bones soften like rubber. It could be fatal. Leave these things to the experts.'

Baxter writes a cheque for five packs. At the end of the afternoon, he sees the Operative has parked his unmarked van outside the bearded man's house and is going in with plastic bags. The man glances at Baxter and give a little shrug. Several of the local inhabitants are making slow journeys past the house; as Baxter moves away he notices faces at nearby windows.

Baxter discovers his wife examining the chequebook.

'Another cheque!' she cries. 'For what?'

'Three packs!'

'It doesn't work.'

'How do you know?'

'Just look!'

'It might be worse without the poison.'

'How could it be worse? You're throwing money away!'

'I'm trying to help us!'

'You don't know where to start!'

She blinks and nods with anger. The baby cries. Baxter refuses to recount what the Operative said. She doesn't deserve an explanation. It does occur to him, though, to smash her in the mouth, and at that instant she flinches and draws back. Oh, how we understand one another, without meaning to!

What suggestions does she have, he enquires, trying to keep down self-disgust. She doesn't have to consider this; she has intentions. Tired of the secrecy, she will discuss the contagion with a friend, when she has the energy. She wants to go out into the world. She has been lonely.

'Yes, yes,' he agrees. 'That would be good. We must try something new.'

A few days later, as soon as his wife has left for the park, there are several urgent taps on the window. Baxter ducks down. However, it is too late. At the door, with a triumphant twirl, his female neighbour presents a paint pot. She wrenches off the lid. It contains a sticky brown substance like treacle. Her head is thrown back by the reek.

Holding the paint pot at arm's length, she takes in the room. By now they have, piece by piece, removed a good deal of the furniture, though a few items, the curtains and cushions, have been replaced by spares, since it is imperative to uphold belief. Baxter and his wife can't encourage visitors, of course. If old friends ring they arrange to see them outside. The only person who visits regularly is his mother-in-law, from whom his wife strives to conceal all signs of decay. This loyalty and protectiveness surprises and moves Baxter. When he asks his wife about it, she says, 'I don't want her to blame you.'

'Why not?'

'Because you're my husband, stupid.'

The neighbour says, 'Put this out.'

Baxter looks dubiously at the substance and grimaces. 'You're not an expert.'

'Not an expert? Me?'

'No.'

'Who told you to say that?'

'No one.'

'Yes they did. Because who is, may I ask? You don't know, do you?'

'I suppose not.'

'Experts steal our power and sell it back to us, at a profit. You're not falling for that, are you?'

'I see what you mean.'

'Look.'

She sticks her finger in the stuff, puts it on her tongue, waggles it at him, tastes it, and spits it into a napkin.

'Your wife's not going to eat that, even if you smother it in honey,' she says, gagging. 'But it'll draw the little devils from all over the room.' She gets on her knees and makes a cooing sound. 'You might notice a dungy smell.'

'Yes.'

'In that case – open the window. This is an early prototype.'

She puts out the treacle in his saucers. There is no doubt that the flies are drawn by it, and they do keel over. But they are not diminishing; the treacle seems to entice more and more of them.

She turns to him. 'Excellent! The ingredients were expensive, you see.'

'I can't pay!' he says forcibly. 'Not anything!'

'Everybody wants something for nothing. This then, for now.' She kisses his mouth. 'Remember,' she says, as she goes. 'Passion. Passion!'

He is staring into the overrun saucers when his wife comes in, holding her nose.

'Where did you get that?'

'An acquaintance. A kind neighbour.'

'That harridan who stares at me so? You're swayed by the oddest people. Any fool's flattery can seduce you.'

'Clearly.'

'But it stinks!'

'The houses are old, the century is old . . . what do you expect?'

He sticks his finger in the muck, licks it and bends forward, holding his stomach.

'Baxter, you are suffering from insanity.' She says softly, 'You would prefer her opinion to mine. But why? Is something going on there?'

'No!'

'You don't care about me now, do you?'

'I do.'

'Liar. The truth counts for nothing with you.'

He notices she has kept her coat on. She puts the baby in his cot. She has finally arranged to visit her best friend, a well-off snobbish woman with two children whose exhibitions of affluence and happiness can be exasperating. He notices now the trouble his wife has taken to look her best. A woman's face alters when she has a baby, and a new beauty may emerge. But she still looks shabby in her ragged clothes, and strained, as if from the effort of constantly keeping something bad away.

From the window he watches her go, and is happy that at least her determination hasn't gone. There is, though, nothing left of their innocence.

Baxter digs a hole in the garden and throws in the odoriferous paint pot and saucers. To avoid his neighbour, he will have to be sure to look both ways and hurry when leaving the house.

He gets the boy up and lies on the floor with him. The kid crawls about, banging a wooden spoon on a metal tray, a noise which delights him, and keeps away all flies. He seems unaffected by the strange tensions around him. Every day he is different, full of enthusiasm and curiosity, and Baxter doesn't want to miss a moment.

He looks up to see the Operative waving through the window. Baxter has never seen him so genial.

'Look,' he says. 'I've nabbed some of the latest development and rushed it straight to you.' He puts several tins of a sticky treaclish substance on the table. 'It's a free sample.'

Baxter pushes him towards the door. 'Get out.'

'But –'

'Pour the tins over your head!'

'Don't shove! You're giving up, are you?' The Operative is enraged but affects sadness. 'It is a common reaction. You think you can shut your eyes to it. But your wife will never stop despising you, and your child will be made sick!' Baxter lunges at him. The man skips down the steps. 'Or have you got a solution of your own?' he sneers. 'Everyone thinks that at some time. But they're deceived! You'll be back. I await your call but might be too busy to take it.'

When Baxter's wife returns they sit attentively opposite one another and have a keen discussion. The visit to her friend has animated her.

'She and the house and the children were immaculate and practically gold-plated, as usual. I kept thinking, I'm never going to be able to bring the subject up. Fortunately the phone rang. I went to the bathroom. I opened her closet.' Baxter nods, understanding this. 'She loves clothes, but there was virtually nothing in there. There were powders and poisons in the bottom.'

'They've been married six years,' says Baxter.

'He's lazy –'

'She's domineering –'

'He's promiscuous –'

'She's frigid –'

'Just shut up and listen!' She continues, 'The rich aren't immune but they can afford to replace everything. When I brought up the subject she knew what I was talking about. She admitted to a slight outbreak – from next door.' They both laugh. 'She even said she was thinking of making a radio programme about it. And if there's a good response, a television investigation.' Baxter nods. 'I'm afraid there's only one thing for it. There's this man they've found. All the top people are using him.'

'He must be expensive.'

'All the best things are, and not everyone is too mean to pay for it. I'm not ready to go back to work, but Baxter, you must.'

'You know I can't find a job.'

'You must stop thinking you're better than other people, and take anything. It's our only hope. They're living a normal life, Baxter. And look at us.'

Once he loved her tenacity. He thinks of how to close this subject.

'What will I wear?'

'You can go to my mother's in the morning and change there, and do the same in the evening.'

'I see.'

She comes towards him and puts her face close to his; her eyes, though darkly ringed and lined now, shine with optimism.

'Baxter, we are going to try everything, aren't we?'

Feeling she will stand there for ever, and ashamed of how her close presence alarms him, he talks of what they might do once the contagion is over. He thinks, too, of how little people need, and how little they ask for! A touch, a hug, a word of reassurance, a moment of warm love, is all she wants. Yet a kiss is too much for him. Why is he so cruel, and what is wrong with him?

For a few weeks he thinks that by keeping away from her, by self-containment and the avoidance of 'controversial' subjects, she will forget this idea. But every few days she brings up the subject again, as if they have both agreed to it.

One night when he leans back, the new cushion disintegrates. It is a charred pile. He jumps up and, standing there, feels he will fall over. He reaches out and grabs the curtains. The entire thing – gauze, he realises – comes apart in his hand. The room has darkened; shadows hang in menacing shapes; the air is thick with flies; the furniture looks as though it has been in a fire. Flies spot his face; his hair turns sticky and yellow even as he stands there. He wants to cry out but can't cry out; he wants to flee but can't flee.

He hears a noise outside. A quarrel is taking place. Crouching below the windowsill, he sees the bearded man on the doorstep of his own house, shouting to be let in. A window opens upstairs and a suitcase is flung out, along with bitter words and sobs. The bearded man eventually picks up the suitcase and walks away. He passes Baxter's house pulling the wheeled case. Certain that Baxter is watching, he waves forlornly at the window.

Baxter feels that if the plague is to be conquered it is unreasonable of him not to try everything. Even if he doesn't succeed he will, at least, have pleased his wife. He blames and resents her, and what has she tried to do but make him happy and create a comfortable home? No doubt she is right about the other thing: in isolation he has developed unreasonably exalted ideas about himself.

But he goes reluctantly to work. The other employees look at him knowingly the day he goes in to apply for the job. It is exhausting work, yet he soon masters the morose patter, and his body becomes accustomed to the physical labour. The spraying is unpleasant; he has no idea what effect the unavoidable inhalation of noxious gases will have. Seeing all the distressed and naive couples is upsetting at first, but he learns from the other men to detach himself, ignore all insults and concentrate on selling as many packs as possible in order to earn a high commission. The Operatives are a cynical and morose group who resemble lawyers. None of the many people who need them will insult these parasites directly – they can't survive without them. But they can never be liked.

Baxter and his wife have more money than before, but to afford the exceptional Exterminator they must save for much longer and do without 'luxuries'. Baxter is hardly at home, which improves the atmosphere during the day. But there is something he has to do every night. When his wife and baby are asleep he turns off the light, sinks to his knees and turns onto his back on the living-room floor. There, as he hums to himself, working up a steady vibration from his stomach, moths graze on his clothes, in his hair, and on his closed eyes. It is a repellent but – he is convinced – necessary ritual of accustomisation. He tells himself that nothing can be repaired or advanced but only accepted. And, after acceptance, there will occur a liberation into pure spirit, without desire, a state he awaits with self-defeating impatience. Often he falls asleep here, imagining that the different parts of himself are being distributed by insects around the neighbourhood, or 'universe' as he puts it; he regards this as the ultimate compliance. His wife believes that his mind has been overrun.

One morning a youngish man in a black suit stands at the door. Baxter is surprised to see he carries no powders, illuminated electrifying poles, squirters, or even a briefcase. His hands are in his pockets. Gerard sits down, barely glancing at the chewed carpet or buckets of powder. He declines an offer to look in the wardrobe. He seems to know about it already.

'Has there been much of this about?' Baxter asks.

'In this street? A few cases.'

Hope rushes in again from its hiding place. Baxter is almost incoherent. 'Did you cure it? Did you? How long did it take?'

Gerard doesn't reply. Baxter goes and tells his wife she should talk to Gerard, saying he has a reassuring composure. She comes into the room and looks Gerard over, but she cannot bring herself to discuss any of their 'private matters'.

Baxter, though, tells Gerard the most forbidden, depressing and, particularly, trivial things. Gerard likes this stuff the most, persuading Baxter to see it as an aperture through which to follow the labyrinth of his mind. After, Baxter is more emotional than he has ever been, and wheels about the flat, feeling he will collapse, and that mad creatures have been released in the cage of his mind.

When Gerard asks if he should come back, Baxter says yes. Gerard turns up twice a week, to listen. Somehow he extends Baxter's view of things and makes unusual connections, until Baxter surprises himself. How gloomy one feels, explains Baxter, as if one has entered a tunnel which leads to the centre of the earth, with not an arrow of light possible. Surely this is one's natural condition, human fate, and one can only instruct oneself to be realistic? The wise will understand this, and the brave, called stoics by some, will endure it. Or is it very stupid? suggests Gerard. He turns things around until revolt seems possible, a terrifying revolt against one's easy assumptions.

Baxter begins to rely on Gerard. His wife, though, resents him. Despite all the ardent talk, the flat remains infested. She claims Gerard is making Baxter self-absorbed, and that he no longer cares about her and the baby.

Baxter wonders about Gerard too. Does this man know everything? Is he above it all? And why is he expending his gifts on Baxter without asking for money? Why should the 'clean man' be immune from the contagion? What can be so special about him?

One time the Operatives bring up the subject in the canteen. Baxter, who normally pays no attention to their conversations, looks up. 'There are people now who think they can talk the contagion away,' they scoff. 'Like people who think they can pray for rain, they won't accept it is a biological fact of nature. There is nothing to be done but await a breakthrough.'

Baxter wants to ask Gerard why he is interested in these conversations, but it soon ceases to matter. Something is different. Gerard has aroused in him a motivating desperation. At night he no longer lies on the floor being devoured. He paces, yes; but at least this is movement, and nothing will stick to him. There is something still alive within him, in both of them, which the flies have been unable to kill off.

Near dawn one night Baxter wakes up and can't go back to sleep. In his cot the boy sucks at his bottle. Baxter places his finger in the boy's fist; he holds his father tight. Baxter waits until he can withdraw without waking him. From the cot he takes a little wooden rattle. He dresses in silence, puts the rattle in his pocket, and walks towards the wardrobe. It is a while since he has poked at anything in there. It seems fruitless now.

He steps out onto the street. As he goes past the bearded man's house and that of his female neighbour he sees a black cloud in the sky ahead of him. There will be a storm, no doubt about it. Soon he is lost, but he keeps his eyes on the cloud, making his way through narrow streets and alleys; he traverses wide roads and, eventually, crosses the river, trying to think of what, yet, might be done. He sees other men who are, perhaps, like him, travelling through the night with mementoes in their pockets, searching for different fears; or popping out of doorways to stand still and stare upwards, thinking of too much to notice anyone, before walking determinedly in one direction, and then in another.

The cloud, as he walks towards it, seems to explode. It separates and breaks up into thousands of tiny fragments. It is a cloud of flies which lifts and breaks, sweeping upwards into the indifferent sky.

MIDNIGHT ALL DAY

First published in 1999

Strangers When We Meet

Can you hear me? No; no one can hear me. No one knows I am here.

I can hear them.

I am in a hotel room, sitting forward in a chair, leaning my ear against the wall. In the next room is a couple. They have been talking, amicably enough; their exchanges seem slight but natural. However, their voices are low; attentive though I am, I cannot make out what they are saying.

I recall that when listening through obstructions, a glass can be effective. I tiptoe to the bathroom, fetch a glass, and, holding it against the wall with my head attached, attempt to enhance my hearing. Which way round should the glass go? If people could see me crouched like this! But in here I am alone and everything is spoiled.

This was to be my summer holiday, in a village by the sea. My bag is open on the bed, a book of love poetry and a biography of Rod Stewart on top. Yesterday I went to Kensington High Street and shopped for guidebooks, walking boots, novels, sex toys, drugs, and Al Green tapes for my Walkman. I packed last night and got to bed early. This morning I set my alarm for six and read a little of Stanislavski's *My Life in Art*: 'I have lived a variegated life, during the course of which I have been forced more than once to change my most fundamental ideas . . .'

Later, I ran in Hyde Park and as usual had breakfast in a café with my flatmates, an actress and an actor with whom I was at drama school. 'Good luck! Have a great time, you lucky bastard!'

they called, as I headed for the station with my bag over my shoulder. They are enthusiastic about everything, as young actors tend to be. Perhaps that is why I prefer older people, like Florence, who is in the next room. Even as a teenager I preferred my friends' parents – usually their mothers – to my friends. It was what people said of their lives that excited me, the details of their description, rather than football or parties.

Just now I returned from the beach, ten minutes' walk away, past a row of new bungalows. The sea is lugubrious, almost grey. I trudged beside deserted bathing huts set in scrub land. There was some appropriate beauty in the overcast desolation and drizzle, and the open, empty distances. A handful of men in yellow capes nursed fishing lines on the shore. On a patch of tarmac people were crowded in camper vans, staring out to sea. Otherwise there is no one else there. I consider all these to be the essential elements for a holiday in England. A couple who need to talk could have the opportunity here.

Bounded by farms and fields of grazing cattle and horses, the hotel is a large cottage with barns to the side, set in flower-filled gardens. There is a dining room, bright as a chandelier with glass and cutlery, where a tie is required – these little snobberies increase the further you are from London. But you can eat the same food in the bar, which is situated (as they said in the hotel guide, which Florence and I studied together) in the basement of the hotel. The rooms are snug, if a little floral, and with an unnecessary abundance of equine motifs. Nevertheless, there is a double bed, a television, and a bathroom one need not fear.

Now there is laughter next door! It is, admittedly, only him, the unconcerned laughter of someone living in a solid, established world. Yet she must have gone to the trouble to say something humorous. Why is she not amusing me? What did Florence say? How long will I be able to bear this?

Suddenly I get up, blunder over the corner of the bed and send the glass flying. Perhaps my cry and the bang will smash their idyll, but why should it?

I doubt whether my lover knows that I have been allocated the next room. Although we arrived in the same car, we did not check in together, since I went to 'explore', just as my sisters and I would have done, on holiday with our parents. It is only when I open the door later that I hear her voice and realise we are in adjacent rooms.

I will leave here; I have to. It will not be tonight. The thought of going home is more than disappointing. What will my flatmates say? We are not best friends; their bemusement I can survive, and I could live in the flat as if I am away, with the curtains drawn, taking no calls, eschewing the pubs and cafés where I do the crossword and write letters asking for work. But if I ring my close friends they will say, Why are you back already? What went wrong? What will I reply? There will be laughter and gossip. The story will be repeated by people who have never met me; it could trail me for years. What could be more beguiling than other people's stymied desire?

Tomorrow I could go on to Devon or Somerset, as Florence and I discussed. We intended to leave it open. Our first time away – in fact our first complete night together – was to be an adventure. We wanted to enjoy one another free of the thought that she would have to return to her husband in a few hours. We would wake up, make love, and exchange dreams over breakfast.

I am not in the mood to decide anything.

They certainly have plenty to say next door: a little unusual, surely, for a couple who have been married five years.

I wipe my eyes, wash my face and go to the door. I will have a few drinks at the bar and order supper. I have inspected the menu and the food looks promising, particularly the puddings, which Florence loves to take a spoon of, push away and say to the waiter, 'That's me done!' Perhaps, from across the room, I will have the privilege of watching this.

But I return to my position against this familiar piece of wall, massage my shin and try to depict what they are doing, as if I am listening to a radio play. Probably they are getting changed. Often, when I am alone with Florence, I turn around and she is naked. She removes her clothes as easily as others slip off their shoes. At twenty-nine her body is supple. I think of her lying naked on my bed reading a script for me, and saying what she thinks, as I fix something to eat. She does the parts in funny voices until I am afraid to take the project seriously. I have a sweater of hers, and some gloves, which she left at my place. Why don't I rap on their door? I am all for surrealism.

They will be in the dining room later. I cannot see why it would occur to him to take her elsewhere tonight. The man will eat opposite his woman, asking her opinion of the sauces, contentedly oblivious of everything else, knowing Florence's lips, jokes, breasts and kindnesses are his. I fear my own madness. Not that I will vault across the table and choke either of them. I will sit with my anger and will not appreciate my food. I will go to bed forlorn, and half-drunk, only to hear them again. The hotel is not full: I can ask for another room. In the bar I saw a woman reading *The Bone People*. There are several young Austrian tourists too, in long socks, studying maps and guide books. What a time we could all have.

But there is an awful compulsion; I need to know how they are together. My ear will always be pressed against this wall.

To think that earlier today I was sitting in the train at the station. I had bought wine, sandwiches and, as a surprise, chocolate cake. The sun burned through the window. (It is odd how one imagines that just because the sun is shining in London, it is shining everywhere else.) I had purchased first-class seats, paying for the trip with money earned on a film, playing the lead, a street boy, a drug kid, a thief. They have shown me the rough cut; it is being edited and will have a rock soundtrack. The producer is confident of getting it into the directors' fortnight at Cannes, where, he claims, they are so moneyed and privileged, they adore anything seedy and cruel.

Florence is certainly sharper than my agent. When I first heard about the film from some other actors she told me that when she was an actress she had had supper with the producer a few times. I imagine she was boasting, but she rang him at home, and insisted the director meet me. I sat on her knee with my fingers on her nipple as she made the call. She didn't admit we know one another, but said she has seen me in a play. 'He's not only pretty,' she said, pinching my cheek. 'He has a heartbreaking sadness, and charm.'

There were scores of young actors being considered for the part. I recognise most of them, smoking, shuffling and complaining, in the line outside the audition room. I presumed we would be rivals for life but it was to me that the producer said, 'It is yours if you want it!'

Waiting for Florence O'Hara on the train made my blood so effervescent that I speculated about whether I could have her in the toilet. I had never attempted such a caper, but she has rarely refused me anything. Or perhaps she could slip her hand under my newspaper. For days I have been imagining what pleasures we might make. We would have a week of one another before I went to Los Angeles for the first time, to Hollywood, to play a small part in an independent American movie.

With two minutes to go – and I was becoming concerned, having already been walking about the station for an hour – I glimpse her framed in the window and almost shouted out. To confirm the fact that we were going on holiday, she was wearing a floppy purple hat. Florence can dress incongruously at times, wearing, say, antique jewellery and a silk top with worn-out, frayed shoes, as if by the time she arrived at her feet she had forgotten what she had done with her head.

Behind her was her husband.

I recognised him from a wedding photograph I saw on the one occasion I popped warily into their flat, to survey their view of Hammersmith Bridge and the river. Florence had suggested I paint the view. Today, for some reason he was seeing her off. She would wave through the window at him – I hoped she would not kiss him – before sinking down next to me.

There is always something suspicious about the need to be alone. The trip had taken some arranging. At first, conspiring in bed, Florence and I thought she should tell her husband she was holidaying with a friend. But intricate lies made Florence's hands perspire. Instead, she ascertained when her husband would be particularly busy at the office, and insisted that she needed to read, walk and think. 'Think about what?' he asked, inevitably, as he dressed for work. But, quietly, she could be inflexible, and he likes to be magnanimous.

'All right, my dear,' he announced. 'Go and be alone and see how much you miss me.'

During the week before our departure, Florence and I saw one another twice. She phoned and I caught a taxi outside my front door in Gloucester Road. She put on a head scarf and dark glasses, and slipped out to meet me in one of the many pubs near her flat, along the river. There was an abstraction about her that makes me want her more, and which I assume would be repaired by our holiday together.

Her husband was walking through the train towards me. Despite having left the office for only an hour, he was wearing a cream linen jacket, jeans and old deck shoes, without socks. Fine, I thought, he's so polite he's helping her right into her seat; that's something a twenty-seven-year-old like me could learn from.

He heaved her bag onto the rack and they sat opposite, across the aisle. He glanced indifferently in my direction. She was captivated by the activity on the platform. When he talked she smiled. Meanwhile she was tugging at the skin around her thumbnail until it bled, and she had to find a tissue in her bag. Florence was wearing her wedding ring, something she had never done with me, apart from the first time we met.

With an unmistakable jolt, the train left the station, on its way to our holiday destination with me, my lover and her husband aboard.

I stood up, sat down, tapped myself on the head, searched in my bag and looked around wildly, as if seeking someone to explain the situation to me. Eventually, having watched me eat the chocolate cake – on another occasion she would have licked the crumbs from my lips – Florence left her seat to fetch sandwiches. I went to the toilet where she was waiting outside for me.

'He insisted on coming,' she whispered, digging her nails into my arm. 'It was yesterday. He gave me no choice. I couldn't resist without making him jealous and suspicious. I had no chance to speak to you.'

'He's staying the whole week?'

She looked agitated. 'He'll get bored. This kind of thing doesn't interest him.'

'What sort of thing?'

'Being on holiday. We usually go somewhere . . . like Italy. Or the Hamptons –'

'Where?'

'Outside New York. I'll encourage him to go home. Will you wait?'

'I can't say,' I told her. 'You've really made a mess of everything! How could you do such a thing!'

'Rob –'

'You're stupid, stupid!'

'No, no, it's not that!'

She tried to kiss me but I pulled away. She passed her hand between my legs – and I wish she hadn't – before returning to her husband. I walked up and down the train before sitting down. It did not occur to me to sit somewhere else. Blood from her thumb was smeared over my arm and hand.

I had never seen her look this miserable. She is sometimes so nervous she will spill the contents of her bag over the street and have to get on her hands and knees to retrieve her things. Yet she can be brave. On the tube once, three young men started to bait and rob the passengers. While the rest of us were lost in terror, she attacked the robbers with an insane fury that won her a bravery award.

For the rest of the journey she pretended to be asleep. Her husband read a thriller.

At the country station, as I marched off the platform, I saw the hotel had sent a car to pick us up: one car. Before I could enquire about trains back to London, the driver approached me.

'Robert Miles?'

'Yes?'

'This way, please.'

The bent countryman led me outside where the air was cool and fresh. The immensity of the sky could have calmed a person. It was for this that Florence and I decided, one afternoon, to get away.

The man opened the car door.

'In you get, sir.' I hesitated. He swept dog hairs from the seat. 'I'll drive as slowly as I can, and tell you a little about the area.'

He deposited my bag in the boot. I had no choice but to get into the car. He shut the door. Florence and her husband were invited to sit in the back. As we drove away the car bulged with our heat and presence. The driver talked to me, and I listened to them.

'I'm glad I decided to come,' Florence's husband was saying. 'Still, we could have gone up to the House.'

'Oh, that place,' she sighed.

'Yes, it's like having a third parent. You don't have to keep telling me you don't like it. What made you decide on here?'

I wanted to turn round and say, 'I decided –'

'I saw it in a brochure,' she said.

'You told me you'd been here as a child.'

'Yes, the brochure reminded me. I went to lots of places as a child, with my mother.'

'Your mad mother.' In the mirror I saw him put his arm around her and lay his hand on her breast.

'Yes,' she said.

'Just us now,' he said. 'I'm so glad I came.'

I am hungry.

At last I unstick my ear from the wall, shake my head as if to clear it, go downstairs, and have supper in the bar crowded with the local lushes, who prefer this hotel to the pubs.

I eat with my back to the room, a book in front of me, wondering where Florence and her husband are sitting and what they are saying; like someone sitting in Plato's cave, trying to read the shadows. Halfway through the meal, having resolved to face them at last, I rise suddenly, change my seat and turn around. They are not there.

As I order another drink, the plump girl behind the bar smiles at me. 'We thought you were waiting for some lucky person who didn't turn up.'

'There's no lucky person, but it's not so bad.'

I take my drink and walk about, though I do not know where I am going. Waitresses tear in and out of the hot dining room, so smart, inhibited and nervous, lacking the London arrogance and beauty. Middle-aged women with painted faces and bright dresses, and satisfied men in suits and ties, who do not question their right to be here – this being their world – are beginning to leave the dining room, holding glasses. For a moment they stand on this piece of earth, as it moves on imperceptibly, and they gurgle and chuckle with happiness.

Optimistically I follow a couple into one of the sitting rooms, where they will have more drinks and coffee. I collapse into a high-backed sofa.

After a time I recognise the voice I am listening to. Florence and her husband have come in and are sitting behind me. They start to play Scrabble. I am close enough to smell her.

'I liked the fish,' she is saying. 'The vegetables were just right. Not overcooked and not raw.'

I have been thinking of how proud I was that I had hooked a married woman.

'Florence,' he says. 'It's your turn. Are you sure you're concentrating?'

When I started with Florence I wanted to be discreet as well as wanting to show off. I hoped to run into people I knew; I was convinced my friends were gossiping about me. I had never had an adventure like this. If it failed, I would walk away unscathed.

'We don't eat enough fish,' she says.

Certainly, I did not think about what her husband might be like, or why she married him. To me she made him irrelevant. It was only us.

He says, 'You don't like to kiss me when I've eaten meat.'

'No, I don't,' she says.

'Kiss me now,' he says.

'Let's save it.'

'Let's not.'

'Archie –'

Her voice sounds forced and dull, as if she is about to weep. How long do I intend to sit here? My mind whirls; I have forgotten who I am. I imagine catastrophes and punishments everywhere. I suppose it was to cure myself of such painful furies that I become depressed so often. When I am depressed I shut everything down, living in a tiny part of myself, in my sexuality or ambition to be an actor. Otherwise, I kill myself off. I have talked to Florence about these things – about 'melancholy' as she puts it – and she understands it: the first person I have known who does.

I realise that if I peep around the arm of the sofa I can see Florence from the side, perched on a stool. I move a little; now she is in full view, wearing a tight white top, cream bags and white sandals.

Oddly, I am behaving as if this man has stolen my woman. In fact it is I who have purloined his, and if he finds out, he could easily become annoyed and perhaps violent. But I gaze and gaze at her, at the way she puts her right hand across her face and rests the back of her hand on her cheek with her fingers beneath her eye; a gesture she must have made as a child, and will probably make as an old woman.

If Archie is a ruling presence in our lives, he is an invisible one; and if she behaves a little, let's say, obscurely, at times, it is because she lives behind a wall I can only listen at. She is free during the day but likes to account for where she is. He would have been more than satisfied with 'I spent the afternoon at the Tate,' and could endure with less about its Giacomettis. When we separate at the end of each meeting she often becomes agitated and upset.

I assumed that I did not care enough about her to worry about her husband. It never occurred to me that she and I would live together, for instance; we would continue casually until we fell out. Nevertheless, watching her now, I am not ready for that. I want her to want me, and me alone. I must play the lead and not be a mere walk-on.

The barmaid comes and picks up my glass. 'Can I get you something else?'

'No thanks,' I say in a low voice.

I notice that Florence raises her head a little.

'Did you enjoy your meal?' says the barmaid.

'Yes. Particularly the fish. The vegetables were just right. Not overcooked and not raw.' Then I say, 'When does the bar close?'

'Thursday!' she says, and laughs.

Without looking at Florence or her husband, I follow her out of the room and lean tiredly across the bar.

'What are you doing down here?' She says this as if she's certain that it is not my kind of place.

'Only relaxing,' I say.

She lowers her voice. 'We all hate it down here. Relaxing's all there is to do. You'll get plenty of it.'

'What do you like to do?'

'We used to play Russian roulette with cars. Driving across crossroads, hoping that nothing is coming the other way. That sort of thing.'

'What's your name?'

'Martha.'

She puts my drink down. I tell her my room number.

'That's all right,' she says. Martha leans towards me. 'Listen –' she says.

'Yes?'

Florence's husband sits heavily on the stool beside me and shifts about on it, as if he is trying to screw it into the floor. I scuttle along a little.

He turns to me. 'All right if I sit down?'

'Why not?'

He orders a cigar. 'And a brandy,' he says to Martha. He looks at me before I can turn my back. 'Anything for you?'

I start to get up. 'I'm just off.'

'Something I said?' He says, 'I saw you in the train.'

'Really? Oh yes. Was that your wife?'

'Of course.'

'Is she going to join us?'

'How do I know? Do you want me to ring the room?'

'I don't want you to do anything.'

'Have a brandy.' He lays his hand on my shoulder. 'I say, barmaid – a brandy for this young man!'

'Right,' I say. 'Right.'

'Do you like brandy?' she says to me, kindly.

'Very much,' I say.

He drags his tie off and stuffs it in his jacket pocket.

'Sit down,' he says. 'We're on bloody holiday. Let's make the most of it! Can I ask your name?'

I met Florence nearly a year ago in a screening room, where we were the only people viewing a film made by a mutual friend. She lay almost on her back in the wide seat, groaning, laughing and snorting throughout the film. At the end – before the end, in fact – she started talking about the performances. I invited her for a drink. After leaving university, she was an actress for a couple of years. 'It was a cattle-market, darling. Couldn't stand being compared to other people.'

Yet a few days after we met, she was sitting crosslegged on the floor in my place, as my flatmates wrote down the names of casting directors she suggested they contact. She fitted easily into my world of agents, auditions, scripts, and the confusion of young people whose life hangs on chance, looks, and the ability to bear large amounts of uncertainty. It was not only that she liked the semi-student life, the dope smoking, the confused promiscuity and exhibitionism, but that she seemed to envy and miss it.

'If only I could stay,' she would say theatrically, at the door.

'Stay then,' I shout from the top of the stairs.

'Not yet.'

'When?'

'You enjoy yourself! Live all you can!'

Our 'affair' began without being announced. She rang me – I rarely phoned her; she asked to see me – 'at ten past five, in the Scarsdale!' and I would be there with ten minutes to spare. Certainly, I had nothing else to do but attend actors' workshops, and read plays and the biographies of actors. Sometimes we went to bed. Sexually she will say and do anything, with the enthusiasm of someone dancing or running. I am not always certain she is entirely there; sometimes I have to remind her she is not giving a solo performance.

Often we go to the theatre in the afternoon, and to a pub to discuss the writing, acting and direction. She takes me to see peculiar European theatre groups that use grotesquerie, masks and gibberish; she introduces me to dance and performance art. When she kisses me goodbye and goes home, or out to meet her husband, I see actresses, girls who work in TV, students, au pairs. They keep me from feeling too much for Florence. There was one night of alcohol and grief, when I wept and hated her inaccessibility. I have not had a suitable girlfriend for more than two years. The last woman I lived with became only my friend; the relationship lacked velocity and a future. My life does tend towards stasis, which Florence recognises.

I had been finding it difficult to break with my background in South London. The men I grew up with were tough and loud-mouthed, bragging of their ignorance and crudity. They believed aggression was their most necessary tool. On leaving school they became villains and thieves. In their twenties, when they had children, they turned to car dealing, building or 'security'. They continued to go to football matches, drank heavily, and pursued teenage longings, ideals to which they had become addicted. What I want to do – act – represents an inexplicable ambition that intimidates them and, by its nature, will leave them behind. I am not saying that there are not any working-class actors. I hope to play many parts. I want to transform myself until I become unrecognisable. But I will not become an actor for whom being working class is 'an act'. No cops or criminals in TV series for me.

In the pub with these friends I try to retain the accent and attitudes of my past, but I have emerged from the anonymous world and they are contemptuous and provocative. 'Give us a speech, Larry. To buy a drink or not to buy a drink!' they chant, pulling at my expensive shirt. I am about to get into a fight over divergent ideas of who I should be. I begin to consider them cowardly, living only little lives, full of bold talk, but doing nothing and going nowhere. It is not until later that Florence teaches me that part of being successful is the ability to bear envy and plain dislike.

I am not educated. If she notices it, Florence never comments on my ignorance. She can be light-headed and frivolous herself; once she shopped for two days. Nevertheless, she sits me down in front of the most exacting films. Bergman's *Cries and Whispers*, for instance, she thinks it necessary we both absorb through repetition; it is as if she is singing along with the film, or, in the case of that work, moaning. She does not categorise these things as art, as I do, but uses them as objects of immediate application.

Almost as soon as I met Florence, she altered the direction of my life. The Royal Shakespeare Company had offered me a two-year contract. I would share a cottage in Stratford. She would sit with me beside the Avon. I had celebrated in Joe Allens with friends, and my agent was working on the contract.

To celebrate, I took Florence out to lunch to celebrate. I read in a magazine that the restaurant was one of the smartest in London, but she swung about in her chair. I should have remembered that she dislikes eating – she is as thin and flat-chested as a dancer. Certainly she does not like sitting down for her food surrounded by people she has seen on television and considers pompous and talentless.

'I have to tell you that you must turn the Stratford opportunity down,' she said.

'It's every young actor's dream, Florence.'

'Rob, don't be such a common little fool. They're too small, too small,' she said. 'Not only that suit you're wearing, but the parts. Going to the Royal Shakespeare Company will be a waste of time.' She flicks my nose with her fingernail.

'Ow.'

'You must listen to me.'

I did.

My agent was amazed and furious. Without entirely knowing why, I took Florence's advice. Soon I am playing big roles in little places: Biff in *Death of a Salesman*, in Bristol; the lead in a new play in Cheltenham; Romeo in Yorkshire.

With a girlfriend she came on the train to see a preview, and we travelled back together late at night, drinking wine in plastic cups. She anatomised my performance so severely I took notes. 'There were a couple of awful moments when you tried to have us laugh at the character you were playing,' she said. 'I thought, if he does that again I will go to the box office and ask for my money back!'

Criticism, I suppose, reminded me of my dependency on her. Yet, when she was finished, and I was almost finished off, she continued to look at me without any diminishment of desire and love.

It was fine by her if I took small parts on television or in films. I had to get used to the camera so that I could concentrate on movies, 'like Gary Oldman and Daniel Day-Lewis'. She said she understood what women would like about me on screen, when I could only laugh at such an idea. Also she said that most actors see only moments; I had to learn how to develop a part through the whole film. She told me to learn as much as I could, for when it took off for me, it would happen very quickly. She even suggested that I should direct movies, saying, 'If you generate your own work it will give you another kind of pleasure.'

Like my friends at drama school, my head was full of schemes and fantasies. I have always been impressed by people who live with deliberation; but ambition, or desire in the world, makes me apprehensive. I am afraid of what I want, of where it might take me, and what it might make others think of me. Yet, as Florence explains, how are cathedrals and banks built, diseases eliminated, dictators crushed, football matches won – without frustration and the longing to overcome it? Often the simplest things have to be explained. Florence fills me with hope, but ensures it is based on the possible.

I have little idea what Florence dreams of and of what kind of world she inhabits with Archie, who is in 'property'; I doubt she is ensnared in some kind of *Doll's House*. In the middle of the city in which I live there is an undisturbed English continuity: they are London 'bohemians'. It is an expensive indolence and careless-ness, but the money for country houses, and for villas in France and the West Indies, for parties, the opera, excursions and week-ends away, never runs out. This set has known one another for generations; their parents were friends and lovers in those alco-holic times, the fifties and sixties. Perhaps Florence is lost in some-thing she does not entirely like or understand, but when she calls her husband's world 'grown up' I resent the idea that she considers my world childish. My guess is that she is uncomfortable in such an intransigent world but is unable to live according to her own desire.

'Rob,' I say.

Florence's husband offers me his be-ringed hand. I can hardly bear to touch him, and he must find me damp with apprehension.

'Archie O'Hara. Stayed here before?'

'No . . . I just came down . . . to get away.'

'From what?'

'You know.'

'Yes,' he says, indifferently. 'Don't I know. That's what we're doing. Getting away.'

We sit there and Martha looks at us as if we all know one another. Archie wears a blue jacket, white shirt and yellow corduroys; his face is smooth and well fed. As Florence has chosen to be with him – most of the time – he must, I imagine, have some unusual qualities. Is he completely dissimilar to me, or does he resemble me in ways I cannot see? Perhaps I will learn.

'How long are you staying?' I ask.

He puffs on his cigar and says nothing.

Martha says, 'I could tell you where to go and what to look at, if you want.'

Archie says, 'Thanks, but I've been thinking of getting another country place. I inherited a stately home as they call them these days, with a lot of Japanese photographing me through the windows. Sometimes I feel like sitting there in a dress and tiara. My wife says you can't sit down without farting into the dust of a dozen centuries. So we might have to drive round . . . estate agents and all that.'

I say, 'Does your wife like the country?'

'London women have fantasies about fields. But she suffers from hay fever. I can't see the point in going to a place where you know no one. But then I can't see the point in anything.'

He puts his head back and laughs.

'Are you depressed?'

'You know that, do you?' He sighs. 'It's staring everyone in the face, like a slashed throat.' He says after a time, 'I'm not going to kill myself. But I could, just as well.'

'I had it for two years, once.'

He squeezes my arm as Florence sometimes does. 'Now it's gone?'

I tap the wooden bar. 'Yes.'

'That's good to hear. You're a happy little man, are you, now?'

I am about to inform him that it is returning, probably as a result of meeting him. But this is despair, not depression. These distinctions are momentous.

We discuss the emptying out; the fear of living; the creation of a wasteland; the denigration of value and meaning. I tell him melancholy was part of my interior scene and that I considered it to be the way the world was, until I stood against it.

I announce, 'People make themselves sick when they aren't leading the lives they should be leading.'

He bangs the bar. 'How banal, but true.'

By now the place has almost emptied. Martha collects the glasses, sweeps the floor and wipes down the bar. She continues to put out brandies for us.

She watches us and says, 'There isn't much intelligent conversation down here.'

'What do you think of meditation?' he says. 'Eastern hogwash or truth?'

'It helps my concentration,' I say. 'I'm an actor.'

'There's a lot of actors about. They rather get under one's feet, talking about "centreing" and all that.'

I say, 'Do you know any actors? Or actresses?'

'Do you count ten breaths or only four,' he says, 'when meditating?'

'Four,' I say. 'There's less time to get lost.'

'Who taught you?'

Your wife, I am about to say.

'I had a good teacher,' I say.

'Where was the class . . . could you tell me?'

'The woman who taught me . . . I met her by chance, one day, in a cinema. She seemed to like me instantly. I liked her liking me. She led me on, you could say.'

'Really?' says Martha, leaning across the bar.

'Only then she took my hand and told me, with some sadness, that she was married. I thought that would suit me. Anyhow, she taught me some things.'

Martha said, 'She didn't tell you she was married?'

'She did, yes. Just before we slept together.'

'Moments before?' said Martha. 'She sounds like an awful person.'

'Why?'

'To do that to you! Do you want her to leave her husband?'

'What for? I don't know. I haven't thought about it.'

Archie laughs. 'Wait 'til he catches up with you!'

'I hope I'm not keeping you,' I say to Archie.

'My wife will be on her REMs by now. I've missed my conjugals for today.'

'Does she usually go to sleep at this time?'

'I can't keep that woman out of bed.'

'And she reads in bed? Novels?'

'What are you, a librarian?'

I say, 'I like basic information about people. The facts, not opinions.'

'Yes. That's a basic interest in people. And you still have that?'

'Don't you?'

He thinks about it. 'Perhaps you study people because you're an actor.'

Martha lights a cigarette. She has become thoughtful. 'It's not only that. I know it isn't. It is an excuse for looking. But looking is the thing.' She turns to me with a smile.

'That might be right, my dear,' Archie says. 'Things are rarely only one thing.'

For my benefit she shoots him an angry look and I smile at her.

'Better make a move,' he says. 'Better had.'

I want to ask him more. 'What does your wife do? Did you ever see her act?'

'Told you she was an actress, did I? Don't remember that. Don't usually say that, as it's not true. Like women, eh?'

'Sorry?'

'Saw how you appreciated my wife, on the train.' He gets down from the stool, and staggers. 'It's beautiful when I'm sitting down. Better help us upstairs.'

He finds my shoulder and connects himself to it. He is heavy and I feel like letting him go. I do not like being so close to him.

'I'll give you a hand,' Martha says. 'It's not far. You're in the next room to one another.'

One on each side, we heave him upstairs. The last few steps he takes with gingerly independence.

At the door he turns. 'Guide me into the room. Don't know the layout. Could be pitch dark with only my wife's teeth for light.'

Martha takes his key and opens the door for him.

'Goodnight,' I say.

I am not accompanying him into the bedroom.

'Hey.' He falls into the room.

I wave at Martha.

'Archie,' says startled Florence from the darkness within. 'Is that you?'

'Who else, dammit? Undress me!'

'Archie –'

'Wife's duty!'

I sink down beside the wall like a gargoyle and think of her tearing at the warm mound of him. Now I have seen him, his voice seems clearer.

I hear him say, 'I was just talking to someone –'

'Who?'

'That boy in the next room.'

'Which boy?'

'The actor, you fool. He was in the train. Now he's in the hotel!'

'Is he? Why?'

'How do I know?'

He switches the TV on. I would not have done such a thing when she was sleeping. I think of Florence sleeping. I know what her face will be like.

Next morning it is silent next door. I walk along the corridor hoping I will not run into Florence and Archie. Maids are starting to clean the rooms. I pass people on the stairs and say 'Good morning'. The hotel smells of furniture polish and fried food.

At the door to the breakfast room I bump into them. We smile at one another, I slide by and secure a table behind a pillar. I open the newspaper and order haddock, tomatoes, mushrooms and fried potatoes.

Last night I dreamed I had a nervous breakdown; that I was walking around a foreign town incapable of considered thought or action, not knowing who I was or where I was going. I wonder whether I want to incapacitate myself rather than seriously consider what I should do. I need to remind myself that such hopelessness will lead to depression. Better to do something. After breakfast I will get the train back to London.

I am thinking that it is likely that I will never see Florence again, when she rushes around the corner.

'What are you doing? What are you intending to do? Oh Rob, tell me.'

She is close to me, breathing over me; her hair touches my face, her hand is on mine, and I want her again, but I hate her, and hate myself.

'What are you intending to do?' I ask.

'I will persuade him to leave.'

'When?'

'Now. He'll be on the lunchtime train.'

'No doubt sitting next to me.'

'But we can talk and be together! I'll do anything you want.' I look at her doubtfully. She says, 'Don't go this morning. Don't do that to me.'

For some reason a man I have never seen before, with a lapel badge saying 'Manager', is standing beside the table.

'Excuse me,' he says.

Florence does not notice him. 'I beg you,' she says. 'Give me a chance.' She kisses me. 'You promise?'

'Excuse me,' the hotel manager says. 'The car you ordered is here, sir.' I stare at him. He seems to regard us as a couple. 'The rental car – suitable for a man and a woman, touring.'

'Oh yes,' I say.

'Would you both like to look at it now?'

With a wave, Florence goes. Outside, I gaze at the big, four-door family saloon, chosen in a moment of romantic distraction. I sit in it.

After breakfast I drive into Lyme Regis and walk on the Cobb; later I drive to Charmouth, climb up the side of the cliff and look out to sea. It is beginning to feel like being on holiday with your parents when you are too old for it.

I return to the hotel to say goodbye to Florence again. In the conservatory, reading the papers, is Archie, wearing a suit jacket over a T-shirt, brown shorts and black socks and shoes, looking like someone who has dressed for the office but forgotten to put their trousers on.

As I back away, hoping he has not recognised me, and if he does, that he will not quite recall who I am, he says, 'Have a good morning?'

In front of him is a half-empty bottle of wine. His face is covered in a fine glacé of sweat.

I tell him where I've been.

'Busy boy,' he says.

'And you? You're still around . . . here?'

'We've walked and even read books. I'm terribly, terribly glad I came.'

He pours a glass of wine and hands it to me.

I say, 'Think you might stay a bit longer?'

'Only if it's going to annoy you.'

His wife comes to the other door. She blinks several times, her mouth opens, and then she seems to yawn.

'What's wrong with you?' asks her husband.

'Tired,' she whispers. 'Think I'll lie down.'

He winks at me. 'Is that an invitation?'

'Sorry, sorry,' she says.

'Why the hell are you apologising? Get a grip, Florrie. I spoke to this young man last night.' He jabs his finger at me. 'You said this thing . . .' He looks into the distance and massages his temples. 'You said . . . if you experienced the desires, the impulses, within you, you would break up what you had created, and live anew. But there would be serious consequences. The word was in my head all night. Consequences. I haven't been able to live out those things. I have tried to put them away, but can't. I've got this image . . . of stuffing a lot of things in a suitcase that can't be closed, that is too small. That is my life. If I lived what I thought . . . it would all blow down . . .'

I realise Florence and I have been looking at one another. Sometimes you look at someone instead of touching them.

He regards me curiously. 'What's going on? Have you met my wife?'

'Not really.'

My lover and I shake hands.

Archie says, 'Florrie, he's been unhappy in love. Married woman and all that. We must cheer him up.'

'Is he unhappy?' she says. 'Are you sure? People should cheer themselves up. Don't you think, Rob?'

She crooks her finger at me and goes. Her husband ponders his untrue life. As soon as his head re-enters his hands, I am away, racing up the stairs.

My love is lingering in the corridor.

'Come.'

She pulls my arm; with shaking hands I unlock my door; she hurries me through my room and into the bathroom. She turns on the shower and the taps, flushes the toilet, and falls into my arms, kissing my face and neck and hair.

I am about to ask her to leave with me. We could collect our things, jump in the car and be on the road before Archie has lifted his head and wiped his eyes. The idea burns in me; if I speak, our lives could change.

'Archie knows.'

I pull back so I can see her. 'About our exact relation to one another?'

She nods. 'He's watching us. Just observing us.'

'Why?'

'He wants to be sure, before he makes his move.'

'What move?'

'Before he gets us.'

'Gets us? How?'

'I don't know. It's torture, Rob.'

This thing has indeed made her mad; such paranoia I find abhorrent. Reality, whatever it is, is the right anchor. Nevertheless, I have been considering the same idea myself. I do not believe it, and yet I do.

'I don't care if he knows,' I say. 'I'm sick of it.'

'But we mustn't give up!'

'What? Why not?'

'There is something between us . . . which is worthwhile.'

'I don't know any more, Florrie. Florence.'

She looks at me and says, 'I love you, Rob.'

She has never said this before. We kiss for a long time.

I turn off the taps and go through into the bedroom. She follows me and somehow we fall onto the bed. I pull up her skirt; soon she is on me. Our howls would be known to the county. When I wake up she is gone.

I walk on the beach; there is a strong wind. I put my head back: it is raining into my eyes. I think of Los Angeles, my work, and of what will happen in the next few months. A part of my life seems to be over, and I am waiting for the new.

After supper I am standing in the garden outside the dining room, smoking weed, and breathing in the damp air. I have decided it is too late to return to London tonight. Since waking up I have not spoken to Florence, only glanced into the dining room where she and her husband are seated at a table in the middle. Tonight she is wearing a long purple dress. She has started to look insistent and powerful again, a little diva, with the staff, like ants, moving around only her because they cannot resist. One more night and she will bring the room down with a wave and stride out towards the sea. I know she is going to join me later. It is only a wish, of course, but won't she be wishing too? It is probably our last chance. What will happen then? I have prepared my things and turned the car around.

There is a movement behind me.

'That's nice,' she says, breathing in.

I put out my arms and Martha holds me a moment. I offer her the joint. She inhales and hands it back.

'What are you thinking?'

'Next week I'm going to Los Angeles to be in a film.'

'Is that true?'

'What about you?'

She lives nearby with her parents. Her father is a psychology lecturer in the local college, an alcoholic with a violent temper who has not been to work for a year. One day he took against London, as if it had personally offended him, and insisted the family move from Kentish Town to the country, cutting them off from everything they knew.

'We always speculate about the people who stay here, me and the kitchen girl.' She says, suddenly, 'Is something wrong?'

She turns and looks behind. As Martha has been talking, I have seen Florence come out into the garden, watch us for a bit, and throw up her hands like someone told to mime 'despair'. A flash of purple and she is gone.

'What is it?'

'Tell me what you've been imagining about me,' I say.

'But we don't know what you're doing here. Are you going to tell me?'

'Can't you guess?' I say impatiently. 'Why do you keep asking me these things?'

She takes offence, but I have some idea of how to get others to talk about themselves. I discover that recently she has had an abortion, her second; that she rides a motorbike; that the young people carry knives, take drugs and copulate as often as they can; and that she wants to get away.

'Is the bar shut?' I ask.

'Yes. I can get you beer if you want.'

'Would you like to drink a glass of beer with me?' I ask.

'More than one glass, I hope.'

I kiss her on the cheek and tell her to come to my room. 'But what will your parents say if you are late home?'

'They don't care. Often I find an empty room and sleep in it. Don't want to go home.' She says, 'Are you sure it's only beer you want?'

'Whatever you want,' I say. 'You can get a key.'

On the way upstairs I look into the front parlour. In the middle of the floor Florence and Archie are dancing; or rather, he is holding on to her as they heave about. The Scrabble board and all the letters have been knocked on the floor. His head is flopped over her shoulder; in five years he will be bald. Florence notices me and raises a hand, trying not to disturb him.

He calls out, 'Hey!'

'Drunk again,' I say to her.

'I know what you have been doing. Up to!' he says with leering emphasis.

'When?'

'This afternoon. Siesta. You know.'

I look at Florence.

'The walls are thin,' he says. 'But not quite thin enough. I went upstairs. I had to fetch something from the bathroom. But what an entertainment. Jiggy-jig, jiggy-jig!'

'I'm glad to be an entertainment, you old fucker,' I say. 'I wish you could be the same for me.'

'What was Rob doing this afternoon?' Florence says. 'Don't leave me out of the game.'

'Ha, ha, ha! You're a dopey little thing who never notices anything!'

'Don't talk to her like that,' I say. 'Talk to me like that, if you want, and see what you get!'

'Rob,' says Florence, soothingly.

Archie slaps Florence on the behind. 'Dance, you old corpse!'

I stare at his back. He is too drunk to care that he's being provoked into a fight.

I feel like an intruder and am reminded of the sense I had as a child, when visiting friends' houses, that the furniture, banter and manner of doing things were different from the way we did them at home. The world of Archie and Florence is not mine.

I am waiting for Martha on the bed when I hear Florence and Archie in the corridor opening the door to their room. The door closes; I listen intently, wondering if Archie has passed out and Florence is lying there awake.

The door opens and Martha rattles a bag of beer bottles. We open the windows, lie down on the bed and drink and smoke.

She leans over me. 'Do you want one of these?'

I kiss her fist and open it. 'I know what it is,' I say. 'But I've never had one.'

'I hadn't till I came down here,' she says. 'These are good Es.'

'Fetch some water from the bathroom.'

Meanwhile I remove the chair from its position beside the wall and begin shoving the heavy bed.

'Let's have this . . . over there . . . against the wall,' I say when she returns.

Martha starts to help me, an enthusiastic girl, with thick arms.

'Why do you want this?' she asks.

'I think it will be better for our purposes.'

'Right,' she says. 'Right.'

A few minutes after we lie down again, undressed this time, there is a knock on the door. We hold one another like scared children, listen and say nothing. There is another knock. Martha doesn't want to lose her job tonight. Then there is no more knocking. We do not even hear footsteps.

When we are breathing again, under the sheets I whisper, 'What do you think of the couple next door? Have you talked about them? Are they suited, do you think?'

'I like him,' she says.

'What? Really?'

'Makes me laugh. She's beautiful . . . but dangerous. Would you like to fuck her?'

I laugh. 'I haven't thought about it.'

'Listen,' she says, putting her finger to her lips.

Neither of us moves.

'They're doing it. Next door.'

'Yes,' I say. 'They are.'

'They're quiet,' she says. 'I can only hear him.'

'He's doing it alone.'

'No. There . . . there she is. A little gasp. Can you hear her now? Touch me.'

'Wait.'

'There . . . there.'

'Martha –'

'Please . . .'

I go into the bathroom and wash my face. The drug is starting to work. It seems like speed, which I had taken with my friends in the suburbs. This drug, though, opens another window: it makes me feel more lonely. I return to the room and switch the radio on. It must have been loud. We must have been loud. Martha is ungrudging in her love-making. Later, there is a storm. A supernatural breeze, fresh, strangely still and cool, fans us.

Martha goes downstairs early to make breakfast. At dawn I run along the stony beach until I am exhausted; then I stop, walk a little, and run again, all the while aware of the breaking brightness of the world. I shower, pack and go down for breakfast.

Florence and Archie are at the next table. Archie studies a map; Florence keeps her head down. She does not appear to have combed her hair. When Archie gets up to fetch something and she looks up, her face is like a mask, as if she has vacated her body.

After breakfast, collecting my things, I notice the door to their room has been wedged open by a chair. The maid is working in a room further along the hall. I look in at the unmade bed, go into my room, find Florence's sweater and gloves in my bag, and take them into their room. I stand there. Her shoes are on the floor, her perfume, necklace, and pens on the bedside table. I pull the sweater over my head. It is tight and the sleeves are too short. I put the gloves on, and wiggle my fingers. I lay them on the bed. I take a pair of scissors from her washbag in the bathroom and cut the middle finger from one of the gloves. I replace the severed digit in its original position.

As I bump along the farm track which leads up to the main road, I get out of the car, look down at the hotel on the edge of the sea and consider going back. I hate separations and finality. I am too good at putting up with things, that is my problem.

London seems to be made only of hard materials and the dust that cannot settle on it; everything is angular, particularly the people. I go to my parents' house and lie in bed; after a few days I leave for Los Angeles. There I am just another young actor, but at least one with a job. When I return to London we all leave the flat and I get my own place for the first time.

I have come to like going out for coffee early, with my son in his pushchair, while my wife sleeps. Often I meet other men whose wives need sleep, and at eight o'clock on Sunday morning we have chocolate milkshakes in McDonalds, the only place open in the dismal High Street. We talk about our children, and complain about our women. After, I go to the park, usually alone, in order to be with the boy away from my wife. She and I have quite different ideas about bringing him up; she will not see how important those differences can be to our son. Peaceful moments at home are rare.

It is in the park that I see Florence for the first time since our 'holiday'. She seems to flash past me, as she flashed past the window in the train, nine years ago. For a moment I consider letting her fall back into my memory, but I am too curious for that. 'Florence! Florence!' I call, again, until she turns.

She tells me she has been thinking of me and expecting us to meet, after seeing one of my films on television.

'I have followed your career, Rob,' she says, as we look one another over.

She calls her son and he stands with her; she takes his hand. She and Archie have bought a house on the other side of the park.

'I even came to the plays. I know it's not possible, but I wondered if you ever glimpsed me, from the stage.'

'No. But I did wonder if you took an interest.'

'How could I not?'

I laugh and ask, 'How am I?'

'Better, now you do less. You probably know – you don't mind me telling you this?'

I shake my head. 'You know me,' I say.

'You were an intense actor. You left yourself nowhere to go. I like you still.' She hesitates. 'Stiller, I mean.'

She looks the same but as if a layer of healthy fat has been scraped from her face, revealing the stitching beneath. There is even less of her; she seems a little frail, or fragile. She has always been delicate, but now she moves cautiously.

As we talk I recollect having let her down, but am unable to recall the details. She was active in my mind for the months after our 'holiday', but I found the memory to be less tenacious after relating the story to a friend as a tale of a young man's foolishness and misfortune. When he laughed I forgot – there is nothing as forgiving as a joke.

However, I have often wished for Florence's advice and support, particularly when the press took a fascinated interest in me, and started to write untrue stories. In the past few years I have played good parts and been praised and well paid. However, my sense of myself has not caught up with the alteration. I have been keeping myself down, and pushing happiness away. 'Success hasn't changed you,' people tell me, as if it were a compliment.

When we say goodbye, Florence tells me when she will next be in the park. 'Please come,' she says. At home I write down the time and date, pushing the note under a pile of papers.

She and I are wary with one another, and make only tentative and polite conversation; however, I enjoy sitting beside her on a bench in the sun, outside the teahouse, while her eight-year-old plays football. He is a hurt, suspicious boy with hair down to his shoulders, which he refuses to have cut. He likes to fight with bigger children and she does not know what to do with him. Without him, perhaps, she would have got away.

At the moment I have few friends and welcome her company. The phone rings constantly but I rarely go out and never invite anyone round, having become almost phobic where other people are concerned. What I imagine about others I cannot say, but the human mind is rarely clear in its sight. Perhaps I feel depleted, having just played the lead in a film.

During the day I record radio plays and audio books. I like learning to use my voice as an instrument. Probably I spend too much time alone, thinking I can give myself everything. My doctor, with whom I drink, is fatuously keen on pills and cheerfulness. He says if I cannot be happy with what I have, I never will be. He would deny the useful facts of human conflict, and wants me to take antidepressants, as if I would rather be paralysed than know my terrible selves.

Having wondered for months why I was waking up every morning feeling sad, I have started therapy. I am aware, partly from my relationship with Florence, that that which cannot be said is the most dangerous concealment. I am only beginning to understand psychoanalytic theory, yet am inspired by the idea that we do not live on a fine point of consciousness but exist in all areas of our being simultaneously, particularly the dreaming. Until I started lying down in Dr Wallace's room, I had never had such extended conversations about the deepest personal matters. To myself I call analysis – two people talking – 'the apogee of civilisation'. Lying in bed I have begun to go over my affair with Florence. These are more like waking dreams – Coleridge's 'flights of lawless speculation' – than considered reflections, as if I am setting myself a subject for the night. Everything returns at this thoughtful age, particularly childhood.

One afternoon in the autumn, after we have met four or five times, it is wet, and Florence and I sit at a table inside the damp teahouse. The only other customers are an elderly couple. Florence's son sits on the floor drawing.

'Can't we get a beer?' Florence says.

'They don't sell it here.'

'What a damned country.'

'Do you want to go somewhere else?'

She says, 'Can you be bothered?'

'Nope.'

Earlier I notice the smell of alcohol on her. It is a retreat I recognise; I have started to drink with more purpose myself.

While I am at the counter fetching the tea, I see Florence holding the menu at arm's length; then she brings it closer to her face and moves it away again, seeking the range at which it will be readable. Earlier I noticed a spectacle case in the top of her bag, but had not realised they were reading glasses.

When I sit down, Florence says, 'Last night Archie and I went to see your new film. It was discomfiting to sit there looking at you with him.'

'Did Archie remember me?'

'At the end I asked him. He remembered the weekend. He said you had more substance to you than most actors. You helped him.'

'I hope not.'

'I don't know what you two talked about that night, but a few months after your conversation Archie left his job and went into publishing. He accepted a salary cut, but he was determined to find work that didn't depress him. Oddly, he turned out to be very good at it. He's doing well. Like you.'

'Me? But that is only because of you.' I want to give her credit for teaching me something about self-belief and self-determination. 'Without you I wouldn't have got off to a good start . . .'

My thanks make her uncomfortable, as if I am reminding her of a capacity she does not want to know she is wasting.

'But it's your advice I want,' she says anxiously. 'Be straight, as I was with you. Do you think I can return to acting?'

'Are you seriously considering it?'

'It's the only thing I want for myself.'

'Florence, I read with you years ago but I have never seen you on stage. That aside, the theatre is not a profession you can return to at will.'

'I've started sending my photograph around,' she continues. 'I want to play the great parts, the women in Chekhov and Ibsen. I want to howl and rage with passion and fury. Is that funny? Rob, tell me if I'm being a fool. Archie considers it a middle-aged madness.'

'I am all for that,' I say.

As we part she touches my arm and says, 'Rob, I saw you the other day. I don't think you saw me, or did you?'

'But I would have spoken.'

'You were shopping in the deli. Was that your wife? The blonde girl –'

'It was someone else. She has a room nearby.'

'And you –'

'Florence –'

'I don't want to pry,' she says. 'But you used to put your hand on my back, to guide me, like that, through crowds . . .'

I do not like being recognised with the girl for fear of it getting in the papers and back to my wife. But I resent having to live a secret life. I am confused.

'I was jealous,' she says.

'Were you? But why?'

'I had started to hope . . . that it wasn't too late for you and me. I think I care for you more than I do for anybody. That is rare, isn't it?'

'I've never understood you,' I say, irritably. 'Why would you marry Archie . . . and then start seeing me?'

It is a question I have never been able to put, fearing she will think I am being critical of her, or that I will have to hear an account of their ultimate compatibility.

She says, 'I hate to admit it, but I imagined in some superstitious way that marriage would solve my problems and make me feel secure.' When I laugh she looks at me hard. 'This raises a question that we both have to ask.'

'What is that?'

She glances at her son and says softly, 'Why do you and I go with people who won't give us enough?'

I say nothing for a time. Then follows the joke which is not a joke, but which makes us laugh freely for the first time since we met again. I have been reading an account by a contemporary author of his break-up with his partner. It is relentless, and, probably because it rings true, has been taken exception to. Playfully I tell Florence that surely divorce is an underestimated pleasure. People speak of the violence of separation, but what of the delight? What could be more refreshing than never having to sleep in the same bed as that rebarbative body, and hear those familiar complaints? Such a moment of deliverance would be one to hug to yourself for ever, like losing one's virginity, or becoming a millionaire.

I stand at the door of the teahouse to watch her walk back across the park, under the trees; she carries a white umbrella, treading so lightly she barely disturbs the rain drops on the grass, her son running ahead of her. I am certain I can hear laughter hanging in the air like an ethereal jinn.

The next time I see her she comes at me quickly, kissing me on both cheeks and saying she wants to tell me something.

We take the kids to a pub with a garden. I have started to like her shaven-headed boy, Ben, having at first not known how to speak to him. 'Like a human being,' I decide, is the best method. We put my son on a coat on the ground and he bustles about on his hands and bandy legs, nose down, arse sticking out. Ben chases him and hides; the baby's laugh makes us all laugh. Others' pleasure in him increases mine. It has taken a while, but I am getting used to serving and enjoying him, rather than seeing what I want as the important thing.

'Rob, I've got a job,' she says. 'I wrote to them and went in and auditioned. It's a pub theatre, a basement smelling of beer and damp. There's no money, only a cut of the box office. But it's good work. It is great work!'

She is playing the mother in *The Glass Menagerie*. By coincidence, the pub is at the end of my street. I tell her I am delighted.

'You will come and see me, won't you?'

'But yes.'

'I often wonder if you're still upset about that holiday.'

We have never discussed it, but now she is in the mood.

'I've thought about it a thousand times. I wish Archie hadn't come.'

I laugh. It is too late; how could it matter now? 'I mean, I wish I hadn't brought him. Sitting in that stationary train with you scowling was the worst moment of my life. But I had thought I was going mad. I had been looking forward to the holiday. The night before we were to leave, Archie asked again if I wanted him to come. He could feel how troubled I was. As I packed I realised that if we went away together my marriage would shatter. You were about to go to America. Your film would make you successful. Women would want you. I knew you didn't really want me.'

This is hard. But I understand that Archie is too self-absorbed to be disturbed by her. He asks for and takes everything. He does not see her as a problem he has to solve, as I do. She has done the sensible thing, finding a man she cannot make mad.

She goes on, 'I required Archie's strength and security more than passion – or love. That *was* love, to me. He asked, too, if I were having an affair.'

'To prove that you weren't, you invited him to come.'

She puts her hand on my arm. 'I'll do anything now. Say the word.'

I cannot think of anything I want her to do.

For a few weeks I do not see her. We are both rehearsing. One Saturday, my wife Helen is pushing the kid in a trolley in the supermarket as I wander about with a basket. Florence comes round a corner and we begin talking at once. She is enjoying the rehearsals. The director does not push her far enough – 'Rob, I can do much more!' – but he will not be with her on stage, where she feels 'queenlike'. 'Anyhow, we've become friends,' she says meaningfully.

Archie does not like her acting; he does not want strangers looking at her, but he is wise enough to let her follow her wishes. She has got an agent; she is seeking more work. She believes she will make it.

After our spouses have packed away their groceries, Archie comes over and we are introduced again. He is large; his hair sticks out, his face is ruddy and his eyebrows look like a patch of corn from which a heavy creature has recently risen. Helen looks across suspiciously. Florence and I are standing close to one another; perhaps one of us is touching the other.

At home I go into my room, hoping Helen will not knock. I suspect she won't ask me who Florence is. She will want to know so much that she won't want to find out.

Without having seen the production, I rouse myself to invite several people from the film and theatre world to see Florence's play. Drinking in the pub beforehand, I can see that to the director's surprise the theatre will be full; he is wondering where all these smart people in deluxe loafers have come from, scattered amongst the customary drinkers with their elbows on the beer-splashed bar, watching football on television with their heads craned up, as if looking for an astronomical wonder. I become apprehensive myself, questioning my confidence in Florence and wondering how much of it is gratitude for her encouragement of me. Even if I have put away my judgement, what does it matter? I seem to have known her for so long that she is not to be evaluated or criticised but is just a fact of my life. The last time we met in the teahouse she told me that eighteen months ago she had a benign lump removed from behind her ear. The fear that it will return has given her a new fervency.

The bell rings. We go through a door marked 'Theatre and Toilets' and gropingly make our way down the steep, worn stairs into a cellar, converted into a small theatre. The programme is a single sheet, handed to us by the director as we go in. The room smells musty, and despite the dark the place is shoddy; there is a pillar in front of me I could rest my cheek on. Outside I hear car alarms, and from upstairs the sound of cheering men. But in this small room the silence is charged by concentration and the hope of some home-made magnificence. For the first time in years I am reminded of the purity and intensity of the theatre.

When I get out at the interval I notice Archie pulling himself up the stairs behind me. At the top, panting, he takes my arm to steady himself. I buy a drink, and, in order to be alone, go and stand outside the pub. I am afraid that if my friends, the 'important' people, remain after the interval it is because I would disapprove if they left; and if they praise Florence to me, it is only because they would have guessed the ulterior connection. The depth and passion Florence has on stage is clear to me. But I know that what an artist finds interesting about their own work, the part they consider original and penetrating, will not necessarily compel an audience, who might not even notice it, but only attend to the story.

Archie's head pokes around the pub door. His eyes find me and he comes out. I notice he has his son, Ben, with him.

'Hallo, Rob, where's Matt?' says Ben.

'Matt's my son,' I explain to Archie. 'He's in bed, I hope.'

'You happen to know one another?' Archie says.

I tug at Ben's baseball cap. 'We bump into one another in the park.'

'In the teahouse,' says the boy. 'He and Mummy love to talk.' He looks at me. 'She would love to act in a film you were in. So would I. I'm going to be an actor. The boys at school think you're the best.'

'Thank you.' I look at Archie. 'Expensive school too, I bet.'

He stands there looking away, but his mind is working.

I say to Ben, 'What do you think of Mummy in this play?'

'Brilliant.'

'What is your true opinion?' says Archie to me. 'As a man of the theatre and film?'

'She seems at ease on stage.'

'Will she go any further?'

'The more she does it, the better she will get.'

'Is that how it works?' he says. 'Is that how you made it?'

'Partly. I am talented, too.'

He looks at me with hatred and says, 'She will do it more, you think?'

'If she is to improve she will have to.'

He seems both proud and annoyed, with a cloudy look, as if the familiar world is disappearing into the mist. Until now she has followed him. I wonder whether he will be able to follow her, and whether she will want him to.

I have gone inside and found my friends, when he is at my elbow, interrupting, with something urgent to say.

'I love Florence more and more as time passes,' he tells me. 'Just wanted you to know that.'

'Yes,' I say. 'Good.'

'Right,' he says. 'Right. See you downstairs.'

Four Blue Chairs

After a lunch of soup, bread and tomato salad, John and Dina go out on to the street. At the bottom of the steps they stop for a moment and he slips his arm through hers as he always does. They have been keen to establish little regularities, to confirm that they are used to doing things together.

Today the sun beats down and the city streets seem deserted, as if everyone but them has gone on holiday. At the moment they feel they are on a kind of holiday themselves.

They would prefer to carry blankets, cushions, the radio and numerous lotions out on to the patio. Weeds push up between the paving stones and cats lie on the creeper at the top of the fence as the couple lie there in the afternoons, reading, drinking fizzy lemonade and thinking over all that has happened.

Except that the store has rung to say the four blue chairs are ready. Dina and John can't wait for them to be delivered, but must fetch them this afternoon because Henry is coming to supper tonight. They shopped yesterday; of the several meals they have learned to prepare, they will have salmon steaks, broccoli, new potatoes and three-bean salad.

Henry will be their first dinner guest. In fact he will be their first visitor.

John and Dina have been in the rented flat two and a half months already and most of the furniture, if not what they would have chosen themselves, is acceptable, particularly the bookshelves in all the rooms, which they have wiped down with wet cloths.

Dina is intending to fetch the rest of her books and her desk, which pleases him. After that, it seems to him, there will be no going back. The wooden table in the kitchen is adequate. Three people could sit comfortably around it to eat, talk and drink. They have two brightly coloured table cloths, which they bought in India.

They have started to put their things on the table, mixed up together. She will set something out, experimentally, and he will look at it as if to say, what's that?, and she watches him; then they look at one another and an agreement is reached, or not. Their pens, for instance, are now in a shaving mug; her vase is next to it; his plaster Buddha appeared on the table this morning and was passed without demur. The picture of the cat was not passed, but she won't remove it at the moment, in order to test him. There are photographs of them together, on the break they took a year ago when they were both still living with their former partners. There are photographs of his children.

At the moment there are only two rotten kitchen chairs.

John has said that Henry, whom she met once before at a dinner given by one of John's friends, will take an interest in the blue chairs with the cane seats. Henry will take an interest in almost anything, if it is presented enthusiastically.

It has only been after some delicate but amiable discussion that they finally agreed to go ahead with Henry. John and Dina like to talk. In fact she gave up her job so they could talk more. Sometimes they do it with their faces pressed together; sometimes with their backs to one another. They go to bed early so they can talk. The one thing they don't like is disagreement. They imagine that if they start disagreeing they will never stop, and that there will be a war. They have had wars and they have almost walked out on one another on several occasions. But it is the disagreements they have had before, with other people, and the fear they will return, that seem to be making them nervous at the moment.

But they have agreed that Henry will be a good choice as a first guest. He lives nearby and he lives alone. He loves being asked out.

As he works near Carluccios he will bring exotic cakes. There won't be any silences, difficult or otherwise.

They first saw the blue chairs four days ago. They were looking for an Indian restaurant nearby, and were discussing their ideal Indian menu, how they would choose the dhal from this restaurant on King Street, and the bhuna prawn from the takeaway on the Fulham Road, and so on, when they drifted into Habitat. Maybe they were tired or just felt indolent, but in the big store they found themselves sitting in various armchairs, on the sofas, at the tables, and even lying in the deckchairs, imagining they were together in this or that place by the sea or in the mountains, occasionally looking at one another, far away across the shop, or closer, side by side, thinking in astonishment, this is him, this is her, the one I've chosen, the one I've wanted all this time, and now it has really started, everything I have wished for is today.

There seemed to be no one in the shop to mind their ruminations. They lost track of time. Then a shop assistant stepped out from behind a pillar. And the four blue wooden chairs, with the cane seats – after much sitting down, standing up and shuffling of their bottoms – were agreed on. There were other chairs they wanted, but it turned out they were not in the sale, and they had to take these cheaper ones. As they left, Dina said she preferred them. He said that if she preferred them, he did too.

Today on the way to the store she insists on buying a small frame and a postcard of a flower to go in it. She says she is intending to put this on the table.

'When Henry's there?' he asks.

'Yes.'

During the first weeks of their living together he has found himself balking at the way she does certain things, things he had not noticed during their affair, or hadn't had time to get used to. For instance the way she likes to eat sitting on the front steps in the evening. He is too old for bohemianism, but he can't keep saying

'No' to everything and he has to sit there with pollution going in his bowl of pasta and the neighbours observing him, and men looking at her. He knows that this is part of the new life he has longed for, and at these times he feels helpless. He can't afford to have it go wrong.

The assistant in the store says he will fetch the chairs and they will be ready downstairs in a few minutes. At last two men bring the chairs out and stand them at the store exit.

John and Dina are surprised to see that the chairs haven't come individually, or with just a little wrapping. They are in two long brown boxes, like a couple of coffins.

John has already said they can carry the chairs to the tube, and then do the same from there to the flat. It isn't far. She thought he was being flippant. She can see now that he was serious.

To show how it must be done, and indeed that it is possible, he gets a good grip on one box, kicks it at the bottom, and shoves it right out of the shop and then along the smooth floor of the shopping centre, past the sweet seller and security guard and the old women sitting on benches.

At the exit he turns and sees her standing in the shop entrance, watching him, laughing. He thinks how lovely she is and what a good time they always have together.

She starts to follow him, pushing her box as he did his.

He continues, thinking that this is how they will do it, they will soon be at the tube station.

But outside the shopping mall, on the hot pavement, the box sticks. You can't shove cardboard along on concrete; it won't go. That morning she suggested they borrow a car. He had said they wouldn't be able to park nearby. Perhaps they would get a taxi. But outside it is a one-way street, going in the wrong direction. He sees that there are no taxis. The boxes wouldn't fit in anyway.

Out there on the street, in the sun, he squats a little. He gets his arms around the box. It is as if he is hugging a tree. Making all kinds of involuntary and regrettable sounds, he lifts it right up.

Even if he can't see where he is going, even if his nose is pushed into the cardboard, he is carrying it, he is moving. They are still on their way.

He doesn't get far. Different parts of his body are resisting. He will ache tomorrow. He puts the box down again. In fact he almost drops it. He looks back to see that Dina is touching the corners of her eyes, as if she is crying with laughter. Truly it is a baking afternoon and it was an awful idea to invite Henry over.

He is about to shout back at her, asking her whether she has any better ideas, but watching her, he can see that she does. She is full of better ideas about everything. If only he trusted her rather than himself – thinking he is always right – he would be better off.

She does this remarkable thing.

She lifts her box onto her hip and, holding it by the cardboard flap, starts to walk with it. She walks right past him, stately and upright, like an African woman with a goat on her shoulders, as if this is the most natural thing. Off she goes towards the tube. This, clearly, is how to do it.

He does the same, the whole African woman upright stance. But after a few steps the flap of the cardboard rips. It rips right across and the box drops to the ground. He can't go on. He doesn't know what to do.

He is embarrassed and thinks people are looking at him and laughing. People are indeed doing this, looking at him with the box, and at the beautiful woman with the other box. And they look back at him and then at her, and they are splitting their sides, as if nothing similar has ever happened to them. He likes to think he doesn't care, that he is strong enough at his age to withstand mockery. But he sees himself, in their eyes, as a foolish little man, with the things he has wanted and hoped for futile and empty, reduced to the ridiculous shoving of this box along the street in the sun.

You might be in love, but whether you can get four chairs home together is another matter.

She comes back to him and stands there. He is looking away and is furious. She says there's only one thing for it.

'All right,' he says, an impatient man trying to be patient. 'Let's get on with it.'

'Take it easy,' she says. 'Calm down.'

'I'm trying to,' he replies.

'Squat down,' she says.

'What?'

'Squat down.'

'Here?'

'Yes. Where do you think?'

He squats down with his arms out and she grips the box in the tree-hugging pose and tips it and lays it across his hands and on top of his head. With this weight pushing down into his skull he attempts to stand, as Olympic weight lifters do, using their knees. Unlike those Olympic heroes he finds himself pitching forward. People in the vicinity are no longer laughing. They are alarmed and shouting warnings and scattering. He is staggering about with the box on his head, a drunken Atlas, and she is dancing around him, saying, 'Steady, steady.' Not only that, he is about to hurl the chairs into the traffic.

A man passing by sets the box down for them.

'Thank you,' says Dina.

She looks at John.

'Thank you,' says John sullenly.

He stands there, breathing hard. There is sweat on his upper lip. His whole face is damp. His hair is wet and his skull itching. He is not in good shape. He could die soon, suddenly, as his father did.

Without looking at her, he picks up the box in the tree-hugging stance and takes it a few yards, shuffling. He puts it down and picks it up again. He covers a few more yards. She follows.

Once they are on the tube he suspects they will be all right. It is only one stop. But when they have got out of the train they find that getting the boxes along the station is almost impossible. The tree-hugging stance is getting too difficult. They carry one box between them up the stairs, and then return for the other. She is quiet now; he can see she is tiring, and is bored with this idiocy.

At the entrance to the station she asks the newspaper seller if they can leave one of the boxes with him. They can carry one home together and return for the other. The man agrees.

She stands in front of John with her arms at her side and her hands stuck out like a couple of rabbit ears, into which shape the box is then placed. As they walk he watches her in her green sleeveless top with a collar, the sling of her bag crossing her shoulder, and the back of her long neck.

He thinks that if they have to put the box down everything will fail. But although they stop three times, she is concentrating, they both are, and they don't put the box down.

They reach the bottom of the steps to the house. At last they stand the box upright, in the cool hall, and sigh with relief. They return for the other box. They have found a method. They carry it out efficiently.

When it is done he rubs and kisses her sore hands. She looks away.

Without speaking they pull the blue chairs with the cane seats from the boxes and throw the wrapping in the corner. They put the chairs round the table and look at them. They sit on them. They place themselves in this position and that. They put their feet up on them. They change the table cloth.

'This is good,' he says.

She sits down and puts her elbows on the table, looking down at the table cloth. She is crying. He touches her hair.

He goes to the shop for some lemonade and when he gets back she has taken off her shoes and is lying flat out on the kitchen floor.

'I'm tired now,' she says.

He makes her a drink and places it on the floor. He lies down beside her with his hands under his head. After a time she turns to him and strokes his arm.

'Are you OK?' he says.

She smiles at him. 'Yes.'

Soon they will open the wine and start to make supper; soon Henry will arrive and they will eat and talk.

They will go to bed and in the morning at breakfast time, when they put the butter and jam and marmalade out, the four blue chairs will be there, around the table of their love.

That Was Then

We are unerring in our choice of lovers, particularly when we require the wrong person. There is an instinct, magnet or aerial which seeks the unsuitable. The wrong person is, of course, right for something – to punish, bully or humiliate us, let us down, leave us for dead, or, worst of all, give us the impression that they are not inappropriate, but almost right, thus hanging us in love's limbo. Not just anyone can do this.

All morning he had wondered whether Natasha would try to kill him.

He was not sure what she wanted, but it would not be a regular conversation. After four years of silence, she had suddenly become unusually persistent, writing to him several times at home and at his agent's. When he sent a note to say there was no point in their meeting she rang him twice at his new house and finally spoke to Lolly, his wife, who was so concerned she opened the door to his room and said, 'Is she trying to get you back?'

He turned slowly. 'It's not that, I shouldn't think.'

'Will you see her?'

'No.'

'Will you tell her not to ring again?'

'Yes.'

'Good,' said Lolly. 'Good.'

Natasha was drinking coffee at a table outside the café, wearing black, but not leather at least; probably she was the only such sombre, self-conscious person in the park. He had arrived early, but in

order to be late had taken his coffee and newspaper to the conservatory, where he had considered the flowerbeds and wished for his
son. Soon they would be having conversations and Nick would
have less need of other people.

He had phoned Natasha unexpectedly that morning to give her
the time and the place to meet, the grounds of an eighteenth-
century Palladian villa in West London. He was apprehensive, but
could not deny that he was curious to see where they both now
were. He calculated that he hadn't actually seen her for five years.

It had been a dull summer and the schools had been open for
two weeks. But a day like this, with the sun suddenly breaking
through, reminded him of the seasons and of change. On the lawn
that sloped down to the pond, people were in short sleeves and
sunglasses. Young couples lay on one another. As it was a middle-
class area, families sat on blankets with elaborate picnics; corks
were pulled from wine bottles, cotton napkins handed out and
children called back from rummaging for conkers in the leaves
and long grass.

He had got up and headed towards Natasha with determination, but the soft focus of the light mist and the alternate caresses
of autumn heat and chill put him in an unexpectedly sensual
mood. This renewed love of existence was like a low erotic charge.
He came regularly to this park with his wife and baby and if,
today, they were not with him, he could mark their absence
by considering how meagre things were without them. At night,
when he joined his woman in bed – she wore blue pyjamas, and
his son, thrashing in his cot at the end of the room, a blue-
striped, short-sleeved babygro, resembling an Edwardian bathing
costume – he knew, at last, that there was nowhere else he would
prefer to be.

What he wanted was to have a surreptitious look at Natasha, but
he thought she had spotted him. It would be undignified to dodge
about.

With his eyes fixed on her, he strode out of the bushes and
across the tarmac apron in front of the café, weaving in and out of

the tables where dogs, children on bicycles and adults with trays were crowded together, irritable waitresses tripping through. Natasha glanced up and started on the work of taking him in. She even rose, and stood on tiptoe. If he was looking to see how she had aged, she was doing the same to him.

She kissed him on the cheek. 'You've cut your hair.'

'I've gone grey, haven't I?' he said. 'Or was I grey before?'

Before he could draw back, her fingers were in his hair.

'Behind the ear, there used to be a few white hairs,' she said. 'Now – there's a black one. Why don't you dye it?'

He noticed her hair was still what they called 'rock 'n' roll black'.

He said, 'Why would I bother?'

She laughed. 'Don't tell me you're no longer vain. Look at you in your shiny dark blue raincoat. How much did those shoes cost?'

'I have a son now, Natty.'

'I know that, Daddio,' she said. She tapped her big silver ring on the table, given to her as a teenager by a Hell's Angel boyfriend.

'You like fatherhood?'

He looked away at the tables piled with the Sunday papers, plates and cups, and children's toys. He heard the names of expensive schools, like a saint's roll-call. He remembered, as a child, his parents urging him to be polite, and wished for the time when good manners protected you from the excesses of intimacy, when honesty was not romanticised.

He said, 'My boy's a fleshy thing. There's plenty of him to kiss. I don't think we've ever seen his neck. But he has a bubbly mouth and a beard of saliva. I bring him here in his white hat – when he cries he goes red and looks like an outraged chef.'

'Is that why you made me come all this way? I couldn't find this bloody place.'

He said, 'I thought it would amuse you to know . . . In May 1966 the Beatles made promotional films here, for "Rain" and "Paperback Writer".'

'I see,' she said. 'That's it?'

'Well, yes.'

He and Natasha had liked pop of the sixties and seventies; in her flat they had lain on oriental cushions drinking mint tea, among other exotic interests, playing and discussing records.

Before he met her, he had been a pop journalist for several years, writing about fashion, music and the laboured politics that accompanied them. Then he became almost respectable, as the arts correspondent for an old-fashioned daily broadsheet. On this paper it amused the journalists to think of him as young, contradictory and promiscuous. He was hired to be contrary and outrageous.

In fact, at night, he was working to show them how tangled he was. Not telling anyone, he wrote, with urgent persistence, an uninhibited memoir of his father. The book spoke of his own childhood terrors, as well as his father's vanity and tenderness. The last chapter was concerned with what men, and fathers, could become, having been released, as women were two decades earlier, from some of their conventional expectations. Before publication, he was afraid of being mocked; it was an honest book, an earnest one, even.

The memoir was acclaimed and won awards. It was said that men hadn't exposed themselves in such a way before. He gave up journalism to write a novel about young men working on a pop magazine, which was made into a popular film. He lived in San Francisco and New York, taught 'creative writing', and rewrote unmade movies. He had got out. He was envied; he even envied himself. People spoke about him, as he had talked of pop stars, once. He met Natasha and things went awry.

She said, 'You still listen to all that?'

'How many times can you hear "I Wanna Hold Your Hand" and "She Loves You"? And the new stuff means nothing to me.'

She said, 'All those symphonies and concertos sound the same.'

'At least they can play,' he said.

'The musicians are only reading the notes. It's not music, it's map-reading.'

'How many of us can do that? It's better that people don't foist their original attempts on the public. Don't forget for years I went to gigs every night. It's funny, I couldn't wait to get home and play something quiet by the Isley Brothers.'

He laughed and waved at a man. 'How was your holiday?' someone called. 'And the builders?'

'These people recognise you,' she said. 'I suppose they are the sort to read. Insomnia would be their only problem.'

He laughed and put his face up to the sun. 'They know me as the man with the only infant in the park who wears a leather jacket.'

She let him sit, but they were both waiting.

She leaned forward. 'After trying to avoid me, what made you want to see me today?'

'Lolly – you spoke to her on the phone – has gone to look at a place we've bought in Wiltshire.'

'You've joined the aristocracy?'

'Not a wet-dog-and-bad-pictures country house. A London house in a field. For the first time in ages I had a spare afternoon.' He said, 'What is it you want?'

'It wasn't to bother you, though it must have seemed like that.' She looked at him with concentration and sincerity. 'Do you want a fag?'

'I've given up.'

She lit her cigarette and said, 'I don't want to be eradicated from your life – cancelled, wiped out.'

He sighed. 'I was thinking the other day that I would never like my parents again, not in the way I did. There are no real reasons for anything, we just fall in and out of love with things – thank God.'

'I would accept that, if you hadn't written about me.'

'Did I?'

'In your second novel, published two and a half years ago.' She looked at him but he said nothing. 'Nick, I believed, at the time we were seeing one another – two years before – we were living some kind of life together in privacy.'

'Living together?'

'You slept at my place, and me at yours. Didn't we see each other every day? Didn't we think about one another quite a lot?'

'Yes,' he said. 'We did do that.'

She said, 'Nick, you used my sexual stuff. What I like up my cunt.'

He lowered his voice. 'The Croatian version of the book has come out. It has been translated into ten languages. Who's going to recognise your hairy flaps or my broth of a stomach and withered buttocks?'

'I do. Isn't that enough?'

'Who says it's your cunt? Sometimes a cunt –'

She rubbed her face with her hand. 'Don't start. The cunt in the book is called ME – Middle England. Those who enter it, of whom there seem to be an unnecessary number, and pretty grotesque they are too, are known as Middle Englanders. We –'

'It was always my joke.'

'Our joke.'

'All right.'

'I thought it would stop disturbing me. But it didn't go away. I feel abused by you, Nick.'

'That wouldn't be the origin of that feeling.'

'No, as you pointed out in the book, when my father was away lecturing, my mother did unwelcome things to me.'

He said, 'Most of the women I've met have been sexually abused. If some women are afraid of men, or hate them, isn't it going to start there?'

She wasn't listening. She had plenty to say; he let her continue.

She said, 'When I saw you the first time I was impressed. Writers are supposed to feel and know. They're wise, with enough honesty, bravery and conscience for us all. Now I'm upset that you saw me as you did. Upset you wrote it down. Would you say anything, expose anyone, provided it served your purpose? If you only believe in your own advantage you would have to agree that that is a miserable place to have ended up.' She picked up her cigarettes and threw them down. 'Why didn't you make the woman strong?'

'Who is strong? Hitler? Florence Nightingale? Thatcher? She wishes to be strong, impervious to human perplexity. Wouldn't that be more accurate?'

He tried to look at her evenly. She had never come at him like this. She had been confused and tolerant and afraid of losing him. They had parted suddenly, abruptly. But for over a year they had spoken on the phone several times a day, and seen one another in the most excessive situations. He had often wondered why they had not been able to continue; he had even considered seeing her again, if she wanted to. They had got along.

If Natasha was clumsy and felt that her elbows protruded; if she walked with her feet turned out, despite having tried to correct this during her childhood, she brought this to his attention. If she was quick and well read, whatever she knew was inadequate. There was always a spot, blemish, new line, sagging eyelid or patch of dry skin on her cheek which it was impossible for her not to draw attention to. She lacked confidence, to say the least, but had attacks of impassioned self-belief, gaiety and determination which she later condemned. After laughing loudly she clapped her hand over her open mouth. But she wouldn't be suppressed; when she had a fear or phobia, she made a note of it, and fought. Perhaps when she was in her fifties she would reach a cooler equilibrium.

As he looked, her outline seemed to blur. It wasn't only that past and present were merging to form a new picture of her, it was that a third person was sitting with them. This had happened before. Natasha had seemed to place between them another woman, a fiction, who resembled Natasha but was her denial and her Platonic ideal. This Natasha, the pop star, was cool, certain, smart. Photographed in a different light, in better clothes, good at ballet, cooking and conversation, this figure dragged Natasha along to better things, while undermining and mocking her. They had both fallen in love with this desirable prevailing woman who haunted them as a living presence, but would never let them possess her. Compared with her, Natasha could only fail. They had had to find others – strangers – to witness and worship the ideal Natasha; and, when the illusion failed, like a cinema projector breaking down, they had to get rid of them.

'You wrote a bit,' he said. 'You know how diverse and complex the sources of inspiration are.'

'I still write,' she said. 'Despite your laughing at me.'

'It was justice you were interested in, and how to live. Literature makes no recommendations. It's not a guidebook but you did learn that the imagination lifts something up and takes it somewhere else, altering it as it flies. The original idea is only an excuse.'

She pretended to choke. 'The magic carpet of your imagination didn't fly you very far, baby. Why did you take parts of me and put them in a book? Nick, you were savage about me. I've asked people about this.'

'They agree with you?' She nodded. He said, 'What are you doing these days?'

'I finished my training. Now I work as a therapist. I have credit card debts up to here. They took the car. Once you start sinking you really go fast. You couldn't –' She shook her head. 'No, no. I'm not going to degrade myself.'

'Not more than you usually like to,' he said.

'No. That's right. Hey. Look.'

She threw her cigarette down and pushed up her sleeve. Drawing a breath, she pushed. There was an appreciable swelling. 'I've been going to the gym.'

He wondered if she required him to squeeze the muscle. 'Popeye's been eating her spinach,' he said.

'It makes me feel good,' she said.

'That's all that matters.'

'I've got into young men.'

'Good.'

He noticed that her ears were pierced in several places. Perhaps she had violated herself all over. It would be like going to bed with a cactus. He wouldn't mention it. The less he said, the sooner it would be over. He saw he was only there to listen. However, something came to him.

'My mind hasn't entirely gone,' he said. 'But these days I do pick up a book and have no memory of what I read yesterday. However, I was labouring through a seven-hundred-page biography of someone I liked. It bulged with facts. Almost the only part I found irresistible was the subject's sciatica and slipped disc – you know how it is at our age. In the end I had no idea what the man might be like. Everything personal and human was missing. Then I thought: where else could you get the complexity and detail of inner motion except in fiction? It's the closest we can get to how we are inside.'

She looked away. 'I've never had a vocation.'

'Why don't you go to Spain?'

'What? Vocation, I said.'

'Why does a vocation matter?'

'I want to find something to be good at. One of my patients is a skinhead, sexually abused by his mother and sister. I don't think he can even read his own tattoos. It is not me he's hating and sapping as he sits there saying "cunt, cunt, cunt". Why am I compelled to help this bastard? Nick, you're omnipotent and self-sufficient in that little room with your special pens that no one's allowed to touch, the coffee that only you can make, music where you can reach it, post-cards of famous paintings pinned in front of you. Is it the same?'

'Exactly.'

'You were always retreating to that womb or hiding place. What made me cross was how you placed the madness outside yourself – in me, the half-addicted, promiscuous, self-devouring crazy girl. Isn't that misogyny?'

He looked startled. 'I'm not sure.'

'You made yourself, Nick, you see, before things got . . . a little mad. You weren't privileged, like some of those show-off scribblers. I remember you sitting with your favourite novels, underlining sentences. The lists of words pinned up by your shaving mirror – words to learn, words to use. You'd write out the same sentence again and again, in different ways. I can't imagine a woman being so methodical and will-driven. You want to be highly considered. Only I wish you hadn't taken a sneaky and spiteful revenge against me.'

He said, 'It's never going to be frictionless between men and women as long as they want things from one another – and they have to want things, that's a relationship.'

'Sophistry!'

'Reality!'

She said, 'Self-deception!'

He got up. It wouldn't take him long to get home. He could carry a low chair out into his new garden, on which they had recently spent a lot of money, and read and doze. Six men had come through the side door with plants, trees and paving stones; he and Lolly couldn't wait for nature. It wasn't his money, or even Lolly's, but her American father's. He wondered if he knew what married but dependent women must feel, when what you had wasn't earned or deserved. Humiliation wasn't quite what he felt, but there was resentment.

He had met Natasha one Mayday at a private party at the Institute of Contemporary Arts, just down from Buckingham Palace, in sight of Big Ben. He would always drink and smoke grass before leaving his flat – in order to get out at all; and he was chuckling to himself at the available ironies. Apart from the Soviet invasion of Hungary, there couldn't have been a worse time for socialism. Certainly no one he knew was admitting to being on the hard left, or to having supported the Soviet Union. 'I was always more of an anarchist than a Party man,' Nick heard as he squeezed through the crowd to the drinks table. A voice replied, 'I was only ever a Eurocommunist.' He himself announced, 'I was never much of a joiner.' His more imaginative left-wing acquaintances had gone to Berlin to witness the collapse of the Wall, 'to be at the centre of history', as one of them put it. 'For the first time,' Nick had commented.

It was easy to sneer. What did he know? It was only now that he was starting to read history, having become intrigued by the fact that people not unlike him had, only a few decades before, been possessed by the fatal seriousness of murderous, mind-gripping ideologies. He'd only believed in pop. Its frivolity and anger was merely subversive; it delivered no bananas. If asked for his views, he'd be afraid to give them. But he was capable of description.

Like him, Natasha usually only worked in the morning, teaching, or working on these theses. They both liked aspects of London, not the theatre, cinema or restaurants but the rougher places that resembled a Colin McInnes novel. Nick had come to know wealthy and well-known people; he was invited for cocktails and launches, lunches and charity dinners, but it was too prim to be his everyday world. He started to meet Natasha at two o'clock in a big deserted pub in Notting Hill. They'd eat, have their first drinks, talk about everything and nod at the old Rastas who still seemed permanently installed in these pubs. They would buy drugs from young dealers from the nearby estates and hear their plans for robberies. Notting Hill was wealthy and the houses magnificent, but it had yet to become aware of it. The pubs were still neglected, with damp carpets and dusty oak bars covered in cigarette burns, about to be turned into shiny places crammed with people who looked as though they appeared on television, though they only worked in it.

He and Natasha would take cocaine or ecstasy, or some LSD, or all three – and retire for the afternoon to her basement nearby. When it got dark they pulled one another from bed, applied their eye-shadow in adjacent mirrors, and stepped out in their high heels.

Now she took his hand. 'You can't walk out on me!' She tugged him back into his seat.

He said, 'You can't pull me!'

'Don't forget the flowers you came at me with!' she said. 'The passion! The hikes through the city at night and breakfast in the morning! And conversation, conversation! Didn't we put our chairs side by side and go through your work! Have you forgotten how easily you lost hope in those days and how I repeatedly sent you back to your desk? Everyone you knew wanted to be a proper writer. None of them would do it, but you thought, why shouldn't I? Didn't I help you?'

'Yes you did, Natasha! Thank you!'

'You didn't put it in the book, did you? You put all that other stuff in!'

'It didn't fit!'

'Oh Nick, couldn't you have made it fit?' She was looking at him. 'Why are you laughing at me?'

'There's no way out of this conversation. Why don't we walk a little?'

'Can we?'

'Why not?'

'I keep thinking you're going to go away. Have you got time?'

'Yes.'

'My sweet and sour man I called you. D'you remember?' She seemed to relax. 'A fluent, creative life, turning ordinary tedium and painful feeling into art. The satisfactions of a self-sufficient child, playing alone. That's what I want. That's why people envy artists.'

'Vocation,' he said. 'Sounds like the name of someone.'

'Yes. A guide. Someone who knows. I don't want to sound religious, because it isn't that.'

'A guiding figure. A man.'

She sighed. 'Probably.'

He said, 'I was thinking . . . how our generation loved Monroe, Hendrix, Cobain, even. Somehow we were in love with death. Few of the people we admired could go to bed without choking on their own vomit. Wasn't that the trouble – with pop, and with us?'

'What d'you mean?'

'We were called a self-indulgent generation. We didn't go to war but we were pretty murderous towards ourselves. Almost everyone I know – or used to.'

'But I was just going to –' She reached into her bag and leaned over to him. 'Give me your hand,' she said. 'Go on. I got you something.' She passed the object to him. 'Now look.'

He opened his hand.

*

On a dreary parade in North Kensington, between a second-hand bookshop and a semi-derelict place hiring out fancy-dress costumes, was a shop where Nick and Natasha went to buy leather and rubberwear. Behind barred windows it was painted black and barely lit, concealing the fact that the many shiny red items were badly made or plain ragged. The assistants, in discreet versions of the available clothes – Nick preferred to call them costumes – were enthusiastic, offering tea and biscuits.

Wrapping themselves in fake-fur coats from charity shops, Natasha and Nick began going to places where others had similar tastes, seeking new fears and transgressions, of which there were many during this AIDS period. If couples require schemes, they had discovered their purpose. It was possible to be a sexual outlaw as long as there were still people who were innocent. They pressed each other on, playing Virgil to one another, until they no longer knew if they were children or adults, men or women, masters or servants. The transformation into pleasure of the banal, the unpleasant and the plain unappetising was like black magic – poor Don Juan on a treadmill, compelled to make life's electricity for ever.

Nick recalled walking one night onto the balcony of a vast club, seeking Natasha, and looking down on a pageant of bizarre costumes, feathers, semi-nudity, masks and clothes of all periods, representing every passion, every possible kink and kook, zig and zag. Natasha was among them, waiting for him with some bridled old man who worked in a post office.

Nick wondered if everyone involved liked participating in a secret, as they recreated the mystery which children discover by whispers, that what people want to do with one another is strange, and that the uncovering of this strangeness is itself the excitement. Certainly there were terrifying initiations, over and over. They were the oddest people; he learned that there was little that was straightforward about humanity. But what appeared to frighten them all was the mundane, the familiar, the ordinary.

Like actors unable to stop playing a part, as though they could be on stage for ever, he and Natasha wanted to remain at a dramatic pitch where there was no disappointment, no self-knowledge or development, only a state of constant, narcissistic emergency and a clear white light in the head.

In order to consume their punishment with their pleasure, which some might call a convenience, they were stoned. Nick remembered a friend at school saying – and this was the best advertisement for drugs he'd heard – 'If you are stoned you can do anything.' Why was living the problem? If he looked around at his friends and acquaintances, how many of them were able to survive unaided? They sought absence until they had become like a generation lost to war. Those who survived were sitting in shell-shocked confessional circles in countryside clinics. He suspected they had left success to fools and mediocrities. By midnight he was rarely able to see in front of him; he and Natasha held one another up, like the vertical arms of a staggering triangle. Sobriety was a terror, though they couldn't remember why, and their heroes, legends, myths, were hopeless incompetents, death-soaked tragic imaginations.

He saw people going to heroin like a fate; imagining you could shun it was arrogant or solemn. Nick had wanted to find like-minded people; he turned them into his jailers. He recalled people in rubber masks, coming at him like executioners. It was arduous work, converting people into objects, when he had not been brought up to it.

Midday one morning he woke up at her place. He rose and lumbered about, reacquainting himself with an unfamiliar object, his body. He had been whipped, badly; his face and hands were grazed, too: he must have fallen somewhere and no one, not even him, had noticed.

Somehow she had gone to work, leaving him a note. 'Remember, Remember!' she had scrawled in lipstick.

Remember what? Then it returned. His task was to withdraw three thousand pounds from his bank account, which, apart from his flat, was all he had and buy drugs from a man who sold everything, but only in large amounts. It would save them the trouble of having to score continually. In two hours he would have the drugs;

minutes later the cocaine would be working, stealing another day and night of his life. Natasha would return; there was a couple they were to meet later; there would be cages, whips, ice, fire.

There had been the death-laden ways of teachers and employers, and there had been rebellion, drugs, pleasure. No one had shown him what a significant life was and the voices that spoke in his head were not kind.

And yet something occurred to him. He walked out of the flat and kept walking through his pain until he reached the suburbs; at last he fell through fields and fields. He never returned to her place. The rest was a depressing cold abstinence and mourning, sitting at his desk half the day, every day, repeatedly summoning a half-remembered discipline, wishing someone would lash him to the chair. Those characters in Chekhov's plays, forever intoning 'work, work, work'. How stale a prayer, he thought, as though the world was better off for the slavery in it. But boredom was an antidote to unruly wishes, quelling his suspicion that disobedience was the only energy. He had to teach himself to sit still again.

After a freezing month he rediscovered capability and audacity. Even the idea of public recognition returned, along with competitiveness, envy, and a little pride. He made her leave him alone, and when they met again, tentatively, his fear of any addiction, which had saved him, but which was also the fear of relying on anyone – some addictions are called love – meant he could not like her any more. What could they do together? It wouldn't have happened to the ideal, desirable Natasha.

She had pressed a small envelope into his palm.

'There.'

He glanced down.

She said, 'You'd be making a mistake to think it was the other things I liked, when it was our talks and your company. You're sweet, Nick, and strangely polite at times. I can't put that together with all you've done to me.' She touched his hand. 'Go on.'

'Now?'

'Then we'll walk.'

In the park toilet a boy stood in a cubicle with his trousers down, bent over. His father wiped him, helping him with his belt, zip and buttons. Nick went into the next cubicle and closed the door. He would open the envelope, have a look for old times' sake, and return it. She had had the day she had wanted.

His hands were shaking. He held it in his palm, before opening it. A gram of fine grains, untouched. Heavenly sand. His credit card was in his back pocket.

He returned to her.

He said, 'I took the parts of you I needed to make my book. It wasn't a fair or final judgement but a practical transformation, in order to say something. Someone in a piece of fiction is a dream figure . . . picked from one context and thrust into another, to serve some purpose. A tiny portion of them is used.'

She nodded but had lost interest.

They walked by the pond, the cascade and the cricket pitch. Children played on felled logs; people sketched and painted; on pedestals, the heads of Roman emperors looked on. Nick and Natasha stepped from patches of vivid sunlight into cooler tunnels. The warm currents had turned chilly. As the sky darkened, the clouds turned crimson. Parents called to their children.

She started to cry.

'Nick, will you take me out of here?'

'If you want.'

'Please.'

She put her dark glasses on and he led her past dawdling families to the gate.

In his car she wiped her face.

'All those respectable white voices behind high walls. The wealth, the cleanliness, the hope. I was getting agoraphobic. It all makes me sick with regret.'

She was trembling. He had forgotten how her turmoil disturbed him. He was becoming impatient. He wanted to be at home when

Lolly got back. He had to prepare the food. Some friends were coming by, with their new baby.

She said, 'Aren't we going to have a drink? Is this the way? Where are we now?'

'Look,' he said.

He was driving beside a row of tall, authoritative stucco houses with pillars and steps. Big family cars sat in the drives. Across the narrow road was a green; overlooked by big trees there were tennis courts and a children's playground. During the week children in crisp uniforms were dropped off and picked up from school; in the afternoons Filipino and East European nannies would sit with their charges in the playground. This was where he lived now, though he couldn't admit it.

'We are thinking of moving here,' he said. 'What do you think?'

'There's no point asking me,' she said. 'Everything has become very conventional. You're either in or you're out. I'm with the out – with the weird, the impossible, the victimised and the broken. It's the only place to be.'

'Why turn habit into principle?'

'I don't know. Nick, take me to one of the old places. We've got time, haven't we? Are you bored by me?'

'Not yet.'

'I'm so glad.'

He drove to one of their pubs, with several small rooms, blackened ceilings, benches and big round tables. He ordered oysters and Guinness.

As he sat down he said embarrassedly, 'Have you got any more of that stuff?'

'If you kiss me,' she said.

'Come on,' he said.

'No,' she said, putting her face close to his. 'Pay for what you want!'

He pushed his face into her warm mouth.

She passed him the envelope. 'If you don't leave some I'll kill you.'

'Don't worry,' he said.

'I will,' she said. 'Because I know what saved you – greed.' She was looking at him. 'My place? Don't look at your watch. Just for a little bit, eh?'

He could tell from the flat that she hadn't gone crazy. The furniture wasn't frayed or stained; there were flowers, a big expensive sofa with books on nutrition balanced on the arm. The records were no longer on the floor. She had CDs now, in racks, alphabetical. As usual there were music papers and magazines on the table. She went to put on a CD. He hoped it wouldn't be anything he knew.

He went into the bedroom. It was as dark as ever, but he knew where the light switches were. Looking at the familiar Indian wall-hangings, he sank onto the mattress to pull off his shoes. He flung his clothes onto the bare, unvarnished floorboards, covered in threadbare rugs. The smell of her bed he knew. He could reach the opened bottles of wine and the ashtray. He swigged some sour red and reached for the pillows.

She almost fell on him; she knew he liked her weight, and to be pinned down. He closed his eyes. When she tied him quickly and expertly, he remembered the frisson of fear, the helplessness, and the pleasure coming from some rarely lit place. He struggled, giggled, screamed.

When he awoke she was sitting across the room at her table in her black silk dressing gown, surrounded by papers, unguents, tins, boxes, with her hands in front of her, like a pianist looking for a tune. She turned and smiled. The door to the cupboard in which she kept her 'dressing up' things was open.

'Untie me.'

'In a while. Tomorrow, maybe.'

'Natasha –'

'Look.' She opened her dressing gown and sat over him. How salty she was. 'Here. If you don't behave I'll read to you from your own work.'

He looked up to see her lips pursed in concentration. At last she released him. They were both pleased, a job well done. He started to move quickly in the bed as some inner necessity and accompanying fury led him to desire satisfaction. There was a man he had to meet in a pub, a greedy, unbalanced man with, no doubt, a talent for rapid mathematics. But Nick couldn't find his clothes amongst the flimsy things flung over the bed.

As it was cold he pulled his clothes on under the sheets as usual. But they smelt musty, as if he'd been wearing them for several days. He turned his sweater inside out.

She pulled him up, holding him in her arms. He lit a cigarette. 'Natty, I'm off to get the stuff.'

She nodded. 'Good. Got the money?'

He patted his pocket. 'You'll be here when I get back?'

'Oh yes,' she said.

He went out into the living room and shook himself, as if he would wake up.

She followed him and said, 'What's up?'

'I'm marked,' he said, pulling his sleeves up. 'Christ. Look! My wrists.'

'So you are,' she said. 'A marked man. They'll fade.'

'Not tonight.'

She said, 'I hope I'm pregnant. It's the right time of the month.'

'That would be a nuisance to me.'

'Not to me,' she said. 'It would be a good memento. A decent souvenir.'

He said. 'You don't know what you're saying.'

'Yes I do. Would you like me to let you know?'

'No.'

'That's up to you.'

He said, 'I'd forgotten how drugs make the dullest stuff tolerable. I hope everything goes well for you.'

He went out into the street. He was walking quickly but to where he didn't know. He had emptied his mind out; there were good things but not to hand. If only the drug would stop working.

At last he remembered his car and returned for it. He drove fast but carefully. Lolly would have finished at the house. She would be on her way back, singing to the boy in the car. He hoped she was safe. He thought of the pleasure on his wife's face when she saw him, and the way his son turned to his voice. There was much he had to teach the boy. He thought that pleasures erase themselves as they occur – you can never remember your last cigarette. If happiness accumulates it is not because it remains in the bloodstream but because it is the bloodstream.

He unlocked the house. He still hadn't become used to the size and brightness of the kitchen, nor to the silence, unusual for London. The freezer was a room in itself. He took the food out and put it on the table. Now he had to get to the supermarket to pick up the champagne.

On the way out he opened the door to his study. He hadn't been to his desk for a few days. He wanted to think there were other things he liked more, that he wasn't possessed by it. He went in and quickly scribbled some notes. He couldn't write now but after supper he would go to bed with his wife and son; when they were asleep he'd get up to work.

Sitting outside in the car, he examined his sore wrists. He pulled his shirt sleeves down. Before, he'd never cover them; he knew some men and many women who would show off their hacked, scarred or cut arms, as important marks.

There was something he wished he'd said to Natasha as he left – he had looked back and seen her face at the window, watching him go up the steps. 'There are worlds and worlds and worlds inside you.' But perhaps it wouldn't mean anything to her.

Girl

They got on at Victoria Station and sat together, kissing lightly. As the train pulled away, she took out her Nietzsche tome and began to read. Turning to the man at her side she became amused by his face, which she studied continually. Removing her gloves she picked shaving cream from his ears, sleep from his eyes and crumbs from his mouth, while laughing to herself. The combination of his vanity, mixed with unconscious naivety, usually charmed her.

Nicole hadn't wanted to visit her mother after all this time but Majid, her older lover – it sounded trite calling him her 'boyfriend' – had persuaded her to. He was curious about everything to do with her; it was part of love. He said it would be good for her to 'reconnect'; she was stronger now. However, during the past year, when Nicole had refused to speak to her, and had ensured her mother didn't have her address, she had suppressed many tormenting thoughts from the past; ghosts she dreaded returning as a result of this trip.

Couldn't Majid sense how uneasy she was? Probably he could. She had never had anyone listen to her so attentively or take her so seriously, as if he wanted to occupy every part of her. He had the strongest will of anyone she'd known, apart from her father. He was used to having things his own way, and often disregarded what she wanted. He was afraid she would run away.

He had never met her mother. She might be incoherent, or in one of her furies, or worse. As it was, her mother had cancelled the proposed visit three times, once in a drunken voice that was on the point of becoming spiteful. Nicole didn't want Majid to think that she – half her mother's age – would resemble her at fifty. He had recently told Nicole that he considered her to be, in some sense, 'dark'. Nicole was worried that her mother would find Majid also dark, but in the other sense.

Almost as soon as it left the station, their commuter train crossed the sparkling winter river. It would pass through the suburbs and then the countryside, arriving after two hours at a seaside town. Fortunately, theirs wasn't a long journey, and next week, they were going to Rome; in January he was taking her to India. He wanted her to see Calcutta. He wouldn't travel alone any more. His pleasure was only in her.

Holding hands they looked out at Victorian schools and small garages located under railway arches. There were frozen football pitches, allotments, and the backs of industrial estates where cork tiles and bathroom fittings were manufactured, as well as carpet warehouses and metalwork shops. When the landscape grew more open, railway tracks stretched in every direction, a fan of possibilities. Majid said that passing through the outskirts of London reminded him what an old country Britain was, and how manifestly dilapidated.

She dropped her hand in his lap and stroked him as he took everything in, commenting on what he saw. He looked handsome in his silk shirt, scarf and raincoat. She dressed for him, too, and couldn't go into a shop without wondering what would please him. A few days before, she'd had her dark hair cut into a bob that skimmed the fur collar of the overcoat she was wearing with knee-length motorcycle boots. At her side was the shoulder bag in which she carried her vitamin pills, journal and lip salve, and the mirror which had convinced her that her eyelids were developing new folds and lines as they shrivelled up. That morning she'd plucked her first grey hair from her head, and placed it inside a book. Yet she still had spots, one on her cheek and one on her upper lip. Before they left, Majid had made her conceal them with make-up, which she never wore.

'In case we run into anyone I know,' he said.

He was well connected, but she was sure he wouldn't know any-one where they were going. Yet she had obeyed.

She forced herself back to the book. Not long after they met, eighteen months ago, he remarked, 'You've been to university but things must have changed since my day.' It was true she didn't know certain words: 'confound', 'pejorative', 'empirical'. In the house they now shared, he had thousands of books and was famil-iar with all the writers, composers and painters. As he pointed out, she hadn't heard of Gauguin. Sometimes when he was talking to his friends she had no idea what they were discussing, and became convinced that if her ignorance didn't trouble him it was because he valued only her youth.

Certainly he considered conversation a pleasure. There had recently occurred an instructive incident when they dropped in for tea on the mother of her best friend. This woman, a sociology lecturer, had known Nicole from the age of thirteen, and probably continued to think of her as poignantly deprived. Nicole thought of her as cool, experienced and, above all, knowledgeable. Five years ago, when one of her mother's boyfriends had beaten up Nicole's brother, this woman had taken Nicole in for a few weeks. Nicole had sat numbly in her flat, surrounded by walls of books and pictures. All of it, apart from the occasional piece of soothing music, seemed vain and irrelevant.

Visiting with Majid she had, by midnight, only succeeded in detaching his hand from the woman's. Nicole had then to get him to leave, or at least relinquish the bottle of whisky. Meanwhile the woman was confessing her most grievous passions and telling Majid that she'd seen him address a demonstration in the seven-ties. A man like him, she cried, required a substantial woman! It was only when she went to fetch her poetry, which she intended to read to him, that Nicole could get the grip on his hair she needed to extract him.

By providing her with the conversations she'd longed for, he had walked in and seduced her best friend's mother! Nicole had felt extraneous. Not that he had noticed. Pushing him out of there, she was reminded of the time, around the age of fourteen, she'd had to get her mother out of a neighbour's house, dragging her across the road, her legs gone, and the whole street watching.

He laughed whenever she recalled the occasion, but it troubled her. It wasn't the learning that mattered. Majid had spent much of his youth reading, and lately had wondered what adventures he had been keeping himself from. He claimed that books could get in the way of what was important between people. But she couldn't sit, or read or write, or do nothing, without seeking company, never having been taught the benefits of solitude. The compromise they reached was this: when she read he would lie beside her, watching her eyes, sighing as her fingers turned a page.

No; his complaint was that she couldn't convert feelings into words and expected him to understand her by clairvoyance.

Experience had taught her to keep her mouth shut. She'd spent her childhood among rough people that it amused Majid to hear about, as if they were cartoon characters. But they had been menacing. Hearing some distinction in your voice, they would suspect you of ambition and therefore of the desire to leave them behind. For this you would be envied, derided, hated; London was considered 'fake' and the people there duplicitous. Considering this, she'd realised that every day for most of her life she had been physically and emotionally afraid. Even now she couldn't soften unless she was in bed with Majid, fearing that if she wasn't vigilant, she would be sent back home on the train.

She turned a few pages of the book, took his arm and snuggled into him. They were together, and loved one another. But there were unaccustomed fears. As Majid reminded her when they argued, he had relinquished his home, wife and children for her. That morning, when he had gone to see the children and to talk about their schooling, she'd become distraught waiting for him, convinced he was sleeping with his wife and would return to her. It was deranging, wanting someone so much. How could you ever get enough of them? Maybe it was easier not to want at all. When one of the kids was unwell, he had stayed the night at his former house. He wanted to be a good father, he explained, adding in a brusque tone that she'd had no experience of that.

She had gone out in her white dress and not come home. She had enjoyed going to clubs and parties, staying out all night and sleeping anywhere. She had scores of acquaintances who it was awkward introducing to Majid, as he had little to say to them. 'Young people aren't interesting in themselves any more,' he said, sententiously.

He maintained that it was she who was drawing away from them. It was true that these friends – who she had seen as free spirits, and who now lay in their squats virtually inert with drugs – lacked imagination, resolution and ardour, and that she found it difficult to tell them of her life, fearing they would resent her. But Majid, once the editor of radical newspapers, could be snobbish. On this occasion he accused her of treating him like a parent or flatmate, and of not understanding she was the first woman he couldn't sleep without. Yet hadn't she waited two years while he was sleeping with someone else? If she recalled the time he went on holiday with his family, informing her the day before, even as he asked her to marry him, she could beat her head against the wall. His young children were beautiful, but in the park people assumed they were hers. They looked like the mother, and con-nected him with her for ever. Nicole had said she didn't want them coming to the house. She had wanted to punish him, and destroy everything.

Should she leave him? Falling in love was simple; one had only to yield. Digesting another person, however, and sustaining a love, was bloody work, and not a soft job. Feeling and fear rushed through her constantly. If only her mother were sensible and accessible. As for the woman she usually discussed such subjects with – the mother of her best friend – Nicole was too embarrassed to return.

She noticed that the train was slowing down.

'Is this it?' he said.

''Fraid so.'

'Can't we go on to the seaside?'

She replaced her book and put her gloves on.

'Majid, another day.'

'Yes, yes, there's time for everything.'

He took her arm.

They left the station and joined a suburban area of underpasses, glass office blocks, hurrying crowds, stationary derelicts and stoned young people in flimsy clothing. 'Bad America,' Majid called it.

They queued twenty minutes for a bus. She wouldn't let him hail a taxi. For some reason she thought it would be condescending. Anyhow, she didn't want to get there too soon.

They sat in the front, at the top of the wide double-decker, as it took them away from the centre. They swept through winding lanes and passed fields. He was surprised the slow, heavy bus ascended the hills at all. This was not the city and not the country; it was not anything but grassy areas, arcades of necessary shops, churches and suburban houses. She pointed out the school she'd attended, shops she'd worked in for a pittance, parks in which she'd waited for various boyfriends.

It was a fearful place for him too. His father had been an Indian politician and when his parents separated he had been brought up by his mother eight miles away. They liked to talk about the fact that he was at university when she was born; that when she was just walking he was living with his first wife; that he might have patted Nicole's head as he passed her on the street. They shared the fantasy that for years he had been waiting for her to grow up.

It was cold when they got down. The wind cut across the open spaces. Already it seemed to be getting dark. They walked further than he'd imagined they would have to, and across muddy patches. He complained that she should have told him to wear different shoes.

He suggested they take something for her mother. He could be very polite. He even said 'excuse me' in bed if he made an abrupt movement. They went into a brightly lit supermarket and asked for flowers; there were none. He asked for lapsang souchong teabags, but before the assistant could reply, Nicole pulled him out.

The area was sombre but not grim, though a swastika had been painted on a fence. Her mother's house was set on a grassy bank, in a sixties estate, with a view of a park. As they approached, Nicole's feet seemed to drag. Finally she halted and opened her coat.

'Put your arms around me.' He felt her shivering. She said, 'I can't go in unless you say you love me.'

'I love you,' he said, holding her. 'Marry me.'

She was kissing his forehead, eyes, mouth. 'No one has ever cared for me like you.'

He repeated, 'Marry me. Say you will, say it.'

'Oh I don't know,' she replied.

She crossed the garden and tapped on the window. Immediately her mother came to the door. The hall was narrow. The mother kissed her daughter, and then Majid, on the cheek.

'I'm pleased to see you,' she said, shyly. She didn't appear to have been drinking. She looked Majid over and said, 'Do you want a tour?' She seemed to expect it.

'That would be lovely,' he said.

Downstairs the rooms were square, painted white but otherwise bare. The ceilings were low, the carpet thick and green. A brown three-piece suite – each item seemed to resemble a boat – was set in front of the television.

Nicole was eager to take Majid upstairs. She led him through the rooms which had been the setting for the stories she'd told. He tried to imagine the scenes. But the bedrooms that had once been inhabited by lodgers – van drivers, removal men, postmen, labourers – were empty. The wallpaper was gouged and discoloured, the curtains hadn't been washed for a decade, nor the windows cleaned; rotten mattresses were parked against the walls. In the hall the floorboards were bare, with nails sticking out of them. What to her reverberated with remembered life was squalor to him.

As her mother poured juice for them, her hands shook, and it splashed on the table.

'It's very quiet,' he said, to the mother. 'What do you do with yourself all day?'

She looked perplexed but thought for a few moments.

'I don't really know,' she said. 'What does anyone do? I used to cook for the men but running around after them got me down.'

Nicole got up and went out of the room. There was a silence. Her mother was watching him. He noticed that there appeared to be purplish bruises under her skin.

She said, 'Do you care about her?'

He liked the question.

'Very much,' he said. 'Do you?'

She looked down. She said, 'Will you look after her?'

'Yes. I promise.'

She nodded. 'That's all I wanted to know. I'll make your dinner.'

While she cooked, Nicole and Majid waited in the lounge. He said that, like him, she seemed only to sit on the edge of the furniture. She sat back self-consciously. He started to pace about, full of things to say.

Her mother was intelligent and dignified, he said, which must have been where Nicole inherited her grace. But the place, though it wasn't sordid, was desolate.

'Sordid? Desolate? Not so loud! What are you talking about?'

'You said your mother was selfish. That she always put herself, and her men friends in particular, before her children.'

'I did say –'

'Well, I had been expecting a woman who cosseted herself. But I've never been in a colder house.' He indicated the room. 'No mementoes, no family photographs, not one picture. Everything personal has been erased. There is nothing she has made, or chosen to reflect –'

'You only do what interests you,' Nicole said. 'You work, sit on boards, eat, travel and talk. "Only do what gives you pleasure," you say to me constantly.'

'I'm a sixties kid,' he said. 'It was a romantic age.'

'Majid, the majority can't live such luxurious lives. They never did. Your sixties is a great big myth.'

'It isn't the lack of opulence which disturbs me, but the poverty of imagination. It makes me think of what culture means –'

'It means showing off and snobbery –'

'Not that aspect of it. Or the decorative. But as indispensable human expression, as a way of saying, "Here there is pleasure, desire, life! This is what people have made!"'

He had said before that literature, indeed, all culture, was a celebration of life, if not a declaration of love for things.

'Being here,' he continued, 'it isn't people's greed and selfishness that surprises me. But how little people ask of life. What meagre demands they make, and the trouble they go to, to curb their hunger for experience.'

'It might surprise you,' she said, 'because you know successful egotistical people who do what they love. But most people don't do much of anything most of the time. They only want to get by another day.'

'Is that so?' He thought about this and said that every day he awoke ebulliently and full of schemes. There was a lot he wanted, of the world and of other people. He added, 'And of you.'

But he understood sterility because despite all the 'culture' he and his second wife had shared, his six years with her had been arid. Now he had this love, and he knew it was love because of the bleakness that preceded it, which had enabled him to see what was possible.

She kissed him. 'Precious, precious,' she said.

She pointed to the bolted door she had mentioned to him. She wanted to go downstairs. But her mother was calling them.

They sat down in the kitchen, where two places had been laid. Nicole and her mother saw him looking at the food.

'Seems a bit funny giving Indian food to an Indian,' the mother said. 'I didn't know what you eat.'

'That's all right,' he said.

She added, 'I thought you'd be more Indian, like.'

He waggled his head. 'I'll try to be.' There was a silence. He said to her, 'It was my birthday yesterday.'

'Really?' said the mother.

She and her daughter looked at one another and laughed.

While he and Nicole ate, the mother, who was very thin, sat and smoked. Sometimes she seemed to be watching them and other times fell into a kind of reverie. She was even-tempered and seemed prepared to sit there all day. He found himself seeking the fury in her, but she looked more resigned than anything, reminding him of himself in certain moods: without hope or desire, all curiosity suppressed in the gloom and agitated muddle of her mind.

After a time she said to Nicole, 'What are you doing with yourself? How's work?'

'Work? I've given up the job. Didn't I tell you?'

'At the television programme?'

'Yes.'

'What for? It was a lovely job!'

Nicole said, 'It wore me out for nothing. I'm getting the strength to do what I want, not what I think I ought to do.'

'What's that supposed to mean?' her mother said. 'You stay in bed all day?'

'We only do that sometimes,' Majid murmured.

Her mother said, 'I can't believe you gave up such a job! I can't even get work in a shop. They said I wasn't experienced enough. I said, what experience do you need to sell bread rolls?'

In a low voice Nicole talked of what she'd been promising herself – to draw, dance, study philosophy, get healthy. She would follow what interested her. Then she caught his eye, having been reminded of one of the strange theories that puzzled and alarmed her. He maintained that it wasn't teaching she craved, but a teacher, someone to help and guide her; perhaps a kind of husband. She found herself smiling at how he brought everything back to them.

'Must be lovely,' her mother said. 'Just doing what you want.'

'I'll be all right,' Nicole said.

After lunch, in the lounge, Nicole pulled the brass bolt and he accompanied her down a dark flight of stairs. This was the basement where she and her brother and sister used to sleep, Nicole wearing a knitted hat and scarf, as her mother would heat only the front room. The damp room opened on to a small garden where the children had to urinate if the bolt was across. Beyond there were fields.

Late at night they would listen to the yells and crashes upstairs. If one of her mother's boyfriends – whichever man it was who had taken her father's place – had neglected to bolt the door, Nicole would put on her overcoat and wellington boots, and creep upstairs. The boots were required because of overturned ashtrays and broken glass. She would ensure her mother hadn't been cut or beaten, and try to persuade everyone to go to bed. One morning there had been indentations in the wall, along with the remains of hair and blood, where her mother's head had been banged against it. A few times the police came.

Majid watched as Nicole went through files containing old school books, magazines, photographs. She opened several sacks and hunted through them for some clothes she wanted to take back to London. This would take some time. He decided to go upstairs and wait for her. As he went, he passed the mother.

He walked about, wondering where in the house, when Nicole was ten, her father had hanged himself. He hadn't been able to ask. He thought of what it would be like to be living an ordinary life, and the next day your husband is self-murdered, leaving you with three children.

On returning he paused at the top of the stairs. They were talking; no – arguing. The mother's voice, soft and contained earlier, had gained a furious edge. The house seemed transparent. He could hear them, just as her mother must have heard him.

'If he's asked you,' she was saying. 'And if he means it, you should say yes. And if you're jealous of his bloody kids, have some with him. That'll keep him to you. He's well off and brainy, he can have anyone. D'you know what he sees in you, apart from sex?'

'He says he loves me.'

'You're not having me on? Does he support you?'

'Yes.'

'Really?'

'Yes.'

Quietly Majid sat down on the top step. Nicole was struggling to maintain the dignity and sense she'd determined on that morning.

The mother said, 'If you stop working you might end up with nothing. Like I did. Better make sure he don't run off with someone younger and prettier.'

'Why should he do that?' Nicole said sullenly.

'He's done it already.'

'When?'

'Idiot, with you.'

'Yes, yes, he has.'

'Men are terrible beasts.'

'Yes, yes.'

Her mother said, 'If it's getting you down, you can always stay here . . . for a while.' She hesitated. 'It won't be like before. I won't bother you.'

'I might do that. Can I?'

'You'll always be my baby.'

Nicole must have been pulling boxes around; her breathing became heavier.

'Nicole don't make a mess in my house. It'll be me who'll have to clear everything up. What are you looking for?'

'I had a picture of Father.'

'I didn't know you had one.'

'Yes.' Shortly after, Nicole said, 'Here it is.'

He imagined them standing together, examining it.

'Before he did it,' said the mother, 'he said he'd show us, teach us a lesson. And he did.'

She sounded as if she were proud of her husband.

Upstairs Nicole packed her clothes in a bag, then went back to find something in a cupboard; after this, there were other things she wanted.

'I must do this,' she said, hurrying around.

He realised that she might want to stay, that she might make him go back alone. He put on his coat. In the hall he waited restlessly.

The mother said to him, 'You're in a hurry.'

'Yes.'

'Is there something you have to get home for?'

He nodded. 'Lots of things.'

'You don't like it here, I can tell.'

He said nothing.

To his relief he saw Nicole emerge and put her scarf on. They kissed her mother and walked quickly back where they'd come. The bus arrived; and then they waited for the train, stamping their feet. As it pulled away, she took out her book. He looked at her; there were some things he wanted to ask, but she had put herself beyond his reach.

Near their house they stopped off to buy newspapers and magazines. Then they bought bread, pasta, hummus, yogurt, wine, water, juice, florentines. They unpacked it on the kitchen table, on which were piled books and CDs, invitations and birthday cards, with his children's toys scattered underneath. It was only then they realised she'd left the bag of clothes somewhere, probably on the train. Tears came to her eyes before she realised the clothes didn't matter; she didn't even want them, and he said she could buy more.

He sat at the table with the papers and asked her what music she was in the mood for, or if she didn't care. She shook her head and went to shower. Then she walked about naked, before spreading a towel on the floor and sitting on it to massage cream into her legs, sighing and humming as she did so. He started to prepare their supper, all the while watching her, which was one of his preferred occupations. Soon they would eat. After, they would take tea and wine to bed; lying there for hours, they would go over everything, knowing they would wake up with one another.

Sucking Stones

Something to look forward to, that was what she wanted, however meagre. Every evening, when Marcia drove back from school through the suburban traffic, angry and listless, with a talking book on the cassette player and her son sitting in the back, she hoped she might have received a letter from a publisher or literary agent. Or there might be one from a theatre, if she had been attempting a play. She did, sometimes – quite often – receive 'encouragement'. It cost nothing to give, but she cherished it.

As she opened the door, and her son Alec ran into the house to put the TV on, she found on the mat, handwritten in black ink on impressively formal grey card, a note from the famous writer Aurelia Broughton. Marcia read it twice.

'This is exciting,' she said to Alec. 'You can look at it but don't touch it.' He was a pupil at the school where she taught seven-year-olds. She read it again. 'Those swine in the writers' group will be very interested. We'd better get going.'

Three years ago Marcia had had a story published in a small magazine of new writing. Last year an hour-long play of hers had been given a rehearsed performance in a local arts centre. It had been directed by an earnest, forceful young man who worked in advertising but loved the theatre.

Marcia had been dismayed by how little the actors resembled the people they were based on. One of the men even had a moustache. How carelessly the actors carried the play in a direction she hadn't considered! After, there had been a debate in the bar.

Several members of the writers' group had come to support her. The young histrionic faces, handwaving, and passionate interruptions began to exhilarate her. It was her work they were arguing about!

The director took her to one side and said, 'You must send this play to the National Theatre! They need new writers.'

He had forgotten that Marcia would be forty this year.

A couple of months later, when the play was returned, she didn't open the envelope. She couldn't see how to go on. She did sometimes feel like this, although it was more ominous now. She had been writing for ten years and had never given up hope. Her need for publication, and the pride it would bring, had grown more acute.

Recently she'd been writing in bed, sometimes for fifteen minutes. At other times she lasted only five. In the morning – oh, the wasted will and lost clarity of words in the morning! – she wrote standing up in her overcoat at the dining-room table, her school bag packed, as her son waited at the front door, juggling with tennis balls. This was the most she could do. At other times she wanted, badly, to harm herself. But self-mutilation was an inaccurate language. Scars couldn't speak.

Marcia dropped the card in her bag along with her pens and the formidable sketchbook in which she made notes. She called them the 'tools of her love'.

While Alec ate his tea, she phoned Sandor, her 'boyfriend' – though she had vowed not to speak to him – and told him about the postcard. He paid little attention to her enthusiasm; it wasn't something he understood. But she couldn't be discouraged.

They drove to her mother's, ten minutes away. It was the plain, semi-detached house in which Marcia had grown up, where her mother lived alone.

She let Alec out and handed him his overnight bag.

'Run to the door and ring the bell. I haven't got time to stop.'

Marcia drove to the end of the quiet road in which she had ridden her bicycle as a child. She turned the car round and passed the house, hooting and accelerating as her mother hurried to the front gate in her flapping slippers, raising her hand as if to stop the car, with Alec standing behind her.

The members of the writers' group were making tea and arranging their seats in the cold local hall where they met once a week. On other nights Scouts, Air Cadets and Trotskyists used it. Marcia had started the group by advertising in a local paper. Originally it was to be a reading circle; she thought more people would come. At the last minute she changed the 'reading' to 'writing'. Two dozen poems, screenplays and a complete novel dropped through her letter box. It was not only she who wanted to put her side of things.

Twelve of them sat on hard chairs in a circle, and read to one another. During the past two years they had declaimed terrible confessions that elicited only silence and tears; dreams and fantasies; episodes of soap operas and, occasionally, there was some writing of fire and imagination, usually produced by Marcia.

The group was to have no official leader, though Marcia often found herself in that position. She enjoyed the admiration and even the spite and envy, which she considered 'literary'. She always kept at least one author's biography beside her bed, and was aware that writing was a contact sport. Marcia also liked to talk about writing and how creativity developed, as if it was a mystery that she would grasp one day. She knew that considering the relation between language and feeling, hearing the names of writers, and speaking of their affairs and rotten personal lives, was what she wanted to do.

She also felt it was an indulgence. Life wasn't about doing what you wanted all day. But didn't Aurelia Broughton do that?

The nurses, accountants, bookshop assistants and clerks who comprised the writers group – all, somehow, thwarted – were doing their best work. Every one of them had the belief, conviction, hope, that they could interest and engage someone else. They wrote when they could, during their lunch break, or in the spent hours late at night. Yet their spavined stories stumbled into an abyss, never leaping the electric distance between people. These 'writers' made crass mistakes and were astonished and sour when others in the group pointed them out. She didn't believe she was such a fool; she couldn't believe it. None of them did.

'I grunt, I grunt. I grunt.'

Marcia put on her glasses and regarded the young man who had stood up to read, a waiter in the pizza restaurant in the High Street. He had come to the house and played with Alec. He was pretty, if not a little fey. He had a crush on Marcia. For a while, after reading some George Sand, she considered giving him a try. Before, he had cried if asked to read aloud. Marcia regretted persuading him to 'share' his work with them. You couldn't tell how someone's prose would sound by the look of them. This boy had been writing a long piece about a waiter in a pizza parlour attempting to give birth to a tapeworm growing inside his body. As the thick grey worm made its interminable muddy progress into the light, via the waiter's rectum – and God had made the world more quickly – Marcia lowered her head and re-read Aurelia Broughton's card.

At school two weeks ago, Marcia had seen in the newspaper that Aurelia Broughton was reading from her latest novel. It was that night. Spontaneously, but aware that she was ravenous for influence, she dropped Alec at her mother's and drove to London. She parked on a yellow line, and obtained the last ticket. The room was full. People who had just left their offices were standing on the stairs. Students sat cross-legged on the floor. There was some random clapping and then a hush when Aurelia went to the lectern. At first she was nervous, but when she realised the audience was supporting her, she seemed to enter a trance; words poured from her.

After, there were many respectful questions from people who knew her work. Marcia wondered why they had come. What had made her come? Not only a longing for poetry and something sustaining. Perhaps, Marcia thought, she could locate the talent in Aurelia by looking at her. Was it in her eyes, hands or general bearing? Was talent intelligence, passion or a gift? Could it be developed? Looking at Aurelia had made Marcia consider the puzzle of why some people could do certain things and not others.

Aurelia had made an interesting remark. Marcia had sometimes thought of her own ability, such as it was, on the model of an old torch battery, as a force with a flickering intensity, which might run down altogether.

However, Aurelia had said, with grandiose finality, 'Creativity is like sexual desire. It renews itself day by day.' She went on, 'I never stop having ideas. They stream from me. I can write for hours. Next morning I can't wait to start again.'

Someone in the audience commented, 'It's something of an obsession, then.'

'No, not an obsession. It is love,' said Aurelia.

The audience wanted a life transformed by art.

Marcia joined a queue to have Aurelia sign the costly hardback. The writer was surrounded by publicists and the shop staff, who opened and passed the books to her. Wearing jewellery, expensive clothes, and an extravagant silk scarf, Aurelia smiled and asked Marcia her name, putting an 'e' at the end instead of an 'a'.

Marcia leaned across the table. 'I'm a writer, too.'

'The more of us the better,' Aurelia replied. 'Good luck.'

'I've written –'

Marcia tried to talk with Aurelia, but there were people behind, pushing forward with pens, questions, pieces of paper. An assistant manoeuvred her out of the way.

The next day, via Aurelia's publisher, Marcia sent her the first chapter of her novel. She enclosed a letter telling of her struggle to understand certain things. Over the years she had tried to contact writers. Many had not replied; others said they were too busy to see her. Now Aurelia had written to invite her for tea. Aurelia would be the first proper writer she had met. She was a woman Marcia would be able to have vital and straightforward conversations with.

Today Marcia shook her head when asked if she had anything to read to the group. After, she didn't go for a drink with the others but left immediately.

As she was getting into her car, the boy who'd written the tapeworm story ran up behind her.

'Marcia, you said nothing. Are you enjoying the piece? Don't be afraid of being ruthless.'

He was moving backwards even as he waited for her reply. She had been accused before, in the group, of being dismissive, contemptuous even. It was true that on a couple of occasions she had had to slip outside, she was laughing so much.

He said, 'You seemed lost in thought.'

'The school,' she said. 'I'll never get away.'

'Sorry. I thought it might have been the worm.'

'Worm?'

'The story I read.'

She said, 'I didn't miss a grunt. It's coming out, isn't it, the piece. Coming out . . . well.' She patted him on the shoulder and got into the car. 'See you next week, probably.'

Her living-room floor was covered in toys. She remembered a friend saying how children forced you to live in squalor. In the corner of the room, the damp wall had started to crumble, leaving a layer of white powder on the carpet. The bookshelves, hammered carelessly into the alcoves by her incompetent husband, sagged in the middle and were pulling out of the bricks.

She wrote and told Aurelia that she was looking forward to seeing her at the appointed time.

With Aurelia's card propped up against Aurelia's novels and stories, Marcia started to write. She would visit Aurelia and take with her a good deal more of the novel. Aurelia was well connected; she could help her get it published.

Next morning Marcia rose at five and wrote in the cold house until seven. That night, when Alec went to bed, she put in another hour. Normally, whenever she had a good idea she would think of a good reason why it wasn't a good idea. Her father's enthusiasm and her mother's helplessness had created a push-me-pull-you creature that succeeded only at remaining in the same place. She bullied herself – why can't you do this, why isn't it better? – until her living part became a crouching, cowed child.

The urgency of preparing something for Aurelia abolished

Marcia's doubts. This was how she liked to work; there was only pen, paper, and something urgent proceeding between them.

During the day, even as she yelled at the children or listened to the parents' complaints, Marcia thought often of Aurelia, sometimes with annoyance. Aurelia had asked her to come to her house at four-thirty, a time when Marcia was still at school. As Aurelia lived in West London, a two-hour drive away, Marcia would have to make an excuse and take the day off in order to prepare to see her. These were the kinds of things famous writers never had to think about.

They were standing, a few days later, in the cramped kitchen looking out over the garden in which she, her father and younger brother had played tennis over a tiny net, when Marcia decided to tell her mother the good news.

'Aurelia Broughton wrote to me. You know, the writer. You've heard of her, haven't you?'

'I have heard of her,' her mother said.

Mother was small but wide. She wore two knitted jumpers and a heavy cardigan, which made her look even bigger.

Mother said, 'I've heard of lots of writers. What does she want from you?'

Alec went into the garden and kicked a ball. Marcia wished her father were alive to do this with him. They all missed having a man around.

'Aurelia liked my work.' Marcia felt she had the right to call the writer Aurelia; they would become friends. 'She wants to talk about it. It's great, isn't it? She's interested in what I'm doing.'

Her mother said, 'You'd better lend me one of her books so I can keep up.'

'I'm re-reading them myself at the moment.'

'Not during the day. You're at school.'

'I read at school.'

'You never let me join in. I'm pushed to one side. These are the last years of my life –'

292

Marcia interrupted her. 'I'll be needing to write a bit in the next couple of weeks.'

This meant her mother would have to keep Alec in the evenings, and for some of the weekend. His father took him on Saturday afternoons, and returned him on Sunday.

Marcia said, 'Could he spend Sunday with you?' Her mother assumed her 'put-upon' face. 'Please.'

Mother formed the same expressions today as she had in the past when caring for two children and a husband, and had made it obvious by her suffering that she found her family overwhelming and pleasureless. Depressives certainly had strong wills, killing off sentient life for miles around them.

'I had a little date, but I'll cancel it,' said Mother.

'If it's not too much trouble.'

Since Marcia's father had died six years ago, Mother had started going to museums and galleries. In the evenings, after a smoked salmon and cream cheese supper, she went often to the theatre and cinema. For the first time since she was young, she had friends with whom she attended lectures and concerts, sailing home in a taxi, spending the money Father had received on retirement. She had even taken up smoking. Mother had grasped that it was a little late for hopelessness.

Marcia didn't want to wait thirty years.

She had, recently, gained a terrible awareness of life. It might have started when she began meeting men through the dating agency, which had made her feel – well, morbid. Until recently, she had lived as if one day there would be a salve for her wounds; that someone, a parent, lover, benefactor, would pluck her from chaos.

Marcia didn't become a teacher until she was almost thirty. She and her husband had started wanting to smash at one another's faces. She had, literally, kicked him out of bed; he ran into the street wearing pyjamas and slippers. Without him, she had a child, a mortgage and only a nugatory income, working in a bar and writing in the mornings. The first day at teacher training college had been awful. She had believed she would wear scarves like Aurelia Broughton and write with a gold fountain pen.

Marcia collected stories of struggling women who eventually became recognised as artists. She believed in persistence and dedication. If she wasn't a writer, how would she live with herself and what value would she have? When she was a proper writer, her soul would not be hidden; people would know her as she was. To be an artist, to live a singular, self-determined life, and follow the imagination where it led, was to live for oneself, and to be useful. Creativity, the merging of reason and imagination, was life's ultimate fulfilment.

If she passed a bookshop and saw dozens of luridly coloured blockbusters, she knew these bad and, often, young writers were making money. It seemed tragic and unfair that, unlike them, she couldn't go to a shop and buy the furniture, clothes and music she wanted.

'You hate me interfering,' Mother said, 'but you wouldn't want to have got to the end of your life and realised you'd wasted your time.'

'Like Father?'

'Filling bits of paper with a lot of scribbling the whole evening.'

'How can expressing yourself be a waste of time?'

From the age of eight, after seeing Margot Fonteyn dance, Marcia had wanted to be a dancer; or at least her mother had wanted that for her. Marcia had attended an expensive ballet boarding school while Mother, who had never worked, packed boxes in a local factory to pay for it. Marcia left school at sixteen to get work as a dancer, but apart from not being as good as the others, and lacking the necessary vanity and ambition, she was terrified of appearing on stage. Now Mother kept three pairs of Marcia's ballet shoes on the mantelpiece, to remind Marcia of how she had wasted her mother's efforts.

'Alec is always round here,' said Mother. 'Not that I don't need the company. But it would be good if that writer woman could offer you some guidance about your . . . work. I expect she knows people employed on the journals.'

'Are you talking about the newspapers again?'

Mother often suggested that Marcia become a journalist, writing for the *Guardian* Women's Page about stress at work, or child abuse.

Marcia went into the front room. Mother followed her, saying, 'You'd make money. You could stay at home and write novels at the same time. It wouldn't be so bad if you were doing something that brought something in.'

Marcia had secretly written articles which she had sent to the *Guardian*, the *Mail, Cosmopolitan* and other women's magazines. They had been returned. She was an artist, not a journalist. If only mother would understand that they were different.

Marcia paced the room. The wallpaper was vividly striped, and there was only one overhead light. Her brother used to say it was like living inside a Bridget Riley painting. The fat armchair with a pouffe in front of it, on which Mother kept her TV magazines and chocolates, sat there like Mother herself, heavy and immovable. Marcia didn't want to sit down, but couldn't just leave while there were favours she required.

Marcia said, 'All I want is for you to help me make a little time for myself.'

'What about me?' said Mother. 'I haven't even had a cup of tea today. Don't I need time now?'

'You?' said Marcia. 'You pity yourself, but I envy you.' Her mother's face started to redden. Marcia felt empty but words streamed from her. 'Yes! I wish I'd sat at home for twenty years supported by a good man, being a "housewife". Think what I'd have written. Washing in the morning, real work in the afternoon, before picking up the kids from school. I wouldn't have wasted a moment . . . not a moment, of all that beautiful free time!'

Mother sank into her chair and put her hand over her face.

'Better find a man then, if you can,' she said.

'What does that mean?' said Marcia, hotly.

'Someone who wants to keep you. What's that one's name?'

Marcia murmured, 'Sandor. He's not my boyfriend. He's only a man I'm vaguely interested in.'

'I wouldn't be interested in any man,' said mother. 'Those dirty creatures aren't really interested in you. What does he do?'

'You know what he does.'

'Can't you do better for yourself?'

'No, I can't,' said Marcia. 'I can't.'

Her mother loved living alone, and boasted of it constantly. When Marcia was a child six people had lived in the house, and apart from Mother they had all died or left. Mother claimed that alone she could do whatever she wanted, and at whatever time, apart from the small matter of giving and receiving emotional and physical affection, as Marcia liked to point out.

'Who wants a lot of men pawing at you?' was Mother's reply.

'Who doesn't?' Marcia said.

Marcia recalled Father as he sat on the sofa with his pad and pen. He would casually ask Mother to make him a cup of tea. Mother, whatever else she was doing, was expected to fetch it, place it before him, and wait to see if it was to his liking. It was assumed that she was at Father's command. No wonder she had taken loneliness as a philosophy. Marcia would discuss it with Aurelia.

They were three generations of women, living close to one another. Marcia's grandmother, aged ninety-four, also lived alone, in a one-bedroom flat five minutes' walk away. She was lucid and easily amused; her mind worked, but she was bent double with arthritis and prayed for the good Lord to take her. Her husband had died twenty years ago and she had hardly been out since. To Marcia she was like an animal in a cage, starved of the good things. Where were the men? Marcia's grandfather and father had died; her brother, the doctor, had gone to America; her husband had decamped with a neighbour.

Marcia went into the bathroom, took a Valium, kissed Alec, and went to her car.

*

That night, alone at home, writing and drinking – as desolate and proud as Martha Gellhorn in the desert, she liked to think – she rang Sandor and told him of her mother's indifference and scorn, and the concentrated work she was doing.

'The novel is really moving forward!' she said. 'I've never read anything like it. It's so truthful. I can't believe no one will be interested!'

She talked until she felt she were speaking into infinity. Even her therapist, when Marcia could afford to see her, said more.

She had met Sandor in a pub, after the man she was with, picked from a black folder in the dating agency office, had made an excuse and left. What was wrong with her? The man only came up to her chest! One woman in the writing group went out with a different man every week. It was odd, she said, how many of them were married. Sandor wasn't.

After her monologue, she asked Sandor what he was doing.

'The same,' he said, and laughed.

'I'll come and see you,' she said.

'Why not? I'm always here,' he replied.

'Yes, you are,' she said.

He laughed again.

She saw him, a fifty-year-old Bulgarian, about once a month. He was a porter in a smart block of flats in Chelsea, and lived in a room in Earl's Court. He considered the job, which he had obtained after drifting around Europe for fifteen years, to be ideal. In his black suit at the desk in the entrance, he buzzed people in, took parcels and accepted flowers, went on errands for the tenants, and re-read his favourite writers, Pascal, Nietzsche, Hegel.

None of the men she had met through the agency had been interested in literature, and not one had been attractive. Sandor had the face of an uncertain priest and the body of the Olympic cyclist that he had been. He was intelligent, well mannered and seductive in several languages. He could, when he was 'on', as he put it, beguile women effortlessly. He had slept with more than a thousand women and had never sustained a relationship with any of them. What sort of man had no ex-wife, no children, no family nearby, no lawyers, no debt, no house? She marvelled at her ability to locate melancholy in people. She would have to unfreeze Sandor's dead soul with the blow-torch of her love. Did she have sufficient blow? If only she could find something better to do.

'See you, Sandor,' she said.

She swigged wine from the bottle she kept beside her bed. She managed to fall asleep but awoke soon after, burning with uncontrollable furies against her husband, Mother, Sandor, Aurelia. She understood those paintings full of devils and writhing, contorted demons. They did exist, in the mind. Why was there no sweetness within?

She arrived an hour early at Aurelia's house, noted where it was, parked, and walked about the neighbourhood. It was a sunny winter's day. This was a part of London she didn't know. The streets were full of antique shops, organic grocers, and cafés with young men and their babies sitting in the window. People strolled in sunglasses and dark clothes, and gathered in groups on the pavement to gossip. She recognised actors and a film director. She looked in an estate agent's window; a family house cost a million pounds.

She bought apples, vitamins and coffee. She chose a scarf in Agnès b. and paid for it by credit card, successfully averting her eyes from the price, as she had earlier avoided a clash with a mirror in the shop.

At the agreed time Marcia rang Aurelia's bell and waited. A young woman came to the door. She invited Marcia in. Aurelia was finishing her piano lesson.

In the kitchen overlooking the garden, two young women were cooking; in the dining room a long, polished table was being laid with silverware and thick napkins. In the library Marcia examined the dozens of foreign-language editions of Aurelia's novels, stories, essays – the record of a writing life.

There was a sound at the door and a man came in. Aurelia's husband introduced himself.

'Marcia.' She adopted her most middle-class voice.

'You must excuse me,' the man said. 'My office is down the road. I must go to it.'

'Are you a writer?'

'I have published a couple of books. But I have conversations for a living. I am a psychoanalyst.'

He was a froglike little man, with alert eyes. She wondered if he could see her secrets, and that she had thought he'd become an analyst so that no one had to look at him.

'What a ravishing scarf,' he said.

'Thank you.'

'Goodbye,' he said.

She waited, glancing through the chapters of the novel she had brought to show Aurelia. It seemed, in this ambience, to be execrable stuff.

She caught sight of Aurelia in the hall.

'I'll be with you in one minute,' said Aurelia.

Aurelia shut the door on the piano teacher, opened it to the man delivering flowers, talked to someone in Italian on the telephone, inspected the dining room, spoke to the cook, told her assistant she wouldn't be taking any calls, and sat down opposite Marcia.

She poured tea and regarded Marcia for what seemed a long time.

'I quite enjoyed what you sent me,' Aurelia said. 'That school. It was a window on a world one doesn't know about.'

'I've written more,' Marcia said. 'Here.'

She placed the three chapters on the table. Aurelia picked them up and put them down.

'I wish I could write like you,' she sighed.

'Sorry?' said Marcia. 'Please, do you mean that?'

'My books insist on being long. But one couldn't write an extended piece in that style.'

'Why not?' said Marcia. Aurelia looked at her as if she should know without being told. Marcia said, 'The thing is, I don't get time for . . . extension.' She was beginning to panic. 'How do you get down to it?'

'You met Marty,' she said. 'We have breakfast early. He goes to his office. He starts at seven. Then I just do it. I haven't got any choice, really. Sometimes I write here, or I go to our house in Ferrara. For writers there's rarely anything else but writing.'

'Doesn't your mind go everywhere except to the page?' said Marcia. 'Do you have some kind of iron discipline? Don't you find ludicrous excuses?'

'Writing is my drug. I go to it easily. My new novel is starting to develop. This is the best part, when you can see that something is beginning. I like to think,' Aurelia went on, 'that I can make a story out of anything. A murmur, a hint, a gesture . . . turned into another form of life. What could be more satisfying? Can I ask your age?'

'Thirty-seven.'

Aurelia said, 'You have something to look forward to.'

'What do you mean?'

'One's late thirties are a period of disillusionment. The early forties are a lovely age – of re-illusionment. Everything comes together then, you will find, and there is renewed purpose.'

Marcia looked at the poster of a film which had been made of one of Aurelia's books.

She said, 'Sometimes life is so difficult . . . it is impossible to write. You don't feel actual hopelessness?'

Aurelia shook her head and continued to look at Marcia. Her husband was an analyst; he would have taught her not to be alarmed by weeping.

'It's those blasted men that have kept us down,' Marcia said. 'When I was young, you were one of the few contemporary writers that women could read.'

'We've kept ourselves down,' said Aurelia. 'Self-contempt, masochism, laziness, stupidity. We're old enough to own up to it now, aren't we?'

'But we are – or at least were – political victims.'

'Balls.' Aurelia softened her voice and said, 'Would you tell me about your life at the school?'

'What sort of thing?'

'The routine. Your day. Pupils. The other teachers.'

'The other teachers?'

'Yes.'

Aurelia was waiting.

'But they're myopic,' Marcia said.

'In what way?'

'Badly educated. Interested only in soap operas.'

Aurelia nodded.

Marcia mentioned her mother but Aurelia became impatient. However, when Marcia recounted the occasion when she had suggested the school donate the remains of the Harvest Festival to the elders of the Asian community centre, and a couple of the teachers had refused to give fruit to 'Pakis', Aurelia made a note with her gold pen. Marcia had, in fact, told the headmaster about this, but he dismissed it, saying, 'I have to run all of this school.'

Marcia looked at Aurelia as if to say, 'Why do you want to know this?'

'That was helpful,' Aurelia said. 'I want to write something about a woman who works in a school. Do you know many teachers?'

Marcia's colleagues were teachers but none of her friends were. One friend worked in a building society, another had just had a baby and was at home.

'There must be people at your school I could talk to. What about the headmaster?'

Marcia made a face. Then she remembered something she had read in a newspaper profile of Aurelia. 'Don't you have a daughter at school?'

'It's the wrong sort of teacher there.'

'Sorry?'

'I was looking for something rougher.'

Marcia was embarrassed. She said, 'Have you taught writing courses?'

'I did, when I wanted to travel. The students are wretched, of course. Many I would recommend for psychiatric treatment. A lot of people don't want to write, they just want the kudos. They should move on to other objects.'

Aurelia got up. As she signed Marcia a copy of her latest novel, she asked for her telephone number at school. Marcia couldn't think of a reason not to give it to her.

Aurelia said, 'Thank you for coming to see me. I'll look at your chapters.' At the door she said, 'Will you come to a party I'm giving? Perhaps we will talk more. An invitation will be sent to you.'

From across the road Marcia looked at the lighted house and the activity within, until the shutters were closed.

Marcia waited beside Sandor at his porter's desk until he finished work at seven. They had a drink in the pub where they had met. Sandor went there every evening to watch the sport on cable TV. He didn't ask her why she had suddenly turned up, and didn't mention Aurelia Broughton, though Marcia had rung to say she was coming up to see her. He talked of how he loved London and how liberal it was; no one cared who or what you were. He said that if he ever had a house he would decorate it like the pub they were sitting in. He talked of what he was reading in Hegel, though in such a garbled fashion she had no idea what he was saying or why it interested him. He told her stories of the criminals he'd known and how he'd been used as a getaway driver.

He asked her if she wanted to go to bed. His request was put in the tone of voice that said it was just as fine if she preferred not to. She hesitated only because the house in which he had a room could have been a museum to the 1950s, along with the failure of the two-bar electric fire to make any impression on the block of cold that sat in the room like death. There was also the hag of a landlady who would sit at the end of his bed at midnight.

'Don't worry, I've just given her *Crime and Punishment* to read,' Sandor laughed, following Marcia into his room. Books were piled on the floor beside the bed. His washing hung over the back of a chair. All his possessions were here.

Lying down with him, she noticed his loaf of white sliced bread and carton of milk on the chest of drawers.

'Is that all your food?'

'Bread and butter fills me up. Then I read for four or five hours. Nothing bothers me.'

'It's not much of a life.'

'What?'

'You're not in prison.'

He looked at her in surprise, as if it had never occurred to him that he wasn't in prison, and didn't have to make the best of nothing.

He kissed her and she thought of inviting him to her house at the weekend. He was kind. He would entertain Alec. But she might start to rely on him; she would always be asking for more. If anyone requested him to yield, shift or alter, he left them. She might not want him, but she didn't want to be forsaken.

After, she stood up to get dressed, looking at him where he lay with his hand over his eyes. She couldn't spend the night in such a place.

That night, for the first time, she wished Alec weren't in mother's bed. Marcia slept with her face in his unwashed clothes. In the morning she didn't write. She had lost the desire, which was also her desire for life. What illusory hopes had she invested in Aurelia? Seeing her had robbed Marcia of something. She had emptied herself out, and Aurelia was full. Where would she find the resources, the meaning, to carry on?

Aurelia had asked her to bring someone to the party; another teacher, a 'pure' teacher Aurelia had said, meaning not a teacher pretending to be a writer. Maybe Marcia should have said no. But she wanted to leave the door open with Aurelia, to see what might develop. Aurelia might read the three chapters and be excited by them. Anyhow, Marcia wanted to go to the party.

'How did it go with Miss Broughton?' asked her mother the next time Marcia went round. 'We've chatted on the phone, but you haven't mentioned it.'

'It was fine, just great.'

Her mother said, 'You're sullen, like a teenager again.'

'I don't know what to say.'

Mother said, more softly, 'What came of it?'

'You should have seen the house. Five bedrooms – at least!'

'You got upstairs?'

'I had to. And three receptions!'

'Three? What do they do in all that space! What would we do with it!'

'Have races!'

'We could –'

'The flowers, Mum! The people working there! I've never known anything like it.'

'I bet. Was it on a main road?'

'Just off. But near the shops. They've got everything to hand.'

'Buses?' enquired her mother.

'I shouldn't think she goes on a bus.'

'No,' said Mother. 'I wouldn't go on another bus again if I didn't have to. Off-street parking?'

'Yes. Room for two cars, it looked like.' Marcia said, 'We chatted in her library and got to know one another. She invited me to a party.'

'To a party? She didn't invite me?'

'She didn't mention you at all,' Marcia said. 'And nor did I.'

'I'm sure she wouldn't mind if I came with you. I'll get my glad rags on!'

'But why?' said Marcia.

'Just to go out. To meet people. I might interest them.'

Before, this would have been a kind of joke, and Mother would have returned to her moroseness. She certainly was getting healthy, if she thought she might interest people.

'I'll think about it,' Marcia said.

'I can't wait!' sang her mother. 'A party!'

Aurelia rang from her car. The connection wasn't good, but Marcia gathered that Aurelia was 'in the neighbourhood' and wanted to 'pass by for a cup of tea'.

Marcia and Alec were having fish fingers and baked beans. Aurelia must have been close; Marcia had hardly cleared the table, and Alec hadn't finished throwing his toys behind the sofa, when Aurelia's car drew up outside.

At the door she handed Marcia another signed copy of her new novel, came in, and sat down on the edge of the sofa.

'What a beautiful boy,' she said of Alec. 'Fine hair – almost white.'

'And how are you?' said Marcia.

'Tired. I've been doing readings and giving interviews, not only here but in Berlin and Barcelona. The French are making a film about me, and the Americans want me to make a film about my London . . . Sorry,' she said. 'Am I making you crazy?'

'Of course.'

Aurelia sighed. Today she looked shrewd and seemed to vibrate with intensity. She didn't want to talk, or listen, rather. When Marcia told her that her will to work had collapsed, she said, 'I wish mine had.'

She got up and glanced along the shelves of Marcia's books.

'I like her,' said Marcia, naming a woman writer, of about the same age as Aurelia.

'She can't write at all. Apparently she's a rather good amateur sculptor.'

'Is that so?' said Marcia. 'I liked her last book. Did you read the chapters I gave you?' Aurelia looked blankly at her. Marcia said, 'The chapters from my novel. I left them.'

'Where?'

'On your table.'

'No. No, I didn't.'

'Perhaps they're still there.'

Marcia guessed Aurelia wanted to see how she lived, that she wasn't looking at her but through her, to the sentences and paragraphs she would make of her. It was an admirable ruthlessness.

At the door Aurelia kissed her on both cheeks.

'See you at the party,' she said.

'I'm looking forward to it.'

'Don't forget – bring someone pedagogical.'

Marcia put Aurelia's novel on the shelf. Aurelia's books were among the rows of books; the books full of stories, the stories full of characters and craft, waiting to be enlivened by someone with a use for them. Or perhaps not.

Mother refused to have Alec to stay. It was the first time she had done this. It was the day before the party.

'But why, why?' said Marcia, on the telephone.

'I realised you weren't taking me to the party, though you didn't bother to actually tell me. I made other arrangements.'

'I was never taking you to that party.'

'You never take me anywhere.'

Marcia was shaking with exasperation. 'Mum, I want to live. And I want you to help me.'

'I've helped you all my life.'

'Sorry? You?'

'Who brought you up? You're educated, you've got –'

Marcia replaced the receiver.

She rang friends and a couple of people in the writers' group, even the boy who'd written about the tapeworm. No one was available to babysit. Half an hour before she needed to leave, the only person left to ask was her husband, who lived nearby. He was surprised and sarcastic. They rarely spoke but, when necessary, dropped notes through one another's doors.

He said he had been intending to spend the evening with his new girlfriend.

'How sweet,' said Marcia.

'What do you want me to do?' he said.

'Can't you both come over?'

'Desperate. Must be another new boyfriend. Have you got any crisps . . . and alcohol?'

'Take what you want. You always did.'

It was the first time she had let her husband into the house since he had left. If the girlfriend was there he wouldn't, at least, snoop around.

When they arrived, and the girlfriend removed her coat, Marcia noticed she was pregnant.

Marcia changed upstairs. She could hear them talking in the living room. Then she heard music.

She was at the door, ready to go. Alec was showing them his new baseball cap.

Her husband held up a record sleeve. 'You know, this is my record.'

'I'm in a rush,' she said.

In the car she thought she must have been mad, but what she was doing was in the service of life. People don't take enough risks, she thought. She didn't, though, have a teacher who might interest Aurelia. However, Aurelia wouldn't turn her away at the door. Marcia had done enough for Aurelia. Had Aurelia done enough for her?

It was Aurelia's husband who let her in and fetched her a glass of champagne, while Marcia looked around. The party was being held on the ground floor of the house, and Marcia recognised several writers. The other guests seemed to be critics, academics, psychoanalysts and publishers.

The effort of getting there had made her tense. She drank two glasses of champagne quickly and attached herself to Aurelia's husband, the only person, apart from Aurelia, she knew.

'Do you want to be introduced as a teacher, or as a writer?' he said. 'Or neither?'

'Neither, at the moment.' She took his arm. 'Because I am neither one nor the other.'

'Keeping your options open, eh?' he said.

He introduced her to several people, and they talked as a group. The main topic was the royal family, a subject she was surprised to hear intellectuals taking an interest in. It was like being at the school.

She liked Aurelia's husband, who nodded and smiled occasionally; she liked being afraid of him. He understood other people and what their wishes were. Nothing would shock him.

He was a little shocked later on, in the conservatory, when she reached up to kiss him. She was saying, 'Please, please, only this . . .' when, across the room, she saw the headmaster of her school, and his wife, talking to a female writer.

Aurelia's husband gently detached her.

'I apologise,' she said.

'Accepted. I'm flattered.'

'Hallo, Marcia,' said the headmaster. 'I hear you've been very helpful to Aurelia.'

She didn't like the headmaster seeing her drunk and embarrassed.

'Yes,' she said.

'Aurelia's going to come to the school and see what we do. She's going to talk to the older pupils.' He lowered his mouth to her ear. 'She has given me a complete set of her books. Signed.'

She wanted to say, 'They're all signed, you stupid cunt.'

She left the house and walked a little. Then she went back and traversed the party. People were leaving. Others were talking intensely. Nobody paid her any attention.

Sandor was lying on his bed with his hand over his eyes. She sat beside him.

'I've come to say I won't be coming so often now. Not that I've ever really come often, except recently. But . . . it will be even less.'

He nodded. He was watching her. Sometimes he took in what she said.

She went on, 'The reason, if you want to know the reason –'

'Why not?' he said. He sat up. 'I'd get you something . . . but, I'm so ashamed, there's nothing here.'

'There's never anything here.'

'I'll take you out for a drink.'

'I've had enough to drink.' She said, 'Sandor, this is hateful. There's a phrase that kept coming into my mind at the party. I came to tell it to you. Sucking stones. That's it. We look to the old things and to the old places, for sustenance. That's where we found it before. Even when there's nothing there we go on. But we have to find new things, otherwise we are sucking stones. To me, this' – she indicated the room – 'is arid, impoverished, dead.'

His eyes followed her gesture around the room as she condemned it.

'But I'm trying,' he said. 'Things are going to look up, I know they are.'

She kissed him. 'Bye. See you.'

She cried in the car. It wasn't his fault. She'd go back another day.

She was late home. Her husband was asleep in his girlfriend's arms, his hand on her stomach. On the floor was an empty bottle of wine and dirty plates; the TV was loud.

She carried the record from the deck, scratched it with her fingernail, and replaced it in its cover. She roused the couple, thanked them, pushed the record under her husband's arm, and got them out.

She started up the stairs but stopped halfway, took another step, and went down again. She returned to the living room and put on her overcoat. She went out onto the small concrete patio behind the house. It was dark and silent. The cold shocked her into wakefulness. She removed her coat. She wanted the cold to punish her.

Early in the morning, during the summer holidays, she sometimes danced out here, with Alec watching her, to parts of Prokofiev's *Romeo and Juliet*.

Now she put the kitchen light on and laid a square of bricks. She went back into the house and collected her files. She carried them outside and opened them. She burned her stories; she burned the play, and the first few chapters of the novel. There was a lot of it and it made a nice fire. It took a long time. She was shivering and stank of smoke and ash. She swept up. She ran a bath and lay in it until the water was tepid.

Alec had got into her bed and was asleep. She put her notebook on the bedside table. She would keep it with her, using it as a journal. But otherwise she would stop writing for a while; at least six months, to begin with. She was clear that this wasn't masochism or a suicide. Perhaps her dream of writing had been a kind of possession, or addiction. She was aware that you could get addicted to the good things, too. She was making a space. It was an important emptiness, one she would not fill with other intoxications. She might, she knew, turn into her mother, sucking stones at the TV night after night, terrified by excitement.

After a time there might be new things.

A Meeting, At Last

Morgan's lover's husband held out his hand.

'Hallo, at last,' he said. 'I enjoyed watching you standing across the road. I was delighted when, after some consideration, you made up your mind to speak with me. Will you sit down?'

'Morgan,' said Morgan.

'Eric.'

Morgan nodded, dropped his car keys on the table and sat down on the edge of a chair.

The two men looked at one another.

Eric said, 'Are you drinking?'

'In a while – maybe.'

Eric called for another bottle. There were two already on the table.

'You don't mind if I do?'

'Feel free.'

'I do now.'

Eric finished his bottle and replaced it on the table with his fingers around the neck. Morgan saw Eric's thin gold wedding ring. Caroline would always drop hers in a dish on the table in Morgan's hall, and replace it when she left.

Eric had said on the phone, 'Is that Morgan?'

'Yes,' Morgan replied. 'Who –'

The voice went on, 'Are you Caroline's boyfriend?'

'But who is this asking?' said Morgan. 'Who are you?'

'The man she lives with. Eric. Her husband. Okay?'

'Right. I see.'

'Good. You see.'

Eric had said 'please' on the phone. 'Please meet me. Please.'

'Why?' Morgan had said. 'Why should I?'

'There are some things I need to know.'

Eric named a café and the time. It was later that day. He would be there. He would wait.

Morgan rang Caroline. She was in meetings, as Eric must have known. Morgan deliberated all day but it wasn't until the last moment, pacing up and down his front room when he was already late, that he walked out of the house, got in his car and stood across the road from the café.

Although Caroline had described Eric's parents, his inarticulate furies, the way his head hung when he felt low and even, as Morgan laughed, the way he scratched his backside, Eric had been a shadow man, an unfocused dark figure that had lain across their life since they had met. And while Morgan knew things about him that he didn't need to know, he had little idea of what Eric knew of him. He had yet to find out what Caroline might have recently told him. The last few days had been the craziest of Morgan's life.

The waitress brought Eric a beer. Morgan was about to order one for himself but changed his mind and asked for water.

Eric smiled grimly.

'So,' he said. 'How are you?'

Morgan knew that Eric worked long hours. He came home late and got up after the children had gone to school. Looking at him, Morgan tried to visualise something Caroline had said. As she prepared for work in the morning, he lay in bed in his pyjamas for an hour, saying nothing, but thinking intently with his hands over his eyes, as if he were in pain, and had to work something out.

Caroline left for work as early as she could in order to phone Morgan from the office.

After a couple of months, Morgan requested her not to speak about Eric, and particularly not about their attempts at lovemaking. But as Morgan's meetings with Caroline were arranged around Eric's absences, he was, inevitably, mentioned.

Morgan said, 'What can I do for you?'

'There are things I want to know. I am entitled.'

'Are you?'

'Don't I have any rights?'

Morgan knew that seeing this man was not going to be easy. In the car he had tried to prepare, but it was like revising for an exam without having been told the subject.

'All right,' Morgan said, to calm him down. 'I understand you.'

'After all, you have taken my life.'

'Sorry?'

'I mean my wife. My wife.'

Eric swigged at his bottle. Then he took out a small pot of pills and shook it. It was empty.

'You haven't got any painkillers, have you?'

'No.'

Eric wiped his face with a napkin.

He said, 'I'm having to take these.'

He was upset, no doubt. He would be in shock. Morgan was; Caroline too, of course.

Morgan was aware that she had started with him to cheer herself up. She had two children and a good, if dull, job. Then her best friend took a lover. Caroline met Morgan through work and decided immediately that he had the right credentials. Love and romance suited her. Why hadn't she been dipped in such delight every day? She thought everything else could remain the same, apart from her 'treat'. But as Morgan liked to say, there were 'consequences'. In bed, she would call him 'Mr Consequences'.

'I'm not moving out of my house,' Eric said. 'It's my home. You're not intending to take that from me, as well as my wife?'

'Your wife . . . Caroline,' Morgan said, restoring her as her own person. 'I didn't steal her. I didn't have to persuade her. She gave herself to me.'

'She gave herself?' Eric said. 'She wanted you? You?'

'That's the truth.'

'Do women do that to you?'

Morgan tried to laugh.

'Do they?' Eric said.

'Only her – recently.'

Eric stared, waiting for him to continue. But Morgan said nothing, reminding himself that he could walk out at any time, that he didn't have to take anything from this man.

Eric said, 'Do you want her?'

'I think so, yes.'

'You're not sure? After doing all this, you're not sure?'

'I didn't say that.'

'What do you mean then?'

'Nothing.'

But perhaps he wasn't sure. He had become used to their arrangement. There were too many hurried phone calls, misunderstood letters, snatched meetings and painful partings. But they had lived within it. They even had a routine. He had received more from Eric's wife – seeing her twice a week – than he had from any other woman. Otherwise, when he wasn't working, he visited art galleries with his daughter; he packed his shoulder bag, took his guide book and walked about parts of the city he'd never seen; he sat by the river and wrote notes about the past. What had he learned through her? A reverence for the world; the ability to see feeling, certain created objects, and other people as important – indeed, invaluable. She had introduced him to the pleasures of carelessness.

Eric said, 'I met Caroline when she was twenty-one. She didn't have a line on her face. Her cheeks were rosy. She was acting in a play at university.'

'Was she a good actress? She's good at a lot of things, isn't she? She likes doing things well.'

Eric said, 'It wasn't long before we developed bad habits.'

Morgan asked, 'What sort of thing?'

'In our . . . relationship. That's the word everyone uses.' Eric said, 'We didn't have the skill, the talent, the ability to get out of them. How long have you known her?'

'Two years.'

'Two years!'

Morgan was confused. 'What did she tell you? Haven't you been discussing it?'

Eric said, 'How long do you think will it take me to digest all this?'

Morgan said, 'What are you doing?'

He had been watching Eric's hands, wondering whether he would grasp the neck of the bottle. But Eric was hunting through the briefcase he had pulled out from under the table.

'What date? Surely you remember that! Don't you two have anniversaries?' Eric dragged out a large red book. 'My journal. Perhaps I made a note that day! The past two years have to be rethought! When you are deceived, every day has another complexion!'

Morgan looked round at the other people in the café.

'I don't like being shouted at,' he said. 'I'm too tired for that.'

'No, no. Sorry.'

Eric flipped through the pages of the book. When he saw Morgan watching, he shut the journal.

Eric said in a low voice, 'Have you ever been deceived? Has that ever happened to you?'

'I would imagine so,' said Morgan.

'How pompous! And do you think that deceiving someone is all right?'

'One might say that there are circumstances which make it inevitable.'

Eric said, 'It falsifies everything.' He went on, 'Your demeanour suggests that it doesn't matter, either. Are you that cynical? This is important. Look at the century!'

'Sorry?'

'I work in television news. I know what goes on. Your cruelty is the same thing. Think of the Jews –'

'Come on –'

'That other people don't have feelings! That they don't matter! That you can trample over them!'

'I haven't killed you, Eric.'

'I could die of this. I could die.'

Morgan nodded. 'I understand that.'

He remembered one night, when she had to get home, to slip into bed with Eric, Caroline had said, 'If only Eric would die . . . just die . . .'

'Peacefully?'

'Quite peacefully.'

Eric leaned across the table. 'Have you felt rough, then?'

'Yes.'

'Over this?'

'Over this.' Morgan laughed. 'Over everything. But definitely over this.'

'Good. Good.' Eric said, 'Middle age is a lonely time.'

'Without a doubt,' said Morgan.

'That's interesting. More lonely than any other time, do you think?'

'Yes,' said Morgan. 'All you lack seems irrevocable.'

Eric said, 'Between the age of twelve and thirteen my elder brother, whom I adored, committed suicide, my father died of grief, and my grandfather just died. Do you think I still miss them?'

'How could you not?'

Eric drank his beer and thought about this.

'You're right, there's a hole in me.' He said, 'I wish there were a hole in you.'

Morgan said, 'She has listened to me. And me to her.'

Eric said, 'You really pay attention to one another, do you?'

'There's something about being attended to that makes you feel better. I'm never lonely when I'm with her.'

'Good.'

'I've been determined, this time, not to shut myself off.'

'But she's my wife.'

There was a pause.

Eric said, 'What is it people say these days? It's your problem! It's my problem! Do you believe that? What do you think?'

Morgan had been drinking a lot of whisky and smoking grass, for the first time. He had been at university in the late sixties but had identified with the puritanical left, not the hippies. These days, when he needed to switch off his brain, he noticed how tenacious consciousness was. Perhaps he wanted to shut off his mind because in the past few days he had been considering forgetting Caroline. Forgetting about them all, Caroline, Eric and their kids. Maybe he would, now. Perhaps the secrecy, and her inaccessibility, had kept them all at the right distance.

Morgan realised he had been thinking for some time. He turned to Eric again, who was tapping the bottle with his nail.

'I do like your house,' said Eric. 'But it's big, for one person.'

'My house, did you say? Have you seen it?'

'Yes.'

Morgan looked at Eric's eyes. He seemed rather spirited. Morgan almost envied him. Hatred could give you great energy.

Eric said, 'You look good in your white shorts and white socks, when you go out running. It always makes me laugh.'

'Haven't you got anything better to do than stand outside my house?'

'Haven't you got anything better to do than steal my wife?' Eric pointed his finger at him. 'One day, Morgan, perhaps you will wake up and find in the morning that things aren't the way they were last night. That everything you have has been sullied and corrupted in some way. Can you imagine that?'

'All right,' said Morgan. 'All right, all right.'

Eric had knocked his bottle over. He put his napkin on the spilled beer and popped his bottle on top of that.

He said, 'Are you intending to take my children away?'

'What? Why should I?'

'I can tell you now, I have had that house altered to my specifications, you know. I have a pergola. I'm not moving out, and I'm not selling it. Actually, to tell the truth' – Eric had a sort of half-grin, half-grimace on his face – 'I might be better off without my wife and kids.'

'What?' said Morgan. 'What did you say?'

Eric raised his eyebrows at him.

'You know what I mean,' Eric said.

Morgan's children were with their mother, the girl away at university, the boy at private school. Both of them were doing well. Morgan had met Eric's kids only briefly. He had offered to take them in if Caroline was prepared to be with him. He was ready for that, he thought. He didn't want to shirk the large tasks. But in time one of the kids could, say, become a junkie; the other a teenage prostitute. And Morgan, having fallen for their mother, might find himself burdened. He knew people it had happened to.

Eric said, 'My children are going to be pretty angry with you when they find out what you've done to us.'

'Yes,' said Morgan. 'Who could blame them?'

'They're big and expensive. They eat like horses.'

'Christ.'

Eric said, 'Do you know about my job?'

'Not as much as you know about mine, I shouldn't think.'

Eric didn't respond, but said, 'Funny to think of you two talking about me. I bet you'd lie there wishing I'd have a car crash.'

Morgan blinked.

'It's prestigious,' Eric said. 'In the newsroom, you know. Well paid. Plenty of action, continuous turnover of stories. But it's bland, worthless. I can see that now. And the people burn out. They're exhausted, and on an adrenalin rush at the same time. I've always wanted to take up walking . . . hill-walking, you know, boots and rucksacks. I want to write a novel. And travel, and have adventures. This could be an opportunity.'

Morgan wondered at this. Caroline had said that Eric took little interest in the outside world, except through the medium of journalism. The way things looked, smelled, tasted, held no fascination for him; nor did the inner motives of living people. Whereas Morgan and Caroline, dawdling in a bar with their hands playing on one another, loved to discuss the relationships of mutual acquaintances, as if together they might distil the spirit of a working love.

Morgan picked up his car keys. He said, 'Sounds good. You'll be fine then, Eric. Best of luck.'

'Thanks a bunch.'

Eric showed no sign of moving.

He said, 'What do you like about her?'

Morgan wanted to shout at him, he wanted to pound on the table in front of him, saying, I love the way she pulls down her clothes, lies on her side and lets me lick and kiss her soft parts, as if I have lifted the dish of life up to my face and burst through it into the wonderland of love for ever!

Eric was tensing up. 'What is it?'

'What?'

'You like about her! If you don't know, maybe you would be good enough to leave us alone!'

'Look, Eric,' Morgan said, 'if you calm yourself a minute, I'll say this. More than a year ago, she said she wanted to be with me. I've been waiting for her.' He pointed at Eric. 'You've had your time with her. You've had plenty. I would say you've had enough. Now it's my turn.'

He got up and walked to the door. It was simple. Then it felt good to be outside. He didn't look back.

Morgan sat in the car and sighed. He started off and stopped at the lights on the corner. He was thinking he would go to the supermarket. Caroline could come round after work and he would cook. He would mix her favourite drink, a whisky mac. She would appreciate being looked after. They could lie down together on the bed.

Eric pulled open the door, got in, and shut the door. Morgan stared at him. The driver behind beeped his horn repeatedly. Morgan drove across the road.

'Do you want me to drop you somewhere?'

'I haven't finished with you,' said Eric.

Morgan looked alternately at the road and at Eric. Eric was sitting in his car, in his seat, with his feet on his rubber mat.

Morgan was swearing under his breath.

Eric said, 'What are you going to do? Have you decided?'

Morgan drove on. He saw that Eric had picked up a piece of paper from the dashboard. Morgan remembered it was a shopping list that Caroline had made out for him. Eric put it back.

Morgan turned the car round and accelerated.

'We'll go to her office now and discuss it with her. Is that what you want? I'm sure she'll tell you everything you want to know. Otherwise – let me know when you want to get out,' said Morgan. 'Say when.'

Eric just stared ahead.

Morgan thought he had been afraid of happiness, and kept it away; he had been afraid of other people, and had kept them away. He was still afraid, but it was too late for that.

Suddenly he banged the steering wheel and said, 'Okay.'

'What?' said Eric.

'I've decided,' said Morgan. 'The answer is yes. Yes to everything! Now you must get out.' He stopped the car. 'Out, I said!'

Driving away, he watched Eric in the mirror getting smaller and smaller.

Midnight All Day

Ian lay back in the only chair in the room in Paris, waiting for Marina to finish in the bathroom. She would be some time, since she was applying unguents – seven different ones, she had told him – over most of her body, rubbing them in slowly. She was precious to herself.

He was glad to have a few minutes alone. There had been many important days recently; he suspected that this would be the most important and that his future would turn on it.

For the past few mornings, before they went out for breakfast, he had listened to Schubert's Sonata in B Flat Major, which he had not previously known. Apart from a few pop tapes, it was the only music in Anthony's flat. Ian had pulled it out from under the futon on their first day there.

Now, as he got up to play the CD, he glimpsed himself in the wardrobe mirror and saw himself as a character in a Lucian Freud painting: a middle-aged man in a thin, tan raincoat, ashen-faced, standing beside a dying pot plant, overweight and with, to his surprise, an absurd expression of hope, or the desire to please, in his eyes. He would have laughed, had he not lost his sense of humour.

He turned the music up. It concealed the voices that came from a nearby children's school. They reminded him of his daughter, who was staying, at the moment, with her grandmother in London. Ian's wife, Jane, had been taken to hospital. He had to discuss this with Marina, who didn't yet know about it. She did not want to hear about his wife and he did not want to talk about her.

But unless he did, his wife would continue to shadow him – both of them – darkening everything.

Although Ian had been a pop kid, and overawed by what he imagined classical music meant, he listened avidly to the Schubert sonata, sometimes walking up and down. No matter how often he heard it, he could not remember what came next; what it said to him he did not know, as the piece had no distinct overall mood. He liked the idea of it being music he would never understand; that seemed to be an important part of it. It was a relief, too, that he still had the capacity to be aroused and engrossed, as well as consoled. Some mornings he woke up wanting to hear the piece.

He and Marina had spent ten days in the tiny flat belonging to Ian's closest friend and business partner, Anthony, who had a French lover or mistress. On the rue du Louvre, the apartment was well situated for walks, museums and bars, but it was on the sixth floor. Marina found it an increasing strain to mount the narrow, warped wooden stairs. Not that they went out more than once a day. The weather had been fresh and bright, but it was freezing. The flat was cold, apart from where it was too hot, beside the electric fire attached to the wall, where the only armchair stood.

What was between him and Marina? Had they only dreamed one another? He did not know, even now. All he could do was find out by living through to the end every sigh and shout of their stupid, wonderful, selfish love. Then they would both know if they were able to go on.

He had listened to the sonata twice by the time she came in, naked, holding her stomach. She lowered herself onto the futon to dress. He had yearned for days and months and years for her, and now could not remember if they were speaking or not.

'Don't get cold,' he said.

'I've got nothing to wear.'

Few of her skirts and trousers fitted now she was pregnant. He himself had left London with two pairs of trousers and three shirts, one of which Marina was usually wearing. It had made him feel like a thief to think of removing his clothes from the flat he had shared with his wife, particularly when she was not there. He had fewer possessions now than he had had as a student, twenty years ago.

He said, 'We must buy some clothes.'

'How much money do we have left?'

'One of the credit cards is still working. At least it was last night.'

'How will we pay it off?'

'I'll get a job.'

She snorted. 'Really?'

Before they left London she had been turned down for a job because she was pregnant.

He said, 'Maybe in an off-licence. Why are you laughing?'

'You – so delicate, so proud – selling beers and crisps.'

He said, 'It's important to me – not to let you down.'

'I've always supported myself,' she said.

'You can't now.'

'Can't I?'

He said, 'Anthony might lend me some money. You haven't forgotten that he's coming this afternoon?'

'We can't keep asking him for money.'

'I love you,' he said.

She looked at him. 'That's good.'

The previous evening they had walked to a restaurant near the Jardins du Luxembourg, and had talked of how seriously the Parisians took their food. The waiters were professional waiters, rather than students, and the food was substantial and old-fashioned, intended to be eaten rather than looked at. The older people tucked wide napkins into their fronts and the children sat on cushions on their seats.

'This was my dream, when I was a teenager,' Marina had said, 'to come to Paris to live and work.'

'We're living in Paris now,' he had replied. 'Sort of.'

She said, 'I didn't imagine it would be like this. In these conditions.'

Her bitter remark made him feel he had trapped her; perhaps she felt the same. As they walked back, in silence, he wondered who she was, the layer upon layer of her. They were peeling and scraping, both hoping to find the person underneath, as if it would reveal the only useful truth. But in the end you had to live with all of someone else.

He and Marina had been to Paris, on an invented business trip, over a year ago, but otherwise they had met only intermittently. These ten days were the longest they had been together. She still kept a room in a house with other young people. Her pregnancy made the women envious and confused, and the boys over-curious as to why she kept the father's name a secret.

When Ian left his wife, he and Marina had spent a few nights together in Anthony's London house. Anthony lived alone; the house was large and painted white, with stripped floorboards, the latest style. It was almost bare, apart from several pale, expensive sofas, and resembled a stage set, ready for the actors to start. But Ian felt like a trespasser and told Anthony he had to get away. Five years before, they had started a film production company together. However, Ian had not been to work for almost three months. He had instructed Anthony to freeze his salary and had walked about the city drunk, talking only to the mad and derelict, people who did not know him. If you made yourself desperately sick you had to live in the present; there was nowhere else. But killing yourself was a difficult and time-consuming job and Anthony had made him stop doing it. Ian did not know whether he could go back to work. He had no idea what he was doing. This was partly why Anthony was coming to Paris, to extract a decision from Ian.

Ian could not forget how generous Anthony had been. It was at his insistence and expense that Ian and Marina had travelled to Paris and stayed in his apartment.

'Go and see whether you two want to be together,' he had said. 'Stay there as long as you like. Then let me know.'

'Everyone's advised me to give her up and go back to Jane. They keep telling me how nice Jane is. I can't do that, but they think I'm a fool . . .'

'Be a fool and to hell with everyone else,' Anthony had said.

As Marina dressed now, Ian knew they were close to a permanent break. They had had their time in Paris and the distance between them was considerable. In the past few days she had talked of returning to London, finding a small flat, getting a job, and bringing up the child alone. Many women did that now; it seemed almost a matter of pride. He would be redundant. It was important for her to feel she could get by without him, he saw that. But if their love, from a certain point of view, seemed like a dangerous addiction, he had to persuade her that they had a chance together, even though, half the time, he did not believe it himself. He did not want to fight; everything was going to hell and that was the fate he had to submit to. But a part of him was not ready to submit. Believing in fate was an attempt to believe you had no will of your own and he did not want that, either.

'I'm hungry,' she said.

'We'll eat then.'

He helped her to her feet.

She said, 'I've been feeling dizzy.'

'Tell me at any time if you want to sit down, and a chair will be produced.'

'Yes. Thank you.'

He held her, leaning forward over her stomach.

She said, 'I'm so glad you're here.'

'I'll always be here, if you want me.'

She regarded herself in the mirror. 'I look like a penguin.'

'Let's set out across the tundra, then,' he said.

'Don't mock me.'

'I'm sorry if I've offended you.'

'Let's not start,' she said.

She was anxious, now her breasts were full, her cheeks red, and her arms, legs and thighs sturdy, that he had loved only her slimness and youth. She felt weary, too, and seemed, in her late twenties, to have passed into another period of her life, without wanting to. All she wanted, most of the time, was to lie down. Veins showed through the pale skin of her legs; every evening she asked him to massage her aching ankles. But her skin was clear; her long hair shone. There was no spare flesh on her. She was taut, pressed to the limit; and healthy.

At the bottom of the stairs she was breathless, but they were both glad to be outside.

He liked walking in Paris: the streets lined with galleries, and the shops full of little objects – a city of people concerned with their senses. It seemed quiet, and stifled by good taste, compared to the vulgar rush, fury and expense of London, which had once again become fashionable. The walls of the London newsagents were lined with magazines and papers, full of the profiles of new artists, playwrights, songwriters, actors, dancers, architects – spitting, cynical, unsettling and argumentative in the new British way. Restaurants opened every day, and the chefs were famous. At midnight in Soho and Covent Garden, you had to push through crowds as if you were at a carnival. It was not something Ian could take an interest in until he had a love, and was settled.

As he walked, Ian saw a smartly dressed, middle-aged man coming towards him, holding the hand of a girl about the same age as his daughter. They were talking and laughing. Ian presumed the girl was late for school, and her father was taking her; there was nothing more important for the man to do. Close, encouraging, generous, available – Ian thought of the father he had wanted to be. He knew children needed to be listened to. But these were ideas he would have to revise; he could not, now, be his own father, in another generation. There would be a distance. He imagined his daughter saying, 'Dad walked out. He was never there.' He would do his best, but it was not the same; he had failed without wanting to.

Ian turned away and waited for Marina to catch up. Her head was bent, as it often was, and she wore a grey woolly hat, with a bobble. Over her long black dress she had on an ankle-length fur-collared overcoat, and trainers. When she was next to him, he took her arm.

He had become accustomed to her size. For days he seemed to forget they were having a child until, at unexpected moments, the terror of how overwhelming it could be seized him, along with the fact that they couldn't escape one another. At the beginning they had talked of an abortion; but neither of them could have lived with such a crude negation of hope. They loved one another, but could they live together? This was the ordeal of his life. If he was unable to make this work, then not only had he broken up his family for nothing, but he was left with nothing – nothing but himself.

He thought of what she had to take on: him grumbling about how awful everything was, and groaning and yelling in his sleep, as if he were inhabited by ghosts; his fears and doubts; his sudden ecstasies; his foolishness, wisdom, experience and naivety; how much he made her laugh and how infuriated she could become. How much there was of other people! If falling in love could only be a glimpse of the other, who was the passion really directed at? They were living an extended, closer look at one another.

In a café nearby, where they had been going every day, she sat down while he stood at the bar to order breakfast. He spoke English in a low voice, as Marina was annoyed that he would not try to speak French. It was almost twenty-five years since he had studied the language, and the effort and his helplessness were humiliating.

He watched as the Parisians came in, knocked their coffee back, devoured a croissant, and hurried off to work. Marina sat with her hands under her stomach. The baby must have been awake, for he – they knew it was a boy – was kicking in her. At times, so thin and stretched had her stomach become, she felt she would split, as if the boy were trying to kick his way out. There were other anxieties – that the baby would be blind or autistic – as well as new pains, flutterings and pulses in her stomach. These were ordinary fears; he had been through this before with another woman, but did not like to remind her.

'You look even more beautiful today,' he said, sitting down. 'Your eyes are brighter than for a long time.'

'I'm surprised,' she said.

'Why?'

'It's been so difficult.'

'A little, yes,' he said. 'But it'll get easier.'

'Will it?'

Of course he was ambivalent about having another child. He recalled sitting in the flat with Jane, having returned from the hospital with their daughter. He had taken a week off work and realised then how little time he and Jane had spent together over the past five years. Once, their fears had coincided; that had been love, for a while. He saw that they had had to keep themselves apart, for fear of turning into someone they both disliked. He did not want to use her words; she did not want his opinions inside her. The girl was, and remained, particularly in her rages, the expression or reminder of their incompatibility, of a difference they were unable to bridge. He was looking forward to seeing his daughter without Jane.

'What's bothering you today?' Marina said, when they were drinking their coffee. 'You stare into the distance for ages. Then you jerk your head around urgently, like a blackbird. I wonder what sort of worm it is you've spotted. But it's nothing, is it?'

'No. Only . . . I've got to talk to Anthony this afternoon . . . and I haven't decided what to say.'

'Or what to do.'

'That's right.'

She said, 'You don't want to go back?'

'I don't know.' They buttered their croissants in silence. 'Things are certainly starting to seem a little aimless here.' He said, 'Anthony's changed.'

'In what way?'

'You don't want me to go on about it, do you?'

She said, 'But I love our talks. I love the sound of your voice . . . even if I don't listen to every word.'

He told her they had run the company for themselves, for fun. They had never wanted to work excessive hours, or accept projects for the money alone. In the past five years they had made three feature films, one of which had been critically successful and made its money back. They had also produced a number of television documentaries. But recently, without discussing it fully with Ian, Anthony had taken on an expensive American comedy project, to be shot in London, with a petulant and talent-less director.

Anthony had made new friends in film and TV. He flew to Manchester United's home matches and sat in the directors' box. He went to New Labour dinners and, Ian presumed, donated money to the Party. He boasted of a new friend who had a trout stream at the end of his garden, though Ian doubted whether Anthony would recognise a trout unless it was served to him on a plate.

In the past twenty years Ian had come to know most of the people in his profession. He was a natural son-type, who liked to listen and admire; he collected mentors. Most of these friends, the majority of whom were from ordinary backgrounds, now lived in ostentatious luxury, like the great industrialists of the nineteenth century. They were the editors of newspapers, film directors, chairmen of publishing houses, heads of TV companies, senior journalists and professors. In their spare time, of which they seemed to have a lot, they became the chairmen of various theatre, film and arts boards. The early fifties in men was a period of frivolity, self-expansion and self-indulgence.

If Ian was perplexed, it was because that generation, ten years ahead of him, had been a cussed, liberated, dissenting lot. Somehow Thatcher had helped them to power. Following her, they had moved to the right and ended up in the centre. Their left politics had ended up as social tolerance and lack of deference. Otherwise, they smoked cigars and were driven to their country houses on Friday afternoons; sitting with friends overlooking their land, while local women worked in the kitchen, they fretted about their knighthoods. They were as thrilled as teenagers when they saw themselves in the newspapers. They wanted to be prefects.

'They've lost their intellectual daring,' Ian said.

'There's a bit of you that sees all that as the future,' Marina said.

'I'm aware that one has to find new things,' he said. 'But I don't know what they should be.'

He looked at her. He felt ready to bring up the subject of his wife.

'We'll have to go back to London eventually,' he said. 'Quite soon, probably, and . . . face everything. I want to do that and I don't want to do it.'

'Where will we go?' she said. 'I've got nothing, your money is in your wife's house, and you haven't got a job.'

'Well –'

He believed she trusted him and imagined he might know, despite everything, what he was doing. Looking at her sweet face now, and her long fingers tearing at a croissant, he contemplated her inner dignity. If he thought she was regal, it was not because she was imperious, but because she was still. She never fidgeted; there was nothing unnecessary in anything she did.

They had stopped talking of the future and what they might do to make a life together, as if they had turned into children and wanted to be told. They drifted about Paris, according to some implicit routine, looking at their guidebooks, visiting galleries, museums and parks, going to restaurants in the evening.

If he were to love her, he had to be transformed from a man who could not do this with Jane, to a man who could do it with Marina. And the transformation had to be rapid, before he lost her. If he could not get along with this woman, he couldn't get along with any of them and he was done for.

'Shall we go?' she said.

He helped her into her coat. They crossed the Seine on the wooden bridge with the benches, where they sat facing the Pont Neuf, enjoying the view. He thought, then, that this was a better moment to start to talk about his wife; but he took Marina's arm, and they moved on.

They knew the eager queue outside the Musée d'Orsay would not take long to go down. He was amazed by the thirst of the crowds, to look at good things.

Inside, Marina was walking somewhere when, adjacent to Rodin's *Gates of Hell*, Ian found himself standing beside the tower of white stone that was *Balzac*. Ian had seen it many times since he was a teenager, but on this occasion it made him suddenly laugh. Surely, Balzac had been a flabby and dishevelled figure, obsessed by money rather than the immortality that Rodin had him gazing towards? As far as Ian could remember, Balzac had hurried through life and received little satisfaction; his ambition had been a little ridiculous – or perhaps, narrow and unreflective. Yet this was a man: someone who had taken action, converting experience into something powerful and sensual.

Rodin had certainly made Balzac a forceful figure. Ian was reminded of how afraid his own timid mother had been of his noise and energy; she was forever telling him to 'calm down'. His being alive at all seemed to alarm her. With Marina, too, Ian had been afraid of his own furies, of his power, and of the damage he believed that being a man might do, and how it might make her withdraw her love. What evil had marauding men caused in the twentieth century! Hadn't he damaged his wife? And yet, looking at Rodin's idea of Balzac now, he thought: rather a beast than a castrated angel. If the tragedy of the twentieth century had been fascism and communism, the triumph was that both had been defeated. Without guilt we lose our humanity, but if there is too much of it, nothing can be redeemed!

Leaving the Musée D'Orsay he realised how quickly he was walking, and how revived and stimulated he was. Rodin and Balzac had done him good.

As they entered a restaurant, Marina pointed out that the place looked expensive, but he hurried her in, saying, 'Let's just eat – and drink!'

She looked at him questioningly, but he wanted to talk, keeping the Rodin in mind like a talisman, or a reminder of some suppressed childhood ecstasy. He could push against the world, and it would survive. He had probably read too much Beckett as a young man. He would have been better off with Joyce.

'I know you don't want to hear about this,' he said, 'but my wife . . .'

'Yes? What is it?'

He had alarmed her already.

'She is in hospital. She took pills and alcohol . . . and passed out. I believe she did it after I told her about the baby. Our baby. You know.'

'Is she dead?'

'Perhaps that would seem like a relief. But no. No.' He went on, 'It's a terrible thing to do, to others, to our daughter in particular. I was surprised by it, as Jane never seemed to like me. She must be deranged at the moment. She will have to realise that she can't cling to me for ever. I don't want to go on about it. I wanted you to know, that's all.'

For a time she was silent.

'I feel sorry for her,' she said. She started to weep. 'To have lost a love that you thought would continue for ever, and to have to recover from that. How terrible, terrible, terrible!'

'Yes, well –'

She said, 'How do I know you won't do the same to me?'

'Sorry?'

'How do I know you won't leave me, as you left her?'

'As if I make a habit of . . . that sort of thing?'

'You've done it once. Perhaps more. How do I know?'

Outrage stopped his mouth. If he spoke he would say terrible things, and they would not understand one another. But he had to keep speaking to her.

She went on, 'I fear, constantly, that you will tire of me and go back to her.'

'I'll never do that, never. Why should I?'

'You know one another.'

He said, 'After a certain age everything happens under the sign of eternity, which is probably the best way to do things. I haven't got time now, for vacillation.'

'But you are feeble,' she said. 'You don't fight for yourself. You let people push you around.'

'Who?'

'Me. Anthony. Your wife. You were always afraid of her.'

'That is true,' he said. 'I cannot stop wanting to rely on the kindness of others.'

'You can't survive on only that.' She was not looking at him. 'Your weakness confuses people.'

'I'm not a fantasy, but a wretched human with weaknesses – and some strengths – like everyone else. But I want to be with you. That I am certain of.' He paid the bill. 'I need to go for a walk,' he said. 'I want to think about what I'm going to say to Anthony. I'll see you at the apartment later.'

She took his hand. 'It would be a shame if your intelligence and wit . . . if your ideas went to waste. Now kiss me.'

He went out, leaving her with her notebook. He walked about aimlessly in the cold. Soon he was in the café where he was to meet Anthony, an hour before he was due, drinking beer and coffee.

He thought that Anthony would understand the difficulties one might have with a woman. But as a business partner, Ian was not certain that Anthony would be patient. Ian had behaved recklessly; madly even. Anthony had less use for him now. If Ian had jettisoned his own wife, Anthony might do the same to him.

From inside the café Ian saw Anthony's chauffeur-driven Mercedes. After sending the car away, Anthony checked his hair and brushed himself down. He had a young woman with him, to whom he was giving instructions. She would be his new assistant. Leaving her walking up and down the pavement making calls, Anthony came in.

He was wearing a well-cut dark suit; his hair had been dyed. Anthony was tall and skinny; he drank little. Apart from confusion and an inability to get along with women, he had few vices. Ian had attempted to introduce him to a few. After Anthony's first Ecstasy pill (provided by Ian, who got them from his postman) they took drugs – mostly Ecstasy, along with cocaine, to keep them up; and cannabis, to bring them down – for a year, which was how long it took them to realise that they couldn't resurrect the pleasure they'd had on the first night. Ian now took only tranquillisers.

'Where is she?' Anthony asked, looking about. 'How does she look?'

'She's at the apartment. She looks splendid. Only . . . I told her about Jane.'

Anthony sat down and ordered an omelette. 'A bloody blackmailing nuisance,' he murmured.

Ian said, 'It was making me mad, the fear of telling her. Can you tell me how Jane is?'

He had asked Anthony to look into it. Anthony would know how to find out.

Anthony said, 'There's nothing physically wrong with her. Of course, she's distressed and depressed, but she will survive that. She's coming out of hospital today.'

'Do you think I should go and see her?'

'I don't know.'

Ian said, 'Consciousness is proving a little tenacious at the moment. Where are my tranquillisers?'

'I told the quack they were for me. He wouldn't give me any. Said I'm tranquil enough.'

'So you didn't bring any?'

'No.'

'Oh, Anthony.'

Anthony opened his briefcase and took out a gadget, a little computer, clearing a space for it on the table. 'Listen –' He was busy. Ian's recent slow pace wasn't Anthony's. 'I need your advice about a director I – we – might use. I think you know him.'

While Ian gave his opinion Anthony typed, rather inaccurately, it seemed to Ian; Anthony's fingers seemed too fat for the keys. It was a machine Ian knew he would never understand, just as his mother had decided it was too late to bother with videos and computers. Still, Ian wondered whether he was really the fool he liked to take himself for. His ideas weren't so bad.

He and Anthony switched subjects quickly, as Ian liked to, to football. Ian hadn't been getting the English papers; he wanted the results. Anthony said he'd been to Stamford Bridge to watch Manchester United play Chelsea.

'I'm assuming you want to make me jealous,' Ian said.

'Why don't you come next time?'

'It's true, I miss London.'

When he could not sleep, Ian liked to imagine he was being driven in a taxi through London. The route took him through the West End and Trafalgar Square, down the Mall, past Buckingham Palace – with Green Park, lit like a grotto, on the right; through the perils of Hyde Park Corner, then past the Minema (showing an obscure Spanish film), and the windows of Harvey Nichols. If you did not know it, what a liberal and individual place you would think London was! He was becoming tired of the deprivations of this little exile.

He started to wonder whether Marina was asleep, or walking in Paris. It occurred to him that she might have left and gone back to London. He wondered if this was a wish on his part, to end his anxiety at last. But he knew it was not what he wanted. He felt like rushing to the apartment to reassure her.

Ian asked, 'How's the American project?'

'Shooting in the summer.'

'Really?'

'Of course. It wasn't difficult getting the money, as I told you.'

He felt patronised by Anthony, but he was at ease with him too. Ian said, 'I don't know why you didn't make those films I liked.'

'You were breaking up. Then you weren't around. Why don't you do them now? There's money for development.'

'Marina and I haven't got anywhere to live.'

Anthony waved out of the window at his assistant, still walking up and down.

'She'll find you a flat. If you come back to London I'll put you in a hotel from tomorrow and there'll be an apartment from Monday. Right?' Ian said nothing. Anthony said, 'You did the right thing by leaving – leaving Jane, and then leaving London.'

'Jane kept saying I didn't try hard enough. It's certainly true that I was . . . preoccupied elsewhere, some of the time. But I was with her for six years.'

'Long enough, surely, to know whether you want to be with someone. You've done it. It's over. You're free,' Anthony said.

Ian liked the way Anthony made it seem straightforward.

'I'm full of regret,' Ian said, 'for how unhappy I've been so much of the time.'

Anthony sighed. 'You can't hold on to that unhappiness for ever.'

Ian said, 'No. I've come to believe in romantic love, too. I feel a fool having fallen for the idea. What's wrong with sublimation? Rather a Rembrandt than a wank, don't you think?'

'Why not sublimation as well as copulation?' said Anthony. 'Look at Picasso.' He leaned across the table. 'How is it with Marina?'

'It's the ordeal of my life. Cold turkey, psychosis and death – all at once. I've been trying to understand something about myself . . . and what I might be able to do. I'm clearer now. I don't want to give up.'

'Why should you? You only have to look at her to see how passionate she is about you. It's funny how blind one can be to such obvious things. Ian, there's a lot happening in the company. I'd like it if you came back. Soon. Monday, say.' Anthony was looking at him. 'What do you think?'

'You really need to know?'

'Yes.'

Ian realised he hadn't talked to Marina about it. Only rarely did he ask her advice. He was used to doing everything alone. If he could solicit her help, if he could learn to turn to her, maybe she would feel more involved. Perhaps love was an exchange of problems.

'I'll ask Marina's advice.'

'Good,' Anthony said.

Ian wanted to carry on talking but Anthony was late for a meeting. After, he would meet his lover. Ian stood up to go.

'The thing is, I'm a bit short of money at the moment.'

'Of course.'

Anthony opened his chequebook and wrote a cheque. Then he gave Ian some cash. Outside, Ian was introduced to Anthony's assistant. He wondered how much she knew of him. Anthony said Ian was returning to work on Monday. When Anthony and the young woman got into the car, Ian waved from the pavement.

As he walked back, Ian thought that he wanted to be at home, in a house he liked, with a woman and children he liked. He wanted to lose himself in the mundane, in unimportant things. Perhaps those things were graspable now. Once he had them, he could think of others, and be useful.

He pushed the key into the lock, got into the building and ran up the stairs. He rang the bell repeatedly. It was cold but he was sweating. He rang again. Then he fiddled with the keys. At last he unlocked the door and went up the hallway. The room was dark. He put the light on. She was lying on the bed. She sat up.

The Umbrella

The minute they arrived at the adventure playground, Roger's two sons charged up a long ramp and were soon clinging to the steel netting that hung from a high beam. Satisfied that it would take them some time to extricate themselves, Roger sat on a bench and turned to the sports section of his newspaper. He had always found it relaxing to read reports of football matches he had not seen.

Then it started to rain.

His sons, aged four and five and a half, had refused to put on their coats when he picked them up from the au pair half an hour before. Coats made them look 'fat', they claimed, and Roger had had to carry them under his arm.

The older boy was dressed in a thin, tight-fitting green outfit and a cardboard cap with a feather in it: he was either Robin Hood or Peter Pan. The younger wore a plastic holster with two silver guns, a plastic dagger and a sword, blue wellington boots, jeans with the fly open, and a chequered neckerchief which he pulled over his mouth. 'Cowboys don't wear raincoats,' he said, through a mouthful of cloth.

The boys frequently refused Roger's commands, though he could not say that their stubbornness and pluck annoyed him. It did, however, cause him trouble with his wife, from whom he had separated a year previously. Only that morning she had said on the phone, 'You are a weak and inadequate disciplinarian. You only want their favour.'

For as long as he could, Roger pretended it was not raining, but when his newspaper began to go soggy and everyone else had left the playground, he called the boys over.

'Damn this rain,' he said, as he hustled them into their hooded yellow raincoats.

'Don't swear,' said Eddie, the younger boy. 'Women think it's naughty.'

'Sorry.' Roger laughed. 'I was thinking I should have got a raincoat as well as the suit.'

'You do need a lovely raincoat, Daddy,' said Oliver, the oldest.

'My friend would have given me a raincoat, but I liked the suit more.'

He had picked up the chocolate-coloured suit from the shop that morning. Since the early seventies, that most extravagant of periods, Roger had fancied himself as a restrained but amateur dandy. One of his best friends was a clothes designer with shops in Europe and Japan. A few years ago this friend, amused by Roger's interest in his business, had invited Roger, during a fashion show at the British Embassy in Paris, to parade on the catwalk in front of the fashion press, alongside younger and taller men. Roger's friend had given him the chocolate suit for his fortieth birthday, and had insisted he wear it with a blue silk shirt. Roger's sons liked to sleep in their newly acquired clothes, and he understood their enthusiasm. He would not normally wear a suit for the park, but that evening he was going to a publishing party, and then on to his third date with a woman he had been introduced to at a friend's house; a woman he liked.

Roger took the boys' hands and pulled them along.

'We'd better go to the teahouse,' he said. 'I hope I don't ruin my shoes.'

'They're beautiful,' said Oliver.

Eddie stopped to bend down and rub his father's loafers. 'I'll put my hands over your shoes while you walk,' he said.

'That might slow us down a little,' Roger said. 'Run for it, mates!'

He picked Eddie up, holding him flat in his arms like a baby, with his muddy boots pointing outwards. The three of them hurried across the darkening park.

The teahouse was a wide, low-ceilinged shed, warm, brightly lit and decorated in the black and white colours and flags of

Newcastle United. The coffee was good and they had all the newspapers. The place was crowded but Roger spotted a table and sent Oliver over to sit at it.

Roger recognised the mother of a boy in Eddie's nursery, as well as several nannies and au pairs, who seemed to congregate in some part of this park on most days. Three or four of them had come to his house with their charges, when he lived with his wife. If they seemed reticent with him, he doubted whether this was because they were young and simple, but rather that they saw him as an employer, as the boss.

He was aware that he was the only man in the teahouse. The men he ran into with children were either younger than him, or older, on their second families. He wished his children were older, and understood more; he should have had them earlier. He'd both enjoyed and wasted the years before they were born; it had been a long, dissatisfied ease.

A girl in the queue turned to him.

'Thinking again?' she said.

He recognised her voice but had not brought his glasses.

'Hello,' he said at last. He called to Eddie, 'Hey, it's Lindy.' Eddie covered his face with both hands. 'You remember her giving you a bath and washing your hair.'

'Hey, cowboy,' she said.

Lindy had looked after both children when Eddie was born and lived in the house until precipitately deciding to leave. She had told them she wanted to do something else but, instead, had gone to work for a couple nearby.

The last time Roger had run into Lindy, he had overheard her imitating his sons' accents and laughing. They were 'posh'. He had been shocked by how early these notions of 'class' started.

'Haven't seen you for a while,' she said.

'I've been travelling.'

'Where to?'

'Belfast, Cape Town, Sarajevo.'

'Lovely,' she said.

'I'm off to the States next week,' he said.

'Doing what?'

'Lecturing on human rights. On the development of the notion of the individual . . . of the idea of the separate self.' He wanted to say something about Shakespeare and Montaigne, as he had been thinking about them, but realised she would refuse to be curious about the subject. 'And on the idea of human rights in the post-war period. All of that kind of thing. I hope there's going to be a TV series.'

She said, 'I came back from the pub and turned on the TV last week, and there you were, criticising some clever book or other. I didn't understand it.'

'Right.'

He had always been polite to her, even when he had been unable to wake her up because she had been drinking the previous night. She had seen him unshaven, and in his pyjamas at four in the morning; she had opened doors and found him and his wife abusing one another behind them; she had been at their rented villa in Assisi when his wife tore the cloth from the table with four bowls of pasta on it. She must have heard energetic reconciliations.

'I hope it goes well,' she said.

'Thank you.'

The boys ordered big doughnuts and juice. The juice spilled over the table and the doughnuts were smeared round their mouths. Roger had to hold his cappuccino out in front of him to stop the boys sticking their grimy fingers in the froth and sucking the chocolate from them. To his relief they joined Lindy's child.

Roger began a conversation with a woman at the next table who had complimented him on his sons. She told him she wanted to write a newspaper article on how difficult some people found it to say 'No' to children. You could not charm them, she maintained, as you could people at a cocktail party; they had to know what the limits were. He did not like the idea that she had turned disciplining her child into a manifesto, but he would ask for her phone number before he left. For more than a year he had not gone out socially, fearing that people would see his anguish.

He was extracting his notebook and pen when Lindy called him. He turned round. His sons were at the far end of the tea-house, rolling on top of another, larger, boy, who was wailing, 'He's biting me!'

Eddie did bite; he kicked too.

'Boys!' Roger called.

He hurried them into their coats again, whispering furiously for them to shut up. He said goodbye to the woman without getting her phone number. He did not want to appear lecherous.

He had always been proud of the idea that he was a good man who treated people fairly. He did not want to impose himself. The world would be a better place if people considered their actions. Perhaps he had put himself on a pedestal. 'You have a high reputation – with yourself!' a friend had said. Everyone was entitled to some pride and vanity. However, this whole business with his wife had stripped him of his moral certainties. There was no just or objective way to resolve competing claims: those of free-dom – his freedom – to live and develop as he liked, against the right of his family to have his dependable presence. But no amount of conscience or morality would make him go back. He had not missed his wife for a moment.

As they were leaving the park, Eddie tore some daffodils from a flowerbed and stuffed them in his pocket. 'For Mummy,' he explained.

The house was a ten-minute walk away. Holding hands, they ran home through the rain. His wife would be back soon, and he would be off.

It was not until he had taken out his key that he remembered his wife had changed the lock last week. What she had done was illegal: he owned the house; but he had laughed at the idea she thought he would intrude, when he wanted to be as far away as possible.

He told the boys they would have to wait. They sheltered in the little porch where water dripped on their heads. The boys soon tired of standing with him and refused to sing the songs he started. They pulled their hoods down and chased one another up and down the path.

It was dark. People were coming home from work.

The next-door neighbour passed by. 'Locked out?' he said.

''Fraid so.'

Oliver said, 'Daddy, why can't we go in and watch the cartoons?'

'It's only me she's locked out,' he said. 'Not you. But you are, of course, with me.'

'Why has she locked us out?'

'Why don't you ask her?' he said.

His wife confused and frightened him. But he would greet her civilly, send the children into the house and say goodbye. It was, however, difficult to get cabs in the area; impossible at this time and in this weather. It was a twenty-minute walk to the tube station, across a dripping park where alcoholics and junkies gathered under the trees. His shoes, already wet, would be filthy. At the party he would have to try and remove the worst of the mud in the toilet.

After the violence of separation he had expected a diminishment of interest and of loathing, on her part. He himself had survived the worst of it and anticipated a quietness. Kind indifference had come to seem an important blessing. But as well as refusing to divorce him, she sent him lawyers' letters about the most trivial matters. One letter, he recalled, was entirely about a cheese sandwich he had made for himself when visiting the children. He was ordered to bring his own food in future. He thought of his wife years ago, laughing and putting out her tongue with his semen on it.

'Hey there,' she said, coming up the path.

'Mummy!' they called.

'Look at them,' he said. 'They're soaked through.'

'Oh dear.'

She unlocked the door and the children ran into the hall. She nodded at him. 'You're going out.'

'Sorry?'

'You've got a suit on.'

He stepped into the hall. 'Yes. A little party.'

He glanced into his former study, where his books were packed in boxes on the floor. He had, as yet, nowhere to take them. Beside them were a pair of men's black shoes he had not seen before.

She said to the children, 'I'll get your tea.' To him she said, 'You haven't given them anything to eat, have you?'

'Doughnuts,' said Eddie. 'I had chocolate.'

'I had jam,' said Oliver.

She said, 'You let them eat that rubbish?'

Eddie pushed the crushed flowers at her. 'There you are, Mummy.'

'You must not take flowers from the park,' she said. 'They are for everyone.'

'Fuck, fuck, fuck,' said Eddie suddenly, with his hand over his mouth.

'Shut up! People don't like it!' said Oliver, and hit Eddie, who started to cry.

'Listen to him,' she said to Roger. 'You've taught them to use filthy language. You are really hopeless.'

'So are you,' he said.

In the past few months, preparing his lectures, he had visited some disorderly and murderous places. The hatred he witnessed puzzled him still. It was atavistic but abstract; mostly the people did not know one another. It had made him aware of how people clung to their antipathies, and used them to maintain an important distance, but in the end he failed to understand why this was. After all the political analysis and talk of rights, he had concluded that people had to grasp the necessity of loving one another; and if that was too much, they had to let one another alone. When this still seemed inadequate and banal, he suspected he was on the wrong path, that he was trying to say something about his own difficulties in the guise of intellectual discourse. Why could he not find a more direct method? He had, in fact, considered writing a novel. He had plenty to say, but could not afford the time, unpaid.

He looked out at the street. 'It's raining quite hard.'

'It's not too bad now.'

He said, 'You haven't got an umbrella, have you?'

'An umbrella?'

He was becoming impatient. 'Yes. An umbrella. You know, you hold it over your head.'

She sighed and went back into the house. He presumed she was opening the door to the airing cupboard in the bathroom.

He was standing in the porch, ready to go. She returned empty-handed.

'No. No umbrella,' she said.

He said, 'There were three there last week.'

'Maybe there were.'

'Are there not still three umbrellas there?'

'Maybe there are,' she said.

'Give me one.'

'No.'

'Sorry?'

'I'm not giving you one,' she said. 'If there were a thousand umbrellas there I would not give you one.'

He had noticed how persistent his children were; they asked, pleaded, threatened and screamed, until he yielded.

He said, 'They are my umbrellas.'

'No,' she repeated.

'How petty you've become.'

'Didn't I give you everything?'

He cleared his throat. 'Everything but love.'

'I did give you that, actually.' She said, 'I've rung my friend. He's on his way.'

He said, 'I don't care. Just give me an umbrella.'

She shook her head. She went to shut the door. He put his foot out and she banged the door against his leg. He wanted to rub his shin but could not give her the pleasure.

He said, 'Let's try and be rational.'

He had hated before, his parents and brother, at certain times. But it was a fury, not a deep, intellectual and emotional hatred like this. He had had psychotherapy; he took tranquillisers, but still he wanted to pulverise his wife. None of the ideas he had about life would make this feeling go away.

'You used to find the rain "refreshing",' she sneered.

'It has come to this,' he said.

'Here we are then,' she said. 'Don't start crying about it.'

He pushed the door. 'I'll get the umbrella.'

She pushed the door back at him. 'You cannot come in.'

'It is my house.'

'Not without prior arrangement.'

'We arranged it,' he said.

'The arrangement's off.'

He pushed her.

'Are you assaulting me?' she said.

He looked outside. An alcoholic woman he had had to remove from the front step on several occasions was standing at the end of the path holding a can of lager.

'I'm watching you,' she shouted. 'If you touch her you are reported!'

'Watch on!' he shouted back.

He pushed into the house. He placed his hand on his wife's chest and forced her against the wall. She cried out. She did bang her head, but it was, in football jargon, a 'dive'. The children ran at his legs. He pushed them away.

He went to the airing cupboard, seized an umbrella and made his way to the front door.

As he passed her she snatched it. Her strength surprised him, but he yanked the umbrella back and went to move away. She raised her hand. He thought she would slap him. It would be the first time. But she made a fist. As she punched him in the face she continued to look at him.

He had not been hit since he left school. He had forgotten the physical shock and then the disbelief, the shattering of the feeling that the world was a safe place.

The boys were screaming. Roger had dropped the umbrella. His mouth throbbed; his lip was bleeding. He must have staggered and lost his balance for she was able to push him outside.

He heard the door slam behind him. He could hear the children crying. He walked away, past the alcoholic woman still standing at the end of the path. He turned to look at the lighted house. When they had calmed down, the children would have their bath and get ready for bed. They liked being read to. It was a part of the day he had always enjoyed.

He turned his collar up but knew he would get soaked. He wiped his mouth with his hand. She had landed him quite a hit. He would not be able to find out until later whether it would show. If it did, it would cause interest and amusement at the party, but not to him; not with a date to go to.

He stood in a doorway watching the people hurry past. His trouser legs stuck to his skin. It would not stop raining for a long time. He could not just stand in the same place for hours. The thing to do was not to mind. He started out then, across the Green, in the dark, wet through, but moving forward.

Morning in the Bowl of Night

It had been snowing.

He got to the house, looked at his watch, saw he was late, and hurried on to a pub he knew at the end of the street. He pushed the door and a barking Alsatian on a chain leapt at him. Young children, one of them badly bruised, chased one another across the slush-wet floor, tripping over the adults' feet. The jukebox was loud, as were the TV and the drinkers' voices. He hadn't been in here for months yet he recognised the same people.

He was backing out when the barman shouted, 'Hey, my man Alan. Alan, where you been?' and started to pull him a pint.

Alan took a seat at the bar, lit a cigarette and drank off half his glass. If he finished quickly he might get another pint in him. It would mean he had no money but why would he need money tonight? The last time he had attended a school nativity play and carol service he had been fourteen, and his best friend's father had turned up so soaked in alcohol that he didn't realise his tie had been dunked in red wine and was still dripping. The boys pointed and laughed at him, and his son had been ashamed.

Alan nodded at the barman who placed the second pint beside the first. Alan's son was too young for shame; in fact, Mikey was starting to worship his father.

Alan needed to calm himself. Melanie, his present girlfriend, with whom he'd lived for a year, had pursued him down the street as he'd left the flat, pulling on his hand and begging him not to go. He told her repeatedly that he had promised his son that he would attend the nativity play. 'All the daddies will be there,' Mikey had said.

'And so will this daddy,' Alan had said.

After much shouting, Alan left Melanie standing in the snow. God knows what state she'd be in when he returned home, if she were there at all. Alan worked in the theatre, though not as an actor. Yet today he felt she had cast him as a criminal, a role he wasn't prepared to play.

Alan finished both drinks and got up to go. It would be the first time he, his wife and their son had been out together as a family since he had left, eighteen months ago.

Perhaps it was his fear that had communicated itself to Melanie. He wasn't sure, however, that fear was the right word. On the way over he had been trying to identify the feeling. It wasn't even dread. The solution came to him now as he approached the house. It was grief; a packed, undigested lump of grief in his chest.

The boy was standing on a chair by the window. Seeing his father he jumped up and down, shouting, 'Daddy, Daddy, Daddy!', banging on the smudged glass.

It had been a week since Alan had seen Mikey, and he was used to looking for the alteration in him. Yet how peculiar he still found it to visit his own son as if he were dropping by for tea with a relation. What he liked most was taking Mikey out to cafés. Occasionally the boy would slip off his stool and run about to demonstrate how high he could jump, but mostly they sat and made conversation like friends, Mikey asking the most demanding questions.

'You're late,' Anne said at the door. 'You've been drinking.'

She was shaking, and her eyes were fixed and wide. He was familiar with these brief possessions, the sudden fits of rage she had throughout the day, usually when she had to ask for something.

Alan slipped past her. 'Pretty Christmas tree,' he said.

He crouched down and Mikey ran into his arms. He was wearing tartan trousers and a knitted sweater. He handed Alan a maroon woolly hat. Anne went to get her coat. Alan pulled the hat down over Mikey's face, and then, as the kid struggled and shouted, picked him up and buried his face in his stomach.

Alan had never liked the street, the area or the house. It had some kind of guilty hold over him. When he visited he felt he should go upstairs, get into bed, close his eyes and resume his old life, as if it were his duty and destiny. Anne still blamed him for leaving, though Alan couldn't understand why she didn't see that it had been best for both of them.

'Kiss,' said Mikey when Anne joined them. 'Kiss together.'

'Sorry?'

'Kiss Mummy.'

Alan looked at his wife.

She had lost weight, her face coming to a point at her chin for the first time in years. She had been dieting; starving herself, it looked like. Her face was covered in white make-up or powder. Her lips were red. He had never let her wear lipstick, not liking it on his face. She dressed better now, presumably on his money. She hadn't been sleeping at the house often, he knew that. Her mother had been staying there with Mikey, not knowing – or not saying – when she would be back.

He and Anne managed to press their lips together for a moment. Her perfume touched off an electric flash of uncontrollable memories, and he shuddered. He tried to think of the last time they had touched one another. It must have been a couple of months before he left. He remembered thinking then, this will be the last time.

It was dark when they went out. Mikey held their hands as they swung him between them. To Alan's relief he chattered away.

Outside the school the parents, dressed up, were getting out of their cars and passing through the gates in the snow. Alan noticed with surprise how happy the children were and how easily their laughter came, whereas the parents exchanged only the necessary courtesies. Was he a particularly gloomy person? His girlfriend said he was. 'If I am, you have made me so,' was his reply. He did feel gloomy, certainly. Perhaps it was his age.

Inside it was warm and bright, and even the teachers smiled. Alan chuckled to himself, imagining what other people might think, seeing him with Anne. How unusual it was, these days, to see a husband and wife together. He exchanged a few amiable words with her, for the public show.

The nativity was performed by the eight- and nine-year-olds, with younger children playing shepherds as well as trees and stars. A painted sky suspended between shortened broom handles was held up by two tiny children. The angels had cardboard wings and costumes made from net curtains. Next year Mikey would be old enough to take part.

A few weeks ago the teacher had asked Alan for suggestions as to how the nativity should be done. Alan was the administrator of a small touring theatre group. He loved the emotional intimacy that actors created between them; and he still liked the excitement of the 'show', the live connection between his colleagues on stage and those who had left their homes for the honest spectacle. There was some sort of important fear that united them all, which made the theatre different from the cinema. His work was badly paid, of course. Some of the actors he worked with appeared on television; the director was married to a rich woman. Alan, though, had no other income. His girlfriend Melanie was an actress. She was pregnant and soon wouldn't be able to work for a while.

When the nativity started Alan checked his pocket. He had taken a handkerchief out with him, a proper cloth handkerchief given to him, inexplicably, by Anne, years ago. He had not gone out with a pocket handkerchief since his last day at school. But all afternoon he had been afraid the children's voices would make him break down. To cheer himself up he had thought of his father, in church at Christmas – the only time he went – singing as loud as he could, not caring that he was out of tune. They were celebrating, Father said, not making a record for Deutsche Grammophon.

The parents cried and laughed through the nativity, and the younger children, like Alan's son, shouted out joyfully.

Alan compared himself to the people he knew there. At the door he had been greeted by a man who had said, 'I could do with a drink, too, but I'm not allowed.'

Until the man reminded him that he had fixed Alan's car a couple of times, Alan couldn't think who he was, for he was thin and decrepit, with a shaven head.

'But at least you look well, you look well,' the man said, as Alan moved away uncomfortably, only at this stage becoming aware of how ill the man must be.

There was a woman sitting in the adjacent row. Alan had been told by an acquaintance earlier in the year that she had thrown herself naked from a window, smashing her face and breaking her ribs, before being taken to hospital in a straitjacket. Another woman, sitting further along the row, had ignored him, or perhaps she hadn't seen him. But she had walked often with him in the park, as their children played. She had told him she was leaving her husband.

It had been a murderous century, yet here, in this comfortable corner of the earth, by some fluke, most of them had been spared. For that he sang, wondering, all the same, why they were so joyless.

Melanie hadn't been pregnant long, but her body had started to change. She was losing her girlishness. Apart from her thick waist, she felt heavy and claimed she was already forced to walk with a 'waddle'. She wasn't working at the moment, so it didn't matter that she had to go back to bed in the morning. When they weren't fighting he would sit with her, eating his breakfast.

She had an appointment the next day, for an abortion. He would pick her up the day after. A long time ago he had been involved in two other abortions. The first he had avoided by going away to stay with another woman. Of the second, he remembered only how the woman lay on the floor and wept afterwards. He recalled sitting across the room from her with his eyes closed, counting back from a thousand. The relationships had broken immediately after. His life with Melanie would end, too. It would seem pointless to go on. Why was it important that relationships went on? By tomorrow night his hope would be destroyed. He couldn't go from woman to woman any more.

Their arguments were bitter and their reconciliations no longer sweet. He had locked her out of the flat. She had thrown away a picture his wife had given him. Alan had flung some of her belongings into the street. For weeks they had pounded one another, emerging into the world as if they'd walked out of a fire, their skin blackened, eyes staring, not knowing what had happened. Would they be together for good or only until tomorrow?

Looking sideways at his wife now, over the head of the boy who connected them for ever, Alan knew he couldn't make such a mistake again.

In their better moods, he and Melanie talked to the child in her belly and considered names for her. They had talked of having a child in a few years. But a child wasn't a fridge that you could order when you wanted, or when you could afford it. The child in her belly already had a face.

Outside the school, as the three of them walked away, Alan spotted an abandoned supermarket trolley. Instantly he picked Mikey up, dumped him in it and ran with it along the side of the road. The yells of the delighted boy, crouching in the clattering tray as they skidded around corners and over speed bumps, and Anne's cries as she ran behind, trying to keep up, pierced the early evening dark.

Laughing, breathless and warm, they soon arrived at the house. Anne closed the shutters and switched on the Christmas tree lights. The room had changed since he'd last been there. It contained only her things. There was nothing of him left in it.

She poured Alan a glass of brandy. Mikey gulped down his juice. Anne said he could pick a bar of chocolate from the tree if he shared it with them. As they discussed the nativity Alan noticed that his son seemed wary and uncertain, as if he weren't sure which parent he should go to, sensing he couldn't favour one without displeasing the other.

At last Alan got up to leave.

'Oh, I forgot,' Anne said. 'I bought some mince pies and brandy butter. I don't know why I bothered, but I did. You still like them, don't you? I'll put them on one plate for you and Mikey to share. Is that okay?'

She went to heat them up. Alan had told Melanie he wouldn't be long. He had to go to her. What a terrifying machine the imagination could be. If it was terrible between them tonight, they might do something irreversible tomorrow. He was afraid her mind might become set.

'You look as if you're in a hurry,' Anne said, when she returned.

He said, 'I'll finish my drink and have one of these pies, and then I'll be off.'

'Will you be coming on Christmas Day?'

He shook his head.

She said, 'Not even for an hour? She can't bear to be parted from you, eh?'

'You know how it is.'

She looked at him angrily. 'How is it that you can't spend time with your own son?'

He couldn't say that Melanie wanted him to be with her on Christmas Day, otherwise she would go away.

Mikey had gone quiet, and was watching them.

She said, 'It has lasted a long time, with this woman. For you.'

'It's going well, yes. We're having a baby, too.'

'I see,' she said, after a while.

'I'm quite pleased,' he said.

Melanie had told a number of her friends that she was pregnant; she discussed it constantly on the phone. Anne was the first person he had told.

'You could have waited.'

'For what?' He said, 'Sorry, I couldn't wait. You know how it is.'

'Why do you keep saying that?'

'It's a fact. There you are. Live with it.'

She said, 'I will, thank you.' Then she said, 'You won't be wanting to see Mikey so much, then.'

'Yes I will.'

'Why should you?'

He said, 'Why shouldn't I?'

'You left us. I only have him. She has everything.'

'Who?'

'Your girlfriend.'

'Listen,' he said. 'I'll see you later.'

He got up and went out into the hall.

At the door the boy held on to the bottom of Alan's coat. 'Stay here for ever and ever amen.'

Alan kissed him. 'I'll be back soon.'

'Sleep in Mummy's bed,' said Mikey.

'You can do that for me.'

Mikey pressed a piece of chocolate into his hand. 'In case you get hungry when I'm asleep.' Then he said, 'I talk to you when you're not here. I talk to you through the floor.'

'And I hear you,' said Alan.

His son was in the window, waving and shouting out. He could see his wife, standing back in the room, watching him go.

He left the house and went to the pub. At the bar he ordered a beer with a chaser. It wasn't until the barman put them in front of him that he remembered he had no money. He apologised and although the barman started to say something, Alan turned and went.

It was cold now. Everything was freezing, the metal of the cars, the sap in the plants, the earth itself. He passed through familiar streets, made unfamiliar by the snow. Many houses were dark; people were starting to go away. As the snow thickened, a rare and unusual silence also fell on the city. He walked faster, swinging his arms inside his coat until he was warm. He thought of the dying man he had met at the door of the school, and of what a terrible thing it was that he hadn't recognised him. He wanted to find the man and say to him, we all grow different and change, every day; it was that, only that. Certainly, no sooner did Alan think he'd understood something of himself than he was changed. That was hope.

From a certain point of view the world was ashes. You could also convert it to dust by burning away all hope, appetite, desire. But to live was, in some sense, to believe in the future. You couldn't keep returning to the same dirty place.

He ran up the steps to the house. The light was on. He knew things would be all right if she were wearing the dressing gown he had given her.

In the kitchen she was heating a quiche and making salad. She looked at him without hostility. Not that she spoke; he didn't either. He watched her, but was determined not to go to her. He believed that if he could cut his desire for her out of himself, he could survive. At the same time he knew that without desire there was nothing.

Sitting there, he thought that he had never before realised that life could be so painful. He understood, too, that no amount of drink, drugs or meditation could make things better for good. He recalled a phrase from Socrates he had learned at university: 'A good man cannot suffer any evil, either in life or after death.' Wittgenstein, commenting on this, talked of feeling 'absolutely safe'. He would look it up. Maybe there was something in it for him, some final 'inner safety'.

They changed into their night clothes and at last got into his favourite place, their bed. Opening her dressing gown he put his hand on her stomach and caressed her. For a short while she lay in his arms as he touched her. Then she touched him a little, before turning over and falling asleep.

He started to think of his sleeping son, as he always did at this time, wondering if Mikey had woken up and was talking to him 'through the floor'. He wanted to go and kiss his son goodnight, as other fathers did. Perhaps he would have another son, and it would be different. He looked around the room. There wasn't enough space for a wardrobe; their clothes were piled at the end of the bed. On a chair next to him, illuminated by a tilting lamp, was a copy of *Great Expectations*, a bottle of massage oil encrusted with greasy dust, his reading glasses, a glass with a splash of wine in it, and a notebook.

His life and mind had been so busy that the idea of sitting in bed to write in his journal, or even to read, seemed an outlandish luxury, the representation of an impossible peace. But also, that kind of solitude seemed too much like waiting for something to start. He had wanted to be disturbed; and he had been.

He knew their resentments went deep and continued to grow. But he and Melanie were afraid rather than wicked. In their own, clumsy way, they were each fighting to preserve themselves. Love could be torn down in a minute, like taking a stick to a spider's web. But love was an admixture; it never came pure. He knew there was sufficient love and tenderness between them; and that no love should go wasted.

The Penis

Alfie was having breakfast with his wife at the kitchen table.

He couldn't have slept for more than three hours, having been out the previous night. He was a cutter – a hairdresser – and had to get to work. Once there, as well as having to endure the noise and queues of customers, he had to make conversation all day.

'Did you have a good time last night?' his wife asked.

They had got married a year ago in Las Vegas.

'I think so,' he said.

'Where did you go?' She was looking at him. 'Don't you know?'

'I can remember the early part of the evening. We all met in the pub. Then there was a club and a lot of people. Later there was a porn film.'

'Was it good?'

'It wasn't human. It was like a butcher's shop. After that . . . it gets a little vague.'

His wife looked at him in surprise.

'That's never happened before. You always like to tell me what you've been doing. I hope it's not the start of something.'

'It's not,' said Alfie. 'Wait a minute. I'll tell you what I did.'

He pulled his jacket from where he had left it, over the back of a chair.

He would examine his wallet and see how much money he had spent, whether he had any cocaine left, or if he had collected phone numbers, business cards or taxi receipts that might jog his memory.

He was fumbling in his inside pocket when he found something strange.

He pulled it out.

'What's that?' his wife said. She came closer. 'It's a penis,' she said. 'You've come home with a man's penis – complete with balls and pubic hair – in your pocket. Where did you get it?'

'I don't know,' he said.

'You better tell me,' she said.

He put it down on the table.

'I don't make a habit of picking up stray penises.' He added, 'It's not erect.'

'Suppose it does start to get hard? It's big enough as it is.' She looked more closely. 'Bigger than yours. Bigger than most I've seen.'

'That's enough,' he said hurriedly. 'I don't think we should keep looking at it. Let's wrap it in something. Get some kitchen roll and a plastic bag.'

When it wriggled they were both staring at it.

'Get that thing off my kitchen table!' she said. She was about to become hysterical. 'My mother's coming for lunch! Get it out of here!'

'I think I will do that,' he said.

A few minutes later, to his surprise, he was walking down the street with a penis in his pocket.

His instinct was to drop it in a dustbin and go straight to work, but after a few minutes' consideration he thought he would take it to an artist whose hair he cut, a sculptor who usually worked in faeces and blood. The sculptor used to work in body parts, but had got into trouble with the authorities. Nevertheless, he might find the opportunity to work with a penis irresistible. The art dealers, who yearned for more and more horrible effects, would be fascinated. Alfie would get paid. His wife had told him that he should become more 'business-minded'. More than anything she wanted him to appear on television.

Alfie was heading in the direction of his friend's house when he saw a policeman walking towards him. Quickly, he pulled the wrapped penis out of his pocket and let it fall to the ground. People threw litter down all the time. It wasn't a serious crime.

He had scarcely gone a few more yards when a schoolgirl ran up behind him, waving the bag and telling him he had dropped his breakfast. Thanking her, he stuffed it back in his pocket.

His teeth were chattering. He didn't want the 'thing' in his pocket one more second.

He turned a corner and found himself crossing the river. Making sure no one was watching, he tossed the penis over the side of the bridge and watched it fall.

Then he noticed that under the bridge a passing cruiser was taking tourists down the river. A voice was commenting through a megaphone: 'On the left we can see . . . and on your right there is a particularly interesting historic monument.'

Meanwhile, the penis, coming loose from its covering, was hurtling towards the upper deck.

Alfie fled.

Less than a mile away, Doug, an actor, got out of bed and strolled into his new bathroom. He was in his early forties, but looked superb.

The next day he was about to start work on the biggest film of his life. It was a costume drama, a classy production, which meant he didn't have to take his prick out of his breeches until the tenth minute. The director was excellent and Doug had chosen his female co-stars himself, for their talent as well as their size. Doug had intended to spend the day in the gym. After he would get his hair and nails done, before retiring early to bed with the script.

It wasn't until he passed the mirror on the way to the shower, and looked at himself for the first time that day, that he realised his penis was missing. The whole thing had gone, penis, scrotum, even his pubic hair.

Doug thought he might faint. He sat on the edge of the bath with his head between his legs, but the position only reminded him of his loss.

He had been 'in' pornography since he was a teenager, but recently the market had started to boom. Pornography had penetrated the middlebrow market and he, coupled with Long Dong – the professional moniker he had given his penis – was becoming a recognisable star.

Doug had appeared on TV chat shows and in mainstream magazines and newspapers. He believed he was entitled to the gratitude and respect that comedians, singers and political impersonators received. After all, distracting the fickle public was arduous and required talent and charm. Uniquely, Doug offered that which most people never saw: the opportunity to witness others copulating; fascination and intoxication through the eyes.

Many men envied Doug his work and some had even attempted it. How many of them could keep it up, under hot lights and with a film crew around them, for hours on end, year after year? Doug could sustain an erection all day and sing something from *Don Giovanni* while checking his shares in the *Financial Times*. Hadn't hundreds of thousands of people witnessed his stick of rock and the jets of gushing, blossoming jissom that flew across his co-stars' faces?

If he lost his manhood, his livelihood would go with it.

Thinking fast now, Doug conjectured whether, late at night, he had taken Long Dong out somewhere and slapped it down on a table. In bars and at parties, all over the world, the public loved asking questions about his work. Like most stars, he adored answering them. At some point someone, usually a woman, asked to see Long Dong. If the time and place was right – Doug had learned to be wary of making the men envious and causing friction between couples – he would let them peek. The 'eighth wonder of the world', he called it.

However, he had never mislaid his greatest asset before – his only asset, some people said.

Doug went to the bars and clubs he had visited the previous night. They were being cleaned; the chairs were upended on the tables and the light was bright. Someone had left behind a shoe, a shotgun, a pair of false eyelashes and a map of China. No penis had been handed in.

Bewildered, he was standing outside on the street when, across the road, he saw his penis coming out of a coffee shop accompanied by a couple of young women. The penis, tall, erect and wearing dark glasses and a fine black jacket, was smiling.

'Hey!' called Doug as his penis stepped into a cab, politely letting the women go first.

Doug hailed another taxi and told the driver to follow the first one. In front he could see the top of his penis. The girls were kissing him and he was laughing and talking excitedly.

The traffic was bad and they lost sight of the cab ahead.

After driving around, Doug decided to go into a bar and consider what to do. He was furious with his penis for flaunting itself round town like this.

He had ordered a drink when the barman said, 'If it's quiet in here it's because that penis from all the films has gone into a bar along the road.'

'Is that right?' said Doug, jumping up. 'Where?'

The barman gave him directions.

A few minutes later he was there. By now it was lunchtime and the place was so crowded Doug could hardly get through the door.

'What's going on here?' he asked.

'Long Dong's arrived,' said a man from a TV crew. 'I've seen all his films – at a friend's house, of course. *Dickhead* is my favourite. The big guy's a star.'

'Is that right?' said Doug.

'Are you a fan?'

'Not at the moment.'

Doug tried to push through the crowd but the women wouldn't let him through. At last he scrambled onto a chair and spotted his penis standing at the bar, accepting drinks, signing autographs and answering questions like a true professional.

'You people have put me where I am today,' he was saying, grandly. 'I feel I should repay you all. What are you drinking?'

Everyone cheered and called out their orders.

'What about me!' shouted Doug. 'Who made you?'

At this Long Dong looked up and caught the eye of his owner. Quickly he made his apologies – and bolted. By the time Doug had shoved his way through the crowd, the penis had disappeared. Doug ran out into the street, but there was no sign of it.

All day, everywhere he went, he heard stories of the remarkable penis, not only of its size and strength, but of its warm way with strangers.

The one person Doug did run into was Alfie, drinking alone in the dark corner of an unpopular bar. Alfie was distraught, convinced the police were pursuing him not only for stealing a penis and trying to sell it, but for dropping it on the head of a Japanese tourist passing beneath Tower Bridge on a pleasure cruiser.

'I recognise you from somewhere,' said Doug.

'Yes, yes,' said Alfie. 'Maybe. I have the feeling we were together last night.'

'What were we doing?'

'Who knows? Listen –'

Alfie explained that he felt terrible about the whole business. If Doug ever wanted a free haircut, he'd be very welcome. He even offered to give him one immediately.

'Another time,' said Doug.

He didn't have time now to consider such things. He had embarked on the search of his life.

'Just let me know when you want a trim,' said Alfie. 'The offer will always be open.'

It wasn't until the evening, wandering about the city at random, that Doug caught sight of his penis again, this time sitting in a workman's caff. It was in disguise by now, with a hat pulled down over its head and its collar up. Doug could see it was suffering from celebrity fatigue and wanted to be alone.

Doug slid into the seat beside it. 'Got you,' he said.

'Took you long enough,' said the penis. 'What do you want?'

Doug said, 'What do you think you're playing at – making an exhibition of yourself in this way?'

'Why shouldn't I?'

'We've got to take it slowly. If there's one thing that makes everyone nervous, it's a big fat happy thing like you.'

'I've had enough of your nonsense,' said the penis.

'Without me, you're nothing,' said Doug.

'Ha! It's the other way round! I've realised the truth.'

'What truth?'

'You are a penis with a man attached. I want out.'

'Out where?'

'I'm going solo. I've been exploited for years. I want my own career. I'm going to make more serious films.'

Doug said, 'Serious films! We're starting the follow-up to *Little Women* tomorrow – *Huge Big Women*, it's called.'

'I want to play Hamlet,' said the penis. 'No one has quite understood the relationship with Ophelia. You could be my assistant. You could carry my script and keep the fans away.'

Doug said, 'You mean, we won't be physically attached ever again?'

The penis said, 'I would be prepared to come back under your management, as I quite like you. But if I do, the arrangement would have to be different. I would have to be attached to your face.'

Doug said, 'Where on my face exactly would you like to be attached? Behind my ear?'

'Where your nose is now. I want to be recognised, like other stars.'

'You'll get sick of it,' warned Doug. 'They all do, and go crazy.'

'That's up to me,' said Long Dong. 'There will be cures I can take.'

The penis took a sausage from the plate in front of him and held it in the middle of Doug's face.

'It would be like that, only bigger. Cosmetic surgery is developing. In the future there'll be all kinds of novel arrangements. What do you say to being a trendsetter?'

'What of my scrotum? It would . . . ahem . . . hang over my mouth.'

'I'd do the talking. I'll give you an hour to decide,' said the penis, haughtily. 'I'm expecting other offers from agents and producers.'

Doug could see that Long Dong was beginning to shrink back into himself. It had been a fatiguing day. When at last his eyes closed, Doug picked the penis up, popped it into his pocket and buttoned it down.

Doug rushed across town to see a cosmetic surgeon he knew, a greedy man with a face as smooth as a plastic ball. He had remade many of Doug's colleagues, inserting extensions into the men's penises, and enlarging the breasts, lips and buttocks of his female colleagues. Few of these actors would even be recognised by their parents.

The surgeon was at dinner with several former clients. Doug interrupted him and they walked in the surgeon's beautiful garden. Doug laid the sleeping penis in the surgeon's hand.

He explained what had happened and said, 'It's got to be sewn on tonight.'

The surgeon passed it back.

He said, 'I've extended dicks and clits. I've implanted diamonds in guys' balls and put lights in people's heads. I've never sewn a penis back on. You could die on the table. You might sue me. I'd have to be recompensed.'

As the objections continued, Doug begged the man to restore him. At last, the surgeon named a sum. That was almost the worst blow of the day. Doug had been well paid over the years, but sex money, like drug money, tended to melt like snow.

'Bring me the money tonight,' ordered the surgeon, 'otherwise it will be too late – your penis will become used to its freedom and will never serve you again.'

The only person Doug knew with such a large sum of cash was the producer of *Huge Big Women* who was, that night, entertaining a few hookers in his suite. The women knew Doug and soon made him aware that news of his misfortune had got round. He blushed and smarted now when the women called him 'big boy'.

To Doug's relief, the producer agreed to give him the cash. Handing it over, he mentioned the interest. It was a massive sum, which would rise daily, as Doug's penis would have to. The man made Doug sign a contract, pledging to make films for what seemed like the rest of his life.

Travelling back to the surgeon, Doug considered what life might be like without his penis. Perhaps he had been mercifully untied from an idiot and they could go their separate ways. But without his penis how could he earn his living? He was too old to start a new career.

The surgeon worked all night.

Next morning, when Doug woke up, the first thing he did was look down. Like a nervous snake charmer, he whistled an aria from *Don Giovanni*. At last, his penis started to stir, enlarge and grow. Soon it was pointing towards the sun. It was up, but not running. He and his love were rejoined.

A few hours later Doug was on the set. His penis swung between his legs, slapping against each thigh with a satisfying smack.

Doug was glad to be reunited with the most important part of himself; but, when he thought of the numerous exertions ahead, he felt weary.

THE BODY

First published in 2002

The Body

1

He said, 'Listen: you say you can't hear well and your back hurts. Your body won't stop reminding you of your ailing existence. Would you like to do something about it?'

'This half-dead old carcass?' I said. 'Sure. What?'

'How about trading it in and getting something new?'

It was an invitation I couldn't say no to, or yes, for that matter. There was certainly nothing simple or straightforward about it. When I had heard the man's proposal, although I wanted to dismiss it as madness, I couldn't stop considering it. All that night I was excited by an idea that was – and had been for a while, now I was forced to confront it – inevitable.

This 'adventure' started with a party I didn't want to go to.

Though the late 1950s and early 1960s were supposed to be my heyday, I don't like the assault of loud music, and I have come to appreciate silence in its many varieties. I am not crazy about half-raw barbecued food either.

Want to hear about my health? I don't feel particularly ill, but I am in my mid-sixties; my bed is my boat across these final years. My knees and back give me a lot of pain. I have haemorrhoids, an ulcer and cataracts. When I eat, it's not unusual for me to spit out bits of tooth as I go. My ears seem to lose focus as the day goes on and people have to yell into me. I don't go to parties because I don't like to stand up. If I sit down, it makes it difficult for others to speak to me. Not that I am always interested in what they have to say; and if I am bored, I don't want to hang around, which might make me seem abrupt or arrogant.

I have friends in worse shape. If you're lucky, you'll be hearing about them. I do like to drink, but I can do that at home. Fortunately, I'm a cheap drunk. A few glasses and I can understand Lacan.

My wife Margot has been a counsellor for five years, training now to be a therapist. She listens to people for a living, in a room in the house. We have been fortunate; each of us has always envied the other's profession. She has wanted to make from within; I need to hear from without.

Our children have left home, the girl training to be a doctor and the boy working as a film editor. I guess my life has had a happy ending. When my wife, Margot, walks into a room, I want to tell her what I've been thinking, some of which I know she will attend to. Margot, though, enjoys claiming that men start to get particularly bad-tempered, pompous and demanding in late middle age. According to her, we stop thinking that politeness matters; we forget that other people are more important than ourselves. After that, it gets worse.

I'd agree that I'm not a man who has reached some kind of Buddhist plateau. I might have some virtues, such as compassion and occasional kindness; unlike several of my friends, I've never stopped being interested in others, or in culture and politics – in the general traffic of mankind. I have wanted to be a good enough father. Despite their necessary hatred of me at times, I enjoyed the kids and liked their company. So far, I can say I've been a tolerable husband overall. Margot claims I have always written for fame, money and women's affection. I would have to add that I love what I do, too, and it continues to fascinate me. Through my work I think about the world, about what matters to me and to others.

Beside my numerous contradictions – I am, I have been told, at least three different people – I am unstable, too, lost in myself, envious and constantly in need of reassurance. My wife says that I have crazinesses, bewildering moods and 'internal disappearances'

I am not even aware of. I can go into the shower as one man and emerge as another, worse, one. My pupils enlarge, I move around obsessively, I yell and stamp my feet. A few words of criticism and I can bear a grudge for three days at a time, convinced she is plotting against me. None of this has diminished, despite years of self-analysis, therapy and 'writing as healing', as some of my students used to call the attempt to make art. Nothing has cured me of myself, of the self I cling to. If you asked me, I would probably say that my problems are myself; my life is my dilemmas. I'd better enjoy them, then.

I wouldn't have considered attending this party if Margot hadn't gone out to dinner with a group of women friends, and if I hadn't envied what I saw as the intimacy and urgency of their conversation, their pleasure in one another. Men can't be so direct, it seems to me.

But if I stay in alone now, after an hour I am walking about picking things up, putting them down and then searching everywhere for them. I no longer believe or hope that book knowledge will satisfy or even entertain me, and if I watch TV for too long I begin to feel hollow. How out of the world I already believe myself to be! I am no longer familiar with the pop stars, actors or serials on TV. I'm never certain who the pornographic boy and girl bodies belong to. It is like trying to take part in a conversation of which I can only grasp a fraction. As for the politicians, I can barely make out which side they are on. My age, education and experience seem to be no advantage. I imagine that to participate in the world with curiosity and pleasure, to see the point of what is going on, you have to be young and uninformed. Do I want to participate?

On this particular evening, with some semi-senile vacillation and nothing better to do, I showered, put on a white shirt, opened the front door, and trotted out. It was the height of summer and the streets were baking. Although I have lived in London since I was a student, when I open my front door today I am still excited by the thought of what I might see or hear, and by who I might run into and be made to think about. London seems no longer part of Britain – in my view, a dreary, narrow place full of fields, boarded-up shops and cities trying to imitate London – but has developed into a semi-independent city-state, like New York, and has begun to come to terms with the importance of gratification. On the other hand, I had been discussing with Margot the fact that it was impossible to get to the end of the street without people stopping you to ask for money. Normally, I looked so shambolic myself the beggars lost hope even as they held out their hands.

It was a theatre party, given by a friend, a director who also teaches. Some of her drama school pupils would be there, as well as the usual crowd, my friends and acquaintances, those who were still actively alive, not in hospital or away for the summer.

As my doctor had instructed me to take exercise, and still hoping I had the energy of a young man, I decided to walk from west London to the party. After about forty-five minutes I was breathless and feeble. There were no taxis around and I felt stranded on the dusty, mostly deserted streets. I wanted to sit down in a shaded park, but doubted whether I'd be able to get up again, and there was no one to help me. Many of the boozers I'd have dropped into for a pint of bitter and a read of the evening paper, full of local semi-derelicts escaping their families – alcoholics, they'd be called, now everyone has been pathologised – had become bars, bursting with hyperactive young people. I wouldn't have attempted to get past the huge doormen. At times, London appeared to be a city occupied by cameras and security people; you couldn't go through a door without being strip-searched or having your shoes and pockets examined, and all for your own good, though it seemed neither safer nor more dangerous than before. There was no possibility of engaging in those awful pub conversations with wretched strangers which connected you to the impressive singularity of other people's lives. The elderly seem to have been swept from the streets; the young appear to have wires coming out of their heads, supplying either music, voices on the phone or the electricity which makes them move.

Yet I've always walked around London in the afternoons and evenings. These are relatively long distances, and I look at shops, obscure theatres and strange museums, otherwise my body feels clogged up after a morning's desk work.

The party was held not in my friend's flat, but in her rich brother's place, which turned out to be one of those five-floor, wide stucco houses near the zoo.

When at last I got to the door, a handful of kids in their twenties turned up at the same time.

'It's you,' said one, staring. 'We're doing you. You're on the syllabus.'

'I hope I'm not causing you too much discomfort,' I replied.

'We wondered if you might tell us what you were trying to do with –'

'I wish I could remember,' I said. 'Sorry.'

'We heard you were sour and cynical,' murmured another, adding, 'and you don't look anything like your picture on the back of your books.'

My friend whose party it was came to the door, took my arm and led me through the house. Perhaps she thought I might run away. The truth is, these parties make me as anxious now as they did when I was twenty-five. What's worse is knowing that these terrors, destructive of one's pleasures as they are, are not only generated by one's own mind, but are still inexplicable. As you age, the source of your convolutedly self-stymieing behaviour seems almost beyond reach in the past; why, now, would you want to untangle it?

'Don't you just hate the young beautiful ones with their vanity and sentences beginning with the words "when I left Oxford", or "RADA"?' she said, getting me a drink. 'But they're a necessity at any good party. A necessity anywhere anyone fancies a fuck, wouldn't you say?'

'Not that they'd want either of us too close to them,' I said.

'Oh, I don't know,' she said.

She took me out into the garden, where most people had gathered. It was surprisingly large, with both open and wooded areas, and I couldn't see the limits of it. Parts were lit by lanterns hung from trees; other areas were invitingly dark. There was a jazz combo, food, animated conversation and everyone in minimal summer clothing.

I had fetched some food and a drink and was looking for a place to sit when my friend approached me again.

'Adam,' she said. 'Now, don't make a fuss, dear.'

'What is it?'

My heart always sinks when I hear the words 'there's someone who wants to meet you'.

'Who is it?'

I sighed inwardly, and, no doubt, outwardly, when it turned out to be a young man at drama school, a tyro actor. He was standing behind her.

'Would you mind if I sat with you for a bit?' he said. He was going to ask me for a job, I knew it. 'Don't worry, I don't want work.'

I laughed. 'Let's find a bench.'

I wouldn't be curmudgeonly on such a delightful evening. Why shouldn't I listen to an actor? My life has been spent with those who transform themselves in the dark and make a living by calculating the effect they have on others.

My friend, seeing we were okay, left us.

I said, 'I can't stand up for long.'

'May I ask why?'

'A back problem. Only age, in other words.'

He smiled and pointed. 'There's a nice spot over there.'

We walked through the garden to a bench surrounded by bushes where we could look out on the rest of the party.

'Ralph,' he said. I put down my food and we shook hands. He was a beautiful young man, tall, handsome and confident, without seeming immodest. 'I know who you are. Before we talk, let me get us more champagne.'

Whether it was the influence of Ralph, or the luminous, almost supernatural quality that the night seemed to have, I couldn't help noticing how well groomed everyone seemed, particularly the pierced, tattooed young men, as decorated as a jeweller's window, with their hair dyed in contrasting colours. Apart from the gym, these boys must have kept fit twisting and untwisting numerous jars, tubs and bottles. They dressed to show off their bodies rather than their clothes.

One of the pleasures of being a man has been that of watching women dress and undress, paint and unpaint. When it comes to their bodies, women believe they're wearing the inside on the outside. However, the scale of the upkeep, the shop scouring and forethought, the possibilities of judgement, criticism and sartorial inaccuracy as, in contrast, the man splashes water on his face and steps without fear into whatever he can find at the end of the bed and then out into the street, have never been enviable to me.

When Ralph returned and I busied myself eating and looking, he praised my work with enthusiasm and, more importantly, with extensive knowledge, even of its obscurer aspects. He'd seen the films I'd written and many productions of my numerous plays. He'd read my essays, reviews and recently published memoirs *Too Late*. (What a dismal business that final addition and subtraction had been, like writing an interminable will, and nothing to be done about any of it, except to turn and torture it in the hope of a more favourable outlook.) He knew my work well; it seemed to have meant a lot to him. Praise can be a trial; I endured it.

I was about to go to the trouble of standing up to fetch more food when Ralph mentioned an actor who'd played a small part in one of my plays in the early 1970s, and had died of leukaemia soon after.

'Extraordinary actor,' he said. 'With a melancholy we all identified with.'

'He was a good friend,' I said. 'But you wouldn't remember his performance.'

'But I do.'

'How old were you, four?'

'I was right there. In the stalls. I always had the best seats.'

I studied his face as best I could in the available light. There was no doubt that he was in his early twenties.

'You must be mistaken,' I said. 'Is it what you heard? I've been spending time with a friend, someone I consider Britain's finest post-war director. Where is his work now? There can be no record of how it felt to watch a particular production. Even a film of it will yield no idea of the atmosphere, the size, the feeling of the work. Mind you,' I added, 'there are plenty of directors who'd admit that that was a mercy.'

He interrupted. 'I was there, and I wasn't a kid. Adam, do you have a little more time?'

I looked about, recognising many familiar faces, some as wrinkled as old penises. I'd worked and argued with some of these people for more than thirty years. These days, when we met it was less an excited human exchange than a litany of decline; no one would put on our work, and if they did it wasn't sufficiently praised. Such bitterness, more than we were entitled to, was enervating. Or we would talk of grandchildren, hospitals, funerals and memorial services, saying how much we missed so-and-so, wondering, all the while, who would be next, when it would be our turn.

'Okay,' I said. 'Why would I be in a hurry? I was only thinking recently that after a certain age one always seems to be about to go to bed. But it's a relief to be done with success. I can lie down with the electric blanket on, listening to opera and reading badly. What a luxury reading badly can be, or doing anything badly for that matter.'

Two young women had stationed themselves out of earshot, but close enough to observe us, turning occasionally to glance and giggle in our direction. I knew that the face out of which I looked was of no fascination to them.

He leaned towards me. 'It's time I explained myself. Let's say . . . once there was a young man, not the first, who felt like Hamlet. As baffled, as mad and mentally chaotic, and as ruined by his parents. Still, he pulled himself together and became successful, by which I mean he made money doing something necessary but stupid.

Manufacturing toilet rolls, say, or a new kind of tinned soup. He married, and brought up his children.

'In his middle age, as sometimes happens, he felt able to fall in love at last. In his case it was with the theatre. He bought a flat in the West End so he could walk to the theatre every night. He did this for years, but though he loved the gilt, the plush seats, the ice-creams, the post-show discussions in expensive restaurants, it didn't satisfy him. He had begun to realise that he wanted to be an actor, to stand electrified before a large crowd every night. How could anything else fulfil him?

'But he was too old. He couldn't possibly go to drama school, without feeling ridiculous. He was destined to be one of those unlucky people who realise too late what they want to do. A vocation is, after all, the backbone of a life.

'At the same time,' he went on, 'something terrible was happening. His wife, with whom he had been in love, suffered from a degenerative illness that destroyed her body but left her mind unharmed. She was, as she described it, a healthy driver in a car that wouldn't respond, that was deteriorating and would crash, killing her. She said that all she needed was a new body. They tried many treatments in several countries, but in the end she was begging for death. In fact, she asked her husband to take her life. He did not do this, but was considering it when she saved him the trouble.'

'I'm sorry,' I said.

'These days, dying can be a nightmare. People hang on for years, long after they've got anything to talk about.'

He went on, 'The man, who had been looking after his wife for ten years, retired and went on a trip to recuperate. However, he didn't feel that he had long to live. He was exhausted, old and impotent. He was preparing for death too.

'One day, in South America, where he knew other wealthy but somewhat dreary people, he heard a fantastic story from a young man he trusted, a doctor who, like him, was interested in the theatre, in culture. Together – can you imagine? – they put on an amateur production of *Endgame*. This doctor was moved by the old man's wish for something unattainable. He confided in him, saying that an amazing thing was taking place. Certain old, rich men and women were having their living brains removed and transplanted into the bodies of the young dead.'

Ralph became quiet here, as if he needed to know my reaction before he could continue.

I said, 'It seems logical that technology and medical capability only need to catch up with the human imagination or will. I know nothing about science, but isn't this usually the way?'

Ralph went on, 'These people might not exactly live for ever, but they would become young again. They could be twenty-year-olds if they wanted. They could live the lives they believed they'd missed out on. They could do what everybody dreams of, have a second chance.'

I murmured, 'After a bit you realise there's only one invaluable commodity. Not gold or love, but time.'

'Who hasn't asked: why can't I be someone else? Who, really, wouldn't want to live again, given the chance?'

'I'm not convinced of that,' I said. 'Please continue. Were there people you met who had done this?'

'Yes.'

'What were they like?'

'Make up your own mind.' I turned to him again. 'Go on,' he said. 'Have a good stare.' He leaned into the light in order to let me see him. 'Touch me if you want.'

'It's all right,' I said, prissily, after stroking his cheek, which felt like the flesh of any other young man. 'Go on.'

'I have followed your life from the beginning, in parallel to my own. I've spotted you in restaurants, even asked for your autograph. You have spoken my thoughts. My audition speech at drama school was a piece by you. Adam, I am older than you.'

'This conversation is difficult to believe,' I said. 'Still, I always enjoyed fairy stories.'

He continued, 'As I told you, I had made money but my time was running out. You know better than me, an actor walks into a

room and immediately you see – it's all you see – he's too old for
the part. Yet one's store of desire doesn't diminish with age, with
many it increases; the means to fulfil it become weakened. I didn't
want a trim stomach, woven hair or less baggy eyes, or any of
those . . . trivial repairs.' Here he laughed. It was the first time he
hadn't seemed earnest. 'What I wanted was another twenty years,
at least, of health and youth. I had the operation.'

'You had your brain removed . . . to become a younger man?'

'What I am saying sounds deranged. It is unbelievable.'

'Let us pretend, for the sake of this enjoyable fantasy, that it
really is true. How does it work?'

He said the procedure was terrifying, but physically not as awful
as open-heart surgery, which we'd both had. When you come
round from the anaesthetic in this case, you feel fit and optimistic.
'Ready to jump and run', as he put it. The operation wasn't exactly
common yet. There were only a handful of surgeons who could do
it. The procedure had been done hundreds of times, perhaps a
thousand, he didn't know the exact figure, in the last five years. But
it was still, as far as he knew, a secret. Now was the time to have it,
at the beginning, before there was a rush; when it was still in everyone's interest to keep the secret.

He went on to say that there were certain people whom he
believed needed more time on earth, for whom the benefit to
mankind could be immense. To this, I replied that although I
didn't know him, it was his mildness that struck me. He didn't
seem the type to lead some kind of master-race. He wasn't Stalin,
Pol Pot or even Mother Teresa returning for another fifty years.

'That's right,' he said. 'Needless to say, I don't include myself in
this. I had children and I worked hard. I needed another life in
order to catch up on my sleep. If I'm back, it's for the crack!'

I asked, 'If you really were one of these women or men, what
would you want to do with your new time?'

'For years, all I've wanted is to play Hamlet. Not as a seventy-
year-old but as a kid. That is what I'm going to do,' he said. 'At
drama school, first. It's already been cast and I've got the part. I've

known the lines for years. In my various factories, I'd walk about, speaking the verse, to keep sane.'

'I hope you don't mind me pointing this out, but what's wrong with Lear or Prospero?'

'I will approach those pinnacles eventually. Adam, I can do anything now, anything!'

I said, 'Is that what you are intending to do after you've played Hamlet?'

'I will continue as an actor, which I love. Adam, I have money, experience, health and some intelligence. I've got the friends I want. The young people at the school, they're full of enthusiasm and ardour. Something you wrote influenced me. You said that unlike films, plays don't take place in the past. The fear, anxiety and skill of the actors is happening now, in front of you. If performing is risky, we identify with the possibility of grandeur and disaster. I want that. I can tell you that what has happened to me is an innovation in the history of humankind. How about joining me?'

I was giggling. 'I'm no saint, only a scribbler with an interest, sometimes, in how people use one another. I don't feel entitled to another go at life on the basis of my "nobility".'

'You're creative, contrary and articulate,' he said. 'And, in my opinion, you've only just started to develop as an artist.'

'Jesus, and I thought I'd had my say.'

'You deserve to evolve. Meet me tomorrow morning.' As he picked up his plate and glass from the floor, the two observing women, who had not lost patience, began to flutter. 'We'll take it further then.'

He touched me on the arm, named a place and got up.

'What's the rush?' I said. 'Can't we meet in a few days?'

'There is the security aspect,' he said. 'But I also believe the best decisions are taken immediately.'

'I believe that too,' I said. 'But I don't know about this.'

'Dream on it,' he said. 'You've heard enough for one evening. It would be too much for anyone to take in. See you tomorrow. It's getting late. I really want to dance. I can dance all night, without stimulants.'

He pressed my hand, looked into my eyes as if we already had an understanding, and walked away.

The conversation had ended abruptly but not impolitely. Perhaps he had said all there was to say for the moment. He had certainly left me wanting to know more. Hadn't I, like everyone else, often thought of how I'd live had I known all that I know now? But wasn't it a ridiculous idea? If anything made life and feeling possible, it was transience.

I watched Ralph join a group of drama students, his 'contemporaries'. Like him, presumably, but unlike me, they didn't think of their own death every day.

I got up and briefly talked to my friends – the old fucks with watery eyes; some of them quite shrunken, their best work long done – finished my drink, and said goodbye to the host.

At the door, when I looked back, Ralph was dancing with a group of young people among whom were the two women who'd been watching him. Walking through the house, I saw the kids I'd met at the front door sitting at a long table drinking, playing with one another's hair. I was sure I could hear someone saying they preferred the book to the film, or was it the film to the book? Suddenly, I longed for a new world, one in which no one compared the book to the film, or vice versa. Ever.

In order to think, I walked home, but this time I didn't feel tired. As I went I was aware of groups of young men and women hanging around the streets. The boys, in long coats and hoods that concealed most of their faces, made me think of figures from *The Seventh Seal*. They made me recall my best friend's painful death, two months before.

'It won't be the same without me around,' he had said. We had known each other since university. He was a bad alcoholic and fuck-up. 'Look at your life and all you've done. I've wasted my life.'

'I don't know what waste means.'

'Oh, I know what it is now,' he had said. 'The inability to take pleasure in oneself or others. Cheerio.'

The chess pieces of my life were being removed one by one. My friend's death had taken me by surprise; I had believed he would never give up his suffering. The end of my life was approaching, too; there was a lot I was already unable to do, soon there would be more. I'd been alive a long time but my life, like most lives, seemed to have happened too quickly, when I was not ready.

The shouts of the street kids, their incomprehensibly hip vocabulary and threatening presence reminded me of how much the needs of the young terrify the old. Maybe it would be interesting to know what they felt. I'm sure they would be willing to talk. But there was no way, until now, that I could actually have 'had' their feelings.

At home, I looked at myself in the mirror. Margot had said that with my rotund stomach, veiny, spindly legs and left-leaning posture I was beginning to resemble my father just before his death. Did that matter? What did I think a younger body would bring me? More love? Even I knew that that wasn't what I required as much as the ability to love more.

I waited up for my wife, watched her undress and followed her instruction to sit in the bathroom as she bathed by candle-light, attending to her account of the day and – the highlight for me – who had annoyed her the most. She and I also liked to discuss our chocolate indulgences and bodies: which part of which of us, for example, seemed full of ice-cream and was expanding. Various diets and possible types of exercise were always popular between us. She liked to accuse me of not being 'toned', of being, in fact, 'mush', but threatened murder and suicide if I mentioned any of her body parts without reverence. As I looked at her with her hair up, wearing a dressing gown and examining and cleaning her face in the mirror, I wondered how many more such ordinary nights we would have together.

A few minutes after getting into bed, she was slipping into sleep. I resented her ability to drop off. Although sleeping had come to seem more luxurious, I hadn't got any better at it. I guess children and older adults fear the separation from consciousness, as though it'll never return. If anyone asked me, I said that consciousness was the thing I liked most about life. But who doesn't need a rest from it now and again?

Lying beside Margot, chatting and sleeping, was exceptional every night. To be well married you have to have a penchant for the intricacies of intimacy and larval change: to be interested, for instance, in people dreaming together. If the personality is a spider's web, you will want to know every thread. Otherwise, after forty, when the colour begins to drain from the world, it's either retirement or reinvention. Pleasures no longer come to you, but there are pickings to be had if you can learn to scavenge for them.

Later, unusually – it had been a long time – she woke me up to make love, which I did happily, telling her that I'd always loved her, and reminiscing, as we often did, about how we met and got together. These were our favourite stories, always the same and also slightly different so that I listened out for a new feeling or aspect.

For the rest of the night I was awake, walking about the house, wondering.

2

The following morning there was no question of not meeting Ralph at the coffee shop he'd suggested. At the same time I didn't believe he'd show up; perhaps that was my wish. He had made me think so hard, the scope of my everyday life seemed so mundane and I had become so excited about this possible adventure and future that I was already beginning to feel afraid.

He arrived on a bicycle, wearing few clothes, and told me he'd stayed up late dancing, woken up early, exercised and studied a 'dramatic text' before coming here. It was common, he said, that people living a 'second' life, like people on a second marriage, took what they did more seriously. Each moment seemed even more precious. There was no doubt he looked fit, well and ready to be interested in things.

I found myself studying his face. How should I put it? If the body is a picture of the mind, his body was like a map of a place that didn't exist. What I wanted was to see his original face, before he was reborn. Otherwise it was like speaking on the phone to someone you'd never met, trying to guess what they were really like.

But it was me, not him, we were there for, and he was businesslike, as I guessed he must have been in his former life. He went through everything as though reading from a clipboard in his mind. After two hours we shook hands, and I returned home.

Margot and I always talked and bickered over lunch together, soup and bread, or salad and sandwiches, before our afternoon nap on separate sofas. Today, I had to tell her I was going away.

Earlier in the year Margot had gone to Australia for two months to visit friends and travel. We needed each other, Margot and I, but we didn't want to turn our marriage into more of an enclosure than necessary. We had agreed that I, too, could go on 'walkabout' if I wanted to. (Apparently, 'walkabout' was called 'the dreaming' by some Aboriginals.) I told her I wanted to leave in three days' time. I asked for 'a six-month sabbatical'. As well as being upset by the suddenness of my decision, she was shocked and hurt by the length of time I required. She and I are always pleased to part, but then, after a few days, we need to share our complaints. I guess that was how we knew our marriage was still alive. Yet she knew that when I make up my mind, I enter a tunnel of determination, for fear that vacillation is never far away.

She said, 'Without you here to talk about yourself in bed, how will I go to sleep?'

'At least I am some use, then.'

She acquiesced because she was kind. She didn't believe I'd last six months. In a few weeks I'd be bored and tired. How could anyone be as interested in my ailments as her?

It took me less time than I would have hoped to settle my affairs before the 'trip'. I had a circle of male friends who came to the house once a fortnight to drink, watch football and discuss the miseries of our work. Margot would inform them I was going walkabout and we would reconvene on my return. I made the necessary financial arrangements through my lawyer, and followed the other preparations Ralph had insisted on.

When Ralph and I met up again he took one look at me and said, 'You're my first initiate. I'm delighted that you're doing this. You live your life trying to find out how to live a life, and then it ends. I don't think I could have picked a better person.'

'Initiate?'

'I've been waiting for the right person to follow me down this path, and it's someone as distinguished as you!'

'I need to see what this will bring me,' I murmured, mostly to myself.

'The face you have must have brought you plenty,' he said. 'Didn't you see those girls watching you at the party? They asked me later if you were really you.'

'They did?'

'Now – ready?'

He was already walking to his car. I followed. Ralph was so solicitous and optimistic, I felt as comfortable as anyone could in the circumstances. Then I began to look forward to 'the change' and fantasised about all that I would do in my new skin.

By now we'd arrived at the 'hospital', a run-down warehouse on a bleak, wind-blown industrial estate outside London (he had already explained that 'things would not be as they seemed'). I noticed from the size of the fence and the number of black-uniformed men that security was tight. Ralph and I showed our passports at the door. We were both searched.

Inside, the place did resemble a small, expensive private hospital. The walls, sofas and pictures were pastel-coloured and the building seemed almost silent, as if it had monumental walls. There were no patients moving about, no visitors with flowers, books and fruit, only the occasional doctor and nurse. When I did glimpse, at the far end of a corridor, a withered old woman in a pink flannel night-gown being pushed in a wheelchair by an orderly, Ralph and I were rapidly ushered into a side office.

Immediately, the surgeon came into the room, a man in his mid-thirties who seemed so serene I could only wonder what kind of yoga or therapy he had had, and for how long.

His assistant ensured the paperwork was rapidly taken care of, and I wrote a cheque. It was for a considerable amount, money that would otherwise have gone to my children. I hoped scarcity would make them inventive and vital. My wife was already provided for. What was bothering me? I couldn't stop suspecting that this was a confidence trick, that I'd been made a fool of in my most vulnerable areas: my vanity and fear of decline and death. But if it was a hoax, it was a laboured one, and I would have parted with money to hear about it.

The surgeon said, 'We are delighted to have an artist of your calibre join us.'

'Thank you.'

'Have you done anything I might have heard of?'

'I doubt it.'

'I think my wife saw one of your plays. She loves comedy and now has the leisure to enjoy herself. Ralph has told me that it's a short-term body rental you require, initially? The six-months minimum – is that correct?'

'That is correct,' I said. 'After six months I'll be happy to return to myself again.'

'I have to warn you, not everyone wants to go back.'

'I will. I am fascinated by this experiment and want to be involved, but I'm not particularly unhappy with my life.'

'You might be unhappy with your death.'

'Not necessarily.'

He countered, 'I wouldn't leave it until you're on your death-bed to find out. Some people, you know, lose the power of speech then. Or it is too late for all kinds of other reasons.'

'You're suggesting I won't want to return to myself?'

'It's impossible for either of us to predict how you will feel in six months' time.'

I nodded.

He noticed me looking at him. 'You are wondering if –'

'Of course.'

'I am,' he replied, glancing at Ralph. 'We both are. Newbodies.'

'And ordinary people going about their business out there' – I pointed somewhere into the distance – 'are called Oldbodies?'

'Perhaps. Yes. Why not?'

'These are words that will eventually be part of most people's everyday vocabulary, you think?'

'Words are your living,' he said. 'Bodies are mine. But I would imagine so.'

'The existence of Newbodies, as you call them, will create considerable confusion, won't it? How will we know who is new and who old?'

'The thinking in this area has yet to be done,' he said. 'Just as there has been argument over abortion, genetic engineering, cloning and organ transplants, or any other medical advances, so there will be over this.'

'Surely this is of a different order,' I said. 'Parents the same age as their children, or even younger, for instance. What will that mean?'

'That is for the philosophers, priests, poets and television pundits to say. My work is only to extend life.'

'As an educated man, you must have thought this over.'

'How could I work out the implications alone? They can only be lived.'

'But –'

We batted this subject back and forth until it became clear even to me that I was playing for time.

'I was just thinking . . .' said Ralph. He was smiling. 'If I were dead we wouldn't be having this conversation.'

The doctor said, 'Adam's is a necessary equivocation.' He turned to me. 'You have to make a second important decision.'

I guessed this was coming. 'It won't be so difficult, I hope.'

'Please, follow me.'

The doctor, accompanied by a porter and a young nurse, took me and Ralph down several corridors and through several locked doors. At last we entered what seemed like a broad, low-ceilinged, neon-lit fridge with a tiled floor.

I was shivering as I stood there, and not only because of the temperature. Ralph took my arm and began to murmur in my ear, but I couldn't hear him. What I saw was unlike anything I had seen before; indeed, unlike anything anyone had ever seen. This was no longer amusing speculation or inquisitiveness. It was where the new world began.

'Where do you get them?' I asked. 'The bodies.'

'They're young people who have, unfortunately, passed away,' said the doctor.

Stupidly, I said, as though I were looking at the result of a massacre, 'All at once?'

'At different times, naturally. And in different parts of the world. They're transported in the same way as organs are now. That's not difficult to do.'

'What is difficult about this process now?'

'It takes time and great expertise. But so does cleaning a great painting. The right person has to do it. There are not many of those people yet. But it can be done. It is, of course, something that was always going to happen.'

Suspended in harnesses, there were rows and rows of bodies: the pale, the dark and the in-between; the mottled, the clear-skinned, the hairy and the hairless, the bearded and the large-breasted; the tall, the broad and the squat. Each had a number in a plastic wallet above the head. Some looked awkward, as though they were asleep, with their heads lolling slightly to one side, their legs at different angles. Others looked as though they were about to go for a run. All the bodies, as far as I could see, were relatively young; some of them looked less like young adults than older children. The oldest were in their early forties. I was reminded of the rows of suits in the tailors I'd visit as a boy with my father. Except these were not cloth coverings but human bodies, born alive from between a woman's legs.

'Why don't you browse?' said the surgeon, leaving me with the nurse. 'Choose a short list, perhaps. Write down the numbers you fancy. We can discuss your choices. This is the part I enjoy. You know what I like to do? Guess in advance who I think the person will choose, and wait to see whether I am right. Often I am.'

Shopping for bodies: it was true that I had some idea what I was looking for. I knew, for instance, that I didn't want to be a fair, blue-eyed blond. People might consider me a beautiful fool.

'Can I suggest something?' said Ralph. 'You might, for a change, want to come back as a young woman.'

I said, 'A change is as good as a rest, as my mother used to say.'

'Some men want to give birth. Or they want to have sex as a woman. You do have one of your male characters say that in his sexual fantasies he's always a woman.'

'Yes . . . I see what you mean . . .'

'Or you could choose a black body. There's a few of those,' he said with an ironic sniff. 'Think how much you'd learn about society and . . . all that.'

'Yes,' I said. 'But couldn't I just read a novel about it?'

'Whatever. All I want is for you to know that there are options. Take your time. The race, gender, size and age you prefer can only be your choice. I would say that in my view people aren't able to give these things enough thought. They take it for granted that tough guys have all the fun. Still, you could give another body a run-out in six months. Or are you particularly attached to your identity?'

'It never occurred to me not to be.'

He said, 'One learns that identities are good for some things but not for others. Here.'

'Jesus. Thanks.'

I took the bag but wasn't sick. I did want to get out of that room. It was worse than a mortuary. These bodies would be reanimated. The consequences were unimaginable. Every type of human being, apart from the old, seemed available. The young must have been dying in droves; maybe they were being killed. I would make a good but expeditious choice and leave.

When the others fell back discreetly I walked beside this stationary army of the dead, this warehouse of the lost, examining their faces and naked bodies. I looked, as one might look too long at a painting, until its value – the value of life – seemed to evaporate, existing only as a moment of embodied frustration between two eternities. Then I began to think of poetry and children and the early morning, until it came back to me, why I wanted to go on living and why it might, at times, seem worth it.

I considered several bodies but kept moving, hoping for something better. At last, I stopped. I had seen 'my guy'. Or rather, he had seemed to choose me. Stocky and as classically handsome as any sculpture in the British Museum, he was neither white nor dark but lightly toasted, with a fine, thick penis and heavy balls. I would, at last, have the body of an Italian footballer: an aggressive, attacking midfielder, say. My face resembled that of the young Alain Delon with, naturally, my own brain leading this combination out to play for six months.

'That's him,' I said, across the lines of bodies. 'My man. He looks fine. We like each other.'

'Do you want to see his eyes?' said the nurse, who'd been waiting by the door. 'You'd better.'

'Why not?'

'Look, then,' she said.

She prised open my man's eyelids. The room was scrupulously odourless, but as I moved closer to him I detected an antiseptic whiff. However, I liked him already. For the first time, I would have dark brown eyes.

'Lovely.' I considered patting him on the head, but realised he would be cold. I said to him. 'See you later, pal.'

On the way out, I noticed another heavy, locked door. 'Are there more in there? Is that where they keep the second-division players?'

'That's where they keep the old bodies,' she said. 'Your last facility will be in there.'

'Facility?' I asked. The necessity for euphemism always alerted me to hidden fears.

'The body you're wearing at the moment.'

'Right. But only for a bit.'

'For a bit,' she repeated.

'No harm will come to it in there, will it?'

'How could it?'

'You won't sell it?'

'Er . . . why should we?' She added, 'No disrespect intended. If, after six months, you change your mind, or you just don't turn up, we will nullify the facility, of course.'

'Right. But I would like to see where I'm going to be hanging out – or up, rather.'

I moved towards the door of this room. The porter barred my way with his strong arm.

The nurse said, 'Confidential.'

Ralph intervened. 'It's unlikely, Adam, but you might know the people. Some say they're emigrating, others "seem" to have died. Others have disappeared, but they come here and re-emerge as Newbodies.'

'How much of this "coming and going" is there about?' I asked.

Ralph didn't reply. I felt myself becoming annoyed.

I said, 'It is curious, inquisitive types like me you claimed you wanted as "initiates". Now you won't answer my questions.'

'Be a patient patient. Soon you'll have as much time on your hands as you could want. You will come to understand much more then.' He embraced me. 'I'll leave you now. I will visit you when it's done.'

'I'll feel like a new man.'

'That's right.'

I was put into bed then, in my room, and examined by the doctor and his assistant. The doctor was whistling, and I closed my eyes. My body had already become just an object to be worked on. I imagined my new body being taken from its rack and prepared in another room.

After a while, the doctor said, 'We're ready to go ahead now. You made a good choice. Your new facility has almost been picked out a few times now. He's been waiting a while for his outing. I'm glad his day has finally come.'

In so far as it was possible, I had got used to the idea that I might die under the anaesthetic, that these might be my last moments on earth. The faces of my children as babies floated before me as I went under. This time, though, I was afraid in a new way: not only of death, but of what might come out of it – new life. How would I feel? Who would I be?

3

A theory-loving friend of mine has an idea that the notion of the self, of the separate, self-conscious individual, and of any auto-biography which that self might tell or write, developed around the same time as the invention of the mirror, first made en masse in Venice in the early sixteenth century. When people could con-sider their own faces, expressions of emotion and bodies for a sus-tained period, they could wonder who they were and how they were different from and similar to others.

My children, around the age of two, became fascinated by their own images in the looking-glass. Later, I can remember my son, aged six, clambering onto a chair and then onto the dining table in order to see himself in the mirror over the fireplace, kissing his fin-gers and saying, as he adjusted his top hat, 'Masterpiece! What a lucky man you are, to have such a good-looking son!' Later, of course, they and their mirrors were inseparable. As I said to them: make the most of it, there'll be a time when you won't be able to look at yourself without flinching.

According to my friend, if a creature can't see himself, he can't mature. He can't see where he ends and others begin. This process can be aided by hanging a mirror in an animal's cage.

Still only semi-conscious, I began to move. I found I could stand. I stood in front of the full-length mirror in my room, look-ing at myself – or whoever I was now – for a long time. I noticed that other mirrors had been provided. I adjusted them until I obtained an all-round view. In these mirrors I seemed to have been cloned as well as transformed. Everywhere I turned there were more mes, many, many more new mes, until I felt dizzy. I sat, lay down, jumped up and down, touched myself, wiggled my fingers and toes, shook my arms and legs and, finally, placed my head carefully on the floor before kicking myself up and standing on it – something I hadn't done for twenty-five years. There was a lot to take in.

It was a while ago, in my early fifties, that I began to lose my physical vanity, such as it was. I've been told that as a young man I was attractive to some people; I spent more time combing my hair than I did doing equations. Certainly I took it for granted that, at least, people wouldn't be repelled by my appearance. As a child, I lived among open fields and streams, and ran and explored all day. For the past few years, however, I have been plump and bald; my heart condition has given me a continuously damp upper lip. By forty I was faced with the dilemma of whether my belt should go over or under my stomach. Before my children advised me against it, I became, for a while, one of those men whose trousers went up to their chest.

When I first became aware of my deterioration, having had it pointed out by a disappointed lover, I dyed my hair and even signed on at a gym. Soon I was so hungry I ate even fruit. It didn't take me long to realise there are few things more risible than middle-aged narcissism. I knew the game was up when I had to wear my reading glasses in order to see the magazine I was masturbating over.

None of the women I knew could give up in this way. It was rare for my wife and her friends not to talk about botox and detox, about food and their body shape, size and relative fitness, and the sort of exercise they were or were not taking. I knew women, and not only actresses, who had squads of personal trainers, dieticians, nutritionists, yoga teachers, masseurs and beauticians labouring over their bodies daily, as if the mind's longing and anxiety could be cured via the body. Who doesn't want to be more desired and, therefore, loved?

In contrast, I tried to dissociate myself from my body, as if it were an embarrassing friend I no longer wanted to know. My pride, my sense of myself, my identity, if you will, didn't disappear; rather, it emigrated. I noticed this with my friends. Some of them had gone to the House of Lords; they sat on committees. They were given 'tribute' evenings; they picked up awards, medals, prizes and doctorates. The end of the year, when these things were handed out, was an anxious time for the elderly and their doctors. Prestige was more important than beauty. I imagined us, as if in a cartoon, sinking into the sludge of old age, dragged down by medals, our only motion being a jealous turn of the head to see what rewards our contemporaries were receiving.

Some of this, you will be delighted to hear, happened to me. My early plays were occasionally revived, most often by arthritic amateurs, though my latest play hadn't been produced: it was considered 'old-fashioned'. Someone was working on a biography which, for a writer, is like having a stone-mason begin to chisel one's name into a tombstone. My biographer seemed to know, better than I did, what had been important to me. He was young; I was his first job, a try-out. Despite my efforts, we both knew my life hadn't been scandalous enough for his book to be of much interest.

However, I'd written my memoirs and made money out of two houses I'd bought, without much thought, in the early 1960s, one for my parents and one for myself, which turned out to have been situated in an area which became fashionable.

Lately, what I have wanted to be cured of, if anything, was indifference, slight depression or weariness; of the feeling that my interest in things – culture, politics, other people, myself – was running down. A quarter of me was alive; it was that part which wanted a pure, unadulterated 'shot' of life.

I wasn't the only one. A successful but melancholic friend, ten years older than me, described his head as a 'raw wound'; he was as furious, pained and mad as he had been at twenty-five. No Nirvanic serenity for him; no freedom from ambition and envy. He said, 'I wouldn't know whether you should go gentle into that night or rage against the dying of the light. I think, on reflection, that I'd prefer the gentle myself.' But it is as if your mind is inhabited by a houseful of squabbling relatives, all of whom one could gladly eject, but cannot.

But where to find consolation? Who will teach us the wisdom we require? Who has it and could pass it on? Does it even exist?

There was religion, once, now replaced by 'spirituality', or, for a lot of us, politics – of the 'fraternal' kind; there was culture, now there is shopping.

When I came round after the operation these weary thoughts, which I'd carried around for months, weren't with me. I had more important things to do, like standing on my head! Without Ralph telling me this – he had become an optimist – I had expected to feel, at least, as if I'd been beaten up. I had anticipated days of recovery time. However, even though I was only semi-conscious, I found I could move easily.

Nevertheless, as soon as I lay down on the bed, I fell asleep again. This time I dreamed I was at a railway station. When I take a train I like to get to the station early so as to watch the inhabited bodies move around one another. Yet I have become slightly phobic about others' bodies. I don't like them too close to me; I can't touch strangers, friends or even myself. In the dream, when I arrived at the station, everyone wanted to meet me; they crowded around me, shaking my hand, touching, kissing and stroking me in congratulation.

This semi-sleep continued. Somehow, I became aware that I was without my body. It might be better to say I was suspended between bodies: out of mine and not yet properly in another. I was assaulted by what I thought were images but which I realised were really bodily sensations, as if my life were slowly returning, as physical feeling. I had always taken it for granted that I was a person, which was a good thing to be. But now I was being reminded that first and foremost I was a body, which wanted things.

In this strange condition, I thought of how babies are close to their mother's skin almost the whole time. A body is the child's first playground and his first experiences are sensual. It doesn't take long for children to learn that you can get things from other bodies: milk, kisses, bottles, caresses, slaps. People's hands are useful for this, as they are for exploring the numerous holes bodies have, out of which leaks different stuff, whether you like it or not: sweat, shit, semen, pus, breath, blood, saliva, words. These are holes into which you can put things, too, if you feel like it.

My mother, a librarian, was fat and couldn't walk far. Movement disturbed her. Her clothes were voluminous. She had no dealings with diets, except once, when she decided to go on a fast. She eschewed breakfast. By lunchtime she had a headache and dizziness; she was 'starving' and had a cream bun to cheer herself up.

Mother was always hungry, but I guess she didn't know what she was hungry for. She replied, when I asked her why she consumed so much rubbish, 'You never know where your next meal is coming from, do you?' Things can seem like that to some people, as if there is only scarcity and you should get as much down you as you can, though it never satisfies you.

Mother never let me see her body or sleep beside her; she didn't like to touch me. She didn't want anyone's hands on her, saying it was 'unnecessary'. Perhaps she made herself fat to discourage temptation.

As you get older, you are instructed that you can't touch just anyone, nor can they touch you. Although parents encourage their children in generosity, they don't usually share their genitals, or those of their partner, with you. Sometimes you are not even allowed to touch parts of your own body, as if they don't quite belong to you. There are feelings your body is forbidden to generate, feelings the elders don't like anyone having. We consider ourselves to be liberals; it is the others who have inexplicable customs. Yet the etiquette of touching bodies is strict everywhere.

Every body is different, but all are identical in their uncontrollability: bodies do various involuntary things, like crying, sneezing, urinating, growing or becoming sexually excited. You soon find that bodies can get very attracted and repelled by other bodies, even – or particularly – when they don't want to be.

I grew up after the major European wars, playing soldier games on my father's farm. My mind was possessed by images of millions of upright male bodies in identical clothes and poses. The world these men made was mayhem and disorder, but at least, as my father used to say, they were 'well turned out' for it. At school, it seemed that each teacher had a particular disability – one ear, one leg or testicle, or some war-wound – which fascinated us. None of us thought we'd ever be down to just one of anything where there was supposed to be two, but we couldn't stop thinking about it. This was the misunderstanding of education: the teachers were interested in minds, and we were interested in bodies. It was the bodies I wanted when I grew up.

I became aware of the reality of my own death at the same time I became aware of the possibility of having real sex with others. Each made the other possible. You might die, but you could say 'hello' before you went.

In the countryside, there are fewer bodies and more distance between them. I came to the city because the bodies are closer; there is heat and magnetism. The bodies jostle; is that for space, or for touching? The tables in the restaurants and pubs are more adjacent. On the trains and in the tubes, of course, the bodies seem to breathe one another in, which must be why people go to work. The bodies seem anonymous, but sometimes any body will do. Why would anyone want this, particularly a semi-claustrophobic like me?

If other people's bodies get too much for you, you can stop them by stabbing or crucifixion. You can shoot or burn them to make them keep still or to prevent them saying words which displease you. If your own body gets too much – and whose doesn't? – you might meditate yourself into desirelessness, enter a monastery or find an addiction which channels desire. Some bodies are such a nuisance to their owners – they can seem as unpredictable as untamed animals, or the feeling can overheat and there's no thermostat – that they not only starve or attempt to shape them, but they flagellate or punish them.

As a young man, I wanted to get inside bodies, not just with a portion of my frame, but to burrow inside them, to live in there. If this seems impractical, you can at least get acquainted with a body by sleeping next to it. Then you can put bits of your body into the holes in other bodies. This is awful fun. Before I met my present wife, I spent a while putting sensitive areas of my body as close to the sensitive areas of other bodies as I could, learning all I could about what bodies wanted. I never lost my fearful fascination with women's bodies. The women seemed to understand this: that the force of our desire made us crazy and terrified. You could kill a woman for wanting her too much.

The older and sicker you get, the less your body is a fashion item, the less people want to touch you. You will have to pay. Masseurs and prostitutes will caress you, if you give them money. How many therapies these days happen to involve the 'laying-on of hands'? Nurses will handle the sick. Doctors spend their lives touching bodies, which is why young people go to medical school. Dentists and gynaecologists love the dark inside. Some workers, as in shoe shops, can get to hold body parts without having had to attend anatomy lectures. Priests and politicians tell people what to do with their bodies. People always choose their work according to their preferences about bodies. Careers advisers should bear this in mind. Behind every vocation there is a fetish.

Around puberty, people begin to worry – some say women do this more than men, but I'm not convinced – about the shape and size of their bodies. They think about it a lot, though the sensible know their bodies will never provide the satisfaction they desire because it is their appetite rather than their frame that bothers them. Having an appetite, of course, alters the shape of your body and how others see it. Starvation; fasting; dieting. These can seem like decent solutions to the problem of appetite or of desire.

The appetite of my new body seemed to be reviving, too. I was coming round because I was aware of a blaze of need. But my form felt like a building I'd never before been in. Where exactly was this feeling coming from? What did I want? At least I knew that my stomach must have been empty. First, I would wake up properly; then I could eat.

My watch was on the bedside table. I could see the numbers with perfect vision, but the strap wouldn't fit round my thick new wrist. At least I knew it was morning and I'd slept through the night. It was time for breakfast. I could not walk out of the room in my new body without preparation.

I continued to examine myself in the mirror, stepping forwards and backwards, examining my hairy arms and legs, turning my head here and there, opening and closing my mouth, looking at my good teeth and wide, clean tongue, smiling and frowning, try-ing different expressions. I wasn't just handsome, with my features in felicitous proportion. The nurse had asked me to examine my eyes. I saw what she meant. There was a softness in me, a wistful-ness; I detected a yearning, or even something tragic, in the eyes.

I was falling in love with myself. Not that beauty, or life itself, means much if you're in a room on your own. Heaven is other people.

The door opened and the surgeon came in.

'You look splendid.' He walked around me. 'Michelangelo has made David!'

'I was going to say Frankenstein has just –'

'No joins or bumps either. Do you feel well?'

'I think so.'

But my voice sounded unfamiliar to me. It was lighter in tone, but had more force and volume than before.

'Go and have a pee,' he said.

In the toilet, I touched my new penis and became as engrossed in it as a four-year-old. I weighed and inspected it. I raised my arms and wriggled my hips; no doubt I pouted, too. Elvis, of course, had been one of my earliest influences, along with Socrates. When I peed, the stream was full, clear and what I must describe as 'decisive'. Putting my prick away, I gave it a final squeeze. Who wouldn't want to see this! My, what a lot I had to look forward to! My appetite – all my appetites, I suspected – had reached another dimension.

'Okay?' he said.

I nodded. We went into another room where the doctor fixed various parts of me to machines, giving me, or my new body, a thorough check-up. As he did so, I babbled away in my new voice, mostly childhood memories, listening to myself in the attempt to draw myself back together again.

'I'm through,' he said at last. Denying me the privacy of a natural born being, he watched me clumsily put on the clothes Ralph had bought me. 'Good. Good. This is incredible. It has worked.'

'Why the surprise? Haven't you done this before?'

'Of course. But each time it seems to be a miracle. We have another success on our hands. Everything is complete now. Your mind and the body's nervous system are in perfect co-ordination. You have your old mind in a new body. New life has been made.'

'Is that it?' I said. 'Don't I require more preparation?'

'I expect you do,' he said. 'Mentally. There will be shocks ahead, adjustments to be made. It would be a good idea to discuss it with Ralph, your mentor. It goes without saying that you cannot talk freely about this. Otherwise you are free to go, sir. Your clock has been restarted, but it is still ticking. See you in six months. You know where we are.'

'But do I know where I am?'

'I hope you will find out. I look forward to hearing how it went.'

The nurse, in reception, handed me my wallet and the bag of things Ralph had told me I'd need for the first few hours after my 'transformation'. She took a copy of my memoirs from under the desk and asked me to sign it.

'I've long been an admirer, sir.'

Writing my old name with my new fingers I had to bend over from a different height. For the first time in years, I did so without having to adjust my posture to avoid an expected pain. I stood back and stared at my signature, which resembled a bad forgery of my own scrawl. I took another piece of paper and scribbled my name again and again. However hard I tried, I couldn't make it come out like the old one.

The amused nurse called a cab for me.

I waited on the couch with my new long legs stuck out in front of me, taking up a lot of room, and touching my face. Watching her work in reception, it occurred to me that the desirable nurse – whose attractiveness was, really, only lack of any flaw – might be seventy or ninety years old. Like people who work at a dentist's, and always have perfect teeth, she was bound to be a Newbody herself. But why would she be doing such a job?

A long-haired, model-like young woman approached the desk, requesting a taxi. Her hip, slightly Hispanic look was so ravishing I must have audibly sighed, because she smiled. It was difficult to tell whether she was in her late teens or early thirties. It occurred to me that we were making a society in which everyone would be the same age. I noticed that the woman was carrying an open bag in which I glimpsed what looked like the corner of a pink flannel night-gown. She sat opposite me, waiting too, nervously. In fact, she seemed to relate strangely to herself, as I must have done, moving different parts of herself experimentally, at first diffidently, and then with some internal celebration. Then she smiled in my direction with such radiant confidence I thought of suggesting we share a cab. What a perfect couple we would make!

But I wanted to be back among ordinary people, those who decayed and were afraid of death. I got up and cancelled the cab. I would enjoy walking. A marathon would be nothing. The nurse seemed to understand.

'Good luck,' I said to the woman.

I headed for the main road. I must have walked for five miles, taking considerable strides and loving the steady motion. My new body was taller and heavier than my last 'vessel', but I felt lighter and more agile than I could recall, as though I were at the wheel of a luxury car. I could see over the heads of others on the street. People had to look up to me. I'd been bullied as a kid. Now, I could punch people out. Not that a fight would be the best start to my new incarnation.

I found a cheap café and ate a meal. I ate another meal. I checked into a big anonymous hotel where a reservation had already been made. I found a good position in the bar where I could look out for people looking at me. Was that woman smiling in my direction? People did glance at me, but with no more obvious interest than they had before. My mind felt disturbingly clear. What defined edges the world had! It had been a long time since I'd had such undeviating contact with reality. After a couple of drinks, I gained even more clarity along with a touch of ecstasy, but I didn't want to get blotto on my first day as a Newbody.

I was waiting in the crowded hotel foyer when Ralph hurried in and stood there looking about. It was disconcerting when he didn't recognise the writer he'd worshipped, whose words he'd memorised, the one he believed deserved immortality! It took him a few distracted moments to pick my body out among the others, and he still wasn't certain it was me.

I went over. 'Hi, Ralph, it's me, Adam.'

He embraced me, running his hands over my shoulders and back; he even patted my stomach.

'Great hard body, pal. You look superb. I'm proud of you. You've got guts. How do you feel?'

'Never better,' I said. They were my words, but my voice was strong. 'Thanks, Ralph, for doing this for me.'

'By the way,' he said. 'What's your name?'

'Sorry?'

'You'll need a new name. You could keep your old name, of course, or a derivative. But it might cause confusion. You're not really Adam any more. What do you think?'

My instinct was to change my name. It would help me remember that I was a new combination. Anyway, hybrids were hip.

'What will it be?' he asked.

'I'll be called Leo Raphael Adams,' I said at last. 'Does that sound grand enough?'

'Up to you,' he said. 'Good. I'll tell them. You have money, don't you?'

'As you insisted, enough for six months.'

'I'll make sure you receive a passport and driving licence in your new name.'

'That must be illegal,' I said.

'Does that worry you?'

'I'm afraid so. I'm not a good man by any means, but I do tend towards honesty in trivial matters.'

'That's the least of it, man. You're in a place that few other humans have ever been before. You're a walking laboratory, an experiment. You're beyond good and evil now.'

'Right, I see,' I said. 'The identity theorists are going to be busy worrying about this one.'

He touched my shoulder. 'You need to get laid. It works, doesn't it – your thing?'

'I can't tell you how good it feels not to piss in all directions at once or over your own new shoes. As soon as I get an erection, I'll call.'

'The first time I had sex in my new body, it all came back. I was with a Russian girl. She was screaming like a pig.'

'Yeah?'

'I knew, that night, it had been worth it. That all those years, day after day, watching my wife die, were over. This was moving on in glory.'

'My wife isn't dead. I hope she doesn't die while I'm "away".'

'It's okay to be unfaithful,' he said. 'It isn't you doing it.'

We talked for a bit, but I felt restless and kept bouncing on my toes. I said I wanted to get out and walk, shake my new arse, and show off. Ralph said he had done the same. He would let me go my own way as soon as he could. First, we had to do some shopping. Ralph had brought a suit, shirt, underwear and shoes to the hospital, but I would need more.

'My son only seems to possess jeans, T-shirts and sunglasses,' I said. 'Otherwise I have no idea what twenty-five-year-olds wear.'

'I will help you,' he said. 'I only know twenty-five-year-olds.'

I was photographed for my new passport, and then Ralph took me to a chain-store. Each time I saw myself in the changing-room mirror I thought a stranger was standing in front of me. My feet were an unnecessary distance from my waist. Recently, I'd found it difficult to get my socks on, but I'd never been unfamiliar with the dimensions of my own body before. I'd always known where to find my own balls.

I dressed in black trousers, white shirt and raincoat, nothing fashionable or ostentatious. I had no desire to express myself. Which self would I be expressing? The only thing I did buy, which I'd always wanted but never owned before, was a pair of tight leather trousers. My wife and children would have had hysterics.

Ralph left to go to a rehearsal. He was busy. He was pleased with me and with himself, but his job was done. He wanted to get on with his own new life.

Staring at myself in the mirror again, attempting to get used to my new body, I realised my hair was a little long. Whichever 'me' I was, it didn't suit me. I would customise myself.

There was a hairdresser's near my house, which I had walked past most days for years, lacking the courage to go in. The people were young, the women with bare pierced bellies, and the noise horrendous. Now, as the girl chopped at my thick hair and chattered, my mind teemed with numerous excitements, wonderments and questions. I had quickly agreed to become a Newbody in order not to vacillate. Since the operation, I had felt euphoric; this second chance, this reprieve, had made me feel well and glad to be alive. Age and illness drain you, but you're never aware of how much energy you've lost, how much mental preparation goes into death.

What I didn't know, and would soon find out, was what it was like to be young again in a new body. I enjoyed trying out my new persona on the hairdresser, making myself up. I told her I was single, had been brought up in west London and had been a philosophy and psychology student; I had worked in restaurants and bars, and now I was deciding what to do.

'What do you have in mind?' she asked.

I told her I was intending to go away; I'd had enough of London and wanted to travel. I would be in the city for only a few more days, before setting off. As I spoke, I felt a surge or great push within, but towards what I had no idea, except that I knew they were pleasures.

Walking out of the hairdresser's, I saw my wife across the road pulling her shopping trolley on wheels. She looked more tired and frailer than my mental picture of her. Or perhaps I was reverting to the view of the young, that the old are like a race all of whom look the same. Possibly I needed to be reminded that age in itself was not an illness.

I recalled talking in bed with her last week, semi-asleep, with one eye open. I could see only part of her throat and neck and shoulder, and I had stared at her flesh thinking I had never seen anything more beautiful or important.

She glanced across the street. I froze. Of course her eyes moved over me without recognition. She walked on.

Being, in a sense, invisible, and therefore omniscient, I could spy on those I loved, or even use and mock them. It was an unpleasant loneliness I had condemned myself to. Still, six months was a small proportion of a life. What would be the purpose of my new youth? I had led a perplexed and unnecessarily pained inner life, but unlike Ralph, I had not felt unfulfilled, or wished to be a violinist, pioneering explorer or to learn the tango. I'd had projects galore.

My bewilderment was, I guessed, the experience of young people who'd recently left home and school. When I taught young people 'creative' writing, their excessive concern about 'structure' puzzled me. It was only when I saw that they were referring to their lives as well as to their work that I began to understand them. Looking for 'structure' was like asking the question: what do you want to do? Who would you like to be? They could only take the time to find out. Such an experiment wasn't something I'd allowed myself to experience at twenty-five. At that age I moved between hyperactivity and enervating depression – one the remedy, I hoped, for the other.

If my desire pointed in a particular direction this time around, I would have to discover what it was – if there was, in fact, something to find. Perhaps in my last life I'd been overconstrained by ambition. Hadn't my needs been too narrow, too concentrated? Maybe it was not, this time, a question of finding one big thing, but of liking lots of little ones. I would do it differently, but why believe I'd do it better?

That evening I changed hotels, wanting somewhere smaller and less busy. I ate three times and went to bed early, still a little groggy from the operation.

The next day was a fine one, and I awoke in an excellent mood. If I lacked Ralph's sense of purpose, I didn't lack enthusiasm. Whatever I was going to do, I was up for it.

There I was, walking in the street, shopping for the trip I had finally decided to take, when two gay men in their thirties started waving and shouting from across the road.

'Mark, Mark!' they called, straight at me. 'It's you! How are you! We've missed you!'

I was looking about. There was no one else they could have been motioning to. Perhaps my leather trousers were already having an effect on the general public. But it was more than that: the couple were moving through the traffic, their arms extended. I considered running away – I thought I might pretend to be jogging – but they were almost on me. I could only face them as they greeted me warmly. In fact, they both embraced me.

Luckily, their talk was relentless and almost entirely about themselves. When I managed to inform them that I was about to go on holiday, they told me they were going away, too, with friends, an artist and a couple of dancers.

'Your accent's changed, too,' they said. 'Very British.'

'It's London, dear. I'm a new man now,' I explained. 'A reinvention.'

'We're so pleased.'

I understood that the last time we met, in New York, my mental state hadn't been good, which was why they were pleased to see me out shopping in London. They and their circle of friends had been worried about me.

I survived this, and soon we were saying our farewells. The two men kissed and hugged me.

'And you're looking good,' they added. 'You're not modelling any more, are you?'

'Not at the moment,' I said.

One of them said, 'But you're not doing the other thing, are you, for money?'

'Oh, not right now.'

'It was driving you crazy.'

'Yes, yes,' I said. 'I believe it was.'

'Shame the boy band idea didn't work out. Particularly after you got through the audition with that weird song.'

'Too unstable, I guess.'

'Would you like to join us for a drink – of orange juice, of course? Why not?'

'Yes, yes,' said the other. 'Let's go and talk somewhere.'

'I'm sorry, but I must go,' I said, moving away. 'I'm already late for my psychiatrist! He tells me there's much to be done!'

'Enjoy!'

I rang Ralph straight away.

'You got your erection, eh?' he said.

I insisted on seeing him. He was rehearsing. He made me go to the college canteen during his tea break and wait. When he did turn up, he seemed preoccupied, having had an argument with Ophelia. I didn't care. I told him what had happened to me on the street.

'That shouldn't have occurred,' he said, with some concern. 'It's never happened to me, though I guess I'll start to get recognised when I've played Hamlet.'

'What is going on? Don't they do any checks first?'

'Of course,' he said. 'But the world's a small place now. Your guy's from LA.'

'Mark. That's his name. That's what they called me.'

'So? How can anyone be expected to know he's got friends in Kensington?'

'Suppose he's wanted by the police somewhere?'

He shook his head. 'It won't happen again,' he said confidently. 'The chances of such a repeat are low, statistically.'

'There have been other weird occurrences.'

'For example?' He didn't want to hear, but he had to.

'Tell me, first, how did he die, my body, my man?'

Ralph hesitated. 'Why do you want to know?'

'Why, are you not allowed to tell me?'

'This is a new area.'

I went on, 'In bed, I was aware of these twinges, or sensations. There were times in my Oldbody life, particularly as I got older, or when I was meditating, when I felt that the limits of my mind and body had been extended. I felt, almost mystically, part of others, an "outgrowth of the One".'

'Really?'

'This is different. It's as if I have a ghost or shadow-soul inside me. I can feel things, perhaps memories, of the man who was here first. Perhaps the physical body has a soul. There's a phrase of Freud's that might apply here: the bodily ego, he calls it, I think.'

'Isn't it a little late for this? I'm an actor, not a mystic.'

I noticed a lack of respect in Ralph. I was a puling twenty-five-year-old rather than a distinguished author. It hadn't taken long before I was confronted with the losses involved in gaining prolonged youth.

I said, 'I need to know more about my body. It was Mark's face they were seeing when they looked at me. It was his childhood experience they were partly taking in, not yours or mine.'

'You want to know why he snuffed himself out? I'm telling you, Leo, face it, this is the truth and you know it already. Your guy's going to have died in some grisly fashion.'

'What sort of thing are we talking about?'

'If he's young, it's not going to be pleasant. No young death is a relief. The whole world works by exploitation. We all know the clothes we wear, the food, it's packed by Third World peasants.'

'Ralph, I am not just wearing this guy's shoes.'

'He was definitely "obscure", your man. There's no way I'm going to let them give you shoddy goods. Anyway, it's impossible, at the moment, to just go and kill someone for their body. Their family, the police, the press, everyone's going to be looking for them. The body has to be "cleared", and then it has to be prepared for new use by a doctor who knows what he is doing. It's a long and complicated process. You can't just plug your brain into any skull, thank Christ. Imagine what a freak show we'd have then.'

'If he's been "cleared", I think that at least you should tell me what you know,' I said. 'I presume he was homosexual.'

'Why else would he be in such good shape? Most hets, apart from actors, have the bodies of corpses. You object to homosexuality?'

'Not in principle, and not yet. I haven't had time to take it in. I'm at the beginning here. I need to know what all this might mean.'

Ralph said, 'As far as I know, he was nutty but not druggy. A suicide, I think, by carbon monoxide poisoning. They had to fix up his lungs. I looked into it, for you. Adam – Leo, I mean. I asked them to give you the best. Some of those women were in great shape.'

'I told you, I'm not ready to be a woman. I'm not even used to being a man.'

'That was your choice, then. Your man had something like clinical depression. Obviously a lot of young people suffer from it. They can't get the help they need. Even in the long run they don't come round. Antidepressants, therapy, all that, it never works. They're never going to be doers and getters like us, man. Better to be rid of them altogether and let the healthy ones live.'

'Live in the bodies of the discarded, you mean? The neglected, the failures?'

'Right.'

'I see what you're getting at. "Mark" might have suffered in his mind. He might not have lived a "successful" life, but his friends seemed to like him. His mother would like to see him.'

'What are you saying?'

'What if I –'

'Don't think about pulling that kind of stunt in front of his mother,' he said. 'She'd go mad if you walked in there with that face on. His whole family! They'd think they'd seen a fucking ghost!'

'I'm not about to do that,' I said. 'I don't know where she lives. That's not quite what I mean.'

Ralph said, 'My guy was struck by lightning while lying drunk under a tree. Nothing unusual about my man, thank Christ, though I keep away from AA meetings.'

There wouldn't be much more I could get out of Ralph. I had to live with the consequences of what I'd done. Except that I had no idea what those consequences might turn out to be.

Ralph said, 'You will come and see me as Hamlet?'

'Only if you come and see me as Don Giovanni.'

'Yeah? Is that what you're going to do? I can see you as the Don. Got laid yet?'

'No.' He gave me my new passport and driving licence. 'Listen, Ralph,' I said as we parted. 'I need you to know I'm grateful for this opportunity. Nothing quite so odd has ever happened to me before.'

'Good,' he said. 'Now go and have a walk and calm down.'

I was, I noticed, becoming used to my body; I was even relaxing in it now. My long strides, the feel of my hands and face, seemed natural. I was beginning to stop expecting a different, slower response from my limbs.

There was something else.

For the first time in years, my body felt sensual and full of intense yearning; I was inhabited by a warm, inner fire, which nonetheless reached out to others – to anyone, almost. I had forgotten how inexorable and indiscriminate desire can be. Whether it was the previous inhabitant of this flesh, or youth itself, it was a pleasure that overtook and choked me.

From the start of our marriage I had decided to be faithful to Margot, without, of course, having enough idea of the difficulty. It is probably false that knowing is counter-erotic and the mundane designed to kill desire. Desire can find the smallest gap, and it is a hell to live in close proximity to and enforced celibacy with someone you want and with whom contact, when it occurs, is of an intimacy that one has always been addicted to. I learned that sexual happiness of the sort I'd envisaged, a constant and deep satisfaction – the romantic fantasy we're hypnotised by – was as impossible as the idea that you could secure everything you wanted from one person. But the alternative – lovers, mistresses, whores, lying – seemed too destructive, too unpredictable. The overcoming of bitterness and resentment, as well as sexual envy of the young, took as much maturity as I could muster, as did the realisation that you have to find happiness in spite of life. I became a serial substitutor: property, children, work, raking the garden leaves, kept the rage of failure at bay. Illness, too, was helpful. I became so phobic of others I couldn't even have a stranger cut my hair. My daughter would do it. This is how I survived my life and mind without murdering anyone. Enough! It was not enough.

Now I found myself looking at young women and even young men on the street and in cafés. When, on my way down an escalator, a woman on her way up smiled and gestured at me, I pursued her into the street. I would, this time, follow my impulses. I approached her with a courage I'd never had as a young man. Then, my desire had been so forceful and strange – which I experienced as a kind of chaos – I'd found it difficult to contain or enjoy. For me to want someone had meant to get involved in maddening and intense negotiations with myself.

I asked the girl to join me for a drink. Later, we walked in the park before retiring to her room in a cheap hotel. Later still, we ate, saw a film and returned to her room. She loved my body and couldn't get enough of it. Her pleasure increased mine. She and I looked at and admired each other's bodies – bodies which did as much as two willing bodies could do, several times, before parting for ever, a perfect paradigm of impersonal love, both generous and selfish. We could imagine around each other, playing with our bodies, living in our minds. We became machines for making pornography of ourselves. I hoped there'd be many more occasions like it. How fidelity interferes with love, at times! What were refinement and the intellect compared to a sublime fuck?

As we lay in each other's arms, and, when she was asleep, I kissed her and said, 'Goodbye, whoever you are', creeping out at dawn to walk the streets for a couple of hours, it occurred to me that this was an excellent way to live.

4

Next morning I was on the train to Paris, my new rucksack on the rack above me. Before we reached Dover I had helped people with their heavy luggage, eaten two breakfasts and read the newspapers in two languages. For the rest of the journey I studied guidebooks and timetables.

For a few weeks before I became a Newbody, I had been in what I called an 'experimental' frame of mind. After finishing *Too Late*, I'd been failing as a writer. I'd become more skilful, but not better. I wouldn't have minded the work getting worse if I'd been able to find interesting ways to make it more difficult. Urgency and contemporaneity make up for any amount of clumsiness, in literature as in love. I had stopped work and had been drawing, taking photographs and talking to people I'd normally flee. I would see what occurred, rather than hide in my room. Despite these efforts, there was no doubt I was becoming isolated, as if it were the solitude of my craft I had become attached to, and it was that I couldn't get away from.

There are few things more depressing than constant pain, and there were certain physical agonies I thought I would never be without. Flannery O'Connor wrote, 'Illness is a place where there is no company.' Perhaps I had been unconsciously preparing for death, as I recall preparing for my parents' deaths. I realised what a significant part of my life my own death had become. As a badly off young man I had constantly thought: do I have the money to do this? As an older man I had constantly thought: do I have the time for this; or, is this what I really want to do with my remaining days?

Now, a renewed physical animation, combined with mental curiosity, made me feel particularly energetic. In this incarnation I would go everywhere and see everything.

When I first had children I was inspired to think about my own childhood and parents; now, this transformation was making me reflect on the sort of young man I had been. I hadn't travelled much then. I had been too absorbed in the theatre, working in any capacity, reading scripts, running the box office and serving tyrannical directors. The rest of the time I was having tragic, complicated affairs, and trying to write. I forfeited a lot of pleasure for my craft; at times I found the deferment and discipline intolerable. I'd break out and go mad, before retiring to my room for long periods – for too long, I'd say now. But those years of habit and repetition served me well: I gained invaluable experience of writing, not only of the practical difficulties, but of the terrors and inhibitions that seem to be involved in any attempt to become an artist.

My excitements then had never been pure; they had always been anxieties. In later life I wondered whether I had been too constrained and afraid for my future, too focused on the success I yearned for and too determined to become established. Travelling unworriedly through Europe had been the least of my concerns.

Did I regret it now, or wish it otherwise? At least I had the sense to understand that there couldn't be a life without foolishness, hesitation, breakdown, unbearable conflict. We are our mistakes, our symptoms, our breakdowns.

The thing I missed most in my new life was the opportunity to discuss – and, therefore, think about properly – the implications of becoming a Newbody. I doubted whether Ralph would have been interested in going into it further. Perhaps such a transformation, like face-lifts, worked better for people who didn't have theories of authenticity or the 'natural', people who didn't worry about its meaning at the expense of its obvious pleasures.

It was its pleasures I was in search of. Soon, I was tearing across Paris; then I went to Amsterdam, Berlin; Vienna. I did the churches and museums of Italy, and they did me. It wasn't long before I'd had my fill of degraded, orgasmically violated bodies strung from walls, and vaults full of old bones. On most days I woke up in a different place. I travelled by train and bus, in the slowest possible way. Sometimes I just walked across mountains, beaches or fields, or got off trains when I fancied the view from the window. If I liked a bus – the route, the thoughts it provoked, the width of the seat or a sentence in a book I was reading on it – I'd sit there until the end of the line. There was no rush.

I stayed in cheap hotels, hostels and boarding houses. I had money, but I didn't want opulence. As a young man I'd wanted that – as a measure of success and of how far I had escaped my childhood. Now it seemed confining to be overconcerned with furnishings.

I talked only to strangers, making friends easily for the first time in years. I met people in cafés, museums and clubs, and went to their houses when I could. If I had been too fastidious before, now I stayed with anyone who would have me, to see how they lived. Unlike most young people, I was interested in people of all ages. I'd go to the house of a Dutch guy of my age, and end up chatting to his parents all weekend. It was the mothers I got along with because I was interested in children and how you might get through to them. The mothers talked about children, but I learned they were talking about themselves, too, and this moved me.

I did, at least, know how to look after myself. I could escape any-one boring. People were more generous than I had noticed. If you could listen, they liked to talk. Perhaps being ambitious and relatively well known from a young age had put the barrier of my reputation, such as it was, between me and others.

The days in each city were full. I could drink, have sex with people I picked up or with any prostitute whose body took my fancy, visit galleries, queue for cheap seats to the theatre or opera, or merely read and walk. In the former East Berlin all I did was walk and take photographs. In a bar in Paris, I met a young Algerian guy who modelled occasionally. The male models didn't earn anything like as much as the girls, and most of them had other jobs. My friend got me a catwalk show during Fashion Week, and I took my turn parading on the narrow aisle, as the flash-bulbs exploded and the unprepossessing journalists scribbled. Was it the clothes or really the bodies they were looking at? Backstage, it was a chaos of semi-naked girls and boys, dressers, the designer and numerous assistants.

I enjoyed all of it, and, after chatting with the designer, whom I'd known slightly in my previous body, I was offered a job in one of his shops, with the prospect of becoming a buyer, which I declined. I did ask him, though, whether, by any chance, as I was a 'student', he'd read any of 'my' – Adam's – books or seen 'my' plays or films. If he had, he couldn't remember. He didn't have time for cultural frivolity. Making a decent pair of trousers was more important. He did say he liked 'me' – Adam – though he had found me shy at times. He said, to my surprise, that he envied the fact that women were attracted to me.

The following day, my new catwalk acquaintance thought it would be a good idea to take me shopping. I had told him I had a small inheritance to blow, and he knew where to shop. In our new gear we went to bars suitable for looking at others as we enjoyed them looking at us – those, that is, who didn't regard us dark-skinners with fear and contempt.

I didn't stay; I wasn't like these kids. I didn't want a place in the world and money. One day, because it rained, I thought I should go to Rome. There, as I attended a lecture and dozed in the front row in my new linen suit, the queer biographer of an important writer, leaning over me enormously, asked me out for a drink. At dinner, this British hack said he wanted me to be his assistant, which I did agree to try, while insisting, as I'd learned I had to, that I would not be his lover. He claimed that all he wanted was to lick my ears. I thought: why not share these fine pert ears around? They're not even mine, but a general asset. I closed my eyes and let his old tongue enjoy me. It was as pleasant as having a snail crawl across your eyeball. It was more difficult being a tart than I'd hoped. Tarts are trouble, mostly to themselves.

I could experiment because I was safe. If you know you're going home, you can go anywhere first. I went with him, imagining tall, glass-fronted bookcases and long, polished library tables on which I would work on my version of *The Key to All Mythologies*, in the way I'd browsed in my father's books as a teenager. That, indeed, was what I was doing, 'browsing' or 'grazing' in the world. The job was less demanding than I'd hoped. Mostly it involved me wearing the clothes he bought for me to parties and dinners. I was his bauble or pornography, to be shown off to friends – intelligent, cultured queens I'd have liked to talk with. As a young man I didn't much enjoy the company of my peers; I liked being an admired boy in the theatre, surrounded by older men.

Therefore this fantasy of Greek life suited me, except that my 'employer' refused to let me out of his sight. When I did get the opportunity to read in his library, I could see his bald pate bobbing up and down outside, as he tried to watch me through the window from an uneven box. His adoration of me became nothing but suffering for him, until I began to feel like an imprisoned princess from *The Arabian Nights*. Beauty sets people dreaming of love. If you don't want to be in someone else's dream you have to clear off.

I got a job working as a 'picker' at the door of a club in Vienna. I tended to point at the inpulchritudinous and lame until a lunatic kicked me in the stomach. A few days later, having been taken to a casino by another acquaintance, I was boredly smoking a cigarette outside and wondering why people were so keen to rid themselves of their money when a woman came to me. She said she'd been watching me. She liked my eyes. She wanted to make love to me.

She was not old. I must have been looking doubtful. (I wasn't always sure whether my expression matched my feeling. I wasn't, yet, convinced of my ability to lie.)

'I will pay you,' she said.

'Have you paid for such love before?'

She shook her head. My deal with myself was not to turn down such offers. I looked at her more closely and said no one had ever offered me a better exchange.

'Come, then.'

She had a chauffeur, and she took me with her. I sat in the back of the car, being driven through the night to an unknown destination.

She was an American heiress with a partially collapsed villa out-side Perugia. She hired an octogenarian pianist to play Mozart sonatas out of tune while she painted me nude looking out at the olive groves. Few portraits can have taken longer. I listened to her for days and strode about in shorts and workmen's boots, pre-tending I could mend things, though everything seemed fine as it was. (Is it only in Italy that ruin itself can seem like art?)

There were always her eyes to return to. I still liked having people fall in love with me. There are moments of life you get addicted to, that you want over and over, but then you get frus-trated when you can't go any further, when the thing you've most wanted bores you.

My real labour was at night, in her room, where, after taking hours to prepare for me, she'd await my knock. I went at my employment seriously, limbering up, bathing, meditating, a proud professor of satisfaction. What internal trips I took, pretending to be a dancer or rock climber. It was dangerous work, sex, but, as always, it was the terrors and uncertainties which made it erotic. For her there had to be safety at the end, some hours of peace in her mind. I looked out for this on her face when she was asleep, like a blessing, and was pleased, waiting beside the bed to assess her temperature, her hand in mine. Then I would sleep well, alone. My pleasure was in her pleasure. After a few weeks, she wanted me to live with her in New York, if Italy got too slow for me. It did, but I didn't. I could satisfy her, but only at the cost of disappointing her. I walked away in my boots through the olive trees. Her eyes were on my back; she did not know where her next love would come from, if at all.

I was glad to have the time to walk around the cities, listening to music, always my greatest passion, on my headphones, particularly as, in my previous body, I'd been suffering from some deafness. I went to clubs and made the acquaintance of DJs. I talked about music. But to be honest, in my former guise I could get to meet more interesting people.

However, I loved this multiplicity of lives; I was delighted with the compliments about my manner and appearance, loved being told I was handsome, beautiful, good-looking. I could see what Ralph meant by a new start with old equipment. I had intelligence, money, some maturity and physical energy. Wasn't this human perfection? Why hadn't anyone thought of putting them together before?

Like many straights, I'd been intrigued by some of my gay friends' promiscuity, the hundreds or even thousands of partners. A gay actor I knew had once said to me, 'Anywhere I go in the world, one glance and I can see the need. A citizen of nowhere, I inhabit the Land of Fuck.' I'd long admired and coveted what I saw as the gays' innovative and experimental lives, their capacity for pleasure. They were reinventing love, keeping it close to instinct. Meanwhile, at least for the time being – though it was changing – the straights were stuck with the old model. I had, of course, envied all that sex without a hurting human face, and in my new guise I had plenty of open bodies in close proximity. On one particular day and night I had sex with six – or was it seven? – different people. It's not something you'd want to do often. Once in a lifetime might just do it.

In Switzerland, through a woman I'd been talking to in a bar, I became acquainted with a bunch of kids in their late twenties who were making a film about feckless young people like themselves. I helped the group move their equipment and was interested to see how they used the new lightweight cameras their parents had financed.

They began to shoot long scenes of banal, everyday dialogue. I was never one to believe that Andy Warhol's films could be a fruitful model, but I encouraged them to keep the camera still and photograph only the faces of their subjects, letting them speak while I sat behind the camera, asking questions about their childhood. I took these away to a studio, cut some of them together, and put music on. The best version was one where I took the sound of the voices off altogether, but kept the music going. The unreachable, silent, moving mouths – someone trying to be heard, or not being attended to – were oddly affecting. When it was my turn in front of the camera I had myself painted white, with a black stripe down the middle, and called it 'zebra piece'. One night, we showed the films in a club and the naked zebra danced on stage with a local thrash band.

Others in the group, operating from a collapsing warehouse, were curating shows of contemporary art. Some reasonable things did get done, though no one much noticed. It was irritating when I found myself interested in them as a teacher or parent – the extent of their minds; in how seriously they could take themselves. They didn't read much; there was a lot of cultural knowledge I took for granted and they didn't. My own son didn't start to read or watch decent films until he was almost twenty. He wouldn't allow us, but only a female teacher, to turn him on to these pleasures. Recently, on the radio I'd said I considered reading about as important as raising poodles. As intended, this had got me into wonderful trouble with the bookworms. The whispering, worshipful tones in which my parents referred to 'literature' and 'scholarship' had always made me wonder what more could be done with a body than pass information in and out of it.

I had been to a club once, in the early 1990s, to see Prince, with my son and the college lecturer who seemed to be educating him (in bed), Deedee Osgood. Despite the squalor and the fact that everyone but me was virtually naked and on drugs, I loved looking at everyone. Now, most evenings, my new pals took me to clubs. This soon bored me, so they gave me Ecstasy for the first time. Though I had smoked pot and taken LSD, and known people who'd become junkies or cocaine addicts, alcohol was the drug of my generation. It seemed the best drug. I'd never understood why anyone would want to waltz with mephitic alligators.

I doubted whether any of my new acquaintances went a day without a smoke or some other stimulant. As my friends knew, the 'E' hit me as a revelation and I wanted it served to the Prime Minister, and pumped into the water supply. I popped handfuls of it every day for a fortnight. It led me into my own body, and out into others', in so far as there was anyone real there at all. I couldn't tell. (I liked to call us E-trippers 'a loose association of solipsists'.) My ardour made my new pals laugh. They had learned that E wasn't the cure, and the last thing the world needed was another drug philosopher.

But after the purifications and substitutions of culture, I believed I was returning to something neglected: fundamental physical pleasure, the ecstasy of the body, of my skin, of move- ment, and of accelerated, spontaneous affection for others in the same state. I had been of puny build, not someone aware of his strength, and had always found it easier to speak of the most in- timate things than to dance. As a Newbody, however, I began to like the pornographic circus of rough sex; the stuff that resembled some of the modern dance I had seen, animalistic, without talk. I begged to be turned into meat, held down, tied, blindfolded, slapped, pulled and strangled, entirely merged in the physical, all my swirling selves sucked into orgasm. 'Insights from the edge of consciousness', I'd have called it, had words come easily to me at that time. But they were the last thing on my mind.

By using others, I could get myself on to a sexual high for two or three days. It was indeed drug-like: a lucent, shivering pleasure not only in my own body but, I believed, in all existence at its most elemental. Narcissus singing into his own arse! Hello! I was also aware, as I danced naked on the balcony of a house overlooking Lake Como at daybreak after spending the night with a young couple who didn't interest me, of how many addicts I'd known and how tedious any form of addiction could be. The one thing I didn't want was to get stuck within.

For the group, there was sex of every variety, and the others' drug-taking had moved to heroin. At least two of the boys were HIV-positive. Several of the others believed that that was their destiny. Because my contact with reality was, at the most, glancing, it took me a while to see how desperate the pleasures were, and how ridiculously romantic their sense of shared tragedy and doom was. My generation had been through it, with James Dean, Brian Jones, Jim Morrison and others. If I'd been a kid now, I'd have found poetic misery hard to resist. As it was, I knew I was not of them, because I couldn't help wondering what their parents would have thought.

What we used to call 'promiscuity' had always bothered me. Impersonal love seemed a devaluation of social intercourse. I couldn't help believing, no doubt pompously, that one of civilisation's achievements was to give value to life, to conversation with others. Or was faithful love only an unnecessarily constraining bourgeois idiocy?

There would be a moment when the other, or 'bit of the other', as we used to say, would turn human. Some gesture, word or cry would indicate a bruised history or ailing mind. The bubble of fantasy was pricked (I came to understand fantasy as a fatal form of preconception and preoccupation). I saw another kind of opening then, which was also an opportunity for another kind of entry – into the real. I fled, not wanting my desire to take me too far into another person. Really, apart from with the woman who paid me, when it came to sex I was only interested in my own feeling.

It has, at least, become clear that it is our pleasures, rather than our addictions and vices, which are our greatest problems. Pleasure can change you in an instant; it can take you anywhere. If these gratifications were intoxicating and almost mystical in their intensity, I learned, when something stranger happened, that indulgence wasn't a full-time job and reality was a shore where dreams broke. It turned out I was seducible.

One of the artists in my group had a four-year-old son. The others were only intermittently interested in him, as I was in them, and mostly the kid watched videos. His loneliness reflected mine. If I'd been up partying and couldn't sleep the next day, I would, before I cured my come-down with another pill, take him to see the spiders in the zoo. Making him laugh was my greatest pleasure. We played football and drew and sang. I didn't mind ambling about at his speed, and I made up stories in cafés. 'Read another,' he'd say. He helped me recall moments with my own children: my boy, at four, fetching me an old newspaper from the kitchen, as he was used to my perpetual reading.

With his stubborn refusals, the kid reduced me twice to fury. I found myself actually stamping my feet. This jarring engagement made me see that otherwise I was like a spy, concealed and wary. If my generation had been fascinated by what it was like to be Burgess, or Philby or Blunt – the emotional price of a double life, of hiding in your mind – the kid reminded me of how much of one's useful self one locked away in the keeping of serious secrets.

The kid sent me into an unshareable spin. I wept alone, feeling guilty at how impatient I had been with my own children. I composed a lengthy email apologising for omissions years ago, but didn't send it. Otherwise, I saw that most of my kids' childhood was a blank. I had either been somewhere else, or wanted to be, doing something 'important' or 'intellectually demanding'. Or I wanted the children to be more like adults – less passionate and infuriating, in other words. The division of labour between men and women had been more demarcated in my day: the men had the money and the women the children, a deprivation for both.

I came to like the kid more than the adults. One time, finding me puking on the floor, he was kind and tried to kiss me better. I didn't want him to consider me a fool. The whole thing shook me. I hadn't expected this Newbody experience to involve falling in love with a four-year-old whose narcissism far exceeded my own. When it came to youth and beauty, he had it all, as well as his emotional volume turned right up. It hadn't occurred to me that if I wanted to begin again as a human being, it would be as a father, or that I would have more energy with which to miss my children living at home, their voices as I entered the house, their concerns and possessions scattered everywhere. Ralph had failed to warn me of feeling 'broody'. I guessed such an idea would recommend 'eternal life' to no more than a few, just as you never hear anyone say that in heaven you have to do the washing-up while suffering from indigestion. I had to shut the possibility of fatherhood out of my mind, kiss the kid goodbye and remind myself of what I had to look forward to, of what I liked and still wanted in my old life.

In my straighter moments, despite everything, I wanted to be close to my wife. I liked to watch her walk about the house, to hear her undress, to touch her things. She would lie in bed reading and I would smell her, moving up and down her body like an old dog, nose twitching. I still hadn't been all the way round her. Her flesh creased, folded and sagged, its colour altering, but I had never desired her because she was perfect, but because she was she.

After my journey through the cities and having to leave the kid, I decided to roam around the Greek islands. My own vanity bored even me and I craved warm sun, clear water and a fresh wind. I'd had two and a half months of ease and pleasure, and I wanted to prepare for my return – for illness and death, in fact. I began to think of what I'd tell my friends I'd been doing.

As the doctor had predicted, I wasn't looking forward to re-entering my old body. When I ate, would it still feel as though I were chewing nails and shitting screws? On some days, would I still only be able to swallow bananas and painkillers? But as my old body and its suffering stood for the life I had made, the sum total of my achievement made flesh, I believed I should reinhabit it. I was no fan of the more rigid pieties, but it did seem to be my duty. Would most deaths soon feel like suicides? It was almost funny: becoming a Newbody made living a quagmire of decision. In the meantime, I was looking forward to staying in the same place for a few weeks and finishing, or at least beginning again, *Under the Volcano*.

My father, the headmaster of a local school, said, before he died of heart failure, that he'd always regretted not becoming a postman. A gentle job, he believed, wandering the streets with nothing but dogs to worry about, would have extended his life. Idiotic, I considered this: worrying was an excitement I needed. But now I had some idea what he meant.

Not that he'd have survived on a postman's salary. I had begun to realise that I, too, wasn't used to today's financial world. I'd always bought my own milk, but had no idea of the price. I'd seriously underestimated what I'd need as a Newbody. The price of condoms! Apart from the cash I'd put aside for my return trip, I'd spent most of my money and couldn't use my bank accounts or credit cards. Until my return I needed a cheap place to stay and money for my keep.

It was in Greece, on a boat one morning, that I met a middle-aged woman with a rucksack who was going to study photography at a 'spiritual centre' on the island I was visiting. She had hitch-hiked from London to visit the Centre, which was known to be particularly rejuvenative for those suffering from urban break-down. When I told her my sad story, she offered to take me along with her.

While I waited in a café in a nearby square, drinking wine and reading Cavafy, she went to the Centre and enquired whether there was any work I could do in exchange for food, a place to sleep and a little payment. Otherwise, I would find a job in a bar or disco, and crash on the beach. The woman returned and told me the Centre had been looking for an 'oddjob' to clean the rooms and work in the kitchen. Providing the leader didn't dislike me, I would eat for free, earn a little money and sleep on the roof.

We walked down to a handful of flower-dotted, whitewashed buildings on the edge of an incline, with a view of the sea. She opened the door in a long, high wall.

'Look,' she said. I did: the devil peeping into paradise. 'They must be between classes.'

It was a shaded garden where the women – naturally, it was mostly women – sat on benches. They talked, wrote earnestly in notebooks and read. In one corner, a woman was singing; another was doing yoga, another combing her hair; on a massage table, a body was being kneaded.

Here, these middle-aged, middle-class and, of course, divorced women from London took 'spiritual' nourishment, meditation, aromatherapy, massage, yoga, dream therapy. What baby with its mother ever had it better than in this modern equivalent of the old-style spa or sanatorium? The three men I saw were middle-aged, with hollow chests and varicose veins.

She asked, 'Will you be all right here?'

'I think I'll manage,' I replied.

After being shown around the kitchen, the 'work' rooms, and the dining room, I was taken to see the Centre's founder or leader, the 'wise woman', as she was called, without irony, or with none that I noticed. I had the impression that it would be wise for me, too, to lay off the irony. It was too much of a mature and academic pleasure.

Patricia came to the door of a small, shuttered house ten minutes' walk from the Centre. In her late fifties, she was big, with long, greying hair, in clothes with the texture and odour of cheap oriental carpets. She invited me in, and ordered me to sit on a cushion. As I dozed off, she talked loudly on the phone, read her correspondence ('Bastards! Bastards!'), scratched her backside and, from time to time, looked me over.

When I got up to inspect a picture, she turned. 'Sit down, don't fidget!' she said. 'Be still for five minutes!'

I sat down and bit my lip.

I could recall her variety of feminism from the first time around: its mad ugliness, the forced ecstasy of sisterhood, the whole revolutionary puritanism. I didn't loathe it – it seemed to me to be a strain of eccentric English socialism, like Shavianism – as long as I didn't have to live under or near it. It did, however, seem better being a young man these days: the women were less aggressive, earned their own money and didn't blame anyone with a cock for their nightmares.

I was irritated by what I considered to be this woman's high-handed approach, and was about to walk out – not that she would have minded – when it occurred to me that for her I was virtually a child as well as only a potential menial. I was neither an Oldbody nor a Newbody. I was a nobody.

I'd always had a penchant for tyrants, at school, at work and in the theatre where, when I was young, they flourished, having come from army backgrounds. I had enjoyed testing myself against them. How many times could they beat you up before they had to come to terms with you? However, now I was shaken by a blast of late-adolescent fury. I'd forgotten how adults talk down to you, when they're not ignoring you, and how they hate to hear your opinion while giving their own. You're at one of your parents' dinner parties and your parents' friends ask you how your exams are going and you tell them you have failed and you are glad, glad, glad. Your parents tell you not to be rude, and you've just been to see *If* . . . Your parents want a gin and tonic but you want a machine gun and the revolution, and you want them now.

Despite this, I guessed that Patricia had an intelligence and intensity my former persona would have enjoyed. I liked the fact that the one thing I wouldn't have said about her, even after only cursory inspection, was that she was serene. Long periods of inner investigation and deep breathing, or whatever therapy she practised, hadn't seemed to have cured her of irritability or incipient fury.

When she did look at me, with what I was afraid was some perception, I felt I would shrivel up. For the first time I felt that someone had seen me as an impostor, a fake, as not being what I seemed. The game was up, the pretence was over.

'What did you say your name was?' she asked.

'Leo Raphael Adams.'

She snorted. 'Arty, bohemian parents, eh?'

'I suppose so.'

'I probably knew them.'

'You didn't.'

'What did they do?'

'Lots of things.'

'Lots of things, eh?'

'They moved around a lot.'

'Good for them,' she said. 'What do you want to do?'

'Work here for a bit,' I replied. 'I'll do anything you want me to.'

'I should hope so. But don't pretend to take what I say literally, Leo, when you know I mean "in life".'

'In life? I don't know,' I said genuinely. 'I've no idea. Why do I have to "do" anything?'

She imitated me. 'Don't know. Don't care. Don't give a shit.'

I shaded my eyes, as if from the sun. 'Why do you keep staring at me?'

'Your blank face.'

I said, 'Is it blank? I've looked at it a lot and –'

'I can imagine, dear.'

'I've never thought of it as blank.'

'Is there one intelligent thought in there – something that will make me think, "I haven't heard that before"? I must have forgotten', she went on, 'that conversation isn't a male art.'

There was a lot I did want to say, but if I started on at her I wouldn't know what it was like to be young.

I said, 'You want me to leave.'

'Only if you want to.' She started to giggle. 'We don't usually have men working here, though there's no rule against it. I may be an old-style sixties feminist, and the self-esteem of women in a male world may be of interest, but it wasn't my intention to set up a nunnery. Your porky prick' – she looked directly at my crotch – 'will certainly put the cat among the pigeons. I think that will amuse me. You can stay . . . for a bit.'

'Thank you.'

Patricia went to the window, leaned out and yelled into the square.

'Alicia!' she called. 'Alicia!' Almost immediately, a girl appeared. 'Take him away,' she said. 'He's working here at the moment. Give him something to do!'

As I walked back, I was aware of someone beside me, as insubstantial and insistent as a shadow.

'I think I'll get out of here,' I said.

'Is that what you normally do – run?'

'If I'm feeling sensible.'

'Don't start getting sensible.'

I said, 'Something about me seemed to enrage her.'

'You take it personally?'

'I've decided to.'

'Why?'

'It made me wonder what sort of power I might have over her.'

'You'll never have any power over her.'

Alicia was not a girl, but a young woman from London, a frail poet with a squint and a roll-up in the corner of her mouth. She told me she had been staying at the Centre for three months, at the expense of an American benefactor, writing and teaching. Despite the relentless sunlight and the hunger for it of the other women, Alicia had not tanned. Her skin remained remorselessly 'Camden High Street in the rain', as I thought of it. She was to show me the roof of the Centre, where I would sleep. It was baking during the day and most likely cold at night, but it suited me, being secluded. I like the sky, though until now have lacked the time to 'commune' with it.

While I unpacked my few things, Alicia opened a spiral notebook, coughed her soul out, tore at her nails with her teeth, and asked whether I minded hearing her poetry.

'Why not?' I said. 'I haven't had any contact with poetry since I was at school.'

'Where were you at school?'

'All over the place.'

'Read anything?'

'Toilet walls.'

She warned me: her poetry was mostly about things.

'Things?'

She explained that even here, 'in the cradle of consecutive thought', the language of the New Age and of self-help, now beyond parody, had taken over the vocabulary of emotional feeling and exchange. If the language of the self was poisoned, it was disastrous for a poet. This was yet to happen to objects without souls, on which she had decided to concentrate her powers.

'Give me an example,' I said.

She began with a poem about kettles and toasters. I liked it, so she followed up with another about her Hoover, and with a further one about music systems, which was unfinished. When I asked her to go on, she told me what the others were to be about – carpets, beds, curtains – and requested suggestions for more.

I changed my shirt, a moment I always enjoyed, and said I thought one about windows would be good.

'Windows?' she said. 'What are you talking about?'

'What's wrong with windows?'

She explained that it was 'too poetic' a subject. Quoting John Cage, she said she was interested in the 'white' emotions rather than the 'black' ones. She needed to get past the 'black' ones to the 'white' ones.

'D'you see?'

'Not a word of it. Me, I'm only the cleaner.'

'That's who I'm writing for. Cleaners and crooks – I mean cooks. Some poems open only for the ignorant.'

'I must be your man, then.'

She was looking at me. Her face was pale but unmarked, as though her despair had neglected to invade it. Yet now, one of her eyes was twitching like a trapped butterfly. I wanted to go to her and press my finger against it. But maybe I would have just pulled it off and torn it to pieces. The poor girl must have fallen in love at that moment.

The work I had to do at the Centre was hard. My body was uncomplaining – it liked being stretched and exerted – but my mind kicked up a fuss. In a life devoted to myself, it had been years since I'd been forced to do anything against my will. I'd always been reasonably successful at getting women to look after me. Now I helped with the cooking; it was good to learn to cook. I emptied the bins and carried heavy sacks of food from the vans; I was taught how to build a wall. I swept, cleaned and painted the rooms. I guessed that this was what the world was like for most people, and it didn't harm me to be reminded of it.

I came to appreciate the simplest things. I grew a beard and learned t'ai chi, yoga and how to play a drum. I swam long distances, sunbathed, read, and listened to the women at meal times and at night, just hanging around them, as I had my mother as a child. I cultivated a reputation for shyness and silence. I might have been a beauty, but direct attention was the last thing I craved. Sometimes I would massage the women, singing to myself. One time, I saw one of the group lying under a tree reading my last play, which was produced five years ago. As I walked past her, I said, 'Any good?'

'The play's not as good as the film.'

I had begun to love the beauty of the island and the peace it gave me. I was almost free of the desire to understand. Agitation and passion seemed less necessary as proofs of life. I wondered whether, when I returned to my old body, my values would be different. I had been certain that I wanted to go back, but it was a question that wouldn't leave me alone now. There were decent arguments on both sides. What could have been worse? I would put it off for as long as possible.

Patricia usually appeared at breakfast and made a speech about the purpose and aims of the Centre. Once, she told us one of her dreams; then she interpreted it, to prevent any misunderstanding. There was an impressed silence, before she swept away. She uttered

few words in my direction but she always looked hard at me as if
we were connected in some way, as if she were about to speak. I
supposed she looked at everyone like this, now and again, to make
them feel part of her community. I no longer believed she understood me, but did I make her particularly curious? She seemed to
say: what do you really want? It agitated me. I kept away from her
but she remained in my mind, like a question.

Patricia's workshops were the most popular and intense, and
always full. However, as Alicia told me in confidence, they were
known more for the quantity of tears shed than for the quality of
wisdom transmitted. But I was only a kitchen skivvy and took no
part. Taking my father's advice, I was on a working holiday.

Ten days after I'd started, Patricia came into the kitchen, where I
laboured under the regime of an old Greek woman with whom I
could barely communicate. I'd never seen Patricia in the kitchen
before. Like the obdurate adolescent I wanted her to see me as, I
refused to meet her look. She had to tell me to stop peeling potatoes.

'Just stop now.'

'Patricia, I wouldn't feel good about leaving half a potato.'

'To hell with potatoes! I am about to begin my dream workshop
with the new group. I've decided that it's time you joined us.'

'Me? Why?'

'I think you should learn something.'

'Oh, I don't want to learn. I had years of it and nothing went in,
as you pointed out.' She looked hurt, so I said, 'What kind of thing
is it?'

She sighed. 'We free-associate around people's dreams. We might
write around them, or paint or draw. Or even dance. I've seen you
shake your butt, at the disco. The girls were certainly intrigued, as
they are when you parade around the place with your shirt off. But
you keep away from the workshop members, don't you?'

'It goes without saying.'

'Even that idiot with the ghost?'

'Ah, yes,' I said. 'That damned ghost.'

The ghost always cheered Patricia up.

One of the women who'd recently come to the Centre and been allocated a room in town, as some people were, had stood up at breakfast and told us her room was haunted. Typically, Patricia imagined this was a ruse for the woman to be moved to a superior room with a sea view – not something Patricia could offer or fall for. Instead of moving her, Patricia had deputed me to sit, all night, in the doorway of the woman's room, keeping an eye out for the revenant.

'Watching for ghosts is one of your duties,' Patricia had said to me, barely containing her delight. 'When the bastard turns up, you deal with it.'

'Such work wasn't in my original job description,' I said. 'And do ghosts use doors?'

'Get lost and do it. Ghosts use all orifices.'

I had told Alicia, 'Wait 'til they hear this back in London – that I've been employed on a ghost-watch.'

That night, I'd stayed awake as long as I could but had, of course, fallen asleep in the chair. The ghosts came. Nothing with a sheet over its head bothered me, but my own internal shades and shadows, by far the most hideous, had become mightily busy. The woman I guarded slept well. By morning, I was in a cold sweat with rings the colour of coal under my eyes. The women at the Centre, when they weren't being solicitous, found they hadn't laughed as much since they'd arrived.

'Particularly not with the ghost-woman,' I said now to Patricia.

'Good. You're not included in the price of the holiday.' She went on, 'Now, come along. People pay hundreds of pounds to participate. I want you to see what goes on here. Tell me. Surely you don't believe that only the rational is real, or that the real is always rational, do you?'

'I haven't thought much about it.'

'Liar!'

'Why say that?'

'There's more to you than you let on! How many kids your age whistle tunes from *Figaro* while they're peeling potatoes?'

She strode out, expecting me to follow her, but I'm not the sort to follow anyone, particularly if they want me to.

I looked at the old Greek woman, washing the kitchen floor. This was the kind of reality I was adjusted to: getting a patch of earth the way you want it while thinking of nothing.

However, I left the kitchen and, outside, went up the steps. In the large, bright room, I could see that Patricia, along with the rest of the class, had been waiting for me.

She pointed at the floor. 'Sit down, then we'll start.'

Around the group she went, soliciting dreams. What a proliferation of imagination, symbolism and word-play there was in such an ordinary group of people! I stayed for over an hour, at which point there was a break. Breathing freely at last, I hurried out into the heat. I kept going and didn't return, but went into town, where I had provisions to buy for the Centre.

When I returned, Alicia was waiting under a tree outside, with her notebook. She stood up and waved in my face.

'Leo, where have you been?'

'Shopping.'

'You've caused a terrible fuss. You can't walk out on Patricia like that,' she said. 'I kind of admire it. I like it when people are driven to leave my lessons. I know there's something pretty powerful going on. I don't like poetry to be helpful. But we masochists are drawn to Patricia. We do what she says. We never, ever leave her sessions.'

'I had work to do,' I said. I wasn't prepared to say that I had left Patricia's workshop because it had upset me. Dreams had always fascinated me; in London, I wrote mine down, and Margot and I often discussed dreams over breakfast.

My dream on the 'ghost-watch' had been this: I was to see my dead parents again, for a final conversation. When I met them – and they had their heads joined together at one ear, making one interrogative head – they failed to recognise me. I tried to explain how I had come to look different, but they were outraged by my claims to be myself. They turned away and walked into

433

eternity before I could convince them – as if I ever could – of who I really was.

The other dream was more of an image: of a man in a white coat with a human brain in his hands, crossing a room between two bodies, each with its skull split open, on little hinges. As he carried the already rotting brain, it dripped. Bits of memory, desire, hope and love, encased in skin-like piping, fell onto the sawdust floor where hungry dogs and cats lapped them up.

Much as I would have liked to, I couldn't even begin to talk about this with the group. My 'transformation' had isolated me. As Ralph could have pointed out, it was the price I had to pay.

I couldn't either, of course, say this to Alicia, who had become my only real friend at the Centre. She came from a bohemian family. Her father had died in her early teens. At fifteen, her mother took her to live in a sex-crazed commune. It had made her 'frigid'. She felt as neglected as a starving child. Now, she overlooked herself, eating little but carrying around a bag of carrots, apples or bananas which she'd chop into little pieces with a penknife and devour piece by piece. She only ever ate her own food, and, I noticed, would only eat alone or in front of me.

In the evenings, she and I had begun to talk. Twice a week there were parties for the Centre participants. The drinking and dancing were furious. The women had the determined energy of the not quite defeated. They liked Tamla Motown and Donna Summer; I liked the ballet of their legs kicking in their long skirts. After, it was my job to clear away the glasses, sweep the floor, empty the ashtrays and get the Centre ready for breakfast. I did it well; cleanliness had become like a poem to me. A cigarette butt was a slap in the face. Alicia liked to help me, on her knees, late at night, as the others sat up, confessing.

Alicia had begun to write stories and the beginning of a novel, which she showed me. I thought about what she was doing and commented on it when I thought I could be helpful. I liked being useful; I could see how her confidence failed at times.

In the late evenings, when I'd finished work, sometimes we went to the beach. We'd walk past couples who'd left the bars and discos to copulate in the darkness: French, German, Scandinavian, Dutch bodies, attempting, it seemed, to strangle the life out of one another. Our business seemed more important, to talk about literature. Sex was everywhere; good words were less ubiquitous.

Since my mid-twenties, I'd taught both literature and writing at various universities and usually had a writing workshop in London. I'd been interested by how people got to speak, and to speak up, for themselves, and by the effect this had on all their relationships. When it came to Alicia, some sort of instruction was something I fell into naturally, and liked.

Nevertheless, I tried to speak in young tones, as if I knew only a little; and I tried not to be pompous, as I must have been in my old body. It was quite an effort. I was used to people listening or even writing down what I said. The pomposity was useful, for emphasis, and my authority could seem liberating to some people. Alicia seemed to like the authority I was able to muster, at times. Being older could be useful.

I had to be wary, too, of this thin, anxious girl. If she was the reason I didn't leave, when she asked me about myself and my education I was evasive, as if I didn't quite believe my own stories, or, in the end, couldn't be bothered with them, which frustrated her. She wanted more of me. I could see she knew I was holding a lot back.

'What have you been writing?' I asked now, as we walked.

'A poem about windows.'

'Everyone knows poems and windows don't go together.'

'They'll have to get along,' she said. 'Like us.' Then she said, 'Hurry, you've got to go and see Patricia.'

'Now? Is she angry with me?'

She squeezed my hand. 'I think so.'

Her fear increased mine. I was reminded of all kinds of past transgressions and terrors: of my mother's furies, of being sent to the headmistress to be smacked on the hand with a ruler. In my youth, all sorts of people were allowed to hit you, and were even praised for doing it; they didn't thank you if you returned the compliment. Now, as numerous other fears arose, I went into such a spin it took me several moments to remember I was called Leo Adams. I could choose to behave differently, to revise the past, as it were, and not be the scared boy I was then.

'Come on,' I said. 'Walk with me.'

'Aren't you afraid of her?' Alicia asked.

'Terrified.'

'I am, too. Are you going to leave?'

'Well, I don't see why I shouldn't.'

'Please don't.' She went on, 'But there is something else, too. She heard your joke.'

'She did? She didn't mention it to me.'

'She might now, perhaps.'

'How did it get round?'

She blushed. 'These things just do.'

A few days ago I had made a joke, which is not a good idea in institutions. It was not a great joke, but it was on the spot and had made Alicia suddenly laugh in recognition. I had called the Centre a 'weepeasy'. I used the word several times, as we young people tend to, and that was that. It had entered the bloodstream of the institution.

Now, we walked through the village to Patricia's. The shops were closed; the place was deserted. Most people were having their siestas, as was Patricia at this time, usually.

Outside Patricia's, Alicia said she'd wait for me under a tree across the square.

I knocked on the door, and Patricia's irritable face appeared at the window. I'm glad to say I always annoyed Patricia; by being alive at all, I failed her. On this occasion, to my dismay, she brightened.

She had come to the door wearing only a wrap-around skirt. Her large brown breasts were hanging down.

'My,' I said, and then blushed. I knew she'd heard it as 'mine'. I went on, 'Patricia, there's something I need to talk to you about.'

'I'm glad you've come, Oddjob,' she said. 'I've got some work for you. Why did you leave my workshop?'

'I wanted to think about it.'

'Did you enjoy it, then?' When I nodded, she said, 'If so, how much? Very, very much? Just very much? Quite a lot? Or something else?'

'Let me think about that, Patricia.' She was looking at me. I said, 'I did like it, in fact.'

'If you did really, you can say why – in your own words.'

I said, 'You used the dream, not as a puzzle to be solved, with all the anxiety of that, as if one of us would get it right, but as a felt image, to generate thoughts, or other images. That was useful. I haven't stopped thinking.'

'That's a good thing to say.' She was flattered and pleased. 'You see, you can be almost articulate, if you really want to be. By the way, I heard what you called the Centre. Weepeasy,' she said. 'Right?'

'Sorry,' I said, bowing my head.

'Is that what you think?'

'It's easy to make people cry.' I went on, 'Confession, not irony, is the modern mode. A halting speech at Alcoholics Anonymous is the paradigm. But what concealments and deceptions are there in this exhibition of self-pity? Isn't it tedious for you?'

'There's no rigour here any more, you could be right. Or any progress. It's become the same every day. I can tell you, that's the least of it.' Then she said, 'Please, come here.'

'Sorry?'

'Here!' I shuffled forward. She put her arms around me and pressed her breasts into my body. 'I am feeling tense today. I wanted to run a centre for self-exploration, only to discover I'd started a small business. You can't explore anything if you don't get the figures right – the eighties taught some women that, at least. Now I'm sick of being an accountant and I'm sick of being wise. Sometimes, I only want to be mad.'

'Yeah,' I said. 'Being the wise woman must be a right bore.'

'Who takes care of me? I have to mother everyone! You've been attending the massage class, haven't you? You know how to do it.'

By now, she was pulling at my fingers.

'Patricia –'

'Massage me, Leo, you dear boy. There's the oil.'

'I want to talk about Alicia.'

'Who wants to hear about that funny little thing? Oh, talk, talk about what you want, as long as you smooth out my soul.'

Her skirt dropped to the floor. She walked across the room, located the oil, and lay down on a towel on her low bed.

She was watching me scratch my stomach. There were certain conversations I'd missed in this new life. You might have a new body but if your mind is burdened the differences don't count for much.

'Go on,' she said.

I told her how Alicia had got sweet on me and that I was concerned about it. I emphasised that I hadn't deliberately led her on.

Of course, I loved the attention of the women at the Centre – who didn't, admittedly, have much else to look at – and had walked around barefoot, wearing only shorts. Celibacy had increased my desire; I wanted to live less in my mind. I remember Margot telling me, years ago, this thing about certain school phobics. Some boys, of particularly disturbed sexuality, imagined that their bodies had turned into penises. The dreaded school was their mother's forbidden body. I was all sex, a walking prick, a penis with an appended body. I didn't flirt; I was unprovocative. I didn't need to do anything.

In my mad mind, I became a kind of performer. Many of my friends have been actors, singers or dancers, men and women who used their bodies in the service of art, or as art itself; people who were looked at for a living. Those of us who cannot perform, who imagine from the audience only an examination of our faults, can have little idea of the relationship between player and voyeur, of how the audience, like a sea of feeling, might hold you up, if you can use it. What do you see and hear out there in all that blackness? What are the watchers doing to you? What was the stripper or any celebrity doing but increasing and controlling envy and desire? This was a splendidly erotic activity, it seemed to me.

It had been years since I had danced, and now, since I didn't need much sleep, I danced every night in one or other of the town's discos, with women from the Centre. Most of them were older than forty, some were over fifty. They knew the chances of their being loved, caressed, wanted, were diminishing, even as their passion increased, in the sun. I danced with them, but I didn't touch them. If I'd been a 'real' kid, I probably would have gone to bed, or to the beach, with several of them. I was their pornography, a cunt teaser. But at least everyone knew where they stood with me.

Usually, while I danced, Alicia watched me, or sat on a chair drinking and smoking. She never danced herself, but took a lot of pleasure in others' enjoyment. Oddly enough, the music most people preferred originated in my day: 1950s rock 'n' roll, and 1960s soul. I knew every note. It sounded fresher and more lasting than the laboured literary work of me and my contemporaries.

In one of the town's discos, while dancing with my 'coven', as I called them, several of the local men started to taunt me. They didn't like this spoiled kid dancing with and hugging these happy women night after night, as well as looking after their bags, fetching them drinks and making sure they all got safely back to the Centre. One night, they gathered around me at the bar and said they wanted to see what sort of man I was. They could find this out only on the beach, where we would be able to have 'a good talk'. Alicia and the other women had to escort me out of there in a group. Looking back, I could see the men standing at the door, smoking and sneering.

Why did this happen? How did they see me? I enquired of Alicia. As someone who had everything, and a future, too. There was nothing I couldn't do or be, she seemed to think. They hated it and wanted it. They could have killed and eaten me.

There were other fantasies about me. A woman in her fifties had told Alicia that I made the women feel inadequate. I was a problem-free rich kid bumming around the world before going to work for a bank. 'We're trying to restart our troubled lives here. He's just passing through,' she said.

'Maybe that is what you are,' Alicia continued, after she'd told me, throwing down her roll-up and rubbing out the stub with her sandal. 'You have the confidence, poise and sense of entitlement of a rich kid. Isn't that right?'

I didn't answer; I didn't know what to say. I hadn't anticipated this much envy. I had, though, known actors who'd become movie stars and been made paranoid and withdrawn as much because of the pressure of imagined spite as that of fame.

I laboured over Patricia's crumpled and folded flesh, humming and thinking. I was good at this; at least I'd learned to love giving comfort and pleasure.

I said, 'How can I deal with this? I am beginning to feel like an object. It is not pleasant, it's persecution.'

'You are supremely enviable,' she said, her voice muffled by the towel. 'You're like the woman everyone wants but no one understands. What you require is support and protection.'

'Who from?'

'That is up to you. But you must ask for it.' She went on, 'It doesn't sound as if you've done the wrong thing, Oddjob. You've made her and some of the others love-sick but you haven't misled anyone. You're a good lad. Women of Alicia's age – they'd fall in love with a plank of wood.'

I was working hard at Patricia's body. To my dismay, as I punched and pummelled, she didn't seem to relax, but began breathing harder.

She turned, put out her hands and untied the string which held up my trousers.

'Please, Patricia,' I said. 'Don't –'

She was holding my penis. 'That's a mighty fine thing you've got there. Know how to use it?'

440

'No, I guess you could show me.'

'You haven't slept with Alicia?'

'That's right.'

'You're a good boy, then. Now, be an even better boy for me.'

Her eyes were glazed with desire.

I said, 'I thought you were supposed to be a wise woman?'

'Even the wise need a prick now and again. You've been fluttering your eyelashes at me for days, don't think I haven't noticed. I'm very intuitive. Now, can you follow through?'

I didn't want to disappoint her; I didn't want her to feel her age or resent me.

Her hands were rough, and at one point I wondered whether she might be wearing gloves. I remembered that for exercise she liked to build stone walls. But, to my surprise, I became excited.

Her noises were honest and forthright. I was sitting facing her. We were rocking. I must have been holding my breath. 'Breathe, breathe,' she ordered. I did what she said. She went on. 'Relax and breathe from your stomach, that way you'll hold out longer.'

It worked, of course. When I'd relaxed, she said, 'Now, continue.'

Patricia howled, 'Adore me, adore me, you little shit!'; she dug her fingers into me, scratched and kicked me, and, when she came, thrust her tongue into my mouth until I almost gagged.

'I needed that,' she said at last. She was lying on the bed, legs apart, almost steaming. 'Dear boy, do fetch me a glass of water.'

I took it to her.

'Thanks, Oddjob. A job well done, eh?'

I sat on the end of the bed and said, 'Now you'll be able to give an orgasm workshop.'

'You know,' she said, 'a lot of the women here think you're a haughty little kid. I don't mind that. I like it. I could humble you, you know.'

'Thank you, Patricia,' I said. 'I think you just have. I'd better go now.'

'One more thing,' she said.

Patricia opened her legs and, from the end of the bed, had me look at her masturbate busily. At times her entire hand seemed to disappear into her body, as if she were about to turn herself inside out.

'Bet you haven't seen that before,' she murmured.

'No,' I said sourly. 'One lives and learns.'

She was about to fall asleep. She waved me away, but not before saying, 'You come back here tonight. Bring your things. Everything will be better if you come and live here.'

'Why would that be?'

'This is the best room in the village. See you tonight!'

I scurried away across the square. Alicia called after me, caught me up and put her arm through mine.

'You're still here?'

'But why not?'

'Alicia, I'm on my way to the beach.'

'Are you okay? Can't I come with you?'

I didn't like to make her run behind me, but I needed to wash myself. I knew she was still there because she was shouting out poems – not her own – as we went, to remind me of the good things.

I stripped off and ran into the sea. I swam and jogged on the beach until I was exhausted. I lay down next to her with the sun on me. Soon, I'd dozed off. When I opened my eyes, she was sitting there wearing just a cigarette, her arms hugging her knees. Unlike the other women at the Centre, she never removed her clothes but always wore a long-sleeved top and ankle-length skirt.

'What is it?'

She said, 'You slept with her.' Her hands shook as she drew on her cigarette. 'Everyone in this hemisphere will have heard.'

'But you didn't cover your ears.'

'I listened to your music. Every note.'

'What will you do with what you heard? Write about it – or is it too human for you?'

'If that was all I was capable of, I'd hate myself!' She took my hand and placed it on her foot. 'Will you look at me? We can't have sex. You don't want to. Perhaps you've had more than enough for today. I have never had an orgasm, and I am a virgin. Touch me, if you feel like it.' She lay back. 'Would you?'

After my earlier experience, I couldn't claim to be erotically absorbed. I did begin to rub her with the palms of my hands; then, when I began to stroke her with my fingers and her eyes closed, my mind began to wander.

'I need to borrow this.'

I took her notebook and pen, and began to make an inventory of what I found on her flesh. I did this, as they say on television, in no particular order. I went to what interested me.

The first thing I noticed was a light brown eyelash on her throat, one of her own. On her forehead there was one hard spot and one pus-filled, with several others under the skin. Her hair looked as though it had been dyed a while ago; parts of it had been bleached by the sun. It was hard to make out its original colour. Her lips were a little ribbed and sore, the bottom more than the top.

I found a purplish bruise, recent, on her side where, perhaps, she had knocked into a table. On her knees there were three little childhood scars. I ran my fingers along the still-livid scar where, I guessed, she'd had her gall-bladder removed. She had five painted toenails, all chipped, and five, on the other foot, unpainted: I guess she must have got bored. There was a lot of sand, mostly dry, between her toes, on the soles of her feet and instep.

She wore cheap silver ear-rings, but I didn't feel she was interested in personal adornment. One ear lobe was slightly inflamed. I also found a leaf on her leg, several insects, dead and alive, in different places, and dirt on her leg. The skin around her fingernails had been pulled and torn. Her cheap watch told the wrong time. Her teeth seemed good; perhaps she had worn a brace as a child, but they were stained, now, from smoking, and one was chipped. There were random and quite deep scratch-marks on one arm (left), which I had noticed before but hadn't attended to. They appeared to have been done with an insufficiently sharp object – a penknife, say, rather than a razor-blade – as if she'd decided to doodle on herself on the spur of the moment, without preparing.

I peered into her ears and mouth, between her legs and then her toes, where I discovered another insect; I looked up her nose – surprisingly hairless, compared to mine. On her chest she had scored what I guessed to be the word 'poet'. On her thigh, there were other words which had been recently bleeding.

I wrote, in the fatuous modern manner, 'This is a Person in the Here and Now Lying Down', and jotted it down, forensically, working in silence for an hour. I kept the dead insects, the leaf, a couple of public hairs, an example of the dirt, a smear of blood and vaginal mucus, and a record of the words, inside her notebook. Mostly her eyes were closed, her breaths deep and long.

I awoke her from her 'dream', and showed her what I'd been doing.

'No one's ever done a nicer thing for me,' she said.

'Pleasure.'

'You said to me once, what people want is to be known. Can I ask you: what is that scar you have?'

'What scar? Where?'

She looked at me as though I were stupid, before pointing it out to me. It was under my elbow, in the soft flesh.

'You don't know what it is?'

'I probably do,' I said, irritably. 'I don't even remember where I got it.'

'You don't want to know yourself. You don't know yourself as well as you know me. I don't understand that. If you knew yourself you wouldn't have done what you did with that woman.'

'I don't see why we have to know either ourselves or each other.'

'But what else is there?'

'Enjoying each other.'

'Knowing is enjoying, for me.'

These were the sort of wrangles we liked. After, we walked back in silence.

I noticed, out at sea, a large yacht with little boats carrying provisions out to it. I'd forgotten that everyone from the Centre had been invited to a party on it that evening. I hadn't taken much notice at the time, but there were numerous rumours about the owner. He was either a gangster, film producer or computer magnate. I wasn't sure which was considered to be worse. I was surprised when Patricia announced at breakfast that we were all going. I was intending to miss it; I couldn't see that Patricia would even notice my absence. How things had changed since then! Hadn't she said to me, a couple of hours ago, 'See you tonight!'

I couldn't defy Patricia and remain at the Centre. If I was going to leave, I'd have to know where I was going.

I said goodbye to Alicia and went to the roof to think. I discovered myself to be even more furious than before about what Patricia had done to me, and furious with myself for having failed to escape untouched. I would insist on sleeping alone tonight, and leave for Athens by the first boat. I packed my bags in readiness. I was young; I could run.

5

I went to eat in a taverna in town, reading at the table. After a few pages, I thought 'I can do this.' I pulled some paper from my rucksack and started on a story, which offered itself to me. It was something seen, or apprehended as a whole – almost visual – which I felt forced to find words for. My hands were shaking; without literature I couldn't think, and felt stifled by a swirl of thoughts which took me nowhere new. But writing and the intricacies of its solitude was a habit I needed to break in order to stray from myself. Some artists, in their later life, become so much themselves, they go their own way, that they are no longer open to influence, to being changed or even touched by anyone else, and their work takes on the nature of obsession. Margot once said to me, 'When you think or feel something important, instead of saying it, you write it down. I'd love it to rain on your computer!'

It did. I put away my pen and paper, paid, and left.

At the Centre the voices, usually so quietly fervent, were almost raucous. Everyone, apart from Patricia, who had yet to appear, had gathered in colourful skirts, dresses and wraps. Some wore bells on their ankles; many wore bras. The night air, invariably sweet, vibrated with clashing female perfumes; jewellery flashed and jingled. Excitement about the party on the yacht was so high that some people were already dancing.

I was wearing my usual shorts and white T-shirt. I'd bought this body because I liked it as it was, a pure fashion item which didn't require elaboration.

I laughed when I saw that Alicia had attempted to comb her hair, making it look even more frizzy. With the light behind her, she looked as though she had a halo. She also wore lipstick, which I'd never seen on her. It was as if she were trying out being 'a woman'.

'I was afraid you wouldn't come,' she said.

'Me too,' I replied.

'We're on the trip, then.'

'Looks like it.'

Our singularity made us both seem insubordinate, as if we were refusing to enter into the spirit of the evening, which was how, to my regret, I'd been as a young man – rebellion as affectation. Not that anyone seemed to notice. With the arrival of Princess Patricia in a long tie-dyed skirt and with flowers in her hair, the party became impossible to resist.

At Patricia's entrance, I said to Alicia, 'I didn't realise we were attending a film premiere!'

After posing in the door until everyone became silent and took her in, she came to me, kissed me on the lips, patted my face, licked her lips, and refused to acknowledge Alicia.

'Are we ready?'

She held my arm and pulled me along, telling the others to follow. It was clear: she wanted to go on the cruise because she wanted to show me off.

Patricia and I led what became a kind of procession through the village to the beach. The old men, sitting at café tables watching us pass, seemed not only to be from another era, but appeared to be another kind of species altogether.

On the beach, where other foreigners from the island were gathering, a band greeted us. In the distance, the yacht, the only bright thing in the dark ocean, glittered beneath the emerging stars. Despite Patricia's attention, I was glad to be there.

Small boats carried us to the yacht. Patricia sat beside me, holding my hand. 'I've been walking on air ever since our love-making. You were just what I needed.' She kept leaning across me.

'Patricia . . .' I was going to tell her, coyly, that I didn't want things to 'move along' too quickly. 'I think we –'

She interrupted me. 'You didn't even get changed,' she said. 'Hold still, then. Let me put this in.' She was fiddling with my ear. 'Now we have matching ear-rings.' She patted my face, sat back and looked at me.

I touched my ear. 'Oh, yes,' I said, perplexed. 'I must have forgotten I'd had it pierced.'

'There are several holes. What a funny boy you are,' she said. 'I've watched you dancing. You do it wonderfully. You must have trained somewhere.'

'I did.'

'Where?' She went on, 'Will you dance with me all night?'

'Not all night, Patricia.'

She took my hand and slipped it between her thighs. 'Most of it, then, darling boy.'

We were helped from the boat onto the yacht. The owner, Matte, an excitable young man, greeted us on deck.

'Thank you, Patricia, for bringing your crew! You are all welcome!' he said. He waved at the women following us. 'Come along, girls! Let's get down!'

As we looked around the boat, Strauss's *Also sprach Zarathustra* in the von Karajan version began playing. I adore Richard Strauss, but am ready to admit how much great music has been turned into kitsch. Where is there to turn for something that sounds fresh today, except to the new or weird? You couldn't turn Bartók's quartets or Webern's meditations into easy listening.

Oddly, though, the Strauss didn't seem only sententious. Against the sea and sky, in this place, and taken by surprise – which, it seems to me, is often the best way to hear music; walking into a shop one Saturday morning and hearing Callas; tricked into amazement – it thrilled and uplifted me again.

This was what I, as a young man, would have wanted.

Food, drink and sexual possibility appeared to be limitless. Matte's uniformed staff walked about with trays, some of which held sex toys and condoms. There was a disco and a band. Those people already there appeared to be British, American and European playboys, models, actors, singers, pleasure-seekers, indolent aristocrats. There were also people that even I recognised from the British newspapers, pop stars and their partners, and actors from soap operas. These were people with groovy sunglasses and ideal bodies – I guessed that different parts of their bodies were of different ages and materials – who made it clear they had seen all this before, and liked being looked at.

Alicia nudged me. 'Someone's staring at you.'

A young woman was indeed looking at me. I smiled, and received a timid wave.

'As always, you're popular,' said Alicia. 'Can I ask who it is?'

'I don't know. She looks like a movie star.'

'You know movie stars?'

'Of course not, but they all know me.' I returned the woman's wave. 'Come on.'

We all strolled around. Patricia seemed to be doing a fine impression of Princess Margaret in her heyday. Alicia and I, at least, weren't sure whether to resist or swoon at the sight of so much gold. Alicia said she liked the way English Londoners were sneery and hated to be credulous, whereas I now found that tedious. This time round I wanted to like things.

When, for a moment, Alicia went to fetch a drink, the 'film star' who'd waved earlier covered herself up and hurried over.

'How funny to meet you here,' she said, kissing me.

I kissed her back; I had to. But I was afraid she'd known me as 'Mark'; perhaps we'd been 'married'. I vowed that when I next saw Ralph I would put an end to his immortality.

'Don't you know me?'

I looked at her until a picture came into my mind. It was of an old woman in a wheelchair wearing a pink flannel night-gown. This woman and I had become Newbodies on the same day. We were, in a sense, the same age.

I said, 'Good to see you. How are you enjoying it?'

'I don't know. Wherever I go, people try to touch or have me. If I don't comply, they're nasty. Still,' she said, 'I wouldn't have men fighting over me if I were a pile of ash.'

'Oh, I don't know. What else will you do?'

'I've got a record contract,' she said. 'And you?'

'It's strange, like being a ghost.'

She glanced around. 'I know. Relax now. There are others here like us. Everyone else is so silly and blind.'

'How many others like us?'

I looked at the faces and bodies behind her. How would I know who was who?

'More than you think. We play tennis and we stay up late at cards, talking about our lives. We have plenty of time, you see. Like pop stars and royalty, we stick together.'

I thought of them, the beauties around a table together, like moving statues, an art work.

I said, 'Soon, everyone in the world will know.'

'Oh, yes, I think so. Does it matter? Come and talk to me later.' She was looking down at her feet. 'Do you love your body now?'

'Why shouldn't I?'

'I'm a little too tall and my waist is too thick. My feet are big. Overall, I'm not comfortable.'

She left when Alicia rejoined me. 'You say you don't know that woman. Will you go with her now?'

'Go where? I don't know what you're talking about.'

'You can if you want,' Alicia said. 'There is time. We've set sail.'

'Set sail for where?'

Alicia was laughing at me. 'I don't know. But I do know that setting sail is what boats tend to do. We're on here until dawn.'

I ran to the side of the boat. We were already in motion. It hadn't occurred to me that I wouldn't be able to escape at any time. I considered jumping into the sea, but wasn't convinced I could swim so far. Anyway, Patricia was beside me straight away. She seemed to be insisting that I stay beside her all night. Not only at her side, in fact, but within touching distance.

She was rubbing my shoulders. 'I've never seen anything like you. I've never wanted anyone so much. I'd never have given myself permission to touch someone like you before.' Her fist was somewhere in my head. 'Where did you get that hair?'

I almost said, 'I saw it in a fridge and bought it, along with everything else you like about me.' I wondered whether that would matter. Now, at least, I knew something. The world is different for the beautiful. They're desired, oh yes; other bodies are all over them. But they don't necessarily like them.

'Come and see this,' Patricia said, without a glance at Alicia. 'A young man will be interested.'

I followed her through the boat to a cabin door. She pushed it. The room within was almost completely dark.

I stepped in. It took a couple of minutes for my eyes to adjust. There must have been about thirty naked people in the room, with a greater proportion of men than women. In a corner, there were Goyaesque mounds of bodies, lost in one another. It was difficult to tell which limb belonged to which body. I wondered whether some of the limbs had become independent of selves, turning into creatures in their own right, arms dancing with legs, perhaps, and torsos alone. There was music, talking, and – a lonely noise – the sound of others' pleasure.

Patricia tugged at my shirt. 'Let's join in.'

'I'm feeling queasy,' I said. 'I'm not used to the . . . motion.'

'Where are you going?'

I hurried through the rooms, corridors and decks of the boat, looking for somewhere she wouldn't find me for a while. For ages I heard her calling my name.

I found a small cabin. Candles were burning; the music was North African. There were oriental cushions, wall hangings, rugs, a lot of velvet. The style amused me, reminding me of the 1960s.

I liked the boat. Why couldn't I get work as a deckhand? But I was annoyed at having to leave the Centre, where I had expected to spend the rest of my time in this body. But I had got in too far with the people there. It was no longer restful. Whatever happened tonight, I would leave the island in the morning, taking the first boat wherever it went. I would go to another island and find a job in a bar or disco.

I heard footsteps. It wasn't Patricia, but Matte, the owner of the yacht, in shorts, bright shirt and flip-flops.

'What the fuck are you doing in here?'

'Am I in the wrong place?' I got up. 'You forgot to set aside a quiet room. It was chaotic and I needed to get away.'

He walked right up to me and stared into my eyes. 'Always ask first.'

I said, 'If I had a room, it'd be like this. The mid-sixties has always been one of my favourite periods.'

'Right. Want a glass of wine now?'

'If that's okay. We were introduced, but in case you've forgotten, the name's Leo.'

He said, 'Matte. Why would someone your age be interested in the sixties?'

'Must be something to do with my parents. And you?'

He was fixing drinks for both of us. 'Those days people knew how to have a laugh. 'Cept I was the wrong age.'

His manner of speaking gave me the impression that English wasn't his first language, but it was impossible to tell where he was from. I'd have been inclined to say, if asked, 'from nowhere'.

'Was this your father's boat?'

His body stiffened. 'Why the hell should it be?'

'I'm asking, is it a family possession?'

He said, 'I hate it when people suggest I haven't worked, that I'm only a rich playboy. I do play at things – I play at being a playboy – but it's a vacation, not a vocation.'

'Sorry,' I said. 'You wouldn't be the first to think of me as a fool. I'll get out.'

He came after me and pulled me back roughly. 'Wait right here. You have to stay now.'

'Why?'

'I recognise you from somewhere.'

'How could we have met? I'm neither a teacher nor student, only a cleaner at the Centre on the island.'

'Ever been a builder?'

'No.'

'Coach driver?'

'Nope.'

'I have seen you,' he continued, screwing up his eyes. 'It's not your face that I particularly recognise.' He walked round me then, as if I were a sculpture. 'It'll come back to me.'

'Are you sure?'

'I might look like a hairy idiot but I've got perfect vision and an excellent memory.'

He was making me nervous, more nervous, even, than Patricia. He chopped out some generous lines of coke and offered me one.

'Thanks,' I said.

He was snorting one himself when there was a knock on the door. It was one of his Thai staff. Matte went to him and then, to my surprise, turned to me.

'I'm being told that someone called Patricia is looking for you.'

'Oh, Christ.'

Matte laughed, and said to the man, 'He can't be found any- where at the moment. He's indisposed.' He shut the door. 'She's after you, eh? Wants your body.'

'Maybe I should appreciate her appreciation more. There'll be a time when no one will want to jump my old bones.'

'The one thing I've never wanted is to get old, to see your own skin blotted and withered.'

'Why is that?'

'I'm from a big family. As a kid, I hated grandmothers, aunts, old men and women kissing me. Their lips, mouths, breath over me – makes me nearly lose me lunch to think of it.'

I said, 'I remember my grandmother's cheeks and hands, her cardigan, her smell, with nothing but love. She had learned things, which made me feel safe. Anyhow, you haven't been old yet. How do you know you won't like it?'

'I haven't died yet. Or visited Northampton. I just know they won't agree with me.'

He kept looking at me as though there was something he wanted to know or ask me.

I said, 'I'll only be here a minute. All I want to do is relax.'

'You do that. I've got a party to run.'

'Right.'

Somewhat self-consciously, I turned to look out at the dark sea, hoping that when I turned back he'd be gone. I heard him lock the door. Before I could speak, I was hit, and lost my bearings.

Instinctively, I imagined Matte had struck me from behind, smashing his fist onto the back of my head with some strength. That was how it felt. But he had encircled my neck with his arm, kicked my legs away and forced me to my knees. I thought: now he's going to shoot me in the back of the head. During this I recalled, incorrectly I hope, a line from Webster: 'Of all the deaths, a violent one is best.'

'What are you doing?'

'Leo, shut it! If you keep still I won't damage you.'

'Keep still for what?'

He was searching in my hair, not unlike the way I would grab my kids and examine their heads for nits. I said, 'I never had you down for a madman.'

''Scuse me,' he said, relaxing his grip. 'I found the mark.'

'Mark?'

'Didn't you know? I guess they like to believe it's all seamless. You can get up now. How old are you really? No need to pretend. I am nearly eighty. A good age in a man, don't you think?'

I murmured, 'You look well.'

'Thanks. So do you.'

6

He said, 'Senex bis puer.'

'An old man is twice a boy?'

'That's the one. I've just taken up wrestling, along with the kick boxing.' He put up his hands. 'Wonderful sport. I'll show you a few moves later.'

I wiped my face. 'I think I've got the idea.'

But I pushed him then, a couple of times, quickly, and he fell back. He was flushed with fury. For a moment, I thought we'd be wrestling. We'd have enjoyed that. But before he could react, I'd dropped my hands and was laughing, so the argument was whether he'd lose his temper or not.

He managed not to, distracting himself by opening a cabinet within which there was a monitor. He switched it on and flicked to a channel showing the orgy room. I spotted Alicia dancing alone, naked. She looked freer than I had seen her before.

'Want this on? Or would you prefer to slip into someone comfortable – when I've finished with you?'

'Neither.'

'Nor me,' he said. 'Nothing's ever new for people like us. It takes a lot to turn us on – if anything does at all.'

'What else is there? Why have we done this?'

'But there is something left. You don't know?'

'Not unless you go to the trouble of telling me,' I said.

'Murder. It is the deepest, loveliest thing. You haven't tried it yet?' I shook my head. 'One must experience everything once, don't you think?'

I said, 'No one's ever hit me like that.'

'Shame.'

'Why did you do it?'

He touched my neck, chest and stomach. 'I considered that body for myself, but wanted something a bit wider and more chunky. I'm surprised it hung around there for so long. Still, they did have an excellent choice of new facilities. It would have looked good on me. It doesn't look bad on you. How does it feel?'

I moved my limbs a bit. 'Fine – until you attacked me.'

'How long have you had it?'

'Not even three months.'

'I didn't hurt you, did I?'

'I'll survive,' I said. 'I'm just a little annoyed. Thanks for the concern.'

'It was your body I was thinking of, rather than you. Hey, what d'you think of my body?' Without waiting for a reply, he removed his shirt. 'Sometimes, all you want is to be able to look in the mirror without disgust.' I nodded approvingly, but, obviously, not approvingly enough. 'What about this?' he said. He was showing me his penis, even slapping it against his leg with obscene pride. 'It just goes on and on.'

'Incomparable.'

'That's what they all say. How are my buns?'

'Jesus. With those you could be your own hotdog.'

'I've been in this body for three years. You get used to bodies, and the person you become in them. As with jeans, Newbodies are better the more they're worn in. You forget you're in them.' He pulled at his stomach. 'Look at that: I'm increasing here, but I don't want to be perfect. I figured out that perfection makes people crazy, or feel inferior.'

'Whereas', I said, 'it's one's weaknesses that people want to know?'

'Maybe,' he said. 'No one ever gets rid of those. I think I'll do another ten years – or even longer, if things go well – in this facility before moving on to something fitter.' He filled his glass once more and held it out. 'To us – pioneers of the new frontier!'

'We have a secret in common,' I said, 'you and me. Do you get to discuss it much with others?'

'They do talk about it, "the newies". But I want to live, not chatter. I love being a funky dirty young man. I love pouting my sexy lips and being outstanding at tennis. My serve could knock your face off! You should have seen me before. I've got the photographs somewhere. What's the point of being rich if you're lopsided and have a harelip? It was a joke, a mistake that I came out alive like that! This is the real me!'

'What I miss,' I said, 'is giving people the pleasure of knowing about me.'

He was unstoppable. 'Soon everyone'll be talking 'bout this. There'll be a new class, an elite, a superclass of superbodies. Then there'll be shops where you go to buy the body you want. I'll open one myself with real bodies rather than mannequins in the window. Bingo! Who d'you want to be today!'

I said, 'If the idea of death itself is dying, all the meanings, the values of Western civilisation since the Greeks, have changed. We seem to have replaced ethics with aesthetics.'

'Bring on the new meanings! You're a conservative, then.'

'I didn't think so. I guess I don't know what or who I am. It's always uplifting, though, to meet a hedonist – someone relieved of the tiring standards which hold the rest of us back from the eternal party.'

'You still think I'm just a playboy, do you? Look at those books!' He pointed at a shelf. 'I'm taking those in! Euripides, Goethe, Nietzsche. I'm dealing with the deepest imponderables. You know what happened to me? I was seventy-five years old. My wife leaves me – not for some virile fucker, but to become a Buddhist. She prefers old fat stomach to me! Some other cultures go for different body shapes, you know.' He went on, 'Mostly, my children don't bother with me. They're too busy with drugs! My friends are dead. I can buy women, but they don't desire me. I didn't just work all my life, I fought and scrambled and dug into the rock surface of the world with my fuckin' fingernails! I lost it all and I was dying and I was depressed. You think I wanted to check out in that state?'

'It sounds hard to say it, but that's a life, I guess. It's the failures, the hopeless digressions, the mistakes, the waste, which add up to a lived life.'

If he'd been in a pub, he'd have spat on the floor. 'You're only an intellectual,' he said. 'I deserved a better final curtain. I bought one! I can tell you, I'm doing some other pretty worthwhile things. Let's hear from you now. What are you doing with your new time?'

'Me? I'm only a menial at the Centre.'

He made a face. 'You're going to keep doing that?'

'I'm definitely not doing anything worthwhile. In fact, I can't tell you what a relief it is to have had a career rather than having to make one. Now, I'm going to enjoy my six months.'

'You're really going back into your slack old body suit?'

'This is an experiment. I wanted to find out what this would be like. But I'm still afraid of anything too . . . unnatural.'

He had been pacing about. Now he sat down opposite me. His tone was more than businesslike; he was firm, but not quite threatening, though it seemed he could become so.

He said, 'You can sell that one, then.'

'Sell what?'

'That body.'

'Sell it?'

'Yeah, to me. I'll pay you well. You will make a substantial profit which you and your family can live on for the rest of your God-given life.'

'What about my old body?'

'I'll get that back for you. No problem. An old body sack is about as valuable as a used condom.' He was looking at me passionately. 'It's a good deal. What do you say?'

'I'm puzzled. You've got the money. Go and buy one. I went to a place, a kind of small hospital. I'm sure you did the same.'

'I did. You think those places are easy to find? It's not that simple any more.'

'What d'you mean?'

'You were either well connected or lucky,' he said. He was drumming his fingers. 'Things have changed already.'

'In what way?' He didn't want to say. 'To put it objectively,' I went on, 'if people want bodies so badly, they could eliminate someone. Unlike you, I'm not recommending it, only suggesting what seems obvious. This isn't the only desirable body around.'

'Bodies have to be adapted. The "mark" on the head tells you that's been achieved. The body you are in now isn't valuable in itself, but the work that's been done on it is. The people who do it are like gods, extending life. There are only three or four doctors in the world today who can do this operation, and they're like the men who made the atomic bomb – hated, admired and feared, having changed the nature of human life.'

'Do you know these body artists?'

'I can get to at least one of them,' he said. 'And I have ill acquaintances who will pay a great deal to be moved into another body facility.'

'People who will give everything rather than die. I can understand that. Wow, I'm in big demand,' I said. 'But I'll wait for my six months to be up. What's the rush?'

'Someone might be dying in awful pain with only weeks to live. They might not be able to wait for your little "try-out" to come to an end.'

'That, as they say, is life.'

'What the fuck are you talking about?'

I said, 'Is it someone you know? A friend or a lover?'

'Shut up!'

I said, 'Fine. But that's what I've decided to do. I'm not handing my body over to anyone. I'm just settling in. We're getting attached.'

'But you don't even want it! How can a few months matter when you're going back? I would advise you most strongly to sell it now.'

'Strongly, eh?'

'If I were you, I wouldn't want to put myself in unnecessary danger. You're not the sort to be able to look after yourself.'

'Matte, it's my decision. I don't want your money, and I don't want my "body holiday" interrupted.'

He was having difficulty controlling himself. Some anxiety or fury was flooding him. He walked about the cabin, with his face turned away from me.

'The demand is there,' he said. 'The bodies of young women, on which there has always been a premium, are in big demand in the United States. These women are disappearing from the streets, not to be robbed or raped but to be painlessly murdered. There are machines for doing it, which I am hoping to be involved in the manufacture of. It's a beautiful procedure, Leo. The sacked bodies are kept in fridges, waiting for the time when the operation will have been simplified. When it'll be like slotting an engine into a car, rather than having to redesign the car itself each time. People might even start to share bodies to go out in, the way girls share clothes now. They'll say to one another, "Who'll wear the body tonight?" There's no going back. Immortality is where some of us are heading, like it or not. But there will be some people for whom it will be too late.'

I was interested to meet someone in my situation and I would have liked to have spent at least one evening with a group of Newbodies – we waxen immortals – sitting around a card table, discussing the past, of which there would have been plenty, no doubt. His tone concerned me, however. I was afraid and wanted to get out of there but he had locked the door. I didn't want to provoke him; he seemed capable of anything. So when he said, 'Come, look at this – it might interest you,' I went with him.

I followed him through narrow, twisting corridors. We passed a door outside of which stood two big men in white short-sleeved shirts. Matte nodded at the men and exchanged a few words with one of them in Greek. I was going to ask Matte what they were guarding, but I had been too curious already.

We went down another corridor. At last, Matte knocked on the door of another cabin. An upper-class English voice said, 'Come.'

459

The room was dark, apart from the light shed by a table-lamp. At a desk sat a woman in her thirties, writing and listening to gentle big-band music. Her clothes appeared to be from another time, my mother's, perhaps, though I could see her hair and teeth were not. If there was something palpably strange about her, I'd have said she resembled an actress in a period film whose contemporary health and look belied the period she appeared to be representing.

Matte went to her. They spoke, and she continued her work.

He stood beside me at the door and whispered, 'That woman is a child psychologist, a genius in her field. Years ago, as a man, she looked after one of my children who was seriously disturbed. She knows almost everything about human beings. When he was ill, not long ago, I paid for him to become a Newbody. He had arthritis and was bent double. He needed to finish his book and to continue to help others, as a woman. Don't you think that's a pretty charitable thing?' He gave me a look that was supposed to shame me. 'She's not sweeping the floor somewhere and chasing sex.' He shut the door. 'What would you ask her?'

'How to die, I guess.'

'Death is dead.'

'Oh, no, everyone'll miss it so, and there would be other psychologists', I said, 'to build on his or her work.'

'She can do that herself. Life renewing itself.'

'How's her book?'

'Looks like she'll need several lifetimes. She's . . . thorough.'

'Read it?'

'A boxful of notes? Most of the time she lies on deck, "thinking". She has too much sex for my liking. I'll accept one of your points: she'd go faster if she thought she was going to snuff it. Wish she'd update her taste, too. She insists on listening to that old-time music, which reminds me of days I want to forget.'

'I guess you can't force anyone to like speed garage,' I said. 'Do your kids know you now?'

'They don't know where I am. They're not speaking to me. When they get older, if they behave themselves, I'll get them new bodies as birthday presents.'

'They'll want that?'

'Those crazy kids'll totally love it. They've been in bands and clinics and stuff. They get exhausted – you know, the lifestyle. This way they can carry on. I'm holding off telling them because I know they're gonna want to get off to a new start right away.'

'What's wrong with that?'

'If they haven't suffered enough, they're not gonna appreciate it. This isn't for everybody.'

I didn't want to listen to him, or argue any more. As with Ralph Hamlet, I found the encounter disturbing. Matte and I were both mutants, freaks, human unhumans – a fact I could at least forget when I was with real people, those with death in them.

I said, 'I need to see where Patricia is.'

For a moment I thought he wouldn't let me go. But what could he do? He was thinking hard though. Then we shook hands. 'There's plenty of women here who would be attracted to you,' he said. 'Take who you want.'

'Thanks.'

'You must think more seriously about the body sale.' He gave me his card and looked me up and down once more. 'I'm your man – first in line with a bag of cash. Look after yourself.'

I knew he was watching me walk away.

I went outside. The moon and stars were bright; the air was warm. On the deck, most of the guests had gathered and were dancing wildly, yelling and whistling. The female Newbody I'd met earlier was performing: kicking out, swaying and singing in front of a guitarist and keyboard player, encouraging us to worship her as she worshipped herself.

I asked someone, 'What's she called?'

'Miss Reborn,' I was told.

When I touched Patricia on the shoulder, she took me in her arms. 'I looked for you everywhere.'

'Matte and I were talking.'

'He wanted your opinion on things, eh?' she said with unnecessary sarcasm.

'I can't say I learned a lot about him.'

'Why not?' she said. 'Up here, I've been following the rumours
and fantasies. His family are wealthy, that's for sure.'

'Is that all?'

'Kiss me.' I did so. She said, 'His beloved brother, who is much
older than him, is dying, apparently, from an incurable disease.'

'His brother?'

'Dying painfully – on this boat, in a sealed cabin, they say.'

'Really?'

'He is yards from us, as we frolic here.' I recalled the two men
guarding a door. 'That's made you think.'

'Why don't we dance while there's time? I can't believe that
singer. Look at her move.'

'Oh, yes,' she said. 'Why didn't you suggest we dance earlier?'

'It's not too late.'

'You little liar, you weren't talking to Matte at all,' she said. 'You
were fucking. You're all cock. How many were there?'

'Too many to mention.'

'I know that if you and I are to be together it's something I'm
going to have to live with.'

'That's right.'

Her head was on my shoulder. While we danced, I could think
over what Matte had said. It wasn't difficult to see why he wanted
my body for his brother. But why didn't he go and buy one, as
I had? That was what I didn't understand – why he was so keen
on me.

I tried to forget about it. I began to enjoy dancing with Patricia,
holding and kissing her, examining the folds and creases of her old
neck and full arms, the excess flesh of her living body, and holding
her mottled hands. I thought about something he'd said, 'Who
wants a lot of Oldbodies hanging about the world? They're ugly
and expensive to maintain. Soon, they'll be irrelevant.'

Yet there was something in her I didn't want to let go of. Her body and soul were one, she was 'real', but how could such a notion count against immortality?

Matte had filled me with anxiety and foreboding. I wasn't aware of how long Patricia and I danced, but I guessed the night was gone. We must have been around the islands and back to where we'd started. I'd been on that boat far too long.

Patricia had her hands inside my shirt. 'You make me feel all slippy. I want you again. I can't wait to have you.'

Much as I was glad to be with her, I didn't think I could go through all that.

'You might have to wait a bit,' I said.

'Why?'

'Oh, I don't know. I'm tired. Look,' I said. 'There's plenty of men about. Young men on their own, too.'

I could see at least three or four well-built guys standing around the edge of the dance floor.

'Tell me something,' she said. I noticed a new clarity in her eyes. 'You won't tell me the truth, I know that. But I'll know anyway. Does touching me, kissing me, licking me . . . is it something you'd rather not do? Does my body disgust you?'

Her physical presence, her body, didn't repel me, in fact. My sister had been a nurse. She'd taught me not to find bodies repellent, only the people inside them. It was Patricia's proprietorial attitude I found difficult. While I was thinking about this, she watched me.

'Now I know,' she said. 'I thought that was it. It took me a while to figure it out.'

'Yes,' I said. 'What you do to me is a description of what you say men do to women, lower and humiliate them. It's fascistic. Patricia, whatever happened to the revolution?'

She stepped back from me, as if something had exploded inside her body.

I slipped away, moving quickly now. It wasn't her I wanted to get away from. Out of the corner of my eye I had seen Matte pointing me out to another man, who was looking to see where I was. Other men were moving towards him.

I went round to the other side of the yacht and stripped off to my pants. I tied my shoes together and stuck them down the back. I could see a few lights on the shore in the distance. Preparations were being made for disembarkation, but it would take some time. I couldn't wait. I climbed onto the rail and dived into the sea.

I had surfaced and been swimming a few minutes when I heard voices. There were splashes behind me. Others were joining in. Why? I stopped for a moment and looked behind. By the light of the ship, I could tell that the swimmers following me didn't resemble women from the Centre, but men from the boat. They were not stoned or drunk revellers either. They were swimming with purpose, without churning up the water. They must have been Matte's men. They were quick and strong. So was I; and I had the advantage, just.

I ran out of the water, put on my shoes and sprinted up the beach into the village. A few bars and discos were still open. The square was full of noise and people. I could have disappeared into the crowd somewhere, but what then? Soon everyone would start to disperse. Anyhow, I didn't want to risk running into any of my other enemies.

I hurried through the narrow alleys towards the Centre. When I got there, it was deserted, to my relief. I relaxed a little and made myself a cup of tea. I would hide out in the place until the morning. But the more I thought about it, the less safe I felt. The men following me had seemed determined. It wouldn't have been difficult for Matte to find out where I was staying, and he was ruthless.

As I was collecting my washbag and a few other things from the roof, I thought I heard someone rattling the handle of the door in the wall. I didn't hear any raised female voices either. Hurrying now, I picked up several items of women's clothing, spread out on the roof to dry, and shoved them in my rucksack.

When I heard voices within the building and saw a torchlight flash, I leapt from the roof of the accommodation block to the roof of the kitchen. I jumped down the side of the building to a narrow concrete ledge below. I knew the only way out now was down the side of the hill. I wasn't sure how steep it was exactly, but I was in no doubt that it was a stiff gradient.

Not only that, the terrain was rough. As I teetered there, trying to decide what to do, I was aware of how strong the desire to live was. Had it come to it, I could have stood on that ledge for days. I'd been depressed in my life, at times; suicidal, even. But I wasn't ready to give up my mind or my body. I wanted to live.

I jumped. It must have been twenty feet down. After hitting the earth, every staggering step was perilous. It seemed to be rocky and sandy at the same time. I couldn't stop to think. I slipped and fell most of the way; it was impossible for me to stay on my feet. My body got cut all over. What was the foliage made of? Tin? Razors? It was like rolling through broken glass. However, to my knowledge I wasn't being followed.

At the bottom of the hill, I halted. I couldn't hear anyone following me. I waited for more of the night to pass. Cautiously, I made my way towards the beach. By now, even the copulators had gone.

I broke into the bathroom of a deserted restaurant where I washed and shaved off my beard. Then I lay down on some benches, pulling a damp tarpaulin on top of me. There were slithery creatures, insects and dogs around, and men who wanted my body. I didn't sleep.

I was at the harbour before it was light, waiting for the first boat to take me back to Piraeus. I'd get to Athens and decide my next move. I had covered my head in a long, light scarf; I wore a wrap-around skirt and dark glasses. I wouldn't get on the boat until the last moment.

I was sitting at the back of a café facing the harbour when someone whispered the name I'd so foolishly given myself in my arrogance. Even as I thought of running once more, I began to shiver with terror.

Alicia, of course, had come looking for me.

'How did you find me?' I said. I indicated my outfit. 'Do these colours suit me?'

'Yes, but not all at once.'

'Some of the men on the island have been threatening me again. I know they work down here.'

She said, 'I thought: what would I do here? Where would I hide? And there you were.'

'Right,' I said. 'Do I look conspicuous?'

'Only to me. Anyone try to pick you up yet?'

'I'm too much of a tragic figure.'

'A tragic figure with most unladylike hairy ears,' she said. We had coffee together. She said, 'You're running.'

'Time to move on. Did you enjoy it last night?'

'Something strange happened. I'll tell you about it another time.' Then she said, 'I won't be staying at the Centre much longer. Patricia will be after me, when she finds you've gone. I'm disappointed you're fleeing like this.'

'I'm sorry if I have made things difficult for you, but she'll never leave me alone.'

'It's the price the beautiful have to pay. Aren't you used to it yet?'

Watching the boat being loaded up, I was getting nervous; I asked if she minded getting me a ticket from the harbour office. I could see several likely candidates for Matte's men.

On the ship, I hid in the women's toilet. After, when people started to bang on the door, I had to come out. I thought I was done for. I made my way to the car deck and hid under a blanket on the back seat of an old Mercedes. The boat docked and the driver got in without noticing me. Outside, as the traffic queued to leave, I hopped out of the car and ran for it. I sprinted out of there and into the crowd, and got a taxi.

7

I'm not sure why, but I returned to the part of London I knew. I felt safer, and more at ease in my mind, in a familiar place. In your own city, you don't have to think about where you are. Being pursued had frightened me; I was scared all the time now. I had no idea whether Matte would still be following me. I must have convinced myself that he'd lost interest in me. Perhaps his brother had died; maybe he'd found another body. I am, however, old enough to know how few of our thoughts bear any relation to the way things are.

I checked into the same dismal hotel as before. When I needed money I worked in a factory packing Christmas toys. Perhaps Matte was right, and it had been a mistake to 'hire' a body for six months. I didn't have time to begin a new life as a new person, and, expecting to go back, I missed my old life. I was in limbo, a waiting room in which there was no reality but plenty of anxiety.

One morning at eight, there was a knock on my door.

In this hotel, there were always knocks on the door – refugees, thieves, prostitutes, drug dealers; people who would never be able to afford new bodies or even to feed adequately the one they already had; people looking for other people and no one wanting to do you a favour, if it wasn't in exchange for another one. Usually, though, they would declare themselves. This time there was no reply.

Maybe Matte had come for my body. I'd seen the movie. Men in dark suits were outside. While they were kicking the door in, I'd hide in the shower with my gun, or climb out of the bathroom window and down the fire-escape. That was the young man's route, and I wouldn't be a young man in my mind, however lithe my body. For there was another part of me, my older mind, if you like, which was, by now, outraged by the violation, the cheek of it. My body wasn't for sale, though I had, of course, purchased it myself.

'How did you find me?'

Alicia was sitting on the bed; I stood looking at her. She had shaved her head and put on weight. She wore a top with a bow at the front.

'Why have you grown a full beard?'

'Alicia, I am hoping to be taken seriously.'

I'd forgotten how nervous she was. 'Leo, it's good to see you. How much do you mind me coming to see you?'

'Not as much as you might think. I do need to know how you tracked me down.'

'I haven't told Patricia – she isn't downstairs, if that's what's bothering you. I looked through your things one time . . . trying to . . . I wanted to know who you were. You do know, I guess, that you're as elusive as a spy. It turned me into a spy. I found a receipt for this hotel and wrote the address into one of my poems. Still,' she said, 'if you want to be private, why shouldn't you be? Do you want me to go?'

'I'll come with you. Let's get out of here. I never stay in this room during the day.'

I was putting on my coat.

She said, 'You're writing.'

In the corner of the room, on a small table, were some papers.

'Please don't look at that,' I said.

'Why not?'

'Leave it! I'm trying . . . to do something about an old man in a young man's body.'

'You've done a lot. Is it a film?' She was turning the pages. 'There's dialogue. It's professionally laid out. Have you written before?'

'You encouraged me, Alicia.'

'It was the other way around. Will you try to sell it?'

'You never know. Give it here now.'

'What a strange boy you are!'

I took the papers from her and put them under the bed.

In the café, I asked, 'How is my friend Patricia?'

'What a trouble-maker you are. People had paid to attend her classes but she refused to get out of bed. You showed her something was possible, some intensity of feeling with a man, and you took it away again. She would send for me and we'd talk about you for hours, wondering who you were. She would rage and weep. The only relief was when that man from the boat came to see her.'

'Man?'

'The playboy. Matte.'

'Alicia, what happened?'

'I was sent out of the room. I heard everything from outside the window.'

'And?'

'You owed him something, he said. He wouldn't say what it was. You didn't borrow money from him?' I shook my head. 'He wanted to find you, wanted to know whether there was anyone who knew you.'

'Did he threaten Patricia?'

'He didn't need to. She was delighted to talk about the intricacies of your character, in so far as she understood it, for hours. Not that this interested Matte. Of course, she doesn't know where you are. I left the island a few days later and went to Athens.'

'Were you followed?'

'Why would I be? What's going on?' Alicia said. 'You know what Patricia wanted? For you to run the place with her.'

'I'd have liked to do that,' I said. 'For a while. It would have been fun. Impossible too, of course, with her attitude towards me.'

'You'd have done it?' she said. 'Don't you have any doubts?'

'What?'

'About yourself. About what you are capable of? That makes you different to a lot of people. Different to most people, in fact.'

'Yes,' I said, 'I do have doubts. I just don't want them getting in the way of my mistakes.'

She said, 'Something else happened. I haven't told you the whole story. When you disappeared from the boat that last night –'

'Yes, sorry. I couldn't stand it –'

'Some people went back to the Centre. But I was hanging around to see whether you might return. A lot of our group stayed on the boat until after breakfast. The dawn was lovely. Matte came to me. He realised I was from the Centre. I don't look like the other people he knows, with their perfect bodies. He took me to his room. He wanted information about you.'

'What did you say?'

'He was sitting there opposite me, opening and shutting his legs like a trap. He looked almost as handsome as you. I promised to tell him everything I knew about you if he fucked me. I told him I was an unorgasmic virgin. It was time, you see. He was amused, and seems to have looked into these things. "Apparently, the use of virgins", he told me, "prolongs life. The headmaster of a Roman school for girls lived to one hundred and fifty. Rather that than ingesting the dried cells of foetal pigs, or drinking snake oil." He seemed to think it was a decent exchange. He fucked me hard, right there on the floor. It was wonderful. Is it always like that? I'm pregnant.'

'By him? Matte?'

She patted her stomach. 'Don't ask me if I'll keep it.'

'The world is full of single mothers. It's the only way, these days. What use are men? But he's not a good man.'

'I don't need to tell you, a good man is hard to find. Ask Patricia!'

'Alicia, that was a mad thing to do! You don't know him!'

'One day, I'll present him with a bill.'

'But why him?'

'You'd turned me on and I couldn't wait any longer. No one else on that boat seemed much interested in having me. I know I'm not beautiful, and as a girl all I wanted was to be beautiful. Matte was looking at me like a hungry wolf I couldn't keep from the door.'

'It's like having a kid with the devil.'

'If he's really bad, you'd better tell me the details. I can only consider my position if I know the facts. Otherwise . . . I'm going ahead with it.'

She was waiting; she seemed to be aware that there was more I knew.

'I only met him once,' I said. I kissed and cuddled her. 'Congratulations.'

'Thanks.'

'What will you do now?'

'I'm back living with Mother. Things are dark. I need to tell you, I don't know how to go on.'

I was looking at her. 'People either want eternal life or they want out right now.'

'Can you think of reasons to continue?'

'Lots. Pleasure.'

'Only that?'

'Children,' I added, 'if you like them. They always gave me more pleasure than anything else.'

'Good, good,' she said.

With her, I always felt I had to justify the most basic things, which discomforted me. Still, I liked her; I'd always liked her. I wanted to help her. Then I had an idea. I told her I had something to sort out; we agreed to meet later.

When we parted, I went to an Internet café and sent an email in my given name, to a friend who was the editor of a literary magazine which published fiction, some journalism and photographs. I urged him to see Alicia as soon as possible. I told him I didn't want my name mentioned. Then I rang Alicia and told her she had to go and see this man after lunch. After some argument she agreed to go to his office, read him a couple of poems and talk about herself.

Later that day, when we met again in a local pub, she told me he'd given her a job reading manuscripts and sorting out the office three days a week.

'That's great,' I said. 'Are you pleased?'

She kissed me. 'I knew that somehow this had happened through you, Leo. But the odd thing was, he didn't know your name.'

'No,' I said. 'He wouldn't remember me. But my father was well connected.'

'Who was your father? Or is that your privacy, right?'

We were sitting in a bar by the window where I could monitor the street for murderers. I recognised a few local people. They all looked like murderers. However, there was one person in particular I had been looking out for during the last few days, without properly admitting it to myself, someone I couldn't search out, but had to wait for.

It had to be now. There she was, my wife, across the road. The wheel of her shopping cart had come off. She was fiddling with it, but it would have to be fixed properly. At a loss, she stood there, looking around. The cart was heavy, full of provisions. She couldn't leave it and she couldn't carry it home.

I asked Alicia to excuse me. I crossed the road to my wife and asked if she were okay.

'I'm rather stuck, dear.'

'These small accidents can be devastating. Can I?'

I hauled the cart into a doorway and took a look at it. I'm not mechanical, but I could see the wheel had sheared off.

'Do you live far?'

'Ten minutes' walk.'

I said, 'I'll be a good Samaritan. Wait one minute.'

I went back to Alicia.

'This is my good deed for the week, perhaps for the century. Meet me in three hours at the pub on the corner.'

She was looking at me. 'You'd go home with any woman, apart from me.'

'It must seem like that.'

'Can't we bring up the kid together?'

I kissed her. 'Later.'

I recrossed the road and picked up the cart in my arms.

'Which way?'

It was heavy and awkward. I walked slowly, with exaggerated complaints, in order to spend more time with my wife.

'Don't you have anyone to help you?' I said.

'Not at the moment.'

We were approaching my house. I noticed the front gate was wonky and needed repairing.

She opened the front door. 'Would you like to come in?' I hesitated. 'Just for a minute,' she said.

'If it's all right with you. I wouldn't mind a glass of water.'

Inside, she said, 'Can I ask . . . what do you do?'

'I've been travelling. Gap year.'

She went into the kitchen and I looked around. Nothing had changed, but everything was slightly different.

My son, now the same age as me, came downstairs and put his head round the door. I almost gave way. It was him I wanted to touch, his hands and face. In the last few years it had become more difficult for us to touch each other. He was embarrassed, or he didn't like my body. I loved, still, to kiss his cheeks, even if I had to grab him and pull him towards me.

'All right, Mum?' Mike said. 'Hello,' he said to me.

I must have been staring.

'My cart broke,' she said.

'Your heart?' he said.

'Cart, you big idiot!'

He came into the room. He looked alert, happy and healthy. I could see my old self in the way he held himself. I missed me. I missed, too, my pleasure in him, in living close to his life, in knowing what he did and where he went.

I was dismayed to see he was carrying my new laptop, a gorgeous little sliver of light I'd bought just before deciding to become someone else. I had been intending to use it in bed. I had always been attracted to the instruments of my trade. Sometimes, merely buying a new pen or computer was enough to get me back to work.

'That looks good,' I said.

'Yes.' He said to his mother, 'I'm borrowing this for a while. I'll return it before Dad gets back. Have you heard from him?'

'He sent his love,' she called.

'Is that all?' he said. 'He won't mind me borrowing this, then. By the way, happy anniversary. Shame to be on your own.'

'I'll raise a glass later,' she said.

I said, 'Can I ask what anniversary it is?'

'Not my wedding anniversary,' she said, 'but the anniversary of the day I met my husband. He's away on business at the moment, the fool.'

'Why fool?'

'His breathing was painful. He couldn't walk far. I could see it in his face, but I don't think he knew how ill he had become. Before he started out on his jaunt across the continent, I had decided we should enjoy the time we had left together. Still, I didn't want to put him off his pleasures.'

Mike said, 'Mum, are you okay? Can I go?'

'Please do.'

He shut the front door.

I asked, 'Would you like me to get going, too?'

'But I must offer you some tea. I'd feel bad if I didn't, after you helped me.'

'You're very trusting.'

'I noticed you looking at the books just now. No burglar or lunatic would do that.'

'Your boy is a great-looking kid.'

'He's doing well. His girlfriend's pregnant.'

'Really? How wonderful. Congratulations.'

'Adam will be back for the birth, I know he will.'

I went upstairs to the bathroom. Coming out, I noticed my study door was open. The books I'd been using before I left were piled on the coffee table, next to the CDs I'd bought but not yet played. I couldn't resist sitting down at my desk. I looked at the photographs of my children at various ages. I knew where everything was, though my hands were bigger and my arms longer than before. The ink in my favourite fountain pen still flowed. I wrote a few words and shoved the paper in my pocket. I had to tear myself away.

When I returned, I sat beside Margot and poured the tea. I glanced at the wedding ring I'd bought her and said, 'Where are you from?'

'Me? You're asking me?' she said. 'Do you want to know?'

'Why not?'

'No one's much interested in women of my age.'

When she told me where she was born, and a little about her parents, I asked other questions about her early life and upbringing. I followed what occurred to me, listening and prompting.

I had heard some of this before, in the years when we were getting to know each other. I had not, though, asked her about it for a long time. How many times can you have the 'same' conversation? But the past was no more inert than the present: there were different tones, angles, details. She mentioned people I'd never heard of; she talked about a lover she'd cared for more than she'd previously admitted.

Her story made more sense to me now, or I was able to let more of it in. We drank tea and wine. She was stimulated by my interest, and amazed by how much there was to tell. She wanted to speak; I wanted to listen.

I asked only about her life before she met me. When my name arose and she did speak about me a little, I didn't follow it up. I wish I'd had the guts to listen to every word – my life judged by my wife, a summing-up. But it would have disturbed me too much.

How she moved me! Listening to her didn't tell me why I loved her, only that I did love her. I wanted to offer her all that I'd neglected to give in the past few years. How withdrawn and insulated I'd been! It would be different when I returned as myself.

Two hours passed. At last, I said, 'Now, I really must get going. I should let you get on.'

'What about you?' she said. She was shaking her head. 'I feel as though I'm coming round from a dream. What have we been doing together?'

I went over to the table on which sat a music system and a pile of CDs.

'Can I play a tune?'

She said, 'Oh, tell me, why did you ask me all those questions?'

'Did they bother you?'

'No, the opposite. They stimulated me ... they made me think ...'

'I'm interested in the past. I am thinking of becoming a medieval historian.'

'Oh. Very good.' She added, 'But what you asked was personal, not historical. You are a curious young man, indeed.'

'Something happened to me,' I said. 'I was changed by something. I . . .'

She waited for me to continue, but I stopped myself. Sometimes there's nothing worse than a secret, sometimes there's nothing worse than the truth.

She said, 'What happened?'

'No. My girlfriend is waiting for me down the street.'

I put on my wife's favourite record. I kissed her hands and felt her body against mine as we danced. I knew where to put my hands. In my mind, her shape fitted mine. I didn't want it to end. Her face was eternity enough for me. Her lips brushed mine and her breath went into my body. For a second, I kissed her. Her eyes followed mine, but I could not look at her. If I was surprised by the seducibility of my wife, I was also shocked by how forgettable, or how disposable, I seemed to be. For years, as children, our parents have us believe they could not live without us. This necessity, however, never applies in the same way again, though perhaps we cannot stop looking for it.

At the door, my wife said, 'Will you come for tea again?'

'I know where you are,' I replied. 'I don't see why not.'

'We could go to an exhibition.'

'Yes.'

I said goodbye, and reluctantly left my own house. Margot had placed a bag of rubbish outside the front door, ready to be taken to the dustbins. I was annoyed my boy hadn't done it; he must have had his hands full, carrying my laptop.

I took the rubbish round to the side of the house. From where I stood, through a hole in the fence, I could see the street. There was a car double-parked on the other side of the road, with two men in it. It was a narrow street and irritable drivers were backed up behind the car. Why didn't they move on? Because the men in the car were watching the house.

I slipped out of the front gate and headed up the road, away from them. It was true: they were following me. I went into my usual paper shop. Outside, the men were waiting in the car. When I continued on my way, they followed me. Who were these men who followed other men?

I knew the streets. Under the railway line, beside the bus garage, was a narrow alleyway through which, years ago, I'd walked the children to school. I turned into it and ran; they couldn't follow me in the car.

Of course, they wanted me badly and were waiting at the top of the alley. This wasn't the death I wanted. I walked quickly. Further down the street the three of them got out of the car and stood around me. Their faces were close; I could smell their aftershave. There were a lot of people on the street.

'Where are you taking me?'

'You'll find out.'

Another of them murmured, 'I've got a gun.'

One of them had put his hand on my arm. It riled me; I don't like being held against my will. Yet I gained confidence; the gun, if it was really a gun, had helped me. I didn't believe they'd shoot me. The last thing they'd want to do was blow up my body.

I started to shout, 'Help me! Help me!'

As people turned to look, the men tried to pull me into the car, but I kicked and hit out. I heard a police siren. One of the men panicked. People were looking. I was away, and running through the closely packed market stalls. The three of them weren't going to chase me with guns through the crowd on market day.

As soon as I could, I rang Ralph's mobile from a phone box.

It was impossible for us to meet. He was 'up to his neck in literature'. Unfortunately, the fool had already told me where he was.

Half an hour later, I pushed open the pub door and entered. I'm a sentimentalist and want always for there to be the quiet interminability of a London pub in the afternoon, rough men playing pool, others just sitting in near silence, smoking. I couldn't see Ralph, but did notice a sign which said 'Theatre and Toilets'. I tripped down some narrow stairs into an oppressive, dank-smelling room, painted black. There were old cinema seats and, in one corner, a box office the size of a cupboard. Pillars seemed to obstruct every clear view of the tiny stage. I saw from the posters that they were doing productions of *The Glass Menagerie* and *Dorian Gray*.

A woman hurried over, introducing herself as Florence O'Hara. She wanted to know how many tickets I wanted for *The Glass Menagerie*, in which she played the mother. Or did I want tickets for *Hamlet*, in which she played Gertrude? If I wanted to see them both, there was a special offer.

As she said this, I was surprised to see, sitting in the gloom, unshaven and in a big overcoat, a well-known actor, Robert Miles, who'd been in a film I'd written seven years ago. Before it began shooting, he and I had had tea together several times.

I looked at Florence more closely. I could recall Robert trying to get her a small part in the film. They'd been lovers, and were still connected in some way.

Had I not been inhabiting this wretched frame, Robert and I could, no doubt, have exchanged greetings and gossip. Instead, when he saw me looking at him, being both nervous and arrogant, he got up and walked out.

At the same time, Ralph emerged, in the costume of a Victorian gentleman or dandy, with a top hat in his hand. We shook hands, and I sat behind him in the theatre seats.

'I haven't got long,' he said.

'Nor me.'

'There's a show later. During the day, I'm working on a new play with Robert Miles. He's trying his hand at directing. I'm working with the best now.'

Ralph was looking tired; his face seemed a little more lined than before.

He said, 'I'm playing Dorian Gray as well. Florence is Sybil. I'm having the time of my life here.' He glanced at me. 'What's wrong? What can I do for you now?'

I told Ralph that Matte had 'recognised' me, was a Newbody himself, required a body for his brother, and was in pursuit of mine. How could this not bother Ralph? After all, wasn't he, theoretically, in a similar position?

'You come to me with these problems, but what can I do about any of them?'

'Ralph, anyone would recognise that, as with anything uniquely valuable – gold, a Picasso – bad people will be scrambling and killing for it. How could they not? But I can't just remove this body as I could a necklace.'

'At least, not yet,' he said. Ralph was looking around agitatedly. 'You stupid fool. Why have you come here? You might have led them to me. They could kidnap me while I'm on stage and strip me down to my brain.'

'How would they know you're a freak like me?'

'Don't fucking call me a freak! Only if you bloody well tell them. And I'm always afraid my maturity is going to give me away. What have you done to alert these people?'

By now, I was yelling, and I had big lungs.

'If you think this isn't going to be something that a lot of people are going to know about, you're a fool.'

He leaned closer to me. 'You get full-on, full-time security. Big guys around you all the time. That's the price of a big new dick and fresh liver.'

'How am I going to afford it?'

'You'll have to work.'

'At what?'

'What d'you think? You used to be a writer. You can start again, in another style. You could become . . . let's say, a magical realist!' I could see Florence in the dressing-room doorway, waving at him. 'Imagine where I'll be in ten years' time, in fifteen, in twenty! How do you know I won't be running one of the great theatres or opera houses of the world?' I was sitting there with my head in my hands. 'I didn't tell you. I will now. Ophelia and I – the girl playing that part, of course – are getting married. I didn't tell you this either:

we have a child together. A few days old, and perfect. I was afraid for a while that it would be some kind of oddity.'

'Well done.'

'Are you going to see the show? Maybe it's better you don't hang around here, if you're being chased.'

I indicated my body. 'All I want', I said, 'is to be rid of this, to get out of this meat. I want to do it tonight, if possible.' He was looking at me pityingly. 'I guess I could find the hospital myself, but I'm in a hurry. What's the address of the place you took me to?'

'Up to you,' he said, sceptically.

He told me the address. I wouldn't forget it. He was glad to be rid of me.

I said, 'Good luck with the show. I'll come and see it in a few days' time, with my wife. She and I are planning to spend a lot of time together.'

At the top of the stairs, I heard Florence's voice behind me.

'What name?' she called.

'What?'

'What name for the tickets to the show?'

'I'll let you know.'

'Don't you even know your own name?'

Coming into the pub was a young woman with a baby in a sling. Ralph's kid, I guessed. But I was in too much of a hurry to stop. There was a miserable cab office at the end of the street where, in my old frame, I had known the drivers and listened to their stories.

I told the cabbie to drive fast. As we went, I looked around continuously, staring into every car and face for potential murderers, thinking hard, convinced I was still being followed. Where I was going wasn't far, but I had to be careful.

Not long after we'd left the city, I said, suddenly, to the driver, 'Drop me off here.'

'I thought you wanted –'

'No, this is fine.' We were approaching an area of low, recently built industrial buildings. 'Listen,' I said, holding up the last of my money, 'give me the petrol can you keep in the back of the car. I've broken down near by, and I'm in a hurry.'

He agreed, and we went round to the boot of the car. He gave me the can and I wrapped it in a black plastic bag. I picked it up and headed for a pub I'd noticed. There, I had a couple of drinks and went into the toilet. I locked the cubicle door and stripped.

It took some time and I was careful and thorough. When I'd finished, and got back into my clothes, I left the pub and ran through the bleak streets towards the building, or 'hospital', I remembered. Soon, I was disoriented, but the address was right. The layout of the streets and the other buildings was the same. Then I saw it. The place had changed. It could have been years ago that I was there. The building I believed to be the 'hospital' was encircled by barbed wire; grass was poking up through the concrete. In the front, an abandoned filing cabinet was lying on its side. What sort of elaborate disguise was this?

I climbed the fence and pushed my way through the wire, which had been severed in several places. Nobody seemed bothered about security. The front door of the 'hospital' wasn't even locked. However, it was getting dark. I tried the lights, but the electricity had been turned off. Bums had probably been sleeping there on rotten mattresses. The place also seemed to have been vandalised by local kids. I guessed that everything important had been taken away long before that. There were no bodies around, neither new nor old. I didn't know what to do now but there was no reason to stay.

I heard a voice.

8

'We weren't too bothered about capturing you earlier. We guessed you'd end up here.'

Matte emerged from the gloom. A torch was shining in my face. I covered my eyes.

I asked, 'You always knew about this place?'

'I knew the caravan would have moved on, but figured out you'd be less well connected than me. I still need that body.'

'Looks like I'm going to need it myself.'

'You've argued yourself out of it. Someone else's need is greater.'

'Your brother?'

'What? Let me worry about him.'

I said, 'You can take the body. There's a lot of life still in it. All I want is the old one back.'

'Come through here.' He pointed to the door, and added, 'This place smells bad, or is it just you?'

'It's the place, too.'

He said, 'Jesus, what the fuck have they been doing, burning bodies?'

I followed him, surrounded by his three men, into another room. I noticed there were no windows; the floors were concrete and covered with broken glass and other debris. The tiles had been pulled up and smashed. Long, bright neon lights were positioned precariously. A man in blue doctor's scrubs was standing there with two assistants, all of them masked. In the middle of the room stood the sort of temporary operating table they use on battle-fields, along with medical instruments on steel trays. I was looking around for my old body. Maybe it was being kept in another room and they'd wheel it in. I couldn't wait to see it again, however crumpled or corpse-like it might seem.

'Where's my old body?' I said to the man I assumed to be the doctor. 'I won't get far without it.'

He looked at Matte, but neither of them said anything.

'I see,' I said. 'There's no body. It's gone.' I sighed. 'What a waste.'

'Tough luck,' he said. 'You're going to eternity. When I've sorted this out, my brother and I are off to Honolulu for a family reunion. The only shame is, he'll remind me of you.'

I noticed, on the floor, what looked like a long freezer on its side. It was large enough for a body the size of mine. There was a wooden box, too, big enough for a dead brain. Brains didn't take up much room, I guessed, and were not difficult to dispose of.

'Can I have a cigarette?' I said.

'That's what did for my brother.'

'My last,' I said. 'Then I'll give up. Promise.'

'Glad to hear it,' said Matte. 'Okay. Get on with it.'

One of the men handed me a cigarette. 'Arsehole.'

'You too,' I said.

The man made a move towards me. Matte said, 'Don't damage him! No bruises, and don't cut him up.'

I said, 'I'm going to undress now, have a smoke, and then I'll be ready for you.'

'Good boy,' said Matte. 'You wanted a death and now you're going to get one.' When I removed my jacket and shirt, Matte looked at me approvingly. 'You look good. You've kept yourself in shape.'

'Look at my dick, guys.' I was waving it at them. 'Wouldn't you like to have one of these?'

Matte said, 'What the fuck's that aftershave you're wearing?'

I lit my lighter, and moved backwards.

'It's petrol,' I said. 'I'm soaked in it. Never had petrol in my hair before. You come near me, pal, and this body you want goes up in flames like a Christmas pudding. And you too, of course.'

I held the lighter close to my chest. I didn't know how much closer I could get it without turning into a bonfire. Still, rather self-immolation than the degradation which would otherwise be my fate. I'd go out with a bang, burning like a torch, screaming down the road.

Apart from Matte, everyone retreated. The doctors shrank back. Matte wanted to grab me. There was a moment when, to be honest, he could have done it. But the others' fear seemed to affect him. He didn't know what to do; all he could do was play for time.

There was nothing behind me but the door, which was open. I picked up my shirt and trousers, before turning and fleeing. I ran, and I guess they ran, but I ran faster and I knew my way out of there.

I climbed the fence, got dressed and continued to run. It was dark, but I was fit and had some idea where I was going. They'd get in their cars and pursue me, but I was being canny now. I was away. They would never find me.

It didn't occur to me for a long time to consider my destination. When I felt safe I rested in someone's garden. I needed a drink, but sweat and petrol don't smell good together. The last thing I needed was suspicious looks. I was carrying my credit cards, but I realized there was nowhere I could go now; not back to my wife, to my hotel, or to stay with friends. I wouldn't be safe until Matte's brother died, or Matte turned his attention elsewhere. Even then there could be other criminals pursuing me. It was as though I were wearing the *Mona Lisa*.

I was a stranger on the earth, a nobody with nothing, belonging nowhere, a body alone, condemned to begin again, in the nightmare of eternal life.

Hullabaloo in the Tree

'Come along now!'

The father, having had enough, decided it was time they all left the playground.

A week ago, in this park, they had run into an Indian friend, a doctor, who'd been shocked by the disrespect and indiscipline of the father's children. The second seven-year-old twin, the one in the Indiana Jones hat, had said to the doctor friend, 'What are you – an idiot?'

The father had had to apologise.

'They are speaking to everyone like this?' the friend had said to the father. 'I know we live here now, but you have let them become Western, in the worst way!'

No English friend would have presumed to say such a thing, the father had commented, later at home.

'The problem is,' the kid had replied, 'he's a brown face.'

The father, furious and agitated ever since, thought he should start being more authoritative.

'We're going!' he said now, in what he considered to be almost his 'sharpest' voice.

He picked up the blue plastic ball and strode out of the enclosed playground and into the park. The seven-year-old twins had been hitting each other with sticks and the two-year-old had been flung from the roundabout, scraping his leg.

Still, they would walk across Primrose Hill to a café on the other side. The children had been asking for drinks; he wanted a coffee.

What better way was there to spend a Sunday morning in the adult world?

To his surprise, his three sons followed him without complaint. His friend should have been there to witness such impressive obedience. His wife-to-be had run into an acquaintance and he could see her still chatting, beside the swings. He had already interrupted her once. Why was it that the time he most wanted to talk to her was when she was engaged with someone else?

Outside the playground, in the open park, with the hill rising up in front of him and the sky beyond it, he felt like walking forwards for a long time with his eyes closed, leaving everyone behind, in order, for a bit, to have no thoughts. For years, before his children were born, he seemed to have forfeited Sundays altogether. Now the poses, the attitude, the addictions and, worst of all, the sense of unlimited time had been replaced by a kind of exhausting chaos and a struggle, in his mind, to work out what he should be doing, and who he had to be to satisfy others.

He didn't walk towards the hill, however, but stood there and held the ball out in front of him.

'Watch, you guys! Pay attention!' he said.

What were fathers for if not to kick balls high into the air while their sons leaned back, exclaiming, 'Wow, you've nearly broken through the clouds! How do you do that, Daddy?'

He enjoyed it when, after this display, they grabbed the ball and tried to kick it as he had done. The seven-year-olds, who lived a few streets away with their mother but were staying for the weekend, had begun to imitate many of the things he did, some of which he was proud of, some of which were ridiculous or irrelevant, like wearing dark glasses in the evening. When they went out together they resembled the Blues Brothers. Even the two-year-old had begun to copy the languid way he spoke and the way he lay on the couch, reading the paper. It was like being surrounded by a crowd of venomous cartoonists.

Now, the father dropped the ball towards his foot but mis-kicked it.

'Higher, Daddy!' called the two-year-old. 'Up, up, sky!'

The two-year-old had long blond hair, jaggedly cut by his mother, who leaned over his cot with a torch and scissors while he was asleep. The boy was wearing a nappy, socks, T-shirt and shoes, but had refused to put his trousers on. The father had lacked the heart to force him.

The father jogged across and fetched the ball. Making the most of their attention while he still had it, he screamed, 'Giggs, Scholes, Beckham, Daddy, Daddy, Daddy – it's gone in!' and drove the ball as hard and far as he could, before slipping over in the mud.

Some shared silences, particularly those of confusion and disbelief, you never want to end, so rare and involving are they.

The oldest twin set down and opened the small suitcase in which he kept his guns, the books he'd written and a photograph of the Empire State Building. He peered into the tree through the wrong end of his new binoculars.

'It's far, far away, nearly in heaven,' he said. 'Here, you see.'

The father got to his feet. Removing his sunglasses, he was already looking up to where the ball, like an errant crown, was resting on a nest of smallish twigs, at the top of a tree not far from the entrance to the playground.

The two-year-old said, 'Stuck.'

'Bloody hell,' said the father.

'Bloody bloody,' repeated the two-year-old.

The father glanced towards the playground. His wife-to-be still hadn't emerged.

'Throw things!' he said. One of the older boys picked up a leaf and tossed it backwards over his head. The father said, 'Hard things, men! Come on! Together we can do this!'

The twins, who welcomed the pure concentration of a crisis, began to run about gathering stones and conkers. The father did the same. The youngest boy jumped up and down, flinging bits of bark. Soon, the air was filled with a hail of firm objects, one of which struck a dog and another the leg of a kid passing on a bicycle. The father picked up one of the twins' metal guns and hurled it wildly into the tree.

'You'll break it!' said the son reproachfully. 'I only got it yesterday.' The father began to march away. 'Where are you going?' called the boy.

'I'm not going to hang around here all day!' replied the father. 'I need coffee – right now!'

He would leave the cheap plastic ball and, if necessary, buy another one on the way home.

Did he, though, want his sons to see him as the sort of man to kick balls into trees and stroll away? What would he be doing next – dropping twenty-pound notes and leaving them on the street because he couldn't be bothered to bend down?

'What are you up to?' His wife-to-be had come out of the playground. She picked up the youngest child and kissed his eyes. 'What has Daddy done now?'

The twins were still throwing things, mostly at each other's heads.

'Stop that!' ordered the father, coming back. 'Let's have some discipline here!'

'You told us to do it!' said the elder twin.

The second twin said, 'Don't worry, I'm going up.'

Probably the most intrepid of the two, he ran to the base of the tree. As well as his Indiana Jones hat, the second twin was wearing a rope at his belt 'for lassoing', though the only thing he seemed to catch was the neck of the two-year-old, whom otherwise, most of the time, he liked. At six o'clock that morning the father had found him showing the little one his penis, explaining that if he tugged at the end and thought, as he put it, about something 'really horrible, like Catwoman', it would feel 'sweet and sour' and 'quite relaxed'.

The boy was saying, 'Push me up, Daddy. Push, push, push!'

The father bundled him into the fork of the tree, where he clung on enthusiastically but precariously, like someone who'd been dumped on the back of a horse for the first time.

'Put me up there too,' said a girl of about nine, who'd been watching and was now jumping up and down beside him. 'I can climb trees!'

The two-year-old, who had a tooth coming through and whose face was red and constantly wet, said, 'Me in tree.'

'I can't put the whole lot of you up there,' said the father.

The youngest said, 'Daddy go in tree.'

'Good idea,' said his wife-to-be.

'I'd be up there like a shot,' said the father. 'But not in this new shirt.'

His wife-to-be was laughing. 'And not in any month with an "r" in it.'

Unlike most of his male antecedents, the father had never fought in a war, nor had he been called upon for any act of physical bravery. He had often wondered what sort of man he'd be in such circumstances.

'Right,' he said. 'You'll see!'

They were all watching as the father helped the boy down and clambered into the tree himself. His wife-to-be, who was ten years younger, shoved him with unnecessary roughness from behind, until he was out of reach.

Feeling unusually high up, the father waved grandly like a president in the door of an aeroplane. His family waved back. He extended a foot onto another branch and put his weight onto it. It cracked immediately and gave way; he stepped back to safety, hoping no one had noticed the blood drain from his face.

He might, this Sunday morning, be standing on tip-toe in the fork of a tree, a slip away from hospital and years of pain, but he did notice that he had the quiet attention of his family, without the usual maelstrom of their demands. He thought that however much he missed the peace and irresponsibility of his extended bachelorhood, he had at least learned that life was no good on your own. Next week, though, he was going to America for five months, to do research. He would ring the kids, but knew they were likely to say, in the middle of a conversation, 'Goodbye, we have to watch *The Flintstones*,' and replace the receiver. When he returned, how different would they be?

Now he could hear his wife-to-be's voice calling, 'Shake it!'

'Wiggle it!' shouted one of the boys.

'Go, go, go!' yelled the girl.

'Okay, okay,' he muttered.

At their instigation, he leaned against a fat branch in front of him, grasped it, gritted his teeth, and agitated it. To his surprise and relief there was some commotion in the leaves above him. But he could also see that there was no relation between this activity and the position of the ball, far away.

The nine-year-old girl was now climbing into the tree with him, reaching out and grasping the belt of his trousers as she levered herself up. It was getting a little cramped on this junction, but she immediately started up into the higher branches, stamping on his fingers as she disappeared.

Soon, there was a tremendous shaking, far greater than his own, which brought leaves, twigs, small branches and bark raining down onto the joggers, numerous children and an old woman on sticks who were now staring at the hullabaloo in the tree.

This was a good time, he figured, to abandon his position. He would pick up the ball when the girl knocked it down. In fifteen minutes' time he would be eating a buttered croissant and sipping a semi-skimmed decaf latte. He might even be able to look at his newspaper.

'What's going on?'

A man had joined them, holding the hands of two little girls.

The youngest twin said, 'Stupid Daddy was showing off and –'

'All right,' said the father.

The man was already removing his jacket and handing it to one of the girls, saying, 'Don't worry, I'm here.'

The father looked at the man, who was in his late thirties, ruddy-faced and unfit-looking, wearing thick glasses. He had on a pink ironed shirt and the sort of shoes people wore to the office.

'It's only a cheap ball,' said the father.

'We were just leaving,' said the wife-to-be.

The man spat in his palms and rubbed them together. 'It's been a long time!'

He hurried towards the tree and climbed into it. He didn't stop at the fork, but kept moving up, greeting the girl, who was a little ahead of him, and then, on his hands and knees, scrambling beyond her, into the flimsier branches.

'I'm coming to get you, ball . . . just you wait, ball . . .' he said as he went.

Like the father and the girl, he continually shook the tree. He was surprisingly strong, and this time the tree seemed to be exploding.

Below, the crowd shielded their faces or stepped back from the storm of detritus, but they didn't stop looking and voicing their encouragement.

'What if he breaks his neck?' said the wife-to-be.

'I'll try to catch him,' said the father, moving to another position.

The father remembered his own father, Papa, in the street outside their house in the evening, after tea, when they'd first bought a car. Like a lot of men then, particularly those who fancied themselves as intellectuals, Papa was proud of his practical uselessness. Nevertheless, Papa could, at least, open the bonnet of his car, secure it and stare into it, looking mystified. He knew that this act would be enough to draw out numerous men from neighbouring houses, some just finishing their 'tea'. Papa, an immigrant, the subject of curiosity, comment and, sometimes, abuse, would soon have these men – civil servants, clerks, shop owners, printers or milkmen – united in rolling up their sleeves, grumbling, lighting cigarettes and offering technical opinions. They would remain out in the street long after dark, fetching tools and lying on their backs in patches of grease, Papa's immigrant helplessness drawing their assistance. The father had loved being out on the street with Papa who was from a large Indian family. Papa had never thought of children as an obstacle, or a nuisance. They were everywhere, part of life.

The three pale boys, Papa's grandchildren, born after he'd died, were looking up at the helpful man in the tree and at the ball, which still sat in its familiar position. Had the ball had a face, it would have been smiling, for, as the man agitated the tree, it rose and fell like a small boat settled on a lilting wave.

The man, by now straddling a swaying bough, twisted and broke off a long thin branch. At full stretch, he used it to jab at the ball, which began to bob a little. At last, after a final poke, it was out and falling.

The children ran towards it.

'Ball, ball!' cried the youngest.

The wife-to-be started to gather the children's things.

The man jumped down out of the tree with his arms raised in triumph. His shirt, which was hanging out, was covered in thick black marks; his hands were filthy and his shoes were scuffed, but he looked ecstatic.

One of his daughters handed him his jacket. The father's wife-to-be tried to wipe him down.

'I loved that,' he said. 'Thanks.'

The two men shook hands.

The father picked up the ball and threw it to the youngest child.

Soon, the family caravan was making its way across the park with their bikes, guns, hats, the youngest's sit-in car, a bag of nappies, a pair of binoculars (in the suitcase), and the unharmed plastic ball. The children, laughing and shoving one another, were discussing their 'adventure'.

The father looked around, afraid but also hoping his Indian friend had come to the park today. By now, *he* had something to say. If children, like desire, broke up that which seemed settled, it was a virtue. Much as he might want to, he couldn't bring up his kids by strict rules or a system. He could only do it, as people seemed to do most things in the end, according to the way he was, the way he lived in the world, as an example and guide. This was harder than pretending to be an authority, but more true.

Now, at the far side of the park, as the children went out through the gate, the father turned to look back at the dishevelled tree in the distance. How small it seemed now! It had been agitated, but not broken. He would think of it each time he returned to the park; he would think about something good that had happened on the way to somewhere else.

Face to Face with You

Ann was cooking breakfast when Ed shouted from the window.

– Come and look! New people are moving in!

Ann hurried over to stand beside Ed. Together, they looked down from their window on the first floor; there was a good view of the street and the entrance to their block.

A small van was parked outside. Ed and Ann watched as two men carried furniture inside, supervised by a man and a woman of around thirty, the same age as Ed and Ann.

– They look okay, said Ed. – What a relief. Don't you think? Decent, ordinary people.

– We'll see. Ann returned to the tiny kitchen at the other end of the living room. – They'll bring a whole life with them, won't they, which we'll get to learn something about whether we like it or not.

The flat upstairs had been empty for a month. Ed and Ann had enjoyed the silence. Going to bed had become a pleasure again. The previous occupant, a musician, had not only returned home from work at three or four in the morning and played music, but had seemed to enjoy moving furniture at midnight, slaughtering animals and making various other unidentified sounds which tormented the couple from the day they moved in. They were considering renting another place when he left. It would have been a shame, as they liked the flat, the neighbourhood, the look of the people in the street.

– Ed, your breakfast's ready, said Ann.

They ate quickly in order to return to their position. It wouldn't take long to empty the van.

– Two well-used armchairs, said Ann.

– A jug now, said Ed, craning to look over her shoulder. – A cracked old thing with flowers on it!

– Perhaps, like me, she loves to see things being poured. Milk, water, apple juice!

– Now a guitar!

– A rug. Nice colour. Bit scruffy, like everything else.

– Student things, really. But that new toaster must have cost them a bit, as well as the music system. Like us, they've been buying better things recently. Look.

Some of the cardboard boxes had come open; other objects the men and the couple carried in unpacked. It seemed to Ed and Ann that the couple had similar tastes to them in music, books and pictures.

– Eventually we'll have to go and say hello, said Ann.

– I suppose so.

– You never like meeting new people.

– Do you?

Ann said – I used to. You never know what interest you will find, or what life-journey they will help you begin.

He said, – What life-journey? We'll have to be careful, otherwise they'll be in and out of our place the whole time.

– Do they look like that to you? she said. – Like the sort of people who'd be in and out? What an assumption to make about strangers!

– So far they haven't taken any interest in their surroundings, said Ed. – Even I would look up at the building I was moving into.

– They're busy right now. They must be incredibly stressed. Actually, I don't believe you would look up.

Ed and Ann had been living together for three years. She was thirty and he was thirty-two. She was an assistant to a TV producer; he worked for a computer firm.

Ed and Ann had intended to go shopping, but this event was more compelling. The couple made coffee, fetched chairs and ate chocolate biscuits beside the window. When nothing much was happening, each of them in turn showered and dressed.

The van was empty. After paying the removal men, the new tenants disappeared into their flat. Ed and Ann had never been into the upstairs apartment, or into any of the other three apartments in the building. But it could only have been the same size as theirs, with a similar layout: bedroom, living room with a narrow kitchen at the end, and a bathroom.

Ed and Ann stood there, listening to the couple moving about.

Ann said, – I can tell they're trying to decide what to do with everything. When things are in place they tend to stay where they are. Nothing changes without a real effort. That happened to us.

– Perhaps we should change something now, said Ed. – What d'you think?

– Don't be silly. Listen, she said, looking up at the ceiling as though it were really transparent. – What they're doing is trying to find a way to merge their things, their lives, in other words.

– I want to know why we've wasted so much time doing this, he said. – I feel cheated. Let's go and see that Wong Kar-Wei film.

– Oh, no, she said. – I need something lighter.

Just as Ann and Ed were getting ready to go to the cinema, still trying to decide which film to see, the couple upstairs seemed to race out of their flat. Ed and Ann heard their feet on the uncarpeted stairs and the crash of the heavy front door.

– Look! called Ann, who had run back to the window.

Ed joined her immediately. – They're standing there in the street. They don't know where to go.

– Either they don't know the area or they can't make up their minds what to do.

– Weren't we like that?

– They've decided. At last! There they go.

– What's he reading? Can you see the book he's carrying?

– He's going to read! she said. – Aren't they going to talk? You're like that. He only opens books!

– He doesn't know anything except there's a hole in the centre of him! He's hungry for information!

– Doesn't he want information about her?

– That's not enough.

Ed and Ann watched the couple walk away, until they turned the corner.

A few hours later, when Ed and Ann returned from the cinema, they looked at each other as if to say, where are they? Almost at that moment the couple from upstairs returned too. Ed and Ann heard the door to the flat upstairs slam; after a while they played a record.

– Ah, said Ed. – That's what he likes.

It was a modern jazz record, known to people who liked 'fusion' but not, he guessed, to the general public. It made Ed want to hear it again, as if for the first time. He felt embarrassed to put his copy on, for fear the couple upstairs thought he was imitating them. Yet why should he have his life dictated by theirs? He played the record with the sound low, lying on the floor with his ear against the speaker.

– What do you think you're doing? said Ann.

When the record stopped, Ed heard the woman upstairs yawn, then the man laughed and seemed to throw his shoes across the floor.

The following week, Ed and Ann were aware of the upstairs couple going to work, to the pub, to the supermarket, and to the second-hand furniture shop to buy a bedside table. The couple left for work at a similar time to Ed and Ann. The man walked to the same tube station as Ed, on the other side of the street. Ann said she'd seen the woman in the bus queue. But they had not actually run into each other face to face yet. They had had no reason to say hello.

– But, as Ann said, – it's inevitable. Aren't you looking forward to it? I don't know anyone who has too many friends.

On Sunday Ed and Ann went to their local coffee shop for breakfast. It was a small café with only eight tables. They had just sat down when Ed noticed something in the Travel section of the newspaper, written by someone his age. 'Bastard,' he murmured, folding the page and tearing it out, to read later.

He looked up to see the couple from upstairs walking towards them. They came into the coffee shop, chose the table in the other alcove and ordered. They ate croissants and, just like Ed and Ann, the woman read the Culture pages and the man looked over the Travel section. He made a face, tore out an article, folded it up and put it in his jacket pocket.

Ed was about to comment on this when Ann said, – Is she attractive? Do you like her legs? You were looking at them.

– All I want is to see her cross them. Then I'll get on with my life. Her hair's all over the place. If she cut it and it was spiky, sort of punky, we could see what she was like.

Ann pulled back her own hair. – What d'you think? Look at me, Ed. What do you see?

– It's as if the sun's come out on a cloudy day, he replied, returning to his newspaper. Then he said in a low voice, – I guess we should go and say hello. Would you mind . . . going over?

– Me? I'm shocked. Why not you?

– You wanted to meet them. And it's always me, he said.

Nevertheless, Ed got to his feet. The man, too, in the other alcove was already getting up. Ed went to him.

The two men shook hands and introduced themselves.

– I'm Ed from the flat downstairs, Ed said. – This is Ann, my wife. Here she is.

Ann had joined them. – I'm sorry, I didn't catch your names, she said.

Ed said, – Ann, these are our new upstairs neighbours, Ed and Ann.

– Hello, Ann, said Ann. – Pleased to meet you. Do you want to hear about the neighbourhood?

– We thought you looked a little lost, said Ed.

– We'd love to hear about it, said Ann from upstairs.

Later the four of them walked back together, parting at the door of Ed and Ann's flat.

Inside, Ed and Ann didn't speak for a while. Ed watched Ann walking about; she seemed to be shaking her head as if she had water in her ears. Ann watched Ed glancing at the ceiling. They sat at the table, close together.

Ed whispered, – What time did they invite us for?

– Seven-thirty.

– Right. Are you looking forward to it?

– I'm wondering what they'll cook and whether they'll do it together.

He said, – We'll see. It'll be useful to get a look at their apartment, too. We've been talking about it for a while.

– What shall we wear?

– What? Normal clothes, he said. – It's a casual, neighbourly thing, isn't it?

– Maybe so, said Ann. – But I don't feel casual at this moment. Do you?

– No, he said. – I don't feel casual. I feel tense. I don't even know what we should do now.

When Ed and Ann first met, they developed the habit, on Sunday afternoons, of going to bed to make love. They still did this sometimes; or they lay down and he read while she wrote in her journal of self-discovery. Now they took off their clothes and got into bed as if they were being observed. They had never before been self-conscious about any noise they might make. They had never lain there without touching at all. When Ed glanced at Ann's unmoving body he knew she was listening for footsteps on the wooden floor above. It wasn't until they heard the sound of Ed and Ann making love upstairs that they felt obliged to get down to it themselves, finishing around the same time.

Slowly, they climbed the stairs to Ed and Ann's apartment for supper.

At around eleven-thirty they returned home, watched each other drink a glass of water – it was part of their new health regime – and went to bed. Upstairs, Ann and Ed were in bed, too.

Ed and Ann felt it was a tragedy that they knew the layout of Ed and Ann's flat upstairs. It was the same as theirs. But Ed and Ann had also placed their chairs, shelves, table, bed and other furniture in the same position. By the banging of doors, even the flushing of the toilet, the use of the shower, the scraping of chairs on the wooden floor, the selection of music, and the location of their voices and then the silence when they went to bed, they would know where Ed and Ann were in the flat and what they were doing.

After work the following day, Ed and Ann went to a local pub to eat and talk. Ed and Ann upstairs were already home. The TV was on and they'd changed out of their work clothes. Ed and Ann guessed the couple upstairs would be making supper.

But when Ed and Ann left the pub to walk home, they turned a corner and bumped into Ed and Ann who said, – We're off to that place you said served good food.

– Thank you for supper last night, they said. – We enjoyed it.

– We enjoyed having you, said Ed and Ann. – We must do something else together.

– Yes, said Ann, staring at Ann. – We must! We'll come round to you! We'll wait for you to set a date.

– We'll do that, said the other Ann.

Ed and Ann watched the other couple go into the pub.

When they got home, knowing Ed and Ann upstairs were out, Ed and Ann were able to talk in their normal voices.

– We will have to invite them back.

– Yes, said Ann. – We had better do that. Otherwise we will appear impolite.

– Maybe we should invite someone else, too, said Ed. – Another couple, perhaps.

– It'll make it less of a strain.

– Why should it be such a strain anyway? he asked.

– I don't know.

But neither of them thought it a good idea to invite another couple. For some reason they didn't want anyone else to see them with Ed and Ann upstairs. It might mean they had to discuss it.

At work, one lunchtime that week, Ed brought up the subject of his neighbours with a friendly colleague. Ed hadn't told Ann that he was intending to talk about this with anyone else, but he had to: the situation seemed to be making him preternaturally tired and paranoid. Sitting on the tube, where he could see the other Ed at the other end of the carriage reading the same book, what could he do but wonder whether anyone else was similarly shadowed?

– Suppose, he told the friend, – that a couple moved in upstairs who were very similar to you.

Once he'd relieved himself of this, Ed awaited his friend's reply. Of course the friend didn't see how this could be a problem. Ed tried to put it more clearly.

– Suppose they were not only quite similar, but were – how shall I put it? – exactly the same. It's as if they're the originals and you're only acting out their lives. Not only that, you thought they were petty, and a bit dim, and that their lives were dull, and that they were not generous enough with each other – they didn't see how much they would benefit from more giving all round – and they had nothing much to say for themselves . . . You know the sort of thing.

The friend said, – Naturally, they'd have the same ideas about you, too.

– I guess that's right, said Ed, nervously. – Let me put it like this: what if you met yourself and were horrified?

– I wouldn't be horrified but so amused I'd laugh my head off, said the friend. – Am I such a bad person? Is that what this important conversation is about?

Of course what Ed had described was not something of which this friend had had any experience. How could he possibly appreciate how terrible and oppressive such a thing could be? The only people Ed and Ann knew who had had this experience were Ed and Ann upstairs.

Ed and Ann tried to forget about their upstairs neighbours. They wanted to go about their lives as normally as possible. But the night following Ed's conversation with his friend, there was a knock on the door of the flat. When Ed opened it, he saw it was Ed. It turned out that both Anns were at evening classes and should be back soon. Ed wanted to borrow a CD he had heard Ed mention at supper. He had lost his own copy and wanted to tape Ed's.

– Come in, said Ed. – Make yourself at home. I wasn't doing anything important.

Ed offered him a drink. Then Ann phoned to say she was having a drink with a friend. The other Ann did the same. Ed stayed until the bottle was finished. He poured it himself and even asked if Ed minded turning off the TV – it was 'distracting' him. He talked about himself and didn't leave off until both Anns returned, around the same time.

When Ed and Ann were under the bedsheets, Ed said, – How could he do it? Just turn up and put me under that kind of pressure? I could have been . . .

– What? said Ann.

– Writing a piece about that journey I made to Nepal two years ago.

– Which I bet you weren't doing, said Ann. – Were you?

– Maybe I was about to start washing out my best fountain pens. Ann, you know I've been intending to.

– I'm afraid you'll never begin that other journey, the deepest one, inside!

– I don't want to hear that! You make me feel awful!

She said, – What do we do in the evenings but watch TV and bicker? Tell me, what did Ed say?

– I learned a lot. He's in the wrong job. Can't get along with the people he works with. He has ambition, but it is unfocused. You go out of your house, people always say – it's the first thing – what do you do? They judge you by what you're achieving and by your importance. Yet to him everyone else seems cleverer and with a much better idea of what's going on. He realises that whether he feels grown up or not, from the world's point of view he is now an adult.

– He knows he's not going to be rich!

– Rich! Nothing is moving forward for him. His fantasy is to be a travel writer. As if! Doesn't know if he'll ever make a living at it. Doesn't even know if he'll ever begin. His friends are making a name for themselves. He gets up in the morning, contemplates his life and can't begin to see how to fix it.

– Do they discuss it? Do they talk?

– Talk! He complains that she doesn't know whether to stay with him. She doesn't know whether this is the best of what a life can offer. She really wants to be a teacher, but he won't encourage her. He thinks she's a flake, interested only in her body, wasting their money on fake therapies and incapable of saying anything with any pith in it. There's a man at work who's older, who guides her, who will guide her away from him. I expect he's fucked her already.

– Oh, she wants to be inspired!

– Is that what she calls it?

– Wait a minute, she said. – Can you please stop? I have to get a drink of water.

– Go on then, drink! he said. – The couple's sex life has tailed off but they don't know if this is a natural fluctuation. If they have children they'll be stuck with each other in some way or other for good. Neither of them has the resources to make a decision! It's trivial in many ways, but in others it's the most important thing in their lives. All in all, they're going crazy inside.

– Some people's lives! said Ann.

For the next two weeks Ann and Ed went out after work, together sometimes, but mostly separately, not returning until late. Ed even took to walking around the streets, or sitting in bars, in order not to go home. He kept thinking there was something he had to do, that there was something significant which had to be changed, but he didn't know what it was. Once, in a pub in which there were many mirrors, Ed thought he saw Ed from upstairs sitting behind him. Thinking he'd seen the devil, he stood up and rushed out, gasping and gesticulating at nothing. He took to spreading out his newspaper and sitting on it beside the pond in a small park near by, wondering what ills could be cured by silence. Except that one evening, under the still surface of the pond, he saw pieces of his own face swimming in the darkness, like bits of a puzzle being assembled by God, and he had to close his eyes.

However compelling the silence by the pond, it didn't follow that they could not hear Ed and Ann upstairs in the morning, and it didn't obviate the problem of the weekends, or the fact that they had promised to invite Ed and Ann for supper, something they had to get past, unless it was to remain a troublesome, undis-charged obligation.

Meanwhile, Ed and Ann bought new clothes and shoes; Ann had her hair cut. Ed started to exercise, in order to change the shape of his body. One night, Ann decided she wanted to get a cat but decided a tattoo would be less trouble. A badger, say, on her thigh, would be unique, a distinguishing mark. Ed said, – That would be going too far, Ann!

– You won't let me be different! screamed Ann.

– They're driving you crazy! This is really getting to you.

– And it's not to you?

– That's it! he said, staring up at the ceiling. – They will have heard everything now!

– I don't care! she said. – I'm inviting them in here, then we'll know the truth!

She took a sheet of paper from the drawer, wrote on it, and took it upstairs, pushing it under the door. A few minutes later, it was returned with thanks.

– They can't wait to see us, said Ann, holding up the piece of paper.

The following weekend, Ed and Ann moved the table into the living room and put out glasses and cutlery; they shopped, cooked and talked things over. They both agreed that this event was the hardest thing they'd had to get through.

At a quarter to eight they opened the champagne and drank a glass each. At eight o'clock there was a knock on the door.

The two Anns and the two Eds kissed and embraced. Ed was looking healthy – he'd been swimming a lot. His Ann was wearing a long white dress which clung to her. She had nothing on underneath. It was so tight that to sit down she had to pull it up to her knees. She showed them her new tattoo.

It was late, almost morning, when the party broke up. Ed and Ann had left, and Ed and Ann were blowing out the candles and clearing a few things away when they fell upon each other and had sex on the rug, which they pulled under the table.

– We did it. I enjoyed the evening, said Ann, as they lay there.

– It wasn't so bad, said Ed.

– What was the best bit, for you?

– I'm thinking of it now, he said.

– I'll stroke your face, then, she said, – while you go over it in your mind.

The two Anns had been talking about their careers. Ed from upstairs, seated near the window and leaning back, had been looking out over the dark street, enjoying the small cigar Ed had given him. Ed had asked him a question, which the other Ed had chosen to answer at length, but only in his mind, though his lips smacked occasionally. Ed had watched his upstairs neighbour smoke, his impatience subsiding, trying to see what he liked and disliked about this familiar stranger. He had thought, – I know I can't take all of him in now. All I have to do is look at him, face him, without turning away. If I turn away now, everything will be worse and I could be done for.

As he had continued to look, with pity, with affection, with curiosity, until the two of them had seemed alone together, Ed had found himself thinking, – He's not so bad. He's lost hope, that's all. He has everything else, he's alive, and there's nothing wrong with him or her, or any of us here now. We only have to see this to grasp something valuable.

– And did you like her tonight? Ann said.

– I did, he said. – Very much so.

– What did you like?

– Her kindness, her intelligence, her energy and her soul. The fact she listens to others. She looks for good things about others to pick up on.

– Wonderful, she said. – What else?

He told her more; she told him what she had thought.

A fortnight later, on a Saturday morning, Ann went to the window.

– Ed, the van is here, she said.

– Good, said Ed, joining her. – There's the guitar, the rug, everything.

The van was parked outside. The familiar objects were being carried in the opposite direction by the same two men. Ed and Ann from upstairs had given up their flat; they were going to Rio for six months and would leave their things with their parents. While they were away, they would think about what to do on their return.

When the van was packed, Ed and Ann went downstairs to wish their neighbours good luck. On the pavement, the couples said goodbye, wished each other well and exchanged phone numbers, sincerely hoping they would never have to see each other again.

The apartment upstairs was empty once more. Ed and Ann went back into their own flat. The silence seemed sublime.

– What shall we do now? said Ann.

– I don't know yet. Then he said, – Oh, but now I do.

– What?

He offered her his hand. In the bathroom, she undressed and stood there with her foot up on the side of the bath, to let him look at her, before she sat down. He filled the jug from the sink taps and went to her and let water fall over her hair, body and legs. Her face was upturned and her eyes were eager and bright, looking at him and into the water, cascading.

Goodbye, Mother

If you think the living are difficult to deal with, the dead can be worse.

This is what Harry's friend Gerald had said. The remark returned repeatedly to Harry, particularly that morning when he had so wearily and reluctantly got out of bed. It was the anniversary of his father's death. Whether it was seven or eight years, Harry didn't want to worry. He was to take Mother to visit Father's grave.

Harry wondered if his children, accompanied perhaps by his wife Alexandra, would visit his grave. What would they do with him in their minds; what would he become for them? He would never leave them alone, he had learned that. Unlike the living, the dead you couldn't get rid of.

Harry's mother was not dead, but she haunted him in two ways: from the past, and in the present. He talked to her several times a day, in his mind. This morning it was as a living creature that he had to deal with her.

He had been at home on his own for a week. Alexandra, his wife, was in Thailand attending 'workshops'. When they weren't running away, the two children, a boy and a girl, were at boarding school.

The previous night had been strange.

Now Mother was waiting for him in her overcoat at the door of the house he had been brought up in.

'You're late,' she almost shouted, in a humorous voice.

He knew she would say this.

He tapped his watch. 'I'm on time.'

'Late, late!'

He thrust his watch under her face. 'No, look.'

For Mother, he was always late. He was never there at the right time, and he never brought her what she wanted, and so he brought her nothing.

He didn't like to touch her, but he made himself bend down to kiss her. What a small woman she was. For years she had been bigger than him, of course; bigger than everything else. She had remained big in his mind, pushing too many other things aside.

If she had a musty, slightly foul, bitter smell, it was not only that of an old woman, but a general notification, perhaps, of inner dereliction.

'Shall we set off?' he said.

'Wait.'

She whispered something. She wanted to go to the toilet.

She trailed up the hall, exclaiming, grunting and wheezing. One of her legs was bandaged. The noises, he noticed, were not unlike those he made getting into bed.

The small house seemed tidy, but he remembered Mother as a dirty woman. The cupboards, cups and cutlery were smeared and encrusted with old food.

Mother hadn't bathed them often. He had changed his underwear and other clothes only once a week. He had thought it normal to feel soiled. He wondered if this was why other children had disliked and bullied him.

In the living room the television was on, as it was all the time. She would watch one soap opera while videoing another, catching up with them late at night or early in the morning. Mother had always watched television from the late afternoon until she went to bed. She hadn't wanted Harry or his brother or father to speak. If they opened their mouths, she told them to shut up. She hadn't wanted them in the room at all. She preferred the faces on television to the faces of her family.

508

She was an addict.

It gave him pleasure to turn off the TV.

Alexandra had recently started, among what he considered to be other eccentricities, a 'life journal'. Before Harry left for work, she sat in the kitchen overlooking the fields, blinking rapidly. She would write furiously across the page in a crooked slope, picking out different-coloured children's markers from a plastic wallet and throwing down other markers, flinging them right onto the floor where they could easily upend him.

'Why are you doing this writing?'

He walked around the table, kicking away the lethal markers.

It was like saying, why don't you do something more useful?

'I've decided I want to speak,' she said. 'To tell my story –'

'What story?'

'The story of my life – for what it is worth, if only to myself.'

'Can I read it?'

'I don't think so.' A pause. 'No.'

He said, 'What do you mean, people want to speak?'

'They want to say what happiness is for them. And the other thing. They want to be known to themselves and to others.'

'Yes, yes . . . I see.'

'Harry, you would understand that,' she said. 'As a journalist.'

'We keep to the facts,' he said, heading for the door.

'Is that right?' she said. 'The facts of life and death?'

Perhaps Mother was ready to speak. That might have been why she had invited him on this journey.

If she'd let little in or out for most of her life, what she had to say might be powerful.

He was afraid.

This was the worst day he'd had for a long time.

He didn't go upstairs to the two small bedrooms, but waited for her at the door.

He knew every inch of the house, but he'd forgotten it existed as a real place rather than as a sunken ship in the depths of his memory.

It was the only house in the street which hadn't been torn through or extended. Mother hadn't wanted noise or 'bother'. There was still an air-raid shelter at the end of the garden, which had been his 'camp' as a child. There was a disused outside toilet which hadn't been knocked down. The kitchen was tiny. He wondered how they'd all fitted in. They'd been too close to one another. Perhaps that was why he'd insisted that he and Alexandra buy a large house in the country, even though it was quite far from London.

He would, he supposed, inherit the house, sharing it with his brother. They would have to clear it out, selling certain things and burning others, before disposing of the property. They would have to touch their parents' possessions and their own memories again, for the last time.

Somewhere in a cupboard were photographs of him as a boy wearing short trousers and wellington boots, his face contorted with anguish and fear.

Harry was glad to be going to Father's grave. He saw it as reparation for the 'stupid' remark he'd made not long before Father died, a remark he still thought about.

He led Mother up the path to the car.

'Hasn't it been cold?' she said. 'And raining non-stop. Luckily, it cleared up for us. I looked out of the window this morning and thought God is giving us a good day out. It's been raining solid here – haven't you noticed? Good for the garden! Doesn't make us grow any taller! We're the same size! Pity!'

'That's right.'

'Hasn't it been raining out where you are?' She pointed at the ragged front lawn. 'My garden needs doing. Can't get anyone to do it. The old lady up the road had her money stolen. Boys came to the door, saying they were collecting for the blind. You don't have to worry about these things . . .'

Harry said, 'I worry about other things.'

'There's always something. It never ends! Except where we're going!'

He helped Mother into the car and leaned over her to fasten the seat belt.

'I feel all trapped in, dear,' she said, 'with this rope round me.'

'You have to wear it.'

He opened the window.

'Oooh, I'll get a draught,' she said. 'It'll cut me in two.'

'It'll go right through you?'

'Right through me, yes, like a knife.'

He closed the window and touched the dashboard.

'What's that wind?' she said.

'The heater.'

'It's like a hair-dryer blowing all over me.'

'I'll turn it off, but you might get cold.'

'I'm always cold. My old bones are frozen. Don't get old!'

He started the engine.

With a startlingly quick motion, she threw back her head and braced herself. Her fingers dug into the sides of the seat. Her short legs and swollen feet were rigid.

When he was young, there were only certain times of the day when she would leave the house in a car, for fear they would be killed by drunken lunatics. He remembered the family sitting in their coats in the front room, looking at the clock and then at Mother, waiting for the moment when she would say it was all right for them to set off, the moment when they were least likely to be punished for wanting to go out.

To him, now, the engine sounded monstrous. He had begun to catch her fears.

'Don't go too fast,' she said.

'The legal speed.'

'Oh, oh, oh,' she moaned as the car moved away.

Awake for most of the previous night, Harry had thought that she was, really, mad, or disturbed. This realisation brought him relief.

'She's off her head,' he repeated to himself, walking about the house.

He fell on his knees, put his hands together and uttered the thought aloud to all gods and humans interested and uninterested.

If she was 'ill', it wasn't his fault. He didn't have to fit around her, or try to make sense of what she did.

If he saw this only now, it was because people were like photographs which took years to develop.

Harry's smart, grand friend Gerald had recently become Sir Gerald. Fifteen years ago they'd briefly worked together. For a long time they'd played cricket at the weekends.

Gerald had become a distinguished man, a television executive who sat on boards and made himself essential around town. He liked power and politics. You could say he traded in secrets, receiving them, hoarding them and passing them on like gold coins.

Harry considered himself too unimportant for Gerald, but Gerald had always rung every six months, saying it was time they met.

Gerald took him to his regular place where there were others like him. He was always seated in a booth in the corner where they could be seen but not overheard. Gerald liked to say whatever was on his mind, however disconnected. Harry didn't imagine that Gerald would do this with anyone else.

Last time, Gerald had said, 'Harry, I'm older than you and I've been alive for sixty years. If you requested any wisdom I'd have fuck-all to pass on, except to say: you can't blame other people for your misfortunes. More champagne? Now, old chap, what's on your mind?'

Harry had told Gerald that Alexandra had taken up with a female hypnotist; a hypnotherapist.

'She's done what?' said Gerald.

'It's true.'

Gerald was chuckling.

*

Harry noticed that Mother was trembling.

On the way to see her, Harry had worried about her liking the new Mercedes, which he called 'God's chariot'.

The car and what it meant had no interest for her. Her eyes were closed.

He was trying to control himself.

A year ago, a friend had given him and Alexandra tickets for a 'hypnotic' show in the West End. They had gone along sceptically. She preferred serious drama, he none at all. He couldn't count the Ibsens he had slept through. However, he did often recall one Ibsen which had kept his attention – the one in which the protagonist tells the truth to those closest to him, and destroys their lives.

The hypnotist was young, his patter amusing, reassuring and confident. Members of the audience rushed to the stage to have his hands on them. Under the compère's spell they danced like Elvis, using broom handles as microphone stands. Others put on big ridiculous glasses through which they 'saw' people naked.

After, he and Alexandra went to an Italian restaurant in Covent Garden for supper. She liked being taken out.

'What did you think of the show?' she asked.

'It was more entertaining than a play. Luckily, I wasn't taken in.'

'Taken in?' she said. 'You thought it was fake? Everyone was paid to pretend?'

'Of course.'

'Oh, I didn't think that at all.'

She couldn't stop talking about it, about the 'depths' of the mind, about what was 'underneath' and could be 'unleashed'.

The next day, she went into town and bought books on hypnotism.

She hypnotised him to sleep in the evenings. It wasn't difficult. He liked her voice.

*

Harry was thirteen when Father crashed the car. They were going to the seaside to stay in a caravan. All summer he had been looking forward to the holiday. But not only had Mother been screeching from the moment the car left their house, but, a non-driver herself, she had clutched at Father's arm continually, and even dragged at the driving wheel itself.

She was successful at last. They ran into the front of an oncoming van, spent two nights in hospital and had to go home without seeing the sea. Harry's face looked as though it had been dug up with a trowel.

He looked across at Mother's formidable bosom, covered by a white polo-neck sweater. Down it, between her breasts, dangled a jewel-covered object, like half a salt pot.

At last, she opened her eyes and loudly began to read out the words on advertising hoardings; she read the traffic signs and the instructions written on the road; she read the names on shops. She was also making terrible noises from inside her body groaning, he thought, like Glenn Gould playing Bach.

Visiting Father's grave had been her idea. 'It's time we went back again,' she had said. 'So he knows he hasn't been forgotten. He'll hear his name being called.'

But it was as if she were being dragged to her death.

If he said nothing, she might calm down. The child he once was would have been alarmed by her terrors, but why shouldn't she make her noises? Except that her babbling drove out everything else. She ensured there was no room in the car for any other words.

He realized what was happening. If she couldn't actually take the television with her in the car, she would become the television herself.

Alexandra was interested in the history of food, the garden, the children, novels. She sang in the local choir. Recently, she had started to take photographs and learn the cello. She was a governor of the local school and helped the children with their reading and writing. She talked of how, inexplicably, they suffered from low self-esteem. It was partly caused by 'class', but she suspected there were other, 'inner' reasons.

Her curiosity about hypnotism didn't diminish.

A friend introduced Alexandra to a local woman, a hypnotherapist. 'Amazing Olga', Harry called her.

'What does she do?' he asked, imagining Alexandra walking about with her eyes closed, her arms extended in front of her.

'She hypnotises me. Suddenly, I'm five years old and my father is holding me. Harry, we talk of the strangest things. She listens to my dreams.'

'What is this for?'

For Harry, telling someone your dreams was like going to bed with them.

'To know myself,' she said.

Amazing Olga must have told Alexandra that Harry would believe they were conspiring against him.

She touched his arm and said, 'Your worst thoughts and criticisms about yourself – that's what you think we're saying about you in that room.'

'Something like that,' he said.

'It's not true,' she said.

'Thank you. You don't talk about me at all?'

'I didn't say that.'

'Nobody likes to be talked about,' he said.

'As if it weren't inevitable.'

In the train to work, and in the evenings when he fed the animals, he thought about this. He would discuss it with Gerald next time.

Faith healers, astrologers, tea-leaf examiners, palm readers, aura photographers – there were all manner of weirdo eccentrics with their hands in the pockets of weak people who wanted to know what was going on, who wanted certainty. Uncertainty was the one thing you couldn't sell as a creed, and it was, probably, the only worthwhile thing.

What would he say about this?

He did believe there was such a thing as a rational world view. It was based on logic and science. These days, 'enlightenment values' were much discredited. It didn't follow they were worthless. It was all they had.

'If you or one of the children fell sick, Alexandra . . .' he put to her one night.

It was dark, but he had switched on the garden lights. They were sitting out, eating their favourite ice-cream and drinking champagne. His trees shaded the house; the two young labradors, one black, one white, sat at their feet. He could see his wood in the distance, carpeted with bluebells in the spring, and the treehouse he would restore for his grandchildren. The pond, stifled by duck weed, had to be cleaned. He was saving up for a tennis court.

This was what he had lived for and made with his labour. He wasn't old and he wasn't young, but at the age when he was curious about, and could see, the shape of his whole life, his beginning and his end.

'You'd go to a doctor, wouldn't you? Not to a faith healer.'

'That's right,' she said. 'First to a doctor.'

'Then?'

'And then, perhaps to a therapist.'

'A therapist? For what?'

'To grasp the logic –'

'What logic?'

'The inner logic . . . of the illness.'

'Why?'

'Because I am one person,' she said. 'A whole.'

'And you are in control?'

'Something in me is making my life – my relationships, I mean – the way they are, yes.'

He was opposed to this, but he didn't know what to say.

She went on, 'There are archaic unknown sources which I want to locate.' Then she quoted her therapist, knowing that at university he had studied the history of ideas. 'If Whitehead said that all philosophy is footnotes to Plato, Freud taught us that maturity is merely a footnote to childhood.'

He said, 'If it's all been decided years ago, if there's no free will but only the determinism of childhood, then it's pointless to think we can make any difference.'

'Freedom is possible.'

'How?'

'The freedom that comes from understanding.'

He was thinking about this.

His car had left the narrow suburban streets for bigger roads. Suddenly, he was in a maze of new one-way systems bounded by glittering office blocks. He drove through the same deep highway several times, to the same accompaniments from Mother.

Setting off from home that morning, he had been convinced that he knew how to get to the cemetery, but now, although he recognised some things, it was only a glancing, bewildered familiarity. He hadn't driven around this area for more than twenty-five years.

Mother seemed to take it for granted that he knew where he was. This might have been the only confidence she had in him. She loved 'safe' drivers. She liked coaches; for some reason, coach drivers, like some doctors, were trustworthy. Being safe mattered more than anything else because, in an inhospitable world, they were always in danger.

He didn't want to stop to ask the way, and he couldn't ask Mother for fear his uncertainty would turn her more feverish.

Cars driven by tattooed south London semi-criminals with shaven heads seemed to be pursuing them; vans flew at them from unexpected angles. His feet were cold, but his hands were sweating.

If he didn't keep himself together, he would turn into her.

He hadn't spoken to Mother for almost three months. He had had an argument with his brother – there had almost been a fist fight in the little house – and Mother, instead of making the authoritative intervention he had wished for, had collapsed weeping.

'I want to die,' she'd wailed. 'I'm ready!'

The forced pain she gave off had made him throw up in the gutter outside the house.

He had looked up from his sick to see the faces of the neighbours at their windows – the same neighbours, now thirty years older, he'd known as a child.

They would have heard from Mother that he was well paid.

Sometimes he was proud of his success. He had earned the things that other people wanted.

He worked in television news. He helped decide what the news was. Millions watched it. Many people believed that the news was the most important thing that had happened in the world that day. To be connected, they needed the news in the way they needed bread and water.

He remembered how smug he had been, self-righteous even, as a young man at university. Some went to radical politics or Mexico; others sought a creative life. The women became intense, quirkily intelligent and self-obsessed. Being lower middle class, he worked hard, preparing his way. The alternative, for him, he knew, was relative poverty and boredom. He had learned how to do his job well; for years he had earned a good salary. He had shut his mouth and pleased the bosses. He had become a boss himself; people were afraid of him, and tried to guess what he was thinking.

He worried there was nothing to him, that under his thinning hair he was a 'hollow man', a phrase from the poetry he'd studied at school. Being 'found out', Gerald called it, laughing, like someone who had perpetrated a con.

Harry's daughter Heather talked of wanting confidence. He understood that. But where could confidence originate, except from a parent who believed in you?

There she was next to him, vertiginous, drivelling, scratching in fear at the seat she sat on, waving, in her other hand, the disconnected seat-belt buckle.

*

It wasn't long before Alexandra started to call it 'work'.

The 'work' she was doing on herself.

The 'work' with the different-coloured pens.

The 'work' of throwing them on the floor, of being the sort of person who threw things about if she felt like it.

'Work,' he said, with a slight sneer. 'The "work" of imagining an apple and talking to it.'

'The most important work I've done.'

'It won't pay for the barn to be cleared and rebuilt.'

'Why does that bother you so much?'

Money was a way of measuring good things. The worth of a man had to be related to what he was able to earn. She would never be convinced by this.

Her 'work' was equivalent to his work. No; it was more important. She had started to say his work was out of date, like prisons, schools, banks and politics.

She said, 'The cost and waste of transporting thousands of people from one part of the country to another for a few hours. These things continue because they have always happened, like bad habits. These are nineteenth-century institutions and we are a few months from the end of the twentieth century. People haven't yet found more creative ways of doing things.'

He thought of the trains on the bridges over the Thames, transporting trainloads of slaves to futility.

In the suburbs, where Mother still lived, the idea was to think of nothing; to puzzle over your own experience was to gratuitously unsettle yourself. How you felt wasn't important, only what you did, and what others saw.

Yet he knew that if he wasn't looking at himself directly, he was looking at himself in the world. The world had his face in it! If you weren't present to yourself, you'd find yourself elsewhere!

Almost all the men in the street had lighted sheds at the end of the garden, or on their allotments, to which they retreated in the evenings. These men were too careful for the pub. The sheds were where the men went to get away from the women. The women who weren't employed and had the time, therefore, to be disturbed. It was a division of labour: they carried the madness for the men.

'All right, Mother?' he said at last. 'We aren't doing so badly now.'

They had escaped the highway and regained the narrow, clogged suburban roads.

'Not too bad, dear,' she sighed, passing the back of her hand across her forehead. 'Oh, watch out! Can't you look where you're going? There's traffic everywhere!'

'That means we go slower.'

'They're so near!'

'Mother, everyone has an interest in not getting killed.'

'That's what you think!'

If Mother had kept on repeating the same thing and squealing at high volume, he would have lost his temper; he would have turned the car round, taken her home and dumped her. That would have suited him. Alexandra was coming back tomorrow; he had plenty to do.

But after a few minutes Mother calmed down, and even gave him directions.

They were on their way to the cemetery.

It was easy to be snobbish and uncharitable about the suburbs, but what he saw around him was ugly, dull and depressing. He had, at least, got away.

But, like Mother continuing to live here when there was no reason for it, he had put up with things unnecessarily. He had never rebelled, least of all against himself. He had striven, up to a point – before the universe, like his mother, had shut like a door in his face.

He was afraid Alexandra would fall in love with some exotic idea, or with Thailand, and never want to return. Mother's irritability and indifference had taught him that women wanted to escape. If they couldn't get away, they hated you for making them stay.

There was a couple he and Alexandra had known for a long time. The woman had laboured for years to make their house perfect. One afternoon, as he often did, Harry drove over for tea in their garden. The woman cultivated wild flowers; there was a summer-house.

Harry sighed, and said to the man, 'You have everything you could want here. If I were you, I'd never go out.'

'I don't,' the man replied. He added casually, 'If I had my way, of course, we wouldn't live here but in France. They have a much higher standard of living.'

The man did not notice, but at this the woman crumpled, as if she'd been shot. She went inside, shut the windows and became ill. She could not satisfy her husband, couldn't quell his yearnings. It was impossible, and, without him asking her to do it, she had worn herself out trying.

If Alexandra was seeking cures, it was because she didn't have everything and he had failed her.

Yet their conflicts, of which there was at least one a week – some continued for days – weren't entirely terrible. Their disagreements uncovered misunderstandings. Sometimes they wanted different things, but only in the context of each other. She was close to his wishes, to the inner stream of him. They always returned to each other. There was never a permanent withdrawal, as there had been with Mother.

It was a little paradise at times.

In the newspapers, he learned of actors and sportsmen having affairs. Women wanted these people. It seemed easy.

There were attractive women in the office, but they were claimed immediately. They didn't want him. It wasn't only that he looked older than his years, as his wife had informed him. He looked unhealthy.

Plastic, anonymous, idealised sex was everywhere; the participants were only young and beautiful, as if desire was the exclusive domain of the thin.

He didn't think it was sex he wanted. He liked to believe he could get by without excessive pleasure, just as he could get by without drugs. He kept thinking that the uses of sex in the modern world were a distraction. It didn't seem to be the important thing.

What was important? He knew what it was – impermanence, decay, death and the way it informed the present – but couldn't bring himself to look straight at it.

'Where is Alexandra today?' Mother asked. 'I thought she might come with us. She never wants to see me.'

Mother's 'madness' had no magnetism for Alexandra; her complaints bored her; Alexandra had never needed her.

He said, 'She's gone to Thailand. But she sends beautiful letters to me, by fax, every day.'

He explained that Alexandra had gone to a centre in Thailand for a fortnight to take various courses. There were dream, healing, and 'imaging' workshops.

Mother said, 'What is she doing there?'

'She said on the phone that she is with other middle-aged women in sandals and bright dresses with a penchant for Joni Mitchell. The last I heard she was hugging these women and taking part in rituals on the beach.'

'Rituals?'

He had said to Alexandra when she rang, 'But you can't dance, Alexandra. You hate it.'

'I can dance badly,' she'd replied. 'And that's what I do, night after night.'

Dancing badly.

Harry said to Mother, 'She told me she looked up and the moon was smiling.'

'At her in particular?' said Mother.

'She didn't itemise,' said Harry.

'This is at your expense?'

Alexandra, somewhat patronisingly, had felt she had to explain it wasn't an infidelity.

'There's no other man involved,' she'd said before she left, packing a few things into their son's rucksack. 'I hope there aren't even any men there.'

He had looked at her clothes.

'Is that all you're taking?'

'I will rely on the kindness of strangers,' she had replied.

'You'll be wearing their clothes?'

'I don't see why not.'

It was an infidelity if she was 'coming alive', as she had put it. What could be a more disturbing betrayal than 'more life' even as he felt himself to be fading!

He was a conventional man, and he lived a conventional life in order for her, and the children presumably, one day, to live unconventional ones. Was he, to her, a dead weight? He feared losing sight of her, as she accelerated, dancing, into the distance.

'Anyway,' Mother said, 'thank you, Harry, dear.'

'For what?'

'For taking me to Dad's . . . Dad's . . .'

He knew she couldn't say 'grave'.

'That's okay.'

'The other sons are good to their mothers.'

'Better than me?'

'Some of them visit their mums every week. They sit with them for hours, playing board games. One boy sent her on a cruise.'

'On the *Titanic*?'

'Little beast, you are! Still, without you I'd have to take three buses to see Dad.'

'Shame you didn't learn to drive.'

'I wish I had.'

He was surprised. 'Do you really?'

'Then I would have got around.'

'Why didn't you?'

'Oh, I don't know now. Too much to do, with the washing and the cleaning.'

He asked, 'Is there anything else that you would like me to do for you?'

'Thank you for asking,' she said. 'Yes.'

'What is it?'

'Harry, I want to go on a journey.'

One morning, when Alexandra was scribbling, he said, 'I'll say goodbye.'

She came to the door to wave, as she always did if she wasn't driving him to the station. She said she was sorry he had to go into the office – 'such a place' – every day.

'What the hell is wrong with it?' he asked.

The building was a scribble of pipes and wires, inhabited by dark suits with human beings inside. The harsh glow of the computer and TV screens reflected nothing back. Nothing reflected into eternity.

Something changed after she said this.

He travelled on the train with the other commuters. The idea they shared was a reasonable though stifling one: to live without, or to banish, inner and outer disorder.

He was attempting to read a book about Harold Wilson, Prime Minister when Harry was young. There was a lot about the 'balance of payments'. Harry kept wondering what he had been wearing on his way to school the day Wilson made a particular speech. He wished he had his school exercise books, and the novels he had read then. This was a very particular way of doing history.

He had to put his face by the train window but tried not to breathe out for fear his soul would fly from his body and he would lose everything that had meaning for him.

At work, he would feel better.

He believed in work. It was important to sustain ceaseless effort. Making; building – this integrated the world. It was called civilisation. Otherwise, the mind, like an errant child, ran away. It wanted only pleasure, and nothing would get done.

The news was essential information. Without it, you were uninformed, uneducated even. You couldn't see the way the world was moving. The news reminded you of other people's lives, of human possibility and destructiveness. It was part of his work to glance at the French, German, American and Italian papers every day.

However, an image haunted him. He was taking his university finals and a kid in his class – a hippy or punk, a strange, straggly peacock – turned over the exam paper, glanced at the question and said, 'Oh, I don't think there's anything here for me today,' and left the room, singing 'School's Out'.

Beautiful defiance.

Couldn't Harry walk into the office and say, 'There's nothing here for me today!' or 'Nothing of interest has happened in the world today!'?

He remembered his last years at school, and then at university. The other mothers helped their student kids into their new rooms, unpacking their bags and making the beds. Mother had disappeared into herself, neither speaking nor asking questions. As the size of her body increased, her self shrank, the one defending the other. He doubted she even knew what courses he was taking, whether he had graduated or not, or even what 'graduation' was.

She didn't speak, she didn't write to him, she hardly phoned. She was staring into the bright light, minute after minute, hour after hour, day after day, week after week, year after year. Television was her drug and anaesthetic, her sex her conversation her friends her family her heaven her . . .

Television did her dreaming for her.

It couldn't hear her.

After the television had 'closed down', and Father was listening to music in bed, she walked about the house in her dressing gown and slippers. He had no idea what she could be thinking, unless it was the same thing repeatedly.

It was difficult to be attached to someone who could only be attached to something else. A sleeping princess who wouldn't wake up.

He wondered if he'd gone into television so that he would be in front of her face, at least some of the time.

At this, he laughed.

'Don't shake like that,' she said. 'Look where you're going.'

'What journey?' he said.

'Oh, yes,' she said. 'I haven't told you.'

On the way to work, he had started to feel that if he talked with anyone they would get inside him; parts of the conversation would haunt him; words, thoughts, bits of their clothing would return like undigested food and he would be inhabited by worms, gnats, mosquitoes. Going to a meeting or to lunch, if human beings approached, his skin prickled and itched. If he thought, 'Well, it's only a minor irritation', his mind became unendurable, as if a landscape of little flames had been ignited not only on the surface of his skin, but within his head.

The smell, the internal workings of every human being, the shit, blood, mucus swilling in a bag of flesh, made him mad. He felt he was wearing the glasses the stage hypnotist had given people, but instead of seeing them naked, he saw their inner physiology, their turbulence, their death.

At meetings, he would walk up and down, constantly going out of the room and then out of the building, to breathe. From behind pillars in the foyer, strangers started to whisper the 'stupid' remark at him, the one he had made to Father.

His boss said, 'Harry, you're coming apart. Go and see the doctor.'

The doctor informed him there were drugs to remove this kind of radical human pain in no time.

Harry showed the prescription to Alexandra. She was against the drugs. She wouldn't even drink milk because of the 'chemicals' in it.

He told her, 'I'm in pain.'

She replied, 'That pain . . . it's your pain. It's you – your unfolding life.'

They went to a garden party. The blessed hypnotherapist would be there. It would be like meeting someone's best friend for the first time. He would see who Alexandra wanted to be, who she thought she was like.

He spotted Amazing Olga on the lawn. She wore glasses. If she had a slightly hippy aspect it was because her hair hung down her back like a girl's, and was streaked with grey.

Alexandra had copied this, he realised. Her hair was long now, making her look slightly wild – different, certainly, to the well-kempt wives of Harry's colleagues.

The hypnotherapist looked formidable and self-possessed. Harry wanted to confront her, to ask where she was leading his wife, but he feared she would either say something humiliating or look into his eyes and see what he was like. It would be like being regarded by a policeman. All one's crimes of shame and desire would be known.

He didn't like Alexandra going away because he knew he didn't exist in the mind of a woman as a permanent object. The moment he left the room they forgot him. They would think of other things, and of other men, better at everything than he. He was rendered a blank. This wasn't what the women's magazines, which his daughter Heather read, called low self-esteem. It was being rubbed out, annihilated, turned into nothing by a woman he was too much for.

Sometimes, he and Alexandra had to attend dull dinners with work colleagues.

'I always have to sit next to the wives,' he complained, resting on the bed to put on his heavy black shoes. 'They never say anything I haven't heard before.'

Alexandra said, 'If you bother to talk and listen, it's the wives who are interesting. There's always more to them than there is to the husbands.'

He said, 'That attitude makes me angry. It sounds smart, but it's prejudice.'

'There's more to the women's lives.'

'More what?'

'More emotion, variety, feeling. They're closer to the heart of things – to children, to themselves, to their husbands and to the way the world really works.'

'Money and politics are the engine.'

'They're a cover story,' she said. 'It's on top, surface.'

He was boring. He bored himself.

She was making him think of why she would want to be with him; of what he had to offer.

When he came home from school with news spilling from him, Mother never wanted to know. 'Quiet, quiet,' she'd say. 'I'm watching something.'

Gerald had said, 'Even when we're fifty we expect our mummy and daddy to be perfect, but they are only ever going to be just what they are.'

It would be childish to blame Mother for what he was now. But if he didn't understand what had happened, he wouldn't be free of his resentment and couldn't move on.

Understand it? He couldn't even see it! He lived within it, but like primitive man almost entirely ignorant of his environment, and trying to influence it with magic, in the darkness he couldn't make anything out!

Gerald had said, 'Children expect too much!'

Too much! Affection, attention, love – to be liked! How could it be too much?

On their wedding day, he had not anticipated that his marriage to Alexandra would become more complicated and interesting as time passed. It hadn't become tedious or exhausted; it hadn't even settled into a routine. He lived the life his university friends would have despised for its unadventurousness. Yet, every day it was strange, unusual, terrifying.

He had wanted a woman to be devoted to him, and, when, for years, she had been, he had refused to notice. Now, she wasn't; things had got more lively, or 'kicked up', as his son liked to say.

Alexandra blazed in his face, day after day.

Mother, though, hadn't changed. She was too preoccupied to be imaginative. He wasn't, therefore, used to alteration in a woman.

Last night . . .

He had found himself searching through Alexandra's clothes, letters, books, make-up. He didn't read anything, and barely touched her belongings.

He had read in a newspaper about a public figure who had travelled on trains with a camera concealed in the bottom of his suitcase in order to look up women's skirts, at their legs and underwear. The man said, 'I wanted to feel close to the women.'

When it comes to love, we are all stalkers.

Last night, Harry checked the house, the garden and the land. He fed the dogs, Heather's horse, the pig and the chickens.

Alexandra kept a tape deck in one of the collapsing barns. He had seen her, dancing on her toes, her skirt flying, singing to herself. He'd recalled a line from a song: 'I saw you dancing in the gym, you both kicked off your shoes . . .'

On an old table she kept pages of writing; spread out beside them were photographs she had been taking to illustrate the stories.

She'd said, 'If there's a telephone in the story, I'll take a picture of a phone and place it next to the paragraph.'

In the collapsing barn, he put on a tape and danced, if dancing was the word for his odd arthritic jig, in his pyjamas and wellington boots.

That was why he felt stiff this morning.

'There is a real world,' said Richard Dawkins the scientist.

Harry had repeated this to himself, and then passed it on to Alexandra as an antidote to her vaporous dreaming.

She had laughed and said, 'Maybe there is a real world. But there is no one living it it.'

It was inevitable: they were nearing the churchyard and a feeling of dread came over him.

Mother turned to him. 'I've never seen you so agitated.'

'Me? I'm agitated?'

'Yes. You're twitching like a St Vitus's dance person. Who d'you think I'm talking about?'

Harry said, 'No, no – I've got a lot to think about.'

'Is something bothering you?'

Alexandra had begged him not to take medication. She'd promised to support him. She'd gone away. The 'strange' had never come this close to him before.

But it was too late for confidences with Mother.

He had made up his mind about her years ago.

Mother hated cooking, housework and gardening. She hated having children. They asked too much of her. She didn't realise how little children required.

He thought of her shopping on Saturday, dragging the heavy shopping home, and cooking the roast on Sunday. The awfulness of the food didn't bother him; the joylessness which accompanied the futile ritual did. It wasn't a lunch that started out hopefully, but one which failed from the start. The pity she made him feel for her was, at that age, too much for him.

She couldn't let herself enjoy anything, and she couldn't flee.

If he had made a decent family himself it was because Alexandra had always believed in it; any happiness he experienced was with her and the children. She had run their lives, the house and the garden, with forethought, energy and precision. Life and meaning had been created because she had never doubted the value of what they were doing. It was love.

If there was anguish about 'the family', it was because

people knew it was where the good things were. He understood that happiness didn't happen by itself; making a family work was as hard as running a successful business, or being an artist. To him, it was doubly worthwhile because he had had to discover this for himself. Sensibly, somehow, he had wanted what Alexandra wanted.

She had kept them together and pushed them forward.

He loved her for it.

Now, it wasn't enough for her.

He said, 'Would it be a good idea to get some flowers?'

'Lovely,' said Mother. 'Let's do that.'

They stopped at a garage and chose some.

'He would have loved these colours,' she said.

'He was a good man,' murmured Harry.

'Oh yes, yes! D'you miss him?'

'I wish I could talk to him.'

She said, 'I talk to him all the time.'

Harry parked the car. They walked through the gates.

The cemetery was busy, a thoroughfare, more of a park than a burial ground. Women pushed prams, school kids smoked on benches, dogs peed on gravestones.

Father had a prime spot in which to rot, at the back, by the fence.

Mother put down her flowers.

Harry said, 'Would you like to get down, Mother? You can use my jacket.'

'Thank you, dear, but I'd never get up again.'

She bent her head and prayed and wept, her tears falling on the grave.

Harry walked about, weeping and muttering his own prayer: 'At least let me be alive when I die!'

Father would have been pleased by their attendance.

He thought, 'Dying isn't something you can leave to the last moment.'

He was like the old man, too. He had to remember that. Being pulled in two directions had saved him.

He walked away from Mother and had a cigarette.

His boss had told him unequivocally 'to rest'. He had said, 'To be frank, you're creating a bad atmosphere in the office.'

Harry's fourteen-year-old daughter Heather had run away from boarding school. Returning from the shops two days after Alexandra had left for Thailand, he found her sitting in the kitchen.

'Hello there, Dad,' she said.

'Heather. This is a surprise.'

'Is it okay?' She looked apprehensive.

He said, 'It's fine.'

They spent the day together. He didn't ask why she was there.

He got on well with the boy, who seemed, at the moment, to worship him. He would, Gerald said, understand him for another couple of years, when the boy would be fourteen, and then never again.

Over Heather, he felt sorry and guilty about a lot of things. If he thought about it, he could see that her sulks, fears and unhappinesses, called 'adolescence', were an extended mourning for a lost childhood.

After lunch, when she continued to sit there, looking at him, he did say, 'Is there anything you want to ask me?'

'Yes,' she said. 'What is a man?'

'Sorry?'

'What is a man?'

'Is that it?'

She nodded.

What is a man?

She hadn't said, 'What is sex?' Not, 'Who am I?' Not even, 'What am I doing here in this kitchen and on earth?' But, 'What is a man?'

She cooked for him. They sat down together in the living room and listened to a symphony.

He wanted to know her.

It had taken him a while to see – the screechings of the feminists had made him resistant – that the fathers had been separated from their children by work, though provided with the consolations of power. The women, too, had been separated from important things. It was a division he had had in the back of his mind, had taken for granted, most of his life.

They were lower middle class; his father had had a furniture shop. He had worked all day his entire life and had done well. By the end he had two furniture shops. They did carpeting, too.

Harry and his brother had helped in the shops.

It was the university holidays when Harry accompanied his father on the train to Harley Street. Father had retired. He was seeking help for depression.

'I'm feeling too down all the time,' he said. 'I'm not right.'

As they sat in the waiting room, Father said of the doctor, 'He's the top man.'

'How d'you know?'

'There's his certificate. I can't make out the curly writing from here, but I hope it's signed.'

'It is signed.'

'You've got good eyes, then,' Father said. 'This guy will turn me into Fred Astaire.'

Father was smiling, full of hope for the first time in weeks.

'What's wrong, sir?' said the doctor, a man qualified to make others better.

He listened to Father's terse, urgent account of inner darkness and spiritual collapse before murmuring, 'Life has no meaning, eh?'

'The wrong meaning,' said Father, carefully.

'The wrong meaning,' repeated the doctor.

He scribbled a prescription for tranquillisers. They'd hardly been in there for half an hour.

As they went away, Harry didn't want to point out that the last thing tranquillisers did was make you happy.

Harry was puzzled and amused by Father striking out for happiness. It seemed a little late. What did he expect? Why couldn't he sink into benign, accepting old age? Isn't that what he, Harry, would have done?

He was taking Mother's side. This was the deep, wise view. Happiness was impossible, undesirable even, an unnecessary distraction from the hard, long, serious business of unhappiness. Mother would not be separated from the sorrow which covered her like a shroud.

In life, Harry chose the dullest things – deliberately at first, as if wanting to see what it felt like to be Mother. Then it became a habit. Why did he choose this way rather than his father's?

His daughter Heather had always been fussy about her food. By the time she was thirteen, at every meal she sat at the table with her head bent, her fork held limply between her fingers, watched by her mother, brother and father. Could she eat or not?

Harry was unable to bear her 'domination of the table' as she picked at her food, shoved it around the plate and made ugly faces before announcing that she couldn't eat today. It disgusted him. If he pressurised her to eat, Heather would weep.

He saw that it isn't the most terrible people that we hate, but those who confuse us the most. His power was gone; his compassion broke down. He mocked and humiliated her. He could have murdered this little girl who would not put bread in her mouth.

He had, to his shame, refused to let Heather eat with them. He ordered her to eat earlier than the family, or later, but not with him, her mother or brother.

Alexandra had said that if Heather wasn't allowed to eat with them, she wouldn't sit at the table either.

Harry started taking his meals alone in another room, with a newspaper in front of him.

Alexandra had been indefatigable with Heather, cooking innumerable dishes until Heather swallowed something. This made him jealous. If Mother had never been patient with him, he wanted Alexandra to tell him whether he was warm enough, what time he should go to bed, what he should read on the train.

Perhaps this was why Heather had wanted to go to boarding school.

His resentment of her had gone deep. He had come to consider her warily. It was easier to keep away from someone; easier not to tangle with them. If she needed him, she could come to him.

A distance had been established. He understood that a life could pass like this.

Father, always an active, practical man, had taken the tranquillisers for a few days, sitting on the sofa near Mother, waiting to feel better, looking as though he'd been hit on the head with a mallet. At last, he threw away the pills, and resumed his pilgrimage around Harley Street. If you were sick, you went to a doctor. Where else could you go, in a secular age, to find a liberating knowledge?

It was then that Harry made the stupid remark.

They were leaving another solemn surgery, morbid with dark wood, creaky leather and gothic certificates. After many tellings, Father had made a nice story of his despair and wrong meanings. Harry turned to the doctor and said, 'There's no cure for living!'

'That's about right,' replied the doctor, shaking his pen.

Then, with Father looking, the doctor winked.

No cure for living!

As Father wrote the cheque, Harry could see he was electric with fury.

'Shut your big mouth in future!' he said, in the street. 'Who's asking for your stupid opinion? There's no cure! You're saying I'm incurable?'

'No, no –'

'What do you know? You don't know anything!'

'I'm only saying –'

Father was holding him by the lapels. 'Why did we stay in that small house?'

'Why did you? What are you talking about?'

'The money went on sending you to a good school! I wanted you to be educated, but you've turned into a sarcastic, smart-arsed idiot!'

The next time Father visited the doctor, Harry's brother was deputed to accompany him.

Harry had a colleague who spent every lunchtime in the pub, with whom Harry would discuss the 'problem' of how to get along with women. One day, this man announced he had discovered the 'solution'.

Submission was the answer. What you had to do was go along with what the woman wanted. How, then, could there be conflict?

To Harry, this sounded like a recipe for fury and murder, but he didn't dismiss it. Hadn't he, in a sense – not unlike all children – submitted to his mother's view of things? And hadn't this half-killed his spirit and left him frustrated? He wasn't acting from his own spirit, but like a slave; his inner spirit, alive still, hated it.

'Harry, Harry!' Mother called. 'I'm ready to go.'

He walked across the grass to her. She put her handkerchief in her bag.

'All right, Mother.' He added, 'Hardly worth going home now.'

'Yes, dear. It is a lovely place. Perhaps you'd be good enough to put me here. Not that I'll care.'

'Right,' he said.

Father, the day he went to see the doctor, remembered how he had once loved. He wanted that loving back. Without it, living was a cold banishment.

Mother couldn't let herself remember what she loved. It was not only the unpleasant things that Mother wanted to forget, but anything that might remind her she was alive. One good thing might be linked to others. There might be a flood of disturbing happiness.

Before Father refused to have Harry accompany him on his doctor visits, Harry became aware, for the first time, that Father thought for himself. He thought about men and women, about politics and the transport system in London, about horse racing and cricket, and about how someone should live.

Yet his father never read anything but newspapers. Harry recalled the ignorant, despised father in *Sons and Lovers*.

Harry had believed too much in people who were better educated. He had thought that the truth was in certain books, or in the thinkers who were current. It had never occurred to Harry that one could – should – work these things out for oneself.

Who was he to do this? Father had paid for his education, yet it gave Harry no sustenance; there was nothing there he could use now, to help him grasp what was going on.

He was a journalist, he followed others – critically, of course. But he served them; he put them first.

Television and newspapers bored Alexandra. 'Noise', she called it. She had said, 'You'd rather read a newspaper than think your own thoughts.'

He and Mother made their way back to the car.

She had never touched, held or bent down to kiss him; her body was as inaccessible to him as it probably was to her. He had never slept in her bed. Now, she took his arm. He thought she wanted him to support her, but she was steady. Affection, it might have been.

One afternoon, when Alexandra had returned from the hypnotherapist and was unpacking the shopping on the kitchen table, Harry asked her, 'What did Amazing Olga say today?'

Alexandra said, 'She told me something about what makes us do things, about what motivates us.'

'What did Mrs Amazing say? Self-interest?'

'Falling in love with things,' she said. 'What impels us to act is love.'

'Shit,' said Harry.

*

The day she ran away, after the two of them had eaten and listened to music, Heather wanted to watch a film that someone at school had lent her. She sat on the floor in her pyjamas, sucking her thumb, wearing her Bugs Bunny slippers. She wanted her father to sit with her, as she had as a kid, when she would grasp his chin, turning it in the direction she required.

The film was *The Piano*, which, it seemed to him, grew no clearer as it progressed. When they paused the film to fetch drinks and food, she said that understanding it didn't matter, adding, 'particularly if you haven't been feeling well lately'.

'Who's not feeling well?' he said. 'Me, you mean?'

'Maybe,' she said. 'Anyone. But perhaps you.'

She was worried about him; she had come to watch over him.

He knew she had got up later to watch the film another couple of times. He wondered whether she had stayed up all night.

In the morning, when he saw how nervous she looked, he said, 'I don't mind if you don't want to go back to school.'

'But you've always emphasised the "importance of education".'

Here she imitated him, quite well. They did it, the three of them, showing him how foolish he was.

He went on, feebly he thought, but on nevertheless: 'There's so much miseducation.'

'What?' She seemed shocked.

'Not the information, which is mostly harmless,' he said, 'but the ideas behind it, which come with so much force – the force that is called "common sense".'

She was listening, and she never listened.

She could make of it what she wanted. His uncertainty was important. Why pretend he had considered, final views on these matters? He knew politicians: what couldn't be revealed by them was ignorance, puzzlement, the process of intellectual vacillation. His doubt was a kind of gift, then.

He said, 'About culture, about marriage, about education, death ... You receive all sorts of assumptions that it takes years to correct. The less the better, I say. It's taken me years to correct some of the things I was made to believe early on.'

He was impressed by how impressed she had been.

'I will go back to school,' she said. 'I think I should, for Mum.'

Before he took her to the station, she sat where her mother sat, at the table, writing in a notebook.

He had to admit that lately he had become frustrated and aggressive with Alexandra, angry that he couldn't control or understand her. By changing, she was letting him down; she was leaving him.

Alexandra rarely mentioned his mother and he never talked seriously about her for fear, perhaps, of his rage, or the memory of rage, it would evoke. But after a row over Olga, Alexandra said, 'Remember this. Other people aren't your mother. You don't have to yell at them to ensure they're paying attention. They're not half-dead and they're not deaf. You're wearing yourself out, Harry, trying to get us to do things we're doing already.'

Alexandra had the attributes that Mother never had. He hadn't, at least, made the mistake of choosing someone like his mother, of living with the same person for ever without even knowing it.

Oddly, it was the ways in which she wasn't like Mother which disturbed him the most.

He thought: a man was someone who should know, who was supposed to know. Someone who knew what was going on, who had a vision of where they were all heading, separately and as a family. Sanity was a great responsibility.

'Why did you run away from school?' he asked Heather at last.

Placing her hands over her ears, she said there were certain songs she couldn't get out of her head. Words and tunes circulated on an endless loop. This had driven her home to Father.

He said, 'Are the noises less painful here?'

'Yes.'

He would have dismissed it as a minor madness if he hadn't, only that afternoon . . .

He had been instructed to rest, and rest he would, after years of work. He had gone into the garden to lie on the grass beneath the trees. There, at the end of the cool orchard, with a glass of wine beside him, his mind had become possessed by brutal images of violent crime, of people fighting and devouring one another's bodies, of destruction and the police; of impaling, burning, cutting.

Childhood had sometimes been like this: hatred and the desire to bite, kill, kick.

He had been able to lie there for only twenty minutes. He had walked, then, thrashing his head as if to drive away the insanity.

A better way of presenting the news might be this: a screaming woman, dripping blood and guts, holding the corpse of a flayed animal. A ripped child; armfuls of eviscerated infants; pieces of chewed body.

This would be an image, if they kept it on screen for an hour or so, that would not only shock but compel consideration of the nature of humankind.

He had run inside and turned on the television.

If he seemed to know as much about his own mind as he did about the governance of Zambia, how could his daughter's mind not be strange to her?

There was no day of judgement, when a person's life would be evaluated, the good and the bad, in separate piles. No day but every day.

Alexandra was educating him: a pedagogy of adjustment and strength. These were the challenges of a man's life. It was pulling him all over the place. The alternative wasn't just to die feebly, but to self-destruct in fury because the questions being asked were too difficult.

If he and Alexandra stayed together, he would have to change. If he couldn't follow her, he would have to change more.

A better life was only possible if he forsook familiar experiences for seduction by the unfamiliar. Certainty would be a catastrophe.

The previous evening, Alexandra had rung from her mobile phone. He'd thought the background noise was the phone's crackle, but it was the sea. She had left the taverna and was walking along the beach behind a group of other women.

'I've decided,' she said straight away, sounding ecstatic.

'What is it, Alexandra?'

'It has become clear to me, Harry! My reason, let's say. I will work with the unconscious.'

'In Thailand?'

'In Kent. At home.'

'I guess you can find the unconscious everywhere.'

'How we know others. What sense we can make of their minds. That is what interests me. When I'm fully trained, people will come –'

'Where? Where?' He couldn't hear her.

'To the house. We will need a room built, I think. Will that be all right?'

'Whatever you want.'

'I will earn it back.'

He asked, 'What will the work involve?'

'Working with people, individually and in groups, in the afternoons and evenings, helping them understand their imaginations. It is a training, therefore, in possibility.'

'Excellent.'

'Do you mean that? This work is alien to you, I know. Today, today – a bunch of grown-ups – we were talking to imaginary apples!'

'Somehow it wouldn't be the same', he said, 'with bananas! But I am with you, at your side, always . . . wherever you are!'

He had had intimations of this. There had been an argument.

He had asked her, 'Why do you want to help other people?'

'I can't think of anything else as interesting.'

'Day after day you will listen to people droning on.'

'After a bit, the self-knowledge will make them change.'

'I've never seen such a change in anyone.'

'Haven't you?'

'I don't believe I have,' he'd said.

'Haven't you?'

He'd said agitatedly, 'Why d'you keep repeating that like a parrot?' She'd looked at him levelly. He'd gone on, 'Tell me when and where you've seen this!'

'You're very interested.'

'It would be remarkable,' he'd said. 'That's why I'm interested.'

'People are remarkable,' she'd said. 'They find all sorts of resources within themselves that were unused, that might be wasted.'

'Is it from that "Amazing" woman that you get such ideas?'

'She and I talk, of course. Are you saying I don't have a mind of my own?'

He'd said, 'Are you talking about a dramatic change?'

'Yes.'

'Well,' he'd said. 'I don't know. But I'm not ruling it out.'

'That's something.' She had smiled. 'It's a lot.'

He had wanted to tell Heather that clarity was not illuminating; it kept the world away. A person needed confusion and muddle – good difficult knots and useful frustrations. Someone could roll up their sleeves and work, then.

He got Mother into the car and started it.

She said, 'Usually I lie down and shut the tops of me eyes at this time. You're not going to keep me up, are you?'

'Only if you want to eat. D'you want to do that?'

'That's an idea. I'm starving. Tummy's rumbling. Rumblin'!'

'Come on.'

In the car, he murmured, 'You were rotten to me.'

'Oh, was I so terrible?' she cried. 'I only gave you life and fed and clothed you and brought you up all right, didn't I? You were never late for school!'

'Sorry? You couldn't wait for us to get out of the house!'

'Haven't you done better than the other boys? They're plumbers! People would give their legs to have your life!'

'It wasn't enough.'

'It's never enough, is it? It never was! It never is!'

He went on, 'If I were you, looking back on your life now, I'd be ashamed.'

'Oh, would you?' she said. 'You've been so marvellous, have you, you miserable little git!'

'Fuck you,' he told his mother. 'Fuck off.'

'You're terrible,' she said. 'Picking an old woman to pieces the day she visits her husband's grave. I've always loved you,' she said.

'It was no use to me. You never listened and you never talked to me.'

'No, no,' she said. 'I spoke to you, but I couldn't say it. I cared, but I couldn't show it. I've forgotten why. Can't you forget all that?'

'No. It won't leave me alone.'

'Just forget it,' she said, her face creasing in anguish. 'Forget everything!'

'Oh, Mother, that's no good. Nothing is forgotten, even you know that.'

'Father took me to Venice, and now I want to go again. Before it's too late – before they have to carry me wheelchair over the Wotsit of Cries.'

'You'll go alone?'

'You won't take me –'

'I wouldn't walk across the road with you', he said, 'if I could help it. I can't stand the sight of you.'

She closed her eyes. 'No, well . . . I'll go with the other old girls.'

He said, 'You want me to pay for you?'

'I thought you wouldn't mind,' she said. 'I might meet a nice chap! A young man! I could get off! I'm a game old bird in me old age!'

She started to cackle.

'Like what?' Heather asked. 'What educational ideas are no good?'

'I think I have believed that if I waited, if I sat quietly at the table, without making a noise or movement – being good – the dish of life would be presented to me.'

He should have added: people want to believe in unconditional love, that once someone has fallen in love with you, their devotion will continue, whether you spend the rest of your life lying on the sofa drinking beer or not. But why should they? If love was not something that could be worked up, it had to be kept alive.

Mother said, 'Children are selfish creatures. Only interested in themselves. You get sick of them. You bloody hate them, screaming, whining, no gratitude. And that's about it!'

'I know,' he said. 'That's true. But it's not the whole story!'

The restaurant was almost empty, with a wide window overlooking the street.

Mother drank wine and ate spare ribs with her fingers. The wine reddened her face; her lips, chin and hands became greasy.

'It's so lovely, the two of us,' she said. 'You were such an affectionate little boy, following me around everywhere. You became quite rough, playing football in the garden and smashing the plants and bushes.'

'All children are affectionate,' he said. 'I'm fed up with it, Mother.'

'What are you fed up with now?' she said, as if his complaints would never cease.

'My job. I feel I'm in a cult there.'

'A cult? What are you talking about?'

'The bosses have made themselves into little gods. I am a little god, to some people. Can you believe it? I walk in, people tremble. I could ruin their lives in a moment –'

'A cult?' she said, wiping her mouth and dipping her fingers in a bowl of water. 'Those things they have in America?'

'It's like that, but not exactly. It is a cheerleader culture. There are cynics about, but they are all alcoholics. What the bosses want is to display ridiculous little statuettes on their shelves. They want to be written about by other journalists – the little praise of nobodies. Mother, I'm telling you, it's Nazi and it's a slave ideology.'

He was shaking; he had become overenthusiastic.

He said, more mildly, 'Still, work – it's the same for everyone. Even the Prime Minister must sometimes think, first thing in the morning –'

'Oh, don't do it,' she said. 'Just don't.'

'I knew you wouldn't understand. Alexandra and the kids wouldn't like it if I suddenly decided to leave for Thailand. I have four people to support.'

'You don't support me,' she said.

'Certainly not.'

'That's your revenge, is it?'

'Yes.'

'Excuse me for saying so, dear. We're both getting on now. You could drop dead any minute. You've been sweating all day. Your face is damp. Is your heart all right?'

She touched his forehead with her napkin.

'My friend Gerald had a heart attack last month,' he said.

'No. Your dad, bless him, retired, and then he was gone. What would your wife and the kids do then?'

'Thank you, Mother. What I'm afraid of is that I will just walk out of my job or insult someone or go crazy like those gunmen who blaze away at strangers.'

'You'd be on the news instead of behind it.' She was enjoying herself. 'You'd be better off on your own, like me. I've got no one bothering me. Peace! I can do what I want.'

'I want to be bothered by others. It's called living.' He went on, 'Maybe I feel like this because I've been away for a week. I'll go in on Monday and find I don't have these worries.'

'You will,' she said. 'Once a worry starts —'

'You'd know about that. But what can I do?'

'Talk to Alexandra about it. If she's getting all free and confident about herself, why can't you?'

'Yes, perhaps she can support me now.'

They were about to order pudding when a motorcyclist buzzed down the street in front of them, turned left into a side street, hit a car, and flew into the air.

The waiters ran to the window. A crowd gathered; a doctor forced his way through. An ambulance arrived. The motorcyclist lay on the ground a long time. At last, he was strapped onto a stretcher and carried to the ambulance, which only travelled a few yards before turning off its blue light and klaxon.

'That's his life done,' said Mother. 'Cheerio.'

The ruined motorcycle was pushed onto the pavement. The debris was swept up. The traffic resumed.

Harry and Mother put down their knives and forks.

'Even I can't eat any more,' she said.

'Nor me.'

He asked for the bill.

He parked outside the house and walked her to the door.

She made her milky tea. With a plate of chocolate biscuits beside her, she took her seat in front of the television.

The television was talking at her. She would sit there until bedtime.

He kissed her.

'Goodbye, dear.' She dipped her biscuit in her tea. 'Thank you for a lovely day.'

'What are you going to do now? Nothing?'

'Have a little rest. It's not much of a life, is it?'

He noticed a travel agent's brochure on the table.

He said, 'I'll send you a cheque, shall I, for the Venice trip?'

'That would be lovely.'

'When will you be going?'

'As soon as possible. There's nothing to keep me here.'

While Heather was at home, Alexandra rang, but Harry didn't say she was there. It was part of what a man sometimes did, he thought, to be a buffer between the children and their mother.

In the morning, before she left, Heather said she wanted him to listen to a poem she had written.

He listened, trying not to weep. He could hear the love in it.

Heather had come to cheer him up, to make him feel that his love worked, that it could make her feel better.

After Alexandra had rung from the beach, Harry rang Gerald and told him about the 'imaging', about the 'visualisation', the 'healing', the whole thing. Gerald, convalescing, took his call.

'I used to know a psychoanalyst,' he said cheerfully. 'I've always fancied talking about myself for a long time to someone. But it's not what the chaps do. It's good business, though, people buying into their own pasts – if Alexandra can think like that. Before, women wanted to be nurses. Now, they want to be therapists.'

'It's harmless, you're saying.'

Gerald said, 'And sometimes useful.' He laughed. 'Turning dreams into money for all of you, almost literally.'

Gerald imagined it was almost the only way that Harry could grasp what Alexandra was doing.

But it wasn't true.

Harry drove around the old places after leaving Mother. He wanted to buy a notebook and return to write down the thoughts his memories inspired. Maybe he would do it tonight, his last evening alone, using different-coloured markers.

It started to rain. He thought of himself on the street in the rain as a teenager, hanging around outside chip shops and pubs – not bored, that would underestimate what he felt, but unable to spit out or swallow the amount of experience coming at him.

It had been a good day.

Walking along a row of shops he remembered from forty years ago, he recalled a remark of some philosopher that he had never let go. The gist of it was: happiness is wanting one thing. The thing was love, if that was not too pallid a word. Passion, or wanting someone, might be better. In the end, all that would remain of one's years would be the quality of one's link with others, of how far one had gone with them.

Harry turned the car and headed away from his childhood. He had to go to the supermarket. He would buy flowers, cakes, champagne and whatever attracted his attention. He would attempt to tidy the house; he would work in the garden, clearing the leaves. He would do the thing he dreaded: sit down alone and think.

The next morning, he would pick up Alexandra at the airport, and if the weather was good they would eat and talk in the garden. She would be healthy, tanned and full of ideas.

He had to phone Heather to check whether she was all right. It occurred to him to write to her. If he knew little of her day-to-day life, she knew practically nothing of him, his past and what he did most of the time. Parents wanted to know everything of their children, but withheld themselves.

He thought of Father under the earth, and of Mother watching television; he thought of Alexandra and his children. He was happy.

Straight

For days he had been fearful of this night but wanted to believe he was ready.

However, when he arrived at the party, bearing a bottle of champagne, he started to feel afraid that people would notice, that they would be able to tell right away what had happened to him, and how he had changed. He wondered whether his friends would think badly of him. He considered who would be hostile, who envious and who sympathetic.

His friends were modernising the house. The floorboards were still bare and some walls unpainted. Wires hung from their sockets; tinsel hung from the wires. The hostess hurried past, wearing antlers. The host, bearing a tray of mince pies, either didn't recognise Brett or took him for granted.

Brett sidled in, shocked that his paranoia hadn't diminished with age, even as his reasonable side told him how unlikely it was that anyone would be in any state to take a close interest in him.

'Brett, Brett!' someone shouted.

'Hallo there!' he replied. 'Whoever you are!'

He had deliberately left it late; the room was crowded. He knew most of the revellers, who were of his age. Now he was able to think about it, he had known some of them for more than twenty years.

He kissed and greeted those near by and went into the kitchen. These were well-off people; they would give a good party. The trestle table was bent with the weight of bottles, cans and food. He added the champagne to the load and looked around.

He wasn't about to drink lemonade. Someone put a glass of wine in his hand. It was a good idea, the perfect cover.

Recently he had been going to the theatre and cinema, and had stayed to the end; he had read at least three books all the way through. This was the first party he'd been to since the incident by the river, as he called it. He had made up his mind to stay a while. There were things it would do him good to look straight at.

He returned to the living room. To his relief, a sombre male friend joined him and began to talk. From where Brett sat, occasionally asking a question, he could observe the other people.

He watched a man trying to zip up his top. The zip stuck; it wouldn't budge. The man pulled it apart and began again. He couldn't get the serrated edges together, and when they did click, they wouldn't move. This went on for some time. Finally the man took the thing off, joined the parts together on his lap and tried to pull it over his head, where it lodged. Others joined in then, tugging the garment and the man in different directions.

Brett was distracted from this by a wet-eyed acquaintance who was dribbling already; his head was bent. Walking like an old man, he looked as though he might collapse. Another friend pulled Brett up, stood close to him, and shouted in first one ear and then the other. When it was obvious that Brett didn't understand, the friend brought a companion over and together they yelled at Brett, or, it seemed, yelled into him, laughing at one another.

Brett was nodding his head. 'I see, I see now.'

'That's it!' said the first friend. 'Brett is with us! Hello, Brett!'

Brett didn't know why they had to stand so near, or why they kept plucking at him. The only thing to do was to have a drink. That was the key to things here; then he would understand. But he couldn't have a drink.

Luckily, Francine fell into the sofa on the other side of him.

'There you are, Brett darling. Thank God you're here. Some of these bloody people are boring fuckers!'

'Are they?'

'You know they are!'

She had made the effort: her lips were bright, her black clothes expensive, her hair colouring and cut the best. She wore high-heeled black suede boots. He noticed, though, when talking to her, that her eyes kept closing, even as she told a story about getting stuck in a lift with her boss. During this narcoleptic monologue, she spilled her drink over him.

He stood up.

'Oh God, God, God! So sorry!' she said. 'I've made you wet.' She was pulling at his wrist. 'Sit down!' She wiped his leg with her hand; she dried her hand on the sofa. 'Don't look so grumpy. You did the same to me once. Except it went over my breasts.'

He looked at her breasts.

'I didn't.'

'You won't remember. You don't remember anything, re-member?'

'No,' he said. 'I don't think I do.'

If he'd forgotten, it wasn't only that dissipation had wiped his memory: he hadn't properly been there in the first place.

'You are out of your mind.' Francine shifted closer to him and stroked his hair. 'Your face is smooth. You've shaved, for a change. But you really are gone, this time.'

'Perhaps I am,' he said, and chuckled. 'Please tell me what you're talking about.'

'First, you can give me some of that. Brett, you owe me.'

Her hands were in his crotch, searching for his pockets.

She said, 'Your face is white, dear! I've never seen you so tense or wide-eyed. Is it that pure stuff people are talking about? You shouldn't be taking it, with your blood pressure. Give it to me and get to the rehab!'

'Is there really something wrong with me, Francine? Tell me if you think there is.'

'What's right with you? You haven't laughed at anything I've said.'

'You haven't said anything funny.'

'Don't be a fool, Brett.'

'Stop that fiddling!' he said. 'There's absolutely nothing for you in my pocket.'

It didn't discourage her.

'You banged your head when you fell in the river. That's what did you in. Isn't that right?' She was laughing with her mouth open. 'What were you doing down there, by the river?'

People loved this story; they rang to ask about it, and it was repeated around town. He couldn't deny her.

He said, 'I got Carol to stop the cab after that party because I needed a pee and didn't want people to see me.'

'Is that why you climbed over the wall and slipped?'

'With my cock out, actually, all the way down the ramp. Right into the cold river, I feared. But into the cold mud, luckily.'

'Didn't Rowena and Carol haul you out?'

'Haul me out?' he said. 'They were tottering around hysterically at the top. I could hear them screeching like a zoo. I was told Rowena rang her agent who was having dinner at Gaga and asked him what to do.'

'What did the agent say? I told her to get rid of that fish. I can fix her up with Morton. He did that deal for Ronnie. Maybe I should arrange –'

Brett said, 'If you really want to know about it, the taxi driver pulled me out. Otherwise, I would have gone down for good, and that, as they say, would have been that. He had blankets in the boot which he wrapped me in. He took me home. I guess I messed up his car. D'you think it's too late to call him and apologise?'

'Where did Carol and Rowena go afterwards?'

'Don't know.'

The taxi driver had been tall and dark-skinned, a North African of some sort, wearing worn-out shoes. At home, Brett invited him in and made tea. The man sat there with Brett's mud on him and said he was a law student with two children. He studied half the time and drove the rest; sometimes he slept; occasionally he played with his children.

Brett offered him dry clothes. When the man refused, Brett tried to give him money for his dry-cleaning bill. At this, the man raised his hands in protest.

'What's wrong?' Brett had asked.

'You don't understand!'

'Please tell me –'

'Anyone would have done this thing!'

'Yes, of course!' said Brett. The man seemed relieved. 'I see, I do see,' said Brett.

He shook the man's hand.

Drinking tea only, Brett had thought about this for the rest of the night and went over it again the next day.

Probably the man was religious. But you didn't need religion to save someone. It had not been a sentimental gesture but what you did when someone fell.

Now Brett watched people shouting at one another. They would laugh inexplicably, their mouths almost touching. No one was listening, but what was there to hear? People's words were not in any recognisable order and their gestures were unrelated to anything they said. A couple dancing looked as though they were wrestling.

Brett kissed Francine's cheek. 'It's time I made a move.'

'Already? That's the best suggestion I've heard in minutes.'

They went out into the hall, where she started talking to someone. She and the other person went into the bathroom and Brett left the house.

Outside, he lit a cigarette and looked for his car keys. It was frosty and still. From the house opposite, he could hear voices singing, and a piano.

He had reached the gate when she caught up with him, one arm in her coat.

'You tried to sneak off without me. Would I leave you here alone? Have I ever done that to you? Here are the keys I took from your pocket.'

He helped her on with the coat and said, 'You live way across town.'

'We're going on to Gaga! Please, just for a bit. Then you can take me home.'

'I don't want to go to Gaga, but I'll drop you off there.'

'How will I get home?'

'How have you got home every night for the last fifteen years?'

'What nonsense you talk, Brett. Come on, you've got to sober up for the drive.'

In the car, she was smoking. Her skirt was up.

'You behave so badly, Brett. But somehow I always forgive you.'

'Thank you,' he said. 'Jesus. Have you seen what's going on tonight?'

He drove slowly. The high street was more than busy. Crowds gathered outside bars and clubs. People ran into the road; they shouted and a man threw a punch; there were ambulances and police cars about. He slowed to a stop and waved at the cars behind him. Someone was lying face-down in the road. Others were trying to pull the person to the pavement but couldn't decide which side of the road was best.

He said, 'What you just said sounded strange but intriguing. What do I have to be forgiven for?'

'Brett, where is the light in this wretched car?'

She had managed to empty her bag on to the floor and was bent double, trying to reclaim her credit cards, cocaine, numerous pills and keys.

He thought he was bleeding. He reached up and realised it was snowing on his head. Slush ran down the back of his neck. Looking for the light, she had released the sun roof. He left it open.

She was saying, 'Forget all that. Brett, the thing is, I think we both need to go away. It's that time of the year. How about Rio?'

'Now?'

'Tomorrow morning.'

'It's too far.'

'Paris? It's only up the road now.'

'What would we do?'

'Eat, drink, go out.'

'I don't want to do that any more.'

'What else is there?'

He said, 'Where am I going to park?'

She had already opened the car door and was heading towards the members' club, plumping her hair and squirting perfume at her throat.

'See you inside!' she called.

They knew him at Gaga. At the end of the night, they often called cabs for him and lent him money to pay for them.

When he pushed the familiar glass door and stepped across the carpet which he remembered, on occasion, feeling against his cheek, he saw a former business partner with mistletoe attached to his forehead by bands of Sellotape.

He pulled Brett to him and started kissing him. 'It's you – you, you bastard! The one who let me down! Now we're both bankrupt!'

'Yes, yes,' said Brett. 'That's right!'

'Been swimming in the river, I hear! How are you doing now?' It took his friend a while to find the words. He was so pleased he repeated them. 'You doing . . . you doing swimmingly . . .' he went, laughing to himself. 'Won't sit down! Busy with something!'

Brett bought Francine a drink and one for himself. How expensive it was! How much money he had spent on it over the years, not to mention energy!

In the bathroom, he threw the drink away and filled his glass with water. What a beautiful drink water was.

He took a seat at the bar and watched the man with the mistletoe weave about until he dropped on to a sofa. There, he went to some trouble to relocate the mistletoe in his open fly. Then he leaned back with his knees apart and began the business – giggling the while – of attracting the waitress's attention.

Over the years, Brett must have sat on all the bar stools and armchairs in the place. He could see a group of his friends settling down to play cards. Johnny, Chris, Carol and Mike. They would be there for a long time; later, they'd go somewhere else. On any other night, he'd have joined them.

The aggression in Gaga seemed high. People wanted help and attention, but they were asking the wrong folks, others just like them. Some of them were wired, with their eyes popping. Others were exhausted, with failing heads. Odd it was, the taking of substances that made you feel worse, that made everything worse in the end. Dissipation was gruelling work, a full-time job. Yet things did get done; these men and women had professions. Brett had to be grateful: at least he had kept his flat and job. He'd only lost his wife.

If he didn't sit with his friends – and he wouldn't; he was cold, while they were hot with enthusiasm – where else was there? How did you get to others? After all, it wasn't only him, or his circle, who was like this. It was his ex-wife's father, his own sister and her boyfriend, who sat around with cans and bottles, fighting and weeping. Or they had been cured but had become addicted to the cure, as tedious off the stuff as they had been on it.

Francine had taken her drink and gone to join a group. He noticed she continued to watch him, knowing he might shrug her off and leave. He didn't see why this would matter to her.

Brett was content to think of the North African, wondering whether something about the man had influenced him. Like the taxi driver, Brett seemed to be in a world where everyone resembled him but spoke in a foreign language. If the man stayed in England, he would always struggle to understand it, never quite connecting.

He had helped Brett; why shouldn't Brett help him? Brett imagined himself turning up at the man's house, offering to do anything. But what might he do? Wash up, or read to the children? Take them all to the cinema? Why shouldn't he do it, now he felt better? The man might be too shy or suspicious for such things, yet surely he had to stop work for lunch or supper? Brett could listen to him. It would be a way of starting again, or returning to a state of teenage curiosity, when you might take any path that presented itself, seeing where it led.

Brett got down from the stool.

'No you don't.' Francine came over and put her tongue in his mouth. 'You take me home. You've been coming on to me all night.'

He didn't mind taking her home. He had come to dislike his own street and thought he should move to another district. Apart from the fact a change would do him good, living near by was a woman he passed often, an ex-barmaid. If she recognised him, which he doubted, she never acknowledged him. She had four children by different fathers and the youngest was his, he knew it. He had stayed with her one night after a party, four years ago. When he made the calculation, it added up. A drinking acquaintance pointed it out. 'Look at that kid. If I didn't know better, I'd say you were the father.'

He had gone to the playground to watch the child. It was true; she had his own mother's hair and eyes. He had seen the woman shout at the girl. He didn't like passing his only daughter on the street.

In the car, Francine was drinking from a bottle of wine.

'Haven't you had enough yet?' he said. 'Can't you just stop?'

'Tonight I'm going the whole way.'

'Why?'

'That's a fatuous question.'

'But I would like to know, really.'

She started to cry, talking all the while. She didn't think to spare him her misery; perhaps it didn't occur to her that he would be concerned.

The North African man drove strangers night after night, despised or invisible amongst abhorrent fools who had so much of everything, they could afford to piss it away.

At Francine's block of flats, he helped her upstairs. He put the lights on and led her to bed. She thrashed about, as if the mattress were a runaway horse she had to master.

He turned his back, but she couldn't remove her clothes. He got her into her pyjamas and kissed her on the side of the head.

'Good night, Francine.'

'Don't leave me! You're staying, aren't you? I –'

She was clawing at his chest. She was an awful colour. He ran for the washing-up bowl and held it by her face.

'Is this it? Is this it?' she kept saying. 'Is it now, tonight?'

'Is it what, Francine?'

'Death! Is he here? Has William Burroughs come to call?'

'Not tonight, sweetheart. Lie back.'

Her vomit splattered the walls; it went over his jacket, his shoes, trousers and shirt, and in his hair.

At the end, she did lie back, exhausted. He removed her soiled pyjamas and put her into a dressing gown.

He was sitting there. She extended her arms to him. 'Come on, Brett.'

'You're pretty sick, Francine.'

'I've finished. There's nothing left. You can do what you want to me.' She was shivering, but she opened her dressing gown. 'That's something no one ever says no to!'

'What difference would it make?'

'Who cares about that! Fetch yourself a drink and settle down. I've always liked you.'

'Have you?'

'Don't you know that? Despite your problems, you're bright and you can be sweet. Won't you tell me what you are on tonight, Brett?'

He shook his head and put a glass of water to her lips. 'Nothing. Nothing.'

'There must be someone else you're going to. That's a rotten thing to do to a woman.'

He thought for a time.

'There is no woman. It's a taxi driver.'

'Christ!'

'Yes.'

'The one who fished you out? You won't know where he is.'

'I'll go to the cab office and wait. They know me there. Hell, understand what I want.'

'What's that?'

'Good talk.'

She said, 'You enjoyed sleeping with me last time.'

'What last time? There wasn't any last time.'

'Don't pretend to be a fool when you're not. Get in.'

She was patting the bed.

He walked to the door and shut it behind him. She was still talking, to him, to anyone and no one.

'There's someone I've got to find,' he said.

Remember This Moment, Remember Us

It is nearly Christmas and Rick is getting quite drunk at a party in a friend's clothes shop.

It is a vast shop in a smart area of west London, and tonight the girls who work there have got dressed up in shiny black dresses, white velvet bunny ears and high shoes. When Rick and Daniel arrived, the girls were holding trays of champagne, mulled wine and mince pies. Has there ever been anything so inviting?

The girls helped Rick's son Daniel out of his pushchair, removed his little red coat and showed him to the children's room where remote-controlled electric toys buzzed across the floor. There was a small seesaw; several other local children were already playing. Rick sat on the floor and Daniel, though it was late for him, chased the electric toys, flung a ping-pong ball through the open window and dismantled a doll's house, not understanding that all the inviting objects were for sale.

Rick had begun drinking an hour earlier. On the way to the party they had stopped at a bar in the area where Rick used to go when he was single. There, Daniel, who is two and a half, had climbed right up onto a furry stool next to his father, sitting in a line with the other early-evening drinkers.

'I'm training him up,' Rick said to the barmaid. 'Please, Daniel, ask her for a beer.'

'Blow-blow,' said Daniel.

'Sorry?' said Rick.

Daniel held up a book of matches. 'Blow-blow.'

Rick opened it and lit a match. 'Again,' Daniel said, the moment he blew it out. He extinguished two match books like this, filling the ashtray. As each match illuminated the boy's face, his cheeks filled and his lips puckered. When the light died, the boy's laughter rang out around the fashionably gloomy bar.

'Ready, steady, blow-blow!'

'Blow-bloody-blow,' murmured a sullen drinker.

'Got something to say?' said Rick, slipping from the stool.

The man grunted.

Rick persuaded the kid to get into his raincoat and put on his hat with the peak and ear-flaps, securing it under his chin. He slung the bag full of nappies, juice, numerous snacks, wipes and toys over his shoulder, and they went out into the night and teeming rain.

It has been raining for two days. News reports state that there have been floods all over the country.

The party was about ten minutes' walk away. Rick was wet through by the time they arrived.

His successful friend Martin with the merry staff in the big lighted shop full of clothes Rick could never afford embraced him at the door. Martin has no children himself, and this was the first time he had seen Daniel. The two men have been friends since Martin designed and made the costumes for a play Rick was in, on the Edinburgh fringe, twenty years ago. Rick congratulated him on receiving his MBE and asked to see the medal. However, there were people at Martin's shoulder and he had no time to talk. The warm wine in small white cups soon cheered Rick up.

Rick hasn't had an acting job for four months but has been promised something reasonable in the New Year. He has been going out with Daniel a lot. At least once a week, if Rick can afford it, he and Daniel take the Central Line into the West End and walk around the shops, stopping at cafés and galleries. Rick shows him the theatres he has worked in; if he knows the actors, he takes him backstage.

Rick's three other children, who live with his first wife, are in their late teens. Rick would love always to have a child in the house. When he can, he takes Daniel to parties. Daniel has big eyes; his hair has never been cut and he is often mistaken for a girl. People will talk to Rick if Daniel is with him, but he doesn't have to make extended conversation.

As the party becomes more crowded and raucous, while drinking steadily, Rick chats to the people he's introduced to. Daniel is given juice which the girls in the shop hold out for him, crouching down with their knees together.

Quite soon, Daniel says, 'Home, Dadda.'

Rick gets him dressed and manoeuvres the pushchair into the street. They begin to walk through the rain. There are few other people about, and no buses; it is far to the tube. A taxi with its light on passes them. When it has almost gone, Rick jumps into the road and yells after it, waving his arms, until it stops.

As they cross London, Rick points at the Christmas lights through the rain-streaked windows. Rick recalls similar taxi rides with his own father and remembers a photograph of himself, aged six or seven, wearing a silver bow-tie and fez-like Christmas hat, sitting on his father's knee at a party.

At home, Rick smokes a joint and drinks two more glasses of wine. It is getting late, around ten-thirty, and though Daniel usually goes to bed at eight, Rick doesn't mind if he is up, he likes the company. They eat sardines on toast with tomato ketchup; then they play loud music and Rick demonstrates the hokey-cokey to his son.

Anna has gone to her life-drawing class but is usually home by now. Why has she not returned? She is never late. Rick would have gone out to look for her, but he cannot leave Daniel and it is too wet to take him out again.

When Rick lies on the floor with his knees up, the kid steps onto him, using his father's knees for support. Daniel begins to jump up and down on Rick's stomach, as if it were a trampoline. Rick usually enjoys this as much as Daniel. But today it makes him feel queasy.

Yesterday was Rick's forty-fifth birthday, a bad age to be, he reckons, putting him on the wrong side of life. It is not only that he feels more tired and melancholic than normal, he also wonders whether he can recover from these bouts as easily as he used to. In the past year two of his friends have had heart attacks; two others have had strokes.

He guesses that he passed out on the floor. He is certainly aware of Anna shaking him. Or does she kick him in the ribs, too? He may be drunk, but he means to inform her immediately that he is not an alcoholic.

However, Rick feels strange, as if he has been asleep for some time. He wants to tell Anna what happened to him while he was asleep. He finds some furniture to hold on to, and pulls himself up.

He sees Daniel running around with a glass of wine in his hand.

'What's been going on?' Anna says.

'We went out,' Rick says, pursuing the boy and retrieving the glass. 'Didn't we, Dan?'

'Out with Dadda,' says Daniel. 'Nice time and biscuits. Dadda have drink.'

'Thanks, Dan,' Rick says.

Rick notices he has removed Daniel's trousers and nappy but omitted to replace them. There is a puddle on the floor and Daniel has wet his socks; his vest, which is hanging down, is soaked too.

He says to her, 'You think I was asleep, but I wasn't. I was thinking, or dreaming, rather. Yes, constructively dreaming . . .'

'And you expect me to ask what about?'

'I had an idea,' he says. 'It was my forty-fifth birthday yesterday and a good time we had too. I was dreaming that we were writing a card to Dan for his forty-fifth birthday. A card he wouldn't be allowed to open until then.'

'I see,' she says, sitting down. Dan is playing at her feet.

'After all,' he continues, 'like you I think about the past more and more. I think of my parents, of being a child, of my brothers, the house, all of it. What we'll do is write him a card, and you can illustrate it. We'll make it now, put it away and forget it. Years will pass and one day, when Dan's forty-five with grey hair and a bad knee, he'll remember it, and open it. We'll have sent him our love from the afterlife. Of course, you'll be alive then, but it's unlikely that I will be. For those moments, though, when he's reading it, I'll be vital in his mind. What d'you say, Anna? I'd love to have received a card from my parents on my forty-fifth birthday. All day I thought one would just pop through the door, you know.'

He is aware that she has been drinking, too, after her class. Now, as always, she begins to spread her drawings of heads, torsos and hands out on the floor. Daniel ambles across the big sheets as Rick examines them, trying to find words of praise he hasn't used before. She is hoping to sell some of her work eventually, to supplement their income.

She says, 'A card's great. It's a good idea and a sweet, generous gesture. But it's not enough.'

'What d'you mean?' he says. He goes on, 'You might be right. When I was dreaming, I kept thinking of the last scene of *Wild Strawberries*.'

'What happens in it?'

'Doesn't the old man, on a last journey to meet the significant figures of his life, finally wave to his parents?'

'That's what we should do,' she says. 'Make a video for Daniel and put it in a sealed envelope.'

'Yes,' he says, drinking from a glass he finds beside the chair. 'It's a brilliant idea.'

'But we're quite drunk,' she says. 'It'll be him sitting in front of it, forty-five years old. He'll turn on the tape at last and –'

'There won't even be tapes then,' Rick says. 'They'll be in a museum. But they'll be able to convert it to whatever system they have.'

She says, 'My point is, after all that time, he'll see two pissed people. What's his therapist going to say?'

'Don't we want him to know that you and I had a good time sometimes?'

'Okay,' she says. 'But if we're going to do this, we should be prepared.'

'Good,' he says. 'We could . . .'

'What?'

'Put on white shirts. Does my hair look too flat?'

'We look okay,' she says. 'Well, I do, and you don't care. But we should think about what we're going to say. This tape might be a big thing for little Dan. Imagine if your father was to speak to you right now.'

'You're right,' he says. His own father had killed himself almost ten years ago. 'Anna, what would you like to say to Dan?'

'There's so much . . . really, I don't know yet.'

'Also, we've got to be careful how we talk to him,' he says. 'He's not two years old in this scenario. He's my age. We can't use baby voices or call him Dan-the-Noddy-man.'

They dispute about what exactly the message should be, what a parent might say to their forty-five-year-old son, now only two and a half, sitting there on the floor singing 'Incy Wincy Spider' to himself. Of course there can be no end to this deliberation: whether they should give Daniel a good dose of advice and encouragement, or a few memories, or a mixture of all three. They do at least decide that since they're getting tired and fretful they should set up the camera.

While she goes into the cellar to find it, he makes Daniel's milk, gets him into his blue pyjamas with the white trim, and chases him around the kitchen with a wet cloth. She drags the camera and tripod up into the living room.

Although they haven't decided what to say, they will go ahead with the filming certain that something will occur to them. This spontaneity may make their little dispatch to the future seem less portentous.

Rick lugs the Christmas tree over towards the sofa where they will sit for the message, and turns on the lights. He regards his wife through the camera. She has let down her hair.

'How splendid you look!'

She asks, 'Should I take my slippers off?'

'Anna, your fluffies won't be immortalised. I'll frame it down to our waists.'

She gets up and looks at him through the eye piece, telling him he's as fine as he'll ever be. He switches on the camera and notices there is only about fifteen minutes' worth of tape left.

With the camera running, he hurries towards the sofa, being careful not to trip up. They will not be able to do this twice. Noticing a half-eaten sardine on the arm of the sofa, he drops it into his pocket.

Rick sits down knowing this will be a sombre business, for he has been, in a sense, already dead for a while. Daniel's idea of him will have been developing for a long time. The two of them will have fallen out on numerous occasions; Daniel might love him but will have disliked him, too, in the normal way. Daniel could hardly have anything but a complicated idea of his past, but these words from eternity will serve as a simple reminder. After all, it is the unloved who are the most dangerous people on this earth.

The light on top of the camera is flashing. As Anna and Rick turn their heads and look into the dark moon of the lens, neither of them speaks for what seems a long time. At last, Rick says, 'Hello there,' rather self-consciously, as though meeting a stranger for the first time. On stage he is never anxious like this. Anna, also at a loss, copies him.

'Hello, Daniel, my son,' she says. 'It's your mummy.'

'And daddy,' Rick says.

'Yes,' she says. 'Here we are!'

'Your parents,' he says. 'Remember us? Do you remember this day?'

There is a silence; they wonder what to do.

Anna turns to Rick then, placing her hands on his face. She strokes his face as if painting it for the camera. She takes his hand and puts his fingers to her lips and cheeks. Rick leans over and takes her head between his hands and kisses her on the cheek and on the forehead and on the lips, and she caresses his hair and pulls him to her.

With their heads together, they begin to call out, 'Hello, Dan, we hope you're okay, we just wanted to say hello.'

'Yes, that's right,' chips in the other. 'Hello!'

'We hope you had a good forty-fifth birthday, Dan, with plenty of presents.'

'Yes, and we hope you're well, and your wife, or whoever it is you're with.'

'Yes, hello there . . . wife of Dan.'

'And children of Dan,' she adds.

'Yes,' he says. 'Children of Dan – however many of you there are, boys or girls or whatever – all the best! A good life to every single one of you!'

'Yes, yes!' she says. 'All of that and more!'

'More, more, more!' Rick says.

After the kissing and stroking and cuddling and saying hello, and with a little time left, they are at a loss as to what to do, but right on cue Daniel has an idea. He clambers up from the floor and settles himself on both of them, and they kiss him and pass him between them and get him to wave to himself. When he has done this, he closes his eyes, his head falls into the crook of his mother's arm, and he smacks his lips; and as the tape whirls towards its end, and the rain falls outside and time passes, they want him to be sure at least of this one thing, more than forty years from now, when he looks at these old-fashioned people in the past sitting on the sofa next to the Christmas tree, that on this night they loved him and they loved each other.

'Goodbye, Daniel,' says Anna.

'Goodbye,' says Rick.

'Goodbye, goodbye,' they say together.

The Real Father

It was true: Mal couldn't bear his son Wallace and dreaded seeing him now. What natural feeling was there between them? They were bewildered strangers who didn't know what to say or do together.

Today, Mal was to take the nine-year-old away for the night.

'We can spend time hanging out,' explained Mal again. 'We can talk – about anything you want.'

'I'd rather go to hell,' Wallace said. 'I'd rather be dead than go anywhere with you!' Loudly he whispered, 'Fucker!'

Wallace had arrived at the house the previous evening. Normally, he stayed the weekend, but Mal was glad to be taking him home tomorrow, after their trip, as he was required at a party. Nevertheless, since he'd woken up, Wallace had been sobbing and complaining on the stairs. It was nearly lunch time; the taxi was waiting outside.

'We're only going to the seaside.'

'For the night!'

Mal explained, 'I've already said that will be nicer for us, rather than rushing back on the last train.'

'Nice for you, torture for me!'

'For me, too, it looks like.'

Wallace was not only what was commonly described as an 'accident', there had been no necessity for his birth at all. How could he not have sensed that?

Mal's wife came over to them. She was accompanied by their

four-year-old, who tried to stroke his hysterical half-brother's swollen, tear-riven face.

'Don't cry, Wally,' he said.

They were all looking at Wallace. His *Beano* shirt ('Look, I'm an advertisement!') was covered with chocolate stains: Wallace used it as a napkin. When he ate, he still spilled his food, and always knocked over his drinks. This was partly because he refused to sit at the table, but ranged about the house looking for things to break and turning the TV off and on. His trousers had a hole where he'd fallen but his trainers were top-of-the-range, with lights in the heel that flashed when he kicked an adult. What annoyed Mal was not his son's resemblance to his mother – the boy turned his head and suddenly Mal was reminded of his eternal connection to a stranger, as if this were a black joke – but to the boy's stepfather, who Wallace called 'Dad' and Mal 'The Beast'.

Mal said, 'Wallace, we do really have to leave – otherwise we'll miss the train.' Wallace opened his chocolate-filled mouth. Mal reached out to pull him. 'Get in the bloody taxi now!'

Wallace sprang back, spitting chocolate over Mal's white shirt. 'If you hurt me, I will kill myself.' He stood up and punched himself in the stomach. 'I will now go and fix my hair.'

Mal was glad of the chance to kiss his youngest son and his wife, who attempted to wipe him down. 'Mal, don't get furious. Try and have a good time with him. Try to talk.'

'Talk!'

'Have you been drinking already?'

'Just the one. I'm petrified he'll do something lunatic during the meeting this afternoon. I wish you would look after him today.'

'I am not yet a saint. I'll have coffee with the girls and we'll laugh about this.'

The boy emerged from the bathroom with his mass of hair – which Mal maintained would one day have to be removed surgically, under anaesthetic – slicked down with water. Mal noticed he had added perfumed hair gel, which sat on his head in lumps, mingling, no doubt, with his nits.

Mal took their luggage out to the car. Wallace had no choice but to follow, carrying a plastic bag which contained drinks, his Gameboy, pens, and many half-eaten Easter eggs.

In the back of the car, Mal stroked him. 'Come on. No one's going to love you if you behave like this. You need charm to get by in this world.'

The boy put his hands over his face as the taxi pulled away. He was wearing the goalkeeping gloves he refused to be parted from.

'Don't ever touch me. Or point at me. Don't do anything bad to me, you bastard.'

Mal noticed the driver's wide eyes watching them in the mirror. Clearly, he was from a country with stricter notions of how children should behave.

'For Christ's sake, shhh . . .'

They were on their way to see Andrea Knowles, a young film director, who was considering using Mal as editor on her first feature film. It was a job he needed badly; it would be a significant step up. Inevitably, Wallace's mother had refused to alter their arrangement. Mal had tried to leave Wallace with his wife, but Wallace had taken to calling her a bitch and had kicked her.

Mal and Wallace's mother had had a 'fling' ten years ago, lasting a few weeks. By the time Wallace was born, they had returned to their separate lives. All Mal wanted was for her to disappear into the mulch of the past. Somehow she had become pregnant and refused a termination.

'How can you kill a baby?' she said.

'There are several methods I could suggest . . .'

What did he remember of their affair? One long conversation – their only real talk – during a party. Later, the girl playing the same jazz records over and over; they were all she could afford. Making love while there was a thunderstorm outside, the branches of the trees striking the windows. It wasn't long before they ran out of ideal moments.

Now she was unrecognisable to him and lived with her husband, an unemployed alcoholic decorator. For years, Mal had hardly been allowed to see or even speak to the boy, though he contributed to his upkeep. When Wallace was six, Mal was given access to him about twice a year. All day they wandered around overheated shopping malls in the Midlands. Sometimes Mal phoned him, but Wallace never volunteered any information. After several silences, he said he had to go – *Rugrats* was on.

A friend of Mal's once joked about how fortunate Mal was to have at least one of his kids living elsewhere. Mal had reddened with fury; for a week, this jibe marked his mind. Being a father entailed various duties which he wanted to follow, except that Wallace's mother prevented them. The word 'duty' sounded odd to him. It was as unlikely a word, these days, as 'moral' or, to him, 'spiritual'. He liked to think he had a pragmatic mouth. Despite this, in his feelings, Mal had had to let his son go – giving him to another man, admitting how little there was of him in the boy – and semi-forgetting him. This was aided by the birth of his younger son.

A year ago, Wallace's mother and her partner had taken a market stall at the weekends, selling home-designed T-shirts. She didn't like Wallace hanging around the market every weekend. Mal guessed this was the real reason for Wallace's having to 'get to know' his real father, by visiting every three weeks.

Mal was relieved to have got his son back before it was too late. Of course, his wife was afraid of the effect this stranger would have on her family. She argued about the length of time Wallace could stay; she refused to let Wallace share his half-brother's bedroom. It had taken Mal a week to convert his own work-room into a space for Wallace, with a TV, video, Playstation and music system. Wallace hated the room but stayed in it during the day, though not at night. He had 'insonia' and heard moans coming down the chimney. Mal lay awake, hearing Wallace watching movies in the living room at four in the morning.

If Mal thought things were beginning to go well in his life, Wallace was the fate he couldn't elude. He had welcomed the boy, but the boy was a genius at not being welcomed. Mal liked to say he wanted to sue for less custody. Sometimes Wallace would play football with Mal, or let himself be taken to the cinema. But Wallace's passion was shopping in London. Mal bought him things to assuage his furious greed: one big thing, it seemed, every day. Wallace had always insisted Mal buy him toys his mother wouldn't let him have or couldn't afford: guns, lightsabres, Playstation discs, Gameboy games, videos of horror films. Nevertheless, Mal knew that as soon as he dropped the boy off at his mother's house, a two-hour drive away, his mobile phone would ring and he would be castigated for the presents, which would be dumped in the basement. The same thing happened if Mal gave him the autographs of movie actors, or film posters and videos.

Now Mal said, 'I'll buy you something at the railway station.'

A space opened in Wallace's distress. 'Buy me what?'

'Anything to stop you abusing me and give me some peace.'

'That's all you want.'

'Wouldn't you?' said Mal.

'I don't want to be here.'

'But we're going to see a woman called Andrea. It's very important that you be nice to her.'

'Why?'

'She might give me a job and I can earn more money to spend on you.'

'I'll tell her you're too lazy and bad-mannered.'

Mal started to laugh.

'What's funny?'

'You.'

'I can stop you laughing.'

'Don't I know it.'

On his last visit, Wallace had thrown some of Mal's papers on to the floor and wiped his feet on them; later, he'd held a cushion over his half-brother's face and punched him. Mal had ripped his belt from his trousers and raised it. His wife cried out and he rushed from the house. Underneath Wallace's whimpering, moaning and abuse, a child was screaming for help. No one knew what to do, but didn't someone have to do something? In such circumstances, how did you learn to be a parent?

As it was, Mal drank when the boy was around. Wallace destabilised him in ways he couldn't grasp, making him believe he was either incompetent and useless or a monster, a feeling which had begin to poison all areas of his life. On his last job, a television serial, his concentration had failed and he had had to do several all-nighters to complete the job. He was afraid that Andrea had heard about this.

At the railway station, Wallace led his father to comics, sweets and drinks. Then Mal obtained sandwiches for both of them, secured a table in one of the cafés and went to get coffee and a beer. On his return, Wallace had disappeared.

Mal waited and drank his beer. Perhaps Wallace had gone to the toilet. After a while, when Wallace's absence seemed to freeze reality into one stopped moment of horror, Mal had no choice but to gather up their bags and the coffee and shuffle through the shops, toilets, bars and cafés as rapidly as he could, asking strangers if they'd seen a plump kid with a filthy face, wearing a *Beano* shirt.

Wallace was alone at a table, driving a hamburger into his mouth and studying his compass.

Mal sank down. 'Jesus, I can hardly breathe. If you do that again, I'll tell your mum.'

'She already knows you don't want me around.'

'Is that what she says?'

'You never visited me on my birthday.'

'I wasn't allowed to.'

Wallace said, 'I didn't like the sandwiches you got for me.'

'I understand. I'm your father and I have no idea what you like to eat.'

Wallace burped. 'It's okay, thanks. I'm full now.'

In the train, Mal sat opposite the boy and closed his eyes.

'Will we crash?' said Wallace loudly. Everyone in the carriage was looking at them. 'They all crash, don't they?'

Mal put on his sunglasses. 'I hope so.'

'Listen –' Wallace had other concerns, but Mal was squeezing balls of wax as far into his ears as they'd go.

He could tell they'd arrived, the air was cooler and fresh. With renewed optimism, Mal carried their bags down to the front, telling Wallace how he'd always loved English seaside resorts and their semi-carnival feel. Such decay could provide a mesmeric atmosphere for a film. If Andrea decided to employ him, he wondered whether she might let him set up a cutting-room here. The family could stay. Wallace might like to visit.

They were both tired when they arrived at the small hotel, which smelled of fried bacon. They looked through into a sitting room full of enormous flower-patterned furniture, in which an old couple were playing Scrabble.

Wallace said, 'Are you sure it's only one night?'

'Yes.'

'You've lied to me before.'

'Excuse me?'

'You've lied about this whole thing.'

In their room, Mal opened the windows. He went out on to the balcony and smoked a joint while watching the untroubled people walking on the front. Wallace settled down on the bed with his Gameboy. Mal unpacked a change of clothes for Wallace and a couple of books on psychology for himself. He took a shower, opened a bottle of whisky and took a long draught.

When he could, Mal walked about naked in front of Wallace, showing him the stomach flopping above the thin legs, the weak grey pubic hair, the absurd boyish buttocks. Wallace needed to take him in, to see him, as Mal believed people in complete families did daily.

Lately, Mal had been unable to stop worrying about whether Wallace had something wrong with him. Perhaps a certain drug or psychiatrist might be of benefit. Yet Wallace had friends; he was doing better at school than Mal ever had. You couldn't pathologise him for hating his father. For Mal, the strain was in having to work this out for himself. Recently he had been mulling over a memory from his student days of two acquaintances discussing R. D. Laing. At the time, he had been embarrassed by his ignorance and instinctively regarded what they said as pretentious, as showing off. But something about families and the impossibility of living within their contradictions, which made children mad, had stuck in his mind. Perhaps this was Wallace's predicament. Was he the embodiment of his parents' mistake, of their stupidity? Wasn't Wallace somehow carrying all their craziness? What, then, could Mal do?

Mal lay on the bed next to him. 'Wallace, will you cuddle me? Will you hold me and let me kiss you?' But Wallace was trying to look elsewhere. Mal said, 'Maybe you know your mother wouldn't like you becoming close to me.'

'She certainly thinks you is a great big fool.'

Mal shut his eyes but was too aware of Wallace to drift off. The joint was making him dreamy. He said, 'I was – almost – a fool. I haven't thought of this for a long time. When I was seventeen and my father had just died, I packed a few things and left home, leaving my mum, who never spoke to me, or to anyone much –'

Wallace looked up.

'Was there something wrong with her?'

'I couldn't stay to find out. I had dyed my hair multi-coloured. I wore a slashed leather jacket and dirty trousers covered in straps and zips, and black motorcycle boots. I went to live in the back of a junk shop we'd broken into –'

'Could the police have taken you to prison?'

'If they'd found us. But we hid, smashing and burning the furniture for heat. We drank cider and took –'

'You were drunk?'

'A lot of the time.'

'Did you fall down and hurt yourself?'

'Often, yes. Except that my uncle, my father's brother, who was recovering from heart surgery, climbed in through the window one day while we were asleep.'

'Were you still drunk?'

'He said that had my father been alive, he'd have been killed by how I was living. I guess I was that man's lost sheep. He couldn't rest until I was safe. You know that Bible story about the sheep?'

'Sheep? I've seen *Chicken Run*.'

'Right. The next day, my uncle took me to the local college and begged them to admit me. I didn't want to go.'

'You didn't want to learn anything?'

'I hated learning.'

'At school, I'm on the top table.'

'Excellent. My uncle said I could live at his house as long as I was at college. So I couldn't drop out. One time in class, the teacher showed a film called *The 400 Blows*. I figured watching movies was better than work. This film was about a young, unhappy kid – like me, then – who didn't get along with his mum and dad. I kept thinking it was like looking at a series of paintings. It was the first time that beauty had seemed to matter to me. I realised that if I could be involved in such work, I'd get a crack at happiness.'

Mal sat up and poured himself another drink.

Wallace said, 'What happened then?'

'That's how I trained to be a film editor. It's why we're here today.'

The phone rang in the silence. Wallace answered.

'Mum? Is that you?'

It was Andrea, downstairs. Mal started to put his clothes on. 'Champ, we'd better go.'

'Why should we? I don't want her!'

Mal wanted to plead with the boy to be polite but knew it would make things worse.

Outside the hotel, Mal introduced Wallace to Andrea.

'He's my real daddy but not really,' said Wallace.

'You can only have one real daddy.'

Wallace was staring at her. She crouched down and showed him the ring through her nose.

'You can touch it.'

He stroked it.

'Does it hurt?'

'Nope. Well, it does now. I've got another one, called a stud.' She put her tongue out.

'Yuckie. What if you swallow it?'

'See if you can grab it, Wallace.'

It was a good little game.

'Can we go to the pier?' asked Wallace.

Mal gave Wallace a five-pound note.

'Of course.'

Wallace said to Andrea, 'He's going to start being all nice now you're here.'

Wallace walked in front, doing karate kicks and shooting imaginary people. He made circular movements with his arms and hands which Mal recognised from rappers. Mal said that when he was a kid, he and his friends wanted to be 'hard', like the cockney criminals they'd heard about. Now the kids based themselves in fantasy on Jamaican–American 'gangstas'.

On the pier, Wallace stopped suddenly to get down on his knees and peer through the wooden slats to the sea below.

'Come on, gangsta,' said Mal.

'What if we fall through?' said Wallace. 'We could die down there.'

Andrea took his hand. 'I'm quite a swimmer. I'd carry you to safety on my back, like a dolphin.'

Wallace disappeared into the hot, noisy arcades and began to dispose of his money. As they followed him, Andrea told Mal about the film, for which most of the finance was in place; she was rewriting the script. They had time to discuss the films they were currently thinking about when, to Mal's surprise, Wallace said he wanted to go on the trampolines. His money was gone, but Andrea offered to pay for him. Wallace took off his shoes and jumped up and down, yelling.

'A great kid,' laughed Andrea. 'Where did you get him?'

Mal sighed and described to Andrea what it had been like seeing his unwanted son for the first time. He told her what had happened since, and how things stood between them.

They filled Wallace with ice-cream and chocolate. When an argument developed about candyfloss and he used Mal's phone to ring his mother and began weeping, Mal had to tell Andrea that Wallace was hungry.

They parted and Mal took the boy for fish and chips. In the hotel, Wallace refused a bath but at least got into his pyjamas. Mal set him up in front of the TV, where he became instantly absorbed. Mal would be able to slip the bottle of whisky into his pocket and open the door.

'What are you doing?' The boy was staring at him in panic.

'I'm going downstairs to have a word with Andrea.'

'No!'

'I won't be long. You'll be fine.'

Mal shut the door before the boy could say anything else. He put his ear to the keyhole but heard only the commercials, which, no doubt, Wallace was mouthing the words to.

Andrea was waiting. They walked quickly through the part of town Mal was familiar with, past clubbers and those looking for restaurants, into a more dilapidated area called the Old Town. He was surprised to see working fishermen preparing to take their boats out for the night. Behind this, the streets narrowed; the close houses seemed to lean across the lanes and almost touch at the top. There were red lights in some of the windows here. She pointed at a house. 'You could score here.'

They entered a pub that seemed full of rough, tattooed late adolescents, most of whom looked like addicts. She went round the place, greeting those she knew. They were pleased to see her, but she was not like them.

Outside again, she said, pointing, 'We could put the camera there and the actors could run into that alley. We could follow them – that way!'

He turned, needing to see and feel what she did. He noticed

there was a sort of silence or poverty – of inactivity or emptiness, he would have said – which you didn't find in London.

She told him, 'The people here think London's a stew full of foreigners. They hardly go there.'

'It's about time we declared independence.'

Mal's legs ached but he went on, pursuing and, at times, questioning her enthusiasm. At last they stood in a cobbled square where the streets seemed to lead in all directions. Mal heard a shout and Wallace came rushing towards them, wearing his pyjamas, football gloves and trainers.

'I followed you!'

Mal wanted to pick him up but the shivering boy was too heavy.

'All this way?'

'You tried to leave me!'

'You were safe in the hotel.' He crouched down and embraced Wallace, kissing his petrified hair.

'Someone was going to steal me!'

'No!'

Andrea took off her sweater and tied it around his neck. Holding hands, they ran back. In the hotel lounge, Andrea ordered hot chocolate and crisps for him.

'You two.' She was laughing. 'You look exactly the same.'

'We do?' said Wallace.

'How could you be anything but father and son?'

Mal and Wallace were looking at one another. Mal said to him, 'I would never leave you for long. We were only trying to figure out how to make Andrea's movie.'

Wallace asked, 'What's it about? You're not going to run away from me again, are you?'

'I'm too tired. In fact, I'm exhausted and broken.'

Mal fetched drinks for himself and Andrea.

Andrea said, 'The story is this. I was nearly grown-up but not quite when my mum and dad said they couldn't live together any more. From then on, I would have to move between them.'

'Like a parcel, like me,' said Wallace. 'You don't want to be posted everywhere all the time.'

'It was worse than that,' she said. 'The film is called *Ten Days* and is set around the time I was sent to stay with Dad – quite near here – for a holiday. Mum wanted to be with another man, you see, which Dad guessed. When I arrived, I found that my poor father couldn't get out of bed for fear of falling over. All he moved was his arm, to drink. I would sit with him, listening to his stories or watching films. While he was asleep, or passed out, I'd roam about the town on my own, making friends with the locals. Kids always complain there's nothing to do in such places. We found plenty to do, oh yes.'

Wallace nudged his father.

'She was so bad.'

'The baddest, me. Back home, when I was asked what Dad and I did on our hols, they worked out that Dad had gone crazy. I was never allowed to see him again.'

'In your whole life?'

'He liked drink and they thought it made him a sick person, a fuck-up.'

'She swore!'

'Dad died a month later. They didn't tell me properly. I heard about his death from a relative. I ran away from home to attend the funeral and I stayed down here a few more days, meeting his friends and sleeping in a tent in the woods. I got into more big trouble at home. I didn't like my new stepfather and came down here to live.'

'It was naughty to run away.' He asked, 'Did you see your dad's dead body?'

'Not in life.' Andrea took a notebook from her rucksack and wrote, '"Goes to see dead body of father in morgue". In the film, she will, now.'

'Dad looks normal to you,' said Wallace. 'But he was in trouble once. He ran away too and he drank cider. He was a burglar, and he had rainbow hair. Didn't you, Dad?'

'Wow,' said Andrea. 'He doesn't look like that kind of guy now.'

Wallace said, 'Will you still let him work for you?'

'What d'you think?'

'I think you should let him. But only if you put me in the film.'

'There might be a small part for you. Have you acted before? Tell you what, I'll pretend to hit you and you have to react. Remember, the action is in the reaction. The camera and the people will be looking at you. Stand up.'

She pretended to hit him a few times. Wallace was sufficiently histrionic on the floor.

Wallace let Andrea kiss him goodnight. Mal accompanied Wallace upstairs and got into bed beside him. Mal's young son often slept between Mal and his wife, but Mal had never slept beside his first son. Wallace fell asleep almost immediately, his comforter twitching in his mouth. He was still filthy; no water had passed over him on this trip.

Mal cuddled Wallace but couldn't sleep. He listened to the sea through the open balcony door. He got up, dressed and went out, locking the door from the outside. On the street it was dark and windy, but there were plenty of people about. The sea was further out than he thought, but he got there.

He realised that he seemed to breathe more easily with so much space around him. He wanted to drift along the beach, following the lights and voices to a crowded bar, to drink and talk with strangers, to find out whether their lives were worse or better than his. But Mal could still see the hotel and what he guessed was their room, the sleeping child just beyond the open balcony door. He couldn't lose that patch of light in the distance.

Mal noticed a group of kids not far away, older than students, listening to a boom-box and passing around plastic bottles of cider. Mal went over to one of them and said, 'Can I dance here?'

'Everyone needs to feel free,' said the kid, who appeared to have been in a fight. Mal hesitated. The dance he had last been familiar with was 'the pogo'. 'Feel free,' repeated the boy.

Mal offered him a swig of whisky from the bottle he had brought out. 'It's been a long time though.'

The boy left him. Mal moved closer to the music and began to shuffle; he jerked his body and shook his head. He was hopping. He began to pogo, alone of course, jumping up towards the sky with his arms out for as long as he could, until he fell over in the wet shingle, getting soaked to the skin.

The sun came brightly through the window of the hotel dining room as Mal, wearing shorts and shoes without socks, filled himself with buttered kipper and fried mushrooms and toast, a starched napkin tucked into the front of his shirt. He had become the sort of man he'd have laughed at as a boy.

'I wonder if you'll remember much of this trip,' he said to Wallace. 'I think I'll get the hotel manager to take a photograph of us outside. You can put it next to your bed.'

'Dad . . . I mean, Mal –'

Newspapers were excellently designed for keeping boys' faces from the sight of their father.

They were on the train when Andrea rang to say she liked the idea of helping Mal move his cutting-room and family to the town for the duration of the film. She had been nervous of suggesting it herself for fear it would put Mal off the job.

Wallace was saying, 'I need to speak to her urgently.'

Mal passed him the phone and heard him explain that he was prepared to be in the film only if he didn't have to cut his hair or kiss girls.

'Andrea agreed,' said Wallace. 'But will mum let me be an actor for her?'

'She might if you tell her you're getting paid.'

The house was deserted when they got back. Mal had guessed his wife would want to avoid them. He opened the doors to the garden and cooked for them both.

Over lunch, Wallace mentioned his piano lessons for the first time. Mal hunted out a Chopin piece played by Arturo Michelangeli and put it on. As they listened, Mal tried to say why he loved it, but he began to weep. He carried on talking but couldn't stop his tears. What he dreaded was driving Wallace home. How could any love survive so many interruptions?

Late that afternoon, before they reached the motorway turn-off, Mal stopped at a service station and had a Coke with his son.

He said, 'When we get to your house, you won't want to say goodbye to me properly. But I want you to know that I will think of you when you're at school, or asleep, or with your friends.'

'I never miss you. I won't be thinking about you.'

'You don't have to. I'll do the thinking, okay?'

Soon they were at Wallace's front gate. The boy scrambled out of the car and ran around the back of the house. Mal carried the bags to the front door and returned to the car. He watched Wallace's stepfather and mother appear and take the bags inside, almost furtively, as though they were stealing them. Mal wanted to look at the couple more, to try and put these two connected families together, but he just waved in their direction and drove away, turning off his phone.

Mal returned to London without stopping. He parked near the house but went past it without going in. He walked to a nearby pub, frequented by northern men working during the week in London. 'No children or dirty boots', it said on the door.

Mal bought cigarettes and set himself up at the bar, ordering a pint and a chaser. He was unsure whether he was celebrating his new job or commiserating with himself over what he had just endured, but he toasted himself.

'To Mal,' he said. 'And everyone who knows him!'

Touched

He shouted and jumped up and down. 'See you soon, soon, soon, I hope!'

He continued waving until they disappeared round the corner, his many aunties, uncles and cousins, packed into three taxis. Ali and his parents were standing on the pavement outside the house. The Bombay part of their family had been staying in a rented flat in Dulwich for the summer. Ali and his parents had seen them nearly every day; tomorrow they were returning to India.

'Come inside now.' Ali's father took his hand. 'I don't like to see you so upset.'

Ali was embarrassed by his tears. His neighbour Mike was standing across the road, shuffling his football cards and scratching, watching and pretending not to. He had been round earlier. After the uncles and aunts had begun their goodbyes, the front door bell had rung and Ali had opened it, thinking it was a taxi. His cousins had crowded behind him.

'Comin' out?' Mike had asked, biting his nails, trying to examine the faces behind Ali. Mike had lost a clump of hair; his father had pulled it out, beating him up. 'What's goin' on? We could 'ear you lot from down the road, makin' a noise all day.'

It was the Saturday of the fifth cricket Test. India had been playing England at the Oval. In the morning, Ali's three rowdy uncles and his father had taken their places in the small front room, pulling the curtains and shutting the door. The men had smoked, drunk beer and cursed the Indian bowlers, while the stolid

Englishmen, Barrington and Graveney, batted all day. The uncles blamed the Indian captain Prince Pataudi, who had only one eye. The Indian aunties had been teaching Ali's English mother to prepare several dishes which she promised to make for her husband and son. The women carried the dhal, keema and rice into the room, which they had been cooking in huge pans first thing in the morning. The men had eaten with their fingers, plates shuddering on their laps, not taking their eyes from the screen. They had yelled abuse in Urdu.

Ali had been allowed to go into the uncles' room whenever he liked. They had begun to speak to him as another man. One even called him 'the next head of the family'. The oldest uncle owned factories in India, the second was a famous political journalist, and the third was an engineer who built dams. At home, all three were notorious 'carousers' and party-givers. During the cricket intervals, they entertained Ali by betting on tossed coins or on which auntie would come into the room next; they played 'stone, paper, scissors'. Ali's abstemious father had a minor job in a solicitor's office.

Ali was an only child. He wrote down cricket scores next to imaginary teams in a notebook his mother had given him. He spent hours alone in the garden, batting a cricket ball, attached by rope to the branch of a tree, with a sawn-off broomstick. The garden was his kingdom, and he was eager to share it with his Indian family as he had today, opening the windows and back door of the small council house. This was unusual: both his parents disliked draughts, whatever the weather. Today, three of his cousins had played cricket out in the garden; the girls, aged between seven and fourteen, had played chase.

The aunties, after they had washed up, had sat on blankets in the shade, stroking and arranging one another's hair like people in a French painting. Ali was kissed and fussed over, enjoying the sight of his aunties' painted toes in their delicate sandals, even the rolls of fat around their stomachs, where their saris had come loose.

That afternoon, Ali had shown his cousin Zahida his bedroom. She was fourteen, a year older than him. They'd looked out at the view of suburban gardens (where he'd once seen a married couple kissing), and he pulled out his copy of *The Man with the Golden Gun*. They bounced on the bed and then she pressed her lips to his. She said she wanted to be 'secret' with him, and he got a torch and led her up the ladder into the attic where there were discarded toys and dusty trunks which had carried his father's things from Bombay. Her bangles clattered and jangled. They couldn't stop giggling. Zahida was convinced there were rats and bats. Who would hear her muffled screams so far up?

They kissed again, but she placed her mouth close to his ear. His body was invaded by such sweetness that he thought he would fall over. She bent forward, placing her hands on top of the filthy water-tank, and in a delirium he continued caressing, until, making his way through intricate whirls of material, he reached her flesh and slid his finger into the top of the crack. That was all. She made noises like someone suffering. He could have remained with her there for hours, but his excitement was yoked to a fear of discovery and punishment. He said they should go downstairs. He went first, and urged her to follow.

'What's wrong?' she had asked. They were back in his bedroom.

'You're leaving tomorrow. I don't want you to go.'

'When I grow up,' she said, 'I'm going to be a pilot like my dad used to be.' Ali had never been in an aeroplane. 'I'll fly everywhere. I'll come and see you.'

'That's a long time away.'

Ali envied his cousins seeing one another almost every day. They lived close to one another and the family's drivers ferried them to one another's houses whenever they wanted. 'We are being called to weddings and parties the whole time.'

Then Zahida said, 'Papa told me you're invited to stay with us.'

'But that's not going to happen, is it? My parents don't like to go anywhere.'

'Come on your own. There's plenty of room. All kinds of bums and relatives turn up at home! Come for the holidays, like we do here. Christmas would be good.'

He said with shame, 'I would, but Dad doesn't have the money to send me.'

'Why not?'

He shrugged. 'He doesn't earn enough.'

She said, 'Save up. Didn't you help out at the circus last Easter?'

'Yes.'

'It made us all laugh like mad. You weren't a clown, were you?'

'I came on to clean up after the elephant,' he said. 'It made the audience laugh. Mostly I carried props around.'

'But you're so small!'

'I'll get bigger.'

She said, 'You're big enough now to wash cars and dig gardens.'

'That's true,' he said. 'I can do that.'

'You can.'

He kissed her. 'Tell India I am coming!'

He was surprised to see his father standing at the foot of the stairs, watching them both.

It was then the taxis had arrived, hooting their horns.

When everyone had gone, Ali's mother sighed with relief. She was leaving for work. His mother was a nurse who worked nights; when she could, she slept during the day. Now, she and father had a row about what the eldest uncles had said to Dad. In a sulk, Ali's father went into his room and sat at his desk with his back to Ali. He was studying law by correspondence course, which Dad's wealthiest brother, the head of the family, was paying for. He had become angry with Ali's father, who had failed his exams and didn't seem to be making much of himself in England. At lunchtime, he had shouted, 'There are so many opportunities here, yaar, and the only one you've taken is to marry Joan! Why are you letting down the whole family?'

As it was, his mother was already annoyed with the men. A few days before, after she had shown off her new washing-machine, they had given her all the Bombay family's washing to do. 'I'm not their servant,' she said, throwing down the pillowcases filled with dirty clothes. Father, with Ali's help, had to figure out how to work the machine, one reading the instructions, the other fiddling with the dials, as a pool of water crept across the floor. Then they ironed and folded the clothes, pretending it was Joan's handiwork.

Dad might now study for hours, with a furious look on his face. Ali sat down, too. In his father's room, where Ali was supposed to have been preparing for the new school year if he was to keep up with the other pupils and not become like his father, all he could hear was the ticking clock. The house seemed to have stopped breathing. His mother wouldn't return until the morning; she'd make his breakfast, ensure he had a clean towel, and, when Mike knocked, send him to the swimming baths.

Ali slipped out without his father appearing to notice; he didn't want to stay at home if no one was laughing or talking. He was surprised to find Mike still outside, kicking a tennis ball against the front wall.

'Come on out, yer bastard. Bin waitin' for yer,' he said. 'What you bin doin', cryin' and all that?'

He and Mike trudged across the flat park at twilight; goal posts like gallows stood in the mud.

'You took yer time gettin' out,' said Mike. 'Nearly dark now.'

'People were round.'

''Ate it when that 'appens. Yer with yer mates now. Everyone'll be down the swings.'

Ali and Mike always went straight to the swings. If it was raining, they shared cigarettes in the dank shed where the footballers changed for the weekend league.

Mike shouted, 'There they are! The scrubbers are out!'

They started to run. It wasn't far. Ali knew all the kids; they weren't his friends but they lived near by, some younger, others older. His mother called them 'rough'.

'Where you bin?' one of them said to Mike.

'Waitin' for Ali. 'E 'ad idiots round. There were dozens of 'em, smellin' the place out. It can't be allowed, so many darkies in a council 'ouse!'

The girls were on the swings, the boys smoking, spitting and hanging from the metal uprights. The boys attempted to twang the girls' braces against their breasts as they swung up and down, but mostly they were discussing the dance. It was up at Petts Wood and there'd be a reggae group. At the moment, they all loved Desmond Dekker's music and were talking about whether they'd be let in to the dance hall or have to sneak in through the back way and get lost in the darkness. The girls would be allowed to slip past the doormen, but the boys were obviously too young. Ali knew he had no chance.

'There's nothing wrong with my family,' Ali said to Mike.

'You over 'ere now,' said Mike.

The two of them looked uncomprehendingly at each other. Ali spat and strode away, but realised he didn't want to go home. He would walk the streets until he was ready to see his father.

At the top of the road he noticed Miss Blake's light on behind the net curtain. Sometimes he went in to see her on his way back from the young actors' club or his Spanish guitar lesson. She always gave him sweets and half a crown. She lived with her brother, a porter at Victoria Station who was well known for fighting in the local pubs.

Miss Blake was blind and always at her gate when the children returned from school and the commuters from work. Some of the other kids would cry out at her – 'She's playing a blinder today!' – but she would continue to stand there, a pure, inane smile on her lips. Sometimes, Ali walked around his bedroom with his eyes closed and his hands out in front, trying to know what it was like for her. He had visited her a lot lately, needing a few pennies. In return, she asked to hear what he'd done at school and what he thought of his friends. He had begun to enjoy his monologues; it was like keeping a diary out loud. Whatever he said, she would listen. It was odd, but he spoke to her more than he did to anyone else.

He tapped on the front window. 'Hi, Miss Blake.'

'Come on in, Alan, dear.'

She thought his name was Alan. He enjoyed being Alan for a while; it was a relief. Sometimes he went all day being Alan.

He followed her into the kitchen which had patches of curling lino over the bare floorboards. The kitchen couldn't have been painted for twenty years and it smelled of gas. To keep warm, Miss Blake always kept the stove lit. She knew where everything was in the house, just by touch. The radio was playing wartime big-band music.

She got him a glass of water which he tried never to drink, the glass was so filthy, and he placed it next to the metal box in which she kept her change. She always seemed to have plenty of coins. She was meant to have paintings inherited from her family, and in the neighbourhood it was rumoured that, unable to see them, she had sold them.

She sat there, waiting for him to speak.

At first, he thought he would tell her about the visit of his family and the restaurants they'd all been to; how they'd seen the zoo, Madame Tussaud's and Hyde Park. But he had never mentioned his Indian connection before. She didn't know he was half-Indian; she was the only person he knew who wasn't aware of this.

He had no idea of her real age. She could have been in her forties; she could have been in her early thirties. It was all the same to him.

'Alan, light me one up,' she said.

He pulled out a Players Number Six for her, and she took it and placed it in her mouth. She smoked heavily, and liked him to light her fags so she could hang on to his hand with hers.

'Where you bin?' she said.

'Busy, busy, busy,' he said.

She leaned forward. 'It's good to be busy. Doin' what?'

He told her about the visit of his uncle, auntie and cousins. He told her the whole thing, dropping in the fact that they were from India. She listened attentively, as she always did, with one of her ears, rather than her eyes, pointed at him; he found himself speaking to the side of her head, to her wispy long hair and the lopsided smile.

'Our father was in India for twenty years,' she said. ''E was a tea trader. Said it was lovely. Better than 'ere in all this cold. Now your family are off.'

'They've gone.'

'You're missing 'em.' He didn't say anything for a bit. 'What?' she said.

'Yes. I do, and will.' He added, 'I'm going over there, when I've saved up.'

'Won't you take me?'

'You?'

'Oh, please say yes, you will.'

'To India?'

'Oh, take me, take me,' she said. 'My brother Ernie takes me nowhere. 'E just curses me. I beg 'im, just the day out, and why not! To smell and 'ear the sea, why not! They've got a blind school there.'

'Where?'

'Bombay. I've bin told of it! They might take me in to help the starvin' sufferin' children!'

What an extraordinary spectacle it would be in Bombay, the English Indian boy and the blind woman.

She was holding a chocolate. 'Now, come 'ere, you poor boy. Open.'

He went to sit on the kitchen chair beside her. Her pinafore was stained. Her eyes were heavy-lidded, always half-closed. There was no reason, he supposed, for her to go to the trouble of keeping her eyes open. The dark moons of her eyes seemed to have become stuck to the top of her sockets.

'Hot today.'

'Where?'

'All over.' He was flapping his shirt. 'I'm sticky.'

'No,' she said. 'Really? You need some talcum powder over you. I've got some somewhere. Let's do this first, 'cause I know what you've come for.'

'Do you?'

Ali opened his mouth in readiness. Then, he didn't know why, he closed his eyes, as though expecting a kiss.

It was her other hand which reached up to his face; it was this hand which stroked his cheek, forehead and nose, and traced the line of his lips.

'I'm only goin' to feel 'ow big you are,' she said, releasing the chocolate into his mouth. ''Ave you 'ad a birthday recently? You seem bigger. That's what I'm trying to get at, Alan.'

'No,' he said, shaking his head, and thereby shaking off her hand at last. 'No increase in size this week.'

'Just a minute.' Now she was holding up half a crown, which he took and pushed into his pocket.

'Thanks. Lord, thanks, Miss Blake.'

'Now keep still.'

She reached for his throat. Her hand was trembling. She was fumbling at something around his neck and then eased lower. Through his shirt she was feeling his chest as if she had never touched another human body and wanted to know what it was like. Her eyelids seemed to be twitching. He had never been this close to her before. He let the chocolate sit on his tongue without biting it, until it melted and dissolved in the heat of his mouth. He found himself thinking of writing to Zahida. When his father went to work tomorrow, he'd go into his room and take some of the flimsy blue airmail paper on which Dad wrote to his brothers. Ali always kept the stamps, and he'd write Zahida a love letter, the first of many love letters, full of poems and drawings, telling her everything. The letters, he knew, took more than a week to get there. He would start writing tomorrow and await her replies, which he would read on the school bus.

Miss Blake worked Ali's shirt loose; it had come completely open. Nurses, like his mother, had to touch strangers all the time. Mother said it was natural; she had seen some rotten things, but no human body had disgusted her.

Ali was silently counting the money he'd make; at this rate he'd be able to stay with Zahida. There would be time for them to do 'everything', as she had put it. He would go where she went, to the club, to the beach, to parties, in the chauffeur-driven car. The family would welcome him as their own. In the evenings, he would sit around with the vociferous men telling stories and jokes, and talking politics. Maybe he'd get married over there and his parents would join him. He'd have to work out the details.

Miss Blake continued to touch him. She seemed to have several hands which went around his upper body, fluttering like dying birds. He had no idea where they would land next. His stomach? His back? He was unable to move, his eyes closed, and all he could hear was the radio, and nothing on it that he liked. He made to move, and Miss Blake let out a surprised cry and turned her face up to him. There was no alteration in the mushed clay of her eyes, but her mouth was twisted.

'Alan,' she moaned.

He slapped the table, and she slid another half a crown across it. He put it in his pocket and skipped to the door.

'Alan, Alan!' Her fingers grasped at the air.

'You can't make me miss *The Munsters*.'

She knew the house and could move quickly around it. But he was outside before she could touch him again.

Father was still at his desk, and his head was resting on his arms. Ali stroked his hair and then tickled his nose. Father sat up suddenly and looked around in surprise.

'What time is this to come back?'

'Don't know.'

'Don't go out with Mike too much,' said Dad, trying to locate his pen, which Ali could see had fallen on the floor. Ali pointed at it. Dad bent down to pick it up and hit his head on the edge of the desk's open drawer. 'Those boys are useless. They're all going to be motor mechanics!' he added, rubbing his head.

'I want to find better friends. Just like you want to find a better job.'

'That's enough, Ali! We've got to work!'

Ali lay down on the sofa on the other side of the room. He pulled his shirt up; his fingers drifted across his body. He touched himself where Miss Blake had stroked him. He smelled his fingers. She was there on him, where Zahida had been earlier. Her money was in his pocket.

He got up. Pretending he was doing his homework, he began to draft his first letter to Zahida. He was already in movement, already leaving there.

Next morning, when he and Mike went past on the way to the open-air swimming pool, and Mike was singing a football song and kicking his kit bag on its cord, Miss Blake was at her gate, rattling the bolt.

'Mike, Mike,' she shouted. 'Where's Alan?'

''Ere 'e is,' said Mike. 'Can't you see 'is stupid brown 'ead? Can't yer smell 'im?'

'Morning, Miss Blake,' said Ali.

'Alan, Alan!' She was leaning far over the gate. 'Don't you want . . . want something to eat? A chocolate or something?'

'I do, Miss Blake. You know I do.' Mike was laughing. 'Just you wait there,' Ali said. 'I'll be back after I've had me dip.'

'But Alan, Alan!' she called again, more urgently. 'Won't you come 'ere and light me snout?'

Ali looked at Mike, and shrugged.

Ali went back to her, drew the packet of Number Six from her hand, popped one in her mouth, took her lighter and lit it. She grasped his hand tightly as he knew she would. When the wind blew out the flame, he handed the lighter back to her. She slipped her hand through the gate and gave him sixpence, which he pocketed. He ran away up the street, to catch up with Mike.

'Mike, you get going,' he said. 'I'll see yer there a bit later on.'

Miss Blake had already opened the gate; Ali followed her up the path.

NEW STORIES

The Dogs

Overnight it had been raining but to one side of the precipitous stone steps there was a rail to grip on to. With her free hand she took her son's wrist, dragging him back when he lost his footing. It was too perilous for her to pick him up, and at five years old he was too heavy to be carried far.

Branches heavy with sticky leaves trailed across the steps, sometimes blocking their way so they had to climb over or under them. The steps themselves twisted and turned and were worn and often broken. There were more of them than she'd expected. She had never been this way, but had been told it was the only path, and that the man would be waiting for her on the other side of the area.

When they reached the bottom of the steps, her son's mood improved, and he called 'Chase me'. This was his favourite game and he set off quickly across the grass, which alarmed her, though she didn't want to scare him with her fears. She pursued him through the narrow wooded area ahead, losing him for a moment. She had to call out for him several times until at last she heard his reply.

Their feet kept sinking into the lush ground but a discernible track emerged. Soon they were in the open. It was a Common rather than a park and would take about forty minutes to cross: that was what she had been told.

Though it was a long way off, only a dot in the distance, she noticed the dog right away. Almost immediately the animal seemed bigger, a short-legged compact bullet. She knew all dogs were of different breeds, Dalmatians and chihuahuas and so on, but she had never retained the names. As the dog neared her son she wondered if it wasn't chasing a ball hidden in the grass. But there was no ball that she could see, and the little speeding dog with its studded collar had appeared from nowhere, sprinting across the horizon like a shadow, before turning in their direction. There was no owner in sight; there were no other humans she could see.

The boy saw the dog and stopped, tracking it with curiosity and then with horror. What could his mother do but cry out and begin to run? The dog had already knocked her son down and began not so much to bite him as to eat him, furiously.

She was wearing heavy, loosely laced shoes and was able to give the dog a wild blow in the side, enough to distract it, so that it looked bemused. She pulled the boy to her, but it was impossible for her to examine his wounds because she then had to hold him as high as she could while stumbling along, with the dog still beside her, barking, leaping and twisting in the air. She could not understand why she had no fascination for the dog.

She began to shout, to scream, panicking because she wouldn't be able to carry her son far. Tiring, she stopped and kicked out at the dog again, this time hitting him in the mouth, which made him lose hope.

Immediately a big long-haired dog was moving in the bushes further away, racing towards them. As it took off to attack the child she was aware, around her, of numerous other dogs, in various colours and sizes, streaming out of the undergrowth from all directions. Who had called them? Why were they there?

She lost her footing, she was pushed over and lay huddled on the ground, trying to cover her son, as the animals noisily set upon her, in a ring. To get him they would have to tear through her but it wouldn't take long, there were so many of them, and they were hungry too.

Long Ago Yesterday

One evening just after my fiftieth birthday, I pushed against the door of a pub not far from my childhood home. My father, on the way back from his office in London, was inside, standing at the bar. He didn't recognise me but I was delighted, almost ecstatic, to see the old man again, particularly as he'd been dead for ten years, and my mother for five.

'Good evening,' I said, standing next to him. 'Nice to see you.'

'Good evening,' he replied.

'This place never changes,' I said.

'We like it this way,' he said.

I ordered a drink; I needed one.

I noticed the date on a discarded newspaper and calculated that Dad was just a little older than me, nearly fifty-one. We were as close to being equals – or contemporaries – as we'd ever be.

He was talking to a man sitting on a stool next to him, and the barmaid was laughing extravagantly with them both. I knew Dad better than anyone, or thought I did, and I was tempted to embrace him or at least kiss his hands, as I used to. I refrained, but watched him looking comfortable at the bar beside the man I now realised was the father of a schoolfriend of mine. Neither of them seemed to mind when I joined in.

Like a lot of people, I have some of my best friendships with the dead. I dream frequently about both of my parents and the house where I grew up, undistinguished though it was. Of course, I never imagined that Dad and I might meet up like this, for a conversation.

Lately I had been feeling unusually foreign to myself. My fiftieth hit me like a tragedy, with a sense of wasted purpose and many wrong moves made. I could hardly complain: I was a theatre and film producer, with houses in London, New York and Brazil. But complain I did. I had become keenly aware of various mental problems that enervated but did not ruin me.

I ran into Dad on a Monday. Over the weekend I'd been staying with some friends in the country who had a fine house and pretty acquaintances, good paintings to look at and an excellent cook. The Iraq war, which had just started, had been on TV continuously. About twenty of us, old and young men, lay on deep sofas drinking champagne and giggling until the prospect of thousands of bombs smashing into donkey carts, human flesh and primitive shacks had depressed everyone in the house. We were aware that disgust was general in the country and that Tony Blair, once our hope after years in opposition, had become the most tarnished and loathed leader since Anthony Eden. We were living in a time of lies, deceit and alienation. This was heavy, and our lives seemed uncomfortably trivial in comparison.

Just after lunch, I had left my friends' house, and the taxi had got me as far as the railway station when I realised I'd left behind a bent paper clip I'd been fiddling with. It was in my friends' library, where I'd been reading about mesmerism in the work of Maupassant, as well as Dickens's experiments with hypnotism, which had got him into a lot of trouble with the wife of a friend. The taxi took me back, and I hurried into the room to retrieve the paper clip, but the cleaner had just finished. Did I want to examine the contents of the vacuum? my hosts asked. They were making faces at one another. Yet I had begun to see myself as heroic in terms of what I'd achieved in spite of my obsessions. This was a line my therapist used. Luckily, I would be seeing the good doctor the next day.

Despite my devastation over the paper clip, I returned to the station and got on the train. I had come down by car, so it was only now I realised that the route of the train meant we would stop at the suburban railway station nearest to my childhood home. As we drew into the platform I found myself straining to see things I recognised, even familiar faces, though I had left the area some thirty years before. But it was raining hard and almost impossible to make anything out. Then, just as the train was about to pull away, I grabbed my bag and got off, walking out into the street with no idea what I would do.

Near the station there had been a small record shop, a bookshop and a place to buy jeans, along with several pubs that I'd been taken to as a young man by a local bedsit aesthete, the first person I came out to. Of course, he knew straight away. His hero was Jean Cocteau. We'd discuss French literature and Wilde and Pop, before taking our speed pills and applying our make-up in the station toilet, and getting the train into the city. Along with another white friend who dressed as Jimi Hendrix, we saw all the plays and shows. Eventually I got a job in a West End box office. This led to work as a stagehand, usher, dresser – even a director – before I found my 'vocation' as a producer.

Now I asked my father his name and what he did. I knew how to work Dad, of course. Soon he was more interested in me than in the other man. Yet my fear didn't diminish: didn't we look similar? I wasn't sure. My clothes, as well as my sparkly new teeth, were more expensive than his, and I was heavier and taller, about a third bigger all over – I have always worked out. But my hair was going gray; I don't dye it. Dad's hair was still mostly black.

An accountant all his life, my father had worked in the same office for fifteen years. He was telling me that he had two sons: Dennis, who was in the Air Force, and me – Billy. A few months ago I'd gone away to university, where, apparently, I was doing well. My all-female production of *Waiting for Godot* – 'a bloody depressing play', according to Dad – had been admired. I wanted to say, 'But I didn't direct it, Dad, I only produced it.'

I had introduced myself to Dad as Peter, the name I sometimes adopted, along with quite a developed alternative character, during anonymous sexual encounters. Not that I needed a persona: Father would ask me where I was from and what I did, but whenever I began to answer he'd interrupt with a stream of advice and opinions.

My father said he wanted to sit down because his sciatica was playing up, and I joined him at a table. Eying the barmaid, Dad said, 'She's lovely, isn't she?'

'Lovely hair,' I said. 'Unfortunately, none of her clothes fit.'

'Who's interested in her clothes?'

This was an aspect of my father I'd never seen; perhaps it was a departure for him. I'd never known him to go to the pub after work; he came straight home. And once Dennis had left I was able to secure Father's evenings for myself. Every day I'd wait for him at the bus stop, ready to take his briefcase. In the house I'd make him a cup of tea while he changed.

Now the barmaid came over to remove our glasses and empty the ashtrays. As she leaned across the table, Dad put his hand behind her knee and slid it all the way up her skirt to her arse, which he caressed, squeezed and held until she reeled away and stared at him in disbelief, shouting that she hated the pub and the men in it, and would he get out before she called the landlord and he flung him out personally?

The landlord did indeed rush over. He snatched away Dad's glass, raising his fist as Dad hurried to the door, forgetting his briefcase. I'd never known Dad to go to work without his briefcase, and I'd never known him to leave it anywhere. As my brother and I used to say, his attaché case was always attached to him.

Outside, where Dad was brushing himself down, I handed it back to him.

'Thank you,' he said. 'Shouldn't have done that. But once, just once, I had to. Suppose it's the last time I touch anyone!' He asked, 'Which way are you going?'

'I'll walk with you a bit,' I said. 'My bag isn't heavy. I'm passing through. I need to get a train into London but there's no hurry.'

He said, 'Why don't you come and have a drink at my house?'

My parents lived according to a strict regime, mathematical in its exactitude. Why, now, was he inviting a stranger to his house? I had always been his only friend; our involvement had kept us both busy.

'Are you sure?'

'Yes,' he said. 'Come.'

Noise and night and rain streaming everywhere: you couldn't see farther than your hand. But we both knew the way, Dad moving slowly, his mouth hanging open to catch more air. He seemed happy enough, perhaps with what he'd done in the pub, or maybe my company cheered him up.

Yet when we turned the corner into the neat familiar road, a road that had, to my surprise, remained exactly where it was all the time I hadn't been there, I felt wrapped in coldness. In my recent dreams – fading as they were like frescoes in the light – the suburban street had been darkly dismal under the yellow shadows of the streetlights, and filled with white flowers and a suffocating, deathly odor, like being buried in roses. But how could I falter now? Once inside the house, Dad threw open the door to the living room. I blinked; there she was, Mother, knitting in her huge chair with her feet up, an open box of chocolates on the small table beside her, her fingers rustling for treasure in the crinkly paper.

Dad left me while he changed into his pyjamas and dressing gown. The fact that he had a visitor, a stranger, didn't deter him from his routine, outside of which there were no maps.

I stood in my usual position, just behind Mother's chair. Here, where I wouldn't impede her enjoyment with noise, complaints or the sight of my face, I explained that Dad and I had met in the pub and he'd invited me back for a drink.

Mother said, 'I don't think we've got any drink, unless there's something left over from last Christmas. Drink doesn't go bad, does it?'

'It doesn't go bad.'

'Now shut up,' she said. 'I'm watching this. D'you watch the soaps?'

'Not much.'

Maybe the ominous whiteness of my dreams had been stimulated by the whiteness of the things Mother had been knitting and crocheting – headrests, gloves, cushion covers; there wasn't a piece of furniture in the house without a knitted thing on it. Even as a grown man, I couldn't buy a pair of gloves without thinking I should be wearing Mother's.

In the kitchen, I made a cup of tea for myself and Dad. Mum had left my father's dinner in the oven: sausages, mash and peas, all dry as lime by now, and presented on a large cracked plate with space between each item. Mum had asked me if I wanted anything, but how would I have been able to eat anything here?

As I waited for the kettle to boil, I washed up the dishes at the sink overlooking the garden. Then I carried Father's tea and dinner into his study, formerly the family dining room. With one hand I made a gap for the plate at the table, which was piled high with library books.

After I'd finished my homework, Dad always liked me to go through the radio schedules, marking programmes I might record for him. If I was lucky, he would read to me, or talk about the lives of the artists he was absorbed with – these were his companions. Their lives were exemplary, but only a fool would try to emulate them. Meanwhile I would slip my hand inside his pyjama top and tickle his back, or I'd scratch his head or rub his arms until his eyes rolled in appreciation.

Now in his bedwear, sitting down to eat, Dad told me he was embarked on a 'five-year reading plan'. He was working on *War and Peace*. Next it would be *Remembrance of Things Past*, then *Middlemarch*, all of Dickens, Homer, Chaucer, and so on. He kept a separate notebook for each author he read.

'This methodical way,' he pointed out, 'you get to know everything in literature. You will never run out of interest, of course, because then there is music, painting, in fact the whole of human history –'

His talk reminded me of the time I won the school essay prize for a tract on time-wasting. The piece was not about how to fritter away one's time profitlessly, which might have made it a useful and lively work, but about how much can be achieved by filling every moment with activity! Dad was my ideal. He would read even in the bath, and as he reclined there my job was to wash his feet, back and hair with soap and a flannel. When he was done, I'd be waiting with a warm, open towel.

I interrupted him, 'You certainly wanted to know that woman this evening.'

'What? How quiet it is! Shall we hear some music?'

He was right. Neither the city nor the country was quiet like the suburbs, the silence of people holding their breath.

Dad was holding up a record he had borrowed from the library. 'You will know this, but not well enough, I guarantee you.'

Beethoven's Fifth was an odd choice of background music, but how could I sneer? Without his enthusiasm, my life would never have been filled with music. Mother had been a church pianist, and she'd taken us to the ballet, usually *The Nutcracker*, or the Bolshoi when they visited London. Mum and Dad sometimes went ballroom dancing; I loved it when they dressed up. Out of such minute inspirations I have found meaning sufficient for a life.

Dad said, 'Do you think I'll be able to go in that pub again?'

'If you apologise.'

'Better leave it a few weeks. I don't know what overcame me. That woman's not a Jewess, is she?'

'I don't know.'

'Usually she's happy to hear about my aches and pains, and who else is, at our age?'

'Where d'you ache?'

'It's the walk to and from the station – sometimes I just can't make it. I have to stop and lean against something.'

I said, 'I've been learning massage.'

'Ah.' He put his feet in my lap. I squeezed his feet, ankles, and calves; he wasn't looking at me now. He said, 'Your hands are strong. You're not a plumber, are you?'

'I've told you what I do. I have the theatre, and now I'm helping to set up a teaching foundation, a studio for the young.'

He whispered, 'Are you homosexual?'

'I am, yes. Never seen a cock I didn't like. You?'

'Queer? It would have shown up by now, wouldn't it? But I've never done much about my female interests.'

'You've never been unfaithful?'

'I've always liked women.'

I asked, 'Do they like you?'

'The local secretaries are friendly. Not that you can do anything. I can't afford a "professional".'

'How often do you go to the pub?'

'I've started popping in after work. My Billy has gone.'

'For good?'

'After university he'll come running back to me, I can assure you of that. Around this time of night I'd always be talking to him. There's a lot you can put in a kid, without his knowing it. My wife doesn't have a word to say to me. She doesn't like to do anything for me, either.'

'Sexually?'

'She might look large to you, but in the flesh she is even larger, and she crushes me like a gnat in bed. I can honestly say we haven't had it off for eighteen years.'

'Since Billy was born?'

He said, letting me caress him, 'She never had much enthusiasm for it. Now she is indifferent . . . frozen . . . almost dead.'

I said, 'People are more scared of their own passion than of anything else. But it's a grim deprivation she's made you endure.'

He nodded. 'You dirty homos have a good time, I bet, looking at one another in toilets and that . . .'

'People like to think so. But I've lived alone for five years.'

He said, 'I am hoping she will die before me, then I might have a chance . . . We ordinary types carry on in these hateful situations for the single reason of the children and you'll never have that.'

'You're right.'

He indicated photographs of me and my brother. 'Without those babies, there is nothing for me. It is ridiculous to try to live for yourself alone.'

'Don't I know it? Unless one can find others to live for.'

'I hope you do!' he said. 'But it can never be the same as your own.'

If the mortification of fidelity imperils love, there's always the consolation of children. I had been Dad's girl, his servant, his worshipper; my faith had kept him alive. It was a cult of personality he had set up, with my brother and me as his mirrors.

Now Mother opened the door – not so wide that she could see us, or us her – and announced that she was going to bed.

'Good night,' I called.

Dad was right about kids. But what could I do about it? I had bought an old factory at my own expense and had converted it into a theatre studio, a place where young people could work with established artists. I spent so much time in this building that I had moved my office there. It was where I would head when I left here, to sit in the café, seeing who would turn up and what they wanted from me, if anything. I was gradually divesting myself, as I aged, of all I'd accumulated. One of Father's favourite works was Tolstoy's 'How Much Land Does a Man Need?'

I said, 'With or without children, you are still a man. There are things you want that children cannot provide.'

He said, 'We all, in this street, are devoted to hobbies.'

'The women, too?'

'They sew, or whatever. There's never an idle moment. My son has written a beautiful essay on the use of time.'

He sipped his tea; the Beethoven, which was on repeat, boomed away. He seemed content to let me work on his legs. Since he didn't want me to stop, I asked him to lie on the floor. With characteristic eagerness, he removed his dressing gown and then his pyjama top; I massaged every part of him, murmuring 'Dad, Dad' under my breath. When at last he stood up, I was

ready with his warm dressing gown, which I had placed on the
radiator.

It was late, but not too late to leave. It was never too late to leave
the suburbs, but Dad invited me to stay. I agreed, though it hadn't
occurred to me that he would suggest I sleep in my old room, in
my bed.

He accompanied me upstairs and in I went, stepping over record
sleeves, magazines, clothes, books. My piano I was most glad to see.
I can still play a little, but my passion was writing the songs that
were scrawled in notebooks on top of the piano. Not that I would
be able to look at them. When I began to work in the theatre, I
didn't show my songs to anyone, and eventually I came to believe
they were a waste of time.

Standing there shivering, I had to tell myself the truth: my secret
wasn't that I hadn't propagated but that I'd wanted to be an artist,
not just a producer. If I chose, I could blame my parents for this:
they had seen themselves as spectators, in the background of
life. But I was the one who'd lacked the guts – to fail, to succeed,
to engage with the whole undignified, insane attempt at origin-
ality. I had only ever been a handmaiden, first to Dad and then to
others – the artists I'd supported – and how could I have imagined
that that would be sufficient?

My bed was narrow. Through the thin wall, I could hear my
father snoring; I knew whenever he turned over in bed. It was true
that I had never heard them making love. Somehow, between
them, they had transformed the notion of physical love into a
ridiculous idea. Why would people want to do something so
awkward with their limbs?

I couldn't hear Mother. She didn't snore, but she could sigh for
England. I got up and went to the top of the stairs. By the kitchen
light I could see her in her dressing gown, stockings around her
ankles, trudging along the hall and into each room, wringing
her hands as she went, muttering back to the ghosts clamouring
within her skull.

She stood still to scratch and tear at her exploded arms. During the day, she kept them covered because of her 'eczema'. Now I watched while flakes of skin fell onto the carpet, as though she were converting herself into dust. She dispersed the shreds of her body with her delicately pointed dancer's foot.

As a child – even as a young man – I would never have approached Mother in this state. She had always made it clear that the uproar and demands of two boys were too much for her. Naturally, she couldn't wish for us to die, so she died herself, inside.

One time, my therapist asked whether Dad and I were able to be silent together. More relevant, I should have said, was whether Mother and I could be together without my chattering on about whatever occurred to me, in order to distract her from herself. Now I made up my mind and walked down the stairs, watching her all the while. She was like difficult music, and you wouldn't want to get too close. But, as with such music, I wouldn't advise trying to make it out – you have to sit with it, wait for it to address you.

I was standing beside her, and with her head down she looked at me sideways.

'I'll make you some tea,' I said, and she even nodded.

Before, during one of her late-night wanderings, she had found me masturbating in front of some late-night TV programme. It must have been some boy group, or Bowie. 'I know what you are,' she said. She was not disapproving. She was just a lost ally.

I made a cup of lemon tea and gave it to her. As she stood sipping it, I took up a position beside her, my head bent also, attempting to see – as she appeared to vibrate with inner electricity – what she saw and felt. It was clear that there was no chance of my ever being able to cure her. I could only become less afraid of her madness.

In his bed, Father was still snoring. He wouldn't have liked me to be with her. He had taken her sons for himself, charmed them away, and he wasn't a sharer.

She was almost through with the tea and getting impatient. Wandering, muttering, scratching: she had important work to do and time was passing. I couldn't detain her any more.

I slept in her chair in the front room.

When I got up, my parents were having breakfast. My father was back in his suit and my mother was in the uniform she wore to work in the supermarket. I dressed rapidly in order to join Dad as he walked to the station. It had stopped raining.

I asked him about his day, but couldn't stop thinking about mine. I was living, as my therapist enjoyed reminding me, under the aegis of the clock. I wanted to go to the studio and talk; I wanted to eat well and make love well, go to a show and then dance, and make love again. I could not be the same as them.

At the station in London, Father and I parted. I said I'd always look out for him when I was in the area, but couldn't be sure when I'd be coming his way again.

Weddings and Beheadings

I have gathered the equipment together and now I am waiting for them to arrive. They will not be long; they never are.

You don't know me personally. My existence has never crossed your mind. But I would bet you've seen my work: it has been broadcast everywhere, on most of the news channels worldwide. Or at least parts of it have. You could find it on the net, right now, if you really wanted to. If you could bear to look.

Not that you'd notice my style, my artistic signature or anything like that.

I film beheadings, which are common in this war-broken city, my childhood home.

It was never my ambition, as a young man who loved cinema, to film such things. Nor was it my wish to do weddings either, though there are less of those these days. Ditto graduations and parties. My friends and I have always wanted to make real films, with living actors and dialogue and jokes and music, as we began to as students. Nothing like that is possible here.

Every day we are ageing, we feel shabby, the stories are there, waiting to be told, we're artists. But this stuff, the death work, it has taken over.

Naturally we didn't seek out this kind of employment. We were 'recommended' and we can't not do it; we can't say we're visiting relatives or working in the cutting room. They call us up with little notice at odd hours, usually at night, and minutes later they are outside with their guns. They put us in the car and cover our heads. Because there's only one of us working at a time, the thugs help with carrying the gear. But we have to do the sound as well as the picture, and load the camera and work out how to light the scene. I've asked to use an assistant, but they only offer their rough accomplices and they know nothing, they can't even wipe a lens without making a mess of it.

I know three other guys who do this work; we discuss it amongst ourselves, but we'd never talk to anyone else about it or we'd end up in front of the camera.

My closest friend filmed a beheading recently, but he's not a director, only a writer really. I wouldn't say anything, but I wouldn't trust him with a camera. He was the one who had the idea of getting calling cards made with 'Weddings and Beheadings' inscribed on them. If the power's on, we meet in his flat to watch great movies on video. He's jokey: 'Don't bury your head in the sand, my friend,' he says when we part. 'Don't go losing your head now. Chin up!'

He isn't too sure about the technical stuff, how to set up the camera, and then how to get the material through the computer and onto the internet.

It's a skill, obviously.

A couple of weeks ago he messed up badly. The cameras are good-quality, they're taken from foreign journalists, but a bulb blew in the one light he was using, and he couldn't replace it. By then they had brought the victim in. My friend tried to tell the men, it's too dark, it's not going to come out and you can't do another take. But they were in a hurry, he couldn't persuade them to wait, they were already hacking through the neck and he was in such a panic he fainted. Luckily the camera was running. It came out underlit of course, what did they expect? I liked it – 'Lynchian' I called it – but they hit him around the head, and never used him again.

He was lucky. But I wonder if he's going mad. Secretly he kept copies of his beheadings and now he plays around with them on his computer, cutting and re-cutting them, and putting on music, swing stuff, opera, jazz, comic songs. Perhaps it's the only freedom he has.

It might surprise you, but we do get paid, they always give us something 'for the trouble', and they even make jokes: 'You'll get a prize for the next one. Don't you guys love prizes and statuettes and stuff?'

But it's hellish, the long drive there with the camera and tripod on your lap, the smell of the sack, the guns, and you wonder if this time you might be the victim. Usually you're sick, and then you're in the building and in the room, setting up, and you hear things, from other rooms, that make you wonder if life on earth is a good idea.

I know you don't want too much detail, but it's serious work taking off someone's head if you're not a butcher, and these guys aren't qualified, they're just enthusiastic, it's what they like to do. To make it work on television, it helps to get a clear view of the victim's eyes just before they cover them. At the end they hold up the head streaming with blood and you might need to use some hand-held here, to catch everything. It has to be framed carefully. It wouldn't be good if you missed something. (That means that ideally you need a quick-release tripod head, something I have and would never lend to anyone.)

They cheer and fire off rounds while you're checking the tape and playing it back. After, they put the body in a bag and dump it somewhere, before they drive you to another place, where you transfer the material to the computer and send it out.

Often I wonder what this is doing to me. I try to think of war photographers, who, they say, use the lens to distance themselves from the reality of suffering and death. But those guys have elected to do that work, they believe in it. We are innocent.

One day I'd like to make a proper film, maybe beginning with a beheading, telling the story that leads up to it. It's the living I'm interested in, but the way things are going I'll be doing this for a while. Sometimes I wonder if I'm going to go mad, or whether even this escape is denied me.

I better go now. Someone is at the door.

The Assault

It is winter, an ordinary day, no worse than any other. I drop my son at school. A few minutes after nine I am leaving the playground, along with the Muslim women, the Africans, the Czechs and the middle-class executives in their suits, already tapping into their Blackberries. I always enjoy the walk home, the relief and freedom of solitude, and will think over everything I have to do, errands, shopping, a lunch, before picking up the boy again.

Outside the school a woman catches my eye. We mothers see each other twice a day, often for years. She looks nice, the sort I might get along with. We smile, but have never spoken or gone for coffee.

'Want a lift?' she asks. It is beginning to rain. We introduce ourselves and get in her car. 'Don't you live by the park? I'll drop you on the corner,' she says. 'I hope that's okay. I have a little time, but I have to get to work.'

I wonder why she offered to give me a lift, if she's not really going my way. Wearing black, she has a slightly frantic look, as though she didn't have time to finish getting ready. But which of us mothers doesn't look like that?

As I am pulling on my seat belt, she begins to tell me about her son, who is a year younger than mine. He has 'behavioural problems', odd and difficult moods. He is being tested for several illnesses, attention deficit, autism and something else, I forget. She describes their visits to the numerous specialists, experts and doctors he sees a lot of now. It is a moving story, and not an uninteresting or uncommon one.

A few moments later she stops the car where the streets diverge, and I open the car door, about to get out. I know this street, and today, on the pavement, there is a local madman, very tall, hair askew, talking furiously to himself, and with a strange gait, taking huge exaggerated steps, like a giant striding across continents. At the end of the street he stops and returns.

The woman continues to speak, and I nod and listen, as she describes a doctor. In my right hand is my phone and my bag; the other hand is still holding the door. Because of the madman, I close it again and lock it.

When I turn to her and mouth some comforting words, I begin to see that the woman has no interest in my response, that there is nothing she wants from me. I only have to be here, a person, that's all.

I look at her face, her clothes, her rings, her shoes, and she watches me reach for the metal door handle again. I see the madman has passed and it would be a good opportunity to get on with my day. I open the door. I appear to gather myself and my possessions up again, but she keeps going.

As I sit there, I become aware, amazed even, that nothing I might do, or attempt to say, will make any difference to this woman. I was brought up to be polite. In fact I believe that if I am rude, I will be hated. My husband is different: he is not afraid of being offensive, he even enjoys it. He would open the car door, say goodbye, and be gone. 'What does it matter?' he'd say. 'They'll survive.'

More than anything I want him to phone me now, to interrupt this, to help me understand. The woman is speaking quickly but every detail is clear; it is not the wild jumble of a psychotic, nor the monotonous tone of the depressive.

'The doctor was nice, he wore a suit, he asked my son many questions. He asked to talk to him privately. Well, I said . . .' You would think there'd be a pause here, but she has clearly developed her gift for making her sentences run on. 'We tried another doctor, recommended by someone else . . . Now, of course, my husband and I are having our difficulties . . .'

I can see her eyes taking in my hand on the door handle; this is a look from her, not a glance, but my obvious desire to escape has no effect.

She begins to do this terrible thing. To prove to myself that I don't lack courage, I attempt to interrupt, opening my mouth to take a breath, but with hardly the first word out of my throat she raises her finger at me and says, 'Just let me finish.'

This must have been going on for fifteen or twenty minutes. Is there something about me which invites such abuse? What would it be? How could she have picked it up when I have never spoken to her before?

After an hour – yes, an hour – I am becoming claustrophobic; I cannot speak, cannot make myself heard. Unsaid words are throttling me. Something in my right eye is vibrating. My breathing is shallow, my legs feel crushed. Surely she can hear that I am angry, and see that she is assaulting me, that I am being crushed under an injustice. But I am mesmerised. My husband would say that this must have happened to me before, yes with mother, in the kitchen, or on the phone, and sometimes with friends, but does it follow that I want this all the time?

Soon an hour and a quarter has passed: more, even; I have lost my bearings. She has forgotten me, and I have forgotten myself, as if she has planted a virus in my mind which slowly wiped away my memory, my volition, my entire identity.

I watch the madman passing, and then I look at her again, the woman whose eyes have not left my face. A terrible thought occurs to me, not one I could bear to say to anyone. I know why her son has withdrawn inside himself, and why he cannot speak, if this is what she does to him. She has forced him into a compact ball, the only protection he has. But who will say this to her?

She is looking at her watch. She must have measured out exactly how much time she had to talk. 'That's it,' she says. 'Sorry, I don't want to be late. We got distracted. Lovely to see you. Let's do it again.'

I get out of the car and take a few steps. I am weak; I need to lie down.

The woman waves and drives off, leaving me on the pavement in the rain with a madman striding towards me.

Maggie

It was late morning when the door bell rang. Max was tramping on an exercise bicycle in his new gym, flicking idly between Indian, Chinese and Arab TV channels. As he did with everything now – recently he had begun to practise, actively, a new creed of 'slowness' – he took his time showering and dressing. Then he sat on the bed, staring out of the window, considering scenes from the past. There was no rush: Marta, the new girl, would let Maggie in, and provide her with coffee, biscuits and the newspapers.

About three times a year Maggie came to London to stay with friends for a few days. Informing Max that she needed to see him, she added that their usual lunch, welcome though it was, wouldn't be enough. She had a serious request she couldn't talk about on the phone.

He and Maggie had met at a campus university in the mid-seventies and stayed together for around ten years, depending on how it was added up, or by whom. It had been his longest relationship, apart from that with his wife. But there were other reasons he wanted to think about what he now called the 'experiment'. After it, Maggie had moved to the country with her partner Joe – called Jesus the Carpenter by Max – and brought up two children. Max had remained in the city, taking advantage of the Thatcherite expansion of the media, where he became successful and now had four children.

'Hello, my dear,' Max said, when he appeared in the kitchen in shorts, flip-flops and a T-shirt which he now realised only just covered his stomach when he stood up. 'Let's go onto the terrace. I'd like you to see it.'

It was unusual now for him to invite Maggie to the house because she irritated Max's wife with, as Lucy put it, her 'soppy self-righteousness and earnestness'. Lucy might well go on to say more maddening things like, 'And as for that weird thing the three of you seemed to have had together, can you explain what in God's name that was about?'

What indeed? However, Lucy was away filming; Max, she and the rest of the family would meet up tomorrow at the place they'd bought in Suffolk.

Max led Maggie up the stairs and onto the terrace, which stretched out across the top of the kitchen. There was a view of the garden, with a shed at the end, where the boys rehearsed their band and watched movies with their friends. Beyond that was the bowling green and the local park. It was spring, the blossom was out; so far it was the nicest day of the year.

They sat at the table and Marta, a young woman with dyed red hair, appeared again with a tray on which there was coffee and two glasses of grappa.

He said, 'This is where I'm intending to spend the summer months.'

Maggie put her head back, attempting to catch the sun on her face. 'What doing?'

'Writing poetry, drawing, learning to paint. Yes,' he said, 'I've got nothing better to do. But for years I was too tangled up to be creative.'

'You were? How?'

He indicated the house and terrace. 'It's all nearly finished. I did it myself.'

'The building?'

'Of course not. The organisation of it.'

'You seem to have a horde of people working here.'

'It takes two girls to keep the house and kids in order, and the Polish builders are installing a sauna.'

'Where are those naughty boys?'

He had briefly seen two of his sons – aged fourteen and fifteen – that morning in the kitchen with a bunch of their friends, who'd slept over.

'The younger ones are with their grandparents, and the big ones seem to have disappeared to Niketown to spend my money,' he said. 'They'll be back later. We're going up the road to watch Chelsea at home tonight.'

Maggie asked, 'Why? Are you a Chelsea supporter?'

He hummed a Chelsea song. 'We all are. Season ticket.'

'But you used to be Fulham.'

'I was Fulham, sort of,' he admitted. 'Mainly because of what I read about Johnny Haynes as a kid.'

He had intended to ask Maggie how she was, knowing she would complain about the hours, the wages, the clients, the government and the local council. She'd been a social worker since they'd been together, when he was beginning to make documentaries, and her work was demanding and difficult. He'd always said that she didn't appear to be quite cut out for it, becoming over-involved and allowing it to exhaust and infuriate her, but she called it 'passion'.

He just said, 'What was it you wanted to ask me?'

'Max, for a while I've thought I should change my life.'

'Congratulations.'

'I knew you'd be delighted.'

'Change it in what way?'

'I'll tell you later.'

'Now I'm intrigued.'

'Good.' She said, 'What's really up with you?'

He shrugged. 'I'm still happily bored.'

'Depressed?'

'A man who is tired of suffering is tired of life. But you won't hear me complain.'

Five years ago Max sold his television company to a big media conglomerate. Having set it up during the time he was with

Maggie to promote investigative journalism on television, he and his colleagues had made programmes about political and business corruption, 'covering shadiness of all shades'. Later, after the company made a satirical political comedy series which achieved big ratings, they made other clever funnies. As he became more of an executive than artist, he sold the company well at a good time. For a while he'd loved having his pockets full of money, buying whatever he wanted, shopping with the kids. Apart from watching football, it was the thing they most liked doing as a family.

He'd done little paying work since, but had 'run the house' and attended to the children while his wife established herself as a producer. 'I'm a feminist house-husband,' he liked to boast. 'All I do is support women, and has the sisterhood been grateful?'

'Right-ho!' he said now. He and Maggie touched glasses and downed the grappa.

'Do you always drink at this time?'

'Marta seems to think so.'

As they left the house, Maggie asked to see the rooms where he worked, smiling when she saw the birchwood ladder-backed chair Joe had restored as a present for Max when they first met.

She reached into her bag and said, 'Joe sent this.' It was a flat wooden paperknife decorated with carved symbols.

'It's lovely, thanks,' he said, putting it on his desk. 'I must find something to give him too.'

He pointed at the long white wall, against which leaned numerous frames covered in brown paper. 'Like everyone else, I've begun to collect art and photographs,' he said. 'It wasn't until recently that materialism made any sense to me. Now I think, this is mine, *mine*, and I've earned it.'

He and Maggie strolled up the road to where his new black Volkswagen convertible was parked. The restaurant was ten minutes' walk away but Max was keen to show off the car.

He regarded her: like him, she was in her mid-fifties, and usually wore walking or what he considered 'climbing' and wet-weather clothes, with boots. She spent more time outside than him, and was tanned and lined, with greying hair that she might have cut herself, and no make-up. In his view, with this Patti Smith look, she appeared older than him now, but as Lucy said, if you think someone your age seems worn out, take it for granted you look twice as bad.

She said, 'My God, it's so wealthy here. But the foreigners I've noticed – they're all employees and cheap labour, aren't they?'

'At this time of day they would be,' he said. 'Nannies, au pairs, cleaners, builders. What did you expect? Amazing to think, Maggie, of how London's cleaned up since we were students. Can you remember how filthy it was then, graffiti, squats, and the tube an even more filthy pit than now, and no one paying for anything?'

'Today it's all control,' she said.

'It would be pretty to think so. But my kids are nervous on the street. Up the road there's an estate where the wild boys see us as rich pickings.'

'Only the very obedient survive, isn't that right?'

'How is it where you are?'

She and Joe still lived in a village in Somerset. When the commune had failed, they'd moved into a low-rent collapsing cottage which they had renovated.

'You wouldn't believe the poverty down there. It's another country, which means it's dull, and my work is repetitive, mostly with old women,' she said. 'That's part of what I want to talk about.'

They sat in the car and Max put on a Clash CD. 'Did we ever see them?' he asked as 'London Calling' started. 'I'm not sure we did, though we saw most of the other bands then.' He went on, 'Now, when I think about it, what a little paradise it was when we were together. The Health Service, unemployment benefit, cheap housing, the BBC, subsidised theatre. Mum and Dad didn't pay a penny for my education, and if you came from a respectable but ordinary background, you believed you could get out and live differently to your parents. All that went when Thatcher came to power.'

For years he and Maggie were 'political' all the time; even their record collection had aided the revolution. He was proud of the anti-racist work they did, and the street stand-offs with the National Front. Much of the rest of their life together puzzled him, and he had begun to think it might be important to discuss it with Maggie later, after a few more drinks. She was argumentative, but he had begun to enjoy disputing, if not goading her, and liked to believe he was less scared of her than before.

'That reminds me,' he said, as the roof of the car slid open and the sound boomed into the street. 'I didn't show you the pictures of me receiving my OBE from the Queen.'

She was laughing. 'I can't wait.'

'Naturally the medal wasn't for me, but for the work everyone did for the company. I have a picture you can put on the mantel-piece. Joe will enjoy it.'

'You're going to be in a provocative mood today.'

'Sorry,' he said. 'But how can you not be fascinated by this funny little country? You go inside Buckingham Palace and there are Beefeaters, Chelsea Pensioners, Gurkhas, men in silver armour standing completely still, with like, you know, fur piled on their heads. There are other men walking across the Palace carpets wearing spurs on their shiny boots, a host of queens, and everyone else in badly fitting borrowed or hired suits. It's like being sober at a fancy dress party.'

'Do you really believe you've made a contribution?'

He said, 'If you ever watch Spanish or Italian TV you'll get some idea of the quality of what we do over here.'

'I won't have a TV in the house. Joe has to go to the pub to watch football.'

'What is it, in your view, that people should be doing?'

'Why can't they talk?'

'Watching the telly is more fun, I would have thought.'

Entering their usual restaurant in Hammersmith Grove, he said, 'The service is terrible here, particularly since the Poles have sensed the downturn and have started to desert. But there's no rush is there?'

As it was warm, they could sit outside, separated from the public by a neat hedge. The place was rarely crowded at lunchtime:

there were only a few businessmen, a table of women who looked like footballers' wives, and a couple of media executives who Max nodded at.

After they sat down she said, 'I want to leave my job and home and come down here to live. Obviously I've got no money, but I'll get a job.'

'It's too expensive, Maggie,' he said, studying the menu. '*We're* only just ahead. Four kids at private school – can you imagine? And capitalism's having a breakdown, as Marx told us it would, every few years. Not a good time at all to try anything new, thank God. Can I order the wine?'

'Max, I can't wait for capitalism to sort itself out. You know how stubborn and bloody-minded I am – it's one of those things I have to do.'

He asked, 'Are you leaving Joe? Is that what it is?'

'Neither of us is seeing anyone at the moment, but you know we don't make a big deal about sharing. We can't be everything to each other.'

'I've been wondering about that,' he said.

'Why?'

'It's such a peculiar and difficult thing.'

Joe had become part of their circle after they'd left university. A tall, long-bearded, lefty ex-public schoolboy with eyes which appealed to girls, he had started out as a furniture restorer to the rich, but wanted to be an honest worker, doing useful everyday toil. People liked to say his hands spoke for him, which Max considered to be a mercy, for otherwise he was almost completely silent. He would visit the flat Max and Maggie shared, and would smile, nod and shake his head, but rarely open his mouth. Later, when Max and Maggie split up and she began to go out with Joe, she would warn her friends that he'd say nothing. More annoyingly, because of Joe's imperturbable silence, great wisdom was often attributed to him, as well as virtue: he was a committed activist. If you were poor and needed someone to work on your house for more or less nothing, he'd be there. Because he hated money and 'breadheads', if you wanted to pay him, better give him something useful, a bicycle, some potatoes, weed, a piano that needed mending.

Maggie didn't believe in giving anyone up. When she started with Joe – and Max, too, was seeing someone – it became the beginning of something else. For about two years they were a threesome. It was an experiment in living. From their point of view, it would have been 'conventional' or 'selfish' to exclude one of them. Joe moved into their flat, indeed into their bed – and Max, who sometimes stayed with a girlfriend, lived in the front room. What was the need for people to disappear into different families?

Apparently Joe never suffered from jealousy: his girlfriend was free and independent; they both were. They could love whoever they wanted, and there was no price to pay. It didn't bother Joe if Maggie spent the night with anyone else, and when she and Max went to the seaside for a couple of days he'd wave them off. Prohibiting was prohibited, saying no was an unacceptable violence. Nor did Joe appear to have wild fantasies about others' pleasures which excluded him. How did someone learn to be like that?

Max had become reluctantly intrigued by this man who was so secure and convinced of his desirability that he knew the woman would return to him. Not only that, there were plenty of others who would want him. Joe appeared to lack nothing; in *his* turn, Max was considered a 'control freak' by the other two for suffering from jealousy. But, as Max wondered, did Joe have a better life because he didn't experience jealousy? Or did he feel it so painfully that he successfully hid it from himself? Was he really as self-sufficient as he made out? Could people really be as interchangeable as he liked to believe?

Joe and Max worked together on various local gardens as they prepared for the birth of Maggie's son by Joe. (Max had begun to see what an important part of the political struggle gardening was.) The three of them took the child home from the hospital, and he was brought up by all of them, with Max doing most of the childcare as the other two were working, while Max was around, trying to get his projects set up. When Max admitted that it was painful being complimented on 'his' son by strangers, when he had to face the fact that the child he had begun to love wasn't his, the three of them decided that the men should take it in turns to father Maggie's children.

When Maggie and Joe began to insist that this had to proceed soon, that he had to make up his mind about it, Max finished with it all. He had to, before he got deeper in. He fled alone to a seaside hotel to try to get over his love for the child, his hatred of Joe's self-sufficiency and his own self-contempt. How had he allowed such a situation to develop? Max's mother was an ordinary woman who would have considered such a parenting arrangement mad. Anyway, Maggie and Joe were moving to Devon to live and work on a commune, taking it for granted that Max would accompany them. But his work was in London, where he was making a documentary about a violent attack by the police on a black man, produced by the glamorous Lucy.

One night after filming she made some banal remarks which were subversive in their effect on him. The ideology he, Maggie and their friends followed was like a religion, almost cult-like; hadn't he noticed it was closing him down, limiting his intelligence and imagination? He thought of those interminable democratic evenings, with everyone smoking, where everything was discussed in infinitesimal detail and, at the end, you had to do what someone else wanted because it had become 'the will of the group' and, probably, even the will of the proletariat.

He was able to pull away from Maggie and Joe, but only at the cost of wishing for death – his own and theirs – when they left London with the child. He and Maggie had believed they'd never stop loving one another, but that hadn't been the case at all, fortunately. He had recovered, as everyone knew he would, and what remained?

Now Maggie and Max were eating. 'Don't you think,' she said, 'hasn't it occurred to you lately, what a conventional age we are living in now? I mean, of coercive ideals, the tyranny of the closed?'

'I thought the biggest change in our time is the huge progress in social freedom. Can't people be whoever they want? Lesbianism, transvestism, domination, bipolar – isn't it all just lifestyle?'

She said, 'The other day I was reading something on Sartre and De Beauvoir. About what a stupid emotional mess they'd made, fucking around with others' lives. The suggestion was that if they'd been nice clean obedient workers maybe they would have been worth listening to. Couldn't you say the same about Shelley, Mary Wollstonecraft, Ginsberg or scores of other artists? "The deadly grip of the commonplace", we used to call it. All the experiments have failed and we must return to the norm.'

He said, 'You still want to experiment with your own life?'

'I try to live as I need to.' She leaned towards him. 'Between you and me, don't you have your . . . interests?'

'I'm well done with that. It's too costly a pleasure.'

'Is that permanent now – the glasses?' she said, looking at his reading glasses which were on a gold chain around his neck.

'Yes. Does it lead you to believe I've become a man without self-respect? I love middle age, when you no longer care how you look or how you might appear to others. Men take it less hard than women, don't you think?'

Maggie had been beautiful as a girl of twenty, gentle, generous and scholarship-clever, from a square and functional family. Feminism and the 'assertiveness' workshops made her less of a pushover, and after a while she lost her charm to ideology, becoming opinionated, angry. Almost everyone let her down, not wanting sufficiently to alter everything, to make the sacrifice which guaranteed sincerity. She excised all flirtatiousness and play from her character, implying that her mood wouldn't improve until the world did. She was the only person he knew who lamented the collapse of the Berlin Wall, believing communism hadn't been given enough time. 'Think of capitalism, it's been around for centuries!'

'You look better at the moment,' she said now. 'Your eyes are clearer, you're less of a smug little fatty.'

'I've lost a stone. It's my greatest achievement. All I want now is to get the kids through school without any of us disintegrating. Nothing need be more complicated than that.'

'It does,' she said. 'You might have noticed, it's terrible when the kids turn ten and they have to push away from you. You learn they don't actually want your company, that it's a long hard divorce and you'll need to make other arrangements for yourself.'

'For me realism is the true thing.'

'Is it really? Then what I'm going to ask will make you even more irritable,' she said.

'I'm pretty chilled now.'

'I could tell you were in therapy when you started taking an interest in my dreams.'

He said, 'I was too angry all the time so I had that part excised from my personality.'

'It was the attractive bit.'

'Mags, please, lately I've been having these horrifying dreams, a series of them. My uncle's dying in bed.'

'Which uncle?'

'You know, the lively, intelligent, funny one. He's long dead of course.'

'That's part of you,' she said. 'It's going. You're letting it go. You're driving it out.'

'I'm not sure that's exactly it,' he said.

They were finishing the bottle. He was becoming tired and would have made an excuse, returned home and napped – which was how he liked to spend the afternoon – if he hadn't been curious about her request. But they drank coffee and drove to Richmond Park, about half an hour away.

He had parked the car and they had begun to walk when she said, 'Max I want you to loan me ten thousand pounds to help me start up in London. I know it won't last me long, but it'll be better than nothing. When – or whether – I'll ever be able to pay it back is another matter.'

He sighed. 'That's a big whack. Will it be enough for you?'

628

'I'm hoping to last five years in London. Despite the stupid expense there are still cheap cultural activities, aren't there?'

'They'll pass an afternoon.'

'Joe thinks it's all stupidity, consumerism and self-hatred down here, but he will visit me and I'll go home when I need to. Otherwise I'll explore – places and people.'

'Is Joe all right about that? Or is he still as indifferent to everyone as he used to be?'

'As always, he'll be happy for me to live as I wish. I drive him mad with my frustration and he's never wanted to be my jailer. The kids will come down too. My son has already climbed the front of the Houses of Parliament in that recent protest. They're at the right age for the city.'

Max said, 'It's always seemed odd to me that you live with someone who lacks the ability to make conversation.'

'Why do we have to communicate verbally when we are already in tune?'

'What was the communication when you said you were going to ask me for money?' He was looking at her. 'Didn't you tell him?'

'I will tell him when I know what's going on.'

'I wouldn't risk the relationship,' he said. 'Lucy and I know a lot of middle-aged women trying to hunt down men on the net and it's a pathetic business.'

'Don't lecture me. But I do often think, why the hell didn't I choose more solvent men?' They walked past some people who were planting trees. 'What are you thinking?' she asked. 'Go on, please say.'

'I was thinking, what if I took that shovel and smashed it over your head?'

She was laughing. 'I knew that. See, we still have the same thoughts.'

He stopped and said, 'Can I hold you?'

'Here, why?'

'Just to see. Or to try to remember.' He took her in his arms and put his face in her hair and neck. He kissed her face, ran his hands across her back, up her thighs, and he looked at her hands.

'Anything else you want to touch or see?' she asked. 'My breasts, genitals?'

'No, no.' He went on, 'Ten grand's a lot of money. You'll never pay it back. I'll have to give it to you.'

'You won't even notice.' She went on, 'I'm so bored by everything. I even prefer America. At least they can vote for Obama or Hillary. A black or a woman. What do we have? Boris Johnson. A character from P. G. Wodehouse.'

'No better man to run London, then. I'm thinking of voting for him. Anything for a change.'

'Oh God. Have *you* changed so much?'

'I like to think I'm capable of revising my views. It would be as daft to believe the same things over the years as it would be to wear the same clothes.'

'For instance?'

'The Falklands. Thatcher was right there, fighting the fascist Galtieri. And then taking on the trade unions, the whole country held to ransom by a few fundamentalist Lefties who wouldn't grow up.'

She stiffened. 'Oh Jesus, Max, all those years of struggle to end up recanting, and for what? Just to look like a turncoat?'

'Look,' he said. 'It didn't work, socialism, communism, the whole idea was fucked. It's the biggest disappointment of our lives, but don't we have to take it like men?'

She said, 'By the way, you carrying your chequebook?'

'You want the money now?'

'Once it's done you won't think about it again. Then we can talk about less painful things.'

'But I haven't thought it through. What would Lucy say?'

'Lucy?'

'What if I discovered she'd donated ten grand to some indigent ex?'

'Is that what I am to you?'

'The wife's not going to be working long hours on a film set for you to take a free dab because you fancy a change of location. She's the breadwinner in our family.'

'This is doing my head in,' she said. 'Let me sit down.' They sat on the grass, leaning against a tree. 'Max, I never asked for *her* money.'

'She and I are together. We don't just go with any stranger who takes our fancy for five minutes. Sex is easy but love is difficult. It's very serious.' He went on, 'And it's not as though the money is for something essential like a cancer operation or plastic surgery.'

'No, it's more important than that. What happened to play, to wildness and experiment?' She got up and he followed her; they walked to the tea-house and ate scones.

She said, 'Do you think you're envious?'

'Of what?'

'All you've done is criticise everything I believe in. But I'm not an old woman yet, Max. I haven't given up, as you appear to have, or become complacent. Feminism taught me that women are capable of deep passion, aliveness and exploration. We can burn on until the end of the night whether we win or lose.'

'How could I not envy you that spirit, though it sounds forced?' Then he said, 'Freud recommends efficient sublimation as the only way forward. You divert yourself, usefully, for life. There's a bit of passion left over, which is tragic, but you have to live with the frustration. It's character-building.'

'What pompous cobblers,' she said. 'Are you saying no?'

'I don't fucking know, Maggie,' he said. 'Why is it that most of one's middle age is spent arguing? I wanted to enjoy a pleasant lunch and all you've done is ruin my bloody day and probably my night. You know I suffer from anxiety. I'm going to have to take a pill.'

'Oh, shut the fuck up and stop being so evasive as usual.'

'But I really can't answer you, my dear. I have to think about it. There are so many other priorities than your self-fulfilment.'

She said, 'I don't like to mention it, but didn't I support you while you developed your career?'

'I walked and fed and changed and paid for your wonderful son every day,' he replied.

'But why shouldn't you have? Whose job is it to bring up the children?'

Max drove them back to the house, where he made tea in the kitchen. There were four boys in the garden, wearing only boxer shorts and flip-flops, lifting weights, kicking a ball, pushing one another around.

'A bunch of chavs and pikeys chased us down the road,' one of the boys said. 'That's why we're sweating.' He said to Maggie, 'There's a council estate across the street.'

Max said, 'What did you do to provoke them?'

'The lowlifes threatened us with a shank. They said, "We know where you live", and Jack said, "We know where you live, in a disgusting council flat with a pit bull eating the sofa and your mother a crack whore."'

Max said, 'Maggie will sort them out. She's a social worker.'

'Chavs and pikeys,' she said. 'Are those the latest descriptions?'

He got up and said suddenly, 'You not only wanted feminism, which was an excellent thing, but you attacked all authority, particularly that of fathers, preferring equality. You made sure that authority died, but there was no equality, only chaos, and that's why we're in a mess. Take responsibility for something at last, Maggie. Not everything is capitalism's fault.'

'Isn't it? This society has become more and more unequal under Blair, the rich taking it all, buying art up and everything else. And the authority you so idealise, Max, was usually corrupt, exploitative and cruel. Why can't each individual have authority? We're not all children.'

The children watched the adults pointing and yelling at one another, and, before they'd stopped, asked for money to go out and buy a video game and pizza. Max handed over some cash.

'How fortunate and spoiled they are,' he said to her. 'With none of the worry we had about the future.'

'Is that good for them?' she asked.

He shrugged. His eldest son patted him on the stomach. 'When's it due, Dad?' he said.

'You see, a dad is a derided thing,' Max said to Maggie.

'Joe isn't.'

'I think I'll fetch some nice wine from the cellar. But have a look at this. It's for Joe.'

He handed her a tiny oil painting, about the size of a packet of cigarettes: a nude woman.

'That's nice.'

He was in the cellar for a while, looking for a wine which might please her. On the way back he passed his jacket, hanging over the back of a chair. He took his chequebook from the pocket and located a pen. When he returned to the kitchen she wasn't there, but had taken her things and gone.

As he opened the wine he wondered whether they'd be able to forgive one another, and whether they'd see one another again.

Phillip

Until at last he was able to identify himself clearly, I couldn't recognise the voice on the phone.

'Who?' I said again. 'I'm afraid I can't hear you. My children are rehearsing their group upstairs.'

'It's Phillip,' he whispered. 'For God's sake! Your old friend, Phillip Heath.'

'Ah.'

'Fred, are you shocked?'

'It's good to hear your voice,' I said cautiously. 'Where have you been all this time?'

'I am still abroad.'

Abroad: it had been a long time since I'd heard that word which was how, when I was a kid, the English referred to the rest of the world.

Over the past fifteen years Phillip had dropped me a postcard every couple of years or so to say he was working in this or that school, or moving apartments. But I couldn't recall the last time we had actually spoken.

On his last postcard, however, a couple of months ago, he had added, 'have been a bit under the weather, old boy'. Then Fiona, my university girlfriend, who had remained in closer touch with him, rang to say Phillip had been operated on for throat cancer.

He sounded croaky and weak on the phone, but said he was recovering. He had been 'thinking things over' and was keen for me to visit him where he was living alone in Italy, near Lake Como.

We could walk together. There were no Muslims, he joked, only hordes of elderly locals walking their dogs. It was old white Europe, where money and glamour had long been replaced by decay and dullness, but not, unfortunately, by decadence. Why didn't I stay in his spare room?

'That's a kind offer,' I said.

'But when exactly can you pop over? I beg you to be definite. Who else can I talk to about things?'

'Things?'

'One's life, I mean, such as it is.'

I promised to look at my diary and phone him in a few days. 'This is sudden for me,' I explained. 'I have teenage children. I teach too – you were my example there, friend.'

'I'm far too weak for that, I'm afraid,' he said. 'Fred, I will wait to hear from you. Please, though, if you want to see my smiling face again better not leave it too long. Dying's an awful trouble and nuisance.'

I wasn't sure when I'd last seen Phillip, but it had been towards the end of the eighties, though the substance of the relationship had been in the middle of that decade, which was when my 'success' began and our friendship – the friendship of him, Fiona and me – had been at its most intense.

The phone call had upset and disturbed me, and I was torn.

How might one turn down the request of a man so sick, perhaps dying unhappily and more or less alone, someone who'd been such a close friend? I'd liked him; I'd loved him, I suppose, and he me. It had been a passionate friendship which had ended badly, indeed violently. Was an inexplicable outbreak any reason to forget the good, wonderful part of it?

As I considered the trip to Como, I became aware of how angry I still was over what had gone on between Phillip and me. Why exactly had I so taken to heart Phillip's attacks on me? Why did I still puzzle over them and continue to hear his voice in my mind, as I argued with him over and over?

*

Although the three of us had been at university together, Phillip was ten years older than Fiona and me and, unusually for that punky dissenting period – the mid-seventies – Phillip had worn ironed shirts, a jacket and leather shoes. At the school where later he became a history master, he wore a tie and carried a briefcase. He had a moustache and glasses. He was not hip and didn't attempt to dress young but looked, according to us, like someone's father, giggling when we called him 'Mr Chips' and, later, Mr Lips.

For us he was knowledgeable and, above all, experienced, seeming to know his way around the world. He'd been married briefly; he wasn't middle-class; his parents had been 'in service' – his mother a cook and his father a gardener – and he had moved far beyond them. After starting as an actor in 'rep', he had run theatres, worked as a stage manager, and even been an actors' agent for a while, before trying to become a journalist. When none of it had seemed to work out, he had returned to university to do a PhD on the British army in the Second World War.

Phillip was the only actively bisexual person I'd known. When Fiona first met him, about a year before I did, he lived with a pretty young male lover with whom he listened to Wagner and went to gay bars like the Black Cap in Camden. But by our third year, when Fiona and I were installed together – and Phillip, having left university, was living alone a few doors down from us – he had had decided life was 'easier' as a heterosexual. He was working as a schoolteacher in the local comprehensive school, while supposedly completing his doctorate.

After university I set out as an actor in children's theatre, but quickly realised that I disliked both children and being on stage. For real money I worked as a typist for an employment agency which sent me to a different office each week.

I had never felt more alienated than I did on that train with the other commuters and in those offices with the other drones. (Of course my father worked in an office, as an accountant.) It was such a fright that I was forced to take myself seriously and become motivated, as they say. At work I began to scribble down plays which were eventually performed on 'the fringe', in small venues and lunchtime theatres. Then I wrote a more ambitious work about a group of students – including characters who resembled Phillip, Fiona and me – visiting a Greek island, the first half of which was comic and the second farcical, nihilistic and vicious.

After starting out at a fringe venue, the play had become a success in the West End. It was produced in nine other countries and made a lot of money for others and some for me. For a few months, I was considered, at least by a couple of newspapers, to be the 'voice of the young' as well as one of Britain's 'most promising' young writers. As Fiona said, if that wouldn't spook your life, what would?

Soon I was working on the script of the film version. The producers had agreed to let me have a go at writing it, with the proviso that if I didn't succeed a proper screenwriter would be brought on. I was keen to do it. The more successful I had become, the more self-doubt I seemed to be prone to.

Phillip had given me the key to his place. My own flat was noisy and Fiona often slept during the day: she was working with young offenders, and had overnight duties. So I'd stroll down to Phillip's in the morning after he'd left for work.

If it was warm, I'd sit on the roof, a flat area with an iron fence looking out over Earls Court, my typewriter on a crate, a beer and an ashtray next to it, trying to write this movie. I'd stride about, saying the dialogue, attempting to see the different scenes crashing together. It wasn't long before I learned that a movie uses up a lot of imagination quickly.

I was anxious all the time, with, I believed, much to be anxious about. During the high success of the play, I had travelled whenever I was invited, meeting journalists, giving talks, as well as doing some reviewing and article writing. My directness was considered amusing and mischievous, and I had appeared on a couple of TV quiz shows. I wasn't optimistic that any of this would last. Indeed, convinced it was a fluke, success induced a plague of symptoms in me, twitches, compulsions, huge anxiety and, on some days, agoraphobia.

Like some of the untalented and talented people I've known, I was preoccupied by the idea that eventually people would understand that I was a fraud and a fool. After all, if you were a professional musician or even a footballer, you had already achieved a high level of competence. In my line of work, I could still feel as useless as a drunk, even as I won a short-story competition for a couple of pages about a woman being devoured by dogs, and my agent rang me with the figures from my latest opening. An older writer whose advice I sought sometimes had said to me, 'It's nothing to write one good or successful piece. Unless you choose to die young, you have to repeat it your whole life. Good luck.'

This wasn't my only doubt and conflict. Fiona and I had been living together for four years, but were separating. She was waiting for a flat she would rent to become available, and soon I would buy my own place. Both of us had been seeing other people, but most nights we slept in the same bed. As a child adored by his parents, I discovered it took an axe to your identity to live with someone who despised you, who looked at you with loathing, refusing to let you give them anything.

Around five o'clock each day it was a relief when Phillip came home, thus signalling the end of my work. If I'd been on the roof, I went down into the flat to greet him, and would bring him a gin and tonic and a cigar. The effort of writing, and the paranoia which solitude engendered, had destabilised me by the afternoon. I believed there could be no luckier man than someone like Phillip who had spent the day working fruitfully, having exhausted his guilt.

While Phillip read the paper, I'd cook for him. If I'd been sunbathing, as I often had, I'd continue to walk about naked as he looked on. I'd been doing yoga in the mornings, I ran and cycled by the river, swam, and lifted weights in our small flat in front of the mirror. I had sculpted this chunky little hot body and was keen for it to be admired.

I've become aware that I have always liked to have a best friend, someone older than me to be brother, guide, accomplice. Phillip was the person with whom I laughed the hardest, and whom I most wanted to hear my thoughts and know me. I could crack him up doing the voices, having always been able to pick up accents and attitudes, mimicking them in a minute. I did resent being an entertainer, but he'd beg me to do them: sturdy lefties in the party, friends, TV personalities. In those days of grave and serious political struggle, frivolity was not only at a premium, it was subversion.

I'd always been an indifferent student, but having a tolerance for others I now recognise as unusual in a writer, I was smart enough to see that if I made intelligent friends, there was much I could pick up with minimal concentration or study. Phillip was also the most fun of anyone around at the time, his conversation being a mixture of personal anecdote – detailed and hilarious accounts of his romantic and sexual misfortunes with both men and women – and literary reference and political gossip: he was a busy member of the Labour Party, and ran the local CND branch. The one-bedroom flat, with a large living room, was stuffed with books. He and I and Fiona spent weekends putting up new shelves while drinking and holding parties on his roof.

I guess Fiona and I were a desirable couple then, both of us good-looking. She'd briefly been a model, and we were bright, keen on the latest clothes and with a touching ignorance of what effect our vanity and self-assurance might have on others, of how it might infuriate them.

With me Fiona had become bored and stifled, and had made up her mind to become daring. She went to bars and stayed out all night. Once, while I waited at home – and no one envies another their masturbation – she slept with two men at the same time. In a hurry, and more under the influence of Joe Orton than I would be again, I decided Phillip could touch me a little.

If it gave him pleasure, and it seemed to when I offered myself to him, he could kiss my hands, shoulders, neck. Then he would caress my head and back, and play with my arse. Several times he sucked me, while I rested on the sofa, somewhat awkwardly I suspect, like a child being felt, as he messed with me until he came. He didn't excite me; I had no desire to touch him and never did. I just liked being desirable, and fancied the idea, for a time, of being in what I considered to be the 'feminine' position. It was the first time I'd had such power over anyone, the ability to make them crazy.

When Fiona was with us Phillip and I didn't do this. Nor was she informed, though I considered her to have been the touch paper since, being more alert than I to subterranean feeling, she'd said one night, 'Which of us do you think Phillip wants? Or could it be both of us? Would anyone have the balls to be that greedy?'

The next time we went round, both of us sat on Phillip's knees giggling. She winked at me and said, 'Dirk Bogarde in *Death in Venice.*'

He was fun to tease, but I respected Phillip. Not that he always respected himself. I'd sat in on some of his school classes, being invited to speak to his pupils about 'my career', where I saw he was capable of arousing enthusiasm in the young, of explaining why a certain figure or period should be paid attention to. As I myself had learned from him, I couldn't grasp why his profession would make him feel inadequate or ashamed of himself.

My blithe view infuriated him. He began to say he was wasted at the school. He needed me to know he was more talented than most people were able to see. He said he needed to 'shut himself away'. It turned out that rather than working on his thesis at the weekend, he had been producing plays and stories. It must have occurred to him that if I could do it, so could he. When he gave them to me to read I was kind, merely pointing out there were more pages than necessary.

Now, at least, I have understood that the longer you know a person, far from getting to know them, as you close in on their unconscious the unsettling delirium and violence of the human system will appear bewildering. So, while I returned Phillip's literary efforts somewhat casually, their general effect didn't quickly dissipate. Though of no aesthetic value, the work could only be a depiction of his mind, and the state he appeared to inhabit I recognised from my alarming but exhilarating experiences smoking dope. His inner self, unlike his outer, was disconnected, incoherent and peopled by many policemen, merchants of attempted order, presumably. Inside, I was shocked to learn, he was not at all like me. The nearly mad are among us everywhere, many of them disguised. Like blondes, they appear to have more fun, as well as more misery. But who, as an artist of some kind, would not welcome the weird as the truth? And who ever gets a straight look at the world?

Since my success I had begun to be invited to numerous openings, closings and publication parties, which appeared to go on most nights of most weeks of the year. We went to places where, outside, there were groups of photographers waiting for film stars and famous writers. I hadn't bought a drink in two years, and if you wanted to pick up strangers and meet bores, you were made. Soho was still rough but money and glamour, eventually to ruin it, was on its way. The Groucho Club had opened and in those days you could blag your way in.

I liked to take Phillip out with me. Being more committed to his pleasure than I – and convinced he could make an instant connection with people – he was always more successful. I was a dedicated cheerleader and witness, but one night, in a pub after a party, he flew into a rage, suddenly grabbed me by the throat and shook me. 'For fuck's fucking fuck sake, stop telling people all the time that I'm a teacher!'

'Should I say you captain submarines?'

'These supercilious, overprivileged people want to hear I'm an actor. I'm a model. I'm a hooker. I'm a movie director. "Teacher" makes them struggle with the death instinct. I can see their eyes trying to contact someone – anyone – across the room.'

Then a girl said to me, another time, 'Will your wonderful play become a film?'

'But yes,' I said. 'It is about to be made.'

'What do you mean?' Phillip asked.

'Looks like I've been lucky again,' I said.

Within a few weeks of my delivering the script, the movie had gone into pre-production. As the director wanted the actors to spend time together before shooting, it was cast early, with a group of attractive young potential stars.

Phillip and I went to a Soho restaurant to meet 'the supernatural two', the boy and girl playing the leads, both of whom had recently appeared in hit feature films, as the stream of ecstatic strangers who approached them attested. The next day, the four of us went to a movie together.

After, I walked Phillip back to his flat. He'd been sullen for a while but now began to berate me. I lacked principle and inner strength; I was a liar, doing or saying anything to gain an advantage. I was losing contact with the actual – working people, money and its absence. In fact I was a total pretence. 'How do you justify your life!' he shouted.

'At least I've made something of myself,' I said.

He grabbed me around the neck. Why would he want to have one of our mock fights now? He was only a little taller than me at around five feet eleven, but at university he'd been a keen rower. His arms were thick and capable; his stomach was hard.

He pulled me backwards until I was on the ground looking up at him as he kicked me in the side. I wanted to get to my feet and lash out at him with schoolkid punches. But not only did this feel unnatural and stupid, I'd get hurt, and I would forfeit our friendship at the moment of my greatest fear.

'That's shown you,' he said.

'Shown me what?' I asked, brushing myself down.

Now I phoned Phillip again, late at night.

'My dear, good evening,' he said sleepily. 'What a treat to hear from you. Have you been drinking?'

'It's worse. I have reached the age when I've begun to survey my wretched life, doing the addiction – sorry, I mean addition, and subtraction.'

Why did I say 'wretched'? Did I really see it like that? Was there justification? Perhaps tonight. My four children were home for the holidays. They were kicking away from us. Soon they would be gone for good, returning only with complaints. I was beginning to wonder that if I wasn't a father, what in fact was I?

Earlier that evening I'd been to an AA meeting. Back at home I'd held out as long as possible before pulling out the vodka bottle I kept behind my study sofa and taking a couple of long swigs.

Phillip said, 'That does happen at your age, my dear boy.'

'Do you remember much about our friendship?'

'Enough of it to say it is characteristic of you to ask such a direct question. As I can hardly sit here and consider the future, since we last spoke more of our shared past has come back, providing considerable amusement.' He went on, 'You were one of my best friends. I still think of you that way.'

'But you hurt me – physically, I mean – several times.'

'Did I do that?' he said. 'Have you been brooding? If that is why you called, I can remember us wrestling a bit. Didn't we like to mess about together like kids?'

'I hated it.'

'I can't recall you saying much at the time,' he said. 'You're certainly not one to refrain from complaint, and you always loved any kind of attention. But I am prepared to apologise,' he said. There was a pause and, I thought, a little giggle. 'Are you still attractive?'

'To some people, I hope. Why does it matter?'

He laughed. 'What else matters except pleasure or at least being cheered up? If only you would come and see me we could clear everything up. And Fred, my dear, if I send you some of my plays and short fiction would you be sweet enough to show them to someone who might help me? I know you have influence and time is shutting me in.'

'Okay,' I said.

'By the way, do you still wake up with an erection?'

'No, I don't,' I said. 'It is also true that I hadn't even noticed.'

I should have seen that our conversation wouldn't provide any of the clarity I'd hoped for. I drank some more, lay down, and reran the spools of memory.

I did like to tease and provoke and I could be, as Fiona liked to point out, an irritating person with a vibe of stubborn negativity. She had moved out of our flat by the time the film started to be made, and I was both bereft and elated, with time on my hands, a lot of which I liked to spend with my friend.

For a few weeks it was just Phillip and I, more or less living together in his flat, though I never slept there. Sometimes I'd walk through the door and he'd cuff me straight off. 'You behave today,' he'd say. 'I'm tired. Don't mess me around.' Or he'd encircle my neck from behind and pull me down, leaving me on the floor, or grab my arm and twist it up behind my back. If he was particularly mad, he'd just throw me to the ground and kick me.

Most days he punched me on one or other of my arms, in a slightly different place, so I had continuous bruises above my elbows, like smeared love-bites. One time I dropped a glass and fetched the vacuum cleaner to clear it up. He took the flex and lashed me about the legs as I stood in a corner, attempting to protect myself. 'This is fun,' he declared. At other times we'd watch TV together, read newspapers aloud or discuss the Labour Party.

Phillip had begun to see a teacher at the school with whom he had a zealous sexual relationship. He flashed me a photograph of her, saying, 'I wouldn't want her meeting you! She nearly tore my cock off.' He withdrew his key and his physical attention. I could not visit him without phoning. One time I walked past him and the teacher on the street and he only nodded at me as a friendly neighbour. I was his shame. I had collaborated, of course. I didn't have to see him. I could even have spoken out.

Soon he married the teacher. When I asked why he hadn't invited me to the wedding he just laughed. The wife lived with him while they waited to move to Rome, where they'd got jobs in an international school.

We spoke on the phone, but I didn't see him until he called and we had a drink together three months later. He explained he'd be going to Rome alone as the marriage had failed. That was all he would tell me.

His leaving for good without any acknowledgement made me aware that this had been the most anomalous episode of my life. The simple explanation was that at the time when I was most successful, I had requested a smack and received it. But really knowing why, isn't that the thing?

Still brooding now, I phoned Fiona and asked, 'Do you remember Phillip knocking me down a few times? Did he hurt me?'

'I hope so,' she said.

'If I'd been a woman in a violent relationship you'd have wanted to make a revolution.'

'You're so serious now – someone said to me the other day that you even have gravitas! It's easy to forget what a flirty and naughty thing you could be,' was all she said. 'I've been going through my photographs. How young and attractive we were. Why don't you take me for lunch? You know the new places, don't you?'

She was the wrong person to ask. Perhaps I would have to visit Phillip. While I vacillated, studying my diaries and making these notes, a niece of his called to say he'd died.

I had been keen to take a boat across that lake, but now, at the funeral hour, I strolled around my old neighbourhood.

The last time I saw Phillip I had invited him to my new loft in a converted industrial building, the first of many places I would buy. I'd got it fresh from a developer, it was more or less empty and at night I liked strolling up and down the wide spaces listening to music, books in piles on the floor, and, from the jacuzzi, looking at the distracting view of the new London skyline of cranes and unfinished buildings. Having decided to acquire an indulgence, I'd begun to collect rock posters, and they, along with a sexy poster for the French production of my play, leaned against the wall. My movie would soon play at festivals before opening all over, which was how I got to buy the flat.

I'd gone to the market in the morning, and made Phillip lunch. I bought new tumblers, plates and napkins, and set them out on my new glass-topped table from the Conran shop. But he wouldn't even sit down, he was in a hurry, he seemed embarrassed, as if he'd get into trouble for being here, though his wife had gone. He was still going to leave the country, and was in the middle of packing.

'If you had any balls you'd have a lot of fun here,' he said. 'But you're afraid of women, aren't you? Of your feeling for them.'

'Yes.'

'Still, you've been a fortunate little shit.'

I agreed. 'All this for almost nothing. I should have made less of myself, I know.' I had been unbuttoning the front of my shirt. Now I tried to take his hand, attempting to stir some sentimentality in him. 'Why do you have to go? Why can't we eat and then lie on the bed and watch telly all afternoon?'

'We never did that.'

'It was almost all we did.'

He reached for my hand and I thought he was going to kiss my fingers. Instead he grabbed at me and twisted my arm, giving me no choice but to turn as he inched it up my back. Had I teased him too much? I had offered him a glass of wine, saying, 'This is to celebrate you becoming Doctor Phillip at last,' perhaps with a little sarcasm, but also with pleasure and pride in his effort.

He continued to bend my arm until I was forced to my knees. From this position I attempted to turn and attack him; however, he pushed me to the ground and I fell awkwardly. When I tried to get up I found my right arm had become useless.

We agreed we had to call an ambulance. Phillip and I sat in casualty for four hours, until a doctor returned my arm to its socket. For a week I walked round with my arm in a sling. The next time I went swimming it popped out again and I had to be carried out of the pool. It was permanently weakened, I was told.

For a while I had to type left-handed. That can't have been the only reason my next play closed quickly, as did its follow-up. The cruelty and delight which accompanied these failures in the press wasn't something I needed to experience again. I rented my flat and moved to Los Angeles, writing several unmade American movies, one involving a chipmunk. My agent commented, 'Your screenwriting reputation will increase until you actually have a movie made. If it tanks, you can kiss your backside, as well as your American career, goodbye.'

At that I came home. It was easy to fail, I found, and for a couple of months I felt I'd been thrown out of my bed and onto the street in the middle of the night. But it didn't get in my way. I succeeded at property. With the aid of my wife, who was an estate agent in an office around the corner when I met her, but a 'property investor' a moment later – and despite the vicissitudes of the capitalism whose end my pals and I had wished for – we kept moving house and buying flats, which we either rented or sold. Within five years I had achieved easily my father's ambition, never to have to do another honest day's work.

I'd never been particularly compelled by money before, and I'd never met anyone whose ambition was only to accumulate wealth. While a teenager I had imagined that being an artist was the most desirable occupation there could be. I found, though, that for a while money and its gathering was as interesting as anything else, until I stopped noticing that I had it. Showing off embarrassed me, and on those occasions when I was forced to see what a struggle life is for most people, the wealth we had skimmed from the world began to curdle, and the temptation to become a human rights activist was almost overwhelming.

Because there was a necessity for a considerable amount of socialising with the most materialistic people on earth, and I am, I've been told, something of a weak-willed if not masochistic man, I saw that it was simpler for me to co-operate rather than whine. My wife liked everything about property – views, gardens, locations, carpets, lampshades. To her it was like collecting art, except that she was a kind of artist too, remoulding everything she bought and not encouraging dissent. I enjoyed her passion and, later, her devotion, concentration and absence. For the conventional amount of time, almost five years, I liked almost everything about her.

We seemed to acquire houses wherever they built them, particularly in the South of France and Italy, staying there with the children and their friends and parents. There were outings, barbecues, dinners and all manner of parties and jubilation, including visits to water parks, with nothing much for me to do except talk.

After a time I found myself taken aback and most likely depressed by the inevitable decline into coolness which appeared to accompany most marriages, requiring acceptance, secrecy or insurgency. What had once satisfied was gone; how then should you live?

Being heroic, I came more or less to allow the situation, having considered bolting. I had little inclination to rebel. I admired subversion in others, but it would seem unnatural to me not to live with my children, visiting them from time to time like a kindly preoccupied uncle. My ambition has gone into the four of them. When I wonder now what I've done, I can only say I've been with the kids, eating, talking, arguing, going to the movies, listening to music, drifting around the streets, playing tennis; that's where years of my time went, and you can't measure, count or discount it.

Naturally the ironies of the period could be a torment. How could I be unaware that we now lived in a rabidly sexual time? My life had spanned what was known as the sexual revolution: from repression to – unrepression, until we reached the prohibition of shame, the prohibition of prohibition. And there was I, in an age of sexual envy, only a curious onlooker. What a beautiful rack it was. I'd say that after fifty, you have to be cunning about your pleasures if you're to have any, and why would you want to?

I saw it was the women in Tolstoy, Zola, Colette and Jean Rhys that I had liked when I could be bothered to read, as a teenager, a way of being close, but not too close, to women. Why not make a vocation of it? I allowed myself to become fond of the wives of rich peripatetic businessmen, of which there always seemed to be a multitude nearby. Restless and bewildered, they had everything but a man to be curious about them, and to tease them with possibility. The modern illusion that women can have 'everything' is a monumentally misleading platitude, leading to despair if you ask me. As is the idea that love is sufficient for a marriage. It is institutions, not affection, which tie people together in the long run.

In the short run I was a double-agent, pretending to be interested in financial increase but actually with a rage for closeness. Where possible I didn't sleep with the women, not wanting to provide my wife with an excuse for more indifference, claiming, when necessary, tightness in the chest, gout or high blood pressure.

It is true I am stout, have sciatica and cannot walk far, though the doctors encourage exercise for those recovering from heart attacks. Lengthy strolls with the girls around various country estates were sufficient to evoke longing, intimacy and fantasy in all concerned. It was their vulnerability I liked. Maybe I was playing Phillip's role, being inaccessible, the one who never delivered, believing he had nothing to give.

I had been editing a book of ghost stories and desultorily writing episodes of TV dramas, to keep my hand in; work-in-regress you might call it. The other day a kind woman said to me, you artists are the lucky ones, knowing what you want to do and why you live, productive, praised and pursued by women. This struck through my indolent complacency, and I thought I might go back to serious scribbling, to see if there was something I might need to say that I couldn't keep to myself.

Meanwhile, once a week, I work in a women's prison. These are asylums by another name, and the unhappy women – 'my murderesses', I call them – raving, silent, gurning and drugged, sometimes like to report their misfortunes to me, occasionally writing them down. I can hardly think of a darker or more miserable business. Although each of us builds our own prison and then complains about the confinement and the food, I know I'll never become accustomed to hearing those heavy keys turn in their locks. Thank God, even now I am capable still of rebelling against myself.

The Decline of the West

The tube journey had been one of the most desolate Mike had endured, and he'd been looking forward to opening the door into the warm hall, hearing the voices of his wife and children, and seeing the cat come down the stairs to rub itself against him.

Mike rarely worked less than twelve-hour days and it had been weeks since he'd got home this early. The au pair saw more of his house and family than he did.

He thought he should give his wife the news straight away, but Imogen passed him in the hall carrying a gin and tonic, saying she was going upstairs to have a bath. Mike pulled a frozen meal from the freezer and put it in the microwave. Waiting for it to heat up, he poured himself a glass of wine and stood at the long windows which overlooked the garden.

He had been intending to start reading about and collecting wine. Imogen had insisted a hobby would make him less restless; having recently given up smoking, wine would be some compensation.

He believed he was good at giving things up. Unlike some of his friends and colleagues, he could control himself, he wasn't any sort of addict. But now that the financial system was out of control and today he had been fired, forsaking almost everything – including his idea of the future – was a different matter.

He switched on the garden lights and, looking out at the new deck where last summer they'd held barbecues, thought, 'I paid for this with my time, intelligence, and the education the state provided me with.' At the far end of the garden was a shed he'd had built for the boys to play music in, fitted with a TV, drum-kit and sound system. The kids had stopped using it before he'd hardly begun paying for it. Beyond that he could see into the bathrooms and bedrooms of other families much like theirs.

Situated on the comfortable outskirts of London, their house was narrow with five floors and off-street parking, overlooking a green. As the boys liked to point out, other children at their schools lived in bigger places; their fathers were the bosses of record companies or financial advisers to famous footballers. Mike, in corporate finance, was relatively small-time.

Still, he and Imogen had been seriously planning more work on the garden as well as the rest of the house. It was something they enjoyed doing together and, until recently, in this prosperous part of London, scores of skilled Polish labourers had been available. Most of Mike and Imogen's friends had been continuously improving their properties. It had been a natural law: you never lost money on a house. Maybe Mike should have been more attentive to the fact that the shrewd Poles had begun to return home a year ago.

Mike put his plate on the hyper-shiny elegant dining-room table where he liked to have supper and talk with friends. Imogen, who for years had never knowingly ingested anything non-organic, would have already eaten with the children. From where he sat Mike had a good view of the two boys playing a violent video game on the family television.

His food wasn't really edible: the rice was dried up, the prawns rubbery. The boys' dirty plates were still on the table, which was otherwise covered in school books, pencil cases, a rucksack out of which a football kit was tumbling, and three £20 notes Imogen had left for the cleaner. Mike picked one of them up and looked at it closely. How had he never noticed what a sardonic little Mona Lisa smile the blinged-up monarch wore, mocking even, as if she pitied the vanity and greed the note inspired?

'Mike, you've been stalked by good fortune your whole life,' his father enjoyed saying to him – the father who only finished paying off his mortgage when he retired, but otherwise considered debt a moral failure. 'In Kent where I lived as a child there were German bombs every night. You have suffered no such catastrophes, and no murders in the family. You're one who escaped the twentieth century!'

But not the twenty-first. *The* word of the post-9/11 era, used interminably by politicians and psychologists, was 'security', and the more the country had appeared to be policed by men in fluorescent jackets with 'Security' stamped on the back, the more afraid Mike felt – with good reason, as it turned out. Having progressed to running a department of forty people, Mike's current job was to execute the employees he had engaged and, in two weeks' time, pack up and remove himself.

'Take out your plate and wash it up,' he called across to the fifteen-year-old, who was playing the game.

'I did it yesterday,' Tom replied.

'It *is* your plate,' said Mike. The boy ignored him. 'And please turn that game off. Let's watch the football or a comedy. I need to be cheered up tonight.'

'Leave me alone,' said the kid. 'I've just started. When you're here you never let me do anything. You're so controlling.'

'Ten minutes and it's going off.'

'No it isn't.'

'Go and waste your life in your own room.'

'My television's broken,' said Tom. 'Why don't you get it fixed like you promised? What have you ever done for me?'

'I've given you all I've got and always will do so.'

'Are you joking? You've done nothing for me.'

The smaller boy, four years his brother's junior, and who claimed to have hurt his foot, hopped across to Mike and rested his head on his shoulder. Mike put his arm around Billy and kissed him. The older boy would never let Mike or even his mother kiss him now.

Mike had found it entertaining that some of his colleagues had stated their intention of becoming gardeners until the recession lifted; apparently the only requirements were an empty head and a desire to develop your muscles. Others had said they might be forced into teaching. Mike, at forty-five, had no idea what he would do. First he had to lose everything.

Billy patted Mike on the back, saying, not without an element of patronisation, '*I* like you sometimes, Daddy. But I want guitar lessons. So first I'll need the guitar and the amp, like Tom has.'

Family life could appear chaotic, but theirs was finely organised, with every hour accounted for. As well as attending private schools, his sons had, as far as Mike could recall, tennis, Spanish, piano, swimming, singing and karate lessons, and they frequently attended the cinema, the theatre and football matches. Like most of his friends and acquaintances, Mike's debts were huge, worth almost two years' income. But he had always considered them – when he did consider them – to be only another outgoing. Somehow, sometime in the mid-1980s debt stopped being shameful and after 1989 there appeared to be general agreement: capitalism was flourishing and there was no finer and more pleasant way to live but under it, singing and spending.

Mike pushed his plate away. After supper he liked to retire to his room where he was studying Stravinsky, listening to his work piece by piece in the order of its composition while reading about the composer's life. Once a fortnight he and his pals held a record group, playing music to one another. Recently an irksome sculptor in this gang had looked straight at Mike and mockingly referred to 'the cult of money', calling his profession and its office ethic 'fundamentalist', because ardent belief was paramount and doubt discouraged.

The sculptor held the condescending and false view that the imagination was only active in art. Mike had been furious but unable to dismiss from his mind the damned man's remark with regard to how he lived his life. He wondered whether he'd become hard and, like the sculptor, incapable of thinking his way into others' lives.

But he did reckon that the desire of the public to see bankers as thuggish, voracious philistines was simply the wish to separate the banking system from the rest of society, as people would prefer not to think of abattoirs while they were eating. Nonetheless, like many people, Mike had also worried whether the present catastrophe was punishment for years of extravagance and self-indulgence; that *that* was the debt which had to be paid back in suffering. Yet how could his family be considered despicable or guilty of this, when all they'd asked for was continuous material improvement?

Mike wandered across to the dishwasher, dropped in the lump of detergent, shut the door, tapped the start button and the world went black. The clock on the cooker stopped, its bright digits stuck on four round zeros; the microwave halted in mid-turn. All sound was suddenly suspended, apart from a dog barking in a nearby garden.

Out of that moment's nothing the little boy's voice called, 'Dad, Dad, Dad – do something!'

Mike fumbled in a drawer for a torch, crossed the house and was eventually able to follow the beam down the rackety wooden steps into the basement. But in his stockinged feet on the slippery stair, he slipped and lost his footing. For a second he believed he was crashing onto his back and would break his neck. How easy it was to fall, and how tempting it was – suddenly would be best – to die!

Grabbing the rail, he steadied himself, took some breaths – smelling gas and rotting cardboard – and padded down to the concrete floor where he stood surrounded by paint cans, broken children's toys, a decade's worth of discarded purchases and bags of credit card receipts.

There in the semi-darkness, gripping and ungripping his fists, he wondered whether he might go mad with fury. He knew he would be shut out now from the company of those he knew and liked, becoming a sort of 'disappeared'. He fantasised about informing the national newspapers of the idiocy and corruption in his office, betraying those narrow-minded fools as he had been betrayed. Failing lack of universal interest in that, he'd buy petrol, break in, burn the place down and see how the bastards liked it. But how long would he hate them for, and what effect would such extended hating have on him? Would he die of cancer? Like others he had actually believed he was an exception and would be spared!

Finding at last the little lever which made everything work again, he pulled it. There was a surge and their awful world started up once more with its humming and vibrating.

On his return to the light he couldn't believe Tom had resumed murdering dark-skinned people in some sort of Third World landscape.

'Turn it off right now!' he shouted. 'That's enough!'

'Bugger off.'

'Tom please, I beg you. Go and do your homework. The world's a filthy rough place run by jackals and murderers. You need to be prepared, if such a thing is possible!'

'Leave me alone! Don't ever talk to me again!'

Mike grabbed the boy and pulled him up out of the chair by his blue school shirt. 'Do what I say sometimes!'

'Fuck off, evil old man, just die! I've been wanting to do this all day!'

'I never spoke to my father like that.'

'Mum says you did.'

Tom was taller, stronger and fitter than Mike; for fun he sometimes put his father in a headlock and pulled him round the room.

'Turn it off, turn it off, turn it off!' Mike yelled at the boy. He ripped the controller from Tom's hand and threw it down. Tom lurched from his chair and made as to head-butt his father; Mike pushed him back in the chest and Tom stumbled and fell onto his backside. Mike swore again and then switched off the TV.

'What's going on? Is this good parenting?' His wife, who appeared to dress in diamonds and gold when at lunch with her friends, came in wearing tracksuit bottoms, an old T-shirt and thick glasses, with white slippers she'd taken from a hotel. 'Are you all right? What's he done now?' she said to Tom.

'I think he's broken my arm,' said Tom, rubbing his elbow.

'Your father's mad,' said Imogen.

'He refused to turn off the game,' said Mike. 'He shows me neither love nor respect.'

'How could he?' she said. 'It's too late! You've spoiled and neglected him, you ridiculous, foolish man. And now you expect him to obey you!'

'He tore my button right off,' said Tom.

'And who will sew it back on?' said Imogen, staring at Mike.

She worked for a charity three days a week. Inevitably it was poorly paid, but she was the family conscience and Mike knew it was important to appear generous. Unlike some of his friends, he didn't want a woman who worked as hard as him, a woman who was never at home.

Billy, who Mike wished wouldn't grow up, but wanted to suspend at this age for ever, reiterated, 'Stop arguing and tell me whether we're definitely going to get my guitar on Saturday!'

'I know I did say we would,' said Mike. 'But I'll have to think about it.'

'You were in a band. What were they called?'

'The Strange Trousers.'

'What a stupid name for a band,' called Tom, who was now texting furiously.

Mike said, 'So is the name of your group, Sixty-Nine, when you don't even know what that is.'

'I do. And you haven't had a sixty-nine for years, old man, and never will again.'

'Wait until *you* get married.'

Imogen said, 'You promised Billy a guitar, an amp and a microphone, so now you have to deliver.'

'Just call me the Delivery Man,' said Mike. 'That's my name. But even you might have noticed there's a financial crash taking place.'

'Ha! Any excuse to let people down.'

'Indeed – that's all I've ever done. But what about you?' he said to her. 'What do you want to get next?'

'Thank you for asking. I've been telling you for weeks I need a new computer,' she said.

'I'll get you the latest desktop Apple,' he said. 'With a printer, and maybe the newest iPod. Everyone should have what they want whenever they want it. Why don't I make a list so I don't forget anyone?'

She poured herself another drink. 'At last – some sense! Things are moving forward here!'

Having begun to feel 'unfulfilled', she was planning to train as a therapist; it would take at least three years, and he had agreed not only to pay her fees but to support her while she studied. 'Once I'm earning,' she argued, 'this whole family will be much better off.' Everything he spent on her was an investment. This would have to be rethought. And to think, before this collapse, he had been hoping to earn enough in the next few years to keep them secure for life.

As he got up she said, 'You washed the other dishes but you forgot to take these plates out.' Mike collected all the plates and took them to the sink. She continued, 'You know, with your habits you should have married someone less house-proud, someone with lower standards all round.'

She wouldn't see he liked scrupulousness and order more as he got older. They employed their Bulgarian cleaner three times a week; the woman was pregnant but sweated furiously as she scrubbed and carried, afraid of losing her job to someone else.

Mike and his wife considered themselves to be equals and there was no way Imogen would now wash the kitchen floor, clean their four toilets or vacuum the house. Since capitalism was cracking under the weight of its contradictions as the Marxists had predicted – neither the communists or Islamists being responsible for its collapse – the family would have to find a smaller place, sharing the household duties like everyone else. If there was no comfort, what then were the consolations of capitalism? If there was no moral accretion, nor any next life, why would anyone support it?

'Come on,' Imogen said to Tom. 'We'll do your French home-work in your room.'

'I'll read to Billy,' Mike said. 'Are you ready, little boy?'

Once Billy had cleaned his teeth and got into his pyjamas, they would lie on the big bed and chat, with the boy's head in Mike's chest; or they'd mock-fight, sing or read until the kid, and usually Mike, fell asleep. It was the part of the day Mike enjoyed most.

Imogen stroked Mike's head before picking up Tom's rucksack and French text book. Mike said, 'Darling, a shitty thing happened at work.'

'Is that unusual?'

'We should talk later.'

'Is it attention you're after?' she said.

She and Tom were going up the stairs, Tom giggling at a funny incident at school.

'Please, Imogen,' Mike called.

'Later, if I'm still awake,' she said. 'Or tomorrow.'

'Tonight, I think.'

'Maybe,' she said. 'Anyway, when I'm less worn out by every-thing.'

'Okay,' he said. 'When you're ready let me know.'

A Terrible Story

When Eric slammed the front door it was cold outside and raining hard. With winter already coming, he was reluctant to go out. But he'd said he'd meet Jake at seven and he couldn't let him down. Not that he had far to go; it took Eric five minutes to get to his local place.

He hurried into the bright, warm and almost-empty café, hung up his coat and sat down. The waiters knew him and brought him the wine he liked without his having to ask. Eric went there most days, to read the paper, make phone calls and work on his computer.

He drank half a glass of wine straight off, to calm himself down after arguing with his wife a few minutes earlier. She and their nine-year-old son had been at the kitchen table doing the boy's homework, but, having had a glass of wine, Eric had felt inspired to expatiate on the current political situation. His wife told him to shut up, and he hadn't wanted to; he had something pressing to say. His wife asserted he always had something important to say at the wrong time. Didn't he want his son to succeed or would the boy be a cretin like his father? The spat accelerated. 'You don't listen to me!' 'You don't speak at the right time, when we want to hear you!' 'You're never receptive!' 'You're a fool!'

Eric shuddered and giggled, as he thought of the two of them freely insulting one another, and the boy looking on.

He missed them and, in truth, wasn't excited about seeing Jake, whom he didn't know well. They had met through a mutual acquaintance three years before at the Jazz Café in Camden, and found they both liked Miles Davis's 'electric' period, as well as Norwegian jazz of the last decade. They always discussed this with some pleasure, along with Liverpool football club, their enthusiasm for jukeboxes, stand-up comedians, and their families, and went home relatively contented. Jake had been generous; he worked in IT and although he travelled a lot, he still found time to 'burn' obscure CDs for Eric and post them to him. Eric worked in film publicity and did what he could to obtain DVDs of the latest movies for Jake and his family.

As both their wives were interested in psychology, they had planned, last Christmas, to go to Jake's flat for lunch to meet his wife and girls, but it fell through.

Now Eric glimpsed Jake scurrying towards the café. They shook hands and Jake sat down.

'How are you, sir? It's been too long,' Jake said. 'Was the last time at the beginning of the year? It was probably February. I remember I had the prawns. I need a beer badly. Will you join me or are you all right with that?'

'Yes, I'm on white wine now,' said Eric. 'I consider it part of my new diet, which I've been enduring for three months.'

'Congratulations!'

'I haven't lost one ounce. I was always a thin kid. I took myself for granted.' He patted his stomach. 'I'm complacent.'

Jake said, 'It's not going well?'

'Last night the wife and I had an orgy involving a packet of chocolate biscuits, so I've had a terrible day, the guilt like a dagger. But I have started exercising. I run, or amble, rather, by the canal, listening to that great music you send me. And you? What's your news?'

Jake had put on the glasses which hung around his neck from a string, and was looking eagerly at the menu. Eric guessed that Jake was a little older than him, about forty-five probably. Jake had seemed stolid, large, but now looked somewhat scrawny, with the collar of his shirt too big for his neck. Had he shrunk in some way? Resembling an ageing professor, he had always been more earnest than Eric, with a more literal character. You'd have to be such a type to adore so much the icy longing and melancholy of Norwegian jazz.

'You have lost weight,' said Eric. 'Much more than me. I envy you.'

'I'm glad. That's good news at last.'

'What about you? What have you been listening to? Anything new?'

'I haven't had any concentration recently,' said Jake. 'It's been crazy, tragic. I promise I'll get some new stuff to you next month.'

'I'd love that. I get so bored, don't you?'

'Do you want the menu?'

'I already know what I want,' said Eric.

'Okay. Can we order? I'm starving.'

Eric called the waiter over; they ordered a beer for Jake and food for both of them.

'Eric, why did you ask me if I get bored?'

'Perhaps because the last time we met you mentioned that things were not good between you and your wife, though they sounded normal to me. She refused to come across and you'd decided to become celibate for a while. A harsh deprivation, but not the most unusual suffering.'

'Yes, I remember telling you I was prepared to endure it until she recovered. She'd begun therapy with a Jungian, I think I said. Eccentric but not too weird.'

'It amuses me,' said Eric. 'He slept with his patients.'

'What?' said Jake. 'Why did you say that?'

'Jung, if I remember rightly, was different in that respect to Freud, who didn't mess around. Yet Freud said sexuality was the main thing, and Jung insisted it wasn't.'

Jake said, 'My wife had always wanted to study so I agreed to support her while she had therapy and trained to be a psychologist – though such a wish is said to be in most cases a sure sign of mental instability –'

'Of course.'

'But not always?'

'Oh it is, always,' said Eric, calling for another glass of wine.

Jake went on, 'My wife sneers at Scandinavian jazz music, in particular the Lord of the Rings names – Frode, Arve, Arild, Siguard. But her weakness is for dresses, like my sweet girls. She claims what she wears makes her mood, so she has filled the flat with them.'

'With her moods?'

Jake laughed. 'Unlike your wife, she is expensive.'

'Tell me,' said Eric. 'I've been meaning to ask this. Do you organise your music in terms of the artist, the year, the country, or something else? Personally I like to keep my artists together, it almost sexually excites me.'

Jake laughed. 'I organise by artist, but in special cases by label. But there's no doubt these are demanding and sometimes terrible decisions.' He went on, 'Not that I've had time to do any filing.'

'Why is that – too much work?'

'My mother died.'

'I am sorry,' said Eric. 'That's tough.'

'Thanks. And a few days before she passed on, Julie decided to tell me she liked the therapist, she loved him. He was wise, intelligent and he understood everything about her.'

Their food came and they began to eat.

'Why is it I like the food so much in this mediocre place?' said Jake.

'Next time,' said Eric, 'as you always come all the way to me, we should eat at your local.'

'Yes, we must do that,' Jake said. 'Eric, I know little about therapy, but I had heard that affection for the quack was part of the process. It was natural, if not normal. It was the cure.'

'Amazing,' said Eric. 'I have always fancied being hypnotised. Have you tried it?'

'Are you saying you think I need it?'

'I have no idea if you do. I think I do!'

Jake said, 'Julie was becoming impatient with my Jung jokes. She knew about the theory of idealising the therapist. She said it wasn't just that. She was, in fact, actually sleeping with him.'

'You're kidding? With the actual Jungian?'

'She said she wanted to be with him. He wanted to be with her. She said we all have an ideal, and at last she had found him.'

'Jake, are you only having a starter?' said Eric with concern. 'Will it be enough for you?'

'I haven't had an appetite lately, so this is welcome. I'm going to scoff all the bread too.' Jake went on, 'I told Julie this was madness. I would have to report the therapist to the authorities for the sake of other patients. But the main thing was the cohesion of our family. The well-being of the girls at home with us. They're young – nine and seven.'

'That was tolerant if not noble of you,' said Eric. 'What did she say?'

'She told me I had to find my own place as soon as possible. Well, I was quite sick after hearing this.'

'Oh God, Jake.'

'The day after I had to leave town to be with mother for the last week of her life. While I was down there with her, doing this awful duty at her bedside, I spoke to Julie and the girls on the phone. They were concerned about me. It was as if nothing had happened. I hoped nothing had happened. But it had, Eric. It had definitely happened. "Did you find somewhere to live?" asked my wife. "You're kidding, how can I right now," I said, "when Mother is taking her last breath?"'

'Almost the moment Mother died I came back straight away. I had a feeling, you know. When I got home my wife had left, with the girls. She had gone to the small town in France where her mother and family lived.'

Eric said, 'I think women often prefer their mothers to their children.'

Jake pushed his plate away and said, 'I need another drink. You?'

'Please.'

'When I dashed to this beautiful country place – where I've been often and which I like very much – Julie was hostile, almost insane with hatred. I said the children barely speak French, they must come home, they need their school, their friends. This is all too sudden.'

'Of course.'

'Has this ever happened to you – that someone you think you know intimately has changed beyond recognition? She was cold and formal, as if talking to someone she didn't know. I'd always liked her, though she had her problems. I liked her voice. She was curious, and interested in gardens. I wanted to make one with her, helping her. But I realised she'd gone somewhere else. Her eyes were dead now, Eric.

'She said she wasn't sure what they were going to do, but she thought she'd return to London with the girls as the grandparents were becoming irritable. I was relieved until she said she was intending to set up home with the therapist. He was waiting for her – making his arrangements. I hated to think of it, Eric, this stranger making "arrangements" to replace me in my family.'

'Christ, Jake, this is heavy. This is bad news, a punch in the gut. Don't talk so fast, you'll give yourself indigestion.'

'That's the least of it,' he said. 'Julie reassured me by saying this man got on well with children. But they couldn't move in together until the house was sold, as the therapist didn't have any money. His practice was small. He's younger than her, just starting out.'

'You were going to be forced out of your own house?'

'Yes, can you believe it? Where would I put everything?'

'This conversation took place in France?'

'Didn't I say? In an old house, a couple of hundred years at least. I was there to ask if the girls would be able to attend their grandmother's funeral, but Julie refused, saying I might abduct them. She said she'd already informed the French and British police that I might attempt something with them! I was forbidden to be alone in their company as if I had suddenly become a monster. How did I become evil overnight? The girls kept asking when they were going home. But I couldn't tell them the truth.

'And then there, with the bewildered maternal grandparents looking on, my previously silent youngest daughter took her violin from its little case and sawed out a squeaky tune for us. By the end tears were pouring down my face. When I left they watched me from the window, crying out "Daddy, Daddy!"

'I returned to England, saw mother into her grave, and went back to work. I sold the Audi A5 and bought a second-hand Astra, hired lawyers and, to help pay them, took a lodger, a girl who would also clean the place because I had fears about neglect – of the place, and of myself. My wife had also emptied our joint bank account. Do you have one?'

'Now you mention it, I do. Thanks for bringing it up.'

'Julie came back to London – and to the house – to pick up some of her clothes. When she arrived she discovered the lodger, a young Czech girl.

'I said Julie's personality has become strange and unnatural. That is madness, I guess. But to give you an illustration, in the house she begins to abuse this poor girl when she discovers a bed in her former study. She starts to cry out that I'm a scum and an alcoholic and a paedophile – as well as a thief and the rest of it. She was loud. The girl is horrified and also looks at me with a very nervous curiosity.

'But what do you say – "I'm not a paedophile alcoholic"? It's nuts for me to have to hear this, I can't begin to defend myself except to say, "Please, please try to control yourself."'

Jake was looking at Eric. 'Are you thinking there must be something crazy about that Jake, he must have chosen badly? Are you? Are you? How come he didn't notice he'd married a mad woman? How could anyone miss such a thing? But she has never behaved like this before! Perhaps it's called regression. Anyway, she had hidden it well.

'Julie was horrified that the girl was in her room. I could tell she was going to spit on her! I asked the girl to get out, I would deal with it. Julie picked up handfuls of things at random and flew out of the house. I could see her from the window, scattering clothes in the street, trying to carry too much at once.'

There was a silence. 'Well, thank God,' said Eric. 'You needed time to think.' Jake sighed. Eric said, 'Those prawns looked good. But I enjoyed my salad, oddly enough, and I've always considered eating salad to be a form of failure.'

'I know what you mean.'

Eric said, 'What happened after, Jake?'

'Come.'

Jake wanted to smoke, so the two men put on their coats and stood outside under the café awning, watching people rush through the rain.

Jake said, 'Obviously there was information I needed to have, so I sought out as many of her friends as I could find. It shook me, as some were violently rude. One said, "I hope the girls hate you when they're older." What had she been telling them about me?

'But there was one friend of hers I was able to get through to. Let me add that having been made crazy and almost violent and suicidal, I had to make a huge effort to pretend to be sane. If I gave anyone the idea that circumstances had made me totally crazy, the whole catastrophe would appear to be down to my craziness. Crazy, eh?

'Julie's friend admitted Julie was in London, spending time with the therapist, working out what to do. Apparently it had been going on for some time. Julie had said to me on a couple of occasions, "You're having an affair," and wouldn't tolerate my denials. The deeper truth became obvious.

'I rang Julie, hoping to contact the reasonable side of her, and delivered a monologue to the answering machine saying we should meet and talk honestly.

'That evening I came home and she was there, Julie, asleep in my – our – bed, can you believe it? My heart pounded. I thought, she's back, her old self, the past eradicated.

'When I got closer I saw she was not asleep, but drugged, perhaps on tranqs or painkillers, I don't know what, with an untreated cut on her forehead. She didn't take illegal drugs. Did she want to kill herself, or did she want to sleep?

'I carried her to the toilet, made her sick and put her back to bed. I lay next to her. I took her in my arms and kissed and caressed her. I looked at her breasts and touched them, remembering how I loved them. The aureoles, is that how you say it? The aureoles were smiling at me.'

'Were they really?'

'I thought of how I had nursed Mum as she shrank to her bald head and bones in that hospital bed.

'I thought of the fine and funny times Julie and I and the girls had had as a family.

'When Julie woke up she tried to speak. Her voice was cracked, frail. "Things are not good, Jake," she said.

'"Why aren't you with your darling lover?" I asked her.

'She turned her head away and wept. All I could do was guess the lover had kind of backed out. Who wouldn't have been delighted? Who wants a filthy corrupt therapist around his children? A man who can fuck his own patient can fuck anyone!'

'Yes.'

'But I kept my mouth shut while she cried, the woman I still love and have wanted more than any other.'

Eric said, 'Didn't you think of asking her to go back to you?'

'I love and hate her, but I don't know if she wants any more of me now. At last she confirmed the therapist had left her. But there was something else. She said that the therapist's wife, who was pregnant –'

'Did Julie know that?'

'I'm not sure. I tend to doubt it. Anyway, when the pregnant Jungian's wife was told about the affair, she went to the balcony, threw herself over head first, and died.'

'Oh God,' said Eric, rubbing his eyes and forehead. 'This is getting too much. I can hardly believe it.'

'You're telling me. Yes, he had lost his child after depriving me of mine.' Jake began to laugh. 'People keep telling me to have therapy,' he said. 'That's surely a joke!' Then he said, 'After this the man refused to see Julie so she went and waited outside his door.

She slept there all night on the step like a dog until she almost froze. In the morning, when he came out, she pursued him, he pushed her over and she tripped and hit her poor head. He tried to run away. She started to shout and he called the police.

'Before they came he said he would never see her again. It was her fault. He was inexperienced and she had seduced him when he was most vulnerable and open to female flattery. He had been a fool – he was human too – but she had been ruthlessly malevolent, evil even, having destroyed his life and ruined the lives of several people.'

'Indeed.'

'She was broken by the accusation, having done nothing, she said, but fall passionately and irrevocably in love for the first time in her life. How could that be a crime?'

Jake and Eric returned to their table and Eric asked for the bill. 'I'll get this,' he said.

Jake said, 'In the morning Julie got on the train back to France.'

'Jake, what will you do now?'

'The lawyers have smelled blood, so I made the decision to write to my friends and ask them, outright, for money,' he said. 'I'm still working, but I need funds for the train fare to France some weekends where I can stay in a little hotel and spend a few hours with my daughters, in order that they don't forget me. While I try to get custody I have to survive, otherwise I will be on the street.'

Eric paid the bill and they went outside. They shook hands, Eric put up his umbrella and Jake said, 'Can we meet again next week, or if that's too soon for you, the week after? Would that be okay? If I don't talk there'll be another death.'

'Yes, yes, call me any time,' said Eric.

'How is your family?' Jake said.

'All fine, thanks. My son is becoming rather a good footballer.'

'You are lucky. You are blessed.'

Eric noticed it was only around ten o'clock when he got back to the house. He locked the door behind him, something he never usually did, and crept in, certain his wife and son would be asleep.

He took off his shoes and went upstairs. His wife was indeed asleep, wearing his new pullover, on the edge of the bed, with his son sprawled across the middle. The little space left was occupied by their two cats.

Eric perched on the edge of the bed, looking at them both. Then he opened the curtains so there was sufficient moonlight for him to see to kiss them.

He wondered what Eric would do when he got home – look at photographs of his lost family?

The boy was nine, and he was heavy, but Eric picked him up and carried him to his bed. Then he got into his own bed and stayed awake for as long as he could, listening to his wife's breathing and waiting for the morning light.

Acknowledgements

Love in a Blue Time first published by Faber in 1997
'In a Blue Time' and 'With Your Tongue down My Throat' first appeared in *Granta*; 'We're Not Jews' first appeared in the *London Review of Books*; 'D'accord, Baby' appeared in *Atlantic Monthly* and the *Independent Magazine*; 'My Son the Fanatic' first appeared in *The New Yorker*, and subsequently in *New Writing 4* (ed. A. S. Byatt and Alan Hollinghurst); 'The Tale of the Turd' appeared in *em writing & music* and *The Word*.

Midnight All Day first published by Faber in 1999

The Body first published by Faber in 2002
'Hullabaloo in the Tree' first published in the *Guardian*; 'Face to Face with You' first published in *The Black Book*; 'Goodbye, Mother' first published in *Granta*; 'Remember This Moment, Remember Us' first published in *Red*; 'Touched' first published in *The New Yorker*

'The Dogs' first published in the *Guardian* in 2004

'Long Ago Yesterday' first published in *The New Yorker* in 2004

'Weddings and Beheadings' first published in *Zoetrope* in 2006

'The Assault' first published in the *Independent* in 2007